An Obsolete Honor

AN OBSOLETE HONOR

A Story of the
German Resistance to Hitler

Helena P. Schrader

To Elizabeth with thanks for years of encouragement.

Helena

iUniverse, Inc.

New York Lincoln Shanghai

An Obsolete Honor

A Story of the German Resistance to Hitler

iUniverse books may be ordered through booksellers or by contacting:

iUniverse
2021 Pine Lake Road, Suite 100
Lincoln, NE 68512
www.iuniverse.com
1-800-Authors (1-800-288-4677)

ISBN: 978-0-595-49088-2 (pbk)

ISBN: 978-0-595-60965-9 (ebk)

Printed in the United States of America

Introduction and Acknowledgments

This novel evolved over three decades, during two of which I lived and worked in Berlin, Germany. It incorporates extensive primary and secondary research conducted in what was then East and West Germany. In fact, I was the first Westerner to gain access to certain relevant materials in East Germany, and conducted interviews with well over 100 survivors of Nazi Germany.

Some of those I interviewed turned into friends, and we carried on year-long dialogues about the subjects and themes described in this book: the nature of evil, the insidious moral corruption that spreads like cancer even to healthy organs in a society ruled by criminals, the power of self-deception, the limits of conscience, God's role in human affairs, and much more. The stories told to me by the witnesses of the period have been worked into the fabric of this novel, as have their understanding and explanations of the entire period, society and regime. Sometimes these perceptions are contradictory. That is the nature of human experience.

Among those survivors of the German Resistance whom I had the privilege to later call friends were, first and foremost: Ludwig Freiherr von Hammerstein, Axel Freiherr von dem Bussche, Philipp Freiherr von Boeselager, Eva Olbricht, Friedrich Georgi, Marion Gräfin Yorck von Wartenberg, and Clarita von Trott zu Solz. It was an honor—which I have yet to earn—that these courageous, bright and warm-hearted people welcomed me into their homes, shared their memories and feelings with me, and encouraged me to persist in this difficult project. Tilly Zerrath and Dorothee Freifrau von Hammerstein went even farther and read early versions of the manuscript, giving me invaluable feedback on even the smallest details described in the novel. Nina Gräfin Stauffenberg, the widow of Claus Graf Schenk von Stauffenberg—the would-be assassin on July 20, 1944—granted me an exceptionally rare interview and received me in the very house where she had lived together with Claus. But, almost as important for this novel, I met with several officers who had opposed the July 20th Plot (Fritz Harnack, Bolko von der Heyde, Hellmuth Reinhardt) and with the widow of Generaloberst Jodl, a man sentenced to death by the International War Crimes Tribunal at Nuremberg for his role in the Nazi war crimes.

Obviously, there are millions of other witnesses whom I was not able to interview. Every person who endured the National Socialist regime, whether as an enthusiastic supporter or as an opponent, has a unique perspective and a personal story that, in its way, is a novel in its own right. This book cannot encompass all their stories, but it does try to provide a spectrum of experiences and attitudes. Furthermore, as someone who lived more than 20 years in Berlin, embedded completely into the society both linguistically and professionally, I am confident that the social and cultural atmosphere portrayed in this novel is authentic. Last but not least, many of the places described were places I have personally visited, usually many times.

I wish to thank my editor, Christina Dickson, for helping me to select from a longer manuscript the essential elements suitable for publication, and for her careful editing of the text. My thanks also go to Charles Whall for a thoughtful and effective cover design.

The front cover shows the room in Berlin's Ploetzensee prison where many of those found guilty of treason by the Nazi regime were executed. Hitler ordered them to be hung with piano wire from meat hooks and slowly strangled. The executions were filmed and Hitler is said to have "enjoyed" watching them. If you look closely at the photo, you can see the hooks from which the condemned were hanged. The back cover shows:

Top left to right: 1) A German officer relaxing at an outdoor café, 2) Female civilian employees of the German Army, 3) Children and their teachers parading before Hitler, 4) Members of the German Armed Forces taking the Oath to Hitler.

Bottom left to right: 1) A German officer and his bride, 2) German wounded being taken from a hospital train, 3) Two Luftwaffe officers relaxing during the summer of 1940, 4) German horse-drawn artillery on maneuvers.

All photos used are in the public domain.

Helena P. Schrader
Oslo, November 12, 2007

Cast of Characters

(Characters marked with * are historical)

Altdorf

Feldburg Family
Philip Freiherr von Feldburg, German General Staff Officer
Sophia Maria Freifrau von Feldburg, his mother
Christian Freiherr von Felburg, his younger brother
Theresa Freiin von Feldburg, his younger sister
Walther Halle, Theresa's fiancé

Staff at the Feldburg Schloss
Josef, the coachman/chauffeur
Heidi, his unmarried daughter and Sophia Maria's maid
Franz, Heidi's illegitimate son, and batman to Philip
Hr. Opitz, the butler, and his wife, Frau Opitz
Martha, the cook
Lucie and Franziska, the kitchen maids
Hr. Lauterbach, the gardener, and his wife, Frau Lauterbach
Jurek Miljewski, one of the Polish workers
Ludmilla, his wife

Local Officials
Father Matthias, the priest
Herr Dettmann, the local party official
Herr Meisterling, the Chief of Police

Berlin

The Feldburgs' Apartment House
Theo Pfalz, the concierge
Prof. Dr. Moldenauer, a tenant
Frau Moldenauer, his wife
Marianne Moldenauer, his daughter
Gottfried Jähring, a tenant
Peter Kessler, a tenant

German General Staff HQ
General Friedrich Olbricht,* Head of the General Army Office
Alexandra von Mollwitz, Secretary to General Olbricht (1941-1943)
Annie Lerche,* Secretary to General Olbricht (1941-1944)
Lotte Koch, Secretary to General Olbricht (1943-1944)
Oberst Reinhard,* his Chief of Staff (1941-1943)
Oberstleutnant Claus Graf von Stauffenberg,* his Chief of Staff
(1943-1944)
Generaloberst Erich Fromm,* C-in-C of the Home Army
Axel Freiherr von dem Bussche,* a young officer on leave

The v. Mollwitz/v. Rantzau Family
Alexandra von Mollwitz
Stefan von Mollwitz, her brother
Albrecht von Rantzau, her stepfather
Louisa von Rantzau, her mother
Grete, her half-sister
Rudi, her half-brother

Miscellaneous
Mr. and Mrs. Silber, a Jewish couple

JG23

Hauptmann Bartels, the squadron commander
Oberleutnant Hartmann, a senior pilot
Dieter Möller, a fighter pilot
Busso Appelt, a fighter pilot
Ernst Geuke, a fighter pilot

Gabrielle Carduner, a French shopgirl
Yvette Dubois, a French shopgirl
M. St. Pierre, their employer

Eastern Front, Army Group Center

Headquarters
Generalfeldmarschall von Kluge,* Army Group Commander
General von Greiffenberg,* Army Group Chief of Staff
Oberst Henning von Tresckow,* First General Staff Officer (Ia)
Heinrich Graf Lehndorff-Steinort,* ADC to the C-in-C (1941)
Carl-Heinz Graf Hardenberg,* ADC to the C-in-C (1941)
Fabian von Schlabrendorff,* ADC to Tresckow
Philipp Freiherr von Boeselager,* ADC to the C-in-C (1943)

144th Infantry Division
General von Rittenbach, Commander (1941)
Oberstleutnant Miersch, CO of the Engineer Battalion
Major Kellermann, Second General Staff Officer (Ib)
Major Krosigk, Staff Officer
Oberleutnant Böttcher, Staff Officer
Leutnant Poncet, Staff Officer
Inspector Benecke, Civil Servant attached to the Staff
General Wittig, Commander (1942)

XXXII Corps
General von Rittenbach, Commanding General
Major Zimmerman, First General Staff Officer (Ia)
Oberleutnant Rolf von Seydlitz, ADC to the Chief of Staff
General Zinsmeister, Commander, 336th Infantry Division
General Lenz, Commander, 294th Infantry Division
General Pickert, Commander, 11th Panzer Division
General Kitzinger, Commander, 6th Panzer Division

CHAPTER 1

▼

Altdorf, Southern Germany
Christmas 1938

Altdorf was a harmonious jumble of half-timbered and plaster façades in predominantly medieval, Renaissance and Baroque styles. The occasional modern structure crouched on the outskirts near the tracks. As the local train from Frankfurt pulled into the little station, the single passenger in the first-class compartment—an officer of the German Army—set his cap firmly on his head. He adjusted the peak to sit just above his rimless glases. He then pulled on his leather gloves and picked up his suitcase by the handle. He shoved back the compartment door and made his way, swaying, to the front of the car. The brakes squealed and the platform whisked past, sparsely populated with citizens awaiting this morning train. Even before the train came to a full halt, the young officer turned the handle and shoved the heavy door open to jump down agilely before the train came to a complete stop.

He looked about the platform expecting Josef, the coachman, and the sight of a slender woman in her early fifties with dark blond hair and a trim wool coat brought him to an abrupt halt. Recovering, he went forward, took her hand, and kissed it. Then he bent and kissed her cheek warmly. "I'm honored, Mamá."

"Don't be cheeky, Philip" she chided.

"But I *am* honored. The last time you met my train must have been …"—he thought back—"over six years ago." That was when his father's illness had started.

"Then it was long overdue," his mother countered, adding with a smile, "You look smashing!" She was looking at him with a mother's unabashed admiration, seeing him for the first time since his promotion to *Rittmeister*, or cavalry captain.

Embarrassed by her admiration, Philip waved her compliment aside with a hasty, "I hardly slept on the train."

His mother had already noticed the imperfection of his shave, no doubt done hastily in the Frankfurt station when changing trains. She was reminded of the many times she'd met her husband in this station during the Great War; he had always arrived unrested and hastily shaved. Philip also had her husband's coloring: dark hair, fair skin and grey eyes. Her husband had been a little taller and more robustly built, but Philip had his seriousness, his self-discipline and his intelligence. "Are you enjoying General Staff training as much as you expected?" she asked, taking his elbow as they proceeded toward the exit.

"More than I expected," came the ready answer. After ten years of working his way up from recruit to *Oberleutnant*, Philip had finally been promoted captain and accepted at the General Staff training college in Berlin, the famous *Kriegsakademie*. He had suffered the early stages of pre-officer and officer existence for this privilege alone.

The stationmaster stood near the exit. He bobbed his head in greeting to the Feldburgs. "Welcome home, *Herr Baron*. Will you be able to stay long?"

"Not as long as I'd like, Herr Leske. Are all your family with you this Christmas?"

"All but Alfred; he's doing his National Labor Service and can't get leave."

Philip nodded sympathetically. All youths were now required to do a year of National Labor Service (*Reichsarbeitsdienst*) before being drafted for two years of compulsory military service. It meant that many families would not be together for Christmas. The strange thing about it was that so few of them seemed to mind.

As he wished Herr Leske "Merry Christmas," Philip noted the huge Nazi flag flapping before the station, and he caught sight of the straw swastikas hung on the Christmas tree at the post office. In one of the store windows, someone had placed a photo of Adolf Hitler and adorned it with greens and a candle as if it were picture of the Virgin or a saint. Something curdled in his stomach, and the sour expression on his face caught his mother's attention.

"Is something wrong, Philip?" She had taken the keys from her leather purse and was unlocking the doors to the black Mercedes.

Philip gestured vaguely toward the photo. "I'd rather hoped that things like that were confined to places like Berlin where Goebbels and the Mob rule! What does Father Matthias have to say?"

"We may not be in the center of things, but we're not entirely immune to the *Zeitgeist* either. The Nazis have been in power nearly six years now, and not everything they've done has been bad." With this, Sophia Maria v. Feldburg slipped behind the steering wheel while her son climbed in on the other side. As she closed her door and backed out of the parking space, she remarked without even looking at her son, "You don't have to look at me like that. I've not turned Nazi and I'm not about to, but the fact of the matter is that this town—no less than any other—has had six years of prosperity and peace. Unemployment is nonexistent, farm prices are up, and—"

"Everybody looks over his shoulder before he dares breathe a word of criticism. Socialists and union leaders are locked away in Concentration Camps. Jews have been forced out of business, prohibited from pursuing the professions, effectively forced to emigrate. The press is muzzled. The currency is worthless abroad—"

"I'm not *defending* them, Philip; I'm only trying to explain what the people of Altdorf see. They didn't hold with Socialism or unions anyway. The townspeople never traveled abroad. Indeed, they never took much interest in the news from farther than 10 miles away. But they all lost sons in the World War, and they are proud that we have 'broken the chains' of Versailles."

"I would have thought the removal of crucifixes from the schools and the crushing of Catholic youth organizations would at least have upset them a little," Philip grumbled. "But I can see our 'devout' neighbors have no compunction about letting their sons serve in a heathen organization." Philip gestured angrily toward a group of five boys approaching along the side of the narrow street. Despite the bundle of scarves, wool mittens and snow boots, it was nonetheless possible to see that the boys wore Hitler Youth uniforms.

"It's compulsory, Philip," Sophia Maria reminded her son.

"Oh, there are ways around it, if you try hard enough."

"Yes, but at the price of attracting attention to yourself, isolating yourself from your classmates, and risking your future. It's hard to get into a high school, much less a college or university, if you haven't demonstrated your 'patriotism' by belonging to the Nazi youth organizations."

At the sight of the car, the boys waved and ran forward. Sophia Maria had to stop as they surged around it. They were in unabashed high spirits, laughing and chatting to each other as they tapped on the windows and shook tin cans. Sophia Maria rolled down the window.

"*Frau Baronin*! Please help us. We want to collect more for the Winter Help than any other Hitler Youth Troop. Please!"

Sophia Maria smiled indulgently, but shook her head. "I don't have any money with me. I only drove to the station. If you come up to the manor later today or tomorrow, I'll make a contribution."

The boys turned their attention to Philip with a silent appeal. When he hesitated, they urged excitedly, "If we collect the most, *Herr Baron*, we win a trip to the North Sea." Philip dutifully took out his wallet and pushed a 10-*pfennig* coin through the slit. The disappointment of the boys was unspoken but tangible. Sophia Maria gave her son a reproving look, and Philip capitulated. He added a one-mark piece to the can. The boys cheered and thanked him. Sophia Maria waved, rolled up the window and drove on.

"You don't really believe that that money goes to help needy families, do you?" Philip demanded angrily. "It goes to pay for the villas and automobiles of the Party leaders!"

"That isn't the youngsters' fault, Philip."

"I know that, but why should I give my hard-earned money to line the pockets of crude, corrupt thugs?"

"Because those boys want a holiday on the North Sea, and because they look up to you and expect you to help and support them. It comes with the manor, Philip."

Philip sighed and said no more.

The manor had been built in the eighteenth century to replace a medieval castle that had outlived its utility. The present structure was neither architecturally outstanding nor historically significant. Built in a rough square around a cobbled courtyard, its only distinctive feature was a central passage, wide enough for a carriage to pass through, which led under the first floor into the courtyard. Otherwise it was a typical baroque manor: solid and symmetrical with a modestly ornate façade. It was free of decoration, unless one counted the coat of arms carved in stone over the carriage passage and the rather functional fountain in the center of the courtyard.

The wood-and-iron doors of the broad carriage entrance were firmly closed. Sophia Maria drove the car around to the garage, which had been added to the barns behind the manor after the Great War. She parked, and then she and Philip crossed the cobbled courtyard and entered the manor by a back door. After greeting the staff, they climbed a flight of service stairs to the first floor. This wing of the manor had been modernized just before the War; it had central heating, hot and cold running water, electricity and a telephone. On the ground floor a fully modernized (for 1910) kitchen and a refrigerated pantry had been installed.

When these practical improvements had been taken care of, there had been only limited resources remaining for purely decorative and luxury alterations. The rooms of the wing were consequently characterized by tasteful but simple furnishings, a stark contrast to the rococo style of the representational rooms in the eighteenth-century main wing.

The breakfast room that Philip and his mother entered was one of the most comfortable rooms in the entire house. It faced south and the sun streamed into it most of the day. The table and cupboards were painted a glossy white, and the floor was tiled with a local imitation of Delft. To their surprise, Philip's younger brother Christian was awaiting them here.

Philip had never known his younger brother to voluntarily rise before 10 am, and he was flattered by the reception. Christian was still in his silk pajamas with a plaid bathrobe thrown over them, but he had hot coffee and tea waiting for them. Christian was 27 years old and a fighter pilot with the *Luftwaffe*.

The brothers embraced heartily. Christian congratulated Philip on his promotion, and then launched into an enthusiastic description of the new fighter his squadron had just received, the Messerschmitt (Me) 109.

Philip listened inattentively as he helped himself to breakfast. He envied Christian his easy charm, which won people's hearts no matter how much he defied customary rules of courtesy. Finished with the topic of airplanes, Christian moved naturally to his next favorite subject: women. "Did I tell you about Bärbel?" he asked his brother.

Philip shook his head without even looking up from the roll he was buttering.

"Well? Aren't you interested?" Christian insisted.

"Not particularly, but I presume you'll tell me about her anyway," Philip returned, pushing his glasses back up his nose. Since Christian had turned fifteen, Philip could not remember a time when Christian had not been "in love." Part of Philip even resented Christian's easy successes with women. He was bothered not so much by the fact that women fell for his brother, as by the way Christian himself seemed to feel no compulsion to avoid scandal or breaking hearts. Christian had always, even as a boy, seemed quite indifferent to what other people thought of him. He had gone his own way, risking the anger of their father, the disappointment of their mother, and the disapproval of the world at large.

Christian was checked only briefly by his brother's indifference. The desire to tell his latest adventure was too great. "She's a photo model! She came to the base for some propaganda photos they were doing. They dressed her up in some uniform and had her pose with us."

Philip glanced up, his glasses glinting. It did not surprise him that they would want to feature his younger brother in a propaganda picture. Christian had their mother's dark blond hair and their father's athletic build. It bothered him, however, that his brother was such a willing participant. "And you were happy to oblige the Minister for Propaganda and Public Enlightenment, Herr Goebbels, it seems."

"If you'd seen Bärbel, even you wouldn't have been able to resist! I've got the photos. Wait 'til I show you!"

Philip nodded, unconvinced, and redirected his attention to his breakfast. He didn't doubt that the girl was attractive in a blonde, sexy way, but he questioned whether she could put two intelligent sentences together. He could not imagine himself wanting anything to do with one of Goebbels' models.

Sophia Maria took advantage of the short lull in the conversation to announce, "There is something I want to discuss with you before Theresa arrives this evening."

Theresa was the youngest of the Feldburg children. Born at the end of the World War, she had just turned twenty and was attending a cooking and housekeeping school. Over a year ago, while doing her compulsory national labor service, she had fallen in love, and ever since then she had been trying to win her parents' permission to marry. Her father had strictly refused until his death.

Philip stiffened at the very mention of his sister's name, and glanced at Christian. Christian did not meet his eye, preferring to pour himself another cup of coffee at this moment.

"I've given my consent to the marriage," Sophia Maria announced. "The invitations will go out after the New Year and the date has been set for March 18th."

Even though half expecting this, Philip still found himself angered by the announcement. Walther Halle was a tradesman's son—an uneducated, self-made man lacking breeding, manners and cultivation. The thought of being related to him, much less to his family, was offensive. "Charming," Philip remarked sarcastically, and dropped his coffee cup down onto the saucer more loudly than necessary.

"I didn't have any choice," Sophia Maria defended herself to her eldest son. "Theresa said she'd marry him with or without my permission. It was a matter of accepting her decision or losing her."

"Is she pregnant?"

"How dare you! You have no right to suggest that about your own sister! Least of all Theresa!"

Philip felt too hostile toward his sister for selling herself so low to apologize, but he mentally acknowledged his mother was right: Theresa was too much of a self-righteous prig to get pregnant before she was married.

"Walther will be joining us for Christmas—" Sophia Maria held up her hand to stop Philip from protesting. "Promise me you will be civil to him. Please don't make this Christmas any more difficult than it already is." Sophia Maria steadied her gaze on her elder son and demanded of him the filial obedience she had always been able to exact. She was briefly conscious of the fact that she could not have brought Christian to heel with a similar request. Fortunately, Christian was less hostile to Walther and more ready to accept him for his sister's sake. Philip, however, cast her a bitter, openly resentful look as he felt the curb of expectations being applied again.

"Please, Philip," Sophie Maria reached out and put her hand on his, "for my sake."

He capitulated, touched as always when his mother favored him with some sign of special affection.

Theresa von Feldburg had Philip's dark good looks but Christian's athletic build. She wore her thick, dark hair braided and wound around her head. She never used makeup, but her face was naturally unblemished, and her eyes were well set off by dark lashes. This afternoon she wore a traditional dirndl with a white blouse and a silk shawl.

The walls of the Halle's apartment were covered with striped wallpaper and hung with paintings and photographs in elaborate frames. The heavy, dark furniture was draped with lace of indecipherable purpose and then laden with things: vases, clocks that didn't work, paperweights, porcelain figurines, photo albums and much, much more. The room was particularly crowded at the moment because of the Christmas tree and its accompanying presents.

While Theresa helped her future mother- and sisters-in-law in the kitchen, her future father-in-law set up the Christmas tree "in secret" in the parlor. At the ringing of a little bell, the women removed their aprons and joined the men in the parlor. The first sight of the tree with all its candles lit brought delighted exclamations from everyone.

The youngest of Theresa's future sisters-in-law recited (as quickly as possible) a poem she had memorized, and then the presents were distributed. Walther's father played Father Christmas, giving out the presents to one and all in a jolly manner appropriate to his role. He even looked the part, being almost as broad as he was tall. Walther claimed that he had a bad temper, but Theresa had never witnessed it. Compared to her own father, Theresa found Herr Halle more congenial. Theresa couldn't remember her father ever losing his temper, but he had rarely shown much warmth, either. Herr Halle, by contrast, had treated Theresa with hearty affection from the first day they met. He was also unabashedly proud of Walther. Theresa found this much preferable to the way her own father had always disapproved of everything Christian did.

Theresa found Frau Halle's uncritical doting and fussing endearing as well. Plump but energetic, Frau Halle had spent the day bustling about the kitchen and the house. She only sat still long enough for the poem. As soon as her husband started to distribute the gifts, she jumped up and rushed back into the kitchen. Thereafter she darted in and out doing this or that. If she did sit down for a moment, she chattered away, rarely giving anyone a chance to reply. A woman who had spent much of her life amusing babies, she seemed not to have fully adjusted to children who could talk back.

Theresa had adopted her future in-laws with a fierce loyalty that allowed no contradiction, no exceptions and no reservations. She looked about herself contentedly and thought: *this* is the way a family ought to be—boisterous, loud, relaxed and natural. She smiled up at Walther, who sat beside her on the sofa, holding her hand.

Ten years older than Theresa, Walther had almost white-blond hair cut short at the neck, parted neatly on the side and combed over the top of his head. His round, red-cheeked and smooth-shaven face was gentler than the fine, high cheekbones of her brothers. Theresa even considered it an advantage that Walther was just 5'7" and tended toward stockiness rather than being tall and lean. Walther was, quite simply, "cuddly." He was warm and soft to snuggle against. Indeed, he encouraged snuggling. Theresa looked forward, with what she considered unseemly eagerness, to losing her virginity to him.

But Theresa was not merely physically attracted to Walther. She was convinced that her choice of husband could not have been better from a genetic standpoint as well. Rather than marrying into another "worn-out" and "decadent" family, Theresa was bringing "fresh blood" into her family. She was sure her children would be stronger and healthier as a result. Besides, Walther represented the future rather than the past. Walther was a self-made man, not the product of privilege and birth.

Walther's father was a common locksmith, a man whose tiny, struggling business in a rented room had been wiped out by the inflation of 1923. He had been reduced to a common laborer and then further humiliated by over eighteen months of unemployment during the last years of the Weimar Republic. Herr

Halle had not seen a reversal of his fortunes until Hitler came to power. In the New *Reich*, he was able to find work, save money, and reopen a locksmith shop. But the years of economic hardship had left their scars—on his and Frau Halle's faces, in the early flight into vocational training of his son, and on Walther's own mentality.

Walther had watched his parents' painfully accumulated savings utterly devalued in a single year when the *Reichsmark* fell to worthlessness. He had seen how honesty and hard work, the sacred virtues of the nineteenth century, were useless in the tides of the twentieth. Walther, blessed with an innate entrepreneurial talent, had chosen to abandon the wisdom of his forefathers. Walther never put his savings in a bank; he reinvested. A natural charmer, he had many "friends," and when he brought friends together for mutually productive business, he expected a little financial return. Best of all, he had vision and the ability to make others believe his vision. A few years back, he had convinced an acquaintance with a little extra cash to invest in the production of a leather pouch with a lock similar to a briefcase lock. This product had been selected by the motorcycle corps of the expanding *Wehrmacht* as a courier pouch. Walther was now manager and half-owner of a prospering factory.

It was this astonishing capability to rise above his heritage that seemed such convincing evidence of Walther's superiority. When Theresa looked at her brothers, it was clear to her that their achievements were paltry by comparison. Regardless of how tiny and exclusive the General Staff was, Philip's admittance could hardly be described as terribly surprising. He had enjoyed every possible advantage—from title, wealth and natural intelligence to the best education money could buy. Walther had had none of that. A comparison to Christian was even more disadvantageous to the Feldburgs. Much as Theresa loved Christian, she had to admit that despite the advantages of birth, education and good looks, Christian hadn't really made much of himself. Theresa's father had once said that a pilot was little more than a "glorified bus driver." And what became of fighter pilots when their reflexes started to deteriorate? Christian's answer "They become Minister of the Interior" might be a clever reference to Hermann Goering, but it was hardly a serious prospect.

Walther's prospects, in contrast, were seemingly endless. If he could rise from saddler's apprentice to small industrialist in just fifteen years—and all without the benefit of a penny of his own capital or a high-school education—then there seemed no limit to where he might be fifteen years from now. Theresa was certain that Walther would be far wealthier than her brothers on their modest officer's salaries and tied as they were to agriculture. Theresa saw Walther and herself as the new elite.

Theresa looked up proudly at the man beside her, and Walther, sensing her gaze, tossed her a wink. Then he turned to his father and announced, "I'm afraid Theresa and I are going to have to get going. The Baroness von Feldburg is expecting us around six."

"Oh, no! Not *yet!*" his mother protested. "You haven't had a single piece of Christmas cake!"

"I couldn't eat another bite," Walther responded, patting his stomach contentedly. "But you could wrap up a couple of pieces for us to take with us."

His mother jumped up to comply, but her husband stopped her. "We should drink a toast first. Walther, pour champagne for everyone."

"Now, Kurt. Not the girls. They're too young."

"Not at all—not with Walther in the family, that is." Herr Halle chuckled happily; Walther had provided the champagne. It was the first time they had had it since the World War.

When everyone stood holding their glasses containing the bubbly, golden liquid, Herr Halle lifted his glass. His expression serious, like a soldier at attention before his commanding general, he declared: "The *Führer!* Who has given the workers work and businessmen business, who has restored national pride and rebuilt our Armed Forces, and who—most important of all—has without war brought all German people together into one New *Reich. Heil Hitler!*"

In the Feldburg manor, the formal rooms had been opened. Candles burned in crystal chandeliers and silver candelabra. The silk wall panels glowed and the parquet floors gleamed. The gilt edgings of the moldings on the ceiling, framing the wall panels, and around the windows glinted. The tall tree in the central window over the carriage entry held tiny honey-wax candles, which cast a soft, tremorous light. The entire household was gathered around the tree in their finest apparel.

Josef, the coachman, and Herr Opitz, the butler, wore livery, and Herr Lauterbach, the gardener, his best (and only) blue suit. The Feldburg brothers were in the dress uniforms of their respective services, with ceremonial swords. Frau Opitz and Frau Lauterbach, the upstairs maids, wore dirndls of only slightly lower quality than Theresa's own. Heidi, Sophia Maria's personal maid and Josef's 42-year-old unmarried daughter, wore a made-over, second-hand evening gown from 1916. Martha, the cook, wore a velvet gown in deep purple that made her look like Queen Victoria. The kitchen maids, Lucie and Franziska, were in cotton dirndls with velveteen vests. Sophia Maria wore an evening gown in black satin and lace, the gown made for mourning her father six years earlier.

As they finished singing "Silent Night," an awkward silence fell on the gathered household. At this point, it was traditional for Baron von Feldburg to read the Christmas story from one of the gospels. "Philip," Sophia Maria called. She held out the Bible to him.

Philip obeyed immediately. He took his father's place with his back to the tree and Sophia Maria to his right and read the holy text. But it was not something he would have chosen to do. He did not read well out loud. He stumbled over the text and lost his place in the dim light, fussing with his glasses as he tried to find his place again. He was glad when it was over, and the others seemed glad, too.

Sophia Maria then distributed a gift to each member of the staff. They were things she had bought herself, things she knew they needed. They were practical gifts that would be used, not shelved. Then the staff withdrew with thanks and best wishes for a merry Christmas, leaving the family to their private gift-giving.

The Feldburg presents were modest, as always. As children they had been encouraged to make things themselves rather than purchase gifts. Although they no longer had time for such efforts, the gifts exchanged still represented the search for something witty or particularly desired rather than something extravagant. Walther's gifts glittered by comparison: a silver cigarette case for Christian, a silver-headed riding whip for Philip, an imported perfume bedded in a silk scarf for Sophia Maria, and a garnet bracelet for Theresa.

Theresa flung her arms around Walther's neck and thanked him profusely. She put the bracelet on at once. Then she took Walther by the arm with the words, "Come see what I've baked!" She led him to a long buffet laden not only with cold cuts, cheese and fresh bread, but also with every imaginable Christmas sweet. A large silver punch bowl suspended over a candle flame contained hot mulled wine with pieces of cinnamon, orange and lemon floating on top. At the other end of the table, a silver tray with cut-crystal champagne glasses waited beside an ice-filled bucket holding a bottle of French champagne.

Sophia Maria nodded toward the champagne and said simply, "Philip."

Philip opened and poured, bringing a glass to each of the others, starting with his mother and Walther. Last of all, he filled his own glass and lifted it. "Merry Christmas."

The others echoed him.

Christian then called for attention and with a smile to Theresa toasted, "Theresa, the most beautiful little sister in the world." Theresa blushed and Walther gave her a quick kiss just below the ear while the others said "Theresa!"

Theresa raised her glass and suggested, "To your new son and brother!"

Without demur Philip, Christian and Sophia Maria raised their glasses along with Theresa and murmured, "Walther"—if somewhat less enthusiastically than they had toasted Theresa herself.

Sophia Maria lifted her glass to Philip: "Herr *Rittmeister* von Feldburg."

They all toasted Philip.

Walther clearly felt it was now his turn and he solemnly suggested, "To the *Führer*, to whom we owe this peaceful Christmas."

Only Theresa raised her glass. Sophia Maria and Christian froze, while Philip abruptly put his glass down. "I won't drink to that," he announced.

Walther was too flabbergasted to respond at once. He had not for a moment thought a toast to the *Führer* might be taken amiss. Although he knew that many aristocrats, and particularly army officers, snobbishly looked down on the new regime, Theresa had never indicated that her family was like that. Quite the opposite, she had seemed every bit as enthusiastic about the Party as he was himself.

"Oh, come on, Philip," Christian urged, trying to restore a festive mood. He lifted his own glass, but Philip remained stubborn.

"Hitler is not responsible for this peaceful Christmas," Philip insisted with a hard, bitter expression.

Walther, recovered from his initial amazement and encouraged by Christian's evident support, risked contradiction—albeit in a jovial, friendly tone. He did not want to offend his future brother-in-law, after all, but he was used to having his opinions applauded by his friends and admiring family. "Who else but the *Führer* could have given us back the Sudetenland without war? You must know better than most of us how close we came to war this past autumn." A little flattery could never hurt, Walther thought.

"My division was deployed on the Czech border," Philip confirmed in a clipped tone, "and that is exactly the point: Hitler brought us to the very brink of an unnecessary, two-front war for which this country is not prepared and which we would have lost at a terrible price. Hitler gambled not only with the lives of our soldiers, who would have been sacrificed, but with the very survival of the nation. Just what kind of peace terms do you think the Allies would have dictated this time?"

Christian was quick to ask, "What makes you so sure we would have lost? We would have had air supremacy in a couple of days and after that—"

"No war ever has been or ever will be won in the air," Philip told his younger brother sharply, annoyed that he was taking Walther's side.

Walther, still working hard to maintain a friendly, even amused, tone, hastened to explain to Philip, "Don't you see? The *Führer* only appeared to risk war. In fact, he'd taken the measure of the spineless Western leaders when he reoccupied the Rhineland. He didn't risk war, he just threatened it—and once again he proved he had assessed the West correctly. He got exactly what he set out to get: the return of the Sudetenland to the *Reich* without bloodshed."

"The Sudetenland never belonged to the *Reich*, so it can hardly return," Philip pointed out coldly, ignoring Christian's groan. "As for making a distinction between risking a war and merely threatening it, you are suggesting that it makes sense to threaten someone who *can* bludgeon you to death on the assumption that he won't *want* to."

"If you know your opponent is bluffing, it makes for brilliant poker," Walther countered with a grin.

"And you find it appropriate for a Head of State to play poker with the national existence?" Philip shot back with raised eyebrows.

Sophia Maria decided it was time for her to intervene. "Enough said, Philip. Let's have supper."

But Walther was now provoked beyond the point where he was willing to let things lie. Ignoring his hostess and Theresa tugging at his elbow, he said to Philip without any attempt to smile, "I think we should respect and admire a Head of State who plays political poker so flawlessly."

"I'm sorry." Philip was determined to make a closing statement. "I can personally only detest a Head of State who is so irresponsible as to risk the national existence for the sake of secondary objectives."

Walther was so shocked by this attitude that for the first time he sounded angry as he demanded, "You consider freeing Germans from Czech tyranny a 'secondary objective'?"

"You'd best check the definition of 'tyranny.' What they have in Czechoslovakia is a good deal farther from tyranny than what we have here in Germany." Philip turned pointedly toward the table to indicate the discussion was over.

Walther did not intend to let any arrogant aristocrat dismiss him as if he were a mere servant. Raising his voice, he demanded, "You prefer Weimar chaos, perhaps?"

"Indeed, I do!" Philip swung back. "Look what happened just six weeks ago!" Suddenly Philip's tone of disapproval and criticism turned to anger. The events of the so-called "*Kristallnacht*" on Nov. 9th had so shaken and shamed him that he continued in a tone of rising agitation, "We won't ever live down the shame of that pogrom."

"If you mean the riots of Nov. 9th—" Walther started, but Philip didn't let him finish.

"There were no riots. Organized mobs, primarily the SA, smashed shop windows and looted like common hooligans. They crammed rings on their fingers and stuffed watches in their pockets. What they couldn't carry away, they broke and left heaped in the gutters. In Berlin!" he stressed in outrage. "The city that welcomed the Jews and Huguenots! The Capital of Germany! I was raised to believe we were a civilized people, a nation that had brought forth great achievements in the arts, music, philosophy and science. And six weeks ago I walked through the wreckage of plunder such as no city in Europe has witnessed since the Thirty Years' War!"

Walther had been appalled by the excesses of Nov. 9th, too, and this—as well as Theresa's increasingly firm hold on his elbow and her strained face—induced him to seek a conciliatory tone. "Well, of course I don't support that sort of thing, but excesses have to be expected when emotions are running high—"

"Emotions? Excesses? We aren't talking about a beer-hall brawl! We're talking about systematic plunder and vandalism—even assault—directed against innocent citizens by the para-military forces of their own state!"

"It's not their state," Walther countered firmly, patting Theresa's hand reassuringly. He could tell how upset she was and he wanted to end the argument—but not by kowtowing to her stuck-up brother. Walther knew he had the forces of history on his side, and he told Philip simply, "We don't want them here. They should have emigrated."

Sophia Maria, too, had noticed Theresa's increasing distress. She was so stunned by Walther's attitude, however, that her intention of preventing Philip from answering died on her lips unspoken. Philip meanwhile shot back, "Where to? Where would you go if you were suddenly told you weren't wanted in Germany anymore?"

Walther frowned and his answer was defensive, "What do you mean!? I'm not a Jew!"

"So?"

"You're not making sense. Only the Jews were attacked. Only the Jews should go."

"Where are Jews born in Germany, the children and grandchildren of Germans, supposed to go, if they can't stay in the country where they were born, educated, employed and served?"

Walther shrugged. "I don't care. America. Why not?"

"The question is why?"

"Stop it, Philip!" Theresa burst out, close to tears. "Why do you have to ruin Christmas?!"

"Walther started this!" Philip told his sister, but his mother and brother both jumped on him. While Christian protested, "It takes two to fight," Sophia Maria simply insisted, "That's enough!"

Christian started talking about his squadron and Bärbel, and Walther took the peace offering gratefully. He chatted with Christian while frequently patting Theresa's hand and sending her little smiles and kisses, until the tears were blinked away and she too joined in the chatter.

They got through supper like that, with Sophia Maria asking Walther polite questions about his family and business and Philip holding his tongue. Finally, when they all insisted they had had enough to eat, Sophia Maria stood to clear the table. Christian and Philip at once jumped up to forestall her. "You sit down, Mamá," Christian ordered. "We'll take care of this." As he spoke, he grabbed a silver tray propped up against the buffet. Almost before Walther could take it in, the Feldburg sons had loaded two trays, blown out the candles, and rolled up the linen tablecloth. With the tablecloth clipped under his elbow, Philip picked up one tray and Christian the other.

Downstairs, as they unloaded the trays, Philip couldn't contain himself any longer. "Theresa's completely under the influence of that ass! She did nothing but spout rubbish all evening: 'The *Führer* doesn't know about the excesses of the SA,' 'The *Führer* is modest and embarrassed when the crowds cheer him,' 'The *Führer* has miraculous visions about the future!' Walther can't believe that stuff himself!"

"I don't think she got it from him. It was her National Service," Christian explained. "Theresa was always lonely. You and I were too much older and besides, we were boys. She couldn't tag along with us when we were home, and Papá made the mistake of not sending her to boarding school. He knew he was dying and he wanted at least one of his children near him. I can't blame him, but it probably wasn't good for Theresa. It's not just that she didn't get a particularly good education, it's that here she couldn't make any friends. The other girls at school were told to 'be careful' around the 'Fräulein Baronin.' They didn't feel at ease with her. It wasn't until Theresa did her National Labor Service that she felt really accepted by anyone. Suddenly she had lots of friends and lots of fun. Naturally, she lapped up everything else, too. She's been taken in by all the slogans about working together for the sake of the common good. She's had her head turned by the feeling of community, and has no reason not to believe everything she's been told by her leaders and teachers."

"You missed your calling as a lawyer," Philip remarked dryly.

"Rubbish," Christian brushed off the compliment. "I just know her better than you do. You're almost ten years older than she is, and you've always looked on and treated her like a child."

Philip didn't answer. He tossed the dirty tablecloth into a dirty-clothes hamper and replaced the perishables in the pantry, while Christian put away the bread and started to run hot water in the sink for rinsing off the dishes. Philip came over and put the plug in the sink. "We might as well wash them properly; I can't stand Walther a minute longer than necessary."

Upstairs, Sophia Maria was having a hard time. Theresa and Walther had seated themselves on the sofa and were cuddling so close together she found it indecent. Not that it really was, but she could tell that Theresa was letting Walther "comfort" her—as if he hadn't been just as much to blame for the argument as Philip. Then again, she resented it whenever Theresa and Walther were overtly affectionate, because in her heart she was still not reconciled to the marriage. Abruptly she understood how her mother-in-law might have resented her own North German, Lutheran heritage as much as she herself now resented Walther's petty bourgeois National Socialism.

Turning to Walther and Theresa, she announced, "I was Lutheran, you know. I only converted to marry Theresa's father, Ferdinand. But we were living in Berlin and were surrounded by my family more than the Feldburgs, so it didn't seem to matter much. Nothing much had really changed. Then the war came and I was sent here. I suddenly discovered I was an outsider, an unwelcome outsider, who could never do anything right as far as my mother-in-law was concerned. The worst of it was that my mother-in-law wasn't content to lecture and bully me; she wrote letters to my husband cataloging all my shortcomings. I had to hear the same criticism and reprimands from Ferdinand by mail. It nearly ruined our marriage."

Theresa stared wide-eyed. She had never known this. She had been born at the end of the war and her Grandma Feldburg had died when she was only five. Walther didn't know what to make of the abrupt confession of his distant and cool-hearted mother-in-law.

Sophia Maria herself continued after an awkward pause, "What I wanted to say, Walther, is that I won't ever do that to you. I won't go behind your back to Theresa. But you mustn't expect us to agree on everything, either, or to evade confrontation. The children have been raised to say what they think."

Walther thanked her and murmured something about being sure everyone would get along just fine in the future. He smiled and patted Theresa's hand as he spoke. Then he suggested it was time for him to turn in. Theresa at once jumped to her feet, saying she'd show him the way (although he'd already taken his suitcase to the guest room and knew where it was). Theresa kissed her mother good night, and Sophia Maria was left alone in the salon.

Philip found her there in the near darkness. All the candles were out and only the dying fire lit up the room. "Is everything all right, Mamá?"

She held out her hand to him with a sad smile.

He came into the room and took her hand. "I'm sorry—"

"Shhh! Christian was right: it takes two."

Philip was tired and depressed. He removed his glasses and pressed his fingers to the bridge of his nose where they'd left their mark. Without directly looking at his mother, he asked, "Do you ever wonder if it's possible that we're the only sane people left in a world gone mad? I mean, if we're right, why are we such a small minority?" There was no answer. The fire was almost out and the room increasingly cold. One of the charred logs broke in two and crumbled into glowing embers on the floor of the fireplace.

Philip shook his head. "Maybe Theresa is right in a way. If you can't fight them...."

CHAPTER 2

▼

Berlin
September 1939

The officer on duty returned and informed Philip that there was no answer to his inquiry. "If I were you, I'd take advantage of the situation," he remarked, with a longing look at the late summer evening outside his office window. "Why not go home early for a change?"

"With suggestions like that, you'll soon be a general's adjutant," Philip quipped. "I'll check in first thing in the morning."

He returned through the warren of interconnected corridors to his own utilitarian office. It was exactly one window wide, with barely room enough for his wooden desk and a visitor's chair. It looked out over a small courtyard that had no other purpose than to provide light to the offices that faced it. The only personal touch in the entire office was a nineteenth-century etching of the Battle of Waterloo. It showed a young French officer on a rearing horse reporting to Napoleon, with an outstretched arm pointing toward the columns of troops visible in the distance. It was titled: "The arrival of the Prussians at Waterloo."

Yet this cramped cubby-hole was a source of pride for Philip, because it was located in the "Bendlerblock." This was the complex of offices that had housed the entire *Reichswehr* Ministry in the inter-war years and was now occupied by a number of key departments of the General Staff. His assignment here represented his probationary assignment to the General Staff. The prestige was particularly great in this case, because most graduates of the War College were sent to staff positions with the troops. It was a rare privilege to be allowed to work in any of the central offices.

Collecting his cap and belt, Philip left the Bendlerblock and went out onto the quiet side street that stretched between the Landwehr Canal and the Tiergarten, the large central park of Berlin. He passed the waiting staff cars with their fender-flags and bored drivers, and reached the canal just as his bus pulled away from the stop on the other side of the bridge. He decided to walk home and turned to stroll along the canal, enjoying the late summer evening.

An excursion boat, its flat, open upper deck crowded with school-children, chugged up the canal. The children, boys and girls of 9 or 10, looked weary as they lined the rail and tossed crumbs to the ducks. They'd probably spent the day on one of Berlin's large lakes, the Wannsee or Tegler See. Some things didn't change even under the Nazis—or ten days into a war.

This sobering thought made Philip sigh. He remembered the outbreak of the last war. His nanny had taken him to Berlin's main avenue, Unter den Linden. She had intended to take him all the way to the royal palace to cheer the Kaiser, but the press of people had been too great. They had found a place on the curb in front of the National Library, and there they had watched as hundreds and hundreds of troops marched past bedecked with flowers. The crowd around them had been jovial, excited, bubbling with good will. A strange man had offered to hold Philip on his shoulders so Philip could see better. Another man had given him a flag to wave. Everyone seemed to have flags to wave or flowers to throw. More than once, women broke from the crowd to rush into the street and bestow a kiss on a passing soldier. Philip asked his nanny if he could run out to his father or uncles if they marched by. His nanny sternly told him he most certainly could NOT. The other people had laughed—but it had been friendly laughter.

It had not been like that on Sept. 1, 1939. The people stood with wary, guarded faces when the news blared from the loudspeakers that "Since the early hours of the morning, German troops have been returning Polish fire." Later, when the Army paraded through the streets, it had been met by silent, sober crowds. Here and there a Party member or an enthusiastic youth had flung out his arm in the Hitler salute, but the masses were eloquently silent. They did not want war and were in no mood to rejoice.

As yet there had not been a single enemy plane in the skies over Berlin, however. There had been no shots fired on the "West Wall" with France. Even the fear of shortages had proved unfounded. German forces continued to slice through Poland, cutting through the country from three directions and mauling the large Polish Army with surprising ease. The only news these days were the Special Armed Forces Bulletins, announced with trumpet fanfares, which reported fresh advances, new victories, or the sinking of unfortunate enemy merchantmen caught at sea.

The sidewalk cafés and bars that Philip passed were filled with customers. They drank their evening beer under the unlit strings of colored lights, indifferent to the blackout. From snatches of overheard conversations, Philip gathered that the mood had shifted from anxiety to overbearing self-satisfaction. Suddenly everyone was a desk-chair strategist who could explain the *Wehrmacht*'s spectacular success, predict the fall of Poland, and dismiss the importance of the French and British armed forces contemptuously.

The Feldburgs' Berlin apartment was located in one of the apartment houses on the canal. The building dated from the 1880s, when this section of Berlin had been relatively new and a large number of officers, civil servants and professionals had made their homes here. Paul *Graf* Walmsdorf, Philip's maternal grandfather, had inherited a sizable fortune from a childless aunt, who had married an "industrial baron." Her husband had not only invested in railways and coal mines, but had also speculated in property in Berlin. Among other properties, he had built this five-story apartment house. The house had been given to Philip's grandfather in 1888. He had redecorated the first floor for himself and his young family and continued to rent out the rest. There were a total of fourteen apartments to let: two on the second floor, and four on the ground and each of the remaining upper floors.

The central entrance was a very ornate doorway at the head of a short walkway flanked by a narrow, well-tended garden. The heavy wooden door with beveled glass opened into a cool, tall entry hall. The floor, walls and curving stairway were all Italian marble. To the left and right, elaborately framed mirrors hung over decorative fireplaces with polished brass grates. The underside of the stairway, as it curved back overhead, had gilded moldings, which framed a romantic hunting scene done in oil on canvas.

Philip let himself in with his house key and would have gone straight upstairs, but he was intercepted by the concierge. The concierge lived in the front ground-floor apartment, accessed by a door behind the stairs. From his front windows he kept an eye on all the comings and goings in the house. "*Herr Baron*!" he called out respectfully, emerging from behind the stairs.

Philip stopped and waited.

Theo Pfalz was a man in his fifties with an ugly burn scar on the right side of his face and neck. This dated from the Great War, when he'd served as an aircraft mechanic. His hands, too, had been so badly burned that he had been reduced to begging after the war until Philip's grandfather gave him the job here. For the last seven or eight years he had appeared only in an SA uniform, which he had already outgrown in girth. The buttons pulled apart on his belly and the leather belt was pushed down so low it was hardly visible.

"What is it, Herr Pfalz?" Philip asked.

"Frau Professor Dr. Moldenauer would like to speak to you, *Herr Baron*. She's been by twice to ask if you were back yet." This was the wife of one of his other tenants, Professor Dr. Moldenauer. They lived in one of the two spacious apartments on the second floor.

"Do you know what this is about?"

"No, but it must be important. She looked very worried."

"Thank you. Please send her up if she asks again." Philip continued up the stairs.

The Feldburg apartment occupied the entire first floor, with grand representational rooms across the front of the house and living rooms stretching back in two wings around the central courtyard. The kitchen, pantry, wash-room and servant quarters occupied the rooms across the back of the house beyond the courtyard. All the rooms looked onto the neatly planted courtyard, and a service entrance from the back of the courtyard provided access for deliveries and servants directly to the rooms at the back.

In the dining room, a cold supper was set out, and Philip's mail was stacked neatly beside the place setting. This was the work of his housekeeper, who came every afternoon to clean, iron and do the laundry. Philip looked through the mail without sitting down. Finding a letter from his mother, he settled himself comfortably in a chair and began to read. Then the doorbell rang.

Philip let Frau Moldenauer in at the front door and led her to the sitting room. Frau Moldenauer was a woman in her early fifties. She had been raised in Hamburg, the daughter of a liberal and successful lawyer. She had studied classics at university, where she had met, fallen in love with, and married one of her professors. The Moldenauers had moved into the gracious ten-room flat on the second floor of the Feldburg apartment house in 1913, when Professor Dr. Moldenauer was appointed to his chair at the Humboldt University in Berlin. Philip switched on the electric chandelier and asked Frau Moldenauer to take a seat.

Frau Moldenauer sat primly on the edge of her chair and held her black leather purse in both hands on her knees. She suddenly felt intimidated by her landlord—particularly his youth and uniform. Raised in a liberal tradition, she did not share the national adulation for the military. Quite the opposite, she associated the military with the arch-conservative, feudal elements she had been raised to distrust. Now she was forced to come begging favors of an officer. And to make it worse, this officer was young enough to be her own son. Her pride could not suffer it, and she abandoned her original scheme.

"What can I do for you, Frau Professor Moldenauer?" the young officer asked politely, with a face that betrayed neither impatience nor curiosity behind his wire-framed glasses.

"Actually, it's just that I'm afraid we will have to move out of the flat, and I've come to give you the requisite six months' notice." She blurted all this out in a rush, to avoid breaking down somewhere in the middle.

The news clearly took her landlord by surprise. He gave her a startled, disbelieving look. "I'm sorry to hear that. You and your family seem so much a part of the house." Philip had been only three, after all, when they moved in.

These words expressed her feelings so exactly, that Frau Moldenauer had a hard time maintaining her composure. The apartment was her home. She had decorated it piece by piece, had raised her children in it, and had expected to grow old and die in it. She hated and dreaded the very thought of looking for another apartment, of moving, of getting to know new neighbors, finding new shops. Worse still, she knew that finding an apartment they could afford meant moving into a smaller apartment in a less fashionable or less convenient part of the city. It meant throwing away beloved possessions and a humiliating reduction in their standard of living—as if the humiliation of her husband's forced retirement in 1933 hadn't been bad enough.

Her husband had been dismissed from the university, forced into early retirement and condemned to living on a pittance, all because he had suggested in a single lecture that the burning of books was "an adolescent gesture unworthy of a great nation." Frau Moldenauer quite agreed with her husband that it was a disgrace for a nation in the twentieth century to engage in book-burning. As a professor of literature, her husband had been quite right to protest the banning and burning of books by such authors as Heinrich Mann or Stefan Zweig. But he should have been more careful about where, when and to whom he protested. He should have known that if he said such things in public, students or jealous colleagues would report him for "disloyal" remarks. He should have known that he would be hounded from his lectern by heckling students and subjected to unpleasant assaults. They had smashed up his car windows and dumped garbage in his office. The university authorities had reacted with a panicked insistence on his immediate resignation—ten years before he was entitled to his pension.

But there was no point in thinking about it. As long as their son had had his law practice, he had been able to pay the bulk of his parents' rent. Frau Moldenauer pulled herself together and told the young army officer opposite her, "Since our son Konrad has been recalled to active service and has had to give up his law practice, he won't be living with us anymore."

"I see; you don't feel you need the space?" Feldburg put the words into her mouth neatly. Frau Moldenauer looked over, startled and relieved by his apparent misunderstanding of her motives. When she met Philip's eyes, however, she had the uncanny feeling that he had not really misunderstood the situation at all. It was rather as if he had missed nothing that she had either said or left unsaid. "Yes," she confirmed, looking down at her purse as she collected herself and got to her feet. "And now I really must run."

Philip also stood, but he stood in her way. "Please, don't be hasty with such a major decision. Obviously, if you really wish to move, I have no say in the matter, but if you should only find yourself in financial difficulties, then perhaps another solution could be found."

Frau Moldenauer looked up, clinging to her purse more fiercely than ever.

"Forgive me, if I have offended you by mistaking the situation—"

Frau Moldenauer sat down again. "No. You have understood perfectly. Konrad has been helping us with the rent, and now that he's been called up.... And the war could go on forever once the French attack...."

Philip smiled faintly. So not everyone was taken in by the early successes. He, too, reseated himself. "I don't wish to pry, but if you could give me a rough idea of what your son has been contributing, it's possible that I could reduce the rent by a comparable amount."

"You'd do that for us?" She looked up at him with wide, wet eyes, her lips almost trembling.

"Frau Prof. Dr. Moldenauer, as I said, you are part of this house. You have been excellent tenants for as long as I can remember. It would be unthinkable for me to throw you out at this stage on account of a few marks a month."

Frau Moldenauer felt ashamed of her earlier negative thoughts about "arch-conservative militarists." Clearly, here was a man whose "conservatism" included viewing profit as incidental or secondary to fairness. Humbled, she calculated the maximum that she and her husband could afford to pay in rent and named the difference between this and her present rent: "20 *Reichsmark*."

"I'd be happy to reduce the rent by that amount. I'll inform my lawyer tomorrow—if that is what you'd like, that is?"

"*Rittmeister* Freiherr von Feldburg! I'd—we'd—be so grateful!"

"Good; consider it done. Was there anything else?"

"No, Herr von Feldburg. I can't begin to tell you how grateful, how *happy* my husband will be—and Marianne!" Marianne was their eighteen-year-old daughter, who still lived at home. "It means so much to her not to be far from the university. She hopes to study medicine, you know, starting next fall, as soon as she's finished her National Labor Service."

"I'm pleased I could be of assistance." They were both on their feet again. Philip escorted Frau Moldenauer to the door and they shook hands. With a last sincere "Thank you so much," she was gone.

∗   ∗   ∗   ∗

Stuttgart

Theresa Halle was in the kitchen of her new apartment, preparing tea while her husband entertained a business visitor in the little parlor. As she was now five months pregnant, she moved less energetically and tired more easily. Even a simple task, like taking the silver tray down from the cupboard, required an effort. The young maid, noting her mistress's little sigh as she went on tiptoe, jumped up from the potatoes she was peeling and rushed over with an alert, "I'll get it!"

Trude had the tray down in a moment and set it on the table for her mistress. Theresa thanked her and sat down at the table. She carefully opened a bag of tarts and cakes she had bought at the bakery. "I just wish I'd had time to bake something myself," she remarked wistfully to Trude. "It seems so lazy to offer bakery goods, but we had no warning at all." She arranged the tarts on a platter, placed it on the tray, and looked around for the creamer and sugar. As she stood to get them, she glanced at Trude and reminded her, "Don't peel the potatoes too thickly." Theresa had received a lecture from her neighbor for being "wasteful" because her potato peelings in the common garbage had been too thick. "Carelessness and wastefulness," her neighbor had reminded her, "are the roots of bad housekeeping. Don't you have more pride in being a German housewife than that?"

Theresa had a great deal of pride in being a good housewife, and she was determined to demonstrate this to her nosy and bitchy neighbor. For a start, she intended to ostentatiously prepare a "single-pot meal" once a week just as the *Führer* recommended. Turning to Trude, she asked, "Did you remember to cut out that new casserole recipe?"

"Oh, yes." Trude dried her hands on her apron and pulled a folded slip of paper torn from a magazine out of her skirt pocket. Beside the recipe was an appetizing picture of the completed dish, and the text admonished: "German Housewives! Remember! Although your only weapon is the kitchen spoon, by the preparation of wholesome and economical meals to nourish your families, you, too, contribute to VICTORY! Prepare this casserole to the delight of your men-folk and give the money you save to the Winter Help!"

"Yes, this looks good," Theresa decided. "We'll try it." She set the recipe aside and took the sugar and creamer from the shelf. From the pantry she took cream and filled the creamer.

The light, popular music that had been playing on the radio was abruptly interrupted by a tense, self-important voice: "Attention! Attention! Stand by for an important announcement!" Both women at once stopped everything and stood motionless, their eyes fixed on the large wooden radio. The blare of trum-pets was followed by another sharp, clear voice which began in precise radio Ger-man: "The Supreme Command of the Armed Forces announces: After the capture early yesterday morning of two of Warsaw's most important defensive fortresses, Polish forces defending Warsaw offered capitulation. At noon today, the documents were signed, ending the siege of the Polish capital. For their part in the capture of the two fortresses ..."

"Thank God!" Theresa exclaimed sincerely. "That means the war is as good as over!"

"What about the French?" Trude asked. Her father had spent three years on the Western Front in the last year and had a healthy respect for the French Army.

"Oh, France won't fight now that Poland is defeated," Theresa assured her blithely. She'd heard Walther say this.

The kettle started to whimper, and Theresa reached for it just as it started to scream. When the tea was ready, she put it on the tray and backed out of the kitchen, pushing the door open with her foot.

Walther's guest, a man his own age, sat in the most comfortable armchair at the head of the coffee table in the Halles' parlor. Theresa had worked hard to give some elegance to the rectangular, low-ceilinged room with its unadorned walls, but she was not satisfied with the results. She noted now that the tall guest banged his knees against the low table as he leaned forward in discussion with Walther, and she felt it was a personal disgrace. Her interest, however, was drawn primarily to the visitor himself. He was a big man already a little thick around the waist, throat and chin, and his features were broad and common. Theresa would have thought him a worker—a miner, perhaps or a farmer—if it had not been for his tailored suit, his manicured hands, and the diamond cufflinks that flashed as he slowly lifted a cigarette to his mouth and back. On his lapel was a gold swas-tika pin. On the table, his cigarette case was enameled with a black, white and red swastika flag.

As Theresa entered, she caught his low but intense words to Walther, "... the opportunity of a lifetime. Those who get in first are going to have the best pickings. Too much hesitation and all you'll get are scraps—if anything at all. I'm only down here out of friendship, Walther, as old teammates and all."

"I appreciate that, Arthur." Walther was sitting on the sofa at the end nearest his guest and leaning forward, his elbows on his knees. His expression was earnest. "But as you've explained it, these *Treuhänder* are employees of the East Trust Agency. They manage the factories entrusted to them, but they don't own them."

"Not yet. We're a holding company of sorts, representing the interests of the State—a temporary wartime expediency to ensure the most rapid and efficient subordination of Polish industrial capacity to *Reich* requirements. But after the Victory, Walther, things will be normalized, and in the meantime—"

Theresa set the tray down at the other end of the coffee table. She smiled at the two men, who had—until then—not noticed her arrival.

Walther sat back, almost as if startled, and smiled broadly. "Sweetheart! How nice!" The other man nodded assent.

"I've just got to get the plates and cups," Theresa apologized, unloading the tray.

"Wonderful," Walther assured her inattentively.

"As I was saying," the other man resumed as she turned to leave, "once the situation has stabilized, all the industries managed by the East Trust Agency will be turned over to German entrepreneurs—but you've got to know the situation, the market, and have the right contacts and connections."

Theresa reentered the kitchen, set the tray down, and started to load it with the cups, saucers, plates, silverware and napkins. Then she backed once more into the hall. The guest was still speaking. "We're talking about practically free labor. No hassles about minimum wage, no hassles about maximum hours—not even for women and minors—and you don't have to worry about safety regulations and the like, either."

Walther snorted skeptically. "That doesn't sound like the *Reich* government I know! A free hand without a shitload of regulations?"

Theresa recoiled to hear her husband use such crude language, but then he didn't know she was within hearing.

"I'm not saying there are no regulations, Walther; only that they work to the advantage of the Trustees, the *Treuhänder*—or can be made to."

Theresa came through the door and both men, who had been leaning forward, at once sat back. "It looks wonderful, darling," Walther praised.

"Yes, wonderful," the guest echoed.

Theresa set the plates, cups and silverware before the men, hoping they would resume their talk, but again they waited until she had exited. This time, however, she did not go back to the kitchen. Instead she lurked in the hall, eavesdropping.

"Did you have something particular in mind?" Walther asked.

"The garment industry in Warsaw is almost exclusively in Jewish hands."

"I don't know anything about clothing! I'm a leather and lock man!"

"You don't have to know anything about clothing. The former owners will be right there running the business for you, making sure it turns a handsome profit, working the late hours while you stay home and enjoy your bride."

"Why should the former owners help me make a profit?" Walther asked skeptically.

Arthur laughed heartily and slapped Walther on the back. "Sometimes you really are naive!" He laughed again, and then patiently explained, "The former owners will work themselves to the bone for you—and on wages hardly good enough to starve on—because they're Jews. If they don't work to your satisfaction, they're going to find themselves out on the street, and winter's coming on fast."

There was a long pause, and then Walther said, "I'd like to think about it."

"Fine, but don't think too long. Warsaw is about to fall, and then we go straight in. The early bird catches the worm."

"I understand."

Theresa had hardly seen Arthur out the door before she asked her husband, "And what was that all about?"

"A business proposition," Walther replied evasively.

"And you think I don't have a right to hear about it?" Theresa challenged indignantly. "Your business decisions affect me and our child," she reminded him sharply, her hand going to her belly.

"I know. I don't make any decisions without thinking about how it will affect you, but it's not your place to interfere," he told her firmly, frowning to show his displeasure.

"Interfere? Who said anything about interfering? I simply asked what this is about," Theresa told him with an air of self-righteous superiority.

"All right," Walther answered with a set face. "It's about a business opportunity in Warsaw once the war is over there."

"It already is. Trude and I heard the announcement while I was fixing tea."

"Are you serious?!" Walther was taken by surprise. He had not expected the war to be over so soon.

"Warsaw capitulated at noon today."

"Damn!" Walther paced away from his wife and gazed out the window into the street. Walther had been born and raised here in Stuttgart. Here he would always be Walther Halle, son of locksmith Kurt Halle who had gone bankrupt in the inflation and been unemployed until the *Führer* eliminated all unemployment. Walther felt that the bankers and businessmen still smiled at him condescendingly. He hated them all, even his partner. It had been Walther's idea, Walther's design, and his know-how that had created the factory. All his partner had ever brought was money—money he had inherited from his father, who had inherited it from his father before him. Yet at every meeting of the Board, the others deferred to his partner. They brushed Walther off like some kind of high-class employee.

He turned back toward Theresa. She was watching him intently from the chair she had lowered herself into, her hand on her bulging belly. Walther did not find her particularly attractive in her present state, but that wasn't the point. She was fertile and he was sure she'd give him lots of children. She was a good housekeeper and hostess. And she was a business asset—a former Baroness v. Feldburg! But she deserved better than this cramped, modern apartment with its discount furniture. "What would you say if I told you I had a chance to make a fortune, but it would require moving to Warsaw?"

"You mean giving up the factory?"

"Well, only the management of it. I'd hold onto my shares, of course. Hire someone to run it. It doesn't require that much skill now that production is routine."

Theresa knew perfectly well that this was not what he would have said two days ago, perhaps not what he would have said two hours ago, and yet she was not surprised. A man who had raised himself so far so fast would not be satisfied with any position for long. "A move to Warsaw?" she asked, to be sure she had understood.

"Well, at least for me—I wouldn't expect you to join me until after the baby is born. That would give me time to get established and find a house and all that."

Theresa pressed her lips together and considered this. The prospect of going to Warsaw was exotic, exciting in its way—if it weren't for wanting good care of the baby. But that could be arranged, she decided, and consented simply, "All right."

Walther was amazed to find it this easy. In an instant he crossed the room, flung his arms around her and gave her big hug and kiss. "You really are the best little wife a man could dream of! And I thought you'd make a fuss about being so far from your family."

"Don't be ridiculous. But we'll need to hire a good German nanny. I wouldn't want some Polish woman looking after our baby."

"No, of course not! And Trude or another maid can come, too, if you want. We'll be able to afford it."

"Then see if you can't find a more comfortable apartment with room for a growing family. I don't intend to stop with one baby, you know."

Walther laughed and kissed her again. "Nor do I!" He felt he was the luckiest man alive.

Theresa felt smug: they were moving up already.

CHAPTER 3

▼

Altdorf
October 1939

Altdorf had suffered from a shortage of medical support ever since the town's Jewish doctor, Dr. Goldberger, had been forced to close his practice as a result of the Nuremberg Laws in 1936. He and his family had silently slipped away, and no new doctor had come to replace him. At the start of the war, one of the two other doctors in town, a reservist, had to join the Army Medical Corps. It was thus not entirely surprising that the day came when an emergency occurred and there was no doctor available.

On gloomy day in late October, a girl from one of the small, outlying villages came breathlessly and desperately to the manor with the news that her mother had collapsed and she couldn't find a doctor anywhere. Sophia Maria telephoned around to neighboring villages until she reached a doctor willing to come, but his own car was in the workshop, so Sophia Maria agreed to fetch him.

Driving the doctor back to his village, the doctor explained in a tone of outrage, "Nothing was wrong with the poor woman but sheer overwork! And that is only one of dozens of cases I've seen this fall! I know the farmers have lost their sons to the army and better-paying jobs in the cities. I know they're going to lose crops or livestock, but, by God, women aren't beasts of burden, and they're not men, either. They can't pick up the slack! They can't do the same work or work the same hours as the 19-year-old son who's not here! These men have got to learn that!"

Sophia Maria, glancing sidelong at the doctor, couldn't help liking him. She liked him because he was angry to see women overworked. Nevertheless, she felt compelled to point out, "I'm going to lose crops, too—and for the same reason: a shortage of labor."

The doctor looked over at her and noted her muddy Wellingtons, her cotton scarf and rough leather gloves. "You look as if you'd been out in the fields yourself, Frau v. Feldburg."

"The barns—but I can't replace a young male laborer, either. I can't even drive a team as well as a young man." She shook her head in disgust at her own incompetence, adding, "It's worse than the last war."

"I know," the doctor nodded. "And it's only just begun."

Sophia knew something was wrong as soon as she turned into the garage. She couldn't put her finger on it until, as she left the garage by the side door, she saw an open truck of substantial age with *Wehrmacht* plates and markings. What could the *Wehrmacht* want here? From the windows of the kitchen, light and the sound of excited voices spilled into the courtyard—although at this time of night, everyone should have been in bed.

Inside, Sophia Maria was confronted by the entire staff, gathered like spectators around the kitchen table where a half-dozen Polish soldiers and a lone *Wehrmacht* guard were sitting.

At the sight of Sophia Maria, everyone got to their feet, first the household staff and then the guard and his bewildered charges. "*Frau Baronin!*" several voices chimed in at once. She held up her hand and addressed the *Wehrmacht* guard. "What is all this about?"

The corporal was an older man, probably a reservist. There was a half-finished beer before his place at the table, and his tunic was unbuttoned at the neck. "I have orders, *Frau Baronin.*" He fished his orders out of his tunic pocket and handed over the dirty, folded document. It was on official stationery and stamped with various official stamps. "I have orders," he repeated, "to bring these five Polish prisoners here and requisition quarters for them. They are to be available to you as agricultural workers."

Sophia Maria looked up from the orders to the prisoners. Their uniforms were dirty, their faces unshaven. They looked exhausted and underfed. Compared to the French prisoners who had worked on the estate during the last war, they were a sorry-looking lot. But they were young men, and probably farmer's sons, because that was the material from which most armies were made. "Thank God!" she thought simply.

✳   ✳   ✳   ✳

Berlin

Rain beat against the windows of the Bendlerblock and pelted the puddles it formed in the courtyard. Throughout the building, the hot-water pipes pinged and hissed in protest against their use, and a slightly musty odor of recycled steam and copper piping filled the offices.

Major Werner Schrader and *Hauptmann* Dr. Kurt Fiedler were temporarily sharing an office together while working on a special project. As Philip entered, Schrader was on the phone nodding and commenting occasionally as he gazed out the window at the sheets of rain. Fiedler bent over a series of tables, checking them against one another.

Fiedler glanced up at the newcomer and gratefully shoved the tables aside with the question, "Did the Order of Battle help?" As he spoke, he removed some papers stacked on his only spare chair and gestured for Philip to sit down.

Philip sat down a little uneasily. Fiedler and he had been in the same class at the Army Staff College, which was the basis of their friendship. Their junior rank and the fact that they were still on probation for the General Staff increased the bond. They made a point of helping one another whenever possible, but Philip was aware he might be crossing the permissible limits of "unofficial" information exchange in the present case. He proceeded cautiously. "If I'm reading this correctly," his eyes on the data Fiedler had loaned him the day before, "our projected dispositions suggest a violation of Belgian and possibly Dutch neutrality."

Unnoticed by Philip, Major Schrader had completed his telephone conversation, and he intervened somewhat sharply in the conversation. "Does that bother you?"

"Doesn't it bother you?" Philip countered, looking over sharply, his glasses glinting.

"Of course, but wouldn't you agree that any offensive in the West is madness?"

"I do, but—"

"—but our revered *Führer* has ordered an offensive." There was just the slightest stress on the word 'revered,' which made Schrader sound very awestruck—or slightly sarcastic.

Philip was not sure which, so he proceeded carefully. "But the Chancellor, as a soldier in the last war, personally saw the misery in the trenches, didn't he? He can't seriously expect us to simply roll over much better prepared defenses. The casualties will be indescribably higher than in the last war."

"Adolf was gassed," Schrader remarked, almost as if making casual conversation. "Poison gas destroys the nerves of the brain, and some claim it can even trigger a slow decay."

Relieved that Schrader was no supporter of Hitler, Philip answered energetically, "Then Brauchitsch and Halder must make Hitler recognize an offensive is madness."

"But what if they can't?" Schrader wanted to know.

"The Commander-in-Chief of the German Army and the Chief of the German General Staff can't convince an Austrian corporal to take their military advice?" Philip could not believe this.

"The C-in-C and Chief of the General Staff advised against the re-occupation of the Rhineland—and it was a glorious, bloodless success. They advised against occupation of the Sudetenland—another bloodless success. They advised against the invasion of the rest of Czechoslovakia—yet another bloodless success. Why should he take their advice now?"

Philip was not given a chance to answer, because the door was flung open and three other officers burst into the room. Rain was dripping from caps and the smell of wet wool clung about them. All were in the process of stripping off leather gloves or unbuttoning their greatcoats. Their pace, faces and tone of voice suggested agitation, if not actual anger.

The three officers already in the room jumped to their feet in startled courtesy at the sight of gold and red collars. Two of the three newcomers were generals, including one of the three Army Group Commanders, *Generaloberst* v. Leeb. The other general, Kuechler, was speaking as they entered: "… if there's one thing the Army's leadership is agreed on—and that is rare these days—then it's the stupidity of an offensive in the West—not to mention in November."

"Agreed, but this incident with General Groppe has necessarily taken precedence," Leeb countered irritably.

"What incident with General Groppe?" General Kuechler asked.

"Didn't you hear?" Leeb asked, surprised. Kuechler shook his head. Leeb explained, "Groppe saw an SS decree ordering all married women with husbands at the front to make themselves available to the SS—"

All the discipline of the German officer corps could not prevent the others from exclamations of outrage and protest. Leeb allowed them to vent their initial shock, and then continued, "General Groppe publicly resigned in protest of the decree."

"He was right! We must all resign!" Kuechler countered. "It must be made clear to that chicken farmer" (he was referring to the Head of the SS, Heinrich Himmler, who had formerly been a poultry farmer) "that German officers and their wives are not livestock for his breeding experiments. That decree must be withdrawn or the entire officer corps will mutiny!"

"Officer corps? This decree affects a common soldier no less than a *Generaloberst*," Leeb countered coldly. "The decree will be withdrawn or the government will fall—and the *Herr Reichskanzler* knows it. Meanwhile, however, General Groppe has been arrested, 'tried' at one of these so-called 'People's' Courts controlled by this riffraff, and sentenced to death."

Again the others burst out with exclamations of shock and fury, which Leeb tolerated until Kuechler pointed out, "That's absurd! General Groppe can only be tried by a court-martial."

"The Gestapo argues that since he had just publicly resigned, he is a civilian and subject to civil law—"

"What law condemns a man for protesting a decree that is nothing less than legislated rape?" Groscurth demanded.

Leeb looked at him, but didn't answer directly; instead he informed them simply, "I've demanded of the *Reichskanzler* that the sentence be immediately reversed, Groppe restored to full honors at once, and the decree suppressed. I was able to make it very clear that otherwise the Army—the whole Army—will no longer accept his leadership. The *Reichskanzler* has personally assured me that all my demands will be met, because it was all really just a terrible misunderstanding."

"Misunderstanding?" Philip scoffed to himself. Unfortunately, the others heard him and turned to stare. He felt compelled to explain himself. "There's more at stake than the fate of one general or the content of one decree. This is no isolated incident, but rather symptomatic of the moral depravity of the entire Nazi—"

"Shut that door!" *Generaloberst* v. Leeb barked, and Groscurth leaped to comply. Then, turning to Philip, he declared in a clipped, hard tone, "The moral depravity of this regime, as you put it, is not the issue. We may deplore it, but Herr Hitler is still the legal Head of State of this country, and, gentlemen, we have all sworn an oath to support him. A soldier's oath is never more sacred than in time of war." He looked at each of the others in turn, making them drop their eyes in shame.

Leeb then continued in a milder but still uncompromising tone, "As soldiers, we have no right to interfere or even question the acts of our legal government on moral grounds. I moved to save the life of one of my divisional commanders, and I objected to the content of that depraved decree—but only because these protests fell within my jurisdiction as a military commander. I was able to argue convincingly that the condemnation of Groppe and the decree itself would have a direct, negative impact on the combat effectiveness of the troops entrusted to me."

Dropping his voice yet again, he continued in an almost fatherly tone, "If we are to have any influence on this government, gentlemen, then we must be very careful. We must not cast ourselves in the role of inveterate opponents. We must try to see the positive and to support it as much as possible. Where it is necessary to protest against the policies of this government, then we must make our objections based on our military expertise. We must be very, very careful not to use moral or political arguments, as these will only discredit us in the eyes of the Party—if not make us look completely ridiculous to them."

Philip felt chastised by the *Generaloberst's* lecture, but General Kuechler was less easily subdued. "I can't agree with the *Herr Generaloberst* entirely. What has been going on in Poland cannot simply be ignored. We must protest, even if the actions of the SS have more to do with—as the young *Rittmeister* so aptly put it—the moral depravity of the regime than with military affairs—"

Leeb waved Kuechler's protest aside. "General Blaskowitz has acted swiftly and decisively to put an end to the atrocities and to bring the responsible SS men to trial. He's already had several of them executed, and I trust him to bring the entire situation under control."

But General Kuechler shook his head. "In the territories attached to East Prussia that fell under my jurisdiction, I also encountered these SS 'cleansing' operations. What has been going on in occupied Poland is not random acts of violence by undisciplined SS troops; it is a deliberate policy."

"That's impossible," *Generaloberst* v. Leeb insisted, unable or unwilling to believe this. "It is senseless."

Kuechler would have liked to be reassured, but he was not. "My own efforts to prevent and punish atrocities were opposed and resisted by the *Gauleiter*" (Regional Party Governor) "of East Prussia at every turn. And I'm the one who has been sent away. *Gauleiter* Koch is still there where he can pursue his policies unimpeded."

"But you were sent away because we need you on the Western Front," Leeb argued, and as the discussion turned to the planned offensive in the West, Philip knew it was long since time for him to leave. He excused himself, but the things he had heard stayed with him.

CHAPTER 4

▼

Altdorf
November 1939

As on every Saturday morning, Heidi came up to Sophia Maria's bedroom to change the sheets. Sophia Maria had washed her hair this morning and sat at her dressing table, still dressed in her bathrobe with her hair in a towel. In the mirror she watched the way Heidi tossed the dirty bed-linens aside and professionally cracked open the fresh sheets. Her movements were young and vigorous, and Sophia Maria imagined she had looked much the same 23 years ago when she had worked as a nurse's aide in a large military hospital.

Heidi had been barely eighteen in 1916 when she had set off in a fresh uniform with a starched apron and veil to serve her king and country. Serious and patriotic, she had said goodbye to her parents at the station and left her parental home and Altdorf for the first time in her life, to serve in a large military hospital on the French border. Sophia Maria could still remember the way a simple gold cross gleamed at the base of her starched white collar. Her parents had shed tears of pride.

Her return a year and a half later had been less glamorous, if no less memorable. She'd had to walk all the way from the station, dragging her canvas suitcase in the rain. The cross was sold and her fingers were bare of rings. Her uniform was gone, and her rough cloak could not hide the fact that she was pregnant.

Heidi's mother, it was said, died of shame. She'd been on her deathbed from TB anyway, and the news of Heidi's disgrace had finished her off. Heidi's father, the coachman Josef, had refused to let his daughter in out of the rain. It was Sophia Maria who had prevailed upon her mother-in-law to take the outcast in.

Heidi had served as Sophia Maria's lady's maid ever since and her son, Franz, had been raised on the estate. With time, the scandal had become less important, and Heidi might have been forgiven if only she'd been willing to play the role of repentant sinner. Instead, she insisted not only that the father of her child had been a flying ace, but also that only his untimely death had prevented him from marrying her. This was too much for the people of Altdorf. They were not prepared to believe such a fairy tale, and still less prepared to forgive a "fallen woman" who wanted to make a heroine of herself for her sin. Heidi remained an outcast in the midst of the household.

Heidi never seemed to mind this, Sophia Maria observed with a certain amusement. Indeed, Heidi truly seemed to consider herself better than her "provincial" colleagues. Whether or not she had been the mistress of a hero, she had "seen something of the world," and she considered her colleagues "country bumpkins." And precisely because of this distance from her colleagues, she was an invaluable source of information to Sophia Maria.

"How are things working out with the Polish workers?" she asked as Heidi started to brush out her hair.

More than a month after the POWs had arrived, a truck full of Polish civilian "volunteers" had arrived in Altdorf. The authorities insisted that these workers would eliminate all labor shortages on the farms. By the time they arrived, however, the slow winter season had started, and many farmers had been reluctant to house and pay these workers through the winter. Sophia Maria was less short-sighted, particularly since housing did not pose a problem for her. The manor complex had been built to house a larger staff and laborers as well. The workers' accommodations behind the manor had lain empty for decades until the POWs arrived. Since the the five prisoners took up only a few of the available rooms, Sophia Maria had taken six Polish civilians.

Only after she had made the decision did she discover what their wages were. The wages were set by the Labor Office at between 18 and 26 *Reichmarks* a month, or less than one-quarter of what German farm workers were paid. Worse still, Sophia Maria had been shocked to learn that of the six workers, five had wives to support, and two had children to support as well—on these pitiful wages. It was impossible. And it was equally impossible to pay them more. Her banking, her taxes, her accounts themselves were subject to audit. A blatant violation of the law would be pointless. This was what she hated most: being forced to take part in a system she considered unjust.

As for being "volunteers," Sophia Maria soon learned from the men, speaking a mixture of German and Polish, that all unemployed laborers had been given the option of "volunteering" for work in the *Reich* or being drafted to do unpaid work for the civil administration of Occupied Poland. Volunteers, indeed!

But by far the worst problem proved the integration of the new workers into the manor community. The six workers combined with the five POWs amounted to eleven Poles—all male—and the regular staff numbered only nine. The cook, Martha, had been the first to protest. She came to Sophia Maria the next day after the men arrived, and politely but firmly asked how she was to make meals for 21 people without more help in the kitchens? It was a fair complaint, and Sophia Maria had agreed that help must be found, but this was easier said than done. Then Josef had complained that the most of the workers knew nothing about handling "decent" horses and listed a half-dozen "crimes" they had committed.

Now Heidi related a new problem. "Frau Opitz objects to the Poles being housed in the manor, *Frau Baronin.*"

"I beg your pardon? How can she object to them living in old, unused quarters?"

"She says it's against the law."

"What law?"

"The one about foreign workers, I suppose. She says that the Labor Office people specifically said the Poles were to be kept separated."

"And so they are." Sophia Maria answered indignantly. "There are no Poles living in the Opitz apartment, are there?"

"No, but she says by letting them live right here in the manor and providing them with sheets and towels and what-not, they might get ideas."

"What do you mean, 'ideas'?"

"Frau Opitz said they might start to think they're as good as we are, and she quoted something from the *Führer* about how we had to protect ourselves against racial inferiors and demonstrate our superiority."

"What rubbish! If Frau Opitz ever says something like that again, tell her from me that one of the telling marks of superiority is generosity. And if she dares to suggest I am breaking the law again, please remind her that her little business with pork sausages is not exactly legal, either!"

Heidi's lips twitched in unmistakable satisfaction at the prospect of making Frau Opitz uncomfortable. She opened her mouth to add something, but the sound of a commotion in the courtyard distracted her. Looking out the window, she reported, "It's Father Matthias."

Sophia joined her at the window. The priest was dismounting from his bicycle (he rode a woman's bike on account of his cassock) and was already surrounded by what looked like all eleven Polish workers. "Heidi, bring me my brown skirt and cream-colored blouse with the tie," Sophia Maria ordered, as she started to tie up her still-damp hair to receive the priest.

Knowing that Father Matthias usually came through the kitchen, Sophia Maria went directly there. The two kitchen maids were washing up after breakfast, but the rest of the staff was still at the table, the men smoking their pipes and the women gossiping over half-drunk cups of coffee substitute. At the sight of the Baroness they started to get to their feet, but Sophia Maria waved them down. "I thought I saw Father Matthias arrive."

"The Polacks have waylaid him, *Frau Baronin*," Frau Opitz explained, with a disgusted nod of her head toward the courtyard.

"Frau Opitz, I forbid you to use that term when referring to my employees—"

The sound of a car in the courtyard distracted everyone. One of the scullery maids, a dish-towel still in her hand, ran over and looked out. In high-pitched excitement she called out, "A BMW! With Party flags on the fenders!" Herr Opitz rose and went to look out the window himself, but the girl continued her narration excitedly for the others. "An SA man is opening the door."

"It's the *Kreisleiter* himself!" Herr Opitz declared, hastily buttoning up his jacket and dusting off his trousers.

"He's gone over to Father Matthias," the girl continued. "Father Matthias just gave the German Greeting!" This aroused comment because Father Matthias had once called the greeting "heathen" and had steadfastly refused to use it up till now. "Now they're shaking hands. Father seems to be getting a lecture; he keeps nodding his head without saying anything. Now the *Kreisleiter* has slapped him on the shoulder and they're looking this way. Father just pointed at us. The *Kreisleiter* is coming this way!"

The household leapt up to hastily clear the leftover dishes from the table. Herr Opitz went forward to answer the knock on the back door as if he were in livery at the front. He stood stiffly and raised his right arm. "*Heil Hitler! Herr Kreisleiter!*"

"*Heil Hitler!*" The stocky man in the brown Party uniform with the red swastika armband replied with the same stiff-armed salute. He wore the Golden Party Badge, which symbolized an early entry into the Party, and a flashy diamond ring suggested what this had brought him with time. His broad face and red nose reflected his affection for beer, and he had the manners of a jolly innkeeper. This was a dangerous illusion. During the so-called "*Röhm-Putsch*" in 1934, this man had personally shot over a dozen men, several of whom were "comrades" and personal "friends." His apparent amiability was a carefully cultivated tool for achieving his objectives.

"The front door was locked, so I had to come round to the back," he explained himself in a friendly tone now. "Father said to come in here." Scowling slightly, he remarked, "He seems awfully friendly with those Polacks. You know it's not allowed for German priests to hear confession or read Mass for Polacks, don't you? You might remind the good Father of that from time to time. I wouldn't want such a nice man to get into trouble on account of some dirty Polacks." His face cleared and he said in a friendly tone, "But today I've come to have a word with Freifrau von Feldburg."

Unnoticed, Maria Sophia had withdrawn, so when Herr Opitz turned around he was momentarily puzzled. Like a good butler, he recovered rapidly. "But of course, *Herr Kreisleiter*, let me take you to the red room and call the *Frau Baronin*."

As Sophia Maria entered the reception room, she held out her hand to the waiting *Kreisleiter*. "Herr Dettmann."

The *Kreisleiter* was visibly confused by this failure to give the German Greeting. He flapped his own hand in a hasty "*Heil Hitler*," and then took Sophia Maria's hand without knowing whether to shake it or kiss it. He ended up bowing over it as he shook it. It was very comical in its way, but Sophia Maria felt only contempt welling up in her.

This man was a nobody! His father had been dismissed from his job at the Post Office for petty embezzlement. Herr Dettmann himself had only a grammar-school education. He'd served as a driver in the war, safely behind the front lines the whole time. After the war he worked as a chauffeur for various war profiteers of the worst kind, men who had profited from the misery of others. He had participated in Hitler's foolish "Beer Hall Putsch" in 1923, but had only risen to power after the so-called "Night of the Long Knives," in which hundreds of people were murdered with impunity by the SS. And now this man was the most powerful political authority in the entire region.

Herr Dettmann, despite the last six years of political power, was still intimidated by the manor and the woman before him. It had been easy to decide to come here, easy to order his chauffeur to drive here, and the entry through the courtyard and kitchen had seemed natural enough. But from the moment Herr Opitz had left him alone in this pompous reception room with dark walnut furniture and red silk panels, he started to regret his decision.

With a graceful gesture of her hand the Baroness offered her visitor a seat, and he lowered his bulk onto the nearest chair—only to regret it as the antique chair groaned under his weight.

"What can I do for you?" Sophia Maria asked in a cool tone.

The *Kreisleiter* cleared his throat and absently scratched behind his ear. "Um, actually, you see," he cleared his throat. "It was brought to my attention that, um, you aren't actually—of course, it might be an oversight—but I was told that, um, you don't belong to the *Frauenschaft*."

"That's true," Sophia Maria conceded readily.

"Um," he cleared his throat again. "Well, you know that the *Frauenschaft* is— that the *Führer* has stressed how important the *Frauenschaft* is, that it's just as important for women as military service is for men. Well, not a duty, of course," he hastened to correct himself, "but the highest form of national service." He looked up at her hopefully.

"I don't doubt what you say, Herr Dettmann. But you must understand that I am a widow. My only daughter is married and both my sons are serving with our armed forces. I have to run this estate alone, and I simply don't have time for membership in any organizations."

"The, um," he cleared his throat yet again and moved uncomfortably, causing the chair to protest, "the *Frauenschaft* isn't just an organization—I mean, this is really not just a personal decision. My wife tells me the Leader of the *Frauenschaft* in this area is—ah—not the right woman."

Sophia Maria smiled faintly. The Leader of the *Frauenschaft* in Altdorf was a shrill, dominant, single woman who had quickly alienated all the other women. "True."

This encouraged Herr Dettmann greatly. He sat up a little straighter, ignoring the creaking of the chair. "My wife says the membership in the *Frauenschaft* is shamefully low here as a result. Now, um, I'm sure you'd agree that it is a disgrace that reflects badly on the Party—and the community—as a whole."

Sophia Maria understood his concern, but since she withheld comment, Herr Dettmann had to continue. "It seems to me—that is, I consider it my duty to— um, well, *Frau Baronin*, I mean, if *you* were to become the Leader of the *Frauenschaft*, I'm sure the membership and participation would dramatically improve."

Sophia Maria stiffened; there was nothing she wanted to do less than become a member of the Nazi Party and lead the local women's organization. "I'm very flattered by your confidence in my influence, Herr Dettmann, but I'm not at all sure I could overcome the lack of enthusiasm for the *Frauenschaft* in Altdorf. You must understand that most of the women here are hard-working women trying to make up for sons and even husbands called up into the armed forces."

"Well, we must all make sacrifices for the country."

"You can be sure, Herr Dettmann, that we here in Altdorf are very willing to make our contribution to the nation, but we see our patriotic duty in doing the jobs we do—running farms and shops in the absence of our men." Sophia Maria was making a conscious effort to argue in terms of the Nazi ideology itself.

"Indeed, indeed," Herr Dettmann agreed. "But the *Frauenschaft* does very important work," he persisted.

"No doubt, Herr Dettmann, but forgive me for being blunt: it doesn't get the cows milked or the bread baked."

"But my wife says it can help women to do these things better, more efficiently. The *Frauenschaft* provides members with all sorts of tips for better housekeeping, my wife says."

"Then perhaps under the right leader the *Frauenschaft* could be made attractive—but I must repeat, I am simply overburdened with my responsibilities here and could not devote the time and energy necessary to do the organization justice. I'm sure there are other women in the community with fewer responsibilities—perhaps your own wife?—who would be challenged and delighted by the opportunity to take over the *Frauenschaft*."

To her intense disappointment, Herr Dettmann did not fall for the bait of making his wife the leader. Instead he insisted, "But no one could ever replace you as the leader of the women in Altdorf. Even if you wished to turn over the actual work of the organization to a deputy, it would be completely inappropriate if anyone but you were honored with the leadership. Surely at this time, when our boys risk their lives every day for our nation, it is not too much to ask you to assume a nominal leadership?"

Trapped, Sophia Maria thought; but inwardly she resisted a moment longer, so distasteful was the idea of joining the Nazi Party. Then again, what was she really sacrificing beyond her pride? Was her pride worth offending this man who—contemptible as he might be—was very powerful? Sophia Maria had no illusions about her own real power. She might still be called "*Frau Baronin*," but she was completely dependent on the good will of the Nazi-controlled organizations. They set prices and wages, regulated which crops could be planted in what quantities, and decided whether she got gasoline, building materials or other rationed goods. She might privately laugh at the self-important "leaders," but she could not afford to provoke their displeasure.

The estate to which she had been "banished" in 1914 had now become her home. More importantly, it was her sons' inheritance and heritage. Feldburgs had controlled the land here for nearly 700 years. Sophia Maria viewed herself as a trustee, holding and maintaining the properties for her sons. She did not feel she had the right to do anything that might endanger their inheritance—certainly not for reasons of personal vanity and pride.

"If you can assure me, Herr Dettmann, that my position will be truly nominal and that I will not be expected to perform any but representational functions, I would, of course, be honored to accept the appointment."

Herr Dettmann smiled with genuine relief and satisfaction. "This is a great win for the Party, *Frau Baronin*." He was certain that he'd be able to brag about this to his superior, the *Gauleiter*.

*   *   *   *

Berlin
December 1939

The letter from the Gestapo, the Secret State Police, had been placed on top of the stack of mail by Philip's housekeeper. Philip picked it up, turned it over, and then reached for the letter opener without sitting down. It was a summons to report to *Kriminalsekretär* (Criminal Inspector) Kuhnfeld in the Prinz Albrecht Strasse, Gestapo headquarters, at 10 the following morning.

"What impudence." Philip walked with the summons to the hall, picked up the telephone, and asked the operator for a connection to the Prinz Albrecht Strasse.

After some delay, the operator in the Prinz Albrecht Strasse reported that Herr *Kriminalsekretär* Kuhnfeld had left his office for the day. (Hardly surprising for 9:30 in the evening.) As no one was willing to take a message, Philip hung up and put the summons with his briefcase so he would remember to call the next day from the Bendlerstrasse.

The next morning, Philip placed the call immediately after his morning ride, but Kuhnfeldt was not yet in his office. This time, however, Philip left a message: *Rittmeister* Freiherr v. Feldburg could not possibly take time to come to the Prinz Albrecht Strasse in the middle of the day, and what was this all about?

In the late afternoon, Inspector Kuhnfeldt reached Philip personally. "*Heil Hitler*! This is *Kriminalsekretär* Kuhnfeldt from the Gestapo."

"Good day. I trust you received my message."

"Indeed, *Herr Rittmeister*, and I quite understand how busy you must be, but we have some very important questions with regard to a case of treason. I'm sure the *Wehrmacht* and the German General Staff is also concerned about eliminating the internal enemy. I don't anticipate this will take very long."

"The trip to the Prinz Albrecht Strasse alone takes a half-hour." Unsaid was the fact that the armed forces were not subject to the Gestapo and that it was a standing, unwritten law that no Army officer would voluntarily set foot in the Prinz Albrecht Strasse except on official Army business.

"I would be happy to come to you, *Herr Rittmeister*, if that is more convenient."

The last thing Philip needed during his probation for the General Staff was a visit from the Gestapo in his office. "Not here in the Bendlerstrasse!"

"Then at home, *Herr Rittmeister?*"

"Only after 9 pm. I'm never home before that."

"Good. Then I will call tomorrow evening at 9:30 pm, shall we say?"

"Just a moment," Philip checked his calendar. "Yes, all right. I've noted that down." The other said "*Heil Hitler*" again, and Philip said "*Aufwiederhören*" and hung up. Then he swore irritably to himself. He still did not know what this was about. He wondered if he should inform or consult his superiors. Indeed, he reflected, he should probably have done so already. Maintaining the Army's autonomy and exemption from Party and police oversight was a high priority. Possibly even this sort of dealing with the Gestapo might compromise it in some way.

Taking the summons, Philip went at once to his direct superior. They consulted and then called the Advocate General's office. It was agreed that an Army lawyer should be present at the meeting with the Gestapo.

Punctually at 9:30 the following evening, the bell to the Feldburg apartment house rang. Theo Pfalz admitted two plain-clothes policemen and escorted them upstairs. Philip admitted them and led them to the "smoking room," once the only room in the apartment where gentlemen had been allowed to smoke. It was decorated in an explicitly masculine style with dark wood panelling, blood-red Turkish carpets, leather chairs and hunting paintings. The two Gestapo men looked around the room as if searching for something, without daring to actually touch or turn over anything.

Philip recognized Inspector Kuhnfeldt by his voice. He was an aging man with a weathered face, deep-drawn lines and gnarled hands. He was short, slight of build, with bowed legs that looked more likely to have come from malnutrition than riding. He wore a poorly tailored, somewhat faded suit under a heavy wool coat that needed cleaning. He was accompanied by a tall, slender young man with fine blond hair and large, owl-eye glasses. The young man wore a new gabardine coat that was far too thin for the weather, over a poor-quality pin-striped suit.

Both men raised their arms in the German Greeting and Philip shook hands reservedly. He then introduced Dr. Karl Sack without explaining who he was. Kuhnfeldt's eyes narrowed at the sight of the lawyer's uniform, however, and Philip suspected he had recognized the insignia of the Advocate General's Corps. Kuhnfeldt showed his own credentials and introduced his colleague as Peter Kessler, who would "take notes." Philip asked them to sit down.

The young Gestapo agent hastily, even nervously, opened his brief-case and fumbled about in it until he found a pad of paper and a pen. He set the briefcase aside and tried to write on his lap, but the pad was too flimsy. He pulled the briefcase back onto his lap and tried to balance it so he could write. Only then did Philip have enough mercy to suggest he take a seat at the secretary. Standing again, he opened the desktop for the young Gestapo agent.

Finally, with everyone settled, Inspector Kuhnfeldt opened the interrogation: "What do you know about Gottfried Jähring?"

Philip's surprise and answer were genuine. "Practically nothing." Jähring was another of Philip's tenants. He rented one of the small apartments on the fourth floor at the back of the house, where access was via the back stairs only. He had also converted the "washing kitchen" in the attic above his apartment into an atelier and paid marginally more rent.

"Could you tell us when he first moved into the flat in this house?"

"I believe it was early 1933, but I'd have to check the exact date."

"Please."

Philip stood and went to the open secretary. The young Gestapo official pulled back hastily, almost tipping over the desk chair in his anxiousness to get out of the way. Philip took a folder with all his rental documents out of a drawer and found the one from Herr Jähring. "March 1, 1933."

Kessler at once jotted this down, as if the information was of immense significance.

Kunfeldt continued his questioning. "What do you know about Herr Jähring's profession?"

"He's an artist."

"What sort of artist?"

"He paints."

"Wouldn't you say it was degenerate art?"

"I really wouldn't know. I'm an Army officer, not an art critic."

"Yes, but do you really consider it likely that he earns sufficient money from his distasteful painting to support himself?!"

"I haven't the faintest idea what an artist can earn from any kind of art, but since he pays his rent punctually, I have no reason to believe he is insolvent, regardless of where the money comes from. He might have family money."

"Do you know his family?"

"I know of it. Ruhr steel interests."

"Money?"

"They own companies."

"Does his family visit often?"

"Never—that I know of."

"Who does Jähring associate with?"

"I don't know."

"Does he have a girlfriend?"

"Not that I know of."

"Does he employ a cleaning woman?"

"Honestly, gentlemen. That's none of my business, and I'm not the least bit interested in knowing."

"Does no one ever visit?"

"I never noticed. I work very long hours, and I'm rarely here. When I am here, I have better things to do than spy on my tenants."

"You have a very fine apartment house, Herr *Rittmeister* Frhr. v. Feldburg— very exclusive and refined." Kuhnfeldt looked pointedly around the room with its bookshelves of leather-bound books, polished furnishings and brass lamps. "Surely you would not be pleased if disreputable individuals were lurking about?"

"Quite correct. But I have neither seen such elements, nor has anyone else complained to me about them. You would do better to question my concierge, Herr Pfalz; he keeps track of everyone who comes and goes."

"We already have," Kuhnfeldt said, looking hard at Philip as if this should make him nervous.

Philip only shrugged and looked straight back at him. "Then you already know more about Herr Jähring's friends and habits than I do."

"Didn't you ask for references when he moved in?"

"At the time, I was a fresh-baked lieutenant. My father was owner-resident of the house. I presume he did request references. I don't know."

"Your father was a Member of Parliament in 1933, wasn't he?"

"No, he did not stand for re-election in the Nov. 1932 elections, because of failing health."

"But he had been an MP. He must have had dealings with Social Democratic and even Communist MPs?"

"What are you implying? My father sat for the Center Party. Any dealings he had with the SPD, much less the KPD, were purely official. As an aristocrat and devout Catholic, my father was not a favorite with the Left."

"Would you consider it impossible that Herr Jähring was recommended to your father by one of his Parliamentary colleagues?"

"I haven't the faintest idea."

"Let me show you something." The Gestapo inspector removed a folded piece of paper from his inside coat pocket and handed it to Philip.

With a puzzled glance at the sphinx-like Dr. Sack, Philip cleaned his glasses on his handkerchief, and then unfolded the paper. He was confronted by a hand-written but duplicated leaflet. In large block letters it started: "THROUGHOUT GERMANY THE FASCIST MURDERERS REIGN!" True enough, Philip thought and read on with interest. "Yet despite the torture chambers of the SA and the Concentration Camps, resistance against this barbaric system is not at an end!" Philip found himself wishing this were true. His eyes skipped to the large print further down the page. "THE NATIONAL SOCIALIST DICTATOR-SHIP IS NEITHER NATIONALIST NOR SOCIALIST!" Right again, Philip thought, and with even more interest he read the underlined text: "The world is very different from the way it is described in Goebbels' lying press." Again he agreed; but conscious of the eyes riveted on him by both Gestapo officials, he passed the leaflet to Dr. Sack and remarked, "Very interesting. But what does it have to do with Hr. Jähring or my father?"

"That is a Communist leaflet, distributed—possibly even produced—by Herr Jähring. We found hundreds of them in his apartment—right here in your apart-ment house."

Philip ignored the implied guilt by location, and remarked with genuine sur-prise, "Communist? But it doesn't have any of the usual slogans—'running dogs of capitalism' and the like."

"We have ways of knowing," Kühnfeldt told him definitively. "Didn't Jähring ever evidence leftist sympathies?"

"I wouldn't know. We never said more to one another than 'good day.'"

"*Herr Rittmeister*, I'm sure you understand that these Communist under-ground cells are a threat to the security of the *Reich*. Is there nothing you can tell us that would help lead us to his traitorous comrades?"

"What makes you so certain he wasn't working alone? I know so little about Herr Jähring in large part because he lived very withdrawn from the world. Like a recluse or hermit, almost."

"We are absolutely certain he had accomplices!" Herr Kuhnfeldt responded, as if Philip had questioned his competence. He added, "Over the years we have learned a great deal about the methods and tactics of these Communist traitors. We know exactly how they operate. Furthermore, since the Pact with Stalin, the Soviet Police have been very cooperative and forthcoming with information on the Communists here in the *Reich*. We have good reason to believe there are at least two other members of Jähring's cell that are still at large."

"I see. May I ask how Herr Jähring managed to escape your notice up to now?"

The inspector frowned. Evidently he resented the question, but he had too much respect for an officer to refuse to answer. "He belonged to the Communist Party under an assumed name. Even his closest associates knew only his false name. Jahring, it turns out, was his real name, which made all his documents foolproof, as they were genuine."

"Interesting."

"Yes." The inspector agreed. "And clever—which is precisely why we must maintain the utmost vigilance in countering the threat."

"I couldn't agree more." Philip glanced at Dr. Sack. "However, I honestly don't know how I can be of assistance. I don't know the man personally and rarely even ran into him in passing."

The inspector seemed to conclude—if somewhat reluctantly—that Philip was telling the truth. He got to his feet and held out his hand. "We appreciate your co-operation, *Herr Rittmeister*. Call if you think of anything—anything at all— that might be useful."

"Certainly." Philip rose.

The younger policeman hastily gathered his notes together and returned them to his briefcase while the others waited. The fact that the others were waiting seemed to make him more nervous, and the paper got stuffed in wrong. He had to pull it out, straighten it and re-insert it.

At the door Kuhnfeldt stopped and looked over at Philip. "There is one last little thing, I'm afraid, *Herr Rittmeister*. Jähring's apartment and atelier must be carefully searched again. We must ask you not to re-rent either until we give notice that we have completed our investigation."

"I understand. How long might that be?"

"I'm afraid I can't say for sure, *Herr Rittmeister*. We will do our best to proceed rapidly, but you must understand that this is a matter of national security. We can leave no stone unturned to find Jähring's accomplices. My colleague, Herr Kessler, will be handling this part of our investigation, but it is his first case. I will, of course, need to check his work. I really must beg for your understanding and patience."

Philip hardly had any choice. He murmured his consent and held out his hand. "Good evening." The two policemen shook his hand, flapped their arms as they answered "*Heil Hitler*" and then departed loudly down the stairs.

Philip closed the door and turned to Dr. Sack with a silent question.

Dr. Sack raised an eyebrow. "Interesting; very interesting. And you never guessed this tenant might be a Communist?"

"Not a clue," Philip admitted.

"Perhaps the most interesting aspect of all is the fact that Stalin considers it worth his while to eliminate German Communists."

"Bitter. They are his loyal servants, and he turns them over to the Gestapo."

Dr. Sack shrugged. "After what he did to his own officer corps or the way he let millions of independent peasants starve during the forced collectivization, can you really wonder that he would sacrifice a few old 'comrades'? You can be sure it is only those who are not completely loyal to him."

Philip hesitated, but Dr. Sack had a reputation as a staunch non-Nazi. He risked remarking, "Everything in that pamphlet was true."

"You sound as if you admire the men who wrote it?"

"Hardly. But it takes courage to fight against this regime, doesn't it?"

"A very great deal of courage," Dr. Sack agreed. "And what for?"

It was mid-January before the Gestapo released the apartment. By then Philip had orders to rejoin his division and had neither the patience for nor interest in interviewing prospective tenants. He informed Theo Pfalz that he intended to leave the apartment vacant, and to his surprise the concierge protested.

Standing unhappily in the smoking room and fidgeting unconsciously with his armband, Theo tried to explain the problem. "It didn't look good, *Herr Baron*, having that Communist living here all these years."

"We can't be expected to know the politics of the residents when even the Gestapo didn't know," Philip argued.

"That may be, *Herr Baron*," Theo admitted, "but it still didn't look good." Theo didn't want to appear disrespectful, but Philip's decision not to rent the apartment put him in an awkward position. He had already promised it to someone. So he pressed ahead, "We have Prof. Dr. Moldenauer living here, who everyone knows got thrown out of the university because he doesn't stand firmly on the basis of National Socialist ideology." (Philip had no idea where he'd acquired this term, but presumably at one of his many SA training courses.) In any case he continued urgently, "It would be better to rent the apartment to someone the Party trusts—to make up for the mistakes of the past, so to speak."

"I don't have to make up for any mistakes." Philip was starting to lose his patience. "Quite the reverse; the Gestapo owes me an apology for keeping my property closed for almost three months."

"I wish you wouldn't talk like that, *Herr Baron*," Theo pleaded. "It could so easily be misinterpreted."

"I cannot spend my life disguising what I think just because some people are so stupid or so fanatical as to misinterpret what I say."

"Yes," Theo agreed, not at all sure what Philip had said. "But couldn't you just rent the apartment to someone the Gestapo would approve of?"

"This is Germany, not Soviet Russia. We still have free private enterprise here, and I have a right to rent my apartments to anyone I like. It is not the State or the police's business." Philip was impatient. He had a lot to do.

"I know, I know," Theo soothed, sensing Philip's mood. "But surely it can't do any harm to choose a tenant they would approve of?"

"Theo, I've already told you, I have no time to look at candidates—much less submit them to the Gestapo for approval—"

"But *Herr Baron*, if I was absolutely certain that this tenant would meet their approval, wouldn't it be a good thing?"

"You mean you have someone in mind?" Philip was astonished. The Gestapo had only given notice on the apartment the day before.

"Yes," Theo confirmed happily. "An educated young man with a good salary who is absolutely above suspicion."

"Well, why didn't you say so at the beginning?" Philip asked with ill-disguised exasperation.

Theo didn't know how to explain his reluctance without leading the conversation in directions he didn't want it to take, so he just shrugged and smiled sheepishly.

Philip, anxious to get the matter over with, continued, "You can tell him to get in touch with my solicitor; the rent has gone up 25 *RM* monthly."

"*Jawohl, Herr Baron!*"

"Anything else?"

"No, *Herr Baron*."

And with that, the matter was closed. Two weeks later the younger of the two Gestapo men moved into Jähring's former apartment, but Philip was no longer in Berlin.

CHAPTER 5

▼

Warsaw
February 1940

Theresa was somewhat unsettled by the increasing evidence of war damage the closer they got to Warsaw. The predominance of military personnel and vehicles and the shabby condition of the buildings, rail stations and population had a yet more negative impact on her. She started to have serious doubts about the wisdom of this move to Warsaw.

When the train finally pulled into the central station at Warsaw, it was almost dusk. Because most of the glass had been destroyed during the siege, boards nailed over the windows blocked out most of the fading light, making it so dingy it exuded insecurity. An icy wind chased discarded tickets and dust down the platforms, and all the refreshment stands were boarded shut.

Four-month-old Siegfried started bawling as soon as the first gust of wind reached him. Around them the other passengers rushed away in all directions, casting disapproving looks at the two women with the crying baby. Even Trude, who was looking after the luggage, had disappeared in the crowds of *Wehrmacht*, railway, police, Party, Civil Servant and SS uniforms. Walther was nowhere to be seen.

"This is unheard of! Unforgivable! I can't speak a word of Polish! How am I to find a taxi?! I don't even have an address!" Although she did her best to sound indignant, Theresa was becoming increasingly terrified. She felt alone and abandoned in a huge ugly world filled with strangers. She was scared.

But just when she felt the tears start to form, she caught sight of Walther at the head of the platform. He was waving to her happily. He wore a new coat with a fur collar and a fur hat—almost like a Russian, Theresa thought disapprovingly. Theresa turned to the woman she had hired as a nanny. "Give him to me," she ordered and held out her arms for Siegfried. When Walther reached her, she was holding their son in her arms.

"I was looking for you everywhere!" Walther excused himself breathlessly. "They announced the wrong platform, but I found Trude and sent her to the car." Walther then gave Theresa a big hug that made Siegfried scream even more furiously.

"Poor darling, you've frightened him!" Theresa drew back from Walther and held up his son. "Isn't he perfect?"

"Perfect," Walther agreed absently. Babies all looked alike to him, and he was much more interested in his wife. "You look lovely, darling."

She did look very pretty in a neat, double-breasted blue coat with gold buttons, and a hat that sat at a smart angle on her piled-up hair. Walther was suddenly very glad that she had joined him. Theresa was inwardly flattered by the compliment, but she felt she should make it very clear just how difficult the journey had been. She returned Siegfried to the nanny and told her husband bluntly, "I'm exhausted and dirty. This has been the most awful trip of my entire life. We've had nothing but problems from the start. I really don't see how you expected three women with a baby to manage everything alone?!"

"But you did, honey," Walther pointed out with a grin. "And now everything is over and you're here. Let me take you to your new home." He slipped his hand under her elbow and led her away. The nanny followed with Siegfried.

In front of the station, a large, shiny Peugeot waited. At the sight of Walther the driver, who had been leaning against the front fender, stood up straight and reached to open the back door. "Here we are, sweetheart; climb in." Walther watched with childlike delight as Theresa looked from the car to him and back again. "It's ours," he told her proudly. "It comes with the factory."

Theresa was impressed, and instantly more reconciled to the prospect of living here than she had been just moments before. Still, she felt that after all she had gone through on the trip, she should not cave in too easily. Without a word she climbed into the back seat.

It was completely dark, and Theresa could neither gain an impression of Warsaw nor see where they were going as they drove. She concentrated on her husband, first passing the greetings from his family and then narrating all the difficulties of the journey—the rude conductors, unhelpful stationmasters, and many inconsiderate fellow passengers. Walther just kept kissing her more and more frequently and passionately as he said again and again, "What a brave little woman I married!" and "See, I knew, you were clever enough to deal with everything!"

Walther snuggled closer and kissed her more and more intimately until Theresa felt compelled to hiss at him, "Walther! We aren't alone!"

The two serving women were sitting opposite and pointedly looked out their respective windows in embarrassment.

Walther whispered, "Okay; later," and then sat back and started chatting in a jovial tone, "You've simply got to meet Max v. Aggstein! He's running the *Deutsche Ausrüstungswerke GmbH* here in Warsaw, and he's on the best terms with the Governor of the Warsaw District." Walther still found it almost unbelievable that he was allowed to move in such illustrious circles. He was also acutely aware that Theresa was a great asset in this regard. Herr v. Aggstein had been notably friendlier ever since he had learned that Theresa had been born a Baroness v. Feldburg. He had said with relief, "My wife will be delighted to finally meet someone of her own kind here in Warsaw."

"What's this *Deutsche Ausrüstungswerke?*" Theresa asked, trying to straighten her hair and skirt and regain her dignity after Walther's "mauling."

"It's part of the SS's economic division. They're into acquiring and running factories, buying and taking over the capital equipment right away. They need highly trained management and have brought in men like Aggstein—he has a degree from the University of Vienna." As a man with only a grade-school education, Walther was very impressed by university graduates. After all, not even his brothers-in-law had degrees. "He said he might drop by with his wife to pay his respects. Frau v. Aggstein is so delighted that a fellow aristocrat is here at last."

"Tonight? But I'm exhausted! And you've hardly met your son, and my hair is filthy! Couldn't you have been more considerate and told him to come another night?"

"You're right." Walther flashed her a wink and grinned—that leering grin that said he had only one thing on his mind. "I'll call and tell him you're too tired for guests tonight. We can have them over for a proper dinner later in the week."

They finally stopped before a modern-looking villa in a quiet suburb. In the darkness all that could be seen was that the neighborhood had neat sidewalks, trees and front gardens; in short, it exuded respectability. Walther led his wife up the front steps and then, to Theresa's surprise, rang the bell.

A minute later she understood why: a maid in uniform opened the door and bobbed a curtsy.

Again Theresa turned a questioning look to the beaming Walther. He announced, "This is Celina, the downstairs maid."

"Does she speak German?" Theresa asked skeptically.

"Yes; that's the reason I hired her, even though she has no experience as a maid. I thought it would be easier for Trude and you to teach her about housework than to struggle with a Polack who can't understand German."

"But couldn't you find someone who both spoke German and had experience?" Theresa asked. Without waiting for an answer, she turned to the girl herself and asked, "And just what sort of work have you done? What are your references?"

"None, ma'am."

"None? But how did you earn your living? You aren't married, are you?" Already Theresa was imagining what a disaster this might be.

"No, ma'am. I'm not married. My father is an officer in the Polish Army, and I never had to work before. But he's been missing since the second week of the war. My mother and I have already sold everything that was left to us."

Theresa was shocked and far from pleased. A girl from good family down on her luck would be not only inexperienced, but spoiled and resentful as well— maybe even sullen. But Theresa knew this wasn't the time to discuss the problem. Walther had meant well. Men were just incompetent when it came to running a household. She would have to take control of things herself.

They continued into the house, and Walther drew Theresa's attention to one thing after another: the fine carpets, the beautiful wood furnishings, the Venetian glass mirror in the entry hall, the china cabinet with Meissen porcelain and Czech crystal. Even the paintings on the walls were oils of excellent quality. Theresa was increasingly astonished, and by the end of the tour quite overwhelmed by the wealth and good taste she found at every turn.

"But, Walther! This must have cost a fortune! And how did you ever find everything? It must have taken countless hours to find and select everything— you can't have managed alone!" Suddenly she was suspicious. Her instinct said that only a woman could have devoted the requisite time and attention to detail necessary to such a perfectly harmonious interior. "Who helped you?" she demanded, full of mistrust.

"No, no. No one helped me. I rented the house completely furnished—as you see, with china, linen, pots and pans—everything."

"Oh, well, that explains why everything matches so well—but can we really afford it?" she asked intently. She was determined that they should not go into debt, and remembered how she had had to count every penny at home to maintain a much smaller apartment.

Walther laughed and beamed, pulling her into his arms again firmly, "Yes, honey." He gave her a quick, teasing kiss on the nose, and enjoyed the way her eyes widened with happiness. She finally realized they were rich. Like a good businessman, he also rejoiced at just what a bargain it had been. He'd simply identified the house he found most suitable among the houses owned and occupied by Jews—and then gone to the police and had the family evicted.

✳   ✳   ✳   ✳

Altdorf
March 1940

The women of the household were gathered in the laundry. Around a pot of tea kept hot over a low candle, they mended and gossiped in a friendly sewing circle. Sophia Maria was sorting through old linens, looking for things she could donate to the Red Cross. A knock on the door drew everyone's attention and Father Matthias put his head around the door. After the murmur of greetings had died down, he looked over at Sophia Maria. "Frau v. Feldburg, may I have a word with you?"

Sophia Maria at once left her work and went out into the hall. Since it was chilly here, however, she suggested they go up to her study, adding, "I might even be able to find a little sherry."

Father Matthias, usually very happy to share a glass with her, hesitated. "Actually, this concerns one of your workers—one of the prisoners—and I really think you should talk to him yourself."

Surprised, Sophia Maria asked, "Is something wrong?" She'd had the impression things were going better recently.

"Yes, something is very wrong—at home in Poland, I mean. I want you to see something." He led her down the hall to the rarely used back entrance of the manor. Here one of the older prisoners was waiting for them, his face tense. He bobbed his head at Sophia Maria and muttered, "*Frau Baronin*," but he kept his eyes fixed pleadingly on the priest.

"Come on," Sophia Maria urged; "this is no place to talk." She took them into the estate office and offered both men a seat.

"Shall I explain?" Father Matthias asked the prisoner. The latter nodded vigorously. Father Matthias began, "Miljewski here received a letter from his wife yesterday—a letter written nearly a month ago! But that's another issue. Frau v. Feldburg, you'd better see this letter yourself." He turned to the prisoner and urged, "Let the *Frau Baronin* read the letter."

The man seemed reluctant, but he took the letter out of his pocket. It was written on poor-quality paper, dirty, and looked as if it had been in the rain at least once. Sophia Maria opened it carefully, so as not to tear it, and held it under the light of the desk lamp. Although her Polish was mediocre, it had improved substantially since the arrival of the Polish workers last fall. Where she stumbled, Father Matthias, who had been born and raised in Breslau, helped her. The text was simple and direct:

> *"My most dearly beloved husband, I am having the priest write to you because I am in complete despair and I don't know what else to do. I hate to trouble you when you must have so many troubles of your own, but no one else can tell me what to do.*
> *You do not know that after the war the Germans threw us off our land. I mean they evicted the whole village—except the Grisas and Konapkas, who are 'German' now. We could take only one bundle of belongings with us and were put on cattle cars. They took us across the new border, but in Tamoszow, where the train stopped, there was no housing. They put us into an old warehouse where there were no beds, no ovens, and no water. Some old stoves were brought, but it is very cold and all the windows are broken. Many children and old people are sick. Some have died. We are all registered as unemployed; otherwise we wouldn't get anything to eat. We also get a couple of zloty unemployment money, but it's not enough to buy warm socks for the children. I have wrapped their feet in my apron, which I tore up. I don't need it, since we don't have anything to cook, only old bread.*
> *But this isn't why I am writing you. I am writing you because now they say I cannot stay here. I must go to work in Germany. If I don't, then I can't get even the bread or the unemployment money. But if I go, what will become of the children? They are too young to work, and everyone here is as bad off as we. Many of the men have been rounded up and sent to Germany. I look for work but there is little, and there are thousands of unemployed because all the Poles who lived in West Prussia or Posen were forced to leave. There is no place to work except in Germany, they say. I thought if I take the children to my aunt in Krakow, then I could find work. But I don't have the money for the train fare. Please tell me what I should do and, if possible, send money so we can go to Krakow. God help and bless you.*
> *Your ever-loving wife,*
> *Ludmilla.*

For several minutes after she had finished reading the letter, Sophia Maria continued to stare at the page, too ashamed to look up. What could she say? There were no words of protest strong enough, no words of outrage adequate, no expressions of sympathy deep enough when it was one's own government and countrymen who had done this. At last she did look up, and at once the prisoner started to speak. In a pleading, desperate tone, the words spilled out in Polish too fast for Sophia Maria to understand—but the meaning was clear, nevertheless.

He had very little money saved. He would have saved more if only he'd known what was happening to his family, but this was the first letter he'd received. Still, he had almost 5 *RM*. Was that enough for the train fare for his wife and three children to Krakow? And how could he get the money to his wife as fast as possible? And if the money wasn't enough, could she advance him what he needed on his wages? He'd work very hard, she'd see.

She waved him silent. "That's not the point." The hope that had been building up in his eyes and voice froze in horrified disappointment. Then she continued, "First we have to find out where your wife is. That letter was written more than a month ago. Perhaps she's already in Krakow, or she may be somewhere in Germany. If they were going to take her rations away, how long could she wait for an answer?"

The man looked back at her in mute despair.

"There has to be some way of getting in touch with the Employment Office in Tomaszov. If she has been receiving unemployment benefits, they will know where she is." The hope was beginning to return to the prisoner's eyes. "We'll take care of that," she said with a glance at her watch, "tomorrow morning. Everything would be closed now." She paused to think and then continued, "If your wife is still there, we'll pay the *Reichsbahn* for the tickets here and have your wife pick them up at the station in Tomaszov. All right?"

The man dropped on one knee and kissed her hand. Then he stood and bowed his head to Father Matthias as well. They wished him good night, and he departed.

When the two Germans were alone, the priest turned to Sophia Maria and asked, "How can they do such things? Drive human beings—women and children—from their homes with only a handful of belongings. In the middle of winter! Freight trains and warehouses! No water, no sanitary facilities, can you imagine what that means?" He shook his head, overcome by images he conjured up from his own childhood in the slums of Breslau.

Sophia Maria could not fully imagine it; it was too far beyond her experience. Still, she was shocked to the marrow of her bones. "Every time I think I've heard the worst, I learn something new. I don't understand how they get away with it. Where is the Army? Why doesn't it do something?"

Father Matthias didn't have an answer. The question was one he'd intended to ask Sophia Maria.

"It's so pointless!" she continued in an angry tone. "What if we can help one woman and her children? What about the others? Miljewski's wife said there were thousands, and if they've really driven all the Poles out of the reincorporated territories, it must be hundreds of thousands, even a million. What do they hope to gain? Don't they realize it will only be the cause of the next war? It doesn't make sense!"

"Inhumanity never makes sense, Frau von Feldburg."

In the morning the tedious struggle with the bureaucracy began. Miljewski sat mutely in Sophia Maria's office as she telephoned. His trusting eyes never left her face as she called the Employment Office in Altdorf, the Employment Office in Tomaszov, the police station at Tomaszov, the SS Command in Tomaszov, the police station again, the Labor Office in Frankfurt am Main, and finally I.G. Farben in Frankfurt. After each call, Sophia Maria explained what she had learned.

Miljewski's wife, Ludmilla, according to the Labor Office in Tomaszov, had "volunteered" for work in the *Reich* just over two weeks earlier. Ludmilla had been found "fit for service in the *Reich*" and transported roughly a week ago to Frankfurt, where the Employment office sent her to the I.G. Farben plant. Sophia called I.G. Farben, and after several connections to offices and employees who disclaimed all knowledge or responsibility for foreign workers, was finally put through to a personnel officer who admitted that, yes, Ludmilla Miljewski was a new employee of the Frankfurt plant.

Miljewski did not know how to react at first. Where were the children? What was his wife doing in a factory? She was a farmer. Was Frankfurt far away? Could he go visit her?

Sophia Maria shook her head. Foreign workers were prohibited from using public transportation or being more than 20 km away from their place of work.

Was there no way? His eyes pleaded. Then he started on a new track. His wife was a good woman, a hard worker, a farmer's wife. She would be one hundred times more useful than the silly RAD girls who were assigned to the estate only for a few months at a time. Miljewski assured Sophia Maria that his wife was a good cook; she could make good food from simple things for the Polish workers.

Sophia Maria listened seriously. He was right. She could use several more women—farm women who knew about pigs and hens, pressing and pickling— women who could cook, clean and look after the "mess hall" of Polish workers. They were managing well enough at the moment, but only because it was winter and the men had time to look after themselves. When spring came, she would desperately need help. Besides, wasn't it a little compensation for all the German government had done to these innocent people, if she could reunite at least one man and wife?

So the telephoning began again. I.G. Farben was willing in principle to release the said worker, but of course there were the costs to consider and the transportation.... In the end it had taken another 3 weeks, 32 *RM* 65 *pf*, and a special train permit from the police and the SS to get Frau Miljewski to Altdorf.

Sophia Maria considered it worthwhile when she saw man and wife fall into each other's arms at the Altdorf station—until her other married Polish workers came to her to ask if their wives couldn't also be brought to Altdorf.

CHAPTER 6

▼

**Berlin
March 1940**

Marianne Moldenauer was trying to carry too much. In addition to her book bag slung over one shoulder, she had an overflowing shopping bag in one hand, her keys in the other, and a loaf of bread under her arm. She made it up to the first landing, but then her book bag fell off her shoulder and jostled the arm with the shopping bag. A cabbage was knocked out of the bag and started bouncing down the stairs. In her haste to try to catch it, she didn't prop up the shopping bag properly and it fell over, spilling its contents onto the landing. "Damn!" Marianne exclaimed heartily, and at once regretted it, as she caught sight of another person at the foot of the stairs.

The young man who looked up at her was slender and tall. He wore round glasses framing gentle, pale-blue eyes. He had very blond, wispy hair over fair skin. He wore a light, tan-colored coat over a light suit, a white shirt and brown tie. Marianne recognized him at once as the Gestapo official who had moved into the apartment upstairs.

Peter Kessler quickly took in the situation and started hurriedly up the stairs. "Let me help," he urged, catching the runaway cabbage and then bending and collecting other items for Marianne as she stonily replaced them in her bag.

When all was once more put away, Marianne muttered an unfriendly "Thank you" without meeting the young man's eyes, and turned to continue up the stairs.

"Here, let me." Kessler at once relieved Marianne of the shopping bag and they started up the stairs together. "Perhaps I should introduce myself," Kessler suggested as they reached the next landing. He promptly shifted the bag to his left hand and held out his right. Despite her reluctance, Marianne had been too well brought up to refuse the gesture. "Peter Kessler," he introduced himself.

Marianne pulled her hand away as quickly as possible with a mumbled "Marianne Moldenauer." Still avoiding his eyes, she started up the stairs again.

"I've seen you several times," Kessler continued, in a valiant effort to start a conversation as he followed in her wake. "I wanted so much to meet you, but you always seem to be in a hurry."

"I'm enrolled in a Red Cross course. It's very demanding."

"I can imagine. Are you interested in nursing, then?"

"I'm interested in medicine," Marianne corrected irritably. "I'm going to study medicine at university as soon as I've finished my compulsory national service next fall."

Kessler looked at her in surprise mixed with wonderment. In the small town he came from, it was rare for boys—let alone girls—to go to university. Girls certainly didn't study medicine. Furthermore, Marianne at 20 was still more girl than woman. She was dressed now in a cardigan sweater over a simple cotton skirt and blouse. She wore ankle socks and practical laced shoes with thick soles. Her brown, wavy hair was clipped out of her face with two barrettes, but hung free to her shoulders.

Taking advantage of Kessler's surprise, Marianne took the bag back from him and with the words, "Thank you again; good day," she turned to unlock her door.

Kessler was hurt by the abruptness of her dismissal. "But—"

She turned back from unlocking the door and waited without encouragement.

"But couldn't we get to know each other better? We could have a cup of coffee or something—it's a beautiful day." His eyes were hopeful.

"I have to put these things away."

"Oh, I'll wait," he agreed happily, a smile breaking out over his face.

"I have to study for my exams. The finals are next week."

"Maybe I can help," he suggested eagerly. "I had to pass a Red Cross test once." Kessler sincerely wanted to help, and had no idea how patronizing he sounded.

Marianne, incensed by his arrogance, told him frankly, "I don't need help studying—just time to do so!"

"Half an hour is all I'm asking for," Kessler countered, with a smile that wavered between hopeful and pleading. "Let me buy you coffee."

"All right; I'll be right out." Marianne spoke with apparent irritation, as if she just wanted to be rid of him. She closed the door behind her and asked herself what on earth she had done. Why hadn't she just said "no"? What did she want with this Gestapo agent? But she was a little breathless with excitement, too. She'd never been asked on a date before by anyone. Her contact with young men had been confined to doing things in mixed groups. A half-dozen young people of both sexes, paying their own way, would go to a movie or concert. She found it flattering as well as confusing that Kessler had asked her out. She wished she could have asked her parents' advice, but they were not at home. In this nice weather, they had probably gone for a walk.

Nervously, she unpacked the groceries in the kitchen and threw her book bag on her bed. Then she grabbed a hairbrush and vigorously stroked her hair. After a few violent strokes, she put the brush down and pulled her hand away. "Why do you want to look nice for that man? You don't want him to be interested in you! Why don't you go and tell him you can't come? You've changed your mind." She almost ran to the door, but stopped with her hand on the handle. What could she say? What excuse could she use?

She opened the door. Kessler was nervously pacing about the landing, apparently distressed that she was taking so long. Relieved to see her, he broke into a bright smile and told her how pretty she looked.

"I brushed my hair," Marianne answered bluntly, trying to deny the effect of the compliment, and added admonishingly, "We mustn't be more than a half-hour."

"Word of honor!" Kessler swore, raising his right hand as if before a court but speaking in a light, playful tone.

"We can go to the café on the corner," Marianne told him, starting down the stairs at her usual fast pace, determined to get this over with.

"Yes, that's a nice place," Kessler agreed. "It must be particularly nice in summer when they have tables outside. They do set up tables in the garden, don't they? I only moved to Berlin last fall, so I don't know. Have you always lived in Berlin?" Kessler was almost running to keep up with Marianne, and talking frantically to her back the whole time.

"I was born here," Marianne replied, reaching the ground floor and casting Kessler the remark over her shoulder.

"How lucky! Maybe you could show me around sometime? There's so much to see and I feel as if I've hardly begun. I hate going to museums and galleries alone. Do you like art?"

"Very much," Marianne told him pointedly.

Something occurred to Kessler. "Did you know Gottfried Jähring very well?" His tone was sympathetic.

"Not very well, but he was always very nice to me, and he let me see his paintings once or twice. I thought they were very interesting."

"Yes. I thought they were interesting, too," Kessler agreed, "but not pretty. Isn't art supposed to be pretty?"

"Not necessarily," Marianne told him with the self-confidence of the freshly educated. "Art is about expression and social commentary and symbolism and many, many other things than just being pretty. Pretty is just kitsch!" she told him definitively.

"Oh," Kessler accepted her judgement meekly. "You see, I never learned about art. I would have liked to, but my father has a small shop in Langen near Frankfurt. I don't suppose you've ever heard of Langen? No reason why you should," he added with a sheepish smile; "nothing ever happens there. Anyway, I'm the first person in our family that could get higher education, and I had to do something practical."

"Oh?" Marianne asked, turning sharply on him, her eyes blazing with fury, "like spy on innocent people and ruin their lives!?"

Kessler was taken aback by her vehemence and hostility. He stopped and caught his breath. His eyes, magnified by his glasses, gazed at Marianne, and the expression in them was one of hurt.

"Well, that's what you do, isn't it?" Marianne challenged him, turning to face him boldly.

"No, Fräulein Moldenauer," Kessler said softly, "that's not what I do."

"Oh? Then how do you describe it?"

"Fräulein Moldenauer," Kessler spoke very softly, his eyes still full of hurt, "my job is protecting innocent people from enemy agents who are trying to undermine our country from within. It is very, very important work, because spies and enemy agents can do as much harm to our Nation as bombers and panzers."

Marianne snorted in disbelief, but Kessler was so sure of his mission that he drew strength and confidence from talking about it. He met Marianne's eyes and said very distinctly and firmly, "I don't mean men like your father, Fräulein Moldenauer. I've read the things he said very carefully, and it's very clear that his remarks were not really treasonous. I'm sure he never wanted—not for one moment—to do any harm to the *Reich*. I think your father—correct me if I'm wrong—but I believe your father is simply misguided. I mean, it seems to me he sincerely believes in liberal democracy such as the English practice it, and has not understood what National Socialism is all about."

Marianne did not find it easy to hear her father discussed, especially by an employee of the Secret State Police; it was a painful subject. Tensely, she flung at Kessler, "If you know he never meant any harm to the *Reich*, why did you hound him from his chair and ruin his reputation?"

"We didn't do that," Kessler pointed out, speaking for the State and Party. "It was the students and faculty who drove him from his chair. But you must understand that if we are to build a National Socialist state, then it is particularly important for the nation's future elite—our future leaders—to be fully indoctrinated with National Socialist ideology. Your father, with his outmoded ideals, couldn't do that. Furthermore, it is the responsibility of all teachers, professors and other educators to strengthen young people's faith in the *Führer*. By suggesting, as your father did, that the *Führer* had made a mistake, he contradicted the entire Leadership Principle on which National Socialism is based. That made him unsuitable to teach future generations of leaders; but, I repeat, it does not make him an enemy of the State. Please believe me when I say I truly respect your father for his integrity and courage. I think it is wonderful that he stood up for what he believed in—even if I have to agree with the University's decision to retire him."

Marianne turned away abruptly and shoved open the heavy door out of the apartment house. She strode down the walk and turned in the direction of the café. Kessler hurried after her, anxiously awaiting her response. She turned into the café and took a seat at an empty table. Only then did she face Kessler. Her expression was set, but her eyes were wet. "My father has so much knowledge and wisdom, and just because of one lecture, he is not allowed to pass that knowledge on to young people! Don't you think that is a waste, Herr Kessler?"

Kessler squirmed a little uneasily, but he met her eyes. "Yes, it is. If only your father could embrace National Socialism—surely you see that it has done so much for our country?" he asked anxiously.

"Yes," Marianne admitted somewhat hesitantly.

Kessler preferred not to hear her doubt. "I knew you were no closed-minded conservative!" Because Kessler had fallen "in love" with the fresh, pretty Marianne from the first time he'd seen her in the courtyard of his new house, he convinced himself that this was enough politics. He changed the subject with an eager smile: "I'll bet you—as a Berliner—have no idea what a thrill it is for a country hick like me just to be here?"

Marianne looked at him uncertainly. She greeted the change of subject, but she was still too tense and upset to share in his happy mood.

Kessler, however, saw what he wanted to see: that Marianne was looking at him with wide, apparently interested, eyes. He was really sitting in a Berlin café with a pretty, sweet city girl! He felt like a man of the world when he waved the waitress over and ordered coffee and cake for two, slipping her the butter stamps without even counting them. Still feeling very worldly, he admitted, "I'm really just like all the country hicks they make fun of in the movies. I still stare with an open mouth when I drive past the *Reichskanzlei* or go through the Brandenburg Gate." His childish delight softened Marianne's hostility to him. It was hard not to like someone who could be so candid about his own provinciality.

Their coffee and cake arrived, heavily laden with whipped cream. Marianne exclaimed in surprise: you needed extra ration cards for cream of any kind. Kessler looked a little embarrassed, but admitted, "We could never have it as children, and I just can't get enough now that I can afford it."

Marianne actually smiled at that. Not a big or long smile, just a quick little smile of understanding. She loved whipped cream, too.

Watching as she—with obvious pleasure—cut into her cake with her fork, Kessler felt himself so in love with her that he couldn't bare to be misunderstood. He burst out, "Fräulein Moldenauer, please believe me, I'm not the monster you take me for. I know the Gestapo has a reputation for harshness, even brutality, but—well—just between the two of us, a lot of that is just propaganda to make people more careful. And if there are abuses, then the only way to stop them is for decent, honest men to go into the Gestapo. We can't leave such important work to uneducated thugs! The more good men go into the Gestapo, the better it will become. It will become better at distinguishing between real threats like the Communist Jähring, and harmless, misguided but well-meaning men like your father. You see that, don't you?"

Marianne nodded her head, but added, "That is, I suppose I understand the theory, but why you?" Marianne couldn't help herself. She liked Peter Kessler, and if only he hadn't been a Gestapo agent, she was sure she would have liked him very much more. Maybe they would even have become friends....

"Please don't think this is arrogant or conceited or anything like that," Kessler pleaded, leaning forward and focusing on her through his glasses. "I truly believe that if I can rise to a position of power, then I can help make the whole organization what it ought to be—a clean and honorable sword of the State—just as good and respected as the Army itself."

Someone older would have laughed at Kessler's naiveté and ambition; but Marianne was just twenty, and she too had secret dreams of making the world a better place by her personal action. Although she could not sympathize with

Kessler's choice of career, she could not remain indifferent to the sincerity and purity of his personal motives. But mostly, she was unconsciously the victim of that inexplicable 'chemistry' that often causes two apparently incompatible people to be attracted to one another. Marianne wanted to believe Peter Kessler. Her answer now was ambiguous: she sighed. But Kessler correctly perceived the softening of her feelings toward him, and he smiled.

"Did you know the *Flying Dutchman* is being performed in the Staatsoper this week?" he asked excitedly.

She shook her head.

"Wouldn't you like to go? If I can get tickets, that is?"

"If you can get tickets ..."

CHAPTER 7

▼

Belgium
May 1940

It had been a good day for the *Luftwaffe*. Called up to soften the defenses of the Allied rear guard, the *Luftwaffe* had provided a squadron of Stukas to do the job and a squadron of Me109s to protect the Stukas. The Stukas had performed their task with textbook precision and devastating effect, while the Me109s held off a single flight of Belgian Hurricanes easily.

The sense of invincibility and victory only mounted when the fighter squadron was ordered to land not at the field from which they had taken off, but at a captured Belgian airfield. They put down amid the wrecks of five Belgian aircraft and the smoke from the burning fuel tanks. An hour later they were taking up quarters in a Mess well stocked with food and drink and filled with the personal belongings of the rightful occupants. It was eerie—but exciting, too.

The officers soon crowded at the unfamiliar bar, all talking at once, anxious to recount their individual adventures, and the intelligence officer was having difficulty getting official reports. Through the open window came the rumble of trucks as the ground crews started to arrive, the shouting of the NCOs directing drivers, and anti-aircraft fire as German crews tried their hand at manning the Belgian airfield defenses.

When it was confirmed that there would be no more flying that day (because their own fuel tankers had not yet reached the new base), Christian was quick to suggest an investigation of the nearest town. Busso went out to organize ground transportation, while Hartmann got the permission of the CO.

When, rather drunk, they arrived back at their temporary base late that evening, Christian was sound asleep in the back of one of the two *Kübelwagen*, squeezed in between Busso and a new pilot, Hans Becker. Dieter was driving with Hartmann asleep beside him in the front. Dieter woke the others as they arrived. Christian remarked, still half asleep, "Not a bad plane, the Hurricane, just not as good as the Emil." (That was the pilot's affectionate name for the Me109e.)

"Yes," Dieter agreed, catching him before he tripped over his own feet.

Becker crawled out of the car after Christian. He had never in his life consumed so much alcohol. "Tomorrow I'm gonna get one," he announced, pulling himself to his feet unsteadily.

"Of course you are," Christian agreed, putting his arm over Becker's shoulder. "We're all going to get one—or two. Come on, Dieter, just leave the car here."

Dieter was feeling the wine, too. His head was light and he was tired in a dreamy, pleasant way. Why not? he thought. No one will care. He locked his side of the car and crawled out the passenger side. "Oops. The lights." He crawled back in to turn them off. The windshield wipers came on. The other officers laughed. Dieter turned off the wipers and then the lights and crawled back out.

They went into the strange mess together. It was dark and quiet.

"SHHHH!" Christian urged loudly.

They laughed and started up the stairs. Becker fell with a clatter. They laughed.

"SHHHH!" Christian repeated. They broke up laughing again.

Finally, after some false turns, they found themselves in their respective rooms; and falling onto his bed, Christian concluded it had been the best day of his life.

Morning came much too early. Christian couldn't rightly call it a hang-over, but his eyes hurt and his stomach was far from enthusiastic about breakfast. The airman who shook him awake only made matters worse.

"The *Herr Leutnant* must get up," he announced solemnly, his youthful face concerned.

Christian turned onto his stomach and waved him to leave, but the airman wouldn't be put off. "You must get up now, *Herr Leutnant*. The *Herr Staffelkapitän* wants to see you at 7.15, *Herr Leutnant*."

"What? The CO? What time is it now?"

"7.03, *Herr Leutnant*."

"*Scheisse!*" Christian was out of bed and rummaging around in the closet for a clean shirt. Everything was wrinkled. "What is this all about? Are we flying this morning?"

The airman shook his head in ignorance.

"*Scheisse!*" Christian repeated, but he rather suspected it had something to do with his kill the day before, and he was elated.

Just outside the Squadron Leader's office, Christian paused and took a deep breath for the first time since he'd been awakened 11 minutes earlier. He gave a quick polishing rub to his boots with his handkerchief before he shoved it in his trouser pocket, smoothed down his tunic, straightened his tie and adjusted the angle of his cap. Then, squaring his shoulders, he knocked sharply on the door.

"Come in!"

Christian stepped in smartly and saluted. The CO did not even look up from his desk. He was reading something. "Feldburg?" He was still reading.

"*Herr Hauptmann!*" Christian was still at attention.

The *Staffelkapitän* slowly raised his head. *Hauptmann* Bartels, a square-faced, heavy-set man, did not exactly put his subordinates at ease when he studied them mirthlessly—as he did now. Christian began to sense he was in trouble. He feverishly tried to work out what it was this time. They hadn't been out that late. Had they made too much noise? Maybe it was leaving the car out in front—that was provocative.

"Feldburg, let me get right to the point."

Christian nodded unconsciously, now very much in a hurry to get any unpleasantness over with.

"I'm going to skip over your usual shortcomings—rudeness, irresponsibility, excessive drinking, arrogance—you were obviously never meant to be a leader in the new Germany, and I'm sure only the pressure of imminent war induced the *Luftwaffe* Personnel Office to accept you in the first place. If I happen to think that was a mistake, there isn't much I can do about it."

Hauptmann Bartels sat up straighter, and his previously disgusted tone turned angry. "The *Luftwaffe* is the finest air force in the world because it has evolved a system of fighting that is disciplined and coordinated—not futile, amateurish and foolhardy like the Belgian. Orders are to be obeyed, *Leutnant* von Feldburg! Are you listening?!"

Christian was still at attention and given the volume of his commander's voice, he could hardly *not* listen. He thought the question stupid, but he replied with the expected, "*Jawohl, Herr Hauptmann!*"

"Then the next time I order you to rejoin the squadron, I expect you to rejoin immediately. You will not go chasing off across the countryside for your personal glory and satisfaction. Is that clear?"

"*Jawohl, Herr Hauptmann!*"

"Now, as to this claim of a Hurricane—"

"Becker can confirm—"

"Don't interrupt!"

Christian swallowed and began to feel defeated. They were going to take away his kill, the most precious achievement of his whole life.

"It is obvious from this report," the CO continued with a contemptuous wave toward the document on his desk, "that you chased a Hurricane and probably damaged it. You did not, however, see either the pilot jump or the aircraft crash. There seems to me no reason to believe that it did not make it safely to another base or at least crash-land safely behind enemy lines. You were already behind enemy lines—if I interpret your sloppy report correctly—when you registered the first hits. You will, therefore, not be credited with it—even if by some chance this entire report is not fabricated."

"Herr Hauptmann—"

"Dismissed!" The *Staffelkapitän* looked down again, and after a moment Christian realized there was nothing he could do but click his heels, salute and leave.

"Heil Hitler!" the *Hauptmann* called out pointedly.

Out in the hall, Christian started swearing furiously under his breath and hoping *Hauptmann* Bartels would soon be shot down.

*   *   *   *

France
May/June 1940

For Philip, the campaign in France was a collage of memories: a stream of days and near-sleepless nights blurred into a background for a few clear images.

Most vivid was May 19, a fine sunny day bordering on turning too warm. By then they had nearly become used to following in the dust of other panzer divisions. They were used to following the war on their radios as other units spearheaded the advance. As town after town passed, the entire campaign was christened *"Blitzkrieg"*—lightning warfare—because of the speed of operations. Philip and his troops had listened with mixed relief and envy as other divisions engaged in fierce fighting crossing the Meuse or clashed with French armor on May 13, 15, and 17.

Philip had been fighting drowsiness as the sun climbed. Behind him, the company groaned along steadily. They were the rear guard of the division's armored and motorized units, as usual, and behind them was nothing but non-motorized infantry and support troops, all trailing by several kilometers. The panzers, as always, were being rushed westward relentlessly.

The voice of the radio operator in the last panzer interrupted his thoughts. "*Herr Rittmeister*, there's something funny going on behind us." This was not the most militarily correct report, but it was typical of the soldier Schill. Schill was the kind of bright, quick-thinking junior NCO who would have been a perfect candidate for officer training if only he had paid more attention to military formalities. But apparently he neither wanted to bother about them nor cared about getting into the officer corps, so he was a simple radio operator.

With binoculars, Philip had rapidly determined that the "funny" activity spotted by Schill was nothing less than French armor pouring up the Moncornet road—and there was no German armor, indeed no troops to speak of, between them and Panzer Corps Guderian's headquarters.

In that instant, Philip saw the entire campaign in the West in jeopardy. He saw it in his mind as if it were laid out in red and blue on a General Staff map. Three German panzer corps had broken through the Ardennes and were racing for the channel in order to trap the British Expeditionary Force and the bulk of the French Army's active divisions in Belgium. These had rushed north to meet the advance of German Army Group B. As the German panzer corps swept westward, their lines of communication and supply stretched out longer and longer. The divisions became increasingly strung out along the length of their advance, and their own flanks were unprotected and vulnerable. Although the British and the bulk of the French forces were pinned down fighting German Army Group B, there were nevertheless still fresh French divisions north of Paris—that is, south of the advancing German panzer divisions.

Philip saw the situation from the perspective of the French General Staff. French forces had to smash through the thin line of German panzers, reestablish contact with the bulk of Allied forces inside Belgium, and then cut off the foolhardy German panzers from their own lines of communication and supply. Cut off from the rest of the German Army, the panzer divisions would be trapped with their backs to the sea and crushed.

As he watched French armor push up the road toward Moncornet through his binoculars, Philip saw this imperative French counterthrust. He saw it piercing the German flank unopposed, rolling over the unprotected Corps HQ, and joining up with the Allied forces in Belgium.

Philip at once turned his panzers around and attacked. He had no orders to do that, but the situation was so clear to him that he had not once considered orders necessary. There was not a minute to lose. He turned his panzer around and in high gear, the engine screaming in protest, rushed back past his company to take the lead while the others reversed their direction in place. He attacked in company strength just a quarter hour after the French panzers had been sighted.

Where he made his mistake was that in his urgency to get his panzers turned around and deployed for an attack, his report to Battalion/Regiment had been too terse and perfunctory. It was not an intentional act. It had been merely been an amateurish mistake—and the fight was between professionals.

Later, Philip learned that the French tanks he had engaged were elements of Colonel Charles de Gaulle's 4th Armored Division. At the time, Philip had only been aware that the French troops were well led, well trained, and better equipped than his own company.

It had been a bloody fight, a fight he could not have won if Stukas hadn't arrived—apparently out of nowhere—and effectively decimated the French. His casualties had been heavy; in less than two hours, 29% of his personnel were dead or wounded and nearly a quarter of his equipment inoperable.

No sooner had the smoke cleared than Regiment demanded an explanation of his action. Colonel Viebranz, the regimental commander, was outraged by what Philip had done. He hadn't made a proper report. He had hidden the magnitude of the attack. He had failed to ask for orders. Obviously, Viebranz concluded, Feldburg was more interested in gaining a personal reputation than in sparing the lives of his troops or even in the outcome of the campaign.

Philip had not defended himself. What could he say? That he had not acted out of personal ambition seemed irrelevant beside the raw fact that his inadequate report had been responsible for Regiment's failure to send reinforcements. Because he had not been reinforced, his company had been vastly outnumbered and correspondingly mauled. His company had suffered 29% casualties, and each and every one of them was his fault.

"Because of your irresponsible behavior," Oberst Viebranz thundered, "enemy tanks came within a few kilometers of Guderian's HQ, and he's breathing fire." Viebranz went on to say that Regiment had no intention of standing between Philip and that fire. Quite the opposite. Philip was ordered to proceed forthwith to Corps HQ and explain his behavior to Guderian personally.

Philip registered with wry cynicism that this was a cowardly and non-military response. Every commander was supposed to take responsibility for his subordinates—particularly for their mistakes. But Viebranz's military experience came from the *Freikorps*, and he had been repeatedly rejected by the *Reichswehr*. Only after Hitler came to power had he been allowed to wear the uniform again. He had taken an instant dislike to Philip—who personified the spirit of the *Reichswehr*—from the day he reported. He was clearly delighted that the aristocratic, *Reichswehr*-trained General Staff candidate had failed after all. Under the shock of the casualties, however, Philip found his career of secondary importance.

Philip was sent by motorcycle to Corps HQ. Here he was escorted by an ADC, with what he took to be looks of guarded sympathy, to General Guderian. Guderian had a reputation for a violent temper. He was known for being abrasive to superiors and blistering to subordinates. Someone had once described him as "a prima donna in the form of a Prussian general."

Philip saluted. "*Rittmeister* von Feldburg reporting as ordered, *Herr General.*"

Guderian looked at him coldly—so coldly that Philip shivered. "You commanded the company that engaged French armor on the Moncornet road today?"

"*Jawohl, Herr General.*"

"Report precisely."

Philip expressionlessly related what had happened, pointedly avoiding all excuses. He knew they would do him no good in this company.

"You reported via Battalion to Regiment and then acted without requesting or awaiting orders?" Guderian summarized.

"*Jawohl, Herr General.*"

There was a long silence and then a slight nod. "Absolutely correct. Regiment should have been able to recognize the seriousness of the situation on its own. Your message was concise, but clear enough." To Philip's amazement he tapped the log of the radio message Philip had sent.

Later the ADC explained to Philip that Guderian had learned of the threat to his headquarters from a frantic courier who had nearly collided with the French and fled back to HQ. Guderian had ordered a response from the 10th Panzer and called for air support. When Guderian had learned that only a single company had been engaged in the action, he had had one of his notorious fits of rage. He had directed this first at Division, but the Divisional Commander replied firmly that he had ordered a response by an entire regiment. A regiment would have been enough. Guderian then turned his fury on *Oberst* Viebranz, who instantly defended himself by claiming that Philip had made a "false" report of the situation. Guderian demanded a copy of the radio log and Philip's personal appearance. When the radio log arrived, however, Guderian had noted that the cryptic message was logged in almost an hour *before* Guderian's HQ had become aware of the threat. This put the entire incident in a new light from Corps perspective.

Guderian informed Philip curtly, "Regiment failed on three counts: they failed to inquire after the strength of forces you reported attacking; they failed to send an observer forward to confirm your report and assess the situation on their own; and, most seriously, they failed to pass on your report to Division or myself. I'm recommending you for the EKII" (Iron Cross Second Class) "and I want you to submit to my Chief of Staff the names of those in your company equally deserving. You can assume that your acceptance into the General Staff is herewith assured."

Before Philip could absorb this fully unexpected twist of events, a call for Guderian from Army Commander v. Kleist terminated the interview. He was dismissed with a hasty handshake.

After that, the circumstances under which he was awarded the EKI (Iron Cross First Class) were less memorable. By mere chance, his company had been the first to break through to the Channel at St. Valéry-en-Caux, one of the last evacuation points for the remnants of the British Army that had not made it out at Dunkirk. The appearance of his Panzers had apparently caused the Royal Navy to withdraw, abandoning literally thousands of British soldiers still on the beach. Since the ships had been far out of range of his cannons and completely invulnerable to the caliber of his guns, Philip had at first been astonished by the flight of the Royal Navy—but relieved as well.

As long as troops were embarking and escaping, he would have been compelled to slaughter them; the withdrawal of the Royal Navy ensured that all the men left behind would be taken prisoner, and so there was no need to fire at them as long as they offered no resistance. Only later did Philip register that this was perhaps the motive for the Royal Navy's withdrawal.

At the time, he found himself massively outnumbered by his "prisoners" and grateful for the cooperation of English officers, who ensured that their men surrendered their arms and then waited patiently and in an orderly manner for further developments. Together with an English sergeant, Philip found himself providing first aid to a seriously wounded English lieutenant. Never had he felt so much respect for the English as in this moment of their worst defeat.

But the memory that most characterized the whole campaign for Philip had been an incident of neither military nor personal importance. It had been only a couple of days after the encounter with de Gaulle's armor, and again the countryside had been rolling by peacefully and harmlessly. They were, yet again, following in the tracks of the lead divisions and keeping track of the spectacular successes of others by radio and map.

Philip periodically pulled out his map and spread it on the top of his panzer to locate the points referred to by other units or to locate his own position. This he had done from the start of the campaign, but on this particular day his gunner kept asking to see the map. The gunner had shown an increasing interest in their progress day by day, but never before had he insisted on being shown their exact location every time they passed a crossroads or a cluster of houses that might have been a village. Philip was beginning to get annoyed, when the gunner cried out, "There!"

The gunner pulled himself halfway out of his escape hatch and was pointing off to one side. Philip followed his finger but saw nothing of particular interest: just a cluster of trees behind a weed-choked graveyard enclosed by a rusting fence.

"That must be where my father's buried." The gunner did not take his eyes off the graveyard as he spoke and he kept his voice level, but his face was tense. Philip hesitated only half a second. Then he quietly told the driver to stop.

The gunner looked up, hopeful but hesitant.

"Go on."

The young man scrambled agilely from his escape hatch with a hurried, "Thank you, *Herr Rittmeister*." He ran to the graveyard and climbed over the fence. From the line of halted panzers, his comrades watched. He looked systematically, pushing the weeds aside and bending over grave after grave. Finally he stopped. He stood for a long moment and then started feverishly up-rooting the weeds and tossing them from the long-neglected grave.

Unobserved, the gunner of another panzer climbed down and went into the field beside the graveyard. When Philip's gunner at last straightened and turned to come back, the other soldier handed him a bundle of wildflowers across the fence. The young man left them on his father's grave and the two soldiers returned to their respective panzers. In five minutes it was over, the graves of their fathers left behind them and a new war pulling them into an unknown future.

CHAPTER 8

▼

Crépon, France (near Cherbourg)
June 1940

Yvette, looking from the window of her fourth-floor flat, sighed at the passing grey trucks of the Luftwaffe. "Horrible!" she exclaimed in a heavy voice as she heard her roommate Gabrielle enter the room.

Yvette and Gabrielle shared the flat under the eaves, which was located over the apartment of their employer, M. St. Pierre. M. St. Pierre, his wife, and their two school-aged children lived over his perfumery, which was located in the fashionable business district of Crépon. Yvette, 21, and Gabrielle, 22, were the two sales clerks at the perfumery, which sold—in addition to the finest French perfumes—gloves, handbags, silk scarves, stockings, and other luxuries. They catered to the provincial elite and the fashion-minded citizens of the little town.

Yvette was petite and pretty in a dark, bright-eyed way. She wore her hair bobbed, and had neat, quick mannerisms that nicely accented her trim, fit figure. Quick in speech and gesture, she usually conveyed cheerfulness and intelligence. Her sadness now, while genuine, did not suit her, nor did her nervous vigil as she watched the *Luftwaffe* convoy roll by endlessly on the street below.

Gabrielle had stayed late in bed, as always on Sundays. She had washed her hair and brushed it dry. As she joined Yvette in their sitting room, she lounged comfortably on the couch and languidly asked "What?" Gabrielle was tall and shapely, with soft coloring. While Yvette's dark eyes and red lips made a sharp contrast to her white skin, Gabrielle had grey eyes, light brown hair and warm-colored, freckled skin. Her hair was long and she wore it loose down her back except at work, when she twisted it loosely onto her head. She was graceful and slow-paced, with the habit of slurring her words slightly and never quite opening her eyes all the way.

In answer to her disinterested "What?" Yvette replied with indignation, "*Les Boches*—the horrible, horrible *Boches*!"

"Are they back?" Gabrielle asked, with a slight show of interest as she looked up from her drying nail polish.

"Are they back?" Yvette parroted angrily. "Hundred and hundreds of them! Didn't you hear? They're setting up an air base next to the inn just outside of town."

"Really?" Gabrielle, with no anger at all, got up and went to gaze from the window with mild curiosity. She looked down on the top of the trucks and then peered with growing interest at the open staff cars. "So this is the fierce *Luftwaffe*. They look delightful, don't you think?"

"Gabrielle! How can you say such things?!"

Gabrielle shrugged again and walked back to the couch. "It's true. Life was boring here before the war. And these 'horrible *Boches*' of yours, weren't they perfectly polite the last time they came through? Frankly, I found them more gentlemanly than most Frenchmen." She smiled. "Especially the officers."

Yvette's father had been killed in the Great War. Completely outraged, she asked, "Have you no patriotism? Don't you love France?"

Gabrielle looked up slowly, but with a set expression around her lips and cold eyes that silenced Yvette. Her nonchalance and mild humor were gone. "Indeed, I love my country very much, and that is exactly why I feel nothing but contempt for our soldiers! Would Napoleon have fled without a major battle? Our fathers defied the Germans for four years! And now? The young men just ran away. I want nothing to do with the weak, cowardly wretches that call themselves French soldiers! I am only interested in real men—and that, apparently, means Germans. So," she shrugged and started to joke softly, "I'm glad there are some Germans to choose from."

Yvette was speechless with anger. Her face grew bright red. Tears came to her eyes and her breath was short, but Gabrielle ignored her.

The *Luftwaffe* base was very good for M. St. Pierre's business. The local clientele was overcome by a sense of uncertainty. Now that the war had turned into an occupation of indeterminate duration, they were uninterested in luxury goods. But the conquering heroes of Germany had no reason to save money, nothing to fear from the future, and lots of incentives to buy feminine luxuries. Most of the young men had never been to France before. They were anxious to send nice souvenirs to mothers, sisters, wives and sweethearts. Victory breeds a generous mentality. The soldiers of the *Wehrmacht* wanted to distribute largess to those unfortunate enough to have to stay home. In addition, there were still many things available in France that had disappeared from Germany years before. The Germans were impressed by anything with a Paris label and an expensive price tag.

Yvette took great pride in being tart to the German customers. This made M. St. Pierre angry and once, when she had been particularly rude, he even threatened to fire her. But Yvette pulled herself to her 5'1" height and faced him courageously. "They are our enemy," she told him self-righteously. "I will not pander to them!"

M. St. Pierre shook his finger at her. "They are our customers. I have built my business—my whole life—on good service." He shook with passion. "Do I ask each person who comes into my shop what his politics are? Do I ask if he is good to his children? If he is faithful to his wife? NO! I don't have to like my customers, but I must be gracious to them—or they won't come back!" He pounded his fist on the counter for emphasis.

"Good!" Yvette retorted. "I don't ever want to serve Germans again."

"If I don't sell my wares, my family starves. How is that patriotic?" M. St. Pierre wanted to know. "Look!" He rolled up his sleeve and showed the scar he had received at Verdun. "I served my country! All I ask now is to be left in peace to earn a living. And if you"—he shook his finger again at Yvette—"are intent on sabotaging me, then go out and get a new job!"

But Yvette did not take his threat seriously. She knew he was very protective of her and would not want her "out on the streets," so she continued to treat the German customers rudely.

Gabrielle was neutral. She did not treat the Germans brusquely or with obvious distaste, but she firmly repulsed their frequent efforts at friendliness. Gabrielle was very cool. She could be an attentive and pleasing sales clerk, but her manner allowed no familiarity. She smiled very distantly and pretended not to even hear personal questions. She told no one her name and never agreed to meet with any German customers after work.

Late one afternoon, in the lull before the closing rush, two *Luftwaffe* officers drifted into the shop. M. St. Pierre had gone into the back to have chocolate with his children, who were just home from school. Their high, happy chatter filtered through the curtain at the back of the shop. Late afternoon sun fell on the floor and across the counters through the open door. A single fly buzzed contentedly around the displays.

Yvette was busily rearranging some silk scarves inside a counter with her deft, shapely fingers; Gabrielle was seated on a high stool behind the opposite counter, dozing. Both girls wore dark dresses with white cuffs and collars; the collars sat primly at the base of their necks with starched neatness and their skirts fell full and limp to well below the knee. Neither girl was expecting customers at this time, and both showed mild surprise when the two officers momentarily darkened the doorway.

The first officer looked very young. He was lean to the point of unattractiveness. His hair and eyes were dark, making his pale skin paler. His serious expression made Gabrielle think he looked artistic. The second officer was an athletic, tanned man, broad-shouldered and quite tall. He had crinkled golden hair and a classically handsome face. Gabrielle could not help smiling—not at him but at her own pleasure. This, she thought, was a man whose arms would feel strong and protective.

Christian did not see her at first. His eyes had followed Dieter, whose attention had been attracted by the scarves Yvette was arranging. Dieter went straight over to that counter and peered at the scarves, while Christian followed leisurely.

Yvette, with a show of obvious contempt, left the scarves in disarray, closed the counter door with a bang, and turned her back on the two men to fuss with some items on the shelves behind the counters. Dieter glanced at her knowingly, and then continued to study the scarves. At last he asked without looking up, "Christian, do you think my sister would like one of these?"

But Christian had noticed Gabrielle and was gazing at her admiringly. Gabrielle looked back with her half-closed eyes, immobile.

"Christian?" Dieter turned around, followed Christian's gaze and sighed.

Christian broke off looking at Gabrielle. "Yes?"

Dieter pointed to the scarves. "Do you think my sister Annie would like one of these?"

Christian gave the scarves only a cursory glance. "Why not perfume? Here," he walked over to Gabrielle's counter, which contained the perfume.

But Dieter was not interested. He lingered over the scarves. "*Mademoiselle, combien ça coûte?*"

Yvette did not turn around. Instead she tossed an answer over her shoulder in French: "Those are very expensive."

"*Combien?*" Dieter persisted.

"350 francs."

Dieter frowned. Gabrielle silently left her stool and moved around beside Yvette. "No, Yvette," she said smoothly in French, "you've made a mistake. These scarves cost only 180 francs."

Yvette at last turned around to face Dieter. Her face grim, she told him in a pinched voice, "These are silk scarves from Marseilles. They are excellent quality." She pulled one out and felt it between her fingers. Dieter reached out to feel it and she snapped her hand back, although their hands had not come near to touching. Dieter looked up at her and held her eyes for a moment. She swallowed, suddenly realizing that she was being childish.

Dieter looked down at the scarf in his fingers. In his excellent French he remarked, "It is certainly fine, but it is not worth 350 francs."

"It costs 180 francs," Gabrielle repeated. She was standing in the sunlight from the door. The light gave her hair bronze highlights, and the breeze lifted the loose strands at the base of her neck. Dieter spared Christian a glance and confirmed his suspicions; Christian was devouring her with his eyes.

Dieter returned his attention to the scarves, this time leaning over the counter to select one for his sister. Christian, whose French was not as good as Dieter's, at last ventured to speak to Gabrielle. "Perfum," he started; "*combien ça la Perfum?*"

"*Quel perfume?*" Gabrielle countered.

Christian returned to the other counter and randomly pointed.

Gabrielle casually followed him to the counter, glanced at the perfume, and answered without interest.

"Do you like it?" Christian tried to ask in French.

Gabrielle shrugged.

"Which perfume do you like?" he continued in his flawed French.

Gabrielle ran her eyes over the display, and then with a soft "ah" selected one, which she set before Christian. "*Pour votre femme?*"

Christian laughed. "*Non, non. Pas de femme!*"

"*Ah, votre maîtresse,*" Gabrielle responded, nodding knowingly.

"*Non, non,*" Christian hastened to correct the misimpression. "*Pas de maîtresse!*" He picked up the bottle and gave it to her. "*Pour vous!*"

Gabrielle looked the bottle, shrugged and started to put it away.

"*Non, non!*" Christian stopped her by laying a hand on her wrist and cried out desperately to his friend, "Dieter! How do I explain to her I want to buy it for her as a gift?"

Dieter looked around and rapidly explained in French.

"Ah," Gabrielle replied with a faint smile and a glance at Christian, who smiled broadly. But she directed her answer to Dieter, "You must tell your friend that I do not accept gifts from strangers." She gently pulled her hand away and replaced the perfume while Dieter translated.

Christian was deterred for only a moment. "Then we must be introduced," he announced. He turned to Gabrielle and with his most charming smile, bowed and introduced himself, "Christian Karl Friedrich Baron de Feldburg. *Et vous, Mademoiselle?*"

To Yvette's astonishment, Gabrielle bowed her head and graciously replied, "*Je m'appelle Carduner et ma amie, Dubois.*"

"May I buy you a drink?" (Christian had this phrase in French well learned.)

Gabrielle laughed lightly. "No. Not tonight."

"Tomorrow?"

"No; I can't say when."

So Christian returned to the perfumery many times. Sometimes he came alone, but more often he came with Dieter. They usually came in mid-afternoon when there were few other customers. They would pretend to look at things if M. or Mme. St. Pierre was there, but just talk if they were not. Christian's staggering French improved in vocabulary, if not in grammar and accent, and Gabrielle frequently laughed at him. Christian deemed this a form of encouragement, even flirting. He argued that she wouldn't care how he spoke French if she were indifferent to him.

While Christian and Gabrielle blundered their way through conversations in which Gabrielle never revealed her first name nor accepted an invitation, Dieter generally looked around the shop or watched passers-by in the street. He politely addressed Yvette if she came near him, but never tried to engage her in conversation.

Yvette, who had looked forward to repulsing his despicable advances, started to feel disappointed, and then insulted, that he failed to show any interest in her. Looking in her mirror at night, she did not see why all men preferred Gabrielle. True, Gabrielle had a fuller figure, but Yvette thought her own dark hair and large eyes prettier than Gabrielle's wishy-washy coloring. It made her bitter to see men fall for Gabrielle again and again. Gabrielle treated all men shabbily. Yvette thought it was unfair that the egotistical Gabrielle won all the men, while someone warm and sweet like herself was neglected. But at this thought she felt a twinge of guilt, because she realized that in Dieter's case she had not been warm and sweet.

So the next time Dieter and Christian came to the shop, Yvette made a point of smiling at Dieter. Dieter, obviously surprised, smiled back. Yvette was delighted by how easy it was. When Gabrielle and Christian had settled down to their strange conversation and Dieter had gone to stand looking out of the window, Yvette timidly approached. "It's terrible weather today," she ventured in a timid little voice.

Dieter jumped in surprise at the sound of her voice next to him, but he recovered quickly and replied, "I like the heavy rain. On days like this we don't have to fly."

"You don't like to fly, *Monsieur*? But you are a pilot, are you not?" Yvette's eyes were bright with amazement.

"I like to fly very much," Dieter corrected, "but not to fight."

"But you are a soldier, *Monsieur*. How can you not like to fight?"

Dieter shrugged. "Perhaps I am a coward, but I think this is all pointless. Why don't the English admit they're beaten and let us have peace? I don't want to kill them. I just want to go home." Dieter had not meant to make such a long speech, but it was said now.

"Are you married, *Monsieur*?" Yvette believed she had discovered the reason for his previous indifference to her.

Dieter, not following her logic, was bewildered. "No; I just want the war to end."

"You are not married? Not engaged?" Yvette persisted, certain this must be the reason why the German pilot wanted the war to end.

"No," Dieter insisted honestly.

Yvette had to admit to herself that she was secretly glad to hear it.

Not long after that day, Gabrielle finally consented to go out with Christian. That is, she said that she *and* Mademoiselle Dubois would be pleased to have dinner with Christian *and* his friend on the following Friday. She glanced a little warily at Yvette as she announced this, but Yvette made no protest. Christian delightedly promised they would call for the girls at 19.00.

Outside the shop, Dieter asked Christian skeptically what he hoped to gain. Christian smiled, "Don't you think she's lovely?"

"I also think she's a nice girl."

"I know that!" Christian snapped back irritably.

"Then where do you think you're going with her?"

Christian was defensive now, "I don't know—I'll see how things go. I didn't hear you protesting," he added with a sharp look.

Dieter looked down and didn't reply at first. Then after a bit he said thoughtfully, "I think you're going to be disappointed."

"We'll see."

On Friday night they found not the girls, but M. St. Pierre, waiting for them. He let them in and like a stern father inspected them both, as if by careful scrutiny of their appearance he could judge their intentions. Finally, he invited them up to the family parlor to wait for the young ladies, who were not quite ready.

In the parlor they encountered Mme. St. Pierre. She was ensconced behind a coffee service wearing a high-necked, lace-trimmed navy-blue dress. She was a formidable figure of respectability who reminded Christian of his Grandmother Feldburg. She inspected the young officers with outright hostility, and only at the husband's hissed command did she deign to offer them a cup of substitute coffee. Dieter made an effort to soften her with compliments about the coffee and the apartment, but her eyes blazed with so much hatred that he gave up. He directed his efforts at small talk to Monsieur St. Pierre instead, asking about his business, while Christian smiled and nodded as politely as he could.

At last the young women came down the stairs together, and the young men sprang to their feet. Gabrielle looked soft and elegant in a cream-colored, loose-fitting dress with a satin sash. She led the way with a slightly whimsical smile, as if there were some joke she was bottling up inside. Yvette had chosen a fitted, rust-colored dress that made her hair and eyes seem richer and deeper than ever. She wore an amber necklace and a much more hesitant expression.

After everyone had exchanged greetings and compliments, the young people were ready to depart. M. St. Pierre turned to the young men. "Where do you intend to take the young ladies?"

Christian mentioned a fashionable restaurant that made Yvette's eyes widen and Gabrielle smile with satisfaction. M. St. Pierre, however, pretended not to be impressed. "You must have them back by midnight—not a minute later—or I will call the police and the base—"

"*Monsieur*," Dieter intervened smoothly, "they will both be back by midnight. Please don't worry." Then, with a bow to *Madame*, he opened the door for the others.

Outside, Christian murmured to Dieter in German that he hadn't been treated like that since he was seventeen.

"Have you dated a virgin since you were seventeen?" Dieter countered.

Their conversation could not continue, however, because the young women were looking at them suspiciously, obviously displeased to be excluded by a language they could not understand.

Christian smiled and moved forward to take Gabrielle's elbow. "You are so enchanting, Mademoiselle, that I was just asking Dieter if you were real or fantasy."

Gabrielle laughed at him because although his meaning was clear his French, as always, was flawed. His admiring gaze needed no translation, however, and it warmed her. Still she teased, "And where are we really going to eat? Café Tati?" She named a disreputable local bar.

"Non, non!" Christian replied in horror, and they both laughed. Soon they were chattering happily.

For Yvette and Dieter the moment was more awkward. They walked along behind Christian and Gabrielle, not touching, and for a long time silence reigned. At last Dieter managed to ask Yvette if she were related to M. St. Pierre. She explained that no, they were not related, but her father and M. St. Pierre's had served together in the last war. M. St. Pierre had promised her father to look after the little girl he left behind when he was mortally wounded. At first, he had even wanted to marry his friend's widow, but her mother chose someone else— an older, more established man. Yvette did not like her stepfather, so she had left home as soon as she was sixteen. She had come to Crépon, to M. St. Pierre.

"And Mlle. Carduner?" he asked.

"She is just his employee," Yvette answered with a little shrug.

After a long pause, Dieter found the courage to ask her her first name. Yvette admitted it, and so Dieter introduced himself, adding with a foolish smile, "And I'm not a Baron or anything."

After dinner they went dancing. Gabrielle let Christian take her onto the floor nearly every dance, and she was not stiff or defensive, but responsive in a ladylike way. Dieter was not a good dancer, however, and so he and Yvette sat most dances out, which suited Yvette. She was still not entirely comfortable to have any man hold her in his arms, much less a German in full uniform. She noticed, however, that the room was full of French girls in the arms of Germans in uniform.

During the last slow dance Gabrielle rested her head on Christian's shoulder, but promptly at 11:30 she insisted along with Yvette and Dieter that it was time to go.

Yvette and Dieter walked ahead of Christian and Gabrielle on the way home. They were no longer having any difficulty talking, and Yvette had slipped her hand through Dieter's arm. His very diffidence had won her more than any amount of ardor. She had had such a lovely evening and Dieter was a wonderful young man—if only he had been French.

Gabrielle and Christian dallied, lagging behind and walking slower and slower. Christian could not stop using her name now that he knew what it was.

"Gabrielle, Gabrielle—truly like an angel." Gabrielle let him hold her hand as they walked.

At last they reached the store. They unlocked the door and slipped inside. Gabrielle told Yvette to "go on up." Yvette gave Gabrielle a disapproving look. Dieter raised his eyebrows, but obligingly wished Yvette "good night" and went back out into the street. He lit up a cigarette and waited by the car.

Gabrielle and Christian lingered in the darkened shop. Gabrielle thanked him for a "lovely evening," but when he caught her in his arms and tried to kiss her, she pushed him away. Christian was puzzled. "Not yet," she told him, and darted up the stairs so fast that M. St. Pierre would hardly notice she had lingered.

Driving back to the base, Christian was silent, and Dieter finally couldn't stand it any longer. "Did you get what you expected?"

Christian grinned. "No."

When Christian did not volunteer any more, Dieter pressed him again, "Well, then? Were you disappointed?"

Christian took his eyes off the road and looked directly at Dieter. "No. Not at all."

*   *   *   *

Altdorf
June 1940

Tuesday, June 25, had been proclaimed a national holiday in order to celebrate the victory over France. Schools, shops and factories were closed and victory celebrations planned in every city and town across the *Reich*. As the staff of the Feldburg estate gathered in holiday spirits in the courtyard, the sound of tolling church bells could be heard all the way from town.

The kitchen maids and the Opitzes' fourteen-year-old son, Bobbie, were in their appropriate uniforms, BDM *(Bund Deutscher Mädel)* for the girls and HJ *(Hitler Jugend,* or Hitler Youth) for Bobbie. Bobbie's excitement expressed itself in exaggerated concern for his uniform, and he kept running to his mother to correct this or that. The girls were more annoyed than delighted to be in uniform. Identical straight navy skirts, white blouses and navy neckerchiefs were not outfits designed to make a girl feel pretty.

The older women had the advantage over the girls of being able to deck themselves in their finery, and they did, wearing their Christmas best. When Sophia Maria appeared in a relatively restrained raw-silk suit, lace blouse, and rakish hat, the sight of her staff in so much splendor surprised her for a moment. Preoccupied as she was by the thought of seeing Philip, who had been given three days' leave to mark his promotion to Major and acceptance into the General Staff, her first reaction was that the others were over-dressed. Then she realized that her own generation had awaited this celebration for more than a quarter century.

The Polish workers stood about in their work clothes or helped hitch the horses to the carriage and the wagon. The women wore their somber shawls over their heads and stood silently in the doorways of the workers' wing. The men—workers or prisoners—stood about in front of the barn. Poles had been expressly forbidden by the police from attending today's celebrations; they were not supposed to mix with Germans. Sophia Maria had stressed, however, that it was a holiday, and there were beer, cheese and sausages for a feast, including strawberries and fresh cream. They were to have their own holiday, she told them, but it was clear they had nothing to celebrate. France had been their best hope, but the powerful, modern French Army had held out no longer than the obsolete Polish one against the *Wehrmacht*. And the British had fled, abandoning the Continent, in which they maintained only a fickle interest. Thus for the Poles, the defeat of France amounted to a second defeat of Poland and, apparently, indefinite exile. As they watched the others depart for their victory parade, they felt themselves condemned to a lifetime of semi-slavery in a strange land, which no amount of strawberries and cream could change.

In Altdorf, the young people jumped down from the wagon and went to join their units, which were already mustering for the parade. The rest of the party joined Sophia Maria as she went into the station to meet the train.

The town, as ordered, was thoroughly "flagged." Flags flew from every flagpole and hung from every window. The huge red banners obscured the flower-filled window boxes that usually gave the town its color. Some people had personally strung special home-made banners, blessing the victory or Hitler, from window to window.

The streets were already crowded with people in their best clothes. They poured out of the houses and flooded in from the surrounding villages and countryside. Most of the women were in traditional dress. The men, in contrast, were predominantly in uniform of one sort or another. No one wanted to be in civilian dress anymore, at least not on a day like this. There were Party, police, SA, postal service, Organization *Todt*, Labor Service (RAD), Forest Service, and railway uniforms everywhere. Only one uniform was conspicuous for its absence: the simple field grey of the Army.

The station was awash with red and white banners, and a radio program describing the ceremonies in Berlin was being piped over the loud-speakers. A hyper-enthused voice narrated: "... and as far as the eye can see, the national banner and our Party banner, blood red between the green leaves of the Tiergarten. In the other direction ..." Sophia Maria tuned out the voice in her mind and checked the station clock. Despite thinking she had left plenty of extra time, they had only just made it.

"I can't imagine why I'm so excited," Martha exclaimed beside her. "I feel just like a young girl again."

Bemused, Sophia Maria glanced at the usually sensible old cook and remarked, "No one has ever accused Herr Goebbels of being incompetent."

But the train was already huffing into the station, its brakes screeching and doors opening as people spilled out. Again, everyone was in their Sunday best and escorted by children in irrepressible high spirits. They poured onto the already crowded platform. The field-grey cap of an officer peeked out of the train, and the crowd on the platform spontaneously cheered. From where Sophia Maria and her staff stood, they could not even see Philip. He was instantly surrounded by well-wishers and admirers. Sophia Maria laughed, knowing how discomfited Philip would be by this reception.

Slowly the crowd started to move toward the station exit, with Philip in the middle. As Sophia Maria expected, he had his cap pulled down to his glasses and was nodding stiffly to the people who clustered around him, thanking and congratulating him. "Thank you, thank you." He caught sight of his mother and shot her a silent plea for relief.

She went forward to his rescue. The crowd parted for her and she gave Philip her hand and then her cheek. As he brushed a kiss on her cheek he murmured in disbelief, "You'd think I'd won the war single-handed."

"Didn't you?" she managed, before Martha and the others pressed forward to congratulate him. Only Heidi hung back a little, smiling knowingly. She was experiencing a sense of déjà vu. She had pictured this scene in her head a thousand times—only her lover, rather than Philip, had been in the central role. Herr Opitz took Philip's suitcase from him and Sophia Maria took his arm, and they started through the station to the buggy and wagon beyond.

"We must proceed directly to the square where seats have been reserved for us—"

Philip recoiled. "You mean to take part in the official celebrations? I was hoping—"

His mother shook her head firmly. "There is no escaping it. My absence would be a scandal—but your absence would be absolutely unforgivable."

"I'm not in dress uniform," he made one last effort to escape.

"Doesn't matter. At least it's grey, and—" she glanced at his left breast pocket and Philip blushed—"the Iron Cross First and Second Class. You're just what the Mayor ordered."

They left the wagon and buggy at the station and proceeded on foot to the square, the crowds getting denser the nearer they got. The approaches and sidewalks around the cordoned-off square itself were packed. They had trouble squeezing their way to the policeman in the middle of the street controlling access to the square and grandstand; but once they were there, he let them through immediately with a heartfelt, "Congratulations and welcome home, *Herr Baron*! *Heil Hitler, Frau Baronin.*"

Embarrassed, Sophia Maria flapped her arm hastily in a Hitler salute, avoiding Philip's astonished look. As she led him to the tribune, she muttered helplessly, "You know, since I became leader of the Frauenschaft here in Altdorf ..." She was very grateful that Philip did not press her.

The maypole in the centre of the square was still in place and bedecked with garlands, flowers and tiny flags. The railing and steps up to the Town Hall were likewise bedecked, and a huge flag, hanging from the first-floor balcony, provided a backdrop for the podium set up on the steps. As Philip and Sophia Maria took their places, the sound of an approaching band could already be heard despite the near-deafening clang of the still-tolling church bells.

A certain ripple of anticipation spread across the crowd pressed around the edge of the square. Eyes focused on the street that ran between the church and the rococo façade of the Fürstenburg bank building. After a moment, the first of the eagle-tipped flag-staffs of the SA standard-bearers emerged. They were followed by the SA band marching—if not playing—in perfect unison. They marched along the width of the square and then turned a neat, square corner and marched directly toward the grandstand. Behind them marched—with notably less precision but no less solemnity—the *Jungmädels* (the Nazi youth organization for girls under fourteen) and the *Jungvolk* (the Nazi youth organization for boys under fourteen). They positioned themselves on either side of the SA. Next came the BDM girls and then the HJ youths. Finally, the men and women of the nearby Labor Service camps marched in. Each organization wore their respective uniform. The tail of the parade was brought up by the city's uniformed civil and Party officials, who marched past the SA to take their places on the grandstand.

At last all the various organizations were drawn up in formation in the square facing the Town Hall. The leaders visibly dressed the lines of the children. The woman standing on Philip's left couldn't resist leaning toward him and remarking, "Don't you think our boys look splendid, *Herr Baron*? Genuine military bearing, don't you think?"

"Splendid drill," Philip agreed readily. "I'm sure my panzer-grenadiers could not parade half so well."

Sophia Maria winced and glanced over to see if the woman had noticed Philip's irony, but fortunately she was beaming happily, oblivious to Philip's barb about the utility of such drill.

A loud bark called all the formations to attention, and while the SA stomped loudly and uniformly into a rigid, stiff-armed salute, the other units followed with more or less smartness. Some of the youngest boys and girls missed the order altogether in the excitement and the tolling of the bells. But when even these stood rigid (and red-faced), the church bells suddenly fell silent and the last clang echoed in the abrupt stillness.

A pause, several seconds of stillness, and then a single trumpeter lifted his instrument and the notes of the National Anthem slipped clear and pure through the hushed square. Only slowly, tentatively, did the crowd start to sing. By the third verse, the whole band played and the crowd was singing fully and joyfully. The words were of peace, and tears flowed down many of the older faces.

When the last notes of the National Anthem died out, there was another thoughtful pause, and then came the strains of the Horst Wessel Song. Only after this had been sung did the mayor mount the steps before the town hall and take up his position behind the podium with its battery of microphones. He spoke in a deep, moderated voice, without the hysteria usual for Party speeches. He spoke of the significance of the day and the celebration. And he spoke of the price Germany had paid: millions of dead, millions of widows and orphans, the reparations that had ruined the economy, the inflation that had ruined the currency and destroyed the savings of the honest and hard-working. He spoke next of the great leader who had risen to lead them from their misery and humiliation. He spoke of the "genius" who had restored Germany's pride, wealth and honor. He spoke of the proud, undefeated German Army, which had been stabbed in the back by the Socialists twenty-two years ago, but now had proved its competence and unbroken will to win.

Abruptly, the mayor cut himself short and announced that he would let a greater speaker than himself deliver the keynote address. Philip looked at his mother, puzzled; the mayor was not generally known for his modesty. Before she could answer, however, the loudspeakers were switched on, and the voice of the announcer in Berlin again dominated the square. A moment later the announcer was replaced by Hitler himself. The familiar haranguing voice bragged and boasted and crowed. It declared the end of the war in the West and proclaimed the most glorious victory of all time. And the crowd went wild. Over the radio from Berlin came the hysterical screams of "*Sieg Heil! Sieg Heil!*" And they were taken up with the same mad enthusiasm by the people of Altdorf. At some point the radio was switched off and for a moment or two it was hardly noticeable, as the formations in the square and the people around them continued to scream "*Sieg Heil!*" on their own. Only gradually did the screaming die away, and the SA band took up their instruments and started playing a merry tune. The cordon was dropped by the police and the formations dissolved as the crowd poured into the square.

Philip and his mother could at last excuse themselves and slip away unnoticed as the dancing started on the wooden platform around the maypole. They collected the buggy at the station, and beyond the town Sophia Maria let the young gelding break into a comfortable canter. She felt happy in the sunny warmth with her son looking masculine and attractive beside her—if only he didn't look so serious. "The shoulder braid suits you—and the red stripes." She referred to the braided epaulettes that were the rank insignia of a Major and the red stripe set in the outer seams of his uniform trousers, which indicated his acceptance into the General Staff. "But did you have to adapt the constantly worried expression of the General Staff as well?"

Philip managed a smile. "I'm sorry. That speech by Hitler put me out of sorts. It's not that I'm not proud of the victory. France deserved to be sharply and soundly defeated after the chauvinistic and vindictive behavior of the last twenty years; but unless we want Franco-German hatred to tear the Continent apart every quarter century, we need a moderate peace. We should show the wisdom and mercy the French failed to show—the wisdom of Metternich and Bismarck. But when I hear that man bragging and crowing, I feel so hopeless. That barroom demagogue isn't interested in a just and enduring peace."

He paused, lost in thought, and Sophia Maria was on the brink of changing the subject when he continued in an even more worried voice, "The worst of it is that we've all sworn a personal oath to him. Like medieval retainers, every single soldier is bound to serve him unto death, regardless of what he does. If I'd had a chance not to take that oath, I don't know what I would have done. But we weren't given a chance to even think about it. No one even told us there was to be a new oath. All they said was that there was to be a memorial to Field Marshal von Hindenburg, and suddenly we were ordered to raise our right hands and repeat the Oath. We repeated the oath and were literally bound to Hitler before we knew what was going on. I'd like to know who was responsible for that! If I'd seen that oath in advance, I might have refused to take it."

"But then you would have had to resign your commission," Sophia Maria pointed out in shock. "Your career would have been finished. You would have been excluded from any form of public service!"

"Yes, exactly; but as it is, I'm saddled with an oath I despise—and I can't break it without despising myself."

"Is it as bad as that?"

"Mother, the Army found Polish prisoners of war who had been crowded together in the open by the SS and left without food or water for days. Synagogues filled with people were burned to the ground. Literally hundreds of civilians were simply machine-gunned to death in some places, and only God and the SS know why. If these things had happened again in France, what would I have done? What could I have done?"

Sophia Maria did not have an answer, so she said nothing. The cool shadows of the pine trees replaced the sun as they turned up the drive.

"How long can we suffer this government?" Philip asked in an almost voiceless murmur.

Sophia Maria drew the horse to a halt and turned to face her firstborn. "Philip, we didn't bring Hitler to power, and we cannot bring him down. All we can try to do is to survive with our personal honor intact—or as untarnished as humanly possible." Philip looked at her rather strangely, and she felt she had to explain. "Look, I think that what our government has done to the Poles is outrageous, but I can't give them back their land. I can't reverse the injustice done to them. All I can do is treat them with as much consideration, kindness and respect as is possible within my own small realm. God knows, that realm is tiny indeed. Technically, I can't even give my workers an old pair of boots. Common decency has been made illegal by this regime, and I have been turned into a 'criminal.' But I must be a criminal if I am to maintain a much higher law: the law of humanity and Christianity."

"Are you trying to tell me I should work inside the General Staff to prevent or at least mitigate Hitler's policies?"

"Yes—as much as you can without landing in a Concentration Camp."

Philip considered this answer. The Army had succeeded here and there in getting orders withdrawn or modified. It had shot the odd SS trooper caught in the act of committing an atrocity. It had even protested against the evident policy of excesses by the SS. And what had it achieved? Not even a postponement of the campaign in the West was to the credit of the Army leadership; only the weather had achieved that. In the face of so much impotence, the Army's leadership had become increasingly fatalistic. Philip had personally witnessed this change of attitude between October 1939 and February 1940. Now Hitler had again proved his military experts wrong: the campaign in France had not been a bloody *Götterdammerung*, but a brilliant success. Just what could the Army leadership do in the face of such "genius"?

Then again, maybe his mother was right. Perhaps he still had to do all he could. If it seemed pitifully insignificant—like giving a man a pair of old boots instead of giving him back his farm—it was still better than nothing. The higher he rose in rank, the more chance he would have to do something positive. Even the Iron Cross was useful, because people—particularly civilians—looked at him differently, with more respect.

But even the C-in-C or the Chief of the General Staff could not change the government, the other half of his brain reminded him. And in the end, that was the only thing that would put an end to the systematic policies of injustice, inhumanity and madness. Suddenly he laughed.

"What?" asked his mother, confused.

"It just struck me that the only hope for ending this dictatorship is revolution, and I find it amusing to think of myself as a revolutionary."

Sophia Maria admitted, "In that sense, I suppose I'm a revolutionary, too. But how is there ever going to be a revolution so long as the people are so contented and self-satisfied? You saw them today—everyone in one uniform or another and feeling self-important. And you heard them roar *Sieg Heil!*"

"You mean they'll support the government, as the French supported Napoleon, just as long as it keeps winning wars?"

Sophia Maria tensed, but then she had to concede, "Yes. I suppose you're right. It is the endless run of victories that has fed the blind faith of our citizens in their *"Führer."*

Philip nodded solemnly and gestured for them to go on. Sophia Maria eased the reins and let the fidgeting horse walk on while Philip asked quietly, "And is the German Army supposed to intentionally lead its country to defeat?"

CHAPTER 9

▼

Cherbourg
August 1940

"Christian?" A timid voice came through his radio. "I'm low on fuel. Hadn't we better turn back?"

Christian checked his own fuel gauge; it read very low. They were over England, having escorted almost 200 bombers in on a raid against British airfields. Unfortunately, they had wasted a lot of time before the attack, because the rendezvous with the bombers hadn't gone according to plan; they had spent more than 20 minutes flying in circles waiting for them. Christian checked his watch and was surprised to find they'd been flying 65 minutes already. That left very little fuel to get back across the Channel. "Right, Ernst." As he spoke, he swung back onto a course for their base.

The lumbering bombers were left behind. The Channel, sparkling and choppy, spread out below them. At one point Christian spotted a small British patrol boat fighting the heavy swells in an ever-changing circle of white foam. He couldn't resist diving down and giving it a quick squirt with his guns. He provoked a croaking bark from its antiquated anti-aircraft gun and flew on.

Over the French coast the red fuel-warning light came on. Christian called ahead to base to report he was trying to make it, but might have to put down in a field. The controller was reassuringly close. Shortly afterwards he spotted the aerodrome itself and started an easy descent. A quick count of planes on the ground suggested that the bulk of the squadron was already back. Christian touched down nicely and trundled over to the spot the ground crew indicated. The Emil, for all its magnificent flying qualities, was a real bitch on the ground. He switched off his engine and shoved the canopy open. His rigger was instantly on the wing beside him.

"Good flight, *Herr Leutnant?*"

"The target was obliterated," Christian answered enthusiastically, aware of a pleasant sensation of relaxation. He flexed his muscles in circles to dispel the stiffness and pulled himself out of the cockpit, relieved to stand even though his legs felt weak and tired for the first few minutes. He pulled his leather helmet off and ran a hand through his damp hair. Then he tossed his helmet onto the wing, asked the fitter to leave it in the cockpit, and asked if there had been any squadron kills.

"*Herr Leutnant* Appelt got a Hurricane." The man seemed to hesitate and then added, "But the *Herr Staffelkapitän* isn't back yet."

"What? He must be. I was practically out of fuel."

The fitter didn't answer or meet his eyes. It dawned on Christian that the bastard might actually have bought it. Out loud he said in a casual, unconcerned voice, "Oh, he's probably put down somewhere else."

Ernst appeared around the Emil's tail, his helmet and parachute in his hand, his jacket unbuttoned over his round belly. Ernst was a short, fat pilot who had joined the squadron straight out of flight school. He had been flying wingman to Christian since they came to France.

Christian quickly glanced around the field and spotted a cluster of pilots smoking over by another plane. "Let's join the others."

Together they strolled over, Christian wriggling out of his parachute and opening his jacket as they went. The other pilots were talking excitedly as Christian and Ernst approached. Hartmann spotted them and called out, "Any luck?"

They both shook their heads, but Christian flung his arm over Busso's shoulders as he came up behind him, saying, "Hear you got a Hurri."

"A flamer," he explained. "Must have hit the fuel tank. It lit up like a torch." He imitated the sound of roaring flame. It was Busso's third kill already.

"Did either of you see what happened to the CO?" Hartmann asked.

"No; what happened?" Christian asked back.

The others shook their heads and shrugged. "We don't know. He's just not back yet, and no radio contact either." They automatically searched the sky, but it was empty.

"He probably ran low on fuel and put down in a field somewhere," Christian repeated his theory.

"Probably," Hartmann agreed. "Funny that there's been no radio contact."

Christian took a long drag on his cigarette and then suggested, "Let's go get a beer." His thoughts were already running ahead to an evening with Gabrielle.

"Let's just hope the field the CO landed in wasn't an English one," Hartmann persisted.

"We won't change things by talking about them," Busso countered. "Let's go get that beer." He was clearly in the mood to celebrate.

Hartmann turned to Dieter and started, "I think—" He cut himself short and went stock still, his head jerked up.

The others instantly did the same. There was an aircraft engine straining somewhere. As one, they turned toward the noise and searched the sky. The sound was low on the horizon and still far off. The irregular throbbing was that of an engine in trouble. It seemed to choke, fade, and then hoarsely cry out again. It was steadily approaching.

"There!" Ernst saw it first and he pointed with his whole arm. "It's a bomber!"

Low to the horizon, the bomber was visibly staggering. Long before they could identify any specific damage, they knew that it was mortally wounded by the way it drunkenly lurched toward them, unable to maintain altitude for any length of time and weaving rather than holding a steady course. By the sound, it had been clear from the start that only one engine was operating, but as it drew nearer they saw that it was dragging one wing—or what was left of it. The pilot was fighting every second to keep the damaged wing from dragging them all down to their deaths.

"That man knows how to fly!" Hartmann whistled with undisguised reverence. The others were equally transfixed, and stared in awe as the plane continued its agonizing progress toward them.

"He'll never put that down in one piece. They've got to get some altitude and jump."

"Get altitude? With that wing?"

The bomber was sinking toward the earth. The engine faltered, roared again. The plane lurched upwards a fraction. Fire trucks and ambulances were rushing along the edge of the field. The ground crews stood like the pilots, still and tense, their eyes riveted on the approaching aircraft.

"They should have jumped."

"Shut up."

They held their breath.

The bomber was sinking again toward the earth, but the damaged wing was lower, threatening to cartwheel the crew to their deaths. They could feel the pilot struggling with it, sweating. Their own hands clenched around imaginary sticks. The engine choked up and stopped. For an instant the plane hung in the air, and then it seemed to drop like a stone. It belly-flopped from 12-15 feet, smacked onto the ground, bounced up leaving its tail behind, and fell back to earth again. It slued forward with a terrible tearing sound.

Christian realized he was running only when he was halfway there. The smell of burning fuel hit him in the face. He kept running, blinking to wet his eyes as dust from the careening plane filled them. He was beside the cockpit before the ambulance or fire truck, Dieter and the others just a few strides behind him.

For an instant, Christian thought all the occupants of the Heinkel were dead. There didn't seem to be any movement inside the cockpit. The windshield was shattered, nothing but fragments of crumbling white glass clinging to the bent metal frame. Lying just beyond the ruptured windows Christian could see the pilot, one half of his face swathed in bandages. He was just sitting there motionless. Then something moved inside the cockpit, and Christian realized that the observer/commander was getting up and leaning over the pilot, trying to help him.

Christian made a move to help as well, but the ambulance had arrived and the medic irritably pulled him out of the way. Christian found himself with the other fighter pilots in a useless group off to one side, while the ambulance crew with serious efficiency extricated the three living crewmen and brought out the dead gunner's body.

The pilot, a very young-looking *Unteroffizier*, was laid on a stretcher, blood soaking through the bandage over his left eye and running down his face, but he was still conscious. His observer, a *Feldwebel*, was holding a shattered arm as if only subconsciously aware of the wound. He limped beside the stretcher, looking down with an unreadable expression at the pilot who had saved his life.

Just as the ambulance crew went to lift the stretcher into the waiting vehicle, the pilot caught sight of the cluster of fighter pilots still in their flying gear. His good eye widened and he reached out an arm to them. The stretcher-bearers hesitated and glanced over their shoulders.

"Why did you leave us like that?" the young bomber pilot asked collectively of the fighter pilots. "There were English all over the place." His tone was uncomprehending, hurt. "They kept coming and coming, and not one bloody Messerschmitt in the whole God-damned sky! One gunner dead over England and the whole Channel to cross, with swarms of Spitfires eating us alive like maggots on a carcass. How—" He broke off, overcome by his own emotion or the pain. He sobbed or gasped, a dry, wrenching intake of breath. His observer signaled for the stretcher-bearers to load him into the waiting ambulance and climbed in after the stretcher, turning his back on the fighter pilots without so much as a glance.

CHAPTER 10

▼

Berlin
October 1940

The wartime headquarters of the General Staff at Zossen outside Berlin was a complex of wooden and concrete barracks lying low among the pines. Flak batteries and interconnected bunkers that allowed the entire business of the General Staff to be conducted underground testified to the General Staff's legendary caution, despite the blustering promises of Goering that no enemy plane would ever reach the skies over Berlin. As long as the skies remained empty, however, work was done in the wooden barracks above ground, and there were plank walkways laid between them. The flak was silent and the dominant sounds were the calling of birds, the wind in the tops of the trees, and the hollow clunk of boots on the wooden boards.

Returning to his office from lunch at the utilitarian mess, Philip was greeted by the sergeant clerk. "*Herr Major*, there was a call for you."

"Any message?"

"No, they said they'd call back. I think—"

The phone rang, and the sergeant answered before handing the receiver over with a smile.

"Feldburg."

His brother's voice came loudly over the receiver. "Philip, can't you get away from that gloomy place and come up to Berlin? I've only got 11 hours before I have to catch the train back to Cherbourg."

In late August Christian had been shot down, and although picked up out of the Channel by a *Kriegsmarine* patrol boat and brought safely to France, he had damaged his eye while bailing out. His squadron leader had, in fact, found that he was blind in one eye, and had sent him back to Berlin for treatment. "Are you really fit to fly?" Philip asked skeptically.

"I've been fit to fly since I arrived!" Christian retorted on the other end of the phone. "I told you I got my second Hurri after I couldn't see out of the right eye. What do we need two eyes for? One's really just a backup for the other."

"Are they letting you out or have you managed to escape?"

"I appreciate your confidence in my ability to escape those sadistic medical jailers, but they actually set me free. I'm calling from a pay phone in front of Schloss Charlottenburg and I'm about to have lunch at that Russian place across the street. I repeat: can you get away and join me?"

"I'll try."

Philip got the afternoon off, and two hours later he met Christian in Berlin.

It was a lovely autumn day, and Christian suggested an excursion to Tegel. The brothers changed into light boating clothes and spent the afternoon on the water. For dinner, however, Christian insisted on the best, and Philip's grumbling about the idiocy and waste of time in changing yet again could not deter him. "After all," Christian quipped, "you can eat at the Esplanade whenever you like, but this may be the last chance of my lifetime." The remark was meant to be funny, but it was tinged with too much truth, and the joke fell flat. Philip dutifully changed into dress uniform.

At the Esplanade the crowd was as elegant as ever, maybe even more so. The ladies were all in evening dress and glittering with jewels. The men were predominately in uniform, whereby the SS, Party and senior civil service were over-represented. Christian was the most junior officer in the room.

They had an aperitif, fine wine, and ignored the prices to feast their whims on non-rationed items, but something was missing from the mood. Christian's impending departure cast a long shadow, and Philip found himself admitting that he actually missed being with the troops and was completely disappointed by his duties at OKH. His long-desired acceptance into the General Staff appeared to be nothing but a Pyrrhic victory.

After dinner Christian wanted to go to a nightclub to keep his thoughts at bay, but Philip retorted with a sour expression, "You know I don't like nightclubs."

"Yes, I know," Christian snapped back with a look at his watch, "but we can't just sit here. It's still two hours 'till my train leaves. Where's the bill? I want to go somewhere else." He twisted around and signaled the waiter.

The bustle of life on the Potsdamer Platz came as a sharp contrast to the sub-dued sounds and grace of the restaurant. Here the crowds jostled each other on the sidewalks. Streetcars, buses and autos clogged the street. A long line of people waiting to get into a movie theater completely blocked the sidewalk, and pass-ers-by had to step into the street to get around them. Cars beeped at the straying pedestrians, and somewhere a police whistle blew.

Christian saw instantly that the blackout was only carelessly observed. True, the neon lights of the advertisements were darkened, the streetlights off, and the headlights of the cars shaded, but as people entered and left the various establish-ments, light spilled from the doors, and many people carried flashlights, which they brazenly used. To Philip's utter amazement, Christian sternly declared, "There's supposed to be a blackout! Don't these people know the regulations?"

Philip could hardly believe his ears. "Since when did you become a believer in regulations?"

Christian ignored his question and continued fuming, "These people act as if the war were over! Don't they realize that we're still dying out there? Don't they care?" Christian was furious.

Philip took his arm and started walking in the direction of home before they attracted any more attention. He tried to explain, "The war doesn't seem very real to the average Berliner—"

"What does it take to make it real to them? We're flying combat sorties twice a day. Some of the pilots are so exhausted, they fall asleep over their dinner. Fighter and bomber squadrons have been decimated. The Me110s have 40% casualties! I don't know if any of my friends will be alive when I get back. I don't know if I'll be alive this weekend! What can be more real than that?"

"Nothing, but how are they to know about it?" Philip gestured vaguely to the crowds around them.

"From the radio, the papers—"

"Christian, all that comes over the radio is victory announcements of the number of British planes shot down, the cities 'obliterated' and the factories 'crushed.' According to the papers, all is going according to plan. The British are being bombed back into the Stone Age, and the *Führer's* unequaled genius is demonstrated daily." Philip sensed that his own bitterness was getting out of hand, and abruptly fell silent.

Christian halted and turned on him. In a rational but demanding tone he asked: "Is the Battle of Britain important or not?"

"It was—but although it's apparently gone unnoticed in the Chancellery, we've already lost it."

"It isn't over!" Christian protested, raising his voice in agitation.

"Yes, it is—"

"The day after tomorrow I'm going to be fighting the bloody battle; don't you dare tell me it's over!"

"Christian." Philip was calm. He met Christian's gaze steadily from behind his wireless glasses. "You may be fighting it every day of whatever life you have left, but the battle is over and lost, because the objective has slipped beyond our grasp."

"Don't talk academically! This is a real war, not a General Staff exercise!"

Christian never realized how much remarks like this hurt Philip, because Philip did not fight back. He simply fell silent for a moment, collected himself and then said softly, "Christian, no matter how you look at it, the purpose of the bombing was to win air superiority in preparation for an invasion. The invasion has been canceled because the *Luftwaffe* failed—"

"WE HAVE NOT FAILED!"

"Christian." Philip's voice was so soft that Christian sensed more than heard it. He realized that he was standing in the middle of a busy sidewalk shouting— and people were staring at him.

"Let's take a taxi home," Christian decided, and stepped off the curb into traffic to hail one.

They did not speak in the taxi, but gradually Christian began to calm down. Philip was right. Of course Philip was right. They had lost the Battle of Britain. But it wasn't their fault and it wasn't over. Tomorrow or the day after, he would be asked to fly and possibly die in a battle that was already lost.

The taxi pulled up in front of the house. Philip leaned forward to pay the driver, and Christian stepped out into the cool, dark street. Here the blackout was strictly enforced and the street was silent and dark in both directions. Christian could hear the lapping of the water in the canal and the rustle of leaves overhead, but his mind was in France.

How had so much sacrifice, courage and hard-won success produced a defeat? The bombers, despite the losses, still went in again and again and they found their targets. "We were winning," Christian declared abruptly, almost belligerently, as Philip unlocked the door. "At high cost, but we were winning. Fighter for fighter, we shot down more of their planes, but their pilots just climbed into new ones and our pilots at best became POWs. Still, the bombers were getting through. Ever since we reorganized the fighter defense to go in in waves and we started flying multiple sorties a day, we've been able to protect them. They were finding their targets and we were knocking out their airfields and aircraft factories. Philip, I swear to you, we would have had air superiority in time for the invasion, if only we hadn't wasted so many men and machines on London. Why did we start bombing London?"

They had reached their own apartment and as Philip closed the door behind them, he asked helplessly, "Why did 'they' stop the panzers miles from Dunkirk?"

"Damn it! I don't want riddles, I want answers! What the hell is going on here in Berlin?"

Philip lost his temper. "An idiot is running the war!"

They stared at each other in the darkness, and then Christian half laughed. Yes, of course, that was it. An idiot was running the war. You couldn't expect rational policy from an idiot. Christian, who had always been able to make fun of Hitler, suddenly didn't find him very funny anymore.

"Do you want cup of *ersatz* before you go?" Philip asked in a weary voice, ashamed of his outburst.

"Tea," Christian countered.

In the kitchen, Philip put the kettle on to boil and then rummaged around until he found cups, saucers, tea and teapot. Christian seated himself at the kitchen table, still in a state of shock. After a bit, however, he started speaking pensively, staring off into space. This was so unlike him that it made Philip look over a little nervously.

"You know," Christian started in a listless, distant voice, "the new pilots arrive so eager and yet so timid. They're anxious to prove themselves, but most of them are afraid they'll fail. They talk to build themselves up, and yet try hard not to make fools of themselves in front of us veterans. They try to make friends with us, too, but we aren't friendly. They think it's because we're snobs. They think we're conceited and look down on them, but it's not that."

The kettle started to whistle and Philip promptly lifted it off the gas before it really screamed. His glasses steamed up. Christian didn't seem to have noticed the kettle or him. He just kept talking, his gaze far away. "It isn't that. It's just that it hurts too much to get to know them. They become people when you know about their families, girlfriends, hobbies and achievements. And when they get shot down, you know what you've lost." His voice was becoming strained. "You're so alone in an Emil. When you're too shot up to help yourself, you just have to sit there and die."

Christian stopped talking, but Philip didn't dare speak or move. He felt like an intruder, as if he were overhearing something Christian did not really intend him to hear. "It's bad," Christian continued, "but to have it all be for nothing...." The anger and the pain blurred together, and Christian fell silent again.

Philip waited a bit and then poured the water into the pot and brought the tea to the table. Christian faced him and spoke clearly and calmly. "I'm not a pacifist, Philip. I know there are just wars. There is nothing absolutely immoral about the sacrifice of some lives for the sake of the nation as a whole. But for nothing? Surely that is institutionalized murder." He was no longer expecting answers from Philip or arguing with him as a representative of the High Command—just expressing his thoughts. And Christian would soon blot out the memory of this conversation, but Philip would remember it the rest of his life.

*   *   *   *

Gabrielle had been awaiting Christian's return with growing impatience. She resented being left to her own devices for so long, a fact aggravated by the discovery that there were no ready replacements for Christian—or none whom she found attractive. Ever since Dieter reported Christian's return to Yvette, she jumped every time the phone rang. When no call came, however, she started practicing scathing speeches, which she intended to deliver if Christian dared call after all. But when she finally heard his voice on the other end of the phone line, she found herself inexplicably out of breath.

"Mademoiselle Carduner?"

"Yes," she managed with what she hoped was cool neutrality.

"This is Christian von Feldburg. You probably don't remember me, but I'm a pilot at the airbase outside Crépon."

Even if Gabrielle suspected Christian was teasing, still—of all the things she had imagined him saying—this was the least expected. She actually stumbled over her answer. "Christian—but—yes, of course, I remember you."

"What a pleasant surprise! And do you also remember the food at the Hotel de Chouan in Quinéville?"

"Yes, of course."

"Well, then, what would you say to dinner there with me on Wednesday?"

"Wednesday?" Why not sooner? What was wrong with today and tomorrow and the day after? But all she managed to say was, "What time?"

"Oh, say 7 pm?"

"Good. Fine," she got out, still a little dazed.

"I'll pick you up at 7 on Wednesday then. *Au revoir.*"

"*Au revoir.*" She hung up. Her heart was beating much too fast, and she was angry with herself—but then she started thinking about what to wear.

Christian could hardly believe it, but he found her more beautiful than he remembered. As always, she managed to be sensuous without being lewd.

Gabrielle, for her part, was quite surprised by the thrill she felt at the sight of Christian. He had never seemed so handsome, so masculine, so strong.

With Gabrielle's permission, Christian left the top down on the *Kübelwagen*, and they drove through the cold, crisp night at high speed to the coast. The wind made conversation impossible, and the stars overhead and the speed on the winding road made it unnecessary. They arrived at the country hotel, nestled among the trees of an old orchard with a view out over the Channel, with heads already light and the blood warming their faces.

Gabrielle had not eaten all day, and the wine went straight to her head. She had long since forgotten that she was angry with Christian. She was exhilarated and sparkling as Christian had never seen her.

After dinner they went onto the dance floor, but soon dancing seemed quite superfluous. They forgot to move to the music as they kissed. Only slowly did Christian become aware that they were on the dance floor and the music had stopped entirely. The other couples around them were chatting and waiting for the next melody or going back to their tables. Christian gently pulled away from Gabrielle, and with his hand on her back he guided her to their table. She was meek and willing. Still Christian hesitated, afraid of Gabrielle's reaction if he misjudged her mood.

"Shall I order more wine? Or are you ready for dessert?"

Gabrielle just slipped her arm through his elbow and put her head on his shoulder. She closed her eyes and murmured, "Um-um."

"Are you tired?" he asked tenderly, his fingers softly stroking her hair.

"Um," she nodded.

He dropped his voice and head so he could murmur directly into her ear, "Shall I take you home?"

"Um-um," she shook her head without opening her eyes.

Christian was momentarily paralyzed by his own excitement. Then he gently brushed his lips against her forehead and whispered, "I'll be right back."

She smiled without opening her eyes and let him go.

When Christian had a room for them, he came back and led her wordlessly out of the restaurant and up the stairs. Gabrielle said not a word.

In the room, Christian did not turn on the light. Instead he closed the door behind them, bolted it and then kissed Gabrielle in the dark. Her mood did not seem to have changed with the change of scene, and that reassured him. He took her purse from her and her coat. He set her purse on a dresser and hung her coat in the closet. When he returned, his eyes were more adjusted to the darkness than before. He found Gabrielle sitting on the bed watching him. He knelt beside her and they kissed again.

"I love you," Christian whispered.

Gabrielle smiled. "I know."

It hurt. He had told himself again and again that she did not love him, but still he had hoped that he was wrong. Her answer now, one he had given in a similar situation, confirmed his pessimism. She did not love him. He was serving some plan of hers. She was allowing him this honor because she wanted it for some reason of her own—not because she wanted him.

He bent and unstrapped her patent shoes one at a time, and carefully placed them side by side at the foot of the bed. "M. St. Pierre will call the military police," Christian whispered teasingly, as he straightened and looked into her fathomless eyes.

Gabrielle laughed softly and kissed him lightly. "He wouldn't dare. He might throw me out—"

"I'll find you a charming little apartment," he promised eagerly.

"I'll be very expensive to keep, *Monsieur le Baron*." She put her arms around his neck and lay back on the bed.

Long after Gabrielle had fallen asleep, her head nestled under his shoulder and her arm across his chest, Christian lay awake staring at the dark. There was nothing he wanted more than for there to be many more nights like this. Yet he feared that such nights would be very few indeed.

CHAPTER 11

▼

West Prussia
October 1940

The Duty Leader woke the girls in the barracks with the usual loud ringing of the bell followed by the shouted, "Wake up, wake up!" To groans and muttered curses, the girls rolled out of their bunk beds, and the usual chaos of nearly a hundred girls rushing to the showers began.

Marianne knew that it paid off to be one of the first, even if the barracks was unheated and so icy cold. She slid off the upper bunk, pulled her panties on under her flannel nightgown, and then replaced the nightgown with her "sports outfit"—one of the three uniforms issued to the girls in the RAD (*Reichsarbeitsdienst*). She grabbed her towel, washcloth and soap, and in wooden clogs joined a horde of other girls pouring out of the wooden barracks.

The toilets and showers were located at the far side of the camp, and the girls found themselves in the frosty gloom of pre-dawn. The sky was just starting to grey behind the tall pines that surrounded the fenced-off perimeter of the camp.

The camp itself was located in West Prussia, one of two provinces which, after the victory over Poland in 1939, had been "reincorporated" into the German *Reich*. Marianne's unit had been sent here three months earlier, allegedly as part of a national effort to help these formerly Polish provinces regain their prosperity. Marianne thought it had more to do with indoctrinating the inhabitants with the spirit of National Socialism. Whatever the reason, the transfer had been a bad blow for Marianne. The girls doing their national labor service usually spent only the first month in camp doing drill, learning songs and receiving "training" in housekeeping, hygiene, racial theory and the like. The remaining months were normally spent working in rural households or assisting mothers with many children. Although the girls were rotated from job to job on a regular basis, and not all employers were pleasant, still Marianne preferred doing useful work to doing mindless drill at the whim of leaders hardly older than herself.

The move to the new provinces had meant a return to the camp life Marianne hated. Marianne's unit had first been assigned to help build the camp, and was then employed in organized groups under their respective leaders on surrounding farms during the harvest. Because they were so far from home and the authorities seemed inordinately concerned about their safety, they were not even allowed the half-day off per week to which the Labor Service girls were entitled.

In compensation, they had been promised a trip to Warsaw, and this trip was scheduled for today. That made all the girls excited, and there was more than the usual pushing and shoving as too many girls tried to use the open showers or wash themselves at the long row of sinks. There was still no warm water, which made showering a hasty affair accompanied by loud shrieks and shrill cries as girls darted in and out under the meager streams of ice-cold water. Marianne preferred to wash herself at a sink with her washcloth. She didn't want to have to travel in the cold with wet hair.

After washing, she rushed back to the barracks to make up her bed, sweep and dust down the room, and be sure all her personal things were neatly stowed (in regulation-sized squares) in her locker before morning assembly. She had once received a sharp rebuke because her towel had been folded with the edges facing inward rather than outward. The "leader" had swept all her things out of the locker and dumped them on the floor. She had had to refold everything, and all the other girls had snickered with delight.

As the only girl in the entire troop who had finished high school and planned to go to university, Marianne was often the butt of ridicule. That was another reason why she hated the camp. At the various houses where she had worked, the farmers' and shopkeepers' wives could tell she came from a "good" family by her educated German, but as long as she did what was asked of her, they made no fuss about it. At the camp, however, the other girls—and especially the leaders— felt it was their duty to teach Marianne that she was "nothing special." According to National Socialist ideology, all healthy German girls were equally valuable to the *Führer*. Their mission as German "maidens" was to marry and bear healthy babies—for which none of them needed a high school, much less a university, education.

But in just a week Marianne would be released from the RAD, her year-long service finally over. Marianne counted the very hours.

Assembly was held in the middle of the camp. The girls lined up in rows by unit and stood facing the flagpoles on which the national and party flags were raised solemnly while the girls sang. Then the camp leader read the "thought of the day"—usually a quote from the *Führer* or one of the other party leaders—followed by a half-hour of calisthenics. Jumping jacks, windmills, and running in place were all carried out to the shouted orders of the leaders at the front. The "senior girls"—one for each unit of six—kept an eye on their charges to be sure there were no "slackers" in the back rows. At last, an hour after they had been woken, the girls had a half-hour for breakfast—as soon as they had changed out of their sports outfits and into the blue "work dresses."

Breakfast was served cafeteria style, of course, and was prepared by the girls on "morning duty." The result was that the scrambled eggs usually had bits of shell in them and the rolls were often burned, while the coffee substitute was either too strong or too weak, but consistently terrible. Still, none of that mattered today. Even before breakfast was over, the sound of heavy engines driving into the camp could be heard, and a cry of excitement went up. "The buses! The buses are here!"

The camp leader loudly called for order. No one would be allowed to leave the camp until after inspection, she warned threateningly. A collective groan filled the cafeteria, but most of the girls, including Marianne, had been expecting it. They hurried back to their respective barracks, changed into their "going out" uniform (blue skirt, white blouse and navy cardigan). Then they stood at attention at the foot of their respective beds while the camp leader and the other "senior" leaders marched through, opening lockers, looking under beds and feeling the windowsills for dust.

At last the girls were released to go to the buses. Here they crowded around, chattering loudly as they squeezed one by one aboard the ancient, battered old buses. The drivers were in the uniform of the *Reichsarbeitsdienst*, but—to the disappointment of many of the girls—they were older men. Marianne heard one of the other girls complaining, "I thought we were finally going to see some real men."

Last to board the buses were the leaders, three per bus. One of the senior leaders tried to make herself heard above the chatter of the girls and the groaning of the ancient engine as the bus bounced its way on the rutted road out of the camp. The girls were "representatives of the New Germany"—easily identifiable by their uniforms. As such, they were expected to demonstrate the superiority of their race. The girls were to stay together. They were not to stray off alone, because the streets of Warsaw were by no means safe, despite the best efforts of the German authorities. Jews and Slavs inhabited the city, the leader reminded her charges, and the rate of crime was "consequently high." On no account were they to engage in conversation with natives—even seemingly harmless conversation might be a prelude to abduction.

"Wouldn't that be a nice change," one of the girls behind Marianne muttered, and the girls around her giggled.

Before the unit had been transferred to West Prussia, the camp had been shaken by the "scandal" of one of the girls getting pregnant. The District Leader and the Provincial Leader and the District Doctor of the RAD had all come. Camp Assembly had been held and there had been long, outraged speeches about Virtue and Discipline and the "shame" of the event. But what had shocked Marianne far more were the conversations she had heard among her comrades. One of the girls from her own unit had worked at the same farm where the girl got pregnant and told the others bluntly, "Gerd is really a good time. I wish he'd got *me* pregnant. Then *I* could have got out of this shitty Labor Service."

"But he's refused to marry Minna," one of the others whispered back in shock.

"Of course. She's got no dowry. Gerd's going to inherit the farm, and he can take his pick of any of the local girls. He's not going to marry a slum-slut like Minna! She was a fool to expect it! She ought to be thankful for the good fucks and the baby."

"But what's she gonna do with a baby and no husband?"

"There are all sorts of places for unwed mothers nowadays. She won't starve." The speaker sounded envious.

In Warsaw their program was rigorous and strictly organized. The girls were taken first to what was left of the Old Town and shepherded officiously from site to site, ending at the Church of the Holy Cross, in which Chopin's heart was reverently preserved. It was then mid-afternoon and the girls were tired and hungry, but Marianne's hope that they would be allowed to eat "someplace civilized" (i.e., in a restaurant) were disappointed. No, they were to be the guests of an SS unit, and the buses pulled to a halt in the forecourt of an ancient yellow-brick barracks that had probably served Russians, Poles and Soviets before it offered a roof to Hitler's SS.

SS officers came out to greet the girls, and Marianne saw the camp leader's usually sour and scowling face light up as she sighted a certain *Sturmhauptführer*. "So that was how we came to this honor," Marianne thought. While she and the other girls were sent to the soldiers' mess, the leaders were taken to the officers' club. Marianne's companions were delighted. It meant that for the first time all day, they were out of sight of their leaders and surrounded by young men.

Before her eyes, her comrades were transformed into completely new people. Some were shy and others bold, but suddenly and despite the uniforms they all seem to exude some kind of femininity. The SS men were no less eager for the exceptional contact with young German women. The word of their arrival spread rapidly through the barracks, and the off-duty SS men streamed into the mess and quickly spread out among the girls. One of them sat directly next to Marianne and asked her name. He was too good-looking, however, and at once one of her comrades jealously intervened. "No point wasting your smiles on Frl. Moldenauer. She is a *high school graduate* and has a boyfriend in Berlin—a Gestapo *Inspector*."

"Sorry," said the young man, and turned to focus his attentions on the girl who had "enlightened" him about Marianne. Marianne wasn't unhappy—she didn't like being chatted up by soldiers—but she resented the way the other girls kept her so isolated. And she resented being here and not in the officers' club. When she thought about her own leader, a young woman whose vocabulary belonged to the gutter, she felt a deep hatred for a system that raised vulgar, brutal people to positions of power and luxury.

It was also soon apparent that their leaders were in no hurry to continue with a tour of Warsaw. Apparently, they did not even care about getting back to the camp before dark. Marianne noted that several girls slipped out of the mess in the company of SS men, including the girl from her unit who had regretted not getting pregnant. No one seemed worried about the girls setting an example of "virtue" here, she noted cynically. The bulk of the girls, however, soon found themselves in the large "common room" of the mess chatting with the off-duty men or, like Marianne herself, sitting around bored and resentful.

Then one of the NCOs asked if they'd had a chance to see the Ghetto. As they hadn't, the NCO decided that he and some of his comrades should organize a little extra trip. "It's not far from here, and you really shouldn't go home without having seen it!"

"The largest concentration of Jews in the whole world," another NCO chimed in eagerly.

"There are over 300,000 of them!" declared a third.

"We're going to build a wall around the Ghetto, and then we won't let them out except with special passes."

"You've really got to see it to believe it!" The SS were so enthusiastic about this unique spectacle that the girls were hardly given a chance to disagree. Soon even an *Obertruppenführer*, the equivalent of a Senior Sergeant, had been found to sanction the outing, and the girls were divided into three groups and escorted by a half-dozen SS per group.

Marianne wouldn't have chosen this outing, but it was better than sitting about in the SS mess. She thought she'd get a chance to see a little more of Warsaw. She was not prepared for what she did see.

Although a wall had not yet been built around the Ghetto, the borders were clearly defined by barbed wire, and huge signs identified the "Jewish Residential Area." German police controlled the identity of those trying to get in or out, and also what they were carrying. There were long lines of people with suitcases, hand-carts and wheelbarrows standing at the control points, and the SS explained that there had been more than 100,000 Jews living in other parts of Warsaw who now had just two weeks to move into the Ghetto. They were prohibited, however, from taking their furniture or any work tools with them. This was why their things had to be searched at entry. Asked why they weren't allowed to take these things with them, the SS explained that they had to be left behind as compensation to the Poles, who had been expelled from the reincorporated territories. The Poles had left their own furnishings and tools behind to enable the resettlement of Germans. It was all very "fair," the SS told the girls.

But what Marianne saw was that worthy-looking gentlemen were being harassed by young policemen, while matrons were frisked rudely by young men with no regard for their sex. To her horror, she noted that what the German policemen were confiscating from these poor people wasn't "tools," but valuables of any kind—and quite obviously for their own enrichment. In outrage, she declared, "But that is outright theft!"

"What the Jews own, they stole from honest Christians," an NCO told her with a wave of his hand. "Besides, what do they need jewels or watches for in the Ghetto?"

Indeed, Marianne thought, she had never seen worse slums in her life. The buildings here were more run-down than the worst parts of Neuköln and Moabit. The façades were more damaged than intact and smeared with graffiti in Polish and Yiddish. Doors were battered, windows broken or boarded up, and there was a pervasive stink, too—burning coal, cabbage, and backed-up toilets. Worst of all, there were people in hopeless little groups, often sitting on the dirty curbstones or their heaps of possessions. One of Marianne's "guides" explained that the Jews moving into the Ghetto were having an increasingly difficult time finding housing.

"But what are they to do?" Marianne asked in distress, as they passed a family of six. The mother was apparently at the end of her strength. She crouched on the curb with elbows on her knees and her arms over her head. A scrawny boy of perhaps twelve in a neat but worn school uniform tried to comfort her with his hand on her shoulder, and a teenager was holding a screaming baby on her hip. A toddler sucking his thumb stared up at Marianne with wide, accusing eyes.

She felt her heart twist. This was impossible! It was October. It was cold already. It would soon start to sleet and snow. But the SS NCO shrugged and said, "That's their problem. Other Jews will just have to make room for them."

Marianne's attention was distracted by harsh shouting. Everyone in her little group looked over to where two German policemen were making an elderly couple unpack everything they had heaped onto a wooden handcart. What attracted Marianne's attention most was that the Jewish man was speaking an educated German—a German better than her RAD leader.

"But, *Herr Wachmeister*," the man addressed the policeman politely, "a violin isn't a tool. It's an instrument." Marianne was reminded of her piano teacher, Herr Silber. He was of a similar age to this man and his wife, too, was a slender, elegant woman, just like the frightened woman clutching the violinist's arm.

"It's prohibited," the policemen insisted in his loud bark. Just like the leaders at her camp. You can't reason with these brainless thugs, Marianne thought; they only understand brute force. Even as she watched, the policeman grabbed the violin. Because the rightful owner at first held on with tenacity, the policeman's arm flew back uncontrolled when he finally broke the old man's resistance. The violin crashed onto the cobbles with a clatter and a last wail of the strings. The old man let out a howl of pain and fell onto his knees. He reached out his hands, no longer possessively, but in a gesture of sheer despair. "My father's violin," he sobbed, "my father's violin."

His wife wrapped her arms around him, but he only stared at the shattered instrument while the police continued plundering their remaining possessions.

Marianne's stomach turned over and tightened. She looked around herself. Where was she? Was she in Europe? Was she in the twentieth century? Was she in the company of Germans? A civilized people? No; the Master Race. A shudder went through her.

The others were already wandering on, the incident "over" and forgotten. The SS were pointing out new points of interest, and the girls nodded and looked about with the pleasantly attentive expression of teenage girls anxious to please the young men escorting them. No one even noticed that Marianne was lingering, rooted to the spot where she had seen the senseless destruction of an innocent and precious instrument. No, she realized a moment later, it wasn't a violin that had been shattered; it was her understanding of civilization itself.

*   *   *   *

Crépon
November 1940

Hearing Christian's voice in the receiver, Yvette at once said, "I'll get Gabrielle." But as she laid the receiver on the counter, she heard the *Luftwaffe Hauptmann* calling out, "No! Wait! Yvette?"

She took up the receiver again. "Yes? What is it?" And suddenly she knew. She felt the earth start to spin under her.

"Yvette, Dieter won't be able to see you tonight. He—"

"No," she tried to stop him, as if it wouldn't be true if only he didn't say it out loud.

"He's not back. He might have put down somewhere else. Or maybe he jumped. It takes weeks before we get the POW lists. Maybe he even made it back across the Channel. We just don't know. He's been posted missing ..." Christian's voice faded away. Then, after a bit, he said, "Yvette? Are you there?"

"Yes."

"Yvette, I'll let you know as soon as we have any more news."

"Yes." She started to replace the receiver, and then she held it to her face again and called out desperately, "Christian! Christian!"

"Yes?"

"Is there a chance? It's not absolutely certain?"

"Yes, of course. Don't worry. He's probably fine. But at the moment, we don't know where he is." Despite his effort to sound positive, Yvette had the feeling he was hiding something from her.

"Thank you." She hung up and just stood there.

Gabrielle was staring at her. "Dieter's been shot down?"

Yvette couldn't bear it. Why Dieter? Why not Christian? Why did Gabrielle have all the luck!? Without answering, she grabbed her coat and plunged out into the pouring rain. She ran without really looking where she was going. Her thin little pumps splashed through puddles and her feet were soon soaking wet. By the time she reached the church, her hair, too, was wet and dripping. Rain—or tears—were dripping off her nose. The church, as usual, was nearly empty, even though Mass was being said. Only a few old women in scarves were sitting scattered about the pews. Yvette bent her knee and crossed herself, slipped into a pew at the back, and pulled out the kneeling bench. She dropped her head on her folded hands and started begging: "God, please, please, please save him! Please let him live! I'll come to Mass every day. I'll buy candles every day! I'll—oh, God, what can I possibly give you that is enough? Don't do it for my sake! Just save him! He's a good man, truly he is, even if he's German. He goes to Mass much more than me. Please, please, please."

*   *   *   *

Berlin
December 1940

Marianne and Peter Kessler had gone out a half-dozen times before she set off for her National Labor Service, and he had been a faithful correspondent the whole time she was away. The fact that she had a young man who wrote her at least once a week had raised Marianne's prestige in the RAD. Nor had it been to her disadvantage that her admirer was a Gestapo inspector; but the year-long correspondence had also brought them closer together than the few dates prior to her departure. It was easier to pour out her heart to a piece of paper than to a handsome young man who consistently managed to make her nervous by his mere proximity.

During her year in the Labor Service, Marianne had found herself writing to Peter the very things she hesitated to tell her parents. She hadn't wanted to distress her parents with the stories of her own humiliation and frustration. Nor had she dared tell her parents how sexually "enlightened" her fellow RAD girls were. So she had confided in Peter instead. She had complained about the absurdity of her peeling potatoes and scrubbing latrines when she could have been in her first semester at university. She had cited the newspapers, which reported a shortage of doctors, and asked if it really made sense for her to delay her training doing tasks that any "idiot" could perform. She had told Peter about the scandal with the pregnancy and reported that "it seems several of the girls here have considerable experience in these matters." Peter had been suitably scandalized by the waste of her time, by the conditions she had to live in, and by the company she was being forced to keep. He had been most upset by her transfer to the reincorporated territories.

For months, Marianne had looked forward to and dreamed about not just going home to her parents or going to university, but also seeing Peter again. As the date for her release drew nearer and nearer, they had closed every letter with the number of days left. Peter had promised her a "welcome home dinner" and hinted that he would spare no expense. Marianne assured Peter that "after the slop I'm forced to eat here" she would find "even an ordinary Berlin café a culinary delight." But she'd fantasized about being taken to one of the famous restaurants—the Adlon, the Esplanade or Kempinski's.

After the visit to the Warsaw Ghetto, however, Marianne told herself she had to break off with Peter. Peter was one of "them." Peter supported the National Socialists, and he sided with those who burned books and broke violins. Marianne was determined never to have anything to do with one of "them" ever again.

The day Marianne returned, her parents met her at the station. She waved with delight from the window, jumped off the train with exuberance, and dropped her suitcase to fling her arms around first her mother and then her father. Her father insisted on carrying her suitcase, and she walked arm in arm with her mother. At home, her father produced a Rhine wine that he had bought specially for this occasion, and her mother made her favorite dinner, chicken fricassee. They spent the whole evening talking and talking and talking. Marianne had never felt so close to her father as when he heard about the shattered violin. He sprang to his feet and paced around the large living room with its grand piano and floor-to-ceiling bookcases. "How did we come to this?" he asked over and over. And then, "What is to become of us?"

Marianne slept in late the next morning, reveling in the luxury of not being woken by a bell and the bellowing of a self-important "leader." She breakfasted with her parents on fresh bread and cheese and marmalade. She went shopping with her mother, happy to carry the shopping bags for the sight and smell of fresh vegetables, fresh-baked bread, preserves and chocolate. Marianne was convinced that there was more on the shelves than ever before—Norwegian salmon, Danish butter, Belgian chocolates and French paté.

In the afternoon she went to the university to inquire into enrollment procedures. She came home footsore and frustrated by the bureaucracy, but her father agreed to do what he had never done before: to ask a favor of one of his former colleagues. An appointment was made for Marianne to meet with him later in the week. And then the doorbell rang.

Marianne's heart leapt, her nerves tensed: Peter. All day she had suppressed thoughts of Peter. She had busied herself and her mind with other things. But now he was there. She couldn't put it off any longer. She had to face him. She had to get it over with.

"I'll go," she told her parents unnecessarily. I'll tell him at once, she decided as she walked determinedly down the hall. There's no need to tell him why. I can say I found someone else. I can say I've fallen in love with an SS NCO … She pulled the door open with a yank of agitation.

Peter stood on the landing with a bouquet of roses so large that it was hard to see him behind them. But she could see him—the narrow face with the big owl-like glasses, the long, fine nose and the thin lips breaking into a timid and yet heartfelt smile. "Welcome home, Marianne!" He held out the red roses to her in a gesture that was meant to be gallant, but reminded Marianne of a schoolboy with a present for his favorite teacher.

And the next thing she knew she had accepted the flowers and was burying her nose in them with an exclamation of "Oh, Peter, they're lovely."

"And I have tickets to the *Staatsoper*!" he declared proudly, pulling the precious tickets from his jacket pocket with an even broader smile. "Herbert v. Karajan conducting *Tristan und Isolde*!" It was one of the musical sensations of the year, and Marianne and her parents had made several unsuccessful attempts to get tickets. How could she possibly say no?

"When?" she asked eagerly—her heart pounding with excitement that was only marginally related to the anticipated musical event.

*   *   *   *

Crépon
December 1940—April 1941

In the days after Dieter went missing, Yvette had looked hopefully at Gabrielle every morning when she came into the shop. Day after day, Gabrielle had shaken her head. "No news."

With each passing day the chances diminished. And then, at the start of December, almost when she had given up hope, Christian called. Without any preliminaries he reported in an excited tone, "We've found him. He went down in the Channel and was picked up by French fishermen. They delivered him to a local civilian hospital in St. Malo and then he was transferred to a central military hospital in Paris. It's taken this long for the bureaucracy to get the news back to us."

"He's alive? He's unhurt?" she asked next, breathlessly.

There was a long, expressive pause.

Oh, God! Why hadn't she prayed for that, too?

"They say he's been pretty badly burned, Yvette. He's going to be in the hospital for months."

"Burned?" The worst nightmare! She'd heard about it. Pilots burned beyond recognition. They had to rebuild their faces with strips of skin taken from other parts of their body—strip by strip. "Where? Where has he been burned?"

"I guess pretty much all over, Yvette. But the doctors say he'll survive. He's out of danger."

"Yes. Thank you."

Months went by. The winter passed. There was no further news. Sometimes Christian came by the shop just to see Yvette, to chat with her. She had the feeling that he was spying on her. Did he think she would just forget Dieter now? Find a new friend? She wasn't that kind of girl! But she wished Dieter would write.

M. St. Pierre also started to make remarks like "Maybe it was all for the best." Or "There are other fish in the sea." But Yvette didn't want the other fish. She wanted Dieter back—and at the same time she was afraid of it. What if she didn't even recognize him? And why didn't he write?

It was a chilly, rainy day in April when she heard a car pull up in the street outside. Not many people had the gasoline rations to drive cars these days—except the officers from the *Luftwaffe* base. A door crunched shut. Somehow she knew. She sat on her stool, clutching her hands in her lap, and waited. A figure darkened the door, and her heart was bashing frantically at her breastbone. A greatcoat hung off his shoulders to mid-calf, a tribute to the rainy weather, and the familiar cap was pulled low. But it was him—recognizably him.

With a cry of joy, Yvette jumped off her stool and ran around the end of the counter, opening her arms. He turned to her, and then she saw it. The other side of his face had been badly burned, up almost to his cheekbone. The right side of his lips and chin was reconstructed, the stitches still very evident, and the skin a patchwork quilt of different colors and texture. She gasped in shock, stopped where she stood. Their eyes met, and she hated herself for hesitating. She flung herself into his arms. "Dieter! Dieter! Dieter!"

He just held her.

She lifted her face, her eyes closed, seeking his lips. He hesitantly obliged. His lips felt so strange, and he winced a little. "Does it hurt?" she asked, opening her eyes in remorse.

"A little," he admitted. Then, with evident difficulty, he asked, "Would you be ashamed to be seen with me?"

"No, no, no! Dieter! Don't you understand? I love you! Why didn't you write?"

He held up his hands.

Yvette cried out again, but this time he knew it was from sympathy, and when she flung herself into his arms again she was crying for him. "Oh, why, why, why? It's so unfair—"

He laid his good cheek on the top of her head, holding her as tightly as he could. "I'm alive, Yvette. I'm standing. I'll even be fit to fly again in another six or eight months. For now, I'm supposed to help the intelligence officer with the paperwork. You're sure you wouldn't mind being seen with me? I thought we could go to dinner, if you like."

"I'll go tell M. St. Pierre!" She was instantly gone, and returned with her hat and coat.

M. St. Pierre followed her out of his apartment and came over to offer his hand to Dieter. His lips smiled as he congratulated the German pilot on his survival and recovery, but his eyes didn't share the sentiments of his tongue.

At dinner, Yvette thought everyone was staring at them, and the more people seemed to stare, the more fiercely she held onto Dieter and the more defiantly she smiled and laughed. She hated the other women who seemed to raise their eyebrows and sniff their noses at her. Did they think they were better than her because they only went out with *handsome* Germans? Yvette hated them! The hypocrites. She had never wanted Dieter more than now. She wanted to comfort him, care for him, cook and clean for him, spoil him. She wanted to be his pillow at night and his sunshine in the morning. "Dieter, I love you," she kept telling him, afraid that he didn't understand.

Dieter was overwhelmed. Christian had reported regularly—and not without a touch of candid jealousy—that Yvette had been faithful to him. But Dieter hadn't expected her to still want him after she saw him. And it made him feel wretched. Finally he couldn't stand it anymore, and he put his arm around Yvette and laid his good cheek on the top of her head. "I love you, too, Yvette. I've never loved like this. I wish I could marry you and take you home to meet my family. I've written home so much about you that both my sisters have threatened to come out here to meet you, but—"

She cut him short, a finger very gently placed on his tortured, reconstructed lips. "I know. I know. The *Luftwaffe*. What do I care about the *Luftwaffe*? If we love one another and we are true to one another, then in the eyes of God we are married."

Yvette was so happy that she hummed and sang snatches of songs as she polished the countertops. "Padam, padam, padam, da da da ..."

Gabrielle took one look at her and declared, "*Ola*, you gave in. Well, let me look at you."

Yvette blushed and cast barely a glance at Gabrielle, but Gabrielle laughed. "Sin suits you, *Chérie*. You've never looked so pretty." Then she went to hang up her coat.

When Dieter called that evening, he insisted on facing M. St. Pierre. "He may not be your father, but he has looked after you. Furthermore, I don't want him to throw you out." Dieter couldn't afford to rent an apartment for Yvette as Christian did for Gabrielle.

Yvette bit her lip and looked up at him with her big, dark eyes. "But he hasn't said anything. Maybe he doesn't know."

"We can't keep it a secret forever. Wait for me here."

Dieter pushed through the curtain at the back of the shop and went up the stairs two at time. He rang the bell and Mme. St Pierre opened. Dieter removed his cap. "May I speak to your husband, *Madame*."

Mme. St. Pierre spat at him, turned her back on him and left him standing. Dieter didn't know what to do and stood, stunned, in the doorway. M. St. Pierre came into the hallway, a newspaper in his hand. "What do you want?" he asked harshly.

"I want to speak to you, *Monsieur*, about Yvette."

M. St. Pierre glanced over his shoulder at his wife, whom Dieter could hear hissing at him in a flood of furious, hate-filled French. But then he signaled Dieter into the formal parlor with its overstuffed furniture and patterned wallpaper. He closed the door behind him. "What do you want? We are conquered. You know you can do as you please. Do you want my approval as well? Well, you can't have it! Yvette was like a daughter to me. Gabrielle—well—what can you expect of a girl like that? If it hadn't been your friend the Baron, it would have been someone else sooner or later. But I wanted something better for Yvette."

Dieter was offended despite himself. "I come from a good family, *Monsieur*. My father is a respected veterinarian. My mother was a nurse in the last war. Both my sisters have higher education, and I am an officer, *Monsieur*—"

"So was Yvette's father!" M. St. Pierre interrupted with a burst of fury. "He was an NCO, an honorable and brave man! He was wounded three times. He fought at the Marne, the Somme, at Ypres. He died fighting for his country, trying to prevent just this: an occupation by you Huns. And now his daughter—

under my very roof—I am so ashamed!" M. St. Pierre broke off. He was so overcome by his own emotions that he could not even look at Dieter. He turned away and stared at his cold fireplace with the polished coal grate.

"Ashamed of what, *Monsieur*?" Dieter asked softly to his back. "That Yvette and I love each other? What is shameful about that? Our hearts wear no uniform. I would—and will—marry Yvette as soon as possible. This is not some cheap affair for me. Don't confuse me with Christian v. Feldburg."

M. St. Pierre turned back and gazed at him. "I know you are a decent young man. That's why I tolerated it. I thought: 'He's a nice young man; he won't dishonor Yvette. It's good for her to have a little fun. She'll only be young and pretty once, and there are so few young Frenchmen here. Why shouldn't she go dancing? Why shouldn't she be taken to expensive restaurants?' But I trusted you not to go too far, *Monsieur*. I trusted you …" He broke off and turned away again. His hands were working, clenching and unclenching, not in rage but in agitation.

Dieter, too, was clutching his cap in his hands in distress. M. St. Pierre had succeeded in making him feel ashamed. But he couldn't undo what he had done. He didn't want to. And nor did Yvette.

M. St. Pierre turned back and faced him. "You are frightened. I understand that. I know what it is to face death and horrible injury day after day." He gestured vaguely to Dieter's mutilated face and hands. "I know that there is no comfort greater than the love of a woman. I do not even know that I would have acted differently in your shoes. But I am no longer a young man, and I see, too, that Yvette will suffer for the rest of her life for this. A collaborator. An unwed mother. Who will look after her and her children when you are killed, *Monsieur*?"

C H A P T E R   12

▼

Berlin
June 1941

In January, Philip had been sent to serve on the staff of the XXI Corps, and in April he found himself fighting Italy's battles in Greece. The episode ended when an RAF Hurricane strafed the narrow road on which they were advancing. The driver tried to dodge the cannon fire by swerving violently. The staff car plunged off the road into a gorge and rolled over several times. The driver and one of General Balck's ADCs were killed in the crash. Philip was found with a broken ankle, several broken ribs and a broken collarbone. After six weeks in various hospitals, he had been given four weeks' convalescence leave in Altdorf. By mid-June, he could walk without a crutch or cane, but was not considered fit enough for front service. He therefore found himself back in a staff position, this time at the General Army Office (*Allgemeine Heeresamt*, or AHA).

Philip was pleased. Despite its innocuous name, the AHA fulfilled all the functions of a peacetime war ministry. Though it possessed no control over operations or intelligence, it was the central organ for the recruitment, organization, training, equipping and supplying of the Army as a whole. Work here thus promised to be interesting and challenging, while offering a welcome return to "civilization." The AHA was located in the heart of Berlin, in the familiar Bendlerblock, situated between the Tiergarten and the Landwehr Canal. Philip could once again walk to work or take a single bus from the family apartment.

Just before 9 am he presented his ID to the sentry at the iron gate leading to the cobbled courtyard, and then proceeded up the well-worn red marble stairs to the second floor. It was sixteen months since his last tour of duty here, but little seemed to have changed. Despite the spectacular victories in France and the Balkans, he was still greeted with military courtesy rather than the Hitler Salute.

Only the national flag hung on the various flagpoles, without the blood-red Party flag beside it. The only significant change appeared to be an increase in the number of female employees. Apparently the NCOs that in peacetime had provided much of the support had been drained off to man garrison posts from Norway to Greece, and women had taken their places.

The receptionist for the Commander of the AHA was a particularly pleasant surprise. She was not objectively prettier than half a dozen other young women working in the building; but whereas the others competed with one another within the narrow confines of Third Reich ideology on feminine beauty, Philip hadn't seen a young lady like this since he'd left Paris. She wore long, dangling earrings, for a start, something one almost never saw in Nazi Germany. Even more unusual, she wore makeup—not heavy makeup (Philip wouldn't have liked that)—just enough not to look tired and bland. Although she wore a simple silk blouse, it had that indefinable extra elegance that could only have come from a Paris designer. Most distinctively, rather than wearing her hair long in back but pulled or coiled away from her face, she had cut it very short and severe at the base of the neck while leaving it long in front. It fell forward, blond and delightfully casual—when she didn't negligently tuck it behind her ears.

Philip noted all this while he introduced himself simply: "Feldburg. I was to report to General Olbricht at 9.15."

"Ja, Major von Feldburg, the General is expecting you. I'll tell him you're here." Her tone was efficient but relaxed. She went to the adjoining office, knocked briefly, and then put her head in to announce him. She left the door open as she returned to her desk, and gestured for him to go on in.

General Olbricht was even more of a surprise. Philip knew him by reputation only. He was one of the first officers to be awarded the newly created Knight's Cross in 1939, and that for personal courage and outstanding leadership in the Polish Campaign. It was said he had rushed forward, loading fighting troops onto his staff car, when he realized the bridges over the Wartha were rigged for demolition but had not yet been blown up. He had personally led this improvised troop against heavy machine-gun fire onto the first of the bridges, although they could have exploded at any minute. The next time Olbricht was confronted with a river crossing, he improvised motorization for all his leading units and again took the bridge by storm before the Polish Army had even evacuated the town of Lowicz. He thereby captured not only the bridges, but also a full troop train.

Philip expected an officer like Guderian, brusquely self-confident, militarily blunt—and chafing at, if not actually bitter about, being tied to a desk rather than leading fighting troops. Instead he was confronted by a mild-looking general with pale-framed glasses and thinning hair.

The long office was comfortably furnished and bright, with four windows. A bust of *Graf* Yorck von Wartenburg caught Philip's attention. During the Napoleonic wars, Yorck had refused to follow orders from Napoleon during his retreat from Russia, forcing his king to break with Napoleon to join the coalition against him. He was revered in the General Staff for the courage to look beyond orders to the overall situation and act in accordance with what was good for the nation—even if it meant disobeying orders from the Supreme Commander.

General Olbricht came around the front of his desk to receive Philip. Philip saluted and the General shook hands, indicating a small round table between two of the windows.

The General opened with the apparently irrelevant remark that Werner Schrader had recommended Philip specifically for the post he was about to assume. Philip hardly knew what to make of this. He hardly knew Schrader and couldn't remember anything he had done that might have impressed the Major—beyond making that remark about the "moral depravity of the Regime" in his presence. Before he could work through the implications of this, however, the General was asking Philip if he was truly fit for his new duties, with such sincere interest that Philip found himself giving more than a perfunctory answer.

The General's eyes flashed with restrained amusement as he replied, "I fear you underestimate the stress of the tasks you are about to assume. You know that the invasion of the Soviet Union is impending?"

Philip started visibly. There had been talk and even some planning for an invasion of the Soviet Union throughout the fall, but he had been told repeatedly that Hitler did not intend to actually invade. All the troop dispositions on the Eastern borders were "preventative" or "bluff." He found himself staring at General Olbricht, unsure whether his opinion was expected or not.

"You don't look delighted," Olbricht observed, with that look of amusement in his eyes that encouraged Philip to be honest.

"*Herr General*, we're overextended as it is—bogged down in a war without visible end with the British Empire, fighting Italy's battles in the Mediterranean; and now, without cause, we're going to take on the largest land army in the world?"

"You aren't familiar with *Mein Kampf*, I gather," came the dry answer.

It was so unusual for an officer to refer to Hitler's book that Philip was instantly on his guard. "The *Führer* denounced a two-front war as the greatest idiocy of the Kaiser's government."

"He denounced the war with England, to be precise—which led to a two-front war—but we already have that. My point was that his writings are filled with demands for 'living space' in the East and saturated with his rabid hatred of Communism, which he frequently equates with international Jewry."

"But it's too late to start a war against the Soviet Union." Philip took refuge in the safety of purely military arguments. "By October our panzers will be immobilized in mud," Philip insisted. "Why not wait until we at least ..." He stopped himself, unable to go on talking nonsense. What was the point of talking weather and postponement? This was yet another war of unjustified aggression that could only end in senseless bloodshed and very probably defeat. "And the non-aggression pact of 1939?"

"Why respect that treaty any more than the others?" the General answered with a shrug. But the next moment his eyes were focused intently on Philip, and for the first time he caught a glimpse of the troop commander who could go straight for an objective with single-minded verve. "Surely you aren't *surprised* to discover our Head of State is disregarding international law?"

"No," Philip acknowledged, "not surprised by the illegality of it, but by the magnitude of the disaster it could bring. We can't possibly win a war against the Soviet Union with the resources we have."

"I'm sorry to report that that appears to be the minority opinion in the High Command. Although I share your opinion, as do Generalobersts Beck and Hammerstein, the majority of active generals, including the gentlemen at OKW, believe that Russia is a paper tiger—as the war against Finland has allegedly proved. They believe we will be in Moscow before the autumn rains mire our panzers in mud."

As he now knew where Olbricht stood, Philip dared asking, "Have they all gone mad?"

"That opinion has also been expressed in certain circles," Olbricht noted, "but I am afraid that it does not change our duties. Perhaps you now understand why your responsibilities here will be more difficult than you imagined."

He proceeded to outline Philip's responsibilities, which—broadly speaking—had to do with guaranteeing that the field and home armies were adequately supplied with all variety of specialists, from medical orderlies to firemen, clerks and barbers. It meant both trying to utilize incoming recruits productively based on civilian training and assuring a steady, regulated flow of specialists out of the Army's training institutions. "Given that there is no way of predicting casualties by specialty, you'll need to be very creative and flexible. But you'll find your most difficult job is the unfriendly competition for resources. Not only with the other armed forces and the SS, but also with the Labor Service, the Hitler Youth, the police and even the Gestapo, all of which make demands on the same labor pool. Another problem looming up is the advisability of increasing reliance on women in certain specialties. But I'd rather not get into that just now. I'll let you get settled into your office and go through your files, and then we can talk again. Any questions so far?"

"No, *Herr General.*"

They stood and the General saw Philip to the door of his office. As Philip went out, Olbricht's attention was drawn to a major standing before the receptionist's desk and talking animatedly with her. "Freiherr von Gersdorff! What brings you to Berlin?"

The major turned to Olbricht and reported in a strained voice, "*Herr General, Feldmarschall* von Bock sent me to 'protest' the Commissar Order—but you can imagine what effect I've had. Brauchitsch and Müller insist it is pointless to protest further."

Olbricht's expression darkened. "Don't the Army Group Commanders realize the blood will be on *their* hands?"

"Tresckow tried to get Bock to fly back personally—but Bock sent me instead." His crooked smile was cynical; who could compare the impact of a General Staff major with a field marshal commanding an Army Group?

"Cowards," was Olbricht's cryptic commentary.

"I don't understand," the receptionist spoke up unexpectedly, and the officers turned to her politely. "Why do you gentlemen put more emphasis on the Commissar Order than the Barbarossa instructions, which are actually worse?"

"The Commissar Order is outright murder!" Gersdorff countered, too shocked to be polite even to a young lady.

"Yes, but directed against a clearly defined and easily identifiable group which is—if nothing else—actively engaged in military operations and ideologically committed to Communism. The status of Commissars as non-combatants is certainly debatable." Gersdorff opened his mouth to protest, but she forestalled him. "Obviously, that is no justification whatsoever for their ordered 'liquidation'; I simply wanted to draw attention to the fact that the victims of the Barbarossa Instructions are unquestionably civilians, and the Instructions effectively suspend at least two hundred years of international law. I am not convinced that the former, merely because it is more systematic, is more objectionable than the latter."

There was a short pause while the officers absorbed this. Gersdorff and Philip were both taken aback by the precise, articulate and confident tone of the receptionist, and astonished that she expressed her opinions on military affairs. Olbricht, however, apparently was not only used to it but even encouraged it. Turning to the visitors, he explained, "Fraulein v. Mollwitz has a law degree and is particularly well versed in international law." Then, turning back to his over-qualified receptionist, he answered, "*Gnädiges Fräulein*, you are, as usual, correct in your assessment. I can only suggest that the emphasis we place on the Commissar Order is a function of the fact that it might cost blood within the very first hours." Olbricht turned abruptly to Philip, remembering, "I don't suppose you've seen either of these orders?"

Philip shook his head, feeling very ignorant.

Olbricht turned back to his receptionist. "Fräulein v. Mollwitz, would you be so kind as to see that Major v. Feldburg has a chance to read them. *Lieber* Gersdorff, maybe you could join me in my office …?"

Olbricht and Gersdorff disappeared into the General's office, and Fraulein v. Mollwitz went over to a safe and removed two manila folders, which she handed over to Philip. "I'm afraid I must ask you to read these here," she apologized. "General Order #1." This was the order Hitler had issued early in the war, prohibiting anyone from knowing anything not directly related to or necessary for his duties. It was ostensibly to increase security, but transparently intended to reduce the ability of any officer to judge the total picture. The order was quietly ignored in the General Staff, as it went against a long tradition of openness for the sake of sound analysis.

Philip set his briefcase down beside the door and seated himself in a wooden armchair. The receptionist resumed her work. The typewriter clacked loudly. Philip read:

> *"In the struggle against Bolshevism, the behavior of the enemy in accordance with the principles of humanity and international law is not to be counted upon … The originators of these barbaric Asiatic methods of warfare are the political commissars."*

Like the pot calling the kettle black, Philip thought. After what the SS had done in Poland, who are we to condemn Soviet "methods of warfare"? He read on:

> *"Commissars are to be immediately, i.e., on the battlefield, identified and disposed of."*

Disposed of? The banality of the phrase was almost the worst of it. They were talking about murder, killing without establishing any crime or guilt—other than the ideological guilt of being Communist—and they used the same language one would use with unwanted documents or furniture.

Philip looked up and focused his attention on the elegant receptionist as she typed away efficiently. "And you said the other order was worse?"

She stopped typing and admitted, "A poor choice of words." She bit her lower lip, not meeting his eyes, and for a moment she seemed unsure of herself. Then she looked at him again and declared in a lucid and self-confident tone: "I didn't mean to imply that there is anything worse than cold-blooded murder; only that because the Barbarossa instructions are more comprehensive and vague, they may in the long run cost many more lives. Here, let me show you." She held out her hand, and he stood and returned both manila folders to her. She flipped the second open and scanned the pages quickly until she found what she was looking for.

"Listen to this: 'Attacks by civilians against the *Wehrmacht*, its personnel or support elements, are to be repressed by the troops with the sharpest methods.' Neither 'attacks' nor 'sharpest methods' are more closely defined. Imagine what an SS division might interpret as 'attacks.' Even the smallest gesture of defiance by youths or children could theoretically be repressed with 'the sharpest methods'—including execution without trial.

"Or here: 'Guerrillas are to be mercilessly eliminated, either in battle or when they attempt to escape ... until the attackers are exterminated.' And now it gets even more delicate: 'Disciplinary action against members of the German Armed Forces and their support elements'—read SD, Gestapo, Party and I don't know who else—'for attacks and excesses against the enemy population'—note, not partisans or even Commissars, just any enemy civilian—'are not necessary, even when these actions constitute a military as well as a civil crime—"

"What?"

"Read it yourself, *Herr Major*." Frl. V. Mollwitz pushed the folder back across the desk toward Philip, her finger marking the passage she had just read. As he read, Frl. v. Mollwitz insisted, "This is a license to barbarity on the part of every individual soldier—impunity from punishment regardless of what he does to Russian civilians, male or female."

"No," Philip told her flatly. "The Officer Corps will not—cannot—allow troops to engage in excesses. Discipline would be utterly destroyed."

Frl. v. Mollwitz fixed her gaze on him for a moment, and Philip felt uncomfortable. The young woman continued politely, "May I draw your attention to one or two more key points?"

Philip wordlessly passed the Instructions back to her. Again she skimmed it quickly, and then read: "In regions where deceitful and insidious attacks of any kind occur, the Battalion or Regimental Commander may instigate collective countermeasures—"

"Thank you; that's enough." Unable to face the young lady's penetrating gaze any longer, Philip picked up his briefcase and with a curt nod limped out of the office. A moment later he was back. "Excuse me; may I see those orders for just one more second."

Frl. v. Mollwitz had been about to replace them in the safe; mutely she handed them back to him.

Philip flipped to the last page of the Commissar Order and paled. "My God," he murmured. Frl. v. Mollwitz was watching him so intently that an explanation seemed unavoidable. In a low voice he remarked, "This is signed by Brauchitsch." (Brauchitsch was the Commander-in-Chief of the German Army.)

She nodded. There was an awkward pause and then she added, "In fairness, I ought to mention that he did issue supplementary orders intended to take the sting out of these," she tapped the folders. "The supplementary orders do place stress on the maintenance of discipline and remind commanders that any actions in accordance with Barbarossa are only to be taken in self-defense. It is the opinion of General Olbricht, however, that the supplementary orders are too weak and will only serve to create widespread confusion. On the other hand, Oberst v. Tresckow argues that they do at least give those officers and commanders who want an excuse for ignoring the Barbarossa Instructions, the option to do so. What concerns me is that the supplemental orders do not significantly minimize the opportunities for excesses by those commanders who share the National Socialist *Weltanschauung*."

Philip gazed at Frl. v. Mollwitz and admitted, "Half an hour ago, I would have assured you that no commander in the German Army would implement those orders, but if Brauchitsch signed them …"

"I have a theory," Frl. v. Mollwitz started, and then broke off.

"Yes?"

"Oh, it's not very scientific, just an observation or an analogy perhaps," she smiled a little apologetically, no longer so sure of herself.

"Yes?"

"It's as if—" She stopped at the sound of someone going by in the hall. Philip stepped back and closed the door.

"Thank you. It's as if Hitler and his close associates were carriers of a disease—a disease which eats away at the moral fiber of the individual. The nearer or longer one is in contact with them, the weaker one's own ethical structure and sense of humanity becomes. Over time, one's entire system of values is corroded to nothing. In the advanced stages of the disease, not only has one's normal sense of human decency been destroyed, but criminal values have replaced healthy ones."

Philip considered this for a moment. "You mean that this is how otherwise—or previously—decent men like Jodl or Brauchitsch ..."

She nodded.

"But if our senior military commanders can't resist the criminal orders of Hitler, then the fate of the entire nation is in the hands of an emotionally unstable, morally degenerate madman."

Frl. v. Mollwitz nodded again.

"This is impossible! There has to be something the generals can do!"

"Freiherr v. Gersdorff says that the Commissar and Barbarossa Orders will be passed on in Army Group Center with verbal orders not to carry them out. Since both orders will be given out only verbally from Army level downward, it all depends on the individual commander in the end."

The words hung in the air for a moment. "Yes, it all depends on the individual." There was another pause. Then Philip took a deep breath. "Frl. v. Mollwitz, I'm afraid I've been a tiresome burden. Please forgive me. Good day." He proceeded to his own office and forced himself to work.

*   *   *   *

Although Alexandra v. Mollwitz had a small apartment of her own in the city, she always went to her parents for dinner on Friday evening. Alexandra's mother and stepfather lived in a modest villa in Grünewald: white stucco with a red tile roof and a single-story semicircular entryway whose roof served as a second-story terrace off the master bedroom. At this time of year the upstairs terrace was protected by a screen of flowers that hung from their window boxes on the railing and reached nearly to the floor of the terrace.

Alexandra rang the bell at the gate just to let them know she was home, and then let herself in. She went rapidly up the four steps to the front door, which opened before she reached it. The housekeeper, who had been with the family more than fifteen years, greeted Alexandra with a smile and declared, "You're looking very pretty today!"

"Thank you, Helga; how are you doing?" Alexandra asked as she removed her earrings from her purse and put them back on her ears before the mirror in the entryway.

Helga closed the door firmly as she answered, "*Ach*! I'm too old for all this bother with ration cards! It's so hard to make sure the family has something decent and different day after day with the restrictions. And the lines get longer every day. The shops all have shortened hours—allegedly because of too little help—but it means they're all open at different times. When is it all going to end?" Because Alexandra worked for a high-ranking general of the General Staff, Helga assumed she understood all the mysteries of the war.

Alexandra could only shake her head slowly. "Helga, I wish I could say something encouraging, but it looks like it will go on forever."

"Alix!" It was her mother's reproaching voice. "I wish you wouldn't say things like that, not even to Helga." Short, plump and matronly, Alexandra's mother displayed no physical similarity to her slender and elegant daughter. From pictures it was evident that even as a young girl it had been her warmth and good humor, rather than her good looks, that attracted admirers. She had first won the love of the dashing dragoon lieutenant Hans-Joachim von Mollwitz and then, after Mollwitz had fallen on the Eastern Front in 1917, conquered the heart of the urbane diplomat Albrecht von Rantzow-Waldbach. She gave her daughter a motherly kiss and got a peck on the cheek in return.

But Alexandra asked at once, "What do you mean? Can't I say what I think even in my own house?"

"Of course you can, dear; it's just that I wish you'd be more careful. You know how Rudi is." Rudi was Alexandra's half-brother. At thirteen, he was a very enthusiastic member of the *Jungvolk*, and he could hardly wait to graduate into the real Hitler Youth. "And what's more important," Frau von Rantzow continued, "Grete has brought home terrible marks in history—for which you and Albrecht are largely responsible." Grete was Alexandra's ten-year-old half-sister. Alix gave her mother a disbelieving look. "You'll hear the whole story when your stepfather gets home. But now, tell me how you're doing. Do you still like the work? I'll never understand why you gave up your good job at the bank to take this purely secretarial position. After all, you are earning less than before! Or have you met a nice young man?"

It was an old controversy. Frau v. Rantzow had viewed her daughter's college education as a "modern marriage market." With each year that Alix did not bring home her future husband, her mother's fear grew that her daughter would end up an old maid. Alix, in contrast, had enjoyed studying and had been enthralled by law itself—which did not mean she was opposed to getting married. She had fallen in love with a fellow student, but after his rejection she had not risked a new relationship. When her mother asked yet again about men, Alix thought briefly of Major v. Feldburg. His response to the Barbarossa Instructions had been so candid and concerned that it had made her like him; but a Catholic nobleman of his age must have married long ago. So she answered her mother by saying, "In the Bendlerstrasse almost all the men are nice, Mutti; and almost all of them are married and have children, if not grandchildren."

Together they went into the spacious living room, which had large windows overlooking a back terrace and garden. Grete, who was setting the table on the terrace, caught sight of Alix. Leaving the napkins in a heap on the table, she ran back inside through the open French doors. "Alix! Alix! You did say that your General" (by which she meant Olbricht) "said that we lost the World War on the front, didn't you? You said there wasn't just a revolution, but that we really and truly lost the war on the front, didn't you?"

Alexandra's mother gave her a you-see-what-I-mean look, and Alexandra sighed. "Yes, Grete, I did say that." Then she added forcefully to her mother, "All the General Staff officers admit that, Mother. It's neither a military secret nor a matter of opinion. It's a fact. The last offensive—"

"You don't have to show off your military knowledge around here, Alix. The point is that Grete innocently takes your word as law and writes such things in a school essay on the 'End of the World War.'"

"But, Mommy," Grete protested, "Alix does know more than that old goat Miss Wenzel! I'll bet Miss Wenzel never in her whole life ever spoke one word with a real General. All she's ever done is teach in that stupid school—"

"Grete! You've got to learn to show more respect for your teachers! I won't have you talking like that about them—or calling your school 'stupid.' Now finish setting the table. Your father could be home any minute."

Indeed, as she spoke, the sound of someone coming in the front door reached them, and Grete darted back onto the terrace, anxious to postpone the inevitable confrontation with her father.

Albrecht v. Rantzow was a tall, distinguished-looking man with greying sideburns and a cultivated English appearance. Colleagues jokingly claimed that he could easily be mistaken for Chamberlain himself—something that he only pretended to dislike. He kissed his wife, gave his stepdaughter his cheek, and then asked the ladies if they wished to join him in an aperitif. Alix and her mother asked for sherry, while he poured himself a cognac.

"Did you have a nice day, dear?" his wife asked.

"As good as can be expected," he answered, with a suddenly sour twist to his lips, turning at the waist to give a reproving look to Alix. She surmised he had learned about the impending invasion of the Soviet Union and no doubt blamed "the Generals" (and so Alix) for it. He turned politely back to his wife, "And you, Louisa?"

"I'm afraid Grete brought home some very disappointing grades," Frau v. Rantzow broke the news to him gently.

Albrecht v. Rantzow's face clouded over at once. "What's the matter with that girl? There's nothing wrong with her intelligence. Why doesn't she apply herself more? She's just plain lazy!"

Alix did not consider this a fair judgment of Grete and would have liked to speak up on her behalf, but she knew her "interference" would not be appreciated. She had been nearly twelve when her mother remarried in 1925. Her relationship with her stepfather had always been marked more by caution. To this day politeness and distance, rather than warmth and sympathy, dominated their relationship. In any case, Alix's mother was quick to defend her younger daughter. "Now, Albrecht! That's not fair. She's just having a hard time adjusting after the five years in Paris."

"We've been back two years now. Plenty of time for her to settle in," Herr v. Rantzow insisted sternly.

"*Naja*, and would you really like it if she had adapted as well as Rudi?" his wife asked, softly but with a raised eyebrow.

Albrecht v. Rantzow was instantly silenced. There was nothing he wanted less than to have another Nazi in the house. After a moment of awkward silence, he asked, "Just where is Rudi?"

"Tonight's his soccer night."

Herr v. Rantzow looked at his watch. "It is nearly 7 o'clock. He should be home by now. He knows we eat punctually."

"It's some sort of special match. Against another *Jungvolk* troop, I think. He did warn me he might be late."

"Warn you? Since when do little boys *warn* their mothers? This is absolutely appalling. I won't tolerate it!" After the bad news about Grete, this was too much, and Herr v. Rantzow lost his temper. "It is bad enough that he's gone twice a week at the damn *Jungvolk* meetings. I will not tolerate him missing dinner a third night in the week. From now on he'll be home on time on Fridays, or he will not be allowed to play football at all!"

"But, Albrecht—" Frau v. Rantzow fell silent as Helga appeared in the doorway.

"Dinner is ready, Frau v. Rantzow."

"Thank you, Helga. You may go ahead and start serving. We'll be right out."

Alix went quickly to the downstairs toilet to wash her hands before joining the others on the terrace. As she joined them, she found Grete already energetically defending herself. "But, Papa, you were the one who said the Jews didn't cause the Inflation. Don't you remember? I asked you how it was the Jews could make the Inflation without hurting themselves since they used the same money as we do, and you said it was all rubbish about them causing the Inflation!"

Herr v. Rantzow looked somewhat embarrassed, while his wife wore the same I-told-you-so look she had used on Alix earlier.

"Grete," her father said sternly, "you are old enough to know that you don't repeat everything you hear at home in school. From now on, in school you repeat exactly what your teachers tell you and forget anything you've heard from your older sister or myself."

"But, Papa, if it isn't true—"

"Don't whine at me like that!"

Grete didn't risk any more open defiance, but she clearly felt she was being unfairly handled. She pushed her hands between her knees and sat with hunched shoulders, pouting at her plate.

Alix, who had taken her place at the table, remarked in what she hoped was a casual tone as she removed her napkin from the silver ring, "Don't you think it's asking a lot of a child to expect her on the one hand to be honest and on the other to give answers she knows are false to her teachers?"

"Alix!" her mother warned, anxious to avoid any confrontation between her eldest daughter and her second husband.

Herr v. Rantzow took the remark surprisingly calmly. "The girl has got to learn how to get along in the real world. I'm afraid that the sooner she learns that survival requires a certain amount of hypocrisy, the better. Hypocrisy and apparent conformity with public opinion have become necessary nowadays."

Alix felt her temper rise. Although she didn't really want to fight with her stepfather, she just couldn't let this remark stand unchallenged. "Adapt instead of resist, you mean?" she asked acidly.

Her stepfather leveled his steel-grey eyes at her and said firmly: "That is exactly what I mean. There is absolutely nothing to be gained by dramatic gestures of defiance. Least of all from a child. I realize, of course, that at your age, your actions are governed by idealism and emotion, but I can assure you, you will outgrow both. In the meantime, I expect you to scrupulously avoid misleading your impressionable younger sister. Now that is the end of the matter."

"May I ask a question?" Alexandra asked, in a tone that clearly reflected her resentment at being talked down to in this fashion.

Frau v. Rantzow sighed; Herr v. Rantzow waited with raised eyebrows.

"Agreeing with you that it is wrong to incite school-age children to futile gestures of defiance, I would nevertheless be curious to know at what point—if any—you consider the refusal to adapt an advisable course—for an adult?"

"At that point where one can effect meaningful change and not merely endanger or disadvantage oneself and one's family."

"One more question, if I may?"

Herr v. Rantzow nodded.

"Was it then your conviction that you could not oppose the Regime in any worthwhile manner—not even at the Embassy in Paris—that induced you to become a member of the Nazi Civil Servants' Association (*Reichsbund Deutscher Beamten*)?"

"Precisely—and the fact that if I had not joined, my career in the Foreign Ministry would have been terminated. I do, after all, have a family to support. Your preference for heroics is a mark of your immaturity and irresponsibility. The head of a family cannot afford either. Is that clear?"

"Perfectly," Alexandra assured him, but he remained acutely aware of her disapproval.

▼

CHAPTER 13

Berlin
June 22, 1941

Philip slept late and woke contentedly in a room bright with sun but cooled by a breeze that made the lace curtains billow and flap. It promised to be a warm and sunny Sunday.

As he went down the corridor toward the bath, the smell of brewing coffee came from the back of the apartment along with the unintelligible cackle of the radio, and Philip indulged in self-congratulation on securing Franz Stadthagen as his batman. Franz was Heidi's illegitimate son, and Sophia Maria had always taken an active interest in him. She used her influence to see that he was admitted to the local gymnasium. She had also promised to finance professional training as soon as he had finished his national labor and military service. Unfortunately, just when he finished the latter, the war started, so that he was still serving in the Army. While on home leave, he had sung his woes to Sophia Maria, who had suggested to Philip that he might be able to arrange "something." When Philip was wounded shortly afterwards, his own batman had transferred away, and Philip was able to get Franz assigned as his replacement. In addition to having a bit of home with him, Franz was an attentive, intelligent orderly and 100% politically "reliable"—from Philip's point of view.

When he joined Franz in the kitchen this morning, the batman met him with a dejected expression. "They've invaded the Soviet Union," he announced in a numb voice.

"They?"

"Well, all right, we've invaded the Soviet Union—if you identify with the bastards who started this damned war!"

Although Philip had known that the invasion was pending, he had not known the exact date. On his hearing the news, the sun seemed to lose its brilliance and the day its charm. Together Philip and Franz listened to the *Wehrmacht* bulletin—repeated every few minutes—until they knew it by heart. It stated little more than the bare bones of the invasion: a preventive war to forestall a massive Soviet attack, it said.

After breakfast, Philip took a long ride, but his thoughts kept drifting back to Russia, to the Commissar Order and the Barbarossa instructions. Were they already being carried out? He wondered, too, about his friends in the 10th Panzer Division, which he knew was slated to go in with the first wave. Philip decided to drop by the Bendlerstrasse to see if he could discover more than was on the radio.

Arriving in the building just after 11 am, he found it unusually quiet. Aside from the duty officers and secretaries, no one else seemed inclined to sacrifice their only free day of the week—certainly not in this fine summer weather. Furthermore, no one seemed to know anything more about the progress of the invasion than what was on the radio. Philip was about to return home himself when he saw Alexandra v. Mollwitz go by in the hall. Impulsively, he stepped out of his office and called after her. "Frl. v. Mollwitz?"

She turned around in surprise.

"Are you expecting the *Herr General*?"

Alexandra shook her head and started back toward Philip so she wouldn't have to shout. "No, I just came to see if I could get any more details of the invasion."

"So did I—but information is scarce, even here."

"In AHA, you mean. I was going to go down to the press center where they translate what's being said in the rest of the world."

"The rest of the world can only repeat what we tell them."

"Radio Moscow and Tass, too?" she asked with a slight smile.

"No; but if they know anything about what is going on, they are not likely to broadcast it. And frankly, even if they claim to have flung us back with severe casualties, I'm not inclined to believe them."

"True, but what about the Finns and Hungarians? They might have slightly different versions. As our allies they may know something, but they certainly have more freedom of expression than we do."

"It's worth trying," Philip conceded, and they started down the hall together, Philip lurching along on his bad ankle. Alexandra at once modified her pace. As the entered the gloomy stairwell, Philip finally ventured to ask the attractive young woman beside him, "Don't you have something better to do on such a lovely Sunday?"

"This won't take that long, and then I thought I'd go down to Wannsee or something." She smiled fleetingly at him. "And you? Doesn't your wife object to you abandoning her on your only free day?"

"I hope she would, if I had one."

In the press center there was no one but a duty corporal whose linguistic abilities did not include either Finnish or Hungarian. "You'll have to wait until tomorrow or the next day," he told them, helplessly indicating a stack of unprocessed material in the in-trays.

"As I said," Alexandra remarked stoically as they left the press center and headed for the exit, "that didn't take long."

Philip laughed. "Well, then, Wannsee or something. Would you care to join me for lunch first?" The question came spontaneously, simply because he wanted to spend more time with this intelligent and attractive young woman, but at the same time he was slightly shocked by his own courage. Attractive women had always been Christian's preserve.

"I'd be delighted—if you aren't ashamed to be seen with me like this." Alexandra indicated her casual attire. Ever since she'd run into Philip she'd been cursing herself for her carelessness. Weekdays she went to considerable trouble to look nice—and not just because she knew General Olbricht expected her to look like a lady. Somehow she couldn't help hoping that she just might meet an eligible young man. And then, on the one day when she dressed only in sandals and a cotton skirt and blouse, she got asked out for the first time since starting work at AHA.

Philip laughed.

Alexandra was at once dismayed and said rather defensively, "I didn't think I looked that bad."

"On the contrary, *gnädiges Fräulein*, I had to laugh because being seen in your company can only redound to my credit."

Alix gave him a skeptical look. Philip's gracious manners reminded her of General Olbricht—or her stepfather's friends and colleagues from the Foreign Service. She wasn't sure if he was just being gallant from habit or if he was sincere.

"You always look as if you'd just been shopping in Paris," Philip explained, and it suddenly occurred to him that perhaps she had someone in Paris who sent her things. He feared an admirer and hoped for a brother, as he continued almost nervously, "It's such a refreshing change from the unimaginative attire of our BDM and *Frauenschaft* 'beauties.'"

"Thank you," Alexandra managed, sincerely pleased, adding in gentle lament, "and to think everything I own predates the war."

"You were yourself in Paris?"

"My stepfather was with the Embassy there from 1934 until the war broke out. At first I was at university in Berlin, but of course I spent all my holidays in France, and from the spring of 1938 until the start of the war, I lived in Paris full time."

"You finished your legal training in 1938?"

"No. I didn't finish. I have the First Exam, not the Second. I only did four of the Legal Internship Stations[1], and then I quit."

"But why did you quit at such a late stage?" If she'd simply failed the second exam, Philip would have understood, but it made no sense to him for her to quit so shortly before taking the second exam. "If you'd finished, you could have worked as a lawyer or judge, rather than typing and filing like the other girls who don't have any university education."

Alexandra's heart lurched slightly, astonished and flattered that a man could picture her as a judge without the least apparent doubt. Not even her stepfather had allowed her to dream of such success. Nevertheless, she answered firmly and without embarrassment, "The reason I quit is something I would rather not discuss in public." Philip suspected instantly that her decision was political rather than personal in nature. Alexandra herself was continuing, "Given the general attitude toward women in the professions, however, it was foolish—or defiant—to go as far as I did. My stepfather thinks I'm a starry-eyed idealist."

"But—if it's true—at least it's in good causes."

"What causes?"

"Women in the professions, humanity in warfare ..."

She was so overwhelmed by this unexpected, open approval that she was speechless.

"Lunch at Kempinski's?"

Alix shook her head. "Too fine. I'd be just as happy at any corner café—as long as they have tables outside."

---

1. A German legal education entails lengthy practical training similar to a medical internship, in which the candidate works as a trainee for a period of three to six months in various legal positions. Certain positions are required (law office, public prosecutors, judge), others optional. The legal internships generally last a total of two years, at the end of which the candidate takes a second set of exams.

Philip was pleased. Few women turned down free meals at expensive restaurants—especially nowadays. Perhaps it was her age. He calculated that if she had had her First Law Exam and four intern stations by the spring of 1938, she was very likely 27 or older. It was older than he would have guessed from her looks—older than he considered ideal—but he was beginning to see advantages in it.

They found an Italian restaurant with tables on the sidewalk, red and white checked tablecloths, and cheap Italian wine. Alix deftly managed to get Philip talking about himself—not an entirely easy task under normal circumstances, but Philip hadn't felt like this in five years or more.

He turned the tables soon, however, and quickly learned about Alix's secondary training as a foreign-language secretary and that she had lived five years in Washington, DC, with her stepfather.

"My half-brother was born there," she confided. "He has dual citizenship until he reaches age eighteen and will have to choose."

"And how old is he now?"

"Thirteen—and his greatest fear is that the war won't last long enough for him to join the SS."

"Waffen—I hope."

Alix sighed, "I don't think he much cares. He's the only Nazi in the family, but his enthusiasm makes up for all the rest of us."

"He's young. He'll probably outgrow it."

"And what did you want to be when you were thirteen?" Alix asked.

"Touché—a General Staff Officer, and that at a time when the General Staff was prohibited by the Treaty of Versailles."

"Which, no doubt, you considered a horrible injustice," she commented with a touch of sarcasm.

"Didn't you?"

"Not particularly. In fact, I approved of the military provisions of the Treaty, but I hated the economic provisions. I can remember 1923 particularly vividly. My mother was trying to make ends meet for a family of three—me, my brother and herself—on a widow's pension that was suddenly worthless. My mother, you have to understand, was the spoiled daughter of a good family. She'd met my father, a lieutenant in the dragoons, at a tea-dance when she was sixteen. She was engaged at seventeen, married at eighteen. Her understanding of financial affairs was—shall we say—limited. Her ability to work was nil. I believe to this day that we only survived because Uncle Erich helped us."

"How old were you then?"

"In the Great Inflation? Nine or ten."

"And living in Berlin?"

"Potsdam, actually, though we frequently came up to Berlin. My mother was having some fight with the bureaucracy. There was something about my father having been promoted to captain just as he went missing, but with a retroactive date. My mother was obsessed with getting a captain's pension rather than a lieutenant's."

"Understandable, if that's all she had to live on. Your father was missing? Not confirmed dead?"

"Only for a couple of months. They later found the body, and he's buried in Poland. My mother never managed to visit the grave, though she used to promise me we would. I was crazy about my father. Maybe because I saw so little of him. My only memories are from his wartime leaves—all dressed up in his best to take my mother out. A dragoon of the *Kaiserreich*. I hope you can appreciate how splendid he looked to a three-year-old girl. I was dazzled."

Philip laughed. "The way I hear it, girls of 23 and 73 were just as charmed."

Alix laughed with him. "I suppose so. He had a Kaiser mustache and a saber, of course, and he let me play with the tassels of his shako, although my mother scolded me." They had finished eating, and Alix sat with her chin in her hand as she narrated unselfconsciously. "And then he bought me the most beautiful dapple-grey rocking horse, which I saw in a display window. It must have cost a little fortune because it was the last one and the shop-keeper didn't want to sell it. My father insisted and refused to leave until it was under his arm. My mother was mortified, and the whole time she kept trying to convince me to choose a pretty doll instead. She said rocking horses were for boys. But I wanted that rocking horse, and my father said that no cavalry officer—in honor—could fail to encourage such a noble preference." She wasn't looking at Philip anymore, but was gazing out across the canal. "You know, I still have that rocking horse—in my tiny apartment here in Berlin." She had meant to make fun of herself, but it didn't come out right; they both knew she was suddenly close to tears. "Silly," she declared with a toss of her head; "I haven't told anyone about that in years."

"I'm honored." Philip was serious, but conscious of her embarrassment, he continued enthusiastically, "Do you like to ride? Disguised under this dull, field-grey uniform is actually a former cavalry officer. We could—"

But Alix was shaking her head. "We couldn't afford it when I was little, and after my mother's second marriage, we moved around too much. I've had a few lessons, but I've never really learned to ride well. My father must be very disappointed in me."

"It's not too late," Philip insisted, adding, "You're lucky to have had a father like that. Mine never really had time for us even when we were adults; he certainly had no patience with children. When I was growing up, I was more afraid of my father than fond of him, and I turned to my maternal grandfather for advice and as a role model. It was my grandfather Walmsdorf who taught me to ride properly and who took me and my brother hunting. Summers on his estate, Wahrnow in Mecklenburg, were the best times of my childhood. And it was because of him that I joined a Prussian cavalry regiment, *Reiterregiment* 3 in Potsdam, rather than the Baden Infantry Guards, in which all my Feldburg ancestors had served. That way I could get up to Wahrnow frequently. I was devastated when my grandfather died of a massive heart attack just after I was commissioned. After that I made an effort to get to know my father better, but we were never close."

"And your mother?"

Philip smiled easily. "She's wonderful. 'Frivolous and self-indulgent' were the words my grandmother Feldburg used, who insisted she spoiled us terribly. You'd like my mother. She's intelligent, principled and competent." Philip would have used the same words to describe Alix to his mother.

At last they left the restaurant and took the *S-Bahn* down to Wannsee with all the other families and couples on an outing from the inner city. They took the ferry over to Kladow, sitting on the open upper deck among the children eating ice cream. In Kladow they had *Berliner Weisse* with raspberry syrup in a beer garden. Then they took the ferry back to Glienecke and the bus into the city. As they parted, Philip thanked Alexandra for the lovely day. "When I heard the news, I never thought I would enjoy the day so much. It's almost perverse when one thinks what must be happening in Russia."

"*Ach, nein,*" she answered. "It wouldn't have changed anything if we'd been gloomy."

Philip had to agree with that, and so they parted, still using the formal form of address.

But that night Philip slept poorly. Partly, of course, it was the invasion of the Soviet Union with its unforeseeable consequences, but mostly it was Frl. v. Mollwitz. She appeared to be everything he had ever wanted in a woman. She was intelligent and educated, came from a good family, and was cheerful, pleasant, and witty. She was also prettier than any other girl he'd ever dated. Philip had never risked rejection or loss to Christian by even trying for really pretty women.

But Christian was far away and Alexandra was so unique that Philip knew he had to take a chance. He had to at least discover if she was all she appeared to be.

She seemed too good to be true. But if she was all that she apeared to be, he would have to find some way of winning her. Women like her were so rare, so special, that he could not expect to find another like her ever again. Even if she was only half of what she appeared to be, he was certain he would be happy with her the rest of his life.

But the risks were daunting, too. What if she was everything she seemed to be and he gave her his heart, and she didn't want it?

*   *   *   *

Berlin
July 1941

Marianne felt nervous and guilty—the way she felt when she left homework unfinished or went to see a film of which her parents disapproved. She clutched the bunch of roses so hard that the thorns broke through the paper protecting them and stabbed into her palm. She felt the scrutiny of the conductor on the bus as if she had been riding "black," though her ticket was valid. And when she changed to the *U-bahn*, she kept feeling the suspicious stares of strangers as she studiously read the advertisements: a film company advertised with a blond soldier smiling at snapshots of a fat baby over a caption that proclaimed: "Photos— the bridge between the front and home." A toymaker promised that building model tanks, planes and guns was an important part of a boy's pre-military upbringing.

When she exited the train in the station, Marianne was at once confronted by a large poster showing a white-haired woman in a checked apron holding out a copper kettle. The print at the bottom proclaimed a metal collection drive, and in eye-catching red the text beside the woman's face proclaimed: "I also help the *Führer*." Marianne was made acutely aware that she herself was not helping him—and didn't want to.

Marianne walked quickly to the address she was seeking—with frequent glances over her shoulder. At the modern apartment house there was no porter, only an electric buzzer beside the nameplates, and again Marianne glanced nervously over her shoulder before pressing the button next to the name she was looking for. A deep buzz announced that the door was being unlocked from within. Her heart pounding, she pushed the door open and disappeared inside.

She hurried up the first flight of stairs to the landing, grateful that the Silbers lived on the first floor. She saw the peephole blink, an indication that someone had bent to look through it. Panicked, she thought: What if the Silbers don't live here anymore? But then the door opened and Dr. Silber himself, his wispy white hair as long and unkempt as ever, stood smiling at her with his pale blue eyes twinkling in surprise behind his glasses. "Fräulein Moldenauer! What a wonderful surprise!"

Embarrassed, she held out her bunch of flowers.

"But, Fräulein Moldenauer! You shouldn't have!" He was backing up as he spoke, letting her in, but also half speaking into the hall behind him. As he closed the door, Frau Silber emerged timidly from the kitchen. "Darling, look!" her husband exclaimed. "Fräulein Moldenauer has come to visit."

Frau Silber hung back and ran her hand through her hair uncertainly. The gesture attracted attention to the grey, which had not been there two years ago. And from her hair, Marianne's attention was drawn to the fact that she was wearing a faded blouse with a button missing and a skirt held together with a safety pin. Frau Silber had been a concert violinist, and even at home she had always been elegantly dressed.

To cover her embarrassment and pretend to her hostess that she hadn't noticed how she was dressed, Marianne started chattering. "Frau Silber, I hope you'll forgive me for not calling first—" No sooner were the words out than she remembered that Jews were no longer allowed to have telephones.

Herr Silber came to her rescue. "Come, come. Let's not stand around in the hall. Join us in the kitchen for a cup of tea."

Marianne advanced toward the kitchen door and handed the flowers to Frau Silber. She took them reverently, as if she had not once received armfuls of flowers after every concert. "Roses!" she exclaimed in undisguised delight. Then she looked around the kitchen, bewildered. "But where are we to put them?"

Marianne had never before been in the Silbers' kitchen. When she had come for her weekly piano lessons, she had always been led directly to the sunny front parlor, where the grand piano sat regally in the middle of a Persian carpet. After her 45 minutes of instruction, Herr Silber would slide back the glass doors to the living room and Frau Silber would join them for tea.

Although the kitchen was spacious and sunny, the table was utilitarian and the straight-backed chairs were mismatched. Herr Silber gestured for Marianne to take a seat, and then took an earthen pottery coffee pot from the shelf over the sink and presented it proudly to the women. "Here's where we'll put the roses," he beamed.

Frau Silber was at once satisfied. "Yes, how inventive," she praised her husband. Herr Silber turned to fill the pot with water and then handed it to his wife, who arranged the roses in the pot with attention, care and skill. In a moment, a beautiful arrangement overpowered the shabby coffee pot, and with a satisfied "there" she set it in the middle of the table. Only then did Frau Silber really seem to remember herself. Urging Marianne to sit down, she declared, "I'll start the water for tea."

Marianne dutifully pulled out one of the chairs and seated herself, still too shocked by the Silbers' impoverished appearance to know where to start. Fortunately, Herr Silber asked how things were going at the university.

Marianne launched into a detailed account of all the trouble she had had getting into the classes she wanted and her problems with the bureaucracy, followed by an enthusiastic report on how wonderful it was to finally start studying after the drudgery of the Labor Service. But there her story faltered a little. She wasn't going to tell the Silbers about Warsaw and the Ghetto. Fortunately, Herr Silber asked, "And do you still find time to play?"

"Piano? Of course. That's the best relaxation in the world—especially after chemistry. I always play at least an hour a day."

"Wonderful! Then come, come! The tea will take another few minutes." Herr Silber jumped up and gestured urgently. Confused but polite, Marianne stood and followed Herr Silber out of the kitchen and into the front parlor. She could not suppress a gasp at the sight of the totally naked room. Not only was the grand piano gone; so were the carpets, the chairs, the bookcases, the paintings and the lace curtains. Even the large chandelier was gone; the naked electrical wiring hung down from the center of the ceiling. All that was left in the room were stacks of sheet music. Glancing through the open doors to the living room, Marianne saw similar desolation.

Herr Silber hurried to one of the stacks of music, and only when he looked back to ask her what music she wanted did he notice how she stood stunned in the middle of the room. "Oh, we had to sell it all," he told her cheerfully. "For the passage."

"Passage?"

"To Chile."

"Chile? You're moving to Chile?"

"Heavens, no! Two old people like us? We could never learn a new language and start life over again. We sent the children."

Only now did Marianne remember that the Silbers had married quite late and had three school-aged children. "You've sent your children to Chile?" She still couldn't quite grasp it, but was beginning to understand Frau Silber's dazed and somewhat disoriented behavior.

"Yes, Chile," Herr Silber agreed, his eyes twinkling as if it were some puzzle which only he had been clever enough to work out. "You see, there aren't many countries in the world willing to take Jews these days. We applied for American visas because we have relatives there. But you see, hundreds of thousands of Jews have relatives in America, and the Americans don't want hundreds of thousands of Jews coming to settle in America. Then we learned that Chile has no barriers against Jewish immigration, so it was just a matter of finding a way to get the children out. Of course, it's very expensive, as you can imagine. At first I thought we would never manage to scrape it all together. Since I'm not allowed to take Aryan pupils and my wife isn't allowed to perform anymore, it's hard to earn a living. The only way to raise the fare was to sell everything of value. Aren't we lucky we had so much!? And you see we can still carry on well enough without all the fancy things."

"The children—they made it safely? All on their own?" Marianne couldn't imagine it: school-age children traveling to the other end of the world without their parents. She hardly risked taking a train across Germany on her own.

"Yes, yes. Everything went splendidly. We found a nice couple who looked after them during the passage, and in Valparaiso they were met by the rabbi. He was expecting them. Wait just a second. I'll fetch the card we had from them." He was gone before she could answer, and a moment later he was back with a bent, dirty postcard. He pushed the card into her hands. "Go on! Read it!"

The card showed the snow-capped Andes with a city in the foreground. She read:

> *Dear Mommy and Daddy, we arrived safely. Everything here is very strange, but the people are very nice. Everyone is kind to us and already we are starting to learn Spanish. You would not believe how much food there is here—none of it is rationed. And Santiago at night is more beautiful than the sky—all the lights! We love you and miss you. Alli, Karl and Hanni.*

Marianne returned the card, but for a moment she couldn't meet his eyes. She kept seeing the elderly gentleman in the Warsaw Ghetto reaching out his hands toward the shattered violin. "But why didn't you go with them?"

He waved his hand irritably. "As I said, we're too old to start life all over again, and there wasn't enough money, anyway."

"But why didn't you come to us! We would have helped, found the money somehow ..." Even as she said it, she knew it wasn't true. Her mother had been compelled to ask Baron v. Feldburg to reduce the rent so that they could stay in their flat. But Baron v. Feldburg was a rich man who didn't know what to do with his money! "I know people who—" again she broke off. Could she really be sure Baron v. Feldburg would have been willing to help Jews? Just because he continued to treat her father with respect didn't mean he actually opposed the Nazis' Jewish policies. After all, he also employed an SA man as his porter and had rented out an apartment to a Gestapo inspector.

Herr Silber patted her arm consolingly. "You see. It isn't so easy."

"But you can't just give up. I want to help—"

"I know you do. You help just by coming to visit, by bringing roses. Come have your tea. My wife has been so lonely now that no one comes to visit anymore—and with the children gone ..."

Marianne wanted to protest. The Silbers had had so many friends; but she only had to remember her father's experience. Before his disgrace, the bell rang frequently with visitors "privileged" to call on the Herr Prof. Dr. Moldenauer, and her mother's frequent dinner parties had been well attended. Now hardly anyone came to see the Moldenauers anymore, either.

Marianne and Herr Silber returned to the kitchen. Frau Silber had set the table with mismatched pottery and glued-together cups and saucers. The tea was waiting. They took their places, and Frau Silber poured with the same elegance with which she had poured from silver.

"You know," Herr Silber admitted wistfully, "what we miss most is a radio. We would so like to hear what is going on in the world."

"But the piano!" Marianne protested. "Surely you miss—"

Herr Silber shook his head. "No; not really." He placed his fingers on the edge of the table and at once began to play. As if they were on the key-board, the fingers danced and stretched—now light, now firm, now rapid, now slow. Herr Silber closed his eyes and a peaceful expression came over his face. Then, without opening his eyes or stopping, he explained to Marianne, "After all, it's the way Beethoven heard his music."

✳   ✳   ✳   ✳

Berlin
August 1942

Alexandra had agreed to meet her best friend Lotte at Dimitri's, a student café in the Charlottenstrasse. Dimitri's was run by a Russian exile. During her first year at university, Dimitri's had been the favorite meeting place of Alexandra's circle of friends. It was dingy, cramped, and full of heavy Russian furniture, had rich carpets and patterned wallpaper, and was decorated with various reminders of Mother Russia, from a balalaika to wooden dolls lined up on the wainscoting. Because of Dimitri's hatred for Communism (he had a peg-leg, a 'gift'—as he put it—from the Bolsheviks), the café had never been popular with Communists, which in turn gave it a certain immunity from SA attack. The SA itself preferred to meet in more proletarian and German Kneipe, and so Dimitri's had been very much the preserve of student intellectuals with leftist but not outright Communist leanings.

When Alexandra had first frequented Dimitri's, it had been the politically turbulent year 1932, and she had been in her first semester. Although she could hardly afford more than a cup of tea (served Russian style in a glass), she had been intoxicated by the atmosphere. The smoke from the cigarettes of her fellow students (even some of the girls smoked!) had swirled like storm clouds amid the waving hands and agitated gestures of the young customers. Everything had been discussed with passion and enthusiasm, often late into the night. It was here that she had first learned to love debate and idealism—and here that she had first fallen in love.

Returning after almost eight years' absence, Alexandra was disappointed. Although the furnishings and decorations had not changed, the students seated around the tables seemed bland. They chatted in polite tones rather than with animation and emotion. The girls were dressed in neat skirts, blouses and lace-up shoes. Most had their hair in braids or curled back from their faces. None wore makeup or earrings, and they certainly didn't smoke. The young men looked very young and unfinished in open-necked shirts, baggy trousers and V-necked sweaters.

Too her utter amazement, however, Dimitri recognized her at once. He broke into a smile at the sight of her and left the glass he was drying on the bar to come out and greet her. "Lady Alexandra!" he exclaimed. "At last you've taken pity on your old friend Dimitri and honored him with your presence!" He bowed low over her hand with the elegance of an old aristocrat.

Alexandra had never dreamed that he missed her, and she was at once embarrassed. "Oh, Dimitri, I didn't mean to neglect you. I just couldn't bear to face Martin and his friends after—never mind. How are you?"

Dimitri balled his fists, raised his hands and shook them in triumph. "Finally those bastards are getting what they deserve! You don't know how long and hard I've prayed for this. Your splendid *Wehrmacht* is shredding the damned Bolsheviks apart. Every day you liberate more and more of my poor, enslaved homeland. If this continues, you will have chased the murdering monsters out of

Moscow before winter. Every day I am closer to going home. My dream of dying on my beloved estate and lying beside my ancestors under the birches may yet come true." His eyes were watering with emotion.

After recovering from her initial shock, Alexandra smiled and took his gnarled hand between both of hers. "I'm so glad some good may come of all this bloodshed."

"Good, Lady Alexandra? This is the best thing that has happened since that anti-Christ Lenin with his abominable Revolution plunged my poor country into misery! The whole world will be freed of the Bolsheviks and Communism forever. The Red Army will never again be able to slaughter innocent people and rape and pillage! But come, come. Sit down. What can I get you? On the house, Lady Alexandra, whatever you like."

"I'm meeting a friend for dinner, Dimitri, but she has never been here before—and she's always late."

He led Alexandra to the table in the window and removed the "reserved" sign. "I'll bring you a nice cup of tea while you wait."

Charlotte "Lotte" Koch was Alexandra's oldest friend. They had known each other since grammar school, and no matter where Alix's stepfather had taken his family, Lotte had visited during the holidays. By the time they were both nineteen and took the *Abitur*, Lotte had grown into an "ideal" Aryan beauty with long platinum-blonde hair, full lips, and an hourglass figure. She also had a lovely voice and had been accepted by the Music Academy. Before completing even one year there, however, she allowed herself to be seduced by the glamor of a film career promised her by some second-level official of the UFA. Her career had lasted only as long as her affair with the married official, and then she had been blacklisted. With no prospects in Germany, she had briefly considered fleeing to Hollywood, but another affair had prevented this, and she had started singing in cabarets. By the time this second affair ended in a dangerous abortion, the war had started, and her escape route was closed.

Lotte claimed that Alix saved her life at this critical point when she had thought of suicide. She took Alix as her example, learned typing and short-hand, and set out on a new career. She secured a position with a record company, where she had promptly met an up-and-coming young opera singer, Eberhard Böll— and started a new affair.

When Lotte arrived at Dimitri's, all heads turned to stare at her. She was dressed in a tight-fitting suit with leg-of-mutton sleeves and a skirt which went to mid-calf but was slit provocatively up the side. Silk stockings, high-heeled shoes and a hat that stood more than sat on her gleaming blonde hair completed her attire. She breezed in, apologized for being late, and kissed Alix on both cheeks. The smell of her perfume filled the entire café, and one of the girls at the adjacent table said in a voice which was clearly meant to be heard: "An honest German woman does not paint herself nor pierce her ears like a primitive Negress."

Lotte turned regally to the plain-faced girl who had sneered and told her in a friendly voice, "My dear, don't you ever listen to what our Propaganda Minister says? Just the other day, he was bemoaning the fact that too few women make an effort to grace our society with charm and beauty." She then opened her purse, extracted a cigarette from a silver case, and lit up. The provocation was too much for the girl at the next table; she angrily called for her bill and left in indignation.

But neither Lotte nor Alexandra was paying attention anymore. Lotte was bursting with her news. "Eberhard's done it, Alix! He's succeeded in getting me an audition with Dr. Steinecke," Lotte announced. "In just ten days! Can you believe it? By next spring I could actually be singing with the *Staatsoper*! Don't you think we should celebrate? Let's order some champagne; and dinner is on me."

Alexandra knew better than to point out that Lotte didn't actually have the job yet. Lotte was far more realistic than she pretended to be. She was simply a firm believer in celebrating at every opportunity. They ordered Crimean *Sekt*, borscht and stroganoff, and Lotte started talking about what she should sing for the audition. "I wanted to sing something from Beethoven, Wagner and Verdi— that's all right, don't you think? I mean, it shows versatility. I'd so like to sing something from *Aida*."

"I can understand. The present staging is inspiring."

"Have you seen it?" Lotte asked, astonished, her spoon partway to her mouth. Alix nodded. "But, Alix! Why didn't you say something?! I've told you hundreds of times I can get you discounts on the tickets, if you just give me enough notice! You can't afford to pay full price on your pitiable salary!" Lotte had been scandalized to learn how little Alexandra earned as a secretary in the *Allgemeines Heeresamt*.

"True; but, you see, I didn't actually buy the tickets. Major v. Feldburg did."

Lotte dropped her spoon and the soup splashed onto her suit. She hastily poured water on her napkin and daubed away the spots. Then she leveled her gaze on Alexandra and demanded, "And who is Major v. Feldburg?"

Alexandra shrugged uncomfortably under Lotte's boring gaze. "He's just one of the officers at AHA."

"Who took you to see *Aida*," Lotte pointed out sternly, "and what else?"

"We've been to the Philharmonic twice and to a couple of films …"

"Alexandra, this sounds serious." In all the years they had known each other, Alexandra had only fallen in love once—and that had ended in a catastrophe. Thereafter she dated only very occasionally, and nothing seemed to really "take off." Lotte knew that Alexandra was still a virgin. In consequence, Lotte felt Alexandra was terribly inexperienced when it came to men, and was instantly protective.

"Is he married?"

"Lotte! You know I wouldn't go out with a married man."

"But I thought all officers married when they were lieutenants or captains or whatever? At least that's what you told me not three months ago," Lotte reminded her. Lotte, like Alix's mother, had immediately assumed that AHA would be an ideal place for Alix to meet a suitable young man, but Alexandra had dismissed the idea on the grounds that the officers with whom she had to deal were too senior not to be married already.

"Most do," Alexandra admitted.

"So what's wrong with your major?—What did you say his name was?"

"Feldburg; Philip Freiherr v. Feldburg."

Lotte whistled and sat back in her chair, her attention focused intently on her friend. "Go on."

"What do you mean?"

"Tell me more. For example, how long has this been going on?"

"There's nothing going on, Lotte. Major v. Feldburg joined the AHA about two months ago. Over the last six weeks, he's asked me out every weekend except the one when he was Duty Officer."

"That sounds good."

Alexandra sighed. "I know, but it isn't what it sounds like. He still uses the formal form, and he's never touched more than my elbow—to help me in or out of a taxi or across a street or whatever."

Lotte frowned. She didn't like the sound of this. Alexandra was an attractive young woman, and it was clear to her that a serious suitor should have been more ardent. Then again, Alexandra's good looks might intimidate an ugly man. "What does he look like?"

"Dark hair, dark-grey eyes, fine classical face, glasses."

"Attractive?"

"Very."

"I suppose he might prefer boys. There are men—"

Alexandra was so indignant in her denials that Lotte instantly knew that Alexandra's heart was lost—even if she didn't know it herself yet. She sipped at her champagne thoughtfully and listened carefully as Alexandra finally started to pour out her heart. Alix was always like that. She needed to be encouraged at first, but when she'd overcome her inhibitions, she would speak with feeling and openness.

"I honestly don't know what to make of him, Lotte. He's everything I thought I hated when I was at university." She gestured vaguely to the room around her to refer to that stage of her life. "He's not only an aristocratic land-owner, he's a General Staff officer, and he's Catholic. There are times when he's so formal that it all but drives me mad! And yet, he's not really the way I thought aristocratic Catholic staff officers were at all. There's nothing haughty about him—or even arrogant. Nor is he the least bit bigoted. I swear, Lotte, he's given more thought to a wider range of topics than most students or even professors. He's amazingly well read, despite his lack of university education, and what's more he tries to analyze and understand concepts—like the key elements of education, the essence of leadership, the relevance of religion in warfare, etc., etc."

Lotte laughed, and Alexandra stopped talking, offended.

Lotte reached out and patted her arm. "I'm not laughing at you, Alix. I just find it amazing how different we are! Can you really picture me raving about some man who wanted to talk about religion and leadership?" Alexandra had to giggle at the thought. Lotte nodded and insisted seriously, "Go on. Tell me what it is that you like best about your young man."

Alexandra hesitated, took her time considering the answer, and then decided, "It's that he has no patent answers and seems genuinely interested in my opinions. He doesn't lecture me, Lotte. He really listens to what I have to say." Alexandra sounded amazed by this, and Lotte knew it was the old wound. Alexandra was continuing, however, unable to restrict Philip's virtues to a single point. "He's reliable. He's trustworthy. He has a strong sense of responsibility, and even if we disagree about this or that on the surface, our basic values are the same."

"So what's wrong with him?" Lotte challenged.

Alexandra shrugged, sighed and played with her empty *Sekt* glass. "He still calls me "Frl. v. Mollwitz," and at times—despite his rank, title and decorations—he seems outright diffident."

"Alexandra." Lotte leaned forward, placed her elbows flat on the table, and folded her hands together. "I want you to give me an honest answer: Have you done anything to encourage him?"

"What do you mean? I've always accepted his invitations."

"Well, does he see you home?"

"Of course."

"To your apartment?"

"Yes."

"And do you invite him up for substitute coffee or a glass of wine?"

"Of course not! He might get the wrong idea! I'm not like you, Lotte; I couldn't deal with having one affair after another. I couldn't go through an abortion to save my life, and being an unwed mother would be even worse." Alix was not so much angry as agitated. Part of her felt that she ought to be more like Lotte. She was 28 years old, and with every day she got older and less "eligible." Her mother had almost despaired, blaming Alix's education. She told Alix she was "too outspoken," adding that men didn't like "clever" women. Alix had started to believe her—until she met Philip. Philip was everything she had ever dreamed of in a husband—except that he was a reactionary Junker. But if he wasn't seriously interested in her, she supposed she ought to at least enjoy an affair with him. The problem was that she simply couldn't imagine sleeping with a man just for the "fun" of it, without any prospects of permanency.

Lotte was making calming gestures. "Relax, Alix. I'm not suggesting you sleep with him. But, you see, men don't like to be rejected any more than we do. Maybe he's afraid you'll reject him, if he goes too far too fast?"

"Lotte! He's a rich baron with an Iron Cross. What has he got to be afraid of?"

"You."

"Me? I'm an old maid—"

"Nonsense. Besides, there must be some reason he isn't married at his age. Maybe he was rejected by the woman of his dreams and hasn't recovered? Or maybe he was just so busy getting his rank and those General Staff stripes and the medals to have time for women? Maybe he's completely inexperienced?"

"I can't imagine that," Alexandra asserted, thinking that Philip was simply too good-looking and charming not to have had lots of experience with women. She combed her hair out of her face with her hand. "You don't really think that's possible, do you?" she tensely asked her experienced friend.

Lotte shrugged. "I admit it's hard to imagine—if he's even half as charming as you make him sound. Maybe he's just too conservative. Don't these Catholic aristocrats usually marry modest maidens straight out of convent schools?—preferably someone they're related to."

"Yes, and that's what I'm afraid of," Alexandra admitted candidly. "I'm afraid that he sees me as a pleasant way to fill his free time until he finds an immature maiden with the right bloodlines."

"And that's not enough for you?" Lotte pressed her. "I know girls who'd sell their souls for just one evening at Kempinski's on the arm of a young, decorated

Baron. But being taken out to expensive restaurants and concerts and films all without any obligations isn't enough for you?" The question wasn't unkind, just very penetrating.

Alexandra paused, her hand still in her hair. Their eyes met. Alexandra shook her head. "No, Lotte. It's ironic, but this reactionary Junker is everything I thought an open-minded, socialist intellectual would be—and wasn't. He's the first man in my whole life who has ever really taken me seriously. He's so much better than Martin was—and he would still be, without his rank, or his title, or his wealth. I'm not saying I'm in love with him," she hastened to stress to Lotte (who knowingly smiled). "It's just that there's nothing I'd like more in the world right now than to get to know him better. I want to know about his personal opinions, not just his public ones. I want to know more about what he feels, not just what he thinks."

Lotte leaned forward and put her hand on Alexandra's wrist. "Then don't let him slip away, Alix. Take a chance."

C H A P T E R 14

▼

Berlin
September 1941

It was pouring rain when Philip and Alexandra finished dinner and went out into the street. The rain had blown in unexpectedly and put an effective end to their plans for a long walk. Alix sighed in disappointment. It was only 8 pm and she did not want to go home yet. She'd looked forward to the evening with Philip all week, not least because he had suggested the walk rather than a concert or movie. Alexandra much preferred his conversation to anything "cultural." Besides, they could not talk uninhibitedly in public places, since there was always the risk of being overheard. The walk had been a means of avoiding those unwanted ears.

With Lotte's advice ringing in her ears, her heart thundering and in her breast, Alix collected all her courage and suggested—without directly looking at Philip—"If you won't get the wrong idea, we could have a glass of wine in my apartment."

Philip, who had been trying to find the courage to make a similar suggestion, agreed at once.

They made a dash for the *U-bahn* and took the underground to Rudesheimer Platz. Although it had now stopped raining as abruptly as it had started, neither of them suggested a change of plans. They walked to the five-story turn-of-the-century apartment house, and Alix took out her key. Philip had often escorted her this far and was familiar with the well-maintained art-deco façade and the balconies overflowing with flowers.

Alix led him into the hallway. Dark wooden paneling, beveled mirrors and heavy marble greeted them. Alix led up two flights of stairs. Before she reached the second landing she called up clearly, "Good evening, Frau Bubner." The door to the left-hand apartment clicked guiltily shut, and Alix and Philip exchanged a conspiratorial smile. Alix had told him about this neighbor, who kept track of her comings and goings more zealously than a watchdog. As there was nothing to stop her looking through the peephole, however, Alexandra registered that the whole house would soon know about her visitor. But having come this far, she refused to be intimidated by an old busybody. She unlocked the right-hand door and held it open for Philip.

The minute the door closed behind her, Alexandra felt a kind of panic. To cover her nervousness, she tried to be casual. "Make yourself at home." She gestured toward the large, dark room on the right. At once she changed her mind. "No, wait, I'd better get the blackout blinds first." She closed the blinds and turned on the lights in the living room, while Philip shook the rain from his cap and hung his coat on the rack by the door. Hardly out of the living room again, she announced, "I'll get the wine," and disappeared down the hall, still wearing her wet raincoat.

Philip entered the living room and stood still for a moment to take it all in. It was sparsely furnished: a table with two chairs, a secretary, a comfortable but very dilapidated reading chair, a standing lamp and bookcases. Through the open door to the left of the secretary, he could just see the end of a bed and a dark wardrobe. All the furnishings looked second-hand. The rugs were badly thread-bare. He wondered if they were cast-offs from her mother or if she had purchased everything herself on her very modest salary.

The secretaries at the Bendlerstrasse were notoriously badly paid. Like the officers themselves, they were expected to work predominantly for the "prestige." Fine for those with family money, but not all the women—not even those from impeccable aristocratic families—had family money. The low salaries had contributed to a situation ending in a tragic execution for treason not very long ago. A Polish officer had exploited the financial difficulties of one of the secretaries to extort military secrets from her. Since Philip by now knew that Alix's father had left only debts and that her stepfather was stingy, he found himself wondering why Alexandra hadn't taken a better paying job. With her language skills and legal training, she could easily have been an executive secretary to a senior manager. Somehow he had never dared asked her why she was at AHA, but he decided tonight might be the time to ask—that and why she hadn't finished her law studies. Then he noticed, almost hidden behind the open secretary, the rocking horse her father had given her.

When Alix arrived carrying two wineglasses, a bottle of wine and a corkscrew, she found him standing beside the rocking horse, absently patting its nose. Hearing her arrival, Philip turned quickly, but seeing that he'd been caught, there was nothing he could do but smile sheepishly and admit, "He is a beautiful grey."

Alexandra laughed. "And considerably better mannered than your colt." Philip had tried to give her a riding lesson on his own horse, but the experiment had almost ended in disaster and had not been repeated. Changing the subject, Alix announced, "Here, I'll let you do the honors," as she turned the bottle and corkscrew over to Philip.

Philip removed the cork and poured. They lifted their glasses "*zum Wohl.*" Then Alix seated herself at the table and Philip followed suit. The table between them was comfortable and reassuring, almost like being in a restaurant or café, as they had been many times.

"The day we went to Wannsee, you said you'd tell me why you never finished your law studies when we weren't in public. Surely this qualifies?" Philip started.

Alix, who had been racking her brain for some neutral topic of conversation, was relieved to have a theme suggested. "Where should I start?"

"The beginning."

"Where's that?" she countered. Then, smiling and tucking her hair behind her ears, she proceeded, "I started my law studies in '32—before the Nazis came to power. So I didn't have to do Labor Service or worry about the quota."

"What quota?"

"The one for women. Surely you know the Nazis limit female enrollment at universities to ten percent?" She sounded offended that he took no interest in discrimination against women.

Philip shook his head. "I didn't know—no one in my family has ever attended university."

That mollified her. She explained, "It's part of their ideology about women being essentially breeding machines. In any case, since I was already enrolled, I didn't have to worry about it." Philip seemed to want to say something, and Alix stopped. "Yes?"

"I was just wondering: How would you characterize the mood at the university when Hitler was appointed Chancellor? Was the news greeted with jubilation or skepticism?"

"Mostly positively. Everyone hoped this would signify a new beginning." She smiled a little wryly. "The Schleicher government was widely viewed as illegal, you know, and the sentiment among students with liberal and leftist leanings was that the grip of the "senile" field marshal and his "reactionary" clique of General Staff Officers had to be broken. Hitler was the leader of the largest party in the *Reichstag*, after all. Even if the NSDAP had no absolute majority, the fundamental principles of parliamentary democracy required that he be asked to form a government. The question is: Why didn't the Army do anything to prevent Hitler from coming to power?" Alix was already so lost in the discussion that she'd forgotten her nervousness.

"As I was only a green lieutenant at the time, it is perhaps presumptuous of me to speak for the C-in-C and Chief of Staff," Philip prefaced his remarks, "but let me remind you that at the time, "the Army" was the 100,000-man *Reichswehr*. In 1933, the SA was at least three times—some say five times—as strong as the Army. They were, of course, essentially untrained hoodlums without heavy weapons of any kind. We probably would have won a direct fight against them. Certainly the mood in my own regiment was militant. We—the young and inexperienced lieutenants—would have welcomed the chance to humiliate the SA. We didn't have the sense to be afraid. But the Army's leadership couldn't afford that luxury. The Army was outnumbered at least three to one, and a very large portion of the population—the largest single faction—stood behind Hitler. So we were talking about civil war—German killing German in the streets of Berlin. And who knows for sure with whom the KPD—or even SPD—would have sided? The KPD might well have sided with the NSDAP, on the principle that chaos leads to revolution and revolution leads to the Dictatorship of the Proletariat.

"Most important, however, is what you just said yourself: Hitler was legally appointed chancellor by the president, Field Marshal von Hindenburg. Any action against his appointment would have been a *coup d'état* against the Weimar Constitution—which all officers had sworn to defend. Remember, too, that the C-in-C at the time was the same Kurt von Hammerstein who had been arrested by his own father-in-law because he refused to join the Kapp Putsch. Hammerstein was one of the few truly loyal generals in the *Reichswehr*. You can't have it both ways. You can't demand that "the generals" be loyal servants of the civilian government and good democrats—and then complain because they don't putsch against the democratically elected government."

"You're good." Alix raised her glass. "If you ever get too shot up to be an officer, you should consider studying law. I never realized General Staff officers had such a highly developed sense of parliamentary democracy."

"Even if I am a "reactionary staff officer," my father was a Member of the *Reichstag* for almost 10 years."

"Really!? You never mentioned that before." Alexandra sat up straighter, tucking her hair back behind her ears again. "He was a Member of the *Reichstag* in 1933? For which Party?"

"The Center, but not in '33. He was in the *Reichstag* from 1924 to 1932, but didn't stand in the November '32 elections because of his failing health and increasing discouragement. He was fed up with the entire political situation—and fairly bitter about it."

"But he was in Berlin. He must have had many friends still in Parliament," Alix pressed him, so absorbed in the conversation that she had completely forgotten that she was alone in her apartment at night with a man.

Philip, by contrast, was finding her increasingly intoxicating. "Of course; but let's not talk about my father. You were going to tell me—"

"I will, I will. Just one more question. Why did the Center vote for the Enabling Law?" She leaned forward on the table and awaited his answer tensely.

"Partly because they were intimidated by the threats against them—"

"Threats?"

"Many MPs received letters in which their death was predicted if they failed to vote for the Enabling Law. But most, like my father, simply felt that Germany wanted a dictatorship."

Alix was obviously shocked. "Who—if not the politicians—is responsible for preserving democracy? The mob can't be allowed to make policy!"

"Not a very democratic attitude, Frl. v. Mollwitz," Philip retorted, amused. "'The mob' is also 'the people'. Even if Hitler had not won an absolute majority and the number of votes in favor of the Nazis declined significantly between the July and November elections, his appointment to Chancellor seemed wildly popular. I remember my father standing with me on the balcony of a friend's house and watching the torchlight procession of the Nazis going by in the street below. He gestured contemptuously at the marching men, shouting more than singing one of their 'fighting songs,' and he said, 'That is the future, Philip. Your future. Thank God I won't be around much longer. I would be nothing but an inconvenient anachronism.'" Philip was slowing turning his empty wineglass between his fingers, lost in the memory. After a moment he added, "So am I—an inconvenient anachronism."

"Thank God!" Alexandra replied with a quick smile.

Philip, who was starting to feel morose from these memories and the sense of utter helplessness, felt that smile lift him up. It warmed him like an unexpected ray of sunshine on a gloomy day. He looked directly at her, half expecting the sunlight to disappear again, a fleeting, insignificant break in the clouds. Instead, Alexandra looked steadily back at him, her chin resting on her hand and the smile still curling her lips. It was almost like an expression of some inner happiness. For a moment he basked in the warmth of that smile, and then he said, "But it is terrible being an anachronism—unable to adjust to new times and unable to change them."

"*Ach*, the times will change," she assured him, sitting back and combing her hair back with her hand, holding the long strands out of her hope-filled face. "Being an anachronism doesn't have to mean you're the remnant of a bygone age. It can also mean you are a representative of a future one—that you are ahead of your time."

"Where do you get your optimism?" Philip asked, amazed and a little jealous.

"Russia: you said yourself that we can't possibly win a war against the Soviet Union."

"And that is a reason to be optimistic?" The officer couldn't believe his ears. He looked at her admonishingly through his glasses, like a schoolmaster.

Alex leaned forward and her fingers drew meaningless figures on the tabletop as she said in a low voice, "Because the only way to cure people of their blind faith in the mad pied piper is for him to stop succeeding."

"Funny," Philip remarked, looking at her sidelong; "that's exactly what my mother said roughly a year ago. But I still find it impossible to welcome a war that we can't win and which will cost us tens of thousands of lives." He paused, thought, and then shook his head. "Never mind; you still haven't told me why you gave up your law studies." He had quite unexpectedly slipped into the familiar form. Catching himself, he at once apologized. "Sorry; is it all right if I use '*du*' with you?"

"I'm honored," Alexandra told him, with a little smile that for a second left him uncertain if he was being mocked. In the next instant, however, her smile broadened and she said with open delight, "*Du*, I better get another bottle of wine before I start on the story of my life."

She was gone and back in a moment with another bottle of wine. Again she handed it to him to open. As he worked to extract the cork, she asked, "Shall I make it long or short?"

"Long, by all means," he assured her, pouring for both of them. Then he leaned back into his chair as if for a truly long evening, but at once noticed that the chair was not comfortable. Boldly he announced, "But you'll have to allow me to make myself comfortable."

Alexandra indicated her one comfortable reading chair, too euphoric to be afraid of what might come of all this. She was in love, and she knew it and welcomed it. Suddenly—for the moment—she didn't care about anything else.

Philip shook his head. "You sit there. I'll be quite comfortable on the floor, if you can spare me a cushion." As he spoke, he settled himself on the floor with his back wedged between the secretary and the wall, his feet propped against the rockers of the rocking horse. "Now, your life story, please."

It took Alix a moment to order her thoughts and tame the excitement that this sudden intimacy evoked. "I took my First Exam in '36, and my first *Referendar* Station was with a civil court. I thought: Now you'll see what justice is in the Third Reich. To my amazement, I found it was very much the same as in the Republic: the same judges, clerks and laws, for the most part.

"My second station was with a Hamburg shipping firm. There I worked in the small legal department, drafting contracts and dealing with issues of international commercial law. Again: very much business as usual. The Third Reich seemed to have had no impact on the legal aspects of the business.

"The third station was a private law practice. Here I ran into some of the more unpleasant aspects of the Third Reich. We had a rash of clients intent on divorcing their Jewish spouses; yet my employers, as much as myself, despised their clients for it. We also had the satisfying task of helping Jewish customers outwit Nazi regulations by finding legal means to salvage some of their capital and get it invested abroad. So despite the confrontation with the injustice, I was more inspired than ever to take to the lists—a white knight, defender of the downtrodden!" She laughed shortly at the memory of her naiveté. Philip raised his glass to her, and she bowed her head graciously.

But the next instant she was deadly serious as she continued, "And then I landed in the office of the public prosecutor." She stopped, considered how to proceed, and then gave up. "*Ach*, Philip, how can I describe what I found there in a way that won't sound dry and legalistic?"

Philip tossed back his head and laughed. When he finished, he explained to the disconcerted Alexandra, "Nothing you've said has even hinted of stodgy legalisms. Don't you realize how passionately you relate things?"

Unknowingly he'd hit the old wound. Inwardly she cringed, and in a hostile voice she challenged, "What do you mean? That I'm a typical emotional female and not suited to law at all?"

Philip answered with an intensity that made her heart stop, "'Typical' is the last word I would ever use to describe you." Then, a little embarrassed by the depth of his feelings, Philip tried for a more neutral tone. "I think it is wonderful if a lawyer isn't cold and calculating, but committed to people and principles. Besides, you're always very cool and professional in the Bendlerstrasse. I was only referring to tonight. Forgive me if I offended you." He bowed his head, and the last remnants of Alexandra's tension melted away. "Please continue. What was it you found at the public prosecutor?"

Alexandra took a deep breath and focused again on the story she was telling. "It was as if my whole house of cards had collapsed on top of me. The entire criminal justice system proved to be nothing but a sham: a highly bureaucratic kangaroo court. To be sure, there were still prosecutors and defense attorneys. All the formalities were carefully observed. But before the stage show started, the judges conferred with the prosecutor and were advised on what verdict and sentence they were expected to produce."

"What?" Philip didn't believe it—and then again, he did.

"And the worst of it," Alix continued, "was that no one was even ashamed of it. I was taken along as if it were the most natural thing in the world, as if there were nothing to even be embarrassed about. The show was for the gullible public, but 'between colleagues' there was nothing to hide. And, you see, suddenly there wasn't any point in being the defender of the discriminated and downtrodden. I would only have been tilting windmills. And then came a case ..." She stopped; her face was deadly serious now, and she looked past Philip.

He noticed her glass was empty, stood, got the bottle and poured for her. She glanced up only as he finished. She gave him a smile and a 'thank you,' but her thoughts were still with this distant trial. Philip filled his own wineglass and Alix finally started again, softly. "The defendant was a skilled welder working for Heinkel. Someone had denounced him, and on a search of his apartment they found multiple copies of 'Free German Youth' and 'Socialist Action.' Those—in case you reactionary Junkers are not familiar with them—were SPD newspapers produced in Czechoslovakia and smuggled across the border by what must have been very courageous and clever men. The vast majority of the workers had by then— early 1938—already adapted to the new regime. Nevertheless, they were reluctant to betray a "comrade," so they turned a blind eye to the Socialist activists. This man, however, was betrayed by a zealous apprentice.

"His wife was left to support the children. She faced endless chicanery when she tried to get permission to visit him, but she didn't collapse or despair. One day she sat herself in my tiny office and told me matter-of-factly of all her vain efforts to get to see her husband. Then she placed a dirty, battered package on my desk and asked if I, as a woman, would deliver it for her—underwear, a comb, a toothbrush, and pictures of the children, she said."

"Did you?" Philip asked anxiously.

"Of course. It was horrible not to be able to do more."

"But what if there had been a letter inside? It could have ruined your career. You might have landed in jail yourself." Philip sounded sincerely distressed.

"But that's the point. What was my career? A sham, a hoax! Delivering that package—and I hope and believe there *was* a letter in it—was probably the most important thing I ever did in my whole life, much less in the cause of justice."

"But if you'd been caught—"

"*Ach*, don't make so much of it. Even if the worst had happened and I'd landed in a Concentration Camp and died there, my death would still have been more meaningful than if that English Hurricane had hit your head rather than the staff car."

"*D'accord*, but—"

"It really wasn't that dangerous," Alex insisted, embarrassed by his evident distress. "Nobody took me seriously at all. I was allowed to see and hear everything precisely because I was insignificant. I only told you the story because I wanted you to know what kind of people these were. No crying, no begging, no apologies, no recriminations." She took wine to strengthen herself. "Philip, I don't know what they did to him, but it must have been horrible. They managed to make him recant, to confess and revile himself—even beg for mercy. But they couldn't tear one name out of him. And since nothing they did could make him betray a comrade, they killed him."

Philip sat unmoving in his corner, his gaze fixed on Alexandra. He thought of his former tenant, Herr Jähring, and supposed that he, too, was dead on account of those leaflets that said nothing but the truth. Then Philip realized that despite his distress, he had drifted into contemplation of how gracefully Alexandra sat curled in the big chair, her feet tucked up under her. He forced his thoughts back to what she was saying.

"… prosecution informed the judges that the State and Party expected the death sentence, and the judges duly delivered it. I called in sick the next day and then got indefinite 'sick leave.' I went to Paris. I hope I never set foot in a courtroom again—until this regime is toppled!"

In the silence that followed, Alexandra felt somewhat embarrassed for the vehemence of her last outburst. Philip was thoughtful. At last he asked, "But given all that, where do you get your optimism? It can't really be the war with Russia." This notion just would not go into his head.

"Ah," she smiled a Mona Lisa smile. "Can't you guess, *Herr Generalstabsoffizier*? It was the contrast between that totally corrupt and cynical prosecutor's office and the AHA. Suddenly I found myself in an environment where Nazi policies weren't enthusiastically cheered or docilely accepted. On the contrary, they were openly criticized, condemned and opposed."

"Unsuccessfully!" Philip shot back, his feet unconsciously setting her rocking horse to galloping.

"Sometimes; not always. And that's not the point. Everywhere I looked, even opponents of the government—like my stepfather—were dutifully carrying out the tasks assigned, pursuing their careers, withdrawing from political life altogether, making peace with the ideology. I interviewed for a number of jobs with major banks and industrial companies. Half of them were more interested in whether I'd been in the BDM and was now a member of "Faith and Beauty" than in my qualifications. Even at those companies where my French secured me attractive offers, it was always the same: Hitler photo in some prominent spot, everyone greeting everyone else with '*Heil Hitler*,' letters signed "*mit deutschem Gruss*." I took a job with the *Depfa*, as foreign language secretary, but I found the atmosphere stifling. I worked in a large office with no less than sixteen other typists. The older women were incredibly unfriendly—as if they thought I would take their jobs away from them. The young women were silly. They got absolutely hysterical whenever Hitler spoke over the radio. I couldn't stand it. So when I got an interview with Olbricht at AHA—"

"Just how did you get an interview with General Olbricht?"

"Oh, chance, I suppose you'd say. I was walking the family dog in Grünewald one Sunday morning when I ran into Uncle Erich—"

"Your father's brother?"

"No, he's not really an 'uncle' at all. He was my father's best friend from the 13th Dragoons, and he felt in some way responsible for us after the war. I suspect he promised my father something. In any case, when I was little he used to bring me presents or take me out for cake and ice cream on my birthday. He came alone because my mother could never get along with his wife, although he had a daughter my age whom I liked. After my mother remarried he visited us rarely, but we never entirely lost contact, and he'd write on birthdays and the like. Anyway, he was out riding and I was walking our dog. He stopped to ask how I was doing, and I'm a terrible actress. My frustration and unhappiness must have come across, because he at once said he might be able to arrange something for me. He called a week later and told me I had an interview with General Olbricht."

"Excuse me. Just who is this 'Uncle Erich' of yours?"

"*Generalleutnant* Erich Hoepner."

"Hoepner," Philip repeated dryly. "Panzer-General Erich Hoepner, who was outside of Warsaw just eight days after the start of the war?"

Alix nodded, "Yes; I read that, too. In any case, he got the Knight's Cross at the same time as Olbricht. I guess they've been friends since then, maybe longer. I'm not sure. Anyway, he'd seen Olbricht recently and knew he wanted to hire a second secretary. I almost canceled the interview, however, because I thought: The pay is insulting, you'll only be an ordinary secretary, you'll have no chance to use your French, and you'll be surrounded by a bunch of reactionary militarists."

"Reactionary militarists," Philip repeated with a sour expression as he sipped his wine.

"Well, my stepfather has never spoken very kindly of the General Staff. He says their interference in foreign affairs has been the cause of all evil, so to speak. I suppose, to a degree, I even shared Hitler's view that the General Staff was like a mad dog that had to be held back by the collar or it would attack everyone."

"Hitler said that?"

"Allegedly. And allegedly he added that he soon discovered that instead of that, it had to be prodded into attacking anything. In my case, the moment I entered Olbricht's office I discovered I was among sane people again for what seemed like the first time in years. I took the job on the spot, and I've never regretted it. No shouted '*Heil Hitler*s,' no hysterical crooning from female colleagues, and no intriguing and scheming, either. The whole atmosphere is one of mutual respect—even for a lowly secretary—"

"That comes from being a bunch of reactionary Junkers," Philip pointed out, and Alex laughed in agreement before adding, "But the criticism of the government is genuine."

"And stops at talk. We talk and curse and complain and we do—can do—nothing."

"Oh, opportunities will eventually come along," she told him blithely. She was too happy to be here, using the familiar form with this man she now knew she was in love with, to worry about any problem at all.

Philip shook his head, unable to believe it. His legs, meanwhile, were cramped from sitting on the floor. He stood to stretch, commenting as he did so, "You really are an incurable optimist."

In confusion, Alexandra also got to her feet. Thinking Philip was preparing to leave, her insecurities returned. Bewildered by his abrupt departure, she asked, "Is that a terrible disease?"

"It's a dreadful disease!" Philip assured her. "I wish I could catch it." They were standing quite close, and Philip was acutely aware of it. When she looked up with a little confused smile, unsure what he wanted, he asked softly, "You don't suppose it might be contagious, do you?"

Alix's heart started beating faster, and her cheeks flushed. "Almost certainly," she assured him. Take a risk, take a risk, her heart cried.

"Should I try to increase the chances of infection?"

"I wish you would."

Philip bent and kissed her. After a moment, he put his glass on the table and kissed her again, taking her in his arms for the first time.

She lifted her face for both kisses and—to her own surprise—she felt comfortable in his arms. When he drew back from the second kiss, she smiled up at him blissfully.

Philip registered to himself, "I'm head over heels for this girl." And kissed her again.

But things were happening too fast and it had been far, far too long since Alexandra had last been kissed—and never like this. She was suddenly frightened again. She pulled back, nervous and confused. "Philip …" She wasn't sure what to say, what she wanted.

"*Ja*, I know. I'll go." He released her, found his glass, finished his wine in a single swallow and put the glass back on the table. He bowed and clicked his heels, "Thank you for a most interesting and enjoyable evening, Frl. v. Mollwitz." He was using the formal form again.

"It was a pleasure, Frhr. v. Feldburg." She held out her hand, trying to disguise her uncertainty with savoir-faire.

He bowed over her hand and started for the door. Wretchedly unsure of herself, Alix followed him. As he put on his coat and set his cap at the right angle, she kept thinking: Lotte would do something to stop him from leaving. But what? Ask him to stay, was the logical answer. But Alix couldn't. She just couldn't. If she did that, he'd expect her to sleep with him.

In the completely darkened hallway he turned to her, and before she knew what was happening they embraced briefly. Using the familiar form again, Philip promised, "I'll call you in the morning."

CHAPTER 15

▼

Crépon, France
November 1941

Dieter had been given a squadron, Ernst had been promoted to *Oberleutnant*, and Christian had ten days' leave. All that had to be celebrated "properly"— which meant that the party at the mess had gone on into the early hours of the morning. Still, knowing that Yvette would be waiting for him, Dieter drank a couple of mugs of coffee and drove himself into Crépon. As always, he parked in the side street beside the shop and let himself in with Gabrielle's old key.

As he mounted the creaking steps to the apartment under the eaves, Dieter felt the burden of his responsibility to Yvette. Her mother had written her a horrible letter, denouncing her in abusive terms, and her stepfather had forbidden her from ever setting foot in his house again. Even if Yvette hadn't been close to her mother, the letter had hurt her deeply, and she'd cried her heart out. There had also been an incident when a young priest refused to let her take communion. The older priest had "straightened things out," but still, it left another wound. Perhaps worst of all, M. St. Pierre increasingly treated both Yvette and Dieter with reserve. He never greeted Dieter anymore, and his tone when talking to Yvette was more that of an irritated employer than of a kindly friend of the family. Yvette suffered under every little slight, and Dieter felt that he had to make up for all of them. Sometimes the burden was wearisome.

Tired and not fully sober, he made a heavy clomping on the wooden stairs with his boots, and he was not really surprised when Yvette opened the door of the apartment to him. She was dressed only in a cotton shift and her hair was in disarray, but she greeted him happily. "*Chéri!* I didn't expect you to come tonight. No doubt the others are still drinking." She could not disguise her contempt for "the others." Her love for him was individual and did not extend to his countrymen or comrades.

Dieter put his arm around her as they went into the room and kissed her without comment. He sank heavily onto the soft bed, which squeaked and bounced under his weight. Dieter leaned forward to remove his boots, and Yvette sprang to help him expertly. He dropped his sidearm, belt and all, beside the bed, and pulled off his tie with a sense of immense relief. Yvette helped him out of his tunic, but he made no further effort to undress. Instead, he just lay back and was instantly asleep.

Yvette lay down beside him, her head on his chest, and listened to the beating of his heart. Then, because of the cold, she fetched the bedspread and spread it out over both of them before drifting off to sleep again.

The loud honking of a horn out in the street wrenched them both back to wakefulness. Yvette sat bolt upright, and Dieter lifted his head to try to see out the window. All he could see was the overcast, drizzling sky. The horn came again; cursing, Dieter dragged himself off the bed. He put his head out of the window.

In the street below, a *Luftwaffe* staff car with a suitcase in the back and a driver in front waited while Christian stood beside it, looking up. Dieter waved to him and Christian waved back. To Yvette, Dieter remarked on his way out of the bedroom, "It's just Christian."

Apparently, M. St. Pierre had already let Christian in, because they could hear his boots pounding up the stairs two at a time. Yvette barely had time to grab her bathrobe and tie it around her waist before he knocked. From the other side of the door he called, "Everybody dressed?"

"*Oui, oui,*" Yvette assured him.

"A pity," Christian replied, coming into the room grinning.

Dieter was frowning. His head ached. He was exhausted, and he felt filthy from sleeping in his clothes. He needed his sleep and resented Christian bursting in on him like this—not to mention that M. St. Pierre would complain about the honking disturbing the whole neighborhood. "I thought you had a train to catch," he reminded his friend.

Christian smelled of shampoo, toothpaste and after-shave. It was obvious to Dieter that he hadn't slept at all, just showered and shaved. Under the circumstances, he looked remarkably fit. "I do," Christian agreed, "but I had to talk to Yvette first."

"Me?" she asked, her hand resting delicately on her chest. She understood more and more German, Dieter noted—along with the fact that she was still flattered whenever "*Monsieur le Baron*" took any interest in her.

"Yes, you," Christian turned to face her, taking his cap off and holding it in his gloved hands. "You've got to talk sense to Gabrielle. She gave me hell last night just because I'm not taking her home with me. You've got to explain to her that it's just impossible. Tell her about all the problems you had."

Dieter had wanted to take Yvette home on his last leave, but the bureaucratic barriers had proved insurmountable. Dieter was told that she needed a document explaining the reason for her journey to the *Reich*, and what reason could he give? Their relationship was officially condemned, even if generally tolerated. Furthermore, she had no passport, and the Vichy authorities said it would take six to eight months (God only knew why) for one to be issued. They'd been compelled to give up the idea. Dieter had gone home only for five days and then spent the remaining five days of his leave with Yvette in Paris.

"But Gabrielle knows about the problems," Yvette told Christian earnestly; "what she's angry about is that you didn't even try. She thinks you don't want to introduce her to your mother."

Behind Yvette, Dieter raised his eyebrows to Christian. He knew perfectly well that Christian would be mortified by the prospect of introducing Gabrielle to Sophia Maria, but Christian lied glibly to Yvette, "That's not true. It's just that after all the trouble you and Dieter had, there wasn't any point in trying. I've promised her four days in Paris; what more does she want?"

"Why not ten days in Paris?" Yvette countered, knowing exactly how angry and insulted Gabrielle had been.

"Gabrielle sees me almost every day, and my mother hasn't seen me in eighteen months," Christian came back in a tone of injured innocence. "You have to make her understand that I owe it to my mother to go home. Please, Yvette, talk sense to her."

A honk came from the car in the street and Christian glanced at his watch. "I've got to go, or I'll miss the connection at Gare du Nord." There was regular service to Paris, but only twice-daily trains from Paris to Berlin. "Please put in a good word for me, Yvette." He caught her hand now, and Dieter watched her blush.

"I'll try," Yvette agreed.

"You're an angel," Christian declared, giving her a quick peck on the cheek. He replaced his cap and started for the door.

"But, Christian," Yvette called, and he looked back expectantly, "the only thing that will really please her—if you can't take her home—is a diamond." She held up her left hand with the diamond ring Dieter had given her.

Christian opened and then closed his mouth. Then he managed a smile and saluted. "*Merci, Mademoiselle, zum Befehl.*" Then he was gone, his boots crashing down the stairs again, as he rushed to catch his train.

Berlin

It was only a short taxi ride from Bahnhof Zoo to the Bendlerstrasse, and Christian decided to surprise his brother. He sent the taxi on to the apartment with instructions to leave his suitcase with Theo, and climbed out at the Bendlerstrasse. The sentries saluted, and Christian went up the red marble stairs against a stream of women and NCOs leaving the house for the day; it was 6 pm. Christian was certain that his conscientious brother would still be chained to his desk. He was therefore surprised to find him already getting into his greatcoat.

"Christian! Where did you come from?!" They embraced and then stood back to look at one another. Christian had slept on the train and was feeling good, but Philip had never looked better. "Do you know a secret I don't know?" Christian challenged. "Like the war is almost over?"

"Don't remind me of the war," Philip countered. "I'm just on my way out to dinner—"

"Aha. Dinner. Not alone, I'm sure." Christian glanced at him sideways with a little smirk. He was both amused and pleased. As far as he knew, Philip hadn't had a girlfriend since the start of the war.

"Anything but alone—tonight was the night I was supposed to meet her mother and stepfather."

Christian whistled. "That serious? So soon? Wait a minute. When did this all start? You've been keeping secrets from me."

"Millions," Philip agreed; but he grabbed his cap, took Christian's arm and closed the door behind them. "How long are you staying?" he asked, as they went out through the narrow anteroom back into the hall and turned away from the stairs.

"I thought 24 hours. I want to take the night train down to Altdorf tomorrow."

"We'll just have to explain. I'm sure Alix will understand. She's one of General Olbricht's secretaries."

Christian now thought he understood. He pictured generals' secretaries as efficient, prudish and unattractive—the kind of women who had failed to catch a husband and posed no threat to jealous generals' wives. All the girls Philip had ever dated had been rather like that—mousy and grey. His last girlfriend had had thick-rimmed glasses over close-set eyes and a pinched mouth.

They were walking along the hall to General Olbricht's office, Christian saluting to the higher-ranking officers passing them. Three doors down, Philip knocked and stepped inside.

"Alix, may I introduce my brother, Christian. Christian, Frl. Alexandra v. Mollwitz."

Alexandra was already in her coat, gloves and hat, expecting Philip momentarily. She looked up, surprised, with her bright blue eyes under a blue hat jauntily set at an angle. Her blonde hair fell beside her cheek on one side and on the other, where she had tucked it behind her ear, her long earring swayed. Christian's jaw all but dropped. After one glance at Alexandra, he turned to gaze at his brother in open admiration. "Congratulations," he told his brother. Then he stepped forward and bowed over Alexandra's hand with an impeccable, "*Enchanté, Mademoiselle, enchanté.*"

Alexandra was taken aback and glanced at Philip with a little puzzled frown. He had mentioned his younger brother in the *Luftwaffe*, but he had not said that he was over six feet tall, blond, and fit for a propaganda poster. He had also not said he was expecting him.

"Christian arrived unexpectedly five minutes ago," Philip explained, watching Alexandra's reaction with an intensity that sharpened his already over-thin features. Ever since he was old enough to take an interest in girls, he had been aware that Christian was more attractive to them. He had never dared compete with Christian for women, and he'd avoided dating anyone Christian might like just to avoid the humiliation of watching Christian take her away from him. But Alix was different. Alix was the woman he loved and wanted—he couldn't change that just because she was also beautiful enough to win Christian's admiration. He found himself resenting Christian's untimely arrival—although rationally, he knew it was better to find out now than later how Alexandra would respond. "He can only stay one night."

"Oh, dear." Alexandra grasped the situation at once and looked disappointed, but she managed to smile and said, "I'm sure my mother will understand. You go ahead and have a happy reunion. I'll arrange another day with Mother—"

"Frl. v. Mollwitz, you cannot think for a moment that I would take my brother away from you. I insist that you join us for dinner." Christian was at his most charming. Philip found himself hoping that Alexandra would decline. She, however, smiled, flattered (of course), and obligingly offered to call her mother about the change of plans.

"Oh, but Alix!" Frau v. Rantzow exclaimed on the other end of the line, loud enough for both officers to hear. "We've gone to so much trouble! Helga has been saving ration cards all week so we could have a proper meal. And Albrecht turned down an invitation to the Argentine embassy—which was quite important—just so he could be here. We've both been so curious—anxious—to meet your young man. You've been talking about him for months and really, you know, you should have introduced him to us long ago—"

Suddenly it was Herr v. Rantzow's voice, sharp and cutting. "Just what is this all about? If this General Staff major is too much of a coward to come home and meet your parents, then—"

Philip and Christian exchanged a glance, but it was Christian who took the receiver out of Alexandra's hand. "Herr v. Mollwitz" (he didn't know Alexandra's stepfather's name), "this is *Oberleutnant* Christian v. Feldburg. I'm Philip's younger brother, and I'm the cause of all the problems. I arrived without giving notice just 15 minutes ago. I only have 24 hours here in Berlin. As I haven't seen my brother in over a year, I very much wanted to spend the evening with him, but before I cause so much distress and inconvenience, I will of course do without the rare pleasure of his company. He and your daughter will leave immediately to join you for dinner as planned. Good evening." Christian hung up without giving Herr v. Rantzow a chance to answer.

The three stood around the phone unhappily. Alexandra was embarrassed and angry that her stepfather had humiliated her like this. She hardly dared look Philip in the eye. Philip was still stunned by the insult, and Christian was disappointed by the prospect of spending the evening alone after all. The phone rang again.

Alexandra picked it up with her usual clipped efficiency. "*Allgemeines Heeresamt, Mollwitz.*"

"Alix, Albrecht didn't know. *Please* invite Philip's brother to join us as well. I couldn't bear to think of him being left out."

Alexandra just looked at Christian, and he nodded.

"All right, we'll be right over."

In the taxi over to the Rantzow villa, Alix explained a little about her stepfather while Philip sat tensely, just listening. At the villa, Philip paid the driver while Christian got out and opened the door for Alix. Christian opened the gate so that Philip and Alix could precede him up the steps. The door to the house opened as they reached it. Helga was in a neat black-and-white maid's uniform, and she dipped a curtsy to the guests before offering to take their hats, sidearms and coats. Alix's mother bustled out of the parlor, dressed in one of her best silk dresses with a large emerald brooch, and welcomed them with excessive exuberance.

The officers bowed over her hand and introduced themselves as Herr v. Rantzow emerged dressed in tails. He looked elegant, distant, and not the least bit embarrassed about what he had said. Of course, he didn't know Philip had heard.

"Freiherr v. Feldburg." He shook hands with first Philip and then Christian: "Freiherr v. Feldburg." Then he indicated the living room with his hand.

In the living room, Grete and Rudi waited, Rudi in his Hitler Youth uniform and Grete in a pretty dirndl. Rudi jumped up at the sight of the officers and flung out his arm with a "*Heil Hitler!*" To his disappointment, the officers both responded with "Good evening." Alexandra introduced "My brother Rudi, and sister, Grete." Grete dipped her knee to the officers.

"An aperitif, gentlemen?" Rantzow asked.

"Thank you," they accepted.

Frau v. Rantzow made a desperate effort to break the ice. "We had no idea that Major v. Feldburg had a brother in the *Luftwaffe*. Are you a pilot?"

"Amazingly enough," admitted Christian, "yes."

"What kind of aircraft do you fly?" Herr v. Rantzau asked politely.

"Fighters—Me109s."

"Do you have many kills?" Rudi asked eagerly, earning a reprimand from his father.

"Eight," Christian answered; then with a glance at Philip, who was still stiff and withdrawn behind his glasses, he decided he had better help things along. He started chatting easily, leaning back in the broad, comfortable armchair and swirling the brandy in his glass. He entertained them with stories about the Battle of Britain that bore little resemblance to the state he'd been in on his last trip to Berlin. Philip almost hated him for his easy charm—even though he knew Christian was trying to help him. And then he risked a glance at Alexandra.

She wasn't hanging on Christian's words as the rest of them were. She was watching him. She caught his glance and smiled. She reached out and touched the back of his hand with her fingers. He caught them and held them, some of the tension easing.

Helga announced dinner and they moved into the indoor dining room. The furnishings were classical, beautifully matched, and the carpet Prussian blue.

Philip noted a signed sketch of Gustav Stresemann and nodded toward the picture. "Did you known Gustav Stresemann?"

Herr von Rantzow glanced at the picture as he shook out his neatly ironed linen napkin. "I had the great honor to be personally acquainted with Foreign Minister Stresemann, yes."

"I only met him a half-dozen times, but he was very impressive. He was never too busy or too self-important to take the time to chat to a mere officer-cadet. I greatly appreciated that."

Philip had scored. While Herr v. Rantzow tried to cover his astonishment, Alexandra and Christian exchanged a glance of shared jubilation. After that, Philip went on the offensive. By the time the officers stood to take their leave after dinner, Herr v. Rantzow was in no doubt about Philip's intelligence and analytical ability.

Alexandra saw Philip and Christian to the door, where a taxi waited for them. In the darkened hall, she flung her arms around Philip and kissed him. "I'm sorry it was such a dreadful evening. Thank you for coming." Then she shook hands with Christian, smiling sincerely. "It was a pleasure meeting you, and I'm sorry we ruined your evening, too."

"*Gnädiges Fräulein*, I have rarely been so entertained in all my life," Christian replied seriously. And suddenly they were all laughing.

Philip leaned forward and kissed Alexandra again, muttering, "I'll call in the morning. We'll all do something together for lunch and the afternoon."

Then they were gone. Alexandra went back into the living room to face her parents.

Herr v. Rantzow was pouring a brandy for himself, having already given his wife an Amaretto. Alexandra looked from one to the other. Her stepfather levelled a questioning gaze at her: "Brandy?"

"Please."

When he handed it to her his look was appraising, as if he were seeing her for the first time. "You astonish me. I thought you'd fall for some pompous pseudo-intellectual like you did the last time."

Alexandra did not like being reminded of her first love affair. She was spared from answering by her mother, who looked outright distressed.

"But he's so serious, Alix, almost gloomy. If only you'd met his brother first! Now there's a delightful young man."

"Philip, if you don't marry her, I will," Christian told his brother simply, as Philip passed Christian his suitcase through the train window. Alexandra had not come onto the crowded platform with them, but waited down in the station, where it was warmer. "Has Mother met her?"

"I volunteered to do duty on Christmas and New Year's, and got the four days off in between. I plan to take Alix down to Altdorf then."

"Mother will like her."

"I hope so. Thank God Rantzow's her stepfather."

"Is she Catholic?" Christian thought to ask.

"Lapsed. Her real father was, and she was baptized and had her first communion in the Church before her mother's second marriage. She hasn't been to mass or confession since, but Father Matthias won't be difficult."

"No, not for you."

"Nor you," Philip countered. Philip, as the acolyte and obedient boy, had been Father Matthias' favorite, but he liked Christian, too. Everyone did. Even Alix. But Philip could think that without jealousy or pain, after watching them together today. She had teased and flirted with Christian as if he were her younger brother, but she had saved all her real smiles for Philip. Philip had not been aware of how much he'd feared Christian would snatch her away until he registered how relieved he was now.

The conductor blew his whistle and Philip stepped back from the edge of the platform. Christian leaned on the edge of the window and looked toward the front of the train. With a loud hiss, the engine pumped black smoke into the already polluted air. The train jerked forward. Christian turned back and waved to Philip, smiling. Philip waved back. It was the second to the last time they saw each other.

When Christian stepped off the train in Altdorf, Sophia Maria was struck by how much he took after her own father. Her father had been nearly six feet tall, broad and blond like Christian—and he, too, had smiled at her like that. Christian flung his arms around her and kissed her firmly on the mouth. With his right arm around her shoulders he led her out of the station, waving with his free hand to the townspeople who greeted him. It made no difference to him whether they said "*Gruss Gott*" or "*Heil Hitler.*"

Christian took no notice of how run down things had become in the town. Wartime shortages made it difficult to do even minor repairs, and paint was almost nonexistent. The forced laborers, furthermore, were careless with the property of their oppressors, and things got broken, cracked and scratched easily. The seats of the buggy in which Sophia Maria collected Christian had somehow become split and cracked, and the stuffing was spilling out. Even the floorboards were cracked, but Christian noted only the fractious horse in the traces and exclaimed, "Mother! Isn't that Meteor?"

"Of course it is. He desperately needs exercise and I don't have time to ride. I hope you'll take him out for a good gallop every day you're here."

"I'd be delighted." Christian took the reins from her.

By the time they were back at the manor, Sophia Maria felt she was ten years younger—or was it thirty? Christian had her laughing like an infatuated school-girl. He delighted her by telling—with obvious admiration—how Philip had danced intellectual circles around Herr v. Rantzow. He insisted that Philip had shown so much detailed knowledge of the Treaties of Rapallo and Larcarno that the diplomat looked dizzy by the end. "There are times when I hate Philip for his precise command of facts and his intolerance of inconsistency, but last night it was pure pleasure." He raved, too, about Alexandra, assuring his mother she deserved Philip's love and returned it. "She'll be a worthy successor to you, Mamá."

Josef came to take Meteor, greeting Christian with a hand on his forelock, but the Poles stood about warily. Most of them had never met Christian before and were clearly uneasy. It was partly his hated uniform, of course, and partly the fear that he might disapprove of his mother's policies of fair treatment. Christian han-dled it well, she thought. He nodded and smiled to each in turn, remarking col-lectively that he knew his mother could not get along without them. Most important, he stressed how much he appreciated their service "until the war is over and we can all go home." The remark won them over, as it suggested hope of a return home and demonstrated sensitivity to the fact that they wanted to leave. Sophia Maria noted that Christian had matured very rapidly during this past year.

Inside the manor they were greeted with notably more enthusiasm by the Ger-man staff. Martha allowed herself a hug, which Christian happily returned. (She never risked that with Philip.) The new kitchen maid and the two RAD girls gazed at him as if he were a movie star. Frau Opitz gave him a '*Heil Hitler*,' but Christian put his arm around her shoulders and teased, "So much formality among old friends?" That melted even her political correctness. Finally Sophia Maria and her son could go up to the breakfast room, and Martha sent up a tray laden with fresh rolls, real butter and eggs, cold meats and cheese on the dumb-waiter. Tea and coffee substitute followed. Alone together again, Christian sat sideways to the table, stretched out his long legs and loosened his tie.

"It's so good to be here."

"Dieter stopped by during his leave. I felt so bad."

"Why?"

"His face."

"Oh, that. He's better off than some. One side is still intact." Sophia Maria was shocked by so much callousness, but Christian looked her straight in the eye. "Most of us in the *Gruppe* don't even notice it anymore, and he has a girl who loves him just the way he is."

Sophia Maria accepted the rebuke gracefully. She bowed her head to Christian, but couldn't resist asking, "And what if it was your face?"

"I've asked myself that many times, and the only thing I'm sure about it is: I'd prefer it to death. And it has its advantages."

"Like what?"

"You know if you're loved for yourself or just your pretty face."

"Aha. Gabrielle only loves you for your pretty face?"

"Gabrielle doesn't love me at all. She sleeps with me for my pretty face, my wallet and my title—in that order."

Sophia Maria stiffened in uncontrollable disapproval, and Christian laughed. Then he caught her hand and kissed it in an apology for offending her sensibilities. "Don't worry about me, Mamá. The point is, I know Gabrielle doesn't love me, and—if you think about it—I'm using her as much as she's using me. It's a fair and honest game of mutual exploitation. I'm not going to ask her to marry me." Christian's encounter with Alix had permanently banished all thought of that. Instead he had bought Gabrielle a diamond pendant. It was bigger and more expensive than the diamond in Yvette's ring, but the mere fact that it was not a ring would give her the message clearly.

Christian changed the subject. "Tell me what you hear from my little sister. She's a terrible correspondent—or I guess I am. I didn't answer her last letter, but that was ages ago. Battle of Britain." He said it lightly—and yet he looked away, checked the teapot to see if the tea was strong enough, and poured himself a cup. His hands weren't quite steady; the teacup rattled in the saucer like the distant chatter of machine guns.

"Theresa?" Sophia Maria distracted him. "She's a terrible correspondent, just as you said. I get a letter from her every month."

Christian looked over, wide-eyed. "You call that bad!? What do you consider a good correspondent?" Christian almost never wrote. He preferred telephoning.

"It's not a matter of how often you write, but whether you communicate. I have the impression I'm just one of Theresa's chores. She has it written in her desk calendar: 'Write Mother.' Once a month, she dutifully sits down and writes me a two-page letter—exactly two pages, one sheet of paper, front and back. And she says nothing."

"What do you mean?" Christian asked, turning to face her with a worried frown around his eyes and his elbows on the table. He could hear the hurt in his mother's voice, and he gave her his full attention.

Sophia Maria shrugged and avoided his eyes. "She talks about *things*—or rather, name-drops about all the important *Gauleiter*, senior civil servants of the Occupation, and SS officers she's entertaining. I'm shocked by how many you would also find in the *Almanach de Gotha*[1]," she noted as an aside.

"Don't be a snob, Mother," Christian shot back. "Neither stupidity nor greed is confined to the lower classes."

"But we ought to have more self-respect and honor, Christian!" And suddenly she wasn't chatting, but indignant. "Theresa's living in a confiscated house. Walther runs his factories with forced labor. She has a maid whose officer father was murdered—not killed in the war but gunned down after he was captured— and apparently Theresa doesn't feel guilty about any of it! She doesn't even question it!" Sophia Maria's voice fell and Christian could hear the despair in it as she whispered, "I've lost her. I let her marry Walther to try to keep from losing her, but I've lost her more than ever. We live in different worlds."

Christian hesitated and then asked, "You mean Walther's financial success has gone to her head?"

"Yes, that too, but what I really meant is that she sees the world differently. It's as if she'd never lived in this house and never learned any of the values I tried to teach all of you. Her world doesn't have people and souls in it, Christian; it is populated with Aryans and Polacks. You'd think she'd never heard the words 'charity,' 'compassion,' 'pity,' or even 'kindness.' Her world is about "struggles"—racial struggles and struggles for resources. She is constantly warning me not to trust my 'Polacks.' She says they're all 'sly and deceitful.' All of them, Christian? Since when are people of any nation all the same? She seems genuinely afraid that they might harm her or her children—but never asks if she has earned their hatred."

Christian, more to comfort his mother than out of conviction, suggested, "Maybe she just feels she has to write that way for the censors. Maybe she thinks it helps Walther's career."

---

1. An almanac of the German aristocracy.

"That would explain her letters, but not the way she acted last summer when she visited …" Sophia Maria shook her head helplessly. "The way she is now, I find it hard to love her."

When Sophia Maria took Christian to the station four days later, she felt as if the sun was being taken away from her. Suddenly she had a long, cold, dark winter and an endless war ahead of her. Christian took her in his arms. "Don't look so gloomy, Mother. Statistically, I stand a better chance of surviving with each hour I spend in the air. And Philip will soon be here with his Alix. Mark my words: you'll soon have Feldburg grandchildren." From the train, Christian leaned out of the window and waved for as long as he could. His mother stood on the platform waving back, but she was crying.

CHAPTER 16

▼

Berlin
December 1941

By early December 1941, fresh Soviet divisions, which had up to then been garrisoning Siberia, arrived on the Moscow front. With these well-trained and well-supplied troops, the Soviet Union went on the offensive against the invading German forces, which had stalled just outside of Moscow. On December 6, ten Soviet armies opened the offensive along a 322-km front, falling upon *Wehrmacht* divisions already exhausted, overextended and seriously short of supplies. Within two weeks, the entire German front held by Army Group Center threatened to collapse.

As a result, the atmosphere in the Bendlerstrasse on Tuesday, Dec. 10 had little trace of Christmas cheer. That it had snowed during the night, making traffic and walking difficult, only contributed to the generally discouraged mood. Alexandra had not thought anything of it when Philip asked to see the General, looking very depressed.

A few minutes later, Philip and Olbricht emerged from the General's office together, looking somewhat better. Olbricht smiled at her and held out his hand. "Congratulations. You'll want the day off, of course." Alexandra, bewildered, glanced at Philip, who was uncomfortably studying the ceiling. "No, it's all right," the General insisted. "Frl. Lerche" (he referred to his second secretary) "can handle everything for the next couple of days, or I'll get help from the typing pool. I won't expect you back until Thursday." Philip meanwhile had taken Alexandra's coat from the rack and held it for her. She thanked the General and left with Philip.

They did not speak as they went along the long hall, up the five steps into the front building, and then down the echoing square stairwell. They walked with difficulty across the trampled snow in the courtyard and out onto the Bendler-strasse. Here Philip turned right toward the canal. With his boot he brushed the dusty snow off the grass beside the sidewalk, and stopped abruptly to contemplate it. "In Russia, they say, the snow is already two meters deep. Two meters."

"You have orders for the Russian front," Alexandra concluded.

Philip nodded. "The invisible but all-powerful hand of the Army Personnel Office is still looking after my 'career'—long after I've lost interest in it." Philip hadn't entirely lost interest in his career, but he was by no means so ambitious that he longed for a new assignment already. He enjoyed his present work, and could not remember ever having had a more congenial superior than General Olbricht. But the real issue was the young woman beside him.

"Army Group Center?" she asked, trying not to show any emotion, even as her stomach cramped up in terror. The casualty figures went across her desk on the way to General Olbricht. She knew that entire divisions had been reduced to almost nothing.

"*Ja*, but only the staff—Army Group staff."

"Ah, Henning v. Tresckow and Co," she said with relief.

"I believe General v. Greiffenberg is the Chief," Philip answered uncertainly. He was in fact certain that Greiffenberg was the Chief, but Olbricht had also made reference to Tresckow. He didn't know why.

"Tresckow is the First General Staff Officer and the more active of the two—according to General Olbricht, of course."

Why were they talking about irrelevancies? Philip took Alexandra's elbow and led her to the canal. The stone banks were white with snow and the slow-moving water seemed black in contrast. They reached a semicircular buttress that jutted out into the canal. It had a rusty railing and a snow-covered park bench. In the late spring it was a favorite place for couples to sit under the blooming chestnut trees. Philip stopped again and drew a deep breath. "I had it all so neatly planned: the four days' leave in Altdorf with my mother. There is some family jewelry I had planned to let you choose from. But with this transfer, of course, my leave has been canceled, and I thought it best to get the General's permission and start the formal request process before I leave Berlin on Thursday. Olbricht naturally assumed I'd already talked to you—which, of course, I should have done."

Alexandra had to laugh. Slipping her arm through his, she pulled him against her and asked teasingly, "Was that a proposal?"

"Not very articulate, was it?"

"Terrible. But, you know, when you're too smooth, all I hear is years of social training; I love it when you're inarticulate."

"Only when I'm inarticulate?"

"Nay." She stood on tiptoe and gave him a kiss. "I love you." It was the first time she had risked saying it to him aloud.

Suddenly and with surprising strength, Philip wrapped her in his arms and kissed her again. When they stopped kissing, he still did not let her go, but held her as he looked across the canal and said simply, "Damn."

Alexandra stood with her head on his chest, and even through his greatcoat she could hear his heart. The wool of the coat was rough on her cheek, and her own heavy coat was awkward and bulky between them. Her wrists were exposed to the cold. Still she hesitated to end the embrace.

At last Philip released her, cocked his head and smiled playfully. "By the way, was that an acceptance?"

"About as clear as your proposal, I admit." They started kissing again, until Philip pulled away and declared: "Now I think we've been a public spectacle long enough. Shouldn't we go drink a bottle of champagne or some such thing?"

Wednesday night, Alix wore her most daring silk cocktail dress and high-heeled sandals, which were perfect nonsense in December. Stunningly attractive even to a stranger, she was magically enchanting to Philip. Still, his impending departure on the next day cast a shadow that neither perfume nor wine could disperse.

They ate too much, drank too much and danced until Alix was all but crippled by blisters and sore feet. It was by then after 1 am, and they took a taxi to Alexandra's apartment. Philip paid off the driver, saying he'd find another, but at the door he lingered.

Alexandra's stomach cramped in panic. She did not want to send Philip away. She did not want to say goodbye, perhaps forever. She dreaded going up to her cold, dark apartment, but she was also terrified of the alternative. If she let him up into her apartment at this time of night on *this* night, he would expect— would have the right to expect—her to sleep with him.

She knew that many women did it. Indeed, in war, it seemed to be expected. But she was afraid of it—and she resented the fact that Philip expected it. She resented the fact that it was so easy for men: a satisfying evening and then off to the front, new duties, new distractions. For men it was neither new nor threatening.

Alexandra was suddenly certain that Philip had had his share of sexual experience. Abruptly, she couldn't stop herself from wondering how many other women there had been. Who had "comforted" him the night before he went to

France with the 10th Panzer Division? Or to Greece? What had become of them? Why hadn't he married them? And what good would an engagement ring do her if she found herself pregnant and widowed before she'd ever been married?

"Alix?" Philip didn't understand why she was hesitating. It was bitterly cold out here, and they had little more than hours before he had to collect his things and catch his train. He wanted to spend those hours with Alexandra—and up to this very minute he had assumed she wanted to spend them with him. "May I come up?" he asked at last, inwardly resentful that he had to ask. He felt she should have invited him up on her own.

Alexandra could not bring herself to honestly say no, and yet her tone was sour as she snapped, "If you insist." Then she turned away from him to unlock the door. She moved as rapidly as she could, taking off her crippling shoes as soon as she was inside, and, although it was probably too late for Frau Bubner, Alix insisted that Philip remove his shoes at the last half-landing as well. Sensing her embarrassment, he dutifully complied.

Inside the apartment, Alix at once switched on the light in the hall, shattering any remnants of romantic atmosphere, and hobbled to the kitchen without taking off her coat. Here, too, she turned on the light and announced, "I'll put the kettle on for tea."

Philip already regretted pressuring her. He felt un-gentlemanly, and her hostility seemed deserved. On any other night he would simply have excused himself, but then on any other night he wouldn't have insisted in the first place. Just as the thought of Russia made him want to spend the night with her, the thought of Russia made it impossible to walk out in the present atmosphere of ill will.

He was still standing uncertainly in his greatcoat and cap, but holding his shoes in his hands, when Alexandra leaned out of the kitchen to see what was keeping him. The sight of him made her relent a little. "I'm sorry, Philip. I'm dreadfully difficult at times."

Philip drew a deep breath. "Let's say, complicated."

"Take off your coat and cap and come have some tea," was Alix's reply as she disappeared back into the kitchen. Philip removed his greatcoat and put his cap and sidearm on the rack above the hangers. He pulled his shoes on again and then followed Alix into the kitchen.

Already the kitchen table was set with cups, saucers, and even biscuits. As he entered, Alexandra was just turning off the gas under the kettle. She poured water into the teapot, and then she turned and faced him. But she was leaning against the stove with her arms crossed—keeping her distance from him.

She was afraid of him, he registered with disbelief. "I don't understand," Philip started.

"Is it really that difficult?!" Alix demanded in a strained voice. Her nerves were close to breaking. "What did you think? That I'm some 'sophisticated woman of the world' who entertains men in her apartment regularly?"

Offended by her tone, Philip snapped back, "If I'd thought that, I wouldn't have asked you to marry me! But I did ask you to marry me and, in case you've forgotten, I leave—"

"Don't say it!" Alix shouted at him. He stopped, completely taken aback by her tone. She had never talked to him like that before. It shocked him. "Don't you see? It sounds like every soldier with the girl he's just picked up in the bar. 'I leave tomorrow for the Eastern Front. Give me one good night.' We're supposed to feel terribly sorry for you when we're the ones being used!"

The comparison was so insulting that Philip lost his temper. "I see! The last six months mean nothing to you!" he snapped furiously. "Well, then, forget they happened! Forget we met at all! Forget everything!" He stormed down the hall and knocked over the coat rack as he tore his coat off it. It crashed to the floor and he had to bend over to retrieve his cap and belt. His hands were trembling as he futilely tried to open the door—he'd forgotten to open the upper lock.

"Philip, stop! Please! Don't go! Please! Stay! Please! Let me explain!"

He looked back. Alexandra was clinging to the kitchen door frame. The sound of her sobs reached him, and tears streamed down her red face. She wasn't pretty in that moment, but the sight of her misery dispelled all his anger. As rapidly as it had ignited, it was extinguished again.

The next instant he closed the distance between them and took Alexandra in his arms. "Don't cry," he begged, as she sobbed miserably, holding both hands over her face. "Please. Don't cry."

She shook her head, tears streaming down her face and dripping off her chin. She tried to wipe them away with her hands without making any attempt to break free of Philip's encircling arms. "I'm sorry, Philip. You have a right to be angry. I'm not being fair. I know. Please don't be angry with me."

"No, I'm not angry," he told her truthfully. It was impossible to be angry with her while she cried in his arms, begging for forgiveness. But he added honestly, "But I don't understand how you could say that."

She drew a ragged breath and looked up at him. "Can't you understand at all? I've never even undressed in front of a man before. And it's always the same—"

Philip cut her short. "Shhh." With an arm around her waist, he guided her to the table and poured them each tea with his free hand. Then he eased her into a chair. "Sit down and let's talk about it."

"You've had lots of other women, haven't you?" she asked in a tight voice, trying ineffectively to wipe away tears with her wet hands as he sat down opposite her.

"Me? Relatively few."

"What does that mean? 'Relatively'? Compared to whom?"

"Christian, for a start."

That brought a weak smile. "That's probably not saying much."

Philip admitted, "Maybe not, but surely what is important is that I haven't slept with another woman since I've met you? In fact, I haven't slept with a woman in the last three years. It's not as easy and insignificant for me as you seem to think."

Philip sensed that this information calmed Alix considerably. She risked sipping her still-steaming tea, and looked with big eyes over the rim of her cup at him. "Will you tell me about the others?"

"I'd rather not. They're insignificant next to you. They mean nothing to me anymore."

"But they were experienced, weren't they?" she insisted, looking at him intensively.

Philip thought back. Most of his adventures dated from the last years of Weimar when, as a cadet, he had finally had the courage to break free of family expectations. Altdorf had been far away and Berlin large enough for him not to fear a confrontation with his father. Of course, a high degree of discretion was *de rigeur* both for his career and because of his father's position, but he had exploited the possibilities offered to the fullest. To Alix's question he answered simply, "Yes."

"Didn't you ever worry that I might not be any good?" Alix countered, clutching her teacup like a shield before her.

Philip had to laugh, but quickly cut himself short and answered her seriously. "Alix, there's no such thing as a woman who isn't good—only men who haven't taken the time to be sensitive. Thank you for reminding me."

"And what if I get pregnant?" she asked in an attempt to be matter-of-fact, not aggressive.

"You know what? I think it would be more sensible if we didn't take any chances. What I'd like more than anything is just to spend the night with you. You don't even have to undress if you don't like. Just let me hold you."

"Are you sure?" she asked very uncertainly.

He nodded.

She put her teacup down. "You aren't angry with me?"

He shook his head and reached out to take her hand in his.

"You thought I was a mature and sophisticated career woman, didn't you? And instead I'm behaving like a sixteen-year-old." She couldn't meet his eyes as she spoke. He sensed she was close to tears again, this time from shame or disappointment in herself.

"That's not the point. What's important is that you feel comfortable—not pressured, frightened and *used*." Some of his outrage over this word still rang in his voice, and Alix squeezed his hand.

"I'm sorry, Philip. I shouldn't have said that. It's just ..."

"What?" he pressed her, wanting to understand.

She shrugged a little awkwardly. "I've heard that line twice before—both times from men who really were exploitative."

Philip was shocked despite himself. Suddenly he realized he knew nothing about Alix's past romances. He had naively assumed that she'd had none. That had been stupid. He should have asked long ago. Now all he could do, however, was ask apprehensively, "When was that?"

"The last time was just over a year ago. I was visiting my maternal aunt in Silesia, and a young man from a neighboring estate showed lukewarm interest in me. I wasn't in love with him, but I wanted to be. After all, I'm not getting any younger, as my mother has pointed out for the last ten years. He was a bomber-commander, had been wounded in the Battle of Britain, and was on convalescent leave. Shortly before he was due to return to his squadron, he tried to seduce me—"

"That's appalling! On your aunt's estate?"

Alix laughed more easily than she had expected. "You'll never be a socialist, Philip. If the Russians win the war, they'll have to shoot you."

"I'll shoot myself first," he quipped back. "And the other time?"

Alexandra sighed. "That was much worse. He was my first love, and I was desperately in love with him as only young students can be." Philip looked so shocked that Alix tightened her hand around his in reassurance. "I don't still love him. Quite the opposite. Because he hurt me as badly as he did, I learned what is really important in a relationship. It's because you are so different from him that I liked you from the start. Martin was someone who had all the answers. He liked 'discussions' only because he liked the sound of his own voice; he never listened to other opinions. He was unreliable in little things—punctuality, paying back debts, returning books. At the time, I was so in love that I told myself he was just too concerned about major issues to remember insignificant details, but I know better now. Your reliability in little things impressed me from the start because I know it's an indication of your reliability in important things. But at the time, as I said, I was infatuated with Martin—only he preferred other girls."

Alix looked Philip squarely in the eye. "Now I know how lucky I was. They all fell for him, and he slept with first one and then another—and eventually abandoned them all." Philip was beginning to understand Alexandra's anxiety. She continued, "Fortunately for me, he scorned me. In fact, he humiliated me publicly—he made fun of me in front of all our friends at a café. He did it so 'wittily' that all my supposed friends laughed along. I was ashamed to see any of them again." She paused, because the memory of this incident still hurt and embarrassed her.

Philip empathized so strongly that he wanted both to comfort and avenge her, but all he could do was stroke the back of her hand in a gesture of sympathy. She thanked him with a timid smile and continued. "After awhile, the shame turned to indignation and anger. I decided I didn't want to have anything to do with his circle anymore. I avoided him after that and made new friends. Several years later, however, he knocked on my door late at night and announced he was off to join the International Brigade—"

"And he expected you to just fall into his arms and sleep with him?" Philip could hardly believe it.

Alix nodded. "More or less. First he let me make him a meal, drank a bottle of my wine, and listened to himself talk about what a hero he was going to be in the cause of Socialism—"

"Alix, you're going to make me an even worse 'reactionary' than I already am. Why did you let him into your apartment at all?"

"I was taken by surprise. Flattered at first. His rejection and ridicule was an unhealed wound, really. It had badly damaged my sense of self-worth. In the first instant, all my earlier infatuation bubbled up, but the longer he talked and the more he drank the more disgusted I became. When he tried to put his arms around me, talking about how he was going to the front and might never return—"

"You threw him out and poured a bucket of cold water over him—I hope."

Alexandra laughed, but shook her head. "I didn't think of the water. But I did show him the door." She paused, looking Philip in the eyes. "I'm sorry. You're so, so different. I—"

Philip leaned across the table and kissed her. Then he stood and pulled her up into his arms. Alix laid her head on his chest and breathed deeply. She felt safe and warm and comforted in his arms, but also very, very tired. "It must be 3 o'clock in the morning."

"There or thereabouts. Thank God for batmen."

Alexandra waited. She thought: 'If he wants to sleep with me now, I'll do it. I'm not afraid anymore.' She almost wanted him to, but Philip had no intention of being like the others. He carried her to her bed, set his glasses aside, and removed his shoes and tunic. Then he lay beside her and held her close in his arms until morning.

*   *   *   *

Berlin-Smolensk

Nothing in Philip's life or training had prepared him for what he found in Russia. The trip itself became a long, unsettling journey into a nightmarish "wonderland."

It had started out cheerfully enough, with the replacement battalions providing a boisterous background to the otherwise tedious trip. The youngsters, mostly conscripts on their way to Russia for the first time, hung out of the windows in every town, where the stations were decked with greens and lights for Christmas. They flirted with the RAD girls who came to pass out substitute coffee, rolls and Christmas sweets. They basked in the admiration of the older citizens, who passed them cigarettes and good wishes through the windows. They sang carols and hiking songs as they rolled steadily through the snow-covered countryside.

When they crossed the old *Reich* border, conditions started to deteriorate, and so did the atmosphere on the train. For one thing, the roadbeds were poor and carrying far more traffic than they had been built to handle. Over and over, the train had to slow to a crawl as it clacked and shook its way over the track. Once they waited four hours in the middle of nowhere while road crews cleared away an earlier train that had gone off the rails. And then there was the war damage. They passed through one totally incinerated village, a ghost town where the train no longer even slowed. Some people claimed that the Poles had burned the village to drive out the *Volksdeutsche* (ethnically German) inhabitants. Others said that the Bolsheviks burned the Polish village. Still others whispered that the SS had been at work—and that the residents had been Jews, burned alive in their houses.

In the re-annexed territories, there was at least evidence of efforts to rebuild. People at the stations were slower to smile, but all the more patriotic. Christmas greens and ribbons were overshadowed by posters and flags celebrating the triumphant return of the "lost territories" to the *Reich* and proclaiming undying devotion to National Socialism. Support services in the stations were less exuberant and more organized, but still cheerful.

In the so-called "Government General" (Occupied Poland), in contrast, only installations and factories of war utility had been repaired. Houses, shops, and cottage industries still showed untended war damage. The residents could occasionally be seen squatting in the partial ruins of their cottages. Shabbily nailed-together debris was all they had to keep out the winter and the snow. No one here had money for, or interest in, Christmas decorations. Everywhere the lean, dull faces of the conquered stared resentfully at the passing troop train. And there were no girls in the stations to pass out sweets and smiles. The boisterous soldiers fell silent.

Just outside Minsk the train was forced to an agonizing crawl as it inched forward right through a maintenance crew resting on their shovels. The crew consisted of POWs—Russians or Poles, it was impossible to tell anymore. Their shabby uniforms hung in rags upon frail, meatless bodies, and their faces were skeletal with dark holes for eyes and hollow cheeks.

In Minsk they were ordered off the train, which then pulled away to some other, apparently more important, task. They spent more than two hours on the windy platform waiting for their next train. Meanwhile another train, caked with snow, gasped into the station and stopped with a heavy sigh. Huge red crosses had been painted on the cars, and almost at once medical orderlies climbed out and started emptying the dead. The stretchers with corpses were lined up along the platform, while from the windows of the train some of the wounded begged the men on the platform for cigarettes. None of the men in the train had winter coats, and the fingers reaching from the windows were frostbitten.

This was a particularly bitter sight for Philip, who knew how hard General Olbricht had fought to get the approval for winter uniforms. The uniforms had been designed and a contractor selected even before Philip joined AHA. The Army could have been completely supplied with winter uniforms by mid-October. But the OKW insisted that there was no need for the uniforms to go into production because "the bulk of the troops would be home before the Russian winter started." By the time the offensive bogged down, production could not be geared up fast enough. The government had resorted to a propaganda offensive, begging civilians to "give up their furs" for the "men on the front." As if the Army were going to issue women's mink coats instead of greatcoats to the troops!

After Minsk, things got worse. It was noticeably colder and the snow was deeper. The war damage was more recent and far less of the debris had been cleared away. Disabled trucks and tanks, shattered rolling stock, and even the wreckage of crashed aircraft were littered about. There were fields of regimented crosses marking *Wehrmacht* graves. There were no civilians in the stations anymore, just soldiers.

The train ground to a halt, for no apparent reason, 80 km short of Smolensk. On either side of the train the snowbanks rose above the windows, leaving the passengers no view but the dirty snow. The word "partisans" was soon being tossed about. Some thought the track had been blown; others claimed an earlier train had "caught" it and was lying strewn across their path. Finally men in snow-caked uniforms came down the track toward them. They were guards from a freight train that was stuck in a snowdrift 1 km ahead. They asked for volunteers and got plenty.

In Smolensk the blackout was being strictly enforced, adding to the sense of chaos. In the darkness, the units embarking and disembarking became mixed together and entangled while the announcer squawked unintelligibly. If Army Group Center had sent anyone to meet Philip, they missed him in the confusion. Philip asked a sentry in front of the station how he could best get to Army Group Center HQ. The sentry politely told him that he would do best to walk. There were no taxis or hacks, because all civilian transportation had long since been requisitioned for the troops. He gave directions.

The streets of Smolensk seemed a continuation of the chaos at the station, only on a grander scale. Here the units that got entangled were motorized and horse-drawn supply columns. One peculiar column was made up of what looked like horse-drawn pontoons, but on closer examination turned out to be ponies harnessed provisionally to panzers.

As soon as Philip and Stadthagen left the main streets, walking became treacherous. In places the snow had been packed or half-melted into ice; elsewhere it had drifted or been shoveled into knee-deep heaps. Cart and hoof tracks crisscrossed chaotically. Nowhere was there a light to help them pick their way across the slippery ruts and ridges.

At last they reached the HQ, which was temporarily housed in what had once been a grand Tsarist palace. Despite the decayed but intact elegant exterior, the interior had been completely remodeled in a functional style. New walls interrupted the ornate moldings of the original ceilings; an elevator shaft cut straight through a mural that had once bedecked the grand entryway. The reception desk, manned by *Wehrmacht* soldiers, sat at the foot of the badly cracked and chipped, yet still grand, marble stairway. On the wall behind the reception desk a plaster relief of Lenin's profile, at least two meters high, had been whitewashed over and a photo of Hitler hung. The nail for the photo pierced Lenin's neck, but the Revolutionary still loomed up ominously above the sickly man with the comical mustache.

Philip sent Franz to find out where their quarters were and then get himself a meal, while Philip went to report to the Chief of Staff. Halfway up the stairs he passed two officers on their way down. They exchanged salutes automatically, absently, and then suddenly the lieutenant turned and grabbed Philip's arm. "Philip! You made it!" It was his cousin, Heinrich *Graf* Lehndorff-Steinort. Philip had not known his cousin was here and could hardly believe his eyes. Lehndorff, in contrast, was clearly expecting him.

Lehndorff turned to his companion, a tall, greying Major of the Reserves, and introduced them. "My cousin, Philip Feldburg. Philip, Carl-Hans Hardenberg." As they shook hands, Lehndorff continued to *Graf* Hardenberg, "Go on without me. I'd like a few words with my cousin."

"No problem," Hardenberg assured him and, with a nod to Philip, continued. Lehndorff took Philip by the arm and ushered him past the Chief of Staff's office and into an anteroom before a door clearly marked: "Commander-in-Chief, Army Group Center, Generalfeldmarschall v. Bock." Philip glanced at the door and back at his cousin.

"Hardenberg and I are the Feldmarschall's ADCs. Philip, I don't have much time. We'll have to exchange personal news later. I just wanted to warn you, or have you already heard?"

"Heard what?"

"Brauchitsch has resigned."

Without thinking, Philip remarked, "Good riddance." Brauchitsch had signed the Commissar Order.

"Not so fast," Lehndorff cautioned. "You haven't heard the end of the story."

Philip felt a chill penetrate to his heart. Evidently Brauchitsch's replacement was someone even worse than the weak-willed C-in-C. "Keitel?" he speculated, trying to think of the worst possible candidate for the job.

Lehndorff shook his head. "Adolf's taken personal command."

"Oh, my God," Philip whispered.

"And the purge didn't stop there. The first thing he did was dismiss all three Army Group Commanders: Bock, Leeb and Witzleben."

Philip glanced toward the door with Bock's name on it, but his thoughts were with Leeb. Ever since that one encounter, he was convinced that Leeb was a decent man. Philip was certain that he would not have signed—or passed on—the Commissar Order. However, his cousin was continuing in his urgent voice, "We think the purge has only begun. Adolf's issued an order that's so incredible—wait, I'll find it for you." He went to one of the desks, searched until he found what he was looking for, and read aloud: "'Every unit is to stand—and if necessary, die—where it is. Any withdrawal is expressly forbidden. The smoking ruins of Russian villages will show the world: here is where German grenadiers fought their last battle.'"

Philip took a moment to absorb the order and then commented, "That's not an operational order, that's a Wagnerian opera."

"Apparently it's going to be the style of orders from now on. We've been ordered to drop all 'courtesies' in orders we issue and use only the imperative. But that's beside the point. Commanders from Leningrad to the Black Sea are in open revolt against this 'stand and die' order."

"Revolution? From the German Officer Corps, at last?"

Lehndorff laughed. "You *will* fit in here, but unfortunately it hasn't gone that far yet. At the moment they are confining themselves to a military protest, but Guderian is one of the loudest. He's popular at home. Maybe his protest will have an impact. Surely Hitler wouldn't dare cashier a popular hero like Guderian?"

Philip shook his head, more in touch with the political realities in Berlin. "Guderian is only a hero if Goebbels lets him be. If he falls from favor, he will disappear from the news and no one will even know why."

Lehndorff clearly didn't want to believe this, but he had no argument against it. He sighed and clapped Philip on the shoulder. "Let me introduce you around."

With a new commander expected momentarily, things were naturally very unsettled—particularly on top of a cataclysmic war situation. Phones were ringing; messengers came in and out. Nevertheless, officer after officer took the time to shake hands and welcome Philip. Last, Lehndorff took him to the Chief of Staff in a large, excessively ornate office. Greiffenberg was leaning against his Louis XIV desk smoking a cigarette, and his First General Staff Officer (Ia), *Oberstleutnant* Henning v. Tresckow, was standing with him. Both turned expectantly toward the junior officers.

Greiffenberg responded to Lehndorff's introduction by coming forward and offering Philip his hand. "We've been expecting you." Although gracious, he looked tired and worried, too.

Tresckow, a man with a fine, mild face, a receding hairline and a sincere, quiet smile, shook hands warmly with Philip. "We're glad to have you with us," he assured him.

There was another knock on the door. Greiffenberg looked at his watch and said tensely, "That may be Kluge." By now Philip knew that *Feldmarschall* v. Kluge had been appointed as Bock's replacement. After a trip to Hitler's HQ to get a briefing from him, he was on his way back to Russia and expected momentarily.

The lieutenant who entered reported instead, "We've just had a call from the 144th Infantry Division. There's been some kind of accident involving the staff— mines or something—"

"Was Rittenbach hurt?" Greiffenberg asked in obvious alarm.

"Yes, but apparently not seriously. He's on the phone and wants to speak with you."

Greiffenberg nodded, "Put him through." He exchanged a look with Tresckow as he went around to the other side of the desk to pick up the phone. "Greiffenberg." They could hear angry rasping on the other end of the line, and Philip made a gesture to Lehndorff, suggesting they should leave. Tresckow waved them to stay. Meanwhile, Greiffenberg had burst out irritably, "What were you all doing in the same staff car? You—"

He was interrupted by a tirade of shouting on the other end. Philip could clearly make out the words "… the whole bridge blew …"

"All right, all right." Greiffenberg now tried to pacify the outraged general on the other end of the line. "But this still has to go through proper channels; why don't you get in touch with the 9th Army—"

Again he was cut off by outraged shouting. "Kluge commanded the 9th Army until he was chosen to take over the Army Group," Tresckow clarified for Philip helpfully. "His replacement, General Model, probably isn't there yet."

Another knock on the door was followed by an officer who put his head in and announced: "The *Herr Generalfeldmarschall!*"

Greiffenberg nodded to him and said into the phone, "Rittenbach, I have to go. *Generalfeldmarschall* v. Kluge has just this minute arrived. Here's Tresckow; he'll handle everything." He handed the phone to his Ia and departed with Lehndorff at his heels.

Philip stood indecisively, on the brink of leaving, but again Tresckow gestured for him to stay. From the other side of the door, Philip could hear what sounded like a large number of boots stomping through the room and a brisk voice saying, "I want to see the entire staff in the operations room a half-hour from now ..." He turned his attention back to Tresckow and noted how much more relaxed Tresckow seemed. His tone was calm and helpful rather than irritated. "All right, and *Herr General's* adjutant (*Ordananonzoffizier*)?" He nodded. "*Herr General's* Ib, Major Kellermann?" Tresckow nodded again. "I see; *Herr General* would prefer that he remains in the post of Ib. All right, just a minute." He covered the receiver with his hand and addressed himself to Philip. "Major v. Feldburg, *Generalmajor* v. Rittenbach has just lost his First General Staff Officer in a partisan attack; he needs an immediate replacement. Do you feel up to it?"

There could only be one reason for this irregular handling of personnel needs, and that was the seriousness of the situation. Under the circumstances, Philip felt he had no choice, although he in no way felt ready for the assignment. "If the *Herr Oberstleutnant* thinks I can manage without any experience on this front, of course, *Herr Oberstleutnant.*"

Tresckow smiled, "Good," and uncovered the receiver again. "*Herr General*, I've got a major here, General Staff, who's just arrived from Berlin ... Yes, I know, but EKI in France and peacetime War College graduate.... Under Beck, yes ... I'll send him right away ... He should reach the 144th tomorrow or the next day ... No, there are no aircraft available.... *Herr General*, it's questionable if I'll be able to find Major v. Feldburg a car ... I have the utmost confidence that the *Herr General* will manage ... May I urge the *Herr General* to see a doctor? ... *Aufwiederhören.*"

Shaking his head with an amused expression, Tresckow hung up the phone. "General v. Rittenbach is a rather impatient, temperamental man, but he's honest, reliable, decent—and a good troop leader. He was, however, never General Staff, and he demanded a 'real' General Staff officer—as if we could produce them out of thin air. Personally, I think highly of him."

Philip was feeling increasingly uneasy. He had no experience fighting the Soviets. He had no overview of the strategic situation anymore—not at the pace things were happening. About the tactical situation of his new division he knew absolutely nothing—except that it was desperate. His predecessor had been killed, so there'd be no orderly transfer of responsibilities. He was being thrown into duties without a clue of how things had been managed up to now. Nor did he know anyone in the division he was about to join. He had no way of knowing who the weak links in the chain were. Worst of all, he was being placed into the position of Deputy Commander. If something happened to Rittenbach after he joined the division, he would be expected to take over command until a replacement arrived. Philip had a healthy sense of self-confidence and did not underestimate his capabilities, but he found it hard to imagine going from company to divisional commander with practically no experience in between. Four weeks as an intelligence officer with a corps in Greece and work at a desk in Berlin didn't seem adequate qualifications to command a division—no matter how briefly or provisionally. He could only pray that the need did not arise. To Tresckow he said, "I only hope I can live up to General v. Rittenbach's expectations."

Tresckow smiled, "Don't worry. The 144th is attached to XXI Corps, 9th Army. You can stop at Corps HQ on the way and they can better fill you in on the tactical situation. Let me show you the strategic overview." Tresckow pulled back the damask curtains behind the desk, revealing a large map of the western Soviet Union. He pointed out the various German and Russian armies, and then located the pin representing the 144th Infantry Division. In a few concise sentences he described the overall situation and pointed out the critical sectors on the front. The entire 9th Army was one of them, threatened from being cut off by breakthroughs both to the north and south of it.

Tresckow returned to the desk. "Now I suggest you get something to eat and try to get some sleep. In the morning I'll have to make arrangements to get you to your division." He paused, cocked his head and said a little wistfully, "I'm sorry about this, actually. I'd been looking forward to working with you—after the good reports Olbricht sent. Maybe another time." He held out his hand. "If I don't see you again before you leave, good luck."

Philip found Franz and broke the news to him. The batman went very pale. Franz had gone to Sophia Maria with his complaints about soldiering without any pretence of courage. He'd said to her flatly, "I'm no hero, *Frau Baronin*. I don't want to be a hero. All I want is to survive the war and have a normal life again."

"Sorry; I know you thought life as my batman would be more comfortable," Philip remarked. He spared his batman the details about the probability of getting cut off and ending in Russian hands in the near future.

Franz swallowed and tried to make the best of it. "I suppose my luck had to turn sometime, *Herr Baron*."

Philip undressed, lay on the narrow cot, and tried to sleep. It wasn't easy, with Hitler's "stand-and-die" order and the red arrows indicating the breakthroughs north and south of the 9th Army so vividly in his mind. His last conscious thought was: "Thank God Alix doesn't know."

CHAPTER 17

▼

Naroforminsk-Obninskaya
December 1941

The operations section of XXI Corps was located in the offices of a large factory. It was impossible to tell what the factory had once produced, because the large rooms with their exposed steel structure had been emptied of equipment by one army or another. It now housed a vehicle maintenance company, but because of the many broken windows, the mechanics worked in their coats and fingerless gloves.

Philip climbed the metal stairs that led from the factory floor to the offices and was directed to an office at the end of the hall whose Cyrillic lettering identified it as the office of the "Director." In the outer office, two corporals occupied the desks of the director's secretaries. It could have been any military office—except for the submachine guns placed within easy reach of both "secretaries." One of these people indicated that Philip should go on through the open door to the next room.

A group of more than a half-dozen officers were collected around a conference table, some standing and some sitting. Photos of Lenin and Stalin had been taken down from the wall and left carelessly standing on the floor. The situation map was spread out on the table. The standing men had rifles over their shoulders, and several other rifles and submachine guns were propped up within easy reach under the window.

The officers looked up expectantly as Philip entered, and he suspected they mistook him for someone else. He saluted to the most senior officer, a colonel of the General Staff whom he presumed to be the Chief of Staff. "Feldburg. I was told to report here on my way to the 144th Infantry Division."

"Ah, yes." The Colonel got to his feet with a slight but audible groan, as if he had been sitting for a long time. He held out his hand. "Glad you made it. Now at least we'll have Rittenbach off our backs. He's been calling every couple of hours to ask where you were."

"I came—"

The Colonel waved him silent. "I know, I know, it's just Rittenbach. He's wounded and has neither ADC nor Ia to assist him. I don't suppose you've eaten?"

"Not since I left Smolensk."

"We'll break and have something to eat," the colonel announced. The men who had been leaning over the map straightened; the others shoved back their chairs with evident relief. The colonel turned to a lieutenant, presumably his ADC, and asked him to see about a meal.

The lieutenant went out and the colonel turned back to Philip. "While we're waiting, would you like to see what the situation is?"

"Please." Philip moved to the table and the colonel turned the map around so it would be easier for him to read. "This was our position when the Russian counteroffensive started." He drew a line with his finger on the map. "They hit us here north of the Vyazma road and broke through quite easily. Why not? Their troops have winter uniforms, full rations and tanks with a wide track-base so they don't get stuck in the snow. Almost simultaneously, they also struck at Balaban-ovo and Maloyaroslavets, but we were able to stop them and throw them back. In the north, however, the Soviets pressed forward, throwing us out of Mozhaysk the day before yesterday. The XXIX Corps counterattacked and retook it—but with heavy losses. Meanwhile, the armies north and south of us are doing worse. Alexsin is now threatened in the south, and—last I heard—the Russians were already in Volokolamsk. That means the whole 9th Army could get cut off if the Russians just turn north from Kaluga and south from Volokolamsk. We were just beginning an orderly withdrawal to new positions along here." The colonel used a pencil and drew the line for Philip on the map. Then he threw the pencil down and his expression became stiff and inscrutable. "But we have orders to stand— and if necessary, die—where we are."

Philip glanced at the other officers. Clearly the prevalent opinion was that they were about to be cut off and duly slaughtered. It would have been too strong to say they were resentful, but it was clear they didn't understand the reasoning of the "stand" order, and some seemed to be expecting Philip to explain it to them.

All he could offer was the information, "The order came from our new C-in-C personally."

"From the *Führer*?" one of the officers asked, startled.

"Yes," Philip confirmed, but the Chief—who evidently had known the source of the order—nipped any discussion in the bud by addressing Philip again. "You may have some difficulty getting to the 144th. I can't spare a vehicle, and fighting is heavy along the nearly impassable roads anyway. You'll have to try following the rail-bed." Again the colonel pointed with his finger on the map, adding, "It's not in use, since we have no time, ties or engineers with which to effect the necessary repairs. Riding, you should be able to reach Rittenbach's HQ in five to six hours."

Philip nodded, but a lieutenant colonel, who he presumed was the Ia, demurred. "Don't you think we should send an escort, *Herr Oberst*?"

The colonel sighed and considered before again turning to Philip. "You understand: alone you'll be a sitting duck for partisans, but an escort will slow you down. I'm willing to provide it, but I tend to think the partisans are distracted right now, aiding the Soviet offensive. I doubt they have time for watching unused rail-beds."

"I'll risk it alone," Philip agreed.

"Good. I'll see that you get a decent mount."

Philip had reason to be grateful for the colonel's consideration regarding the horse when he saw the animal provided for Franz. It had dull eyes, was piteously thin and moved with the unsteady, clumsy step of an animal without the strength or will to go much further. Nearly all the horses serving with the 9th Army had been pushed beyond their endurance and were dying in droves.

It was dusk as they reached the HQ of the 144th Infantry Division, and Franz's horse was stumbling and swaying. Directed to a wooden villa on the outskirts of a partially destroyed village, they jumped down onto feet like blocks of ice on the end of half-paralyzed legs. Philip stumbled awkwardly as he tried to walk and nearly tripped; Franz caught him.

"Just think," he reminded his batman, "if you hadn't complained to my mother you could have been eating figs and olives on Crete." Philip referred to the current position of Stadthagen's former division. He was feeling increasingly guilty for dragging Heidi's only son into this mess. He was all she had, and it didn't look very likely that she would ever see him again.

"With my luck, I would have drowned with the half of the division that got sunk by the Royal Navy on the way there," Franz assured him.

"See if you can find some feed for these poor beasts, and I'll find out what the situation here is."

The house apparently serving as the divisional HQ was not the typical wooden cottage of the region. Although only a single story, it stretched lengthwise into a substantial structure and was graced with a veranda across the front. It had a chimney at each end, front steps leading to the veranda, and four dormer windows. It was also in deplorable condition; unpainted, the veranda rotting, broken glass in the dormer windows—the damage of neglect, not war.

Inside the dim entryway, a rickety wooden staircase climbed, turned at eye level and continued overhead. To the left and right were doorways and a hallway ran along the back. Randomly, Philip opened the door to his left and found himself in a room that seemed stuffy after the cold outside. A fire was blazing in an open fireplace, fed by a man in the uniform of an *Oberzahlmeister*. In the unsteady light of the fire, a jumble of makeshift desks and antique furniture stood still amid the restless, apparently senseless turmoil of officers and civil servants.

Directly before Philip, looming out of the half-light, was a priest in the uniform of an Army chaplain. He did not take note of Philip, but scowled as his colleague, the Protestant chaplain, argued heatedly with the paymaster. "… we're talking about your comrades! Think what this would mean! I simply can't believe I'm talking to a German civil servant—"

"Excuse me, *Herr Pfarrer*, but do you have any idea what our casualties have been in the last seven days?—"

"I probably have a better idea than you! I've been closing their eyes and seeing that they get a proper burial!" The pastor raised his voice.

"Yes, but have you seen the figures? Do you realize we're talking about 8 officers dead and another 13 wounded? 131 men have been killed and nearly 400 wounded. At that rate I can calculate for you the precise date on which this division will totally cease to exist—"

Philip didn't hear the end of the conversation, because an officer entered from behind him in a gust of cold air. Taking no notice of Philip, he rushed past, shouting, "*Oberleutnant* Weber! It's impossible! It's simply impossible! I've just been down to the workshop myself. They've been at it for 24 hours straight and it can't be done. There aren't any spare parts, and they've cannibalized everything they have—even the captured vehicles."

The officer thus addressed let off a stream of oaths and threats in which the phrase "the *Herr General* will have your guts" was repeated frequently.

A telephone rang insistently on the empty desk next to Philip. No one in the crowded room took the least notice of it, clearly considering it someone else's responsibility. Philip reached it in two steps and picked up the receiver. "Feldburg, 144th Infantry Division."

There was a stunned silence on the other end of the line, and then a distant voice said, "*Oberstleutnant* Miersch. I wanted to report reestablishment of telephone communication to Balabanovo … Is Inspector Benecke there?"

"I have no idea. I'm the new Ia, and I just arrived this minute. I don't know anyone, but I'll pass on your report to General v. Rittenbach."

The *Justizinspektor* at the next desk looked up and stared at Philip, and then looked about the room to see why no one else was taking note of his arrival. In the telephone the voice suddenly became more forceful. "Excellent! I'm the CO of the Engineer battalion. I'm halfway to Balabanovo, and I've been awaiting orders concerning the rail bridge over the River Protva—"

"I'm sorry; I haven't had time to orient myself, nor have I spoken to General v. Rittenbach. I'll consult with the *Herr General* and get back to you as soon as possible. Wait a minute." A man in the uniform of an Army engineer inspector had just come up to the desk and was gazing at Philip as if he were an apparition. "I believe Inspector Benecke has just returned. I'll turn you over to him." He turned the receiver over to the stunned inspector and was at once greeted by a stocky, exhausted-looking major of the reserves. The major had thick bags under his eyes and clay-colored skin. "Major Frhr. v. Feldburg, I presume?"

"Yes."

The other major held out his hand, "Krosigk, IVa. I gather you just got in from Corps? They told us you were on your way. Let me take you across to the operations section. We're nothing but administration and support here." He was already gesturing toward the door, but the chaos was momentarily paralyzed as everyone stared at the new First General Staff Officer and Deputy Commander of the division.

As the door closed behind them, Major v. Krosigk remarked in a low voice, "The last 24 hours have been perfect hell. It was during a relocation of the divisional command post that we lost—in one blow—the Ia, the Ic, the divisional adjutant and the General's ADC. It's a miracle the General himself walked away with only minor injuries."

"What happened?"

"Partisans must have had wind of our move. They laid mines—not regular pressure mines but fused ones—and blew them up just as the staff vehicles crossed a bridge. The General and Ib were thrown clear into deep snow, but the others …" He shrugged. "The first car was completely demolished and burst into flames. All the survivors were in the second car."

Krosigk gestured for them to go outside. "The General thinks this is too obvious a place for an HQ, since it is the largest building in the village. He's set up his command post in the cottage across the street." They went out the door and down the steps as Krosigk continued, "Since the partisan attack, staff work has been crippled, but the Russians haven't let up in the least. We even had to recall the military police sent after the partisans. They're our headquarters reserve."

They crossed the snowy street and Krosigk led Philip into one of the typical wooden cottages, which was guarded by two sentries. Although much smaller than the villa opposite, this cottage bore signs of loving care. The steps and roof were in good repair, the shutters were freshly painted, and there were even snow-filled flower boxes under the windows. Inside they were again greeted by heavy warmth, this time from a large tile oven. Light was provided by smoking oil lamps, and the smell of fried onions and boiled potatoes filled the air.

In what had evidently been the Russian family's best parlor, a make-shift operations room had been set up. The situation map was spread out on a table, held down by a field manual and a couple of revolvers; the fourth corner curled up unheeded. At a secretary, an officer worked with the aid of a lighted candelabrum. Two other officers worked together on a couch, materials scattered around on the floor.

Everyone looked up as Krosigk and Feldburg entered, and here everyone immediately realized who the strange major had to be. They got to their feet as best they could, but none with more alacrity than the major on the sofa. He was the only other man in the room—and apparently the division—with the distinctive uniform of the General Staff. "Kellermann." He held out his hand. "You must be Feldburg." As they shook hands, the Second General Staff Officer, responsible for supply, declared, "General v. Rittenbach just went to lie down, but I'm sure he wants to see you. I'll take you right in." He led Philip back into the hall, past the kitchen where a meal was in preparation, and to a closed door.

Kellermann knocked loudly to be heard over the chatter of the Russian women in the kitchen, and Philip felt his stomach tighten. On the other side of the door was not just his new direct superior, but the man Philip would have to live with, work with, advise and represent. Philip was expected to be his alter ego—and for all Philip knew, this was a man who had carried out the Commissar Order or believed Hitler was the "greatest military genius of all time."

At a barked "Come in," Kellermann opened the door and stepped aside for Philip. The General had stretched himself out fully clothed. He sat up expectantly, instantly alert, his eyes bloodshot but attentive above his unshaven face. His arm was in a sling that stood out white against his grey uniform, and a *Pour le Mérite* glinted in the light of the single oil lamp. Philip came to attention and saluted. "Major v. Feldburg—"

"Thank God."

*   *   *   *

Obninskaya-Maloyaroslavets

In the eight days since Philip had joined the 144th Infantry Division, he had not once been out of his clothes, and he was beginning to get used to having a beard. Though Hitler's "stand and die" order still held, he and Rittenbach had almost immediately agreed to remove all the support activities of the division behind the Protva River. Furthermore, the engineers had been tasked to repair and convert the downed railroad bridge to facilitate the rapid withdrawal of the fighting units when the time came. Neither Philip nor Rittenbach doubted that the time would come.

For eight days, Philip had also not left the divisional command post. Napping when he could and solicitously cared for by Franz and the Russian women whose house they had commandeered, he tried to maintain a calm, objective overview of the division's situation. Rittenbach, meanwhile, rushed from crisis point to crisis point, providing leadership and securing a first-hand impression of conditions.

It was now clear to Philip both why Rittenbach's division had held while others crumbled under the pressure, and why he had been so desperately insistent on getting an immediate replacement for his First General Staff Officer. Rittenbach was a general who led very much from the front. His junior officers and troops knew that the more desperate their situation, the more likely he was to appear. He could be trusted to show up, assess the situation from his greater experience, and make an instant decision on what to do. Officers and men knew that he would ask neither the impossible nor the unnecessary of them. The result was a fighting morale that Philip admired more from day to day.

This style of leadership, however, demanded mobility and extended periods away from the command post. Rittenbach could not keep track of all the various developments, nor could he chart them on a map. He had no time or nerves for sorting through the dozens of reports and requests until he found the critical cries for help or the essential information. He needed someone who did all that for him. He needed a strategic-thinking individual who kept an eye on the "big picture," sorted through the "snow" of information, and could provide him with concise reports of the essentials, enabling him to make decisions from "up front."

Philip had quickly grasped what Rittenbach wanted of him, and already they were a well-functioning team. Yet for all his admiration of the General's active leadership, Philip still thought there were times when he carried things to extremes. The General had been away from the command post for 36 hours and out of communication for 6 when the newly relocated Divisional Support HQ reported Soviet units operating behind them.

Philip stared at the telegraph and was momentarily lamed. After all their efforts, after 8 days of holding their own, filling gaps and throwing back attacks, they had—after all—been cut off. Somewhere else, some other division along the long, wriggling front had failed to hold. There had been a breakthrough, and the 144th was already caught in the trap. But then the initial panic receded and he asked the lieutenant who had handed him the message, "Did you confirm this?"

"It just came in, sir."

"Get confirmation and more details."

While *Oberleutnant* Böttcher withdrew, Philip set aside his glasses and rubbed the bridge of his nose. Then he reached for the strong black tea with which their Russian hostess kept them supplied. If the report was true, it most likely meant a breakthrough southwest of them; but in that case they should have heard something about it either from the 105th Division on their right flank or from Corps HQ.

Oberleutnant Böttcher was back. "A patrol reports evidence of strong Soviet troop movements to the west and south of Maloyaroslavets."

"What evidence? How strong? Panzers or infantry? Moving in what direction? I need precise information, Böttcher." Philip tried not to sound as annoyed as he felt. Böttcher had absolutely no staff training and had been dropped into his present position because he was still recovering from a bout of jaundice. "Also— no, I'll do that myself." Philip put his glasses back on and reached for his telephone. He demanded a connection to the 105th Division. Moments later he had his counterpart at the 105th on the other end of the line. "Pahnke? Feldburg here. Has there been a breakthrough in your division?"

"Of course not—or you would have been the first to hear."

His tone, as much as his words, reassured Philip. Although they had never met, they had talked so frequently in the last days that Philip felt he knew Major Pahnke well enough to trust him now. He explained, "My Support HQ is reporting enemy units behind Maloyaroslavets."

"Must have come from the north. Our front is currently stable."

"Thank you." He hung up and tried Corps HQ, but they reported the same: the entire front of the Corps was holding under moderate pressure.

Böttcher was back, and he read aloud: "No evidence of armor. Estimate at least a division, as there are strong mounted reconnaissance patrols screening." Böttcher handed Philip the telegram.

Philip got up and went to the telegraph operator. "To our support HQ: In which direction are the enemy troops moving?"

The answer came back: "To the north."

"That doesn't make sense," Philip said out loud.

Around him the rest of the little operational staff had gathered. Böttcher had evidently told the others the content of the message, and Philip could smell the growing alarm. Böttcher, standing nearest to him, kept licking his lips and staring at the telegram. *Leutnant* Poncet, another convalescing front officer temporarily given staff duties, wore the rigid expression of a young man trying to disguise his fear. *Hauptmann* Blankenstein, the replacement Third General Staff Officer responsible for intelligence, who had only arrived four days ago, was nervously shuffling the index cards he held. The technical sergeants at the telegraph and encoding machines watched the officers intently.

Philip shook his head and remarked with emphasized calm, "Something's not right about that report. Ask them to send out another patrol."

He returned to his desk, but behind him he heard the others whispering around the map. Philip stood again and went over to them, carrying his tea. "Gentlemen." The three officers looked up guiltily, stepping back from the map and expecting a reprimand. "Let me explain something. The way the front is running, enemy units that broke through north of us would attempt to join up with the enemy units thrust forward here." He set his finger on the map. "That way they would encircle the largest number of our units. That encircling movement would bring them nowhere near Maloyaroslavets—and in any case they would be headed south. Likewise, enemy units that swung up from the bulge south of us would swing wide of Maloyaroslavets, probably following the road over Medyn. The most likely explanation would thus be a breakthrough in the sector held by the 105th, but I've already checked with them and with Corps. There has been no breakthrough. So where did this Soviet division come from? And where is it going to?"

"I don't see that that matters at the moment, *Herr Major*," Blankenstein retorted impatiently, almost irritably. In civilian life, Blankenstein was an assistant of Russian studies at the University of Heidelberg. Philip sensed his disdain for the intellectual qualifications of officers and his resentment at not being more highly appreciated by them. He continued, in a tone that suggested he thought he was the only one in the room who had grasped the essentials of the situation:

"The point is, they're there, and as a consequence we are about to be cut off. The General should be informed at once so that a withdrawal can be effected in time."

That the others shared this view—without having to be told—was evident. Poncet shifted uneasily, and Böttcher nodded unconsciously.

"By no means does it mean we are cut off," Philip countered firmly. "Assuming there are indeed Soviet Army units—and not merely partisans mistaken for military forces—behind our support HQ, then they are probably just cavalry with the explicit task of disrupting our supply lines and causing panic. But even if they were part of an encircling movement, their success would only be complete when they hooked up with other enemy units and cut off our withdrawal toward Barovsk and Polotnyany—as well as toward Medyn. Furthermore, they would have to be so firmly entrenched that we could not simply roll through them. As yet, there is no evidence that any of those conditions are met."

While Poncet and Böttcher seemed satisfied with this explanation, Blankenstein retorted with tight lips and obvious skepticism, "I certainly hope the *Herr Major* is right."

Philip ignored his tone and said evenly, "I think we all have work to do."

Nevertheless, he was glad to see Rittenbach when the General arrived shortly afterwards. Rittenbach looked as if he had not slept since he'd left the command post 36 hours earlier. He pushed the door open heavily, stomped snow off his boots, and banged it off his greatcoat with wooden gestures. He sent his orderly to get him something to eat from the kitchen and entered the parlor/operations room. Here he removed his hat and gloves, nodded to the officers, and said only, "Feldburg, if you would be so kind ..." Then he turned and made for his own room.

Here Rittenbach put his cap and gloves aside, removed his greatcoat and sank onto the bed. He looked up at Philip. Despite his appearance, his tone was forceful when he spoke. "What is the latest report from *Oberstleutnant* Miersch?"

"His troops are working in exposed and windy conditions so extreme that no one can stand it longer than 35-40 minutes. What is more, they are working in such precarious positions that he feels it is only a matter of time before someone falls into the river and is lost. He complains of inadequate tools, inadequate blankets, and inadequate shelter, and says it is criminal to expect his troops to make the kind of sacrifices we're asking of them when we can't even provide a hot meal—"

Rittenbach waved Philip silent. "Miersch is absolutely correct. It *is* criminal. Now, how soon does he think the bridge will be ready for troops, if not vehicles?"

"Another 12 to 24 hours—for vehicles. I didn't ask about foot or horses only. Work could be speeded up, he says, with non-specialist support, although such troops would be more likely to fall into the river—"

"Whatever he wants. And the hot meal?"

"Already taken care of—along with the blankets."

Rittenbach looked amazed. "How did you manage that?"

"Major Kellermann organized a voluntary—I mean genuinely voluntary—drive among the local population."

Rittenbach stared at him for a moment. "For all they know, we've killed their sons and husbands, and they still sacrifice for us? It can't all be for the sake of a few reopened churches. I'll never understand them." He shook his head, baffled.

"Our hostess says she hopes German women would do the same for Russian boys in the same circumstances."

Rittenbach's eyes bore into Philip. "Do you think they would?" Before Philip could answer, he shook his head as if to clear it. "*Naja*, we don't have time to worry about it. But one thing I will not do is burn this village when we pull out!" He spoke aggressively, as if expecting contradiction from his First General Staff Officer. "*Führer* Order or no *Führer* Order, the Military Code explicitly forbids the implementation of senseless orders, regardless of who issues them. I would like to draw your attention to Paragraph—" He stopped as he realized that his Ia—far from raising objections—was grinning at him.

"I was afraid I was going to have to convince *Herr General* of the stupidity of it."

Rittenbach smiled for the first time since Philip had met him, and for a moment they both felt better. The scorched-earth policy had preyed on each of them separately, and the uncertainty of how the other would react had increased the strain. This, at least, was one less problem to worry about.

But then the rest of the situation pressed in on them again, and Rittenbach asked, "Anything I should know about before catching some sleep?"

"Unfortunately, yes, *Herr General*. We've had a report from our Support HQ of enemy patrols operating behind Maloyaroslavets."

Rittenbach, who had been bending over to pull off his boots, sat upright. "Where has there been a breakthrough?"

"No one is reporting a breakthrough. I talked to 105th and Corps personally. In my estimation, these are either isolated cavalry patrols that have slipped through the lines with the express intention of harassing our rear, or they are partisans mistaken for regular units. Then again, *Herr General*, I'm not really in a position to make that judgment. I don't know the officers reporting well enough."

"Who is reporting? Kellermann?"

"No; Krosigk, based on the reports of a *Leutnant* Mönch." Philip had no idea who this *Leutnant* Mönch might be.

Rittenbach, however, evidently knew him, and made a face. "Mönch is an amateur. Have them send out another patrol. When did the first report come in?"

"Just over an hour ago. I've already ordered a second patrol."

"Good." Rittenbach bent to pull off his second boot, and his batman entered with a bowl of steaming stew and bread.

"Herr General, if I'm wrong ..." Philip started.

Rittenbach kicked his boots to one side, and looked again at Philip. He thought for several minutes, absently scratching at his bearded chin. Then he asked, "Orders for the withdrawal have all been prepared?"

"Yes, *Herr General*, and kept up to date."

"Then, if you feel like it, take my eight-wheeler and the radio truck and go back yourself. You can use the opportunity to check on the preparations for receiving the fighting troops. If it should prove to be a serious attempt at encircling us, send a code-word at once."

Philip nodded, satisfied, and left the room. Another weakness of the General's leadership style was an unintentional neglect of the support troops. He welcomed this opportunity to check up on them.

After days of uninterrupted work in the stuffy Russian cottage, Philip found the cold, clear air refreshing and invigorating. Although it was nearly midnight, the full moon and fresh snow muted the darkness. The stars seemed particularly near, and the Milky Way was a grey smudge. Ahead of them the trees opened up on the glitter of the icy Protva. From the frozen edges laden with snow, the ice grew thinner until it completely broke, and black water ran swift and forceful between the icy banks. Directly ahead of them, the iron girders of the rail-bridge swept up majestically. Ice-encrusted and lightly dusted with snow, they sparkled in the moonlight. It was a magnificent sight, but as they drove nearer Philip searched in vain for *Oberstleutnant* Miersch and his engineers. The bridge was utterly abandoned. He looked in alarm at the driver, who at once stomped on the brakes.

Around them was littered the evidence of recent camping and working, but not a living creature stirred. Even more mysteriously, there was no evidence of violence—no corpses, no weapons, no bloodstains on the snow.

"There's someone on the other side of the river, *Herr Major.*" The driver drew Philip's attention to two small figures waving at them. Philip swung open his door and jumped down, going toward the bridge to meet the figures coming toward him. Without orders, the drivers of both vehicles drew their rifles and covered him.

The men coming toward him were in *Wehrmacht* uniforms: engineers. They called out, breathless with exertion or excitement, "*Herr Major!*" The sergeant saluted with a glance toward the General's eight-wheeler, apparently disappointed that it was not Rittenbach himself. "Did you get our message? We couldn't get any acknowledgment, so *Oberstleutnant* Miersch took the battalion back on his own initiative—"

"Back? Where? Why?"

"Maloyaroslavets!" The sergeant gestured with his arm toward the southwest. To his horror, Philip noticed a dull red hue to the sky.

"We tried to establish contact with the Support HQ, but the lines were dead—"

"Soviet cavalry," Philip concluded, and ran back to the radio truck.

By the time Philip reached Maloyaroslavets, the Soviets had been driven off by *Oberstleutnant* Miersch's engineers. They had, however, already achieved their apparent objective of causing havoc in the rear. At least a half-dozen houses burned, and various *Wehrmacht* vehicles were also in flames. An increasing number of corpses—all *Wehrmacht*—greeted the eight-wheeler as it slowly rolled deeper and deeper into the town.

A Lt. Colonel stepped into the street and signaled the eight-wheeler to halt. Philip opened his door and jumped down. "*Oberstleutnant* Miersch?"

"Major von Feldburg, I presume. Are you alone or is the General with you?" He, too, glanced hopefully toward the General's familiar eight-wheeler.

"Rittenbach is trying to get some sleep. What happened?"

"I don't know entirely. We noticed the light from the flames, but as there was no sound of explosions or gunfire, we weren't immediately alarmed. I tried to put a call through just to see if they needed help fire-fighting, and when the lines were dead I became suspicious. I decided to investigate—in force. As we approached, we saw horses milling about in the streets, and soon realized that most of the riders had dismounted to attack the various buildings." He pointed in succession toward what had been the maintenance depot, the field hospital, the mess, the communications center, the military post office and the HQ itself. The snow was trampled and dirty. Miersch was continuing, "We didn't take time for finesse,

Herr Major. I took the battalion right up the road—rather like the Old Fritz—firing volley after volley to disguise our own weakness. The Soviets blew a bugle signal and the riders poured out of the buildings, vaulted on their mounts and were gone. I did not pursue, but I've set up sentries. You were challenged, I hope?"

Philip nodded. "Is Major Kellermann alive?"

"Yes; he's trying to organize materials for the wounded. What I don't understand, *Herr Major*, is that—from what I can see—not even the most elementary precautions had been taken against this kind of attack."

"Was there no defense?"

"Major v. Krosigk tried to defend the HQ itself, but most of the civil servants and *Herr Doctors* don't know how to use a rifle—certainly not with their trousers full."

"What are your own casualties?"

"None—as I said, the Russians fled, offering no resistance at all when we appeared."

In the HQ building, a former school, the destruction was less serious than might have been expected. From the look of things, the room facing the street had not been defended. Apparently the staff had taken refuge in the stairwell beyond, which had no windows. The door leading to the stairwell was splintered with bullet holes, and just beyond the door were heavy bloodstains. The banister had been ripped or otherwise broken off from the stairway, and again there was blood on and beside the stairs.

As Philip stood and surveyed the scene, Major v. Krosigk came up behind him and stood silently for a moment. Finally Philip turned to face him and hardly recognized him: he had gone grey.

"This is where *Intendanturrat* Lambrecht died." He indicated the bloodstain on the wooden floor. "He tried to delay them as they broke in, so the others would have time to get upstairs. But even so, *Stabszahlmeister* Dr. Domkirche and *Heeresjustizinspector* Schemmer didn't make it. You see," he pointed to the shattered banister. "They shot Schemmer in the back and he fell off the stairs, taking the banister with him. Look, there are his glasses." Krosigk went forward and lifted a pair of wire-framed glasses off the floor near the shattered banister. One of the two lenses was broken, but the other was whole despite the twisted frame. Philip remembered the officious-looking inspector who had stared at him in amazement on the day of his arrival.

"Where is the rest of your staff?" Philip asked the IVa a little harshly.

Krosigk was snapped out of his contemplation of the glasses. He looked up and gestured vaguely, "Major Kellermann has them doing various things."

"Where is Major Kellermann?" As the Second General Staff Officer, Philip thought that Kellermann ought to have been more in evidence. He seemed to have played no role in the "engagement" at all.

Philip's disapproval must have been evident, because Krosigk answered by saying, "Dear Feldburg, you must understand, Major Kellermann is a genius at organization. Anything the division needs he'll somehow manage to find and provide, but he's not a combat commander." Krosigk's gaze strayed to Philip's Iron Crosses. "It's something you and the *Herr General* will have to remember: all the men here are basically civilians—regardless of what uniform you dress them up in. *Kriegsgerichtsrat* Dr. Niesse is 48 years old! *Oberzahlmeister* Ebling has a heart problem. *Inspektor* Benecke has a stomach ulcer. These are middle-aged men with children and grandchildren. They belong in some provincial town working in offices—not fighting Communist cavalry in the middle of nowhere at night." Although Krosigk said "they," Philip had no doubt he meant "we."

Philip was not without sympathy, but he didn't have the time or words to give comfort. Furthermore, it was clear to him that Germany had started this war, and if all the Krosigks and Beneckes and Eblings now regretted it, it was too late. Like every professional soldier, Philip felt a certain contempt for amateurs, who from the safety of their pubs were always more jingoistic and militant than the professionals who had to pay the price. Hadn't these Sunday soldiers cheered and applauded when Hitler promised them "living space" in the East?

"Major v. Krosigk, we have a division that is still—at this very moment— engaged against a much superior enemy. That division requires the support that this HQ is supposed to provide. You had better collect your staff at once and get to work becoming operational again."

If Philip seemed callous, Rittenbach was furious. Arriving early the next morning when much progress had already been made on getting back to "normal," he was nevertheless unappeasable. The Support HQ had been perfectly aware of the danger, as they had reported it themselves, but they had taken no precautions whatever! Kellermann, Krosigk, the Commander of the Military Police, and the entire staff were subjected to Rittenbach's rage as he swept through the village of Maloyaroslavets distributing insults and threats of court-martial with equal abundance and vehemence. For Rittenbach there could be no "mitigating circumstances" and no excuses. They were in a struggle for their survival, and mistakes were fatal. It was a side of Rittenbach Philip had never seen before, but he quickly recognized that this, too, was part of Rittenbach's effectiveness. His officers and men found his rage unpleasant enough to want to avoid it—even if it meant going to extra effort.

Nevertheless, when they were alone together, Philip admitted, "*Herr General,* these men are amateurs. We should have checked up on them sooner." Philip was remembering how General Olbricht claimed that it was a frequent error of commanders to simply "assume" that the support echelons would function like machines. "Support troops have to feel appreciated if they are going to give their best effort," Olbricht had told him once. "That means checking up on them now and again, and praising them for good work."

Rittenbach nodded with resignation, his anger burned out, but added, "When have either you or I had time to check up on them in the last week? There's only so much any man can do, Feldburg. The question is: how much more can this division take?"

CHAPTER 18

▼

Berlin
January 1942

Alix felt she had handled Philip's transfer to the 144th well—as a future officer's wife should. Rather than showing her fear, she had managed to say something like, "That's a great deal of responsibility, isn't it?" General Olbricht had assured her that the Ia of a division was one of the most challenging jobs in any staff officer's career, "and one of the most rewarding." Unfortunately, Alix also had access to the situation map. Olbricht's map did not break down the units below Corps, but Alix could see for herself that the entire 9th Army was projecting eastward, while the armies to the north and south had given much more ground. The risks were obvious.

And then came the letter from Stefan.

Stefan was Alix's younger brother. He had been born shortly before his father went missing in 1917. He had been just seven when their mother met Albrecht v. Rantzow, and it was perhaps natural that the diplomat made considerable efforts to win the affection of his bride's son. Even as a child, Alix felt that her stepfather favored Stefan, and this had added to her resentment of her stepfather. But she had never blamed Stefan, who so wanted a father, for accepting Albrecht v. Rantzow in place of the father he had never known.

It was probably just as natural that Stefan soon dreamed of a diplomatic career, like that of his stepfather, as he grew up. After the *Abitur* and Labor Service, Stefan had completed his compulsory military service and just managed to get in one semester at university before the war came and he was recalled. He served as an officer candidate in Poland and—although he claimed he had done nothing to deserve it—was commissioned second lieutenant just before the French campaign.

He was still serving as lieutenant with the 46th Infantry Division, XXXXII Corps, 11th Army, Army Group South. With her attention riveted on Army Group Center, Alix had not followed the developments on this front with the same attention. As a result, the letter from Stefan found her somewhat unprepared, particularly because it arrived in record time. A wounded friend of his had brought it with him to Berlin, and the nurses had obligingly put it in the Berlin post. Just two weeks after the events described, Alix found herself reading about how her brother's division had nearly been trapped on the Kertsch Peninsula.

Although she'd never heard of the peninsula before, a look at the atlas quickly showed a peninsula between the Sea of Asowsch and the Black Sea with a narrow neck just 18 km across. Stefan described how his corps had taken the peninsula in mid-November at high cost. "The division was down to roughly 50% of official strength," Stefan wrote, "and 90% of our vehicles needed repairs of one kind or another, while the horses could hardly move in the snow since they have no spiked shoes. We still have no winter uniforms."

In early December, the corps had been weakened by the withdrawal of two divisions to help with the siege of Sewastopol. All that remained of the "corps" was the weakened 46th Division and a Romanian cavalry brigade. On December 26, the Soviets landed more than two divisions at eight different points along the north shore and at the tip of the peninsula. Stefan's division was concentrated to eliminate these bridgeheads; and although it succeeded partially, it was not possible to eliminate them all. The Soviets reinforced the surviving bridgeheads and then on the 29th landed four more divisions at the neck of the peninsula, roughly 100 km behind Stefan's division. It was now clear that the first landings had been a diversion to draw the Germans deep into the peninsula, and that this landing at their rear was the real threat. Stefan's division and the Romanian cavalry brigade could not possibly cope with six enemy divisions at once. The Corps commander, *Generalleutnant Graf* Sponeck, therefore, gave the order to pull back off the peninsula entirely.

Stefan wrote in his neat, elegant handwriting:

"Over Christmas the weather had been mild and most of us had soaking wet feet when suddenly temperatures dropped to minus 30 degrees. Our feet froze inside our boots. The gasoline froze in the vehicles, even when the motors were left running. The horses slipped and fell until their knees were torn open, and they didn't have the strength to get up again. The blizzard was blowing in our faces the whole time, which made it impossible for the artillery to provide effective protection for the withdrawal. The MGs jammed in the cold. But because of the earlier thaw, the apparently frozen swamps that we tried to cross sometimes gave way, swallowing man, horse and wagon—particularly the vehicles. Before we'd gone half the

distance, we had so few operational vehicles left that the only way we could get the wounded out was by abandoning some of our equipment. It was so bad, we even discarded some of our machine guns—particularly the ones that had jammed. But we did get the wounded out, and do you know what thanks we got? GFM v. Reichenau says our "retreat was incompatible with the honor of the German Army." An order was issued saying that we had disgraced ourselves and in conse-quence, no one in the division is entitled to decorations, promotions or leave!

"They can keep their damned decorations! And I never asked to be called Herr Leutnant *and don't give a damn if there's an "Ober" in front of it or not. But, Alix, we've been out here for 9 damned months, and only the thought of eventually going home has kept us going at all. If we get no leave, it is like being condemned to death. We might just as well lie down and die right now.*

"Now we've heard that Graf Sponeck is going to be court-martialed for giving the order to pull back. Do you realize what that means? He's going to be punished for saving our necks. People are even saying he's going to be shot. If they start shooting generals for saving their troops, we might as well desert to the Soviets right now!"

Alix was unable to sleep that night. More than once she got up, turned on the light, and reread the letter. In the morning, she tucked it into her purse and took it to work with her.

Annie Lerche was collecting the dirty cups and saucers from the General's office when Alix arrived. As she backed out with the dirty dishes on a tray, she saw Alix and greeted her. "Morning—Alix! What's happened? Philip isn't—"

Alix shook her head and turned her back to unwind her shawl and take off her coat. She was not pleased that her state of mind was so obvious, but no doubt it had something to do with her not washing her hair and forgetting to put on makeup. "No, I had a letter from my brother. Isn't General Olbricht here yet?"

"He's here, but he and *Oberst* Reinhardt have been summoned to *General-oberst* Fromm." Reinhardt was Olbricht's Chief of Staff and Fromm was the C-in-C of the Home Army, i.e., Commander of all troops stationed inside Germany.

It was two hours before Olbricht reappeared, and he looked so dispirited that Alix hesitated to approach him. Reinhardt came out of the other adjoining office and went into Olbricht's, where they were closeted together for almost another hour. By then, Alix had enough material typed for Olbricht's signature to have a legitimate reason to go in to him. She knocked, and he called "please" as usual.

She stepped into his office and closed the door behind her, the signature folder on her arm. Olbricht was sitting at his desk, resting on his elbows, and he looked at her through his glasses with eyes that were dull. He looked, she thought, as if he had just suffered a personal defeat.

"Is something the matter, *Herr General?*"

"Hitler's just thrown Erich Hoepner out of the Army in disgrace—stripped him of rank, command, right to wear the uniform, pension, everything! Without even giving him a chance to explain himself!"

"Erich Hoepner?" Alexandra gasped, disbelieving. "Uncle Erich" was too famous, too successful, too good for this. On the personal side, he had always been her favorite "uncle," and if he hadn't arranged this job with AHA, she would never have met Philip. Suddenly Alix was aware of just how much she owed him. "But why?" she asked the General.

"He ignored Hitler's stupid "stand and die" order and pulled his 4th Panzer Army back to defensible positions!" Suddenly Olbricht jumped up and started pacing behind his desk. "That man owes Erich Hoepner his victory in Poland! It was Hoepner's armor that threatened the Polish capital just eight days after the start of the war. He received the Knight's Cross at the same time I did! If he can no longer wear it, I don't want it, either! I'm ashamed to wear this very uniform." Olbricht struck angrily at the eagle with the swastika in its claws on his own breast. Then, in an obvious effort to get control of himself, he went to look out of the window and stood with his hands behind his back.

A moment or two later he turned around and with a little, crooked smile and sad eyes begged, "Please forgive me for my outburst, *gnädiges Fraulein*. Erich Hoepner has become a good friend in the last few years. He's not only a first-class soldier; he's an intelligent, open-minded, and honest man. I hate to think of him humiliated like this—and for doing exactly what I would have done in his shoes. He was right, Frl. v. Mollwitz. He was absolutely right to do what he did." Olbricht sighed. "Now, what can I do for you? Signatures?"

"Not really; they were just an excuse." Alix laid the signature folder on the desk, but she took Stefan's letter from the pocket of her skirt. As she handed it to Olbricht, she explained, "It's from my brother. Please read it."

Olbricht frowned slightly, but he took the letter and, still standing, read it by the window. When he finished, he turned back to her and remarked admonishingly, "That letter should never have gotten past the censors."

"It didn't come by military mail. It was carried personally by one of my brother's wounded comrades."

Olbricht nodded without further comment and then added, "I'll see what I can find out about Sponeck. At least he's been given a chance to defend himself—unlike Hoepner."

"But he could be shot," she reminded him.

"No!" Olbricht burst out. "The Officer Corps will not allow that. Have Dr. Karl Sack call me at once." With a gesture toward the folder, he added, "I'll ring when I'm finished with that." Alix withdrew.

*   *   *   *

Berlin
February 1942

Marianne stood helplessly in the doorway and watched Herr and Frau Silber close their overstuffed suitcases. When Frau Silber couldn't force the clasps to close, Marianne sprang forward and helped. With her youthful strength, she pressed the suitcase tighter, and Frau Silber got it shut. Still, it bulged and strained so much that Marianne looked at it skeptically, certain it would spring open again.

Herr Silber smiled and held up a finger. "Wait!" In a second he was back with a roll of twine. He wound the twine around both his wife's and his own suitcases as if they were packages to be sent through the mail. He carried both suitcases into the hall and then went into the kitchen to collect two shopping nets filled to bursting with bread, cheese, salami and bottles of water. He handed the two nets to his wife, took two envelopes off the table and stuffed them into his jacket pocket, and looked around the kitchen. "That's it. I rather suspect the authorities will be disappointed."

Marianne helped the Silbers into their shabby coats. It wasn't easy because both were already wearing at least two layers of sweaters. Hats and scarves went on next and finally gloves, the latter gifts from the Moldenauer family. They were made of real leather with rabbit-fur linings. At last, dressed for the outside, they opened the apartment door and went out onto the landing. Herr Silber closed the door behind them and locked if fastidiously. Marianne took one of the suitcases and started down the stairs.

In the entryway, Herr Silber stopped to place his envelopes neatly on top of the mailbox with the addressee face up: *Die Geheime Staatspolizei*—the Gestapo. Inside one of the envelopes was a meticulously completed questionnaire describing the contents of the apartment they had left behind. Working by candlelight and wrapped in their overcoats against the cold, Marianne and Herr Silber had checked the appropriate boxes and filled in the blanks. Herr Silber had chuckled and chortled to himself the whole time. "Won't they be disappointed!" he declared in delight. "'Rugs, number and size in square meters: none.' 'Curtains: none.'" Et cetera, et cetera. When it came to "china," Herr Silber had made Marianne bring him each piece and describe it to him as he wrote out the description on the form: "One dinner plate with blue rim, glued together. One saucer with pink rose pattern, chipped. One plain green teacup, no handle." And so it had gone until late into the night.

In the other envelope were a letter and a complete set of keys to the apartment with tags identifying them: front door, upper lock; front door, lower lock; pantry, etc. The letter stated simply, politely but proudly, that "Herr Dr. Silber and his honored wife" did not allow themselves to be collected as if they were criminals or stray animals. They would appear at the appointed time and place for deportation of their own accord, like the adults and reasonable citizens they were.

The questionnaire had appeared two weeks earlier, and by then every Jew in Berlin knew that it meant deportation "to the East". Silber had not been surprised. The deportations had been going on for some time and were clearly directed at all "useless" and "unprotected" Jews—i.e., those not doing forced labor in some war industry, married to Aryans, or friends of prominent Nazi officials. The *Reich* was to be made "Jew-free" by transporting all Jews to the mammoth and growing ghettos established throughout the occupied territories in Eastern Europe—Warsaw, Riga, Krakow and Lublin. "To the Pale," as Herr Silber described it. "First the Russians sent us there and now the Germans, always to the Pale. Funny—I just said 'the Germans' as if I weren't German, too. All that propaganda eventually seeps into your brain, even if you don't want it to."

Marianne had seen the Ghetto in Warsaw, and she'd tried to talk the Silbers into attempting an illegal existence in Berlin. Herr Silber refused to even consider it. He refused to endanger the people who would have to hide them and feed them. He refused to live like a wanted criminal. Instead he had obtained from the Jewish Council the date of their scheduled deportation and asked if he couldn't report for deportation voluntarily.

The official of the Jewish Council had stared at him in disbelief. No one went voluntarily into the deportation machine. Herr Silber insisted, "I won't be picked up like a common criminal. They can force me to leave my home and country only because they are stronger than I am. But they cannot—not even with their guns—take away my dignity. If I cannot avoid deportation, then I am going to embark on it like a man."

On the street, the light was murky behind the heavy winter fog mixed with coal dust. The air smelled of burning coal, and coal ash was sprinkled on the icy sidewalks to reduce the slipperiness. It was so early that hardly anyone stirred on the streets in this still-fashionable neighborhood.

Marianne carried one suitcase, Herr Silber the other and one of the shopping bags, and frail Frau Silber managed a shopping bag and her purse. Together they started their long walk to the Eastern Station. Because Jews were not allowed to use public transportation, the Silbers had to cover the whole distance on foot. At the first bus stop, however, Marianne took the two suitcases and went on ahead.

At the station, Marianne had breakfast and read magazines until the time she expected the Silbers. But they did not show. She waited with increasing nervousness. The Jewish Council had impressed upon them the dire consequences, not only to themselves but to the Council as well, if they failed to appear. No matter what their excuse, if they failed to arrive in time, it would be assumed that they had tried to "evade" the authorities. They would be treated like traitors—which meant shot. So Marianne fretted, paced, and chewed her nails as the clock jumped forward minute by minute. The trains came and went to the metallic announcements.

At last she caught sight of them. Poor Frau Silber was limping, and Herr Silber red and breathless. Marianne ran down the steps, leaving the two suitcases unattended for a moment. "It's almost time," Marianne lied. (It was, in fact, already five minutes past the appointed time.)

"We got a little lost …" Herr Silber panted, but he didn't have the breath to explain as he pulled himself up the steps, and Marianne didn't have the patience to listen. They were back to the suitcases.

On the other side of the room, a slow snake of people entered at the door from the street and worked its way down a stairway to the tunnel leading under the tracks to the next platform. The people in the column carried suitcases, bundles or knapsacks, and all wore the Star of David.

The Silbers hurried toward the now visible end of the column of deportees. A representative of the Jewish Council, catching sight of them, gestured urgently for them to come faster. They broke into a crippled, footsore and overburdened run.

The representative of the Jewish Council was explaining to an SS *Untersturmbannführer* as they panted up, "This is the couple we agreed about, Silber and his wife."

The SS *Untersturmbannführer* looked annoyed and impatient. "Who's the girl?"

"I don't know."

"Papers!" he demanded of Marianne as the man from the Jewish Council insistently ordered the Silbers to join the column.

Marianne set down the suitcase she'd been carrying, and at once Herr Silber grabbed it. Marianne found her ID and handed it to the SS *Untersturmbann-führer*. Her heart was pounding in her ears; she couldn't seem to catch her breath. The *Untersturmbannführer* scrutinized her picture, then her face, and then the ID again. He held the ID closer, turned toward the light to see better, turned it over and studied the back. He scratched with his nail around the photo, and finally decided it was genuine after all.

He handed it back to Marianne, adding in a stern voice, "You'd do well to have less to do with these Jewish swine!" He advised, "An Aryan beauty like you ought to be comforting some of our lonely troops!" Then he turned away. His duties were to see this transport to its destination, not fuss about students foolish enough to be seen helping Jews.

The last thing Marianne saw of the Silbers was Herr Silber's disappearing hat. For a long time she just stood staring at the spot where it had disappeared, feeling lost and suddenly alone. Only gradually did it dawn on her that not only would she never see the Silbers again, but her own life had just become empty and meaningless as a result.

CHAPTER 19

▼

Yukov, Soviet Union
March 1942

General v. Rittenbach succeeded where Hoepner and Sponeck failed. He pulled back his division so incrementally and unobtrusively that his withdrawal went unnoticed at *Führer* Headquarters. To be sure, he frequently clashed with General Model and their relationship was more strained than ever, but by the end of March the entire XXI Corps had managed to extricate itself from the exposed positions it had held when the "stand and die" order was issued. Furthermore, their present positions were chosen for their relative defensibility, while a notable easing of the pressure from the enemy had enabled them to dig in and establish reliable lines of communication and supply. Life at Divisional HQ had even started to assume a degree of routine that included regular meals, a full night's sleep, even baths and changes of clothes. The routine also included the daily intelligence briefing.

Based on intercepted enemy radio messages, the interrogation of prisoners and enemy civilians, the reports of reconnaissance patrols and *Luftwaffe* observations, the Ic pieced together a picture of enemy units, strength and intentions as best he could. *Oberleutnant* Blankenstein officiously spread the maps before Philip and commenced the briefing. As always, Blankenstein adopted his lecturing tone when he delivered this information. He consistently managed to rub Philip the wrong way with his combination of condescension and infallibility. Against this, Philip had only the weapon of extreme courtesy. He feared that outright criticism or sarcasm would impair Blankenstein's efficiency. He'd had just about as much lecturing as he could take when the fresh young face of his adjutant appeared in the doorway.

Philip had not fully adjusted to the luxury of having an adjutant, and König seemed hardly old enough to be out of school, but in fact he had had substantial combat experience as an officer candidate in NCO rank before being promoted lieutenant. He was also endowed with what appeared to be perpetually good humor. Even now, with a routine task, he sounded cheerful. "The *Herr General* requests *Herr Major* to join him in his office. *Oberleutnant* Beier is there."

Beier was regimental adjutant of the 52nd Infantry Regiment under *Oberst* Albrowski. As Philip entered Rittenbach's office, the General was already pulling on his gloves and reaching for his gun belt. Not even waiting for Philip to report, he opened, "*Oberst* Albrowski insists on me traipsing through this abominable thaw to pay a visit to him for reasons he has not seen fit to disclose." Rittenbach was clearly in a foul temper.

Philip glanced at *Oberleutnant* Beier. The lieutenant's face was dirty, and he stood very stiff and looked decidedly uncomfortable.

"*Oberst* Albrowski is not accustomed to making frivolous requests, *Herr General*," Philip remarked evenly.

Rittenbach cast Philip a peeved look. "I knew you'd say something like that. Well, see how you like the idea of accompanying me, then."

Philip had much to do and no desire to travel about the countryside, but he knew when he was trapped. "As the *Herr General* wishes."

"Well, then?" the General signaled impatiently, "Get your hat, gloves and greatcoat. It may be warmer than it was, but it is hardly tunic weather."

With a suppressed sigh, Philip did as he was ordered. Five minutes later he found himself climbing into the staff car as *Oberleutnant* Beier remounted the horse on which he'd arrived.

For over a week the temperatures had held above freezing during the day. The melting snow shrank together or turned to slush and water, which froze again during the night. Where the snow had been packed hardest, it melted most slowly. The roads were a combination of water-coated ice and mud during the day and frozen ruts and sheets of ice at night. Dirty straw had been thrown onto the roads—allegedly to improve traction for man, beast and vehicle—but as far as Philip could tell, it only made it more unpleasant.

They pulled up at Regimental HQ and were met by *Oberst* Albrowski. His face was set and grim as he saluted Rittenbach and held out his hand to Philip. He spoke even before Rittenbach. "I'm sorry to drag *Herr General* all the way out here, but this is something that cannot be described." Already he was leading them down the alley that ran beside the official building converted into a HQ.

They walked rapidly despite the mud on which their boots slipped, sank and stuck.

His attention on his footing, Philip hardly saw where they were being led until abruptly, Albrowski halted. Philip looked up and saw a thick, dark mound in the middle of a field of snow. At first he could make nothing of it all, and then he recognized, with a qualm of distaste, that this was another heap of unburied corpses such as had been coming to light more and more as the snow receded. Strewn across the entire countryside were these piles of casualties from both armies, which the earth had been too frozen to receive at the time of their death. They had been stacked like cordwood and left behind, covered rapidly by blizzards and forgotten by comrades who had gone on to die somewhere else.

Yet even as these thoughts went through him, he noticed that there was something odd about this mound of dead. The uniforms were strange. He forced himself to focus. There were no uniforms at all. These weren't soldiers, they were civilians. The long white beard of an old man, the tangled hair of a young woman, and—falling off the end of the pile—the unfinished shape of a child of 6 or 7. "Holy Mother of God!"

Rittenbach seemed to take it all in at the same instant as his First General Staff Officer. His head jerked and his voice came out harsh and brutal. "What is this?"

"The Jewish population of Zubovo," Albrowski answered in a brittle voice.

Rittenbach's head whipped around. "What do you mean?" It was like a snarl.

Albrowski was striding forward again, pulling Rittenbach and Feldburg in his wake, taking them nearer the corpses. Albrowski was pointing, narrating, his anger pouring forth viciously. "... more than 100. I don't know exactly. I haven't counted. How can I expect my soldiers to deal with that?!" His finger pointed to a round-faced baby clutched in the crook of his mother's arms. Beside her was an old couple still holding hands even in death. Philip tasted bile in his throat and fought it back down. Rittenbach cast him a glance and asked the *Oberst*, "Who did it?"

"*Einsatzkommandos*! *Einsatzgruppen*! Who else?"

"In Lemberg the Soviets murdered some 2,000 of their own citizens," Rittenbach reminded him.

Albrowski shook his head. "This is our work. Germans did this. Germans! Does *Herr General* think it matters to anyone in the world if they wore the eagle here or here?!" He indicated first the eagle on his own breast and then the sleeve of his upper arm, where the SS units wore their eagle. "We did this!" he insisted. "Their blood is on our hands, and I don't care if there was a Jewish conspiracy responsible for the lost war and the inflation and God knows what else. We still have no right to murder! God will punish us for this! He will—"

"Pull yourself together!" Rittenbach ordered. He decisively turned his back on the corpses and strode back the way they'd come.

"You can't turn your back on this!" Albrowski shouted after him. "These people demand justice!"

Rittenbach spun back on Albrowski, "If you don't pull yourself together, I will relieve you of your command immediately!" When this had sunk in, he added in a lower, but still rough voice, "What good will that do these people?"

"What good does turning my back do?"

Rittenbach went back to Albrowski and spoke in an intense undertone. Philip could not hear exactly what was said; he didn't try. He'd fought down the initial nausea, but he still felt queasy still. Suddenly Rittenbach grasped him firmly by the upper arm and marched him away. Albrowski followed silently. Back on the street, Philip stumbled and slipped in the mud. Rittenbach caught him and stopped. After a moment he asked, "All right?" His tone was fatherly. Philip nodded and started forward to prove his point. "Slowly," Rittenbach urged, and then turned to Albrowski and ordered, "Start from the beginning."

"One of the HQ motorcycle couriers saw them first. He went over, thinking they might be some of our own dead who needed identification and burial. When he saw what it was, he burst in here in an agitated state and insisted that we come out and see it. He's a 12-year volunteer from the *Reichswehr*, German Cross in Gold, EKII, twice wounded—and there were tears of rage or pity in his eyes. Some of the young troops of the anti-tank company who had drifted over out of curiosity were sick. Beier, too. It speaks well for them. One has the feeling they wouldn't have been able to do it. But some of our young men did it—shot helpless, unarmed civilians of both sexes. Can *Herr General* tell me how that is possible? The young men who did that went to German schools and German churches. Where did they learn to point guns at naked women and children and fire at point-blank range?"

"In SS training," Rittenbach answered. "The SS prides itself on being Godless. It recognizes no authority other than the orders of the *Führer*. Its self-appointed task is racial warfare."

"Does *Herr General* think a man is thinking about the survival of his race when he blows the brains out of a baby's head?!" Albrowski had raised his voice again, and Rittenbach instantly stopped. Albrowski dropped his voice. "*Herr General*, protectiveness toward women, respect for old people, and love for children are basic human instincts. What does it take to suck the most elemental feelings of sympathy out of a young man?"

"Maybe not as much as you think," Rittenbach countered. "Murders are committed in every society. If all the moral force of church, law and society is not enough to prevent such things, what can you expect from men given justification and orders for murder? We should not be so surprised when men turn back into the sadistic, bloodthirsty beasts they really are."

"Is *Herr General's* opinion of mankind really so low?" Albrowski was astounded.

"After what I've just seen, yes," Rittenbach told him. "The only difference between the young men who committed that bestial atrocity and our own troops is a few months of training and service. We must be aware of how easily and quickly troops can be turned into murderers. The threads that hold them to civilized behavior are—it seems—very thin indeed. Let that be a lesson to us." After a moment to let this sink in, he urged Albrowski, "Go on. How did you find out what happened?"

Albrowski hesitated a moment and then resumed his narrative. "We called some of the civilians over and asked them what had happened. They were reluctant to talk, so I got angry and accused them of doing it. They denied it and insisted we had done it. I got even angrier and pointed out that we had never been here before. Eventually we got out of them that the massacre had occurred in late November. By then the front was almost to Moscow and the only troops operating back here were SS *Einsatzkommandos*. According to the inhabitants they only stayed three days, just long enough to round up and kill the entire Jewish population of Zubovo."

They had reached the HQ building again, and Beier came out. "*Herr General,* a meeting of all divisional First General Staff Officers has been called by the Army. I have ordered my own horse saddled for Major Frhr. v. Feldburg."

Rittenbach nodded and the next thing Philip knew, he was mounting the unfamiliar grey gelding.

Six hours later, Philip was delivered back at his own HQ with the latest Army instructions in his head. Inside the HQ, he went directly to the operations room to write down the verbal orders just received and start converting them into divisional orders. He did not want to give his mind time to think about the massacre of the Jews at Zubovo. He was consciously repressing the memory and thoughts of it. All day he had managed to tell himself: you can't deal with that now.

In the operations room he found Major Kellermann and briefed him concerning the new orders. The others slowly gathered around, and Philip went to the

map to outline the reallocation of the front sectors. 144th ID had been transferred
to another Corps. "Where's the *Herr General*?" Philip asked generally. "Isn't he
back yet?"

"He's been here for hours but hasn't shown himself. He seemed in a bad
mood." Kellermann waited expectantly, obviously hoping Philip would enlighten
them. Philip just bent over the map again and continued as if there had been no
interruption. He couldn't resist remarking, "I'm afraid the Army does not share
your complacency about the Soviet inability to field new divisions, Herr Blankenstein."

"Major v. Feldburg?" *Leutnant* König called from the doorway.

Philip stood upright. "*Ja, bitte*?"

His adjutant gestured for him to come out into the hall. With a slight frown
of annoyance, Philip left his colleagues and went into the hall. König backed up
as he came, drawing him farther out of the room into the dark of the unlit corridor. "*Herr Major*, the *Herr General* would like to see you in his quarters."

"Fine; why didn't you just say so?"

König looked embarrassed, "It's—the *Herr General*—I think—it sounds as if
he's been—well—drinking." König hardly dared meet Philip's eyes as he made
this unheard-of accusation. Rittenbach had never before shown an inclination to
heavy drinking. In fact, Philip could not remember seeing him take more than a
single shot of vodka, very occasionally, to warm up.

"Does anyone else know?"

"Dammerow." That was the General's ADC.

"But not the others?"

König shook his head. Philip went back to the doorway and announced he
was going to report to the General, adding that he was not to be disturbed unless
it was absolutely necessary. He saw the exchanged look and knew that they would
soon be engaged in all sorts of wild speculation about what was going on. Outside
the General's door, Philip took a deep breath and then knocked.

"Who's there?" the General snarled in one of his most unfriendly tones.

"Feldburg."

"Come in!"

But when Philip tried the door, he found it bolted. He heard Rittenbach
approach from the other side and shoot the bolt back. Suddenly he was standing
in the door, bowing Philip in like an obsequious host. "Heartily welcome, my
dear Baron." He gestured for Philip to take a seat and flung the door shut behind
him, bolting it again. The room was dark—the shutters and curtains shut. A bot-

tle stood beside the heavy reading chair. "Please, please, sit down, Dear Feldburg. May I offer you some cognac?" Rittenbach was still playing host.

"I have some new orders from Army, *Herr General*; we've—"

"Damn Army!"

Not knowing how to reply to this, Philip stood mutely where he was until Rittenbach came toward him, pressed a glass into his hand and poured the cognac for him. "Do you for a moment think," Rittenbach started, standing so close that his liquor-laden breath was warm on Philip's face, "that that ass-licker Model would lift a finger to protest the murder of Jews? Never! The only thing that matters to that lackey is the favor of an Austrian corporal! I spent all afternoon trying to word a protest strong enough for what we saw." He gestured angrily toward his desk. "Do you think any words are strong enough? No. First, there are no words, and second, even if there were, Model wouldn't listen. It took me hours, but I finally realized an hour or so ago that all my efforts were pointless. Nothing I say will have the slightest impact on Model. Do you know why? Because Model doesn't give a damn about the Jews, or International Law, or God, or even his own troops, because his *Führer* doesn't give a damn about any of those things!"

Philip drank his cognac and held out his glass for more. Rittenbach poured obligingly. Then he returned to his chair and seated himself comfortably. Philip offered, "I could report via the General Staff." Since the establishment of the General Staff, staff officers had possessed the right to report behind the backs of their superiors to the next senior General Staff officer. Over the years, there had been more than one incident where a disagreement between commanding generals and their staff officers had resulted in the commander getting sacked. Philip did not have to report to Model but to his Chief of Staff, a much more reasonable and decent man.

"I thought of that, too," Rittenbach admitted, "but then I realized it wouldn't do any good. All protest is pointless—"

"It worked in Poland," Philip started. "Blaskowitz—"

"I know what Blaskowitz did—and it did not work. It only resulted in the control of occupied territory being removed from Army to SS jurisdiction. Now we have responsibility for only the combat zones themselves—and behind our backs the *Einsatzgruppen* roam at will, slaughtering whole villages. Protest is pointless, my dear Feldburg, because the Supreme Commander himself has ordered these murders, and our protests only make us incompetent and contemptible in his eyes. Our protests have made us weaker, not stronger."

Philip started to speak, but Rittenbach held up his hand and stopped him. "Look at the Commissar Order! If we had protested, it would only have resulted in the SS being asked to come forward, find the Commissars, and 'take care' of them. Instead, we have the responsibility for 'taking care' of them ourselves—which at least gives us the chance to remove their insignia and report to higher HQ that we 'didn't find' any Commissars. If that starts to arouse too much suspicion, we can always say 'x number of Commissars taken care of'—who ever bothers with a body count? Or we can, as I know some commanders have done, report the total number of Soviet officers killed in combat as 'Commissars taken care of.' Nobody checks the graves to see if the corpses wear the right insignia. All in all," he reflected, his eyes sharp and focused, "it seems to me we would have done better to pretend ideological enthusiasm."

"We can't!" Philip burst out. "That would mean the betrayal of our entire value system! It would be an insult to our nation, our people, our uniform! It would mean dishonor—"

"*Ja, ja,*" Rittenbach waved him silent. "Honor. But what have we left of our honor now?" He let it sink in. "You heard what Albrowski said: those people didn't even notice the difference between our uniforms and theirs. Do you think anyone else in the world will? Do you think they should?"

"I don't know, but I know the difference, and as long as I live by my own code of honor I can stand before my God tonight with a clean conscience."

"Can you?" Rittenbach asked earnestly, and then continued slowly and deliberately, "I envy you." He left Philip in discomfort for a moment and then continued, "I keep thinking that our hand-washing turns us into accomplices."

"But if *Herr General* is right and protest is futile, what else can we do?" Philip sank onto the chair behind him as a sense of despair closed over him.

"What if we volunteered to 'take care' of the Jewish population—just as we do the Commissars?" Rittenbach asked, a smile playing around his lips as he swirled his cognac in his glass.

Philip was horrified—but at the same time he could follow Rittenbach's logic. That gave him pause. Then he shook his head. "It wouldn't work. The Party bosses may be too cowardly to come to the front to check on the Commissars, but they'd have no such hesitation about checking on our 'success' in the villages far behind the lines. We'd have to produce bodies."

"Perhaps. But wouldn't it be better to sacrifice some to save the rest?"

"What does *Herr General* mean?" Philip asked, not wanting to believe what he thought Rittenbach was suggesting.

"Wouldn't it be better to kill 50 Jews and let 50 go free than to 'preserve our honor' by letting the SS kill all 100?"

"Could you do that?!" Philip demanded, so shocked that he forgot to use the third person. "Herd helpless people together, old and young, and then gun them down? My God! They can't even all have died at once. They would have had to—" Philip downed his cognac, reached for the bottle and poured himself another glass. All the thoughts he had been suppressing bubbled up into his consciousness and crowded in on him. He would not be free of them now.

"No," Rittenbach answered simply. "No, I would not be able to do that—or even order it. I am old and foolish. I'm too weak—but let's hope others among us are not so squeamish."

"We're out of cognac and I'm not drunk yet."

"Don't worry, I have another bottle."

✳   ✳   ✳   ✳

Berlin
March 1942

As Alix turned the corner on the landing leading up to her flat, she caught sight of a figure sitting before her door. She caught her breath in surprise and then the man stood up, towering over her. Six feet of lean body, dirty greatcoat, muddy, cracked and near-ruined boots. Alix let out an inarticulate, half-suppressed cry and took the stairs two at a time to fling herself into the outstretched arms of her brother.

"Stefan! When did you get here? Why didn't you cable? How did you get leave? You haven't gone AWOL, have you? God, it's wonderful to see you!" She looked straight into his face. He had aged years. He was too thin. His skin was rough and dry, his face lined. But he was alive, and he was here. "Here; get your bag out of the way so I can let us in." Over her shoulder to the door opposite she called, "It's my little brother, Frau Bubner!" Then she had the door to her own apartment open, and she and Stefan crashed inside together.

Stefan gave her another hug, and then Alix ordered him to take his coat off and stay awhile. "Or do you want to go straight home to Mother?"

"No, I thought it would be good to see you alone first. We can call Mother in an hour or two." He paused. "Did you tell Mother—I mean, did you show her that letter?"

"Stefan! How could I? Soaking feet that froze inside your boots. Throwing away your MGs. No leave—you aren't really AWOL, are you?"

Stefan shook his head. "No. They lifted the whole 'dishonor' thing."

"Who did? When?"

"*Feldmarschall* v. Bock as soon as he took over from Reichenau, but mostly it was Manstein. Manstein came out to the division and called all surviving officers of the 46th together. He told us that even though he disagreed with *Graf* Sponeck's decision tactically, he still considered the decision legitimate. He wanted us to know that he had not been informed of *Graf* Sponeck's trial in advance, that he had been denied the right to testify when he learned of it, and that he was 100% opposed to the verdict and sentence. Manstein said that he would make every effort to see that *Graf* Sponeck is rehabilitated 'as soon as the atmosphere in *Führer* HQ allows it'—whatever that means." Stefen gave his sister a questioning look.

Alix shook her head. "How should I know? I have as little to do with *Führer* HQ as possible. Go on. What did Manstein do? Let some of you go on leave?"

"Exactly. He even gave out some medals."

"Oh, Stefan! I'm sorry. Congratulations!" Stefan was wearing the EKII. She gave him another kiss. "Come on! Let's have a bottle of *Sekt* together or something." She led him to the kitchen. "Are you hungry?" she asked over her shoulder, and before he could answer, "When did you get to Berlin?"

"Oh, about three o'clock—"

"Stefan!" Alix spun around, disappointed to have missed four whole hours with him. "Why didn't you come to the Bendlerstrasse? I could have introduced you to everyone!"

Stefan pulled out one of the kitchen chairs and settled into it with his legs outstretched. "I did go to the Bendlerstrasse. I stood on the far side of the street for at least ten minutes watching all the generals and colonels going in and out, and decided I didn't want to make all those salutes."

"*Ach*, Stefan!" Alix looked at him admonishingly. "I so want you to meet General Olbricht, and Annie Lerche, of course."

"I know. But what's wrong with tomorrow when I can go in civvies?"

"All right," Alix agreed readily, knowing that nothing would bring back the lost hours. "Now, did you want something to eat?"

"No; Mother will stuff me. Is that apple juice?" He had caught sight of something in the cupboard as she opened it to get glasses.

"Yes. Do you want some?"

"I'd sell my soul for some!" She put the juice and a glass before him, and Stefan started talking as he poured for himself. "Alix, you can't imagine what heaven it is to be here! Apple juice and balconies with flowers, and girls—when did the skirts get so short? It would be scandalous if it weren't so delightful. You know what I thought? If it's a nice day tomorrow, we could go to the zoo. I know it sounds silly, but—"

"Stefan, I have to work tomorrow ..."

"But you must get a lunch break, and the zoo is just five minutes away by bus. We could meet at the Elephant Gate and afterwards, I promise, I'll come back and meet your General. But now, tell me about your baron instead. I always knew you'd do well, regardless of your pretensions of socialism!"

"What makes you think that just because he's a baron, he's a good catch?" Alix challenged.

"Well, General Staff, major, EKI ..."

"That sounds disgustingly militaristic! Where is all your liberal idealism?"

Stefan laughed. "In the closet at home. Tomorrow in civvies I'll be myself again. Don't you have a photo of him?"

Alix readily fetched the few snapshots she had of Philip. She didn't like any of them, she told Stefan; none did him justice.

"Does he have a sister?" Stefan asked hopefully.

"She's married."

"Don't you know any girl you could introduce me to?"

"You're too young."

"Thank you, beloved sister; but if I'm old enough to die for *Führer* and Fatherland, I'm old enough to fall in love."

"I meant for my friends," she explained, as she started running cold water over the bottle of champagne to cool it down. She also launched into a subject near to her heart that she didn't dare discuss with anyone but Stefan. "Mother wants grandchildren. She wants me to stop working after I'm married."

"Do you want to work? I thought you said the work was boring?"

"Yes and no. The work itself is boring—typing, typing, typing—but I do get to hear and see a lot of fascinating developments. If I swallow my pride and look at it as an opportunity to learn things, it's actually quite exciting. Besides, can you really picture me as a housewife? It's a good thing Mother never gets here. She'd be appalled to see I haven't washed the windows since last fall!"

"That is not the point," Stefan countered. "The point is whether Freiherr v. Feldburg would be scandalized by the state of your windows." He turned to look at them, shaking his head in mock disgust.

"Mother says I'm marrying 'under false pretenses' if I let Philip think I'm a good housewife, when all the time I can hardly fry an egg. She wants me to settle down and learn to cook properly and all that." Stefan rolled his eyes sympatheti- cally. He knew how hard Alix had struggled to avoid being turned into a housewife. "So I wrote to Philip and said: Look, I'm a terrible cook and housewife. Do you still want me?'"

"And?"

Alix grinned at her younger brother. "He said: if he was concerned about cooking and cleaning, he'd hire someone—but he didn't intend to marry them."

When he finished laughing, Stefan remarked, "Money is wonderful. I hope we win the war, or it might not be that simple."

"I'll worry about that tomorrow."

"You're right: enjoy the war, the peace is going to be terrible! I'll get that." He took the bottle of champagne from her and opened it over the sink. Alix held the glasses ready, and they lost very little.

After another hour or so, their consciences got the better of them. They called Frau v. Rantzow, told her Stefan had "just that minute" arrived, and set off for home.

*   *   *   *

Valognes, France
April 1942

For her 20th birthday Yvette asked Dieter to take her to dinner and dancing at "Le Chateau," a very exclusive restaurant housed in an eighteenth-century manor house. She expressly asked Gabrielle and Christian to come with them.

Christian and Gabrielle were fighting more and more these days. Gabrielle openly flirted with other men, usually higher-ranking officers, but that did not stop her from letting Christian support her. Christian complained more and more about the expense of keeping her, and the whole squadron knew that he spent many off-duty nights in the mess these days. But this balmy spring night had started out well, because Yvette's happiness bubbled over and infected both Gabrielle and Christian.

Yvette had never looked prettier. She wore red lipstick and nail polish and a wine-red velvet gown that clung without being tight. Christian noticed for the first time that she was fuller-figured than she had been, which made her more attractive in his eyes. But what made her most attractive was the way she still looked at Dieter. They danced almost every dance together, and Yvette turned down every attempt to cut in on her, even from a colonel with a Knight's Cross and oak leaves. Christian was the only other man whom she let dance with her, and that only once. "I can tell you our secret," she told him smiling as they spun slowly to the strains of a Strauss waltz. "I'm going to have a baby!"

She was so obviously happy about this that—despite all his own qualms about the implications—Christian could only congratulate her. But his doubt and worry were reflected on his face, causing Yvette to lean closer and whisper in his ear, "We found a priest willing to marry us secretly. My baby will not be born a bastard."

Christian twirled her to the music with a wider smile. "A pleasure to make your acquaintance, Frau Möller."

Yvette beamed back at him.

Gabrielle, meanwhile, was dancing with the colonel with the Knight's Cross and oak leaves, but Christian knew the colonel moved from mistress to mistress rapidly. If Gabrielle was stupid enough to fall for him, she'd only come crawling back to him in a month or two. Maybe it would even do her good to get discarded, Christian told himself, sitting alone at the table and watching her lean her head on the colonel's shoulder.

At the end of the dance, the colonel brought her back to Christian with his arm around her satin-clad waist. "I really must congratulate you, *Herr Oberleutnant*; you have excellent taste. May I join you?" He didn't wait for the junior officer to reply, but pulled out the chair vacated by the still dancing Dieter and sat down. He took out cigarettes and offered them around. He lit Gabrielle's for her gallantly. "What Group are you with?"

"JG 23."

"Aha." The contempt of the bomber pilot for fighters was very obvious. "Many claims?" the bomber pilot asked, blowing smoke toward the ceiling.

"Enough."

"How many is that?" he asked with raised eyebrows, letting his eyes scan Christian's empty chest contemptuously.

Dieter and Yvette came up behind him, and the *Oberst* glanced up with apparently no intention of vacating his seat. Then he saw Dieter's face and sprang to his feet, somewhat embarrassed.

"Thank you, *Herr Oberst*," Dieter said, politely but frostily.

The colonel bowed to Gabrielle with a smile and asked her for another dance. Gabrielle went off with him without a second's hesitation.

Just after midnight, they left the restaurant. Gabrielle opted to stay longer, her colonel promising to bring her home. Christian refused to make a scene, bowing to his rival as graciously as he could. Then in a casual tone to Gabrielle he added,

"I'll give notice on the apartment, then. You can have 'till the end of the week to move your things out." He turned and walked away without a backward glance.

At the car, he offered to drive. He was more sober than usual, and that way Dieter and Yvette could cuddle in the back seat. Although the night was chilly, he asked if he could leave the top down. Yvette, snuggled happily inside Dieter's greatcoat, agreed.

Christian pulled out of the drive, the gravel crunching, and turned onto the tree-lined country road. He stepped on the gas, accelerating as if he were taking off in his fighter. The road curved around toward a slight rise. He gave more gas, mentally lifting his sights toward a bomber flown by the colonel with the Knight's Cross. The car topped the rise and almost immediately afterwards the road was blocked by a barricade. Christian slammed on the brakes and automatically ducked down under the windshield. The brakes grabbed unevenly. The car swung to the left and smashed diagonally into the barricade, the right fender crumpling against the heavy tree trunk.

The punching sound of objects hitting the left-hand side of the car made Yvette scream. Dieter had already flung her down onto the floor of the car and was covering her with his body. Christian kicked open the right-hand door and dived out of the car, drawing his sidearm. Two more crashes came, and Christian fired from cover at something moving near the trees without being able to see exactly what it was.

The crack of his pistol made two men take flight. They ran stupidly away from the cover of the trees and into an open field. Christian took aim, his arm outstretched. He had been an enthusiastic hunter ever since childhood and was a first-class shot. He took his time. The clouds that had been partially blocking the moon slipped off to one side, and suddenly he could see his targets brilliantly. He at once bent his elbow so the pistol pointed into the air, slipped on the safety and put it back into his belt. "Just a couple of kids," he told Dieter, who was gazing up at him.

While Christian inspected the damage done to the car, Dieter extricated himself from Yvette's arms and clambered out. There were a half-dozen dents in the left side of the car, and the fist-sized rocks that had caused them lay in the road. The fender was bent in from the collision with the tree trunk, but otherwise no real damage had been done.

The two officers together pulled the tree trunk and various branches out of the way and then climbed back into the car. Dieter took a shivering and shaken Yvette into his arms, while Christian started the engine without problems.

"Shit!" Christian exclaimed vehemently. "No one is going to believe there was a barrier in the road! No doubt I'll be accused of drunk driving and charged for the damages!" He was trying to ease the tension by joking, but it didn't work. All three of them knew that this was just the beginning. The hostility to the Occupation Forces was only going to increase from here.

CHAPTER 20

▼

Yukov, Soviet Union
April 1942

General Model came, as he so often did, unexpectedly and enraged. Ritttenbach considered the Army Commander crude, brutal and self-indulgent. Philip knew of more than one incident where Model had ripped the medals and rank insignia from officers, NCOs or soldiers for some petty fault. He was feared and hated by his subordinates, and apparently that was the way he wanted it.

Now Generals Model and Rittenbach were at each other's throats, and the staff sat helplessly in the outer office. They held their breath and avoided each other's eyes as the generals argued audibly in the adjoining room. While no one could hear exactly what was being said, the intensity of the dispute was obvious.

Before being told to leave the room, Philip had pointed out that the division's strength had fallen from 14,000 to just over 5,000 in the last six months. Model had screamed at him that this was not the point, and Rittenbach had replied caustically, "What else is the point? You can't honestly believe that we, with our decimated divisions, can conquer a continent?"

"That is defeatism! To doubt victory is treason!" Model shouted back.

"This has nothing to do with treason, but with reason," Rittenbach scoffed, and at that point Model had ordered both Philip and his own ADC to leave the room.

Model's ADC had a miserable job. He went to await his General beside their car. Philip joined the rest of Rittenbach's staff in the operations room, and his sense of foreboding grew with each passing minute. Unable to concentrate, he cleaned his glasses on his handkerchief and looked blindly at the maps.

The argument came to an abrupt end. The shouting stopped. Those waiting in suspense exchanged a look. The door opened and the two generals appeared, stony-faced. The junior officers sprang respectfully and expectantly to their feet. Model strode through them, shouting for his ADC, as if the room were empty. Rittenbach watched him go and with a dry "Feldburg," he returned to his office. Philip followed unwillingly, dreading what he was about to hear. He closed the door.

Rittenbach stood with his back to him, and Philip waited wordlessly until at last Rittenbach turned around. Philip found himself checking to see if Rittenbach's *Pour le Mérite* still hung at his neck. It did. Evidently Model's anger had not reached the requisite level for medal stripping.

"I've been relieved of my command," Rittenbach announced simply, and Philip caught his breath. It was the worst scenario possible. "You can expect my replacement in the next 24 to 36 hours."

"If this has anything to do with the *Herr General's* protest over—"

Rittenbach waved him silent and shook his head. "It has virtually nothing to do with that; that was just the proverbial straw that broke the camel's back."

"But there is not one single decision *Herr General* has made since I was appointed Ia of this division that I did not support. Any criticism of the command of this division is criticism of me, as well as of *Herr General.*"

Rittenbach smiled wanly and shook his head. "My dear Feldburg, General Staff Officers have no names, remember? To the commander go both the fame and the shame. Besides, we're not still serving in the Royal Prussian Army."

"*Herr General.*" Philip stood at attention and spoke very precisely and emphatically. "Whether I have a name or not, I supported every decision you made. If General Model feels they were incorrect, then I must also resign—"

"You'll do nothing of the sort! You'll remain at your post and serve this division and your new commander with as much loyalty and skill as you have served me! If anyone had wanted your removal, they would have asked for it!"

Philip looked so resentful that Rittenbach relented. His tone became fatherly. "Don't take it so personally. This has nothing to do with military competence. It is part of a wider purge that started, God knows, with Schleicher and Hammerstein, Fritsch and Brauchitsch. They don't want old generals like me anymore. We come with too much baggage like 'decency' and 'honor' and 'legality.' And, oh yes, let's not forget we've 'failed to grasp the spirit of the times' and don't appreciate 'the *Führer's* unequaled genius.'"

"A political dismissal," Philip summarized.

"Not exactly. I'm accused of lacking 'offensive spirit' and 'vigor.' I'm being relieved and sent back to the leadership reserve. Possibly I'll be given another command at a later date. Maybe I'll be given some new assignment like training female auxiliaries …" Rittenbach choked on his own bitterness and fell silent. After a long pause he resumed in a resigned tone, "Maybe it is all for the best. After all, I'm tired." For the first time Philip heard not just physical exhaustion in his voice, but defeat. "More than once during this past six months I've been prepared to die or be taken prisoner. But after 35 years of military service, I never thought I'd simply be discarded like an old coat."

Philip hesitated, but then—unable to think of anything clever—he said honestly, "*Herr General* will always be an example of a good commander, which I will try to emulate as long as I wear this uniform."

Rittenbach seemed to consider this and then he nodded. "Thank you. I'm honored. Now we must each do our duty as it is assigned to us."

Rittenbach's replacement was *Generalleutnant* Wittig. A man a good five years younger than his predecessor, he exuded vigor and self-confidence. His first order was to remove the HQ from the somewhat dilapidated State Bank building where Rittenbach had located it. The HQ was relocated in a spacious and elegant villa on the edge of town, reputed to have once been the home of a Soviet Secret Police chief. Philip pointed out that Rittenbach had intentionally avoided the villa because it was such an obvious choice and would thereby invite air and partisan attack.

Wittig brushed the objection aside with contempt. "I'm not afraid of the Red Air Force, much less partisans."

The operations room was set up in the billiard room. The maps were tacked onto the green felt table. General Wittig spent several hours studying the division's situation on his own before calling Philip in to him.

"I want to know where the division stood at the start of the Soviet offensive last December."

Philip cast him a quick, questioning look and then wordlessly pulled out a larger-scale map showing all of the western Soviet Union. "Here."

"And now we're here." Wittig himself found Yukov on the new map and jabbed his finger at it.

"That's right. On December 6, Army Group Center's front ran roughly like this." Philip drew it for him with his finger. "And now it runs so." Again he drew the front with his finger.

Wittig stood up with a disgusted click of his tongue. "And all while under orders not to retreat, regardless of the cost."

"Correct," Philip agreed. "*Feldmarschall* v. Bock wanted to withdraw to positions running along here." Philip drew this line on the map. "Instead we were ordered to stand and die. You can see for yourself that the result has been to all intents and purposes the same—except that the order to stand cost over 235,000 German officers and soldiers their lives." Philip studiously avoided any trace of emotion as he spoke.

"So you disapprove of the *Führer* Order," Wittig concluded with a sour twist of his lips.

"I disapprove of the futile waste of lives."

"If the *Führer's* orders had been properly carried out, there would have been no waste of lives. We would have held our positions before Moscow and been in a position to take it this spring. Instead, as a result of this shameful incompetence—if not outright disloyalty—the *Führer* has ordered the entire Army Group to go on the defensive. He will seek a decision in the South instead. Did you know that?"

Philip had not known it, but he considered it good news. Maybe he would live to see his wedding after all. Wittig, however, clearly did not share his sense of gratitude for being out of the main theater of operations. Philip glanced at him, noting that he wore no more medals than Philip did himself. In his head he heard Rittenbach's scoffing voice say: "sore throat." To Wittig he remarked in his most polite tone of voice, "I deeply regret that *Herr General* will as a result have fewer opportunities to earn the Knight's Cross."

*   *   *   *

Berlin
April 1942

Alexandra had been left with the responsibility for all the formalities of preparing her wedding, even if there was no set date. She had to file their documents (including proof of "Aryan" descent) with the *Standesamt* (County Clerk). She had to be sure that the impending wedding was officially announced without a specific date. She had to see that invitations were printed up with a blank for the date to be written in by hand. She had to find a variety of hotels with suitable rooms for the reception in hope that one or the other would be available on short notice. Et cetera, et cetera, et cetera.

Quite aside from the usual strain of trying to please everyone (including a mother-in-law she had never met and could only reach by telephone), Alexandra found the entire business of organizing her wedding emotionally exhausting. She couldn't overcome the superstitious fear that the more she prepared, the more likely it was that the wedding would never take place.

She finally wrote a letter to Philip in which she confessed she didn't want to plan anything at all. When he returned to Berlin, they could improvise, she suggested. But she ripped the letter up. From his letters, it seemed that Philip liked hearing about the wedding plans—as if hearing about the plans made him believe it would happen. As a result, Alix gave priority to everything that Philip could be consulted on and kept putting off finding a dress.

Her mother nagged her about this increasingly, but it was Lotte who finally took things in hand. "Alix," she lectured over tea at Dimitri's, "I'm not going to just sit here and watch you ruin your own wedding. I mean, if I'm to be your witness, I insist on you wearing something that won't disgrace me. Eberhard will be with me, after all. Now, I won't take 'no' for an answer. I've arranged for one of the dressmakers who design the opera costumes to show you some patterns and material."

"Lotte! I'm marrying a reactionary Catholic baron! I can't appear in an opera costume!"

"Of course not. Trust me. This dressmaker is a genius. Besides, you could never afford the material we get allocated. Imported Japanese silk and French brocades. Really exquisite!"

"Won't you get in trouble for letting me have some of it?"

"Nonsense, everyone does it—at least all the officials from the Propaganda Ministry. No one will even notice."

Three days later she met with the dressmaker and let herself be talked into a gown in French Empire style, all in white on white. The price was more than two months' salary, but she didn't have the nerve to bargain. It was Stefan's second-to-the-last night in Berlin and she couldn't bear to be apart from him, even if she did have to work the next day. She rushed out of the dressmaker's and ran to catch the *S-Bahn*. At S-Bahnhof Grünewald, she missed her bus and had to walk the rest of the way. She was late, of course, but Helga assured her it was all right. "Your stepfather isn't home yet. He called to say he'd be late."

Frau v. Rantzow had heard her daughter arrive and came out of the library/study. "Good that you came by, Alix. I've been going through the guest list again, and we just can't leave out the Heidenbluts. Too many of your father's other colleagues will have invitations. They are sure to hear about it."

Alexandra bristled instantly. "I really don't care if they know they weren't invited. If they come, they will only find fault with everything anyway." The real problem was that these convinced Nazis would inhibit everyone else.

"But your father fears Hr. Dr. Heidenblut could be promoted shortly. If he becomes more powerful, it could even be bad for your father's career if we are seen to be excluding him. It's not as though two people more or less will make any difference to the budget."

"No; the point is, I don't want to have to watch everything I say at my own wedding," Alix answered hotly. Choosing friends on the basis of what might be 'good' for her stepfather's career was an old wound; Alix had always objected to it as hypocritical. Fortunately, the door banged open and Rudi burst in breathlessly. He was still in his soccer uniform, which was filthy, and his hair was standing on end with sweat. "We won!" he announced loudly. "3 to 2!"

Stefan was behind him, grinning with brotherly pride. Apparently he had attended Rudi's game. At the sight of Alix, he came and gave her a hug, while his mother exclaimed in horror about all the mud Rudi was tracking into the front hall. She made Rudi remove his shoes and sent him to change as rapidly as possible before his father saw him. Just minutes later, Hr. v. Rantzow arrived and Helga announced dinner.

Over dinner Rudi described the game, play by play, to an indulgent mother and sisters. Then Frau v. Rantzow launched into more wedding issues, including whether Grete should sing. She had recently been at another wedding, and the bride's sisters had all sung a pretty little song. Grete pleaded with Alix not to make her do this. Stefan noticed that his stepfather had hardly said a word all evening, and interrupted his mother and sister's squabbling. "*Vati*, is something bothering you?"

"No, of course not." Herr v. Rantzow dismissed him with an irritable wave of his hand. He reached for his wine, avoiding Stefan's eyes. "Just a busy day," he insisted.

"That's no reason for sulking," Stefan teased.

"You'll never make a diplomat with that approach," his stepfather retorted, with a warning glance over the rim of his wineglass.

"I concede I've been schooled more in the direct approach lately," Stefan admitted, unperturbed by his stepfather's tone. "I've also been taught tenacity— or the Red Army would be in Berlin by now. So do tell us what's bothering you. Why were you so late?"

Herr v. Rantzow took a deep breath. "Since you insist: it is the situation in the Pacific."

"But we've—or our allies the Japanese have—just won a spectacular victory!" Rudi announced, anxious to show off to Stefan how much he knew about military affairs. "A whole American army on the Philippines has just surrendered. More than 50,000 Americans were made prisoners."

"Exactly," Rudi's father snapped. "This means the Americans have no bases in the Pacific west of Hawaii. No place to refuel their ships. And who can guess what psychological impact this blow will have on the morale of a luxury-loving people like the Americans?"

"You make it sound as if the Americans were our allies!" Rudi protested, completely confused.

"I wish they were! Or at least that they weren't our enemies. Never in my life have I witnessed greater stupidity, greater madness, than the declaration of war on the United States!" This burst out of Herr v. Rantzow in an exceptionally loud voice. He was himself surprised what a relief it was to finally say out loud what had been whispered for months. But now the floodgates were open and he continued in an angry rush, "How could anyone be so stupid as to declare war—without the slightest provocation!—on the most powerful industrial nation on earth! This one act of madness has doomed us to defeat!"

Alix listened almost in amusement. Her stepfather had not once been willing to admit that Hitler was personally to blame for the disastrous military decisions taken over the last year—they were the fault of the "the generals." When it came to foreign policy, however, it did not occur to him to blame "the diplomats." Hitler alone was to blame.

Rudi couldn't believe what he was hearing. "But the Americans were just defeated," he insisted, confused.

"No," his father turned to him in a suddenly cold and precise tone. "The Americans suffered a setback. They lost 50,000 men. How many have we lost in Russia? Five times that many!—and with a population many times smaller than that of America. What the Americans suffered in the Philippines is not—by any means—a defeat. It was a setback which will only prolong this war. I fear it will last for years now."

"How can you say that? We're going to beat the Russians this summer, and the Japanese will take care of the Americans, and then the British will give up."

"You don't know what you're talking about," Rudi's father told him contemptuously.

"I do know what I'm talking about," said Rudi, raising his voice. "And you know I'm right. You shouldn't be saying these defeatist things—"

"I'll say whatever I like in my own house," Herr v. Rantzow told his son, in a tone bordering on a threat. He put down his knife and fork and glowered at his impudent offspring.

"It's my house, too!" Rudi flung back. "I have a right to say what I think, too!"

"You don't think at all," his father sneered. "You say whatever the Minister for Public Enlightenment and Propaganda, that maniac Goebbels, tells you to think."

"No, I don't! I just believe in the *Führer*. He's the greatest genius of all time, and I know I can trust him! Whatever he does is right, even if we can't understand it, because we're not as intelligent—"

"Don't talk such rubbish at my dinner table. It makes me sick." Herr v. Rantzow picked up his knife and fork again with the intention of resuming his meal. His son, however, was bright red with agitation. He burst out furiously, "It's not rubbish! Look at all the *Führer* has done for our Fatherland! Why won't you admit it?" Rudi was desperate for some concession. The contradiction between his father's view of the world and the picture presented everywhere else was increasingly unbearable.

But Herr v. Rantzow's patience was also at an end. He snapped back, his knife and fork still poised at ready, "Because your *Führer* is nothing but the bastard son of an Austrian customs official with a demonic gift for rabble rousing. We would all be better off if the *Führer* were shot!"

Stefan and Alix both recoiled, and Frau v. Rantzow was horrified. She cried out, "Albrecht!"

Rudi leapt to his feet. "That's treason!" he shouted. "I should go to the police and report you!"

There was a stunned, deathly silence. Then, without another word, Herr v. Rantzow stood and left the dining room. A moment later they heard the front door to the house slam shut. The others stared in horror at Rudi.

Rudi looked around the table desperately. His expression was no longer angry, but frightened. "I didn't mean it!" he whined. "Honestly, I wouldn't do that. You know I wouldn't do it." He begged for understanding.

Frau v. Rantzow jumped up and ran after her husband. They heard her go out the front door.

The four children sat facing each other, the other three still staring at Rudi. He repeated miserably, "I didn't mean it," and sank back into his chair.

"But you said it," Alexandra observed dryly, "and it *has* been done—at least the papers report that children have turned in their own parents for 'treasonous' remarks."

Stefan looked at her, scandalized, but he said nothing.

Rudi protested again, "I would never do anything like that, NEVER. It's just that he's so unfair!"

Alix sighed. Rudi was just a boy. Stefan hadn't been easy at fourteen either, and although Alix had no use for Rudi's naive politics, she could sympathize with his frustration in dealing with his father. She stood, and without comment took her plate and glass to the kitchen. Grete leaped up to do the same.

In the kitchen they found Helga red-eyed and terrified. "Oh, Miss Alix! He won't really report your father, will he?"

Alix patted the maid on her shoulder. "No, Helga, he won't." She was very sure of this.

Back in the dining room, Stefan was talking to Rudi in a calm, soothing man-to-man tone. "… so you've got to think of this as a test, preparation for the future. No matter what he says, Rudi, just keep calm. Close your ears if you can. If you know you're right, then you don't have to say it—time will prove you right."

"*You* believe in the *Führer*, don't you, Stefan?" Rudi pleaded for reassurance.

Stefan took a deep breath and glanced at Alix. "Certainly; but I can't help thinking he made a terrible mistake in starting this war—and a worse one in invading the Soviet Union. You have to see it to believe it. Their reserves are endless. It just doesn't matter how many prisoners we take or how many men we kill—there are always more. More troops, more guns, more tanks, more planes."

"But their soldiers and tanks and planes aren't as good as ours!"

Stefan shook his head, "I'm not so sure, Rudi."

"You mean, you really think we could lose the war?" Rudi asked incredulously.

"Yes, I mean even that," Stefan confirmed seriously.

"But if we all work together. If the German people really get behind the *Führer*—instead of people like *Vati* always complaining and criticizing.…"

"It won't change the number of Russian tanks there are," Stefan told him gently. Rudi was speechless. He just couldn't grasp that his hero brother didn't think the same way his leaders and teachers said soldiers thought. The *Wehrmacht* wasn't allowed to doubt its own invincibility. "And you know," Stefan continued, conscious of the influence he had on his younger brother, "if there weren't informers and house searches without warrants and secret police and Concentration Camps, then maybe Father wouldn't be so critical."

"But there wouldn't be informers and secret police if there weren't so many people who were against the government. A government has to be able to protect itself against opponents. Good citizens have nothing to fear from the police and informers."

"Do you really believe that, Rudi? That no one is ever reported out of jealousy or hate or on the basis of a misunderstanding? You know, Rudi, I think a lot of people just want to be left alone to live their lives in peace—without worrying about being arrested by over-conscientious or hostile fellow citizens just because of something they said in a moment of weakness. You don't really think *Vati* wants Hitler dead, do you?"

"No, of course not; but that's not what the Gestapo and KZs are there for. They protect us from the real enemies of the State—the ones like the Communists and the Jews who want to destroy Germany. And before the Seizure of Power, everyone just fought with everyone else and there was chaos. Only the *Führer* got us all working together for the common good—now that the Jews and Communists are out of the way. And now we have leaders who show us all how to work for the common good instead of all the factions just following their own interests." Rudi had learned his lessons well.

"But what happens if the leaders are wrong?" Stefan insisted.

Rudi looked puzzled. That wasn't a question anyone asked in school or in the Hitler Youth. "But only the very best people should become leaders," he reminded Stefan.

"And is that always true? Didn't you tell me just the other night that some of the boys in your *Jungvolk* troop got promoted because their fathers are big shots in the Party?" He'd struck a nerve. In Rudi's eyes was the first inkling of doubt. "Besides, even the best people make mistakes sometimes."

"But we don't have a choice," Rudi tried again. "Democracy doesn't work."

"It works in other countries. The US, England, Switzerland, even France. Do you want me to believe that Germans are less intelligent than the English or Americans, Rudi?"

This time Rudi was out of answers.

CHAPTER 21

▼

Berlin
May 1942

After days of rain it was suddenly sunny and warm, and everyone in the Bendler-strasse seemed to be finding some excuse for getting away early. Annie Lerche already had her coat and hat on, but nevertheless she asked guiltily, "You don't mind me going a little early, do you? I've finished all the documents that General Olbricht gave me. They're ready for his signature."

Alix cast a wistful glance over her shoulder at the bright day outside, but what good was it to her with Philip still in Russia? Annie had a young man who wanted to take her to dinner. "It's fine. I'll see that he gets your signature folder."

Annie left without further urging and Alix tried to find her place again. The door to the General's office opened and Olbricht stood in it. He seemed to watch Alix work for a minute before addressing her. "Has Frl. Lerche left already?"

"Yes, *Herr General.* She had a date, and with the weather …"

"Quite all right," he assured her, but he seemed to hesitate before continuing. "And what are your plans this evening, Frl. v. Mollwitz?"

Alix shrugged and tried to smile. "Nothing particular."

"Would you care to join us for dinner? Eva just called and suggested I bring you along." Eva was Olbricht's wife. Alix had met her perhaps a half-dozen times over the last year, but always in a larger gathering with the entire staff of the AHA. This sounded like a more intimate affair.

"I'd be honored, *Herr General.*"

Olbricht smiled his more impish smile and added, "Wait 'till you find out what it may cost you."

"I beg your pardon, *Herr General?*"

"I have some extra work that I'd like you to handle—for officers only and all that."

"I see."

"I won't be able to leave for another hour or so. Maybe you could look through the files while you wait for me? That can wait until tomorrow." He indicated the document she was currently typing.

"As you wish, *Herr General.*"

He went back into his office and returned with a thick file folder. As he handed it to Alix, he seemed to look at her with particular intensity. "If you feel this extra work is too much, you must tell me. It is important material that, for reasons you will soon see, I'd rather not entrust to Frl Lerche. But you must be very honest with me. I will not think the less of you if you decline to take on this work." Alexandra assured him she would be honest with him, went to her desk, and opened the file folder. Olbricht returned to his office, closing the door behind him.

"Operation Valkyrie." Leave it to Hitler, she thought, to come up with these Wagnerian names. Who were they planning to attack this time? To her amazement, however, she soon discovered that these plans were *defensive*. More than that, they were for the defense of the *Reich*—a purely Home Army plan to put down a revolt by forced laborers or eliminate a threat by enemy paratroopers. In the current war situation it made no sense at all. The *Wehrmacht* was on the offensive everywhere. Neither England nor Russia had the air power to land paratroops in or near Berlin. Surely not even Stalin would be so foolhardy as to waste troops on a mission doomed to failure? The idea of a revolt by forced laborers was almost more absurd. The laborers at the factories were heavily guarded, and those who worked in private households were mostly frightened women and youngsters. Alexandra could imagine isolated uprisings against bad treatment or inadequate food or simply to run away, but not a coordinated attack against the German government that required a *Wehrmacht*—rather than a police—response.

Yet the plans were very meticulously worked out, with exact listings of the troops available in and around Berlin—from the training and replacement battalions of the Army to *Reichsbahn*, civil police, SS and SA units. There were maps showing the locations of the various ministries and the Party organizations. There was even a discussion of the various communications networks that needed to be protected. Alix became so engrossed in the plans that she started when Olbricht again opened his door and suggested she pack her things to accompany him.

Alexandra closed the Valkyrie folder and returned it to General Olbricht for him to lock in his own safe. "What do you think?" he asked as he spun the combination.

"It doesn't make any sense, *Herr General*. The alleged threat, I mean. Who ordered such a plan?"

"My dear Frl. v. Mollwitz, that is truly the beauty of it. The good Admiral Canaris managed to frighten our beloved *Führer* into requesting these plans himself. *Generaloberst* Fromm, anxious as always to outdo his rival Himmler, instantly volunteered to draw up the plans—by which, of course, he meant that I was to work out details. For which, I admit, I have not shown the *Generaloberst* sufficient gratitude." Olbricht sounded sincerely delighted rather than irritated, and Alexandra understood none of it.

"But it is a terrible waste of time. Who do you have working out these plans?"

"Major Lubben, at the moment; but if I ever get your future husband back, I thought he'd be the best officer for the job." Olbricht pulled on his leather gloves as he spoke and reached for his cap. He was smiling like the cat that had just swallowed the canary, and Alix knew that she was missing something.

She had no time to think about it, however. She fetched her coat and purse to accompany General Olbricht down to the courtyard where his car was waiting. The driver opened the door for them and Alix settled into the back seat. As they drove out the gate, Olbricht inquired how Alix's riding lessons were going. She wanted to surprise Philip by being halfway competent on horseback when he returned. Olbricht had recommended a stables and instructor. After they had crossed the Canal and drove along the near-empty streets, however, he changed the subject. "Frl. v. Mollwitz, we've known each other roughly a year—isn't that so?"

"Yes, *Herr General*; and in all that time I've never had reason to regret taking the job."

"I'm pleased to hear that. You have, of course, heard me complain more than once."

"About my work, *Herr General?*" Alexandra was startled; she had always thought he was pleased with her.

"Good heavens, no! I meant with the war, the leadership."

Relieved, Alexandra flashed him a smile and remarked, "But that's one of the reasons I so enjoy working for you, *Herr General*." He had to laugh.

Then, serious again, he asked, "But if I were to say that a restructuring of the leadership might be necessary, how would you feel about it?"

Suddenly it started to dawn on her what this was about. Tense and excited, she answered very clearly: "I would ask if there were any way I could help."

"You already are," came the answer, with that cat-that-swallowed-the-canary smile again. Then he added, "But you do see that if that was to be necessary—the change in leadership structure, I mean—then we would have to secure the Chancellory to protect it from reactionary elements. Indeed, it would be necessary to cordon off *all* the ministries from elements disloyal to the government. You see?"

Alexandra first felt cold and then hot from sheer excitement. She gazed at General Olbricht as she ventured to suggest, "And it would be very important to control the radio stations, so that no one could broadcast misinformation, I presume."

"Quite. And the lines of communication generally would have to be secured."

"I see. And all the various installations that are in the hands of unreliable troops would have to be taken over by patriotic units."

"Exactly." They were both starting to grin. But then Olbricht became very serious and formal. "Nevertheless, Frl. v. Mollwitz, I am asking a great deal of you to take on this extra work. I repeat: this work is entirely voluntary. I would understand perfectly if you feel that—at a time like this, just before your marriage—you could not handle the extra burden."

"*Herr General*, I would rather do this work than all the rest." She met his eye as she said this.

"And your fiancé? Our good Frhr. v. Feldburg? I know his patriotism is above question, but would he approve of your involvement in this matter?"

"*Herr General*, since I cannot ask him, I must act in accordance with my own conscience, and trust that his love for me and for Germany is great enough to accept my decision."

*   *   *   *

Yukov, Soviet Union
June 1942

Philip soon abandoned the practice of expressing his opinion on secondary matters such as the location of HQ or the censorship of mail. In the long run, these were minor issues. He could not afford to irritate Wittig any more than necessary if he wanted his opinions on important matters to carry any weight at all. Thereafter, things went quite smoothly for more than a month. They were both pleasantly surprised to discover tactical competence in the other, and their relationship was actually starting to improve when the crisis broke.

The crisis did not at first appear to have the makings of a crisis. Philip, going through the log of the previous day's communications, noted a message from one of the battalions passing on a request for support to the SS. Philip felt the saliva flow in his mouth and beat back thoughts of Zubovo. But he calmed himself with the thought that the SS would hardly need Army support for that kind of work. It was probably legitimate anti-partisan activities, he reasoned.

The following morning, however, the battalion commander called. "Has Division heard anything about what my 9th company was used for?"

"The company lent to the SS?"

"Yes."

"What?"

There was a long pause and then a reluctant, "One of the lieutenants of the company just made a report to me which, if true, would indicate a serious breach of the rules of war."

Philip stiffened and then suggested, "I don't think this should be discussed over the phone. You'd better come here."

Major Geyer arrived within the next couple of hours. He was accompanied by a weathered but nervous-looking lieutenant. The lieutenant was thin and was missing two fingers on his left hand. Philip led the visitors to Wittig's office. Wittig had been warned and was expecting them.

Wittig sat behind a huge desk and listened passively as Geyer first reviewed the military situation in his sector. "In recent weeks we've lost almost 20 men—and all to traps and booby traps. My men are becoming increasingly unnerved. They are more and more reluctant to move about in the dark and to trust strangers— even children. We were anxious to fight back against the partisans and if the SS had information, it seemed sensible to cooperate."

"By all means," Wittig agreed, and Philip bit his tongue. "So what is the problem?"

"*Leutnant* Neuchterlein reported to me this afternoon that they have not been engaged in anti-partisan activities, but rather misused for racial warfare against Gypsies and Jews."

"What is that supposed to mean?" Wittig demanded of the lieutenant.

"We were asked to kill defenseless, unarmed people, *Herr General*. Mostly women and children."

"Where? When? Make a proper report!"

Philip could see that the lieutenant was shaking; he cleared his throat several times before being able to speak. If Philip had been with Rittenbach, he would have intervened to calm Rittenbach's impatience. With Wittig, however, he didn't dare play the same role.

"The SS had located an overgrown cellar. Not just one cellar but a maze of underground rooms, which must have belonged to some large building many years ago. Nothing was left of the building, but smoke betrayed the cellars and the fact that they were occupied. Because there were multiple entrances, and because we had no way of knowing what the layout was underground, the plan was to use flame-throwers to flush the inhabitants out. My company was to shoot them as they came out. But when the people ran out, they were waving anything white to indicate they were surrendering. I held my fire and arrested them instead."

"Correct," Wittig agreed with a shrug. "What's the problem?"

"They were mostly women and children; a few old people. All were very thin and filthy. They looked like they had been living in those cellars for months with hardly anything to eat. They weren't armed. But when the SS saw what we'd done, they insisted that we kill them."

"Kill them? Why?"

"They said they were Jews and Gypsies, and they said they have orders to exterminate them."

"Then it is not our affair," Wittig declared immediately.

The other three officers were stunned by this hasty dismissal of the problem. Geyer spoke for all of them. "They were Army prisoners, *Herr General.*"

"Yes—or no," Wittig decided conveniently. "It was an SS operation. What happened next?"

"The acting company commander, *Oberleutnant* Arndt, and the SS commander moved out of hearing and consulted. When they came back, Arndt ordered us to shoot the prisoners."

At last Wittig seemed shocked. "Ordered *you* to shoot them?"

"Yes, *Herr General.*"

"And?"

"I protested, *Herr General,* but Arndt insisted. We shot them. Even the little girls."

There was a long silence. Then Wittig turned to Philip. "You'd better send for *Oberleutnant* Arndt."

Arndt duly arrived a couple of hours later, and again they used the General's office. Wittig, in the presence of Philip, Geyer and Neuchterlein, asked for

Arndt's version of the incident. Arndt also started by stressing the amount of partisan activity in his sector, but Wittig cut him short. Arndt stood very straight, his face blank and his gaze fixed over the General's shoulder: the perfect soldier. "With respect, *Herr General*, I only wished to remind *Herr General* that partisans don't take prisoners. Permission to ask: why do we take prisoners?"

"I presume you have heard of the Geneva Conventions?" Wittig asked sarcastically.

"*Jawohl, Herr General*; but as *Herr General* knows, the partisans don't respect them. Could *Herr General* tell me why we should do so?"

"Because we are signatories," came the clear answer. After allowing this to sink in, Wittig continued. "But that is not the issue. According to *Leutnant* Neuchterlein, the prisoners you took included women and children."

"*Jawohl, Herr General.*"

"You ordered women and children shot?" Wittig was clearly baffled by Arndt's utter lack of shame.

"*Jawohl, Herr General.* What were we supposed to do with female or child prisoners, *Herr General?*"

"Send them back to the prisoner collection point and let the rear echelons worry about it," Wittig retorted in an exasperated tone.

"With all due respect, *Herr General*, that seemed an unnecessary risk. *Herr General* must be aware that women are frequently active partisans or spies."

"And the children, too, I presume, you consider partisans and spies?" Wittig's tone was sneering.

Arndt's face reddened for the first time, but Philip's assumption that he was finally ashamed of himself proved wrong. "At 8 or 9—even younger—these Russian brats are perfectly capable of throwing hand grenades. These are Bolshevik fanatics! Children of Revolution! They can't be compared to German children of the same age."

"*Leutnant* Neuchterlein claims that the SS clearly identified your prisoners not as partisans but as 'Gypsies and Jews.'"

Arndt cast Neuchterlein a look that was part suspicious, part hostile, and part surprised. Then he turned to General Wittig and said in a firm, decisive tone: "I never heard anything of the kind. They were always referred to as partisans."

Philip looked quickly at Neuchterlein. The lieutenant looked deathly pale. He licked his lips. Wittig also glanced at him and then continued his interrogation of Arndt. "You are convinced the prisoners were partisans?"

"Completely convinced, *Herr General.* The SS had excellent intelligence." His tone was confident and precise.

"All right; you and Neuchterlein can wait outside." Wittig dismissed the junior officers and turned his attention to Geyer. "Tell me about your officers."

"Arndt has been a daring and effective officer. That's why I named him acting commander to replace *Hauptmann* Hampel, who was killed last month."

"And Neuchterlein?"

"He was wounded before I took over the battalion and did not return from hospital until a few weeks ago."

"What is your recommendation, Geyer?"

Geyer took a deep breath. "They must be disciplined, of course; but allow me to plead for leniency. The conditions of partisan warfare are such as to wear down a man's patience and fill him with helpless rage. These men have been under extreme pressure for too long. That has to be taken into consideration."

To Philip's horror, Wittig eagerly agreed. "Exactly my view. As I see it, this is precisely the kind of situation for which the Barbarossa Instructions were issued. I trust you to find a suitable means of reprimanding Arndt for overstepping the bounds, and I don't want to hear any more about it." Wittig was on his feet and had seen Geyer out the door before Philip could pull his thoughts together.

Philip, still reeling from the pace of events, at last managed a lame-sounding protest: "*Herr General* can't just leave it at that."

"What do you mean, I can't?" Wittig reacted as if Philip had just challenged his authority.

"I mean that the incident cannot just be swept under the carpet. We are talking about the murder of women and children, an atrocity—"

"I'm sick of that word," Wittig replied with a wave of his hand. "It's melodramatic. War is ugly, and ugly things happen in it. Leave the name-calling to the journalists."

"Fine," Philip agreed, intellectually disgusted by this facile evasion. He pushed his glasses up his nose and proceeded, "Then we won't use the word, but that changes nothing of the substance. Shooting prisoners, much less women and children, is a crime."

"It is entirely debatable whether the Geneva Conventions apply in this situation," Wittig retorted in an academic tone. He lectured Philip, "Partisans wear no uniforms and do not themselves respect the rules of war. The Conventions make a clear distinction between those combatants who wear uniforms and are organized, etc., and those who don't. The latter can, according to the Conventions, be treated like bandits."

The longer Wittig lectured, the more difficult Philip found it to remain calm. He wished he had had better legal training—or that Alix were here—but without either, all he could do was argue somewhat shallowly, "There is no evidence that they were partisans. All we know with certainty is that they were hiding in a cellar, underfed, filthy, frightened—and that they surrendered to us!"

"I don't understand what you are upset about, Major von Feldburg," Wittig told him in a very superior tone, as if he found Philip's behavior unprofessional or even childish. "I have ordered disciplinary action. What more do you want?"

"I want a court-martial," Philip replied challengingly, raising his voice for the first time, "for all officers involved and the troops that actually carried out those illegal orders!"

Wittig was aghast. "Are you mad? You can't court-martial troops for shooting the enemy!"

"Since when are starving women and children the enemy?"

"Since the Soviets started using women and children to help fight their partisan battles!" Now Wittig also raised his voice.

"We do not know they were partisans!" Philip insisted. "There's no evidence!"

"We've been through all this before. Arndt overreacted. He will be disciplined. A court-martial, however, would be too extreme under the circumstances!"

"Extreme? For murdering unarmed women and children who had surrendered!?"

"You heard the testimony! These troops have been under intense partisan pressure. Time and again they have lost comrades in cowardly ambushes, and they have had little chance to hit back. It was a natural reaction for Arndt to take revenge on any ones he thought might be partisans. These troops have been under pressure for too long—"

"I know exactly what pressure the troops have been under." Philip made it very clear that he considered himself a better judge of how much the troops had endured than the newcomer Wittig.

"Then you should understand that clemency is appropriate! A full court-martial might actually result in the death sentence. Military justices are nothing but a bunch of lawyers and judges dressed up in uniform! Most have no understanding of the hell our troops have been through. Did you ever think of that!?" Wittig had lost his temper.

It was Philip's turn to enjoy the superiority of calm. "Yes," he said icily, "that may be necessary."

"Necessary!? Necessary to shoot good combat officers merely for taking revenge against the enemy? How can you say that?" Wittig demanded hotly.

"Precisely because the pressure on the troops to commit such acts of so-called vengeance is so great. If there is no countervailing pressure on the troops to obey the Military Code, then such acts of lawless violence will become more common until they are no longer disciplined troops at all, but rather a band of murdering mercenaries. That can only be prevented if we—the commanding officers, the Staff, the High Command—make it absolutely clear that crimes will be punished without exception!"

"If we show no understanding of the pressure the troops are under," Wittig shouted at him, "they will lose faith in us, even start to hate us!"

Philip had never heard anything so ridiculous in his life, and he too lost his temper. "Troops respect discipline and consistency! As long as the military code is in effect—"

"Actually," Wittig remarked with sudden composure, "there are orders suspending the Military Code."

Trapped. The Barbarossa Instructions. Wittig had him and Philip knew it, but he couldn't bring himself to just give in. He tried one last time to defend his position. "If the German Army tolerates murder, it is not an army anymore, but a barbarian horde!"

"War is not a civilized business."

"It is as civilized as we make it!"

For several seconds the two men stared at each other. Both were furious and utterly committed to their convictions. There was no common ground anymore.

Then Wittig seemed to abruptly remember his superior rank. He broke eye contact, moved stiffly back behind his desk, and declared, "The decision has been made. The matter is closed."

But Philip knew it was too late to return to a normal tone of voice, and he knew too that the "matter" could not be closed as long as the war lasted. "No, *Herr General,*" he stated flatly. Inflated with indignation, Wittig would have delivered a withering rebuke if Philip had not forestalled him by remarking, "Because it is impossible for me to accept *Herr General's* decision or *Herr General's* attitude in this matter, I must request permission to resign."

Wittig was stunned by this turn of events. "You'd resign over this minor incident?" Evidently he did not find the issue important.

"Yes."

Wittig reflected briefly and then shrugged. "As you wish. Submit your request in writing and I will pass it on with my approval."

Philip nodded and came to attention. "If the *Herr General* has no further requests …"

"Not at the moment."

As Philip passed through the outer office, everyone looked extremely busy. Too busy. If they had not heard the confrontation, someone would at least have glanced up.

Philip felt totally isolated.

CHAPTER 22

▼

Smolensk, Soviet Union
June 1942

Oberst i.G. Henning von Tresckow greeted Feldburg in a relaxed manner, offering him a cigar. Then he settled himself casually, half-seated on the front of his desk, and started to chat about inconsequential things.

Tresckow had only met Feldburg once, on that day in December of the previous year when Philip had passed through Army Group Center. Nevertheless, Tresckow had since had ample opportunity to observe him from a distance. Aside from the official orders and reports, both written and verbal, Tresckow had spoken at length with Rittenbach about his Ia and heard reports from the officers of the neighboring divisions, from Corps, and from the 9th Army as well. Up to now Feldburg had appeared to be a competent, alert and outspoken officer. Tresckow had been impressed by his incisive analytical ability and convinced of his sound character. He was now confronted by a listless officer wearing chipped glasses smeared with fingerprints.

Feldburg answered Tresckow's questions with extreme reticence—almost reluctance—although the questions themselves were harmless. Disappointed by his failure to establish some rapport between them, Tresckow stopped trying and asked directly, "Could you tell me something more specific about the circumstances that led you to request a transfer back to Army Group?"

"It's very simple, *Herr Oberst*," Feldburg replied, with a shrug and no greater reluctance than with the previous questions. "One of our companies was loaned to the SS for what were ostensibly anti-partisan operations. Instead they were used for 'racial warfare' against Gypsies and Jews." Feldburg was not looking at Tresckow as he spoke. He gazed blankly at nothing. He did not notice that Tresckow stopped smoking his cigar and stared at him. Feldburg continued in his monotone. "Women, children and old people who had surrendered to us were shot without investigation or trial."

Tresckow leapt to his feet, went around the back of his desk, reached for the phone, and then stopped himself. He sat down in his chair. "Go on," he urged.

Feldburg stared at him, confused. "But there isn't any more."

"You're telling me a company of the 144th ID shot women and children in cold blood—not by accident in the midst of a fight with partisans?"

"Correct, *Herr Oberst*. They had surrendered and were begging for mercy."

"Why wasn't this reported immediately? Why wasn't there a court-martial?"

"General Wittig explicitly rejected my demand for a court-martial. That was why I offered my resignation."

"You submitted your resignation, but you didn't say why! You didn't pick up the phone and inform me!" Tresckow was angry. "Why didn't you call me at once?!" He looked distressed, as if *he'd* failed in some way.

Feldburg only shrugged. "What could *Herr Oberst* have done? The people were already dead, and protests are pointless. From Blaskowitz to Rittenbach—all our protests against these policies have been a waste of breath. Women and children were gunned down mercilessly, and I resigned like some small-town councilman distressed over the traffic ordinances."

"If only the field marshals would show so much decency!" Tresckow flung back at him. "If the Army Group Commanders had all resigned, maybe we wouldn't have Commissar Orders or Barbarossa Instructions!"

"Of course we would, *Herr Oberst*," Feldburg told him flatly. "If Leeb, Bock and Rundstedt had resigned, it would only have saved him the trouble of firing them later. There will always be ambitious generals—Models and Wittigs—happy to take the place of the men who quit. And regardless of who commands our divisions and corps, the SS will continue to do as they please behind our lines. What's the point of protesting anymore?"

"By God, Feldburg! Are you seriously suggesting we should just resign ourselves to the injustice? That we should close our eyes to these atrocities? That we should accept crimes of this magnitude?"

"What choice do we have, *Herr Oberst*? Nothing will change until there is a change at the source of these policies." Feldburg meant this argument as final. It was clear to him that no change was possible.

Tresckow appeared to misunderstand him. "Correct. Do you think you're the first person intelligent enough to recognize that?"

The shock of the answer was dizzying. Philip was shaken from his apathy. He stared at the senior officer. "What does *Herr Oberst* mean?"

"In the words of Friedrich II: 'A people is no longer bound by its oath of loyalty if a ruler violates his highest duty to serve the interests of his subjects.' Hitler has not only failed to serve the interests of the people, he has led them into a morass of misery and amorality. He must be removed from power."

"That will never happen without a revolution," Philip scoffed; "and the masses idolize him!" His contempt for the complacent citizens at home who adored their *Führer* was easy to hear in his bitter tone.

"We are not democrats dependent on majority will, but German officers with a responsibility to our country. The entire nation—the innocent along with the guilty—will be held to account for the crimes committed by that man in our name. The individual innocence will be drowned in the collective guilt."

"To hold the innocent responsible for the crimes of the guilty is like shooting a whole village because one or two villagers are partisans."

"You're absolutely right, but don't deceive yourself that our conquerors will be so discriminating or just. Each innocent victim we murder today will cost the lives of other innocent victims later. You swore an oath, Freiherr v. Feldburg, to defend your country and countrymen. A madman is threatening the very existence of the nation and virtually the entire population as well! You have a duty to stop him."

"And what am I supposed to do to stop him?" Philip snapped back. "Christ himself couldn't stop this war alone!"

"But you're not alone," Tresckow repeated softly.

"How many are we? A platoon? A company? Even a battalion? Against the SS? The SA, the Gestapo, the police and the majority of the population? God is always on the side of the bigger battalions!"

"You're too fine a General Staff Officer to believe that. You know as well as I that sometimes a surgical strike, with just a few troops, can achieve what divisions and armies cannot."

"Cut off this monster's head and its limbs will fight blindly and brutally—to save their own necks and privileges!"

Tresckow smiled faintly. "Have you so little faith in your own profession?"

"If *Herr Oberst* had spent the last months fighting with Generals Wittig and Model, *Herr Oberst* would certainly share my low opinion of the moral fiber of our fellow officers." Philip's answer was acid.

Tresckow registered how bitter he was and then said softly, "I meant your profession as a staff officer: precise planning and clear, unambiguous orders. It's precisely the Models and Wittigs of the world who generally carry out orders without thinking about them."

Although this appeared to give Philip pause, he answered simply with the words of Field Marshal v. Moltke the Elder: "'No plan survives contact with the enemy.'"

"True," Tresckow conceded; "the question is simply whether you personally prefer to continue your zombie-like obedience to this anti-Christ or want to take a chance working against him."

"When the chances of success are so slight, then all I can possibly achieve is the destruction of my own life and that of my innocent bride! I won't do that!" His words hung in the air. Philip came to himself. He became painfully aware that he had just shouted at his direct superior for no good reason at all.

Tresckow stood and walked over to the window. Ashes fell from his cigar as he held it behind his back. He turned around. "I didn't realize you were married."

Philip sighed, "I'm not. I was engaged in December. We wanted to marry on my first leave."

"Why don't you take it now? Go home for a month. Get married. The leave papers will be issued at once."

Philip, surprised by the abrupt change in Tresckow's tone, was too unsettled to feel properly grateful or delighted. Even as he left the HQ for the train, he was pursued by depression rather than joy. He was nagged by the feeling that he had deeply disappointed Tresckow.

*   *   *   *

Warsaw, Poland
June 1942

Although Walther had been given very little warning of his brother-in-law's impending stopover in Warsaw, he was determined to roll out a very lush red carpet. It was now roughly three years since he had last seen his wife's eldest brother. In that time a great many things had changed. Walther mentally winced to think what a small, insecure man he had been back then—awed by the manor and the title and the General Staff training. But now the roles were reversed. In three years Philip had crept up only a single rank, while Walther had leapt from part-owner of an obscure provincial factory to owner of a booming and diversified industrial empire in the *Reich*'s most important colony.

Philip's rank of Major seemed lowly to a man who daily had contact with *Gruppenführer* and *Kreishauptleute* and even occasionally had business with the Governor General himself. Nowadays Walther had many "friends" who were powerful figures of the administration and Party in the Government General. Walther's sense of superiority was strengthened by the fact that Philip was only now marrying, while Walther had three children. Financially, of course, Walther considered himself beyond comparison: Walther's income exceeded that of an Army major many times, while his financial worth had soared far beyond that of the Feldburg properties and was growing rapidly.

In his security and self-satisfaction, Walther was prepared to be generous. He had not forgotten that embarrassing and unseemly fight of Christmas 1938. Nor had he forgotten that Philip had refused to toast the *Führer*. But Walther was determined to let bygones be bygones. For one thing, Philip was no doubt embarrassed by his shortsighted inability to recognize the *Führer's* genius, and it would be bad manners to remind him of it. Last but not least, Walther knew that Theresa still craved her brother's approval, and Walther wanted to be sure she won it.

Walther was shocked by how bad his brother-in-law looked when they met him at the station. He remembered a handsome man with clean, regular features under fine, dark hair. The man who got off the train was no longer handsome. He was too gaunt, his face too angular, and his hair shaved too close by a military barber. He was so thin that he no longer looked athletic and trim, but outright ill. To a man like Walther, used to life among the elite of occupied Warsaw, Philip didn't look German at all, but rather like the one of the "subhumans" who worked in Walther's factories. Philip's chipped glasses and shabby uniform completed the picture. Walther's shock quickly turned to outright pity.

"Ah, there you are!" he called out with forced joviality, as Philip waved solemnly at them and separated himself from the other disembarking passengers. Walther thumped Philip heartily on the back and exclaimed, "Wonderful to see you!"

Philip and Theresa exchanged a brotherly kiss.

"It's very kind of you to receive me at such short notice, but I thought since I would be passing directly through—"

Walther didn't let Philip finish, saying, "Not at all, not at all."

"We would never have forgiven you if you hadn't stopped," Theresa insisted. "We want to hear everything—especially about this mysterious bride of yours. I was so surprised when Mother wrote at Christmas that you'd become engaged so suddenly! I hope you have some pictures with you."

Philip nodded and gestured toward the briefcase he was carrying. Then because Theresa made no move to even greet Franz, who was carrying his suitcase, Philip pointedly said, "You remember Franz Stadthagen, Heidi's son."

"Oh, yes, hello." Theresa cast the soldier a negligent smile, but did not give him her hand. Instead she looped her arm through her brother's and started to lead him out of the station.

Outside, the chauffeur leaped to open the back door of the car. Walther was certain he had made a good impression: the shiny black BMW, the uniformed driver, the leather interior. Walther saw Philip's eyes sweep over the car and then turn in silent question to him. "I've got these five factories now, and they're spread out all over the city. Then, too, I often have to go to Krakow to consult the Governor General and the like, so a car is really essential." He tried to sound casual and not show how proud he was. Because of fuel rationing, very few civilians could support an auto nowadays.

Philip nodded, and at Walther's gracious gesture climbed into the back seat. Walther leaned across his wife to ask Philip, "Now I presume you're tired and hungry, so if you want, we can go straight to the house; but I thought you might be interested in seeing a bit of Warsaw or my factories?"

"Oh, honey! Don't you think we could eat first? I'm starving," Theresa protested in a sugary voice.

"I thought we could eat downtown—if your brother agrees—maybe the Victoria or the Excelsior?" He named two of the most fashionable hotel restaurants in Warsaw.

"Oh, yes, that would be lovely," Theresa agreed at once. Then remembering her brother, she turned to him solicitously. "But Walther's right; we can go straight home if you prefer."

Philip managed to smile, "Please. I'm happy with whatever you choose." Fearing this sounded unappreciative, he added, "I'd very much like to see Walther's factories, maybe even some of Warsaw. But let's have lunch first so Theresa won't starve." It was meant as a joke, but it fell flat because neither of his companions was aware how far from starving they looked in Philip's eyes. While they missed the unkind irony, they were pleased with his decision. They assumed his less than enthusiastic tone was an indication of sheer weariness. Husband and wife decided between them on the Excelsior and the driver was given his instructions.

Theresa took over the conversation, declaring, "I must say, you don't act like a man on the way to his wedding. At least, I hope Walther didn't look so depressed!" She tossed her husband a teasing smile. He laughed heartily and patted her well-padded thigh. "Not at all, sweetie, not at all."

"You aren't having second thoughts or something, are you, Philip?" Theresa asked in a concerned, sisterly tone that rubbed Philip very much the wrong way. Who was she to play marriage counselor? His reply was tinged with irritation.

"No, not for a second—but I'm afraid I've been on the Front for the last six months. It's not something I can just forget."

"But surely things are better now, on the Front, I mean," Theresa asked her brother innocently, unable to understand his mood. "I mean, we're doing splendidly."

"That's in the south, honey. Your brother is with Army Group Center," Walther corrected his wife.

Theresa waved it aside. "Oh, I can never keep track of these things. So many unpronounceable Russian place names and a lot of numbers for our units! I can never keep them straight. Show me some pictures of my future sister instead," she urged.

Philip willingly obliged, pulling his briefcase onto his knees and removing his precious, somewhat dog-eared snapshots of Alix. Theresa was consciously positive. Was she one of the Westphalische Mollwitzes? And she already had a law degree? But why was she working as a secretary? Was Olbricht so important? And how old was she? 28 already? She certainly didn't look that. She was really very pretty. Didn't Walther think she was simply lovely?

Although Walther denied she was one whit prettier than his wife, the photos seemed to have a calming effect on Philip. Some of the tension left him, and his answers gradually became longer, more relaxed and informative.

At the chosen hotel, the liveried doorman opened the car door for the passengers in the back. The driver was instructed to take Philip's luggage and Stadthagen to the house and then return for them. They went into the hotel.

The reception hall was heavy with gold décor, massive crystal chandeliers, plush carpets and overstuffed furniture. They passed on into the nearly empty dining room. The tables and chairs were neo-rococo in white and gold. The walls were of red silk brocade, and the other guests were in a bright—almost confusing—array of uniforms, from familiar Party and SS to the green-grey uniform of the officials of the Government General and a variety of more exotic inventions for local police, railway, and Labor Service.

"You must order whatever your heart—or rather your stomach—desires," Walther instructed his brother-in-law. "Cost is absolutely no object."

Philip smiled faintly. "I never doubted it." He opened the menu, scanned for the most expensive item and then, ashamed of himself, backed off a bit. "Freshwater crabs would be very nice."

"Freshwater crabs it is! And you, darling?"

Theresa made her choice. The champagne was served. Walther proposed a toast to the bride and groom, and Theresa cast him an adoring look. How right she had been to put her faith in this man. Here he sat, able to play the grand *seigneur*, generous and forgiving, while her brother was really a pitiful wreck of a man. She could almost feel sorry for Philip, seeing him like this, except that she was too busy feeling smug. All that false Feldburg pride that had been so high-and-mighty at her wedding was humbled now. She was almost ashamed of how low Philip had sunk: a shabby uniform, chipped glasses and ill-kept hands.

Aloud, Theresa declared, "Did you know Christian was having an affair with some French woman?"

Philip smiled, "Of course. When has Christian ever been without a woman?"

"But French! Why not one of our patriotic Auxiliaries?"

"The uniforms of the Auxiliaries wouldn't appeal to Christian."

Walther laughed at that, and Theresa could only look from husband to brother, a touch annoyed. She changed the subject, returning to Philip's wedding. "I'd so like to meet your Alexandra—after all, she's the first sister I've ever had. Maybe I could join you in Altdorf for the last week of your leave? What do you think, Walther? Could you spare me for a short little week?" she smiled coyly.

"Well, maybe," Walther answered, with an intimate smile.

Philip wondered if they were putting on this show especially for him, or if they truly had not outgrown this juvenile display of dependency. Did they really not know that most married couples now prayed for a week together rather than fussing about a week apart? A look at the plush surroundings, the waiters in white dinner jackets and the fat customers convinced him that maybe they really didn't know.

After lunch they set off on a tour of Walther's factories. In the outer office of the first factory, Walther noted with satisfaction that his two elderly secretaries (Theresa made sure that no pretty young girls worked in his immediate proximity) were working hard. They clacked away at the typewriters, returning the carriage with brisk jerks. Their entire demeanor was enough to make any derogatory remarks about "Polish economics" ludicrous. Philip thought that the women looked nervous and harassed.

On the factory floor, Walther explained above the noise that the capital equipment was the very best available in the world. Because of the noise and Philip's technological ignorance, specific attributes of the equipment were lost on him. Philip saw only that the workers looked underfed, shabby and bone weary. After they had inspected one factory, Philip said that he was sorry, but he was more tired than he'd thought. He asked to go home to rest.

Walther and Theresa (who was bored anyway) readily agreed. Walther had been pleased by how intently Philip had looked at everything in this one plant, and he felt confident that he had made an impression. As they got back into the car, Theresa finally broached a subject she had been avoiding up to now. "Philip, I should warn you that we're having a little dinner party tonight. It's been planned for weeks and the invitations were sent out ages ago. It was just out of the question to cancel on such short notice."

"I wouldn't have expected that, but please allow me to retire early. I need a good night's sleep."

Theresa and Walther assured him that they understood perfectly, while Theresa went on to list all the "important" guests. Unfortunately, Philip did not know enough about politics in Occupied Poland to be impressed.

It was not until the following morning, after Walther had left for the office, that Philip and Theresa were alone together. They sat over the remnants of breakfast, drinking the last of the (real) coffee. The nanny had taken the children away, and Philip had less than an hour before he had to leave to catch his train.

"I hope we didn't keep you awake last night," Theresa remarked as she poured the coffee. "You're still looking rather tired."

Philip was unsure how to answer this, and at first he avoided his sister's eyes. She had indeed kept him from his sleep, but not in the way she meant. It was not the noise of the party, but rather the impressions from the whole day, that had plagued him into the night. Finally he took a deep breath and looked straight at her. "Theresa, how can you live like this without the slightest shame?"

Theresa nearly dropped her coffee cup. Up to this very minute she had been convinced that she had at last impressed her older brother. "What do you mean?" she demanded indignantly.

Philip gestured vaguely to the room around them. "I mean living here, fat and warm, while the people around you starve and freeze? You eat off the china and use the silver of people driven into the squalor of the Ghetto. You wear clothes and jewels paid for by the profits of forced labor. Doesn't your conscience ever bother you?"

Theresa saw red. "I'm not fat!" she told him furiously. "It's normal to put on some weight after a pregnancy, and I've given the Fatherland three children in as many years! And you're mad to think this house has anything to do with the people in the Ghetto! Walther found it years ago—"

"Theresa! How do you think he found it? From reading an announcement in a newspaper? Since when do people rent—much less sell—houses furnished down to the crystal, the linen and the quartz ashtrays? Use your head!"

"How should I know why someone would do it, but they did, that's all I know! How dare you presume to know better—"

"Because Walther told me exactly what happened! He, at least, is no hypocrite. Indeed, I think he was rather proud of himself for getting such a good 'deal.' Good deal, indeed! This house wasn't bought, it was stolen, and the rightful owners were literally thrown out onto the street!"

"That's not true! You just hate Walther so much you're not willing to admit he's a success! You're ashamed to admit that he's made more of himself than you ever will! That's why you can't accept him! You're jealous!"

"Oh, but I do accept him," Philip retorted. "Walther is what he is—an ambitious, clever, unscrupulous—but definitely gifted—businessman. He believes in getting ahead any way he can. I understand that, and I accept it. In a way, I even admire him. Given his background, he's come a long way. My question is how can you, who were raised to think of something other than your own pleasure and comfort, live in a stolen house and profit from slave labor?"

"You're absolutely crazy! Walther pays his workers a very decent wage for Polacks—"

"A decent wage? For Polacks? Do you even know what they're paid? Have you ever asked?"

"I don't have to ask! All these things are carefully regulated, and you don't understand anything about business anyway! You don't seem to realize what a terrible time we have here. You don't see how dangerous and difficult it is here. All you see is the luxury. You have no idea of how hard Walther has had to work for it. And do you think it's a pleasure living here? So far from home? Raising babies in this backward country? Always worrying what will happen if one of them gets sick? You can't trust these Polacks further than you can throw them. Every week we hear of murders carried out in the dark—even servants who kill their German employers in their own beds!"

Philip sighed and swished his cold coffee around in his cup. He saw that it was pointless. Or rather, he didn't have the energy to fight.

*   *   *   *

Berlin
June 1942

As the eastern industrial slums of Berlin slipped past, the passengers excitedly collected their belongings, donned caps and belts, and pushed out into the aisles. The windows were shoved down and soldiers leaned out. Their luggage blocked the passageways, and a euphoric, anticipatory mood swept through the train. Strangers talked to one another. Friends laughed over nothing. No one complained.

The train started to brake. The wheels screeched in protest. Soldiers leaned still farther out of the windows. "Ost Bahnhof," they confirmed and re-confirmed. The train slipped under the dirty glass roof. It crawled forward. Doors opened. Everyone crowded toward the exits—their luggage, helmets, and rifles banging against the compartments, the frames of the doors, and each other.

As Philip stood, he caught sight of himself in the mirror over the middle seat opposite. He saw what his brother-in-law had seen. He was no longer a handsome man, but one with overly pronounced features and sunken eyes under a military haircut. His glasses sat crooked, the wire frames loose from too much rough handling, and one lens was chipped. He wasn't even properly shaved, because the restrooms had been blocked for hours. What woman in her right mind would want to kiss such a face?

Shaking himself free of his thoughts, he put his cap on without daring another glance in the mirror. He left the compartment following Stadthagen, who had already manhandled their luggage down the aisle. Stadthagen jumped onto the platform, grabbed the suitcases from the train, and then grinned up at Philip. "Any objection if I make my own way home, sir? I'll see that the luggage gets there safely, and surely you don't need me around for your reunion with Frl. v. Mollwitz?"

"Do you have money for a taxi?"

Stadthagen gallantly waved the offer aside and was lost in the crowds. He must have some girl of his own, Philip registered—a little amazed not to know more, but unable to think about it just now.

The public was not allowed on the platform, and the disembarked passengers bunched together at the top of the stairs and down into the hall. Philip took his place at the back of the crowd, and then lost his nerve and sat down on a bench. It was painted green with white lettering: "For Aryans Only".

Alexandra would be waiting for him in the hall below, and he suddenly didn't feel he could face her. So much had changed since they'd parted. It wasn't just his face. He couldn't remember the last time he'd laughed. And he was a failure. He'd failed Rittenbach, who had ordered him to stay and serve the division; and he'd failed Wittig, who had expected him to be a competent First General Staff Officer; and he'd failed Tresckow …

He glanced toward the stairway. The last of the crowd was starting down. He stood and started after them, his heart beating and his hands sweating in anticipation. He started to look for Alix as soon as he could see into the hall. He could see people pressed up against the railing separating passengers from non-passengers. They called and reached out and waved. Women were crying. Children were bouncing up and down. But Alix wasn't there.

At once he came up with a ream of excuses for her—she hadn't received his cable from Smolensk, Olbricht hadn't given her the time off, she'd missed a bus. But they were empty excuses; the fact was, she wasn't there.

Ever since he had been given leave so unexpectedly, he had made multiple attempts to reach Alix, but all had failed. He had sent a cable and left messages. It was hard to imagine that she didn't know about his arrival, but it was possible that she had had second thoughts about the marriage. Maybe she no longer wanted to marry him?

He looked down, following the men ahead of him as they squeezed one by one through the turnstile. Ashamed to be one of those forlorn-looking people who search desperately and vainly for someone who isn't there, he did not search the crowd again.

Around him his fellow passengers were embraced by every conceivable type of loved one, from grizzled old men to cupid-like children. Mothers wept, girl-friends made public love, children jumped up and down. Philip pushed past them, his mind on a taxi home, where he could hide away.

"Didn't you expect me?" Alexandra asked, suddenly beside him. He started, and then did something he had never expected himself to do: he pulled her into his arms and kissed her like every common soldier.

Only when they were finished did he murmur, "I didn't see you."

She pulled back a little to look at him. She was smiling from the depth of her soul—an unconscious, uncontrollable smile. "I can't believe it," was all she managed to say. "I was so afraid this day would never come."

Philip was too busy drinking in the sight of her to remember his horror at his own face. She looked different than he remembered. She looked stronger and her hair was different—lighter, shorter. But he had no time for her exterior appearance; he was absorbed by her eyes. He fell into them, drowned in them. She loved him!

"*Ach*, Philip," she said helplessly, as incapable of taking her eyes off him as he from her. But then she reached out her hand and traced a scar in front of his left ear.

Philip seized her hand and kissed the palm. "Nothing heroic," he answered her finger's question. "Saturn shied at the sound of our own 8,8s."

"You didn't write me about that."

Philip laughed. "What cavalry officer writes home about the times he's thrown?" Then he realized he'd laughed, and laughed again to think how easy she made it.

Although Alexandra didn't know what he was laughing about, she joined in. She was happy just to have him here, happy to see him laughing. Philip slipped his arm around her waist and they started toward the exit, suddenly both talking at once.

CHAPTER 23

▼

Berlin
June 1942

"Alexandra, you can't wait any longer. The Justice of the Peace has the next wedding in 20 minutes. You must let *Vati* or Herr Böll be a witness," Frau v. Rantzow urged.

The little party of guests was collected in the antechamber of the Justice of the Peace in Berlin-Smargendorf. Lotte was there with her opera singer, Eberhard Böll, and the Rantzows, but Christian had failed to show up as he had promised just the night before. Philip had gone in search of a public phone to try to put a call through to his squadron.

Alexandra was dressed for the civil ceremony in a flowing light-blue chiffon dress and high-heeled white shoes. She wore pearls and white gloves. A single lily had been pinned at her left ear. Her father and Eberhard Böll were in tails, her mother in a green raw-silk suit with a corsage of orchids. Lotte, of course, outdid them all in a striking black-and-red suit, black stockings and red shoes.

Lotte volunteered to go fetch Philip, adding, "Let's hope he didn't refuse at the last jump."

"What nonsense!" Frau v. Rantzow rebuked, irritated as usual with Lotte's flippancy in such a solemn situation.

Before Lotte could start down the stairs, however, they heard voices echoing loudly in the stairwell above the thump of hurried footsteps. Philip and Christian emerged.

Christian was pulling off his flying jacket, and his dark-blond hair was damp with sweat from his flying helmet, which Philip was carrying for him. "Fog in Cherbourg," was all he said collectively. Alix rushed over to welcome him with an uninhibited hug and kiss on his cheek.

"Thank you for coming!"

Under his flying gear he was in the dress uniform of a *Luftwaffe Hauptmann*; and Alexandra, attuned to rank insignia from work, noticed even before Philip, "You've been promoted!"

"Mollwitz and Feldburg?" The clerk from the Justice of the Peace called from the door. "This is your last—"

"We're here," Philip answered, and taking Alexandra away from Christian, he escorted her into the little hall used for civil ceremonies. In just ten minutes it was officially over. Philip and Alexandra were legally recognized by the Government of the German *Reich* as man and wife. They were given a copy of *Mein Kampf* as a state wedding present and shooed out of the office to make room for the next couple.

Frau v. Rantzow took over. She directed Philip and Alix down to a hired open carriage laden with white roses and drawn by a white horse. There was only enough room in the back for the bride and groom, so Christian had to crawl into the back of Eberhard's Volkswagen as they followed the Rantzows to the *Schloss* Hotel Gerhus, where the reception was to be held. Here many of the guests had already started to collect, being served champagne by the white-coated waiters. They clapped as Philip, in dress uniform with white gloves and sword, helped Alexandra out of the carriage. The guests were in tails for the most part and the ladies in cocktail dresses. Even Alexandra felt as if she hardly knew half of them; they were mostly friends and colleagues of her stepfather. But Uncle Erich was there, and she gave him a hug and kiss on both cheeks before proudly introducing him. "Philip, this is Uncle Erich."

Although Erich Hoepner was in civilian dress (his dismissal from the *Wehrmacht* had included a prohibition against wearing uniform), Philip pulled himself up into his smartest salute. "*Herr General*, I'm honored."

Around them the civilians stared in confusion. Hoepner grasped Philip's hand with so much strength that his knuckles cracked. "Thank you for that, young man." The friendship was sealed.

Eva Olbricht came over to congratulate them next. "Fritz will come as soon as he can," she assured them, "but it probably won't be until dinner or later. He'll bring Frl. Lerche with him." With Alexandra on leave, someone had to do the work at the office.

"We understand," Alexandra assured her. "Thank you for being here. Philip, have you met Frau Olbricht?"

Philip clicked his heels and bowed over her hand. Eva Olbricht looked him in the eye. "I hope you appreciate what an intelligent young woman you have and will encourage her to finish her legal training."

Philip was at little taken back by this direct approach, and he was reminded of the way some of his fellow officers spoke derogatorily about the "*Frau Generalin*." He answered sincerely, however, "It is Alix's decision. If she chooses to resume her training, I will not stand in her way."

"Well said," Frau Olbricht nodded, satisfied. Then she smiled up at him sideways, and Philip saw the beautiful young woman who had captured the General's heart a quarter of a century earlier. "I think we're going to get along splendidly."

Frau v. Rantzow interrupted, insisting on introducing Philip and Alexandra to the people she thought "important." Once or twice Philip glanced across the crowd to Christian with a look of helplessness. The only person he wanted to talk to was his brother, and they were being kept apart by dozens of strangers making small talk to him. Then the photographer arrived. The guests were herded into one of the halls where light snacks waited for them, while Philip and Alexandra were shooed into another for the photos. Photos were posed with Alexandra's family and then with the witnesses. The photographer managed everything "just like an opera director," according to Eberhard, telling them exactly where to stand, what pose to take, and even turning their heads this way and that or arranging their hands and accessories.

While they were standing together with the photographer pushing them about, Philip finally got a chance to ask his brother, "When were you promoted to *Hauptmann*?"

"When I got a *Staffel*."

"Congratulations!" The flashlight flashed, catching that moment when Philip turned in delighted surprise to Christian. "When did you get the *Staffel*?"

"Yesterday."

"In JG 23?"

"Yes, but in Africa."

"What?" Philip's smile froze.

"We've had a *Gruppe* there for more than a year. The commander and two squadron leaders were shot down in this latest offensive. I've been given one of them. Should be an exciting change from the drudgery over the Channel."

In the face of Christian's efforts to make light of the dangers, it was impossible for either Philip or Alexandra to say what they were thinking. Alexandra remembered, however, that Christian had bought an extravagant diamond pendant for a girlfriend the last time he'd been in Berlin. She remarked, "Your girlfriend must be heartbroken."

"Gabrielle won't even notice I'm gone. She's got a new friend. I'll miss Dieter, though. It will be odd flying with strangers. I don't know a single one of the pilots stationed in Africa."

"How did you get leave if you're under orders for Africa?" Philip registered that Christian was replacing a commander shot down in combat and must be under urgent orders.

Christian grinned. "I didn't. Officially I'm on my way to Africa right now."

"You're flying your own plane down?" Philip started to grasp why Christian had arrived in flying jacket and boots over his uniform.

Christian nodded. "They're as short of aircraft as they are of pilots. I had to refuel anyway, but I can't stay much longer. I should change and be on my way."

"Of course," Philip agreed, but he had his arm around Christian and seemed stunned. Alexandra turned to the photographer and gestured for him to take another picture. The shutter clacked loudly to the flashes of light, and then Christian and Philip walked out together.

"Wait, we're not finished yet!" Frau v. Rantzow protested. "I want some pictures with—"

"That's enough, Mother!" Alexandra snapped. "Didn't you hear?"

The dinner seemed interminable; and despite the best efforts of the bride and groom to forget their respective brothers, the absence of Christian and Stefan seemed weightier than the presence of all the others. There was a brief moment of real joy when General Olbricht arrived with Annie Lerche just before dessert was served. He asked to make a toast to the newlyweds, and soon had everyone laughing as he fell into his native Saxon dialect to give a highly embellished account of their "unseemly" courtship directly under his nose in the dingy corridors of the AHA. He ended by presenting the bride and groom each with a mock evaluation with the official stamps and signatures of his Chief of Staff and himself, describing their "unusual dedication to duty as evidenced by the hours spent together after duty" and the like.

Philip and Alix had time for only a couple of dances before they had to change to leave for the station. They slipped out as unobtrusively as possible, since the party would go on for several hours without them. Alexandra changed into low shoes and a comfortable skirt and blouse, Philip into his everyday uniform. Since Stadthagen had already checked their luggage for them the day before, they could travel light; Philip carried only his briefcase and Alix had a small suitcase for her toiletries.

At Anhalter Bahnhof there was the usual chaos. With so much rolling stock needed to keep the lines of communication open to the overextended *Wehrmacht*, there were too few locomotives or cars to serve domestic needs. Some trains had been cut entirely, others shortened. It had been impossible to reserve a sleeping car or even a seat at such short notice.

The platform was so crowded, however, that it proved impossible to move up and down in search of Stadthagen. All they could do was join the crowd and wait. As soon as the train pulled into the station, the crowd surged forward, pushing, shoving and cursing one another. Soldiers on leave, traveling businessmen, women with children, youths from the Labor Front, BDM girls and factory workers suddenly all turned into wild beasts. "Where's your respect for a woman with the Mother Cross?!" "I've only got three days' leave!" "We're already late back to camp!" "Serves you right, then!" "We're serving the Fatherland!" "Do you think we're not?! Who do you think makes the guns you use?!"

Someone trampled so hard on Alexandra's foot that she crumpled up in pain and could hardly limp forward. "This is madness," Philip declared and pulled her out of the crowd. He started up along the length of the train, looking for a car that was less wildly assaulted. Alix limped behind him, increasingly afraid that they would not get on the train at all.

Then from one of the windows, Stadthagen's head emerged and he waved to them, shouting loudly, "*Herr Baron*! Here! Come quick!" He was clearly fighting to hold onto the seats he'd claimed.

Philip ran forward, grabbed onto the window, and hauled himself in through it. Then together, he and Franz pulled Alexandra up through the window into the train. One of her sleeves tore under the arm in the process, and she lost one of her shoes. Stadthagen clambered out, retrieved the shoe, and climbed back in just in time. Already the announcer was squawking. The train lurched forward and slowly eased out of the station.

They looked around. Stadthagen had been at the station early enough to position himself where a first-class car was due to stop. He had claimed three seats for them in the first compartment behind the sleeping cars. They shared the compartment with a sour-looking, hefty woman in the uniform of the RAD, a thin civilian with spectacles and a prominent Party badge, and a clergyman of the German Church. All three looked aghast at the newcomers, but it was the man with the Party badge who challenged them first. "Just who do you think you are?

Clambering in through the window like thieves! Good Germans are orderly and come through the door!"

The RAD woman nodded rigorously and turned on Alexandra. "You slut! Everyone in the station must have seen up your skirt as you climbed in!" She turned to the clergyman for support. "Shouldn't we call the conductor and have these personages removed?"

Philip pointedly ignored the comments, but Franz was more impudent. "I wouldn't talk like that to the *Herr Baron*. He's first cousin to the Armaments Minister."

"Stadthagen," Philip warned. This was an outright lie.

But Stadthagen had judged their fellow passengers correctly, and they were instantly put on the defensive—whether because of the alleged connection or because of the title. Unsure of themselves, the other passengers chose to simply ignore their presence. Philip, seated in the middle, turned sideways so Alix, at the window, could lean against him, and he held her in his arms. There was nothing to see because the blackout blinds had already been lowered completely. Alix closed her eyes and tried to concentrate on the fact that she was in Philip's arms at last. Nothing else mattered, she told herself; but the woman from the RAD was talking in such a loud voice with the clergyman that she was forced to listen.

They were jointly lamenting the deplorable deterioration in public morals. Soon the other civilian, a teacher, picked up the thread. The train clacked and clattered and Alexandra tried not to listen, but their indignant, complaining voices were very penetrating. The clergyman insisted that his Church was "God's SA," and complained about the increasing spread of pagan rituals. "And it's not just the SS anymore. Ordinary citizens are turning their backs on the Church—as if we of the German Church did not wholeheartedly support the *Führer!*" The pastor was indignant.

Altogether, it seemed like every second sentence uttered by their fellow passengers referred to "the *Führer*." "The *Führer* said …" "The *Führer* would be scandalized if he knew …" "The *Führer* expects …" This wasn't the way Alix had pictured her wedding night …

Eventually Alexandra fell asleep in Philip's arms, and the conversation of the others gradually petered out. Stadthagen had long since curled up in his corner, with his head on his bunched-up coat. Philip, too, folded his glasses away in his breast pocket and tried to sleep, but too many thoughts plagued him.

In unproductive confusion, his mind wandered from the increased danger to Christian, to the emptiness of the civil ceremony that left him feeling as if he weren't married yet. He thought with fondness of the way Olbricht had cheered up a depressing dinner, and then started puzzling over the Tresckow-Olbricht connection. Ever since his conversation with Tresckow, Philip had found himself remembering that Olbricht had often referred to Tresckow, a far too junior officer for Olbricht to know in an official capacity. Tresckow was a lieutenant colonel; Olbricht a three-star general. But what if the plans Tresckow referred to were being developed by Olbricht?

The slamming of doors and high-pitched giggles pierced his consciousness. Frowning, Philip looked toward the sound. A girl dressed only in her slip, her hair falling from what had once been a braid, was running down the aisle, pursued by a man in even fewer clothes. He caught up with her just beyond the door to Philip's compartment. He flung her against the glass window and pressed against her, cutting off her hysterical giggles with his smothering kiss.

From the open door to the sleeping compartment came the sound of other voices and laughter. Another man wearing the brown trousers of some Party uniform, the suspenders hanging down to his knees and his tie loosened unevenly, emerged in the doorway. One arm was around a BDM girl whose blouse had been opened almost to the waist, clearly exposing her bra. He held a bottle of champagne in the other hand. The girl reached for the bottle and he held it out of her reach, saying, "Nay, nay, open up!"

She dutifully opened her mouth and stuck out her tongue. He shook the bottle with his thumb over the nozzle, and then squirted the frothy and expensive liquid in the direction of the girl's mouth. Most of it naturally landed somewhere else. It ran down off her chin, soaked her neck and frothed in her décolleté. She giggled and wriggled in drunken excitement.

The kissing couple looked over and the girl in the slip demanded, "Hey, leave some for me!" She staggered forward with her tongue out to get her "share" of the champagne.

Then the four passengers disappeared back into the sleeping compartment, leaving Philip seething with rage. So that was the kind of person who had booked the sleeping car, leaving him to spend his wedding night sitting up! In agitation, he eased out from under a sleeping Alexandra and went to pull the curtains closed between the compartment and the aisle. Before he did, he went out into the aisle and looked into the sleeping car. To his horror, he saw that an orgy seemed to be in progress. The doors to all the sleeping compartments were open. Men and young girls in various states of undress were wandering in and out with bottles and cigarettes in their hands. He had never seen anything like it in his life—much less in a first-class sleeping car of the *Reichsbahn*!

For a moment he considered calling a conductor, but the fat, balding men in their brown uniforms were too self-assured. Philip sensed without evidence that these men must be Party VIPs of some kind, some of the increasingly legendary "golden pheasants" about whom more and more jokes circulated. Indignantly, he turned his back on them, closed the door to the compartment, and pulled the curtains shut.

He must have drifted off to sleep for a bit, but he was woken by the sound of something thudding against the glass of the compartment. He sprang up in instinctive alarm, waking Alexandra. In a stride he was at the door to the compartment, sharply shoving the door back. A girl fell onto his feet. Her hair looked as if it had been torn from her two braids. Lipstick was smeared all over the lower half of her face. All that was left on her torso was her BDM tie, made fast around her naked neck and hanging between her still pubescent breasts. She wore her BDM skirt, but had lost one of her socks and both her shoes. She grunted and rolled over onto all fours. She swayed as she crawled into the aisle and then started vomiting.

The door to the sleeping car crashed open, and a man with a huge paunch over pitiable naked genitals cooed, "Mäuschen? Where are you, my little sweetie-pie? Why did you run away from Uncle B-B?" He saw her gagging on the floor at his feet and reached down, grabbed her arm and pulled her to her feet. "Come back to beddy-bye, Mäuschen," he cooed.

As he led her away, her eyes met Philip's. She was completely dazed, her gaze empty. Philip's stomach turned over and he slammed the compartment door shut. When he turned back into the compartment, he came face to face with Alexandra, her eyes wide with horror. She had seen it all.

Sophia Maria needed only one look at the disembarking passengers to guess that they had had a terrible night. Her new daughter-in-law had bags under her eyes, a torn blouse, a crushed skirt and her stockings bunched around her ankles. Philip looked even worse. She gave him a hug and a kiss and embraced the clearly nervous Alexandra as well. Then she hustled them into the waiting Mercedes. She was glad she'd had the foresight to use some of her precious gasoline rations for this occasion. In the Mercedes they were less exposed to view than in an open buggy. She drove to the carriage entrance and told Philip to take Alexandra straight up to the guest suite, thereby avoiding a reception from the staff, who waited in the courtyard and kitchen. She sent a breakfast tray up to them.

Philip bathed, shaved and changed into his dress uniform, but he told Alexandra to take her time, even a nap if she liked. They had three hours until the Wedding Mass. "I'll go down to the church, and my mother will bring you in the car," he told her. He found his mother in her study.

"Are you all right?" was all she asked.

Philip took a deep breath. "I will be. I want to go talk to Father Matthias. You'll bring Alix down to the church?"

"Father Matthias is here. You know he doesn't like marrying couples he doesn't know. He wanted to have a chat with your Alexandra before the sacrament."

"We got almost no sleep on the train. There was an orgy going on in the sleeping car—middle-aged men in Party uniforms of some kind helping themselves to dazed BDM girls."

"Philip!"

"I'm serious. Alix, unfortunately, saw what was happening. On our wedding night."

"Is she all right?"

"I don't know."

"Would you please go down and greet the staff? They are feeling insulted and neglected."

Philip smiled coldly, "I know. I have to play 'Herr Baron.' Have I ever disappointed you?" It was a rhetorical and bitter question.

Sophia Maria shook her head, hurt and frightened by his apparent state of mind. He was almost a stranger to her in this dark, bitter mood, but she felt she had something more important to do right now. While Philip dutifully went downstairs, she knocked at the door to the guest suite.

"Who's there?" came the timid voice from beyond the gilded door.

"Sophia Maria."

A moment later the door opened and Alexandra stood before her, wearing a bathrobe and with a towel wrapped around her wet hair. She looked up with large blue eyes over the streaks of blue from the sleepless night. Sophia Maria was struck by how fragile she seemed.

"Forgive me for intruding, but I wanted to be sure you were comfortable and to see if there was anything you needed."

Alexandra shook her head. "Thank you; everything's fine."

"But you need help getting into your gown and with your hair. No woman should be alone when she prepares for her wedding. I feel very badly that none of your family could be here with you. Not even your mother or a best friend. I realize we don't know each other, but I'd like to help."

Put like that, Alexandra could hardly refuse. She backed up uncertainly into the room. She was feeling very small and intimidated by her surroundings. Although she had occasionally been invited to the homes of family friends, including some rambling manor houses, none had been as "feudal" as this. Philip had not prepared her for his wealth in any way. Furthermore, as she had been raised in north German austerity, the baroque/rococo décor made her feel as if she were in a film or a hotel. Nor had she recovered from the shock of the night before. She couldn't shake the image of the BDM girl in her dazed stupor.

Sophia Maria closed the door and offered, "Shall I dry your hair? Sit down." She indicated a dresser with a low stool before a large gilded mirror.

Alexandra dutifully took her place on the stool, facing the mirror; and Sophia Maria, standing behind her, started to massage her head through the towel. She spoke in a soft, low voice. "The first time I came to Altdorf, I was horrified. The people were closed and hostile, and the manor was over-laden with an alien history and tradition. I felt completely out of place.

"I met Philip's father in Berlin, you see. We saw one another at various balls and soirées in Berlin and Potsdam. For some reason I don't remember, his mother even came up to Berlin to meet me. We married on my father's estate in Mecklenburg. It was not until the Great War started that I came down here, because Ferdinand insisted that I spend the war with his mother. I don't know if he really thought I couldn't be trusted on my own in Berlin, or if it was some illogical 'protectiveness.' In any case, I was packed off on a train and suddenly found myself in this little provincial town amid narrow-minded and hostile strangers. I was 'that Prussian woman' who had 'seduced' the Young Baron—and I wasn't even Prussian!"

Alexandra was so startled that she turned to look up at Sophia Maria. "But what could they have against you? A Countess Walmsdorff—"

"As far as they were concerned, I was Prussian and Protestant, and people here were very resentful of both. Bismarck's "*Kulturkampf*" was a vivid and hated memory. Sometimes I was made to feel as if I'd personally been responsible for it—especially by my mother-in-law. Whatever Ferdinand intended by sending me down here, what he achieved was the end of our romance. His mother systematically poisoned him against me. Even after the war and after she was dead, we were never close again. I could never forgive him for taking his mother's side in everything." Her hands stopped massaging Alexandra's head, and in the mirror their eyes met. "I swore I would never be that kind of mother-in-law."

Without giving Alix a chance to reply, she resumed her monologue. "Not that I could be. I don't have the same influence over either Philip or Christian that my mother-in-law had on Ferdinand.

"Ferdinand was an only child, you see. At his birth there was some complication, and the doctors advised my mother-in-law not to risk another pregnancy. Since an heir had been secured, her husband accepted this decision, and he never visited his wife's bed again.

"In my old age," Sophia Maria admitted with a whimsical smile, "I have come to feel more charitable toward my mother-in-law. She wanted a nursery full of children, and had only the one boy instead. It was natural that she doted on and soon dominated him. What I can't forgive, even now, is that she also used my children as weapons against me."

"What do you mean?" Alexandra asked, enthralled already by what her mother-in-law was telling her.

"She used their behavior as a measure of my competence. It is hard enough trying to be a good mother without having everything your children do analyzed for the mistakes you made. But of course, the worst of it was what it did to the children. I am convinced to this day that much of Christian's irresponsibility was nothing more than unconscious rebellion against his grandmother. He resented her efforts to make him into a marionette, and his apparent disobedience was really just a fight for independence. In retrospect, I understand him, but at the time he made life very difficult and often reduced me to tears."

Sophia Maria paused, her thoughts turned inward. When she continued, she sought Alexandra's eyes in the mirror. "Only now, twenty years later, do I realize that Philip was the one who suffered most. You see, he tried to shield me from my mother-in-law's criticism by being 'good.' Between us, his grandmother and I ruined his childhood," Sophia Maria concluded with a sad, twisted smile.

Alexandra turned around and sought direct eye contact. "I'm sure Philip doesn't see it like that! He speaks so highly of you!"

"Thank you." Sophia Maria rested her hand tentatively on Alexandra's shoulder. She smiled with her lips, but her eyes remained troubled. She was feeling guilty for what she'd done to Philip, always demanding the obedience she had come to expect. She winced inwardly as she recognized the double standard she had applied, allowing Christian freedoms she had denied Philip. She drew a deep breath. "Something else my mother-in-law did was to try to turn the boys against me."

Alexandra again turned around to look directly at her mother-in-law in shock. "That's horrible!"

Sophia Maria shrugged. "I suppose she wanted them to replace the children she had never had."

"What did she do?" Alexandra asked, still looking up.

Sophia Maria turned her firmly back toward the mirror, removed the towel, and with a silver comb that waited on the dresser, started combing out Alexandra's hair. "Various things. I can remember Christmas 1917. The rationing had become increasingly stringent, and the children could hardly remember sweets. We went into town to do some Christmas shopping, and in the *Konditorei* there were cookies with icing in the window. At once a choir of voices went up: 'Please, Mamá, please!' I melted at once and took one step in the direction of the door, but got no farther. My mother-in-law started lecturing me in a voice that made everyone up and down the whole street stop to stare. What was I thinking? How could I even dream of buying the boys sweets? Hadn't I seen the price? And the icing would ruin their teeth! Besides, giving in every time they begged was turning them into spoiled weaklings, a disgrace to their proud name. What was ever to become of the poor things with a mother like me? There was no question of defying her—not in front of half the town.

"That was bad enough, but also quite typical. The reason I remember the incident was because Philip—he was only seven at the time—came to me in a rage a few days later. His grandmother had called him into her room and offered him one of those glazed cookies—on the condition that he not tell anyone about it. Philip was furious. His grandmother, he told me—shaking in childish indignation—had tried to bribe him! He turned the cookies down, telling his grandmother that they were 'bad for his teeth.'

"Christian, incidentally, took the cookies without a qualm, but continued to refer to his grandmother in disrespectful language behind her back. In his way, he was just as incorruptible as Philip—only he didn't see why he should go without the cookies."

Suddenly they were both laughing. "They're very close, aren't they?" Alix ventured as the laughter died.

Sophia Maria looked at her in pleased surprise. "Yes, they are. Most people assume that their relationship is poor, because they are so different and often quarrel over little things. How did you guess the truth?"

"Christian diverted from an operational flight to be at our wedding yesterday. He didn't have leave."

"Diverted from France?" Sophia Maria couldn't picture it.

"No; on his way to Africa." In the mirror, Alexandra saw Sophia Maria's eyes widen, and realized too late that Sophia Maria did not know about Christian's transfer. She turned around and caught her mother-in-law's hand. "I'm sorry! You didn't know."

Sophia Maria had already recovered. "I had to find out sometime." She added, in a voice strained by trying to sound casual, "Then he won't be joining us for Mass here in Altdorf." All morning she had been expecting his arrival momentarily.

Alexandra shook her head. She could see how disappointed her mother-in-law was. As if reading her thoughts, Sophia Maria looked straight at Alexandra. "It's not what you're thinking: I don't love Christian more than Philip. I had just so looked forward to seeing them together." She fell silent, obviously thinking about her sons. Alexandra hesitated to speak.

Sophia Maria resumed, saying, "It's so like Christian to ignore regulations and risk punishment for his brother's sake. Philip wouldn't do the same for Christian, but he would literally give his life for his younger brother."

Alexandra's hair was almost dry from the combing, and it was getting late. "It's almost noon," Sophia Maria declared. "Could I persuade you to talk to our priest for a few minutes? He has a policy against marrying people he doesn't know. He made an exception for Philip, but …"

Alexandra had been warned. "No, I don't mind talking to him—if you don't think he'll back off after meeting me?"

"Not a chance in the world," Sophia Maria assured her with a wide, sincere smile. "When you're finished with Father Matthias, let me know. I'll help you change into your wedding dress." She started for the door, but with her hand on the handle she stopped. She turned back. "Alexandra?"

"Yes?"

"What's eating at Philip?"

There was no greater compliment that a mother could give her daughter-in-law than this implicit acknowledgment that Alexandra knew Philip better than she did. Alexandra was flattered enough to give an honest answer without thinking: "*Einsatzkommandos.*"

"What?" Sophia Maria had never heard the term.

"They're SS special forces that operate behind the front lines with the explicit objective of exterminating the Jewish and Gypsy populations."

"What?!" Sophia Maria took a step deeper into the room.

"They conduct systematic mass murder, and Philip saw the remnants they left behind: a mass grave with old people, women and little children—all shot in the back of the head. And then one of the companies of his division shot civilians who had surrendered to them. *Generalleutnant* Wittig refused to let him even call a court-martial. That's why he resigned as Ia."

Sophia Maria sank into a chair and stared at Alexandra, still trying to grasp what she had just been told. "You mean the SS is murdering Jews on a large scale, and no one is willing to stop or even report them?"

"No," Alexandra answered very clearly and distinctly, in a low, almost inaudible voice. "I mean the SS has *orders* to exterminate the Jews and no one *can* stop them. Not as long as Hitler is our *Führer* and Supreme Commander."

Sophia Maria crossed herself without taking her eyes off her daughter-in-law. After she had recovered from her initial shock, she whispered, "Poor Philip."

Alexandra wore a wreath and carried a bouquet, both made of flowers from the garden and arranged and bound in bright ribbons by Ludmilla. The entire German staff and half the town crowded into the church or waited outside to congratulate the "*Herr Baron.*" The *Kreisleiter* was there along with the police chief, the head of the nearby RAD camp, the station master and postmaster, and the local leaders of the Hitler Youth and BDM. Alexandra knew she would never remember any of the names, and she had never shaken so many hands in her life. She felt as if she were play-acting or impersonating someone important. Philip had slipped into his most inaccessible formality, smoothly thanking everyone by name, the right phrases readily on his tongue. Alix was very relieved when Sophia Maria finally signaled for them to return to the car.

Up at the manor the circle of guests was much more exclusive, intimate and relaxed. In contrast to the party Alexandra's parents had organized, at this gathering no one had been invited because it would "be the right thing" or to impress anyone else or further anyone's career. The arrival of two Jesuits, however, caused a minor sensation. Philip broke off the conversation he was engaged in and went across the room to show his respect, with a humility Alexandra had never seen in him before. One of the Jesuits was old and fragile, with almost no hair left and few teeth. The other was a still-vigorous man with steel-grey hair and a limp. "That's Father Georg, the rector, and Father Lucas, one of the teachers from the boys' boarding school," Sophia Maria explained to the astonished Alexandra.

Following Philip hesitantly, Alexandra saw the old man embrace Philip, and as she came up she heard him saying in a scratchy voice, "I was released two weeks ago. You mustn't look so distressed. At my age, a few hairs or teeth less is no tragedy." The old man brushed his fragile hand over his near-naked scalp, smiling, but Philip was staring at him as if he were looking at a ghost.

"But why, Father? What did you do?"

The priest shrugged, "You've heard of Bishop *Graf* Galen's sermons, I hope?"
Philip frowned. "No."
The older priest turned to the younger. "You see, Lucas? I did not do too much, but rather too little!" Then, turning back to Philip, he asked, "Have you never heard of the so-called Euthanasia Program?"

Philip shook his head.

"Well, that is a program in which allegedly incurably ill mental patients—helpless souls dependent on care—are forcibly removed from the hospitals and asylums for the sole purpose of exterminating them. According to Bishop *Graf* Galen, tens of thousands of innocent patients have been murdered.'"

A little crowd had collected around the Jesuits, including Sophia Maria and an elderly nun. The nun, an aunt of Philip's, crossed herself and covered her mouth with a trembling hand. Sophia Maria and several others exclaimed in shock. Only Philip seemed unmoved. He gazed expressionlessly at the old Jesuit and asked, "Did Bishop Galen protest?"

"First he protested. Then he made an official report to the police, charging the authorities with murder. But it had no effect. The innocent victims were still collected and slaughtered like cattle. So Bishop Galen sought to arouse widespread public opposition to the policy. He exposed this secret program in a public sermon on August 3 of last year, and—"

"August of last year?" Philip interrupted. "Why didn't I hear about it? I was still in Berlin at the time!"

"Yes, but the authorities did all they could to keep the sermon secret. That's why those of us who learned about it felt we had to reproduce and distribute the text as widely as possible. We at the school produced several hundred copies of the text, and I sent it out to the parents of all our boarders. I planned to send it to alumni next," he added with a smile at Philip, "but the Gestapo was faster."

Philip was so tense, Alexandra thought he might explode. He asked only, "When were you arrested?"

"August 15 of last year, but I was lucky. I was only sentenced to Concentration Camp. I escaped the death sentence, my lawyer says, only because I had not yet tried 'to undermine the fighting morale of our troops.' But I was wrong, Philip; I should have written to you and the others fighting with the *Wehrmacht* first. You have a right to know what awaits you if you are too seriously wounded to be considered 'productive' citizens anymore. The fate of mental illness could happen to all and any of us—from wounds, illness or simply old age."

The younger priest informed them, "The school was closed immediately. We were given just two hours to get out, and the buildings have been turned over to the *Lebensborn* Program. You know what that is?"

Philip looked uncertainly from the old priest to the younger one. "What?"

"Human stud farms. So-called racially suitable girls are paired with racially suitable SS men, and their children are then given to 'deserving'—read racially acceptable—childless couples."

"These policies amount to nothing less than a denial of the immortal soul," the rector told his former pupil firmly. "They treat people like soulless, conscienceless, mindless animals."

Philip nodded. "Yes. That's what we have become. Mindless, conscienceless animals."

The old Jesuit at once put his arm around Philip and insisted, "Not you, Philip. I know that you have a conscience and that you will always listen to it." However, Philip's face remained hard, his thoughts impenetrable.

After the horror of the night before, it was a relief to find the local train—old and run down as it was—relatively empty. They arrived in Baden-Baden without incident and had no difficulty getting a taxi to the spa hotel. Here, however, they discovered that they had again been displaced by a "golden pheasant"—in this case, the recently appointed *Generalbevollmächtigter* for Labor, Sauckel. Sauckel had called an urgent meeting of experts and senior officials of his organization— and, of course, the hotel had to put the bridal suite at his disposal. Alexandra, feeling Philip stiffen beside her, was quick to say that they didn't mind at all. They were shown to a modest room that nevertheless had a private adjoining bath and a balcony over-looking the park. It was furnished with quality antiques. The carpet was deep and soft. A dozen roses greeted them from the dresser and, in a bucket of ice, a bottle of champagne waited—compliments of the house.

Alexandra opened the French doors to the balcony and went out into the night. "Come look at the stars, Philip! Aren't they magnificent?"

Philip slowly followed her onto the balcony, still trying to smother his resentment at the downgrading of their accommodations. He folded his arms around her so she could lean back against his chest. She folded her arms over his. "The most beautiful stars I've ever seen were in the night skies of the Russian winter." He rested his chin on the top of her head.

"Don't think about Russia, Philip, not tonight," she pleaded.

Philip bent and kissed her. "I'm sorry," he sighed. He was sorry for everything: the horrible trip of the night before, the downgrading in accommodations here, and most of all his own depression, which he could not seem to shake off even now. Alexandra turned around and lifted her arms around his neck to kiss him properly. Her intention was to signal complete surrender—to assure him wordlessly that she was not going to make a silly scene this time. She wanted him to take her tonight.

Philip was astonished by the electrifying feel of her in his arms, soft and seductive. He had never wanted any woman as much as he wanted Alexandra. Not one of the girls of his youth, no matter how provocatively they had dressed or how expertly they had teased, had ever aroused in him a similar feeling of desire. Now his own words about there being no such thing as a woman who "wasn't any good" came back to haunt him. He felt that he alone was responsible for making tonight a success.

He slowly backed off the balcony and into the hotel room without disengaging from Alexandra's embrace. He felt his way hesitantly to the bed and then turned and eased Alix down. When she sat on the edge looking up at him expectantly, he kissed her on the nose, and then went and closed the door to the balcony. Next he locked and chained the door to the hall and turned off all but one of the lights. He set his spectacles aside, opened the bottle of champagne, poured two glasses, and brought one back to Alexandra. He sat beside her and kissed her under the ear. After that, things took care of themselves.

It was raining the next morning, which encouraged them to stay in bed. They called room service for breakfast, and lay in bed talking and making love alternately until the sun came out at about noon. Then they decided to go down for lunch and a walk. They bathed, dressed and went downstairs. It was a mistake.

Sauckel and the men meeting with him had just started their lunch break. The lobby was awash with brown uniforms, and the unfortunate other guests passing in and out felt compelled to raise their arms and bark "*Heil Hitler!*" Philip's mood was instantly shattered. Alix watched with concern and a growing sense of helplessness as his face closed and his lips grew thin.

In the dining room there was not one table free, and the waiter offered to seat them at a table for four at which one man was sitting alone. As it was already quite late and the lone man was a civilian, Philip agreed. They were taken over by the waiter and introduced themselves. The man stood, bowed to Alexandra, and shook hands with Philip. "Heinrich Fröhlich," he introduced himself; "Chief of Personnel at Siemens."

"And what brings you to Baden-Baden?" Philip asked politely.

"The gentlemen behind us," the businessman answered candidly. "If we aren't to be starved of labor, I have to ensure the good will of Sauckel and his underlings. That can't be done nowadays without personal contact—and, of course, the appropriate payments."

"Bribes, you mean," Philip corrected acidly.

The businessman shrugged. "It's the way it is."

From the neighboring tables, the conference participants complained about the lack of fresh strawberries and the limitations of the wine menu. Philip lost his appetite, and there was nothing Alexandra could do but cut lunch short and depart.

Outside, Alexandra took her husband's hand and smiled at him, trying to break through his gloom. He smiled back, but it was an absent smile—an alibi while his thoughts lingered elsewhere. They walked hand in hand through the park. Alexandra tried chatting to distract Philip. He made an effort to at least listen, but after a while he gave up and admitted, "Alix, I can't stand it. Even here everything has been poisoned by that brown filth." He indicated two bent old women in headscarves raking the grass in the park. Their clothes were a miserable patchwork of old things, their cracked feet were bare, and they wore the distinctive badges of forced laborers. His hand then took in the benches with "for Aryans only" painted on them, the troop of little boys in the uniform of the *Jungvolk*, and the SS soldiers opening the doors of the black Mercedes disgorging brown-uniformed passengers and "glamorous" women before the Casino.

"Is this what so many men are dying for out there? A Germany where only the corrupt have any power? Where helpless patients are murdered and young girls are turned into whores by the nation's 'leaders'? Is this what Christian and I are supposed to die for?" He was looking at his wife as if he expected her to give him an answer.

Alexandra's first reaction was sheer panic. How could she answer such a question? But if she didn't find an answer, their precious time together was going to be ruined by the oppressive shadow of the Regime. Then she realized that she did have an answer: she had to tell him about Valkyrie. She had to tell him that decent people were working to put an end to this rule of terror. She had to share with him the reason she felt hopeful for the future. She had to tell him what she was risking, or their whole marriage would be based on a lie.

But she was afraid he might not approve of what she was doing. She avoided his sharp, penetrating eyes by putting her arms around him and leaning her head on his chest. "No, Philip," she whispered, "it's not what you are meant to die for. The war has to be stopped …"

Philip took her words for a helpless attempt to deny reality. He tightened his arms around her, ashamed of himself for ruining her honeymoon. Alexandra clung to him; her heart was beating rapidly. She was suddenly very, very afraid of Philip's reaction. Philip could sense her fear, and he assumed it was just his talk of death. He gently tried to pry Alexandra away from his chest so he could look into her face, but she resisted tenaciously. He would have had to use more force than he was willing to use with her, so he gave up and said, "Forgive me."

"It's not that. It's …"

Philip asked gently, "What is it, Alix? Tell me."

"I have a confession to make."

"I'm listening." He waited, holding her patiently.

"Philip," she started in a timid voice, very frightened that he would angrily order her to stop her activities. If he did that, she would never forgive him. "General Olbricht asked me to type up some top-secret plans—plans for putting down a forced laborers' revolt or to eliminate an enemy commando raid in the center of Berlin. But that's not what they're really about …" Her voice faded away, afraid to be more articulate.

Philip hesitated and then asked sharply, "Is Tresckow part of these plans?"

"Yes, but I don't know Tresckow's role. There are lots of things I don't know. I don't know the civilians who are working on the plans for what comes afterwards. I don't know what Admiral Canaris and *Oberst* Oster have to do with things. And although I know that Tresckow is kept informed of developments, I don't know why. The plans themselves are being worked out in AHA."

Philip had stopped breathing. Then, speaking very slowly and softly, he told her: "Tresckow wants me to help him with these plans … Would you approve of that?"

Alexandra looked up, hardly daring to believe her luck. Philip wasn't just willing to let her continue; he would be part of it. They would be working together. "Of course."

"What do you mean, 'of course'—we are talking about breaking my oath and High Treason," he rebuked her.

"It may be treason against the government—but not against the nation, Philip. We're talking about putting an end to the murder of innocent people and stopping the senseless sacrifice of others—like Christian and Stefan."

"Only if we succeed. The chances of success are pitiable."

"Maybe. Personally, I think General Olbricht is brilliant. And the supplemental orders—things like the closing of the Concentration Camps and the arrest of *Gauleiters*—are being handled by Uncle Erich and Generaloberst Beck."

"Beck? Ludwig Beck is involved?" Philip took a step back, holding Alexandra at arm's length and searching her face intently.

She nodded, meeting his eyes. "Olbricht always refers to him as the CO of the Operation."

"Beck, Olbricht, Hoepner, Tresckow—good company to die in." Philip managed a little twitch of his lips as if he were trying to smile.

"Better than for the *Führer*," Alexandra insisted.

"There's a difference. On the front I die alone. As a traitor, I drag you down with me."

"I'm already there, Philip."

"No, you're not. As Olbricht's secretary you can always claim you were just doing your job—following orders. You can claim you never had any reason to think the plans had a use beyond their official purpose. But if I join this conspiracy, they'll never believe that. You'll pay the same price as I. You could be tried for treason and beheaded."

In an impulsive and passionate gesture, Alexandra reached up and took Philip's head in her hands. She went on tiptoe to kiss him. "That you would hesitate on my account is flattering, but I can't love you because you're a man of conscience and character, and then expect you to behave like an opportunist. In the midst of so much death, I want to believe there is something worth dying for, and you can't go on as you have been. You can't continue to serve a criminal regime without it destroying you. Don't you see, Philip? Only this can give our lives meaning."

"What about our love?"

"What chance has our love in a world poisoned by moral depravity on this scale? Just think of the last two days: all our love couldn't change the world around us, and it has ruined our wedding. Without hope of a better future, why should we go on living at all—much less have children?"

She was right, Philip realized with a touch of surprise. How could he have been so stupid? She was right, and so was Tresckow. The fight against the Nazis was not a military confrontation where only operations with a chance of success should be risked. It was the only means of rescuing his sanity and soul.

Philip took Alexandra more firmly into his arms and rested his cheek on the top of her head. "What would I do without you, Alix?"

CHAPTER 24

▼

Berlin
August 1942

As soon as she reached her bike, Marianne pulled the scarf off her head and shook out her hair. She ran her fingers through it and sighed. It was still six weeks until her compulsory work in the armaments factory would be over and the winter semester would begin. It seemed an interminable time.

She bent and deftly spun the dial of the combination lock on her bicycle chain. Around her the other workers streamed past, chatting and gossiping. Polish and Russian were as common as German. As Marianne looped the bicycle chain around the seat for the journey home, someone jostled her roughly. Annoyed, she looked up. The other woman was already apologizing profusely, and Marianne's frown dissolved as she recognized one of the Jewish workers.

The woman didn't seem to notice her smile. She just kept apologizing, brushing imaginary dirt off Marianne's work smock, and then she disappeared back into the crowd before Marianne could stop her. For a moment Marianne gazed after the disappearing figure, and then she let her hand run casually down her smock into the pocket. Yes, there was a piece of paper there. She left the note where it was. Taking the handlebars of the bike, she kicked up the stand. She rolled the bike to the factory gate and out into the street. Then she mounted her bike and set off as usual.

Only after she reached a main intersection with a traffic light several blocks from the factory did she risk removing the note from her pocket. On the back of a canned-goods label was scribbled anonymously: *Oldenburgerstr. 71, 2nd court-yard, left wing, fourth floor, right.*

Marianne felt a leap of nervous excitement. The traffic light changed. She stuffed the note hastily back into her pocket and cycled automatically. This could only be a plea for help, and it filled her with irrepressible joy. She had succeeded. She had managed to convey her sympathy to her Jewish colleagues and win their trust. And someone needed her help. Her life could become meaningful again, as it had not been since the Silbers' deportation.

But the note also made her nervous. She could not know what would be asked of her or by whom. Assisting Jews was a crime. She could not even be entirely sure it wasn't a trap of some sort. But she did not hesitate.

She cycled immediately—albeit by an indirect route—to the Oldenburgerstrasse. She chained her bike to a struggling sapling in front of #67. She then walked across the street to a tobacconist and bought a women's magazine. When she came out again, she went into #71. She walked under the front building by the vehicle entrance, crossed the first courtyard, and passed under the next building into the second courtyard. She took the door to the left and mounted the stairs to the fourth floor.

The stairwell was shabby and dirty, with both childish and obscene graffiti scribbled on the dirty paint. Heavy, unpleasant cooking odors hung in the air, and the stink of a stopped toilet greeted her on the second half-landing. On the fourth floor, right, a yellow Star of David informed all visitors of the religion of the residents. Although Marianne had met no one on her way up, she looked about guiltily before knocking. Her heart was thudding in her chest.

She could hear someone behind the door and knew they were looking through the peephole. The door opened a crack and a voice whispered, "What do you want?"

"My name is Marianne Molde—"

"SSSSHHHH!!!" The door opened wider and a hand gestured her inside.

Marianne found herself in a narrow, darkened hallway, confronted by an elderly man in a long, flowing white beard. This took Marianne a little aback; she had never had anything to do with Orthodox Jews before. The man was bowing his head slightly and gesturing for her to go into the kitchen. In a whisper he assured her, "You must believe we would never have bothered you if it weren't an emergency. We are at our wits' end and don't know where else to turn. My daughter," the man indicated a woman who was standing behind the vapor of boiling water from a pot on the stove, "heard that you—that you were—" He couldn't seem to find the right words.

"Decent," his daughter supplied the word sharply.

"It's about a child. A five-year-old child. Its whole family was picked up two days ago. A neighbor saw what was happening when she glanced out of the window. She saw the truck and the guards that were loading the neighbors into the truck. Without thinking she ran out, grabbed the youngest child—the five-year-old—and saved her."

"But how?" Marianne asked.

"She shouted at the guards, asking them what they were doing," Marianne's colleague from the factory explained. "She told the SS that the child was her own.'" The woman gave Marianne a piercing look. "You're not old enough to have children of your own. Maybe you can't understand."

"Of course I can!" Marianne protested without thinking, without knowing exactly what it was she was supposed to understand.

Her protest did not impress the hard-bitten woman behind the steam. "Do you know what it is for a mother to watch another woman grab her small child away from her? Can you know what a mother feels when a virtual stranger takes her child away with the words, 'This is *my* child'? I wonder! The real mother had to shrug, to show indifference to the tears and fright of her own little girl. Only her indifference could convince the guards that a lie was the truth. But it worked. The guards slammed the tailgate shut and drove away. The child, holding the hand of a semi-stranger, watched her mother and sisters and brothers disappear in the truck—and she hasn't spoken a word since."

There was an uncomfortable silence in the narrow kitchen. The woman looked down at the potatoes in the boiling water. Marianne did not know where to look.

At last the old man spoke. "But the woman who rescued the child couldn't keep her. Too many people in the house knew the truth. She would have been reported immediately."

The man's daughter took over the narrative. "The fear that someone had seen what she had done seized her almost at once. She had acted spontaneously, impulsively, without thinking. If she had thought about what came afterwards, she would not have done it."

The man continued, "She knew she had to take the child somewhere where it wouldn't be recognized. She brought the child to us."

"But we're Jews," the woman said harshly. "Tomorrow or the next day, they'll come for us, too. This child wasn't taken away from her own family only to die with strangers."

The word "die" made Marianne start.

"Didn't you know that?" the woman challenged. "What did you think happened to all the deported Jews?" The woman's tone was contemptuous. "Did you really believe we were "resettled"? Of course we're "resettled"—to work camps and worked to death! And what do you think they do with those of us who are too young or too old to work? What do you think happens to the sick and disabled?" She shook her head and then spat out, "They let them starve to death."

Marianne stared at the woman, resisting understanding. The Silbers. Were they too old to work? And what kind of work would be expected of them? Herr Silber was a gifted musician, his wife a concert pianist.

"The child doesn't look Jewish." The old man spoke in a soft, calm voice. "We need a family, a Christian family, who can take her in. Would you know of one?"

"Of course I'll take her—we'll take her. We'll invent some story. Of course, of course. Where is she?"

The man looked at his daughter. She scrutinized Marianne for several more seconds before she silently left the stove and pushed past Marianne out of the room. A moment later she was back with a small, wide-eyed child. Wisps of fine, dark hair fell over her high forehead; she clasped her hands together.

Marianne dropped into a squat and smiled at the little girl, but the child did not smile back. "What's your name?" Marianne asked the most obvious and natural question for opening a conversation with a strange, shy child.

She was rewarded with a sharp, violent rebuke from the older woman. "You must never ask that! Never! You must never remind this child of her past! She has no past! You have to invent a name and background and a history for her, and you have to believe it yourself! You must never, never refer to reality!"

Marianne sensed that this woman didn't think she was up to the responsibility entrusted her. She could hear the man sigh behind her. Marianne blushed, ashamed of her stupidity. Anxious to make good, to prove she wasn't either as stupid or as irresponsible as she seemed, she said, "Yes, of course; I just wanted to know for myself."

"No! The less you know, the better. You don't know our names or the name of the woman who brought her here. It's best if you go now. Is it dark yet?" Her father pushed the blackout blinds aside and peered out. "Almost," he announced.

"Almost isn't good enough. I'll give the child something to eat."

"That's not necessary!" Marianne didn't want this couple to have to go with less food; Jewish rations were much less than those of other citizens. "I'll buy something on the way home—or at home there are lots of wonderful—"

"She's not used to sweets or fruit. You'll have to be careful."

"Yes, of course." Marianne burned with frustrated humiliation. Why was everything she said wrong? She meant well. She only wanted to help.

"You'd better go now after all," the woman decided and showed Marianne and the child to the door.

To Marianne's astonishment, her parents received the strange child with sur-prising warmth and a minimum of questions. All of Frau Moldenauer's grandpa-rental instincts seemed to come to the fore. With touching tenderness she got the silent child to eat, undress and go to bed. But no sooner was the child out of sight and hearing than the questions began. Marianne's concocted story was torn to shreds. When she told the truth, her parents stared at her in stunned disbelief. Helping the Silbers with extra rations and old clothes was one thing; this was something else again.

"Marianne, I don't know what you were thinking!" her father began. "We can't possibly keep her. We can't suddenly have a child here. We'd have to explain it to everyone, and she'd have to be registered with the police. What could we possibly tell them? She has no papers."

"We'll have to say her papers got lost. We can go to the police and apply for new papers—"

"Don't be ridiculous! If she's not in the birth registry, no one is going to issue an ID. I can't believe that a girl as intelligent as you could get herself into such a mess."

"But what else could I do? I couldn't just leave her there, knowing she might get picked up and killed—"

"Don't get carried away! These deportations of the Jews are unpleasant, but they are only part of a resettlement scheme. I've even heard reports that they have orchestras and theater groups in the ghettos. It's a ridiculous exaggeration to claim that the Jews are killed."

Just a few hours earlier, Marianne would have agreed with her father, but the strange woman's eyes had been too convincing. She knew that that woman would not have entrusted the child to her care if she hadn't felt compelled by the cer-tainty that deportation meant death. Marianne was certain, but she knew she could not convince her father of it. He was too logical, too much of a careful scholar. He would demand documentation, reliable sources, evidence. Marianne sighed.

"I really would have expected more maturity and rational thinking from you," her father was continuing. "Tomorrow you will take the child back and say it would be better off among its own kind."

"I can't do that! I can't go back there and face those people! I won't go back there!"

"Well, the child can't stay here!" her father told her definitively, his whole authority as head of the house in his words, tone and expression.

Marianne held her hands together. "*Vati*, please! At least let her stay a couple of days until I can find another home for her. Whether it's true or not, the Jews believe the children are allowed to die in the East. If I take her back, they'll look at me like a murderer. I'll feel like a murderer."

"Just what do you think your friend Peter Kessler is going to think of you keeping a little Jew-girl under your roof?"

"Why should he learn she's a Jew? We can say she's the daughter of a relative who had to go into the hospital suddenly. That would explain why she came without warning, and also why she disappears later."

"And she is a sweet child." Frau Moldenauer entered the conversation for the first time, to the surprise of husband and daughter. "Imagine being torn away from her own mother like that! And she's so thin and timid. After all she's been through, I couldn't bear to just throw her out again. She needs kindness and comfort."

"I admire your motives and honor your feelings, my dear," Prof. Dr. Moldenauer told his wife with a look of dismay on his face, "but, you are being irrational nevertheless. We cannot keep her here. It is too dangerous. We must find another solution tomorrow."

"Tomorrow," as Marianne hoped, stretched into two, three and even four days. Meanwhile, Marianne had had time to think about what needed to be done. Clearly, even the story of the sick relative would arouse suspicion if the child stayed too long. Either she would have to remain totally hidden, like a forbidden pet, in constant danger of discovery, or a believable and documented story to explain her presence had to be invented. The first solution was easier in the short run, but how long could a child be expected to hide? To remain perfectly silent? To live cut off from fresh air and children its own age? The better long-term solution was, therefore, a new, fictitious identity that would allow her to grow up openly and normally. But that was only possible if they could buy or forge documents that would enable them to register her with the police.

When Marianne suggested this course of action to her parents, her father raged and her mother broke down entirely. "I can't go on," she sobbed. "It's too much for me. If we had to go to the police—I can't. I just can't. I'm too old to become a criminal," she admitted miserably, ashamed of her weakness.

Marianne didn't need her father's stern lecture about how she should show more concern for her mother's health. Over the past few days, Frau Moldenauer's nerves had come all too obviously near to collapse. Dark bags under her eyes attested to her sleepless nights. Her hands shook. She jumped and sucked in her breath every time the phone or doorbell rang. Even Marianne had to face the fact that her mother, despite her feelings and good intentions, just couldn't bear the strain of this "illegal" existence much longer.

Marianne had to find another home for the child. She mentally searched her list of acquaintances and friends. One person after another was dismissed as unsuitable; but at last she remembered a university friend who had admitted to being one-quarter Jewish. Marianne took the *S-bahn* to her friend's house in Wannsee, and they went to the beach to sun and swim. When they were out swimming away from the crowds, Marianne risked telling her the story. Before she had even finished, her "friend" cut her off angrily. "Why are you telling me this? I have troubles enough, always hiding my Jewish grandmother! How could you think I would help? Life is hard enough as it is!" She swam quickly away, kicking her feet vigorously in Marianne's direction. When Marianne reached the beach, the other girl had already taken her towel and disappeared.

Marianne broke down and wept. After she had cried for a while, she felt better. She went back into the lake and splashed the cool water onto her face. Then she lay in the sun and dozed for awhile before she dressed and started for home.

But in the crowded *S-Bahn*, the uneasiness started to build up again. The child and her parents were waiting for her at home, and she was no closer to a solution than ever. Her mother was having heart pains and looked so ill that even the cleaning woman, Frau Wendt, had commented on it.

Marianne's head went up sharply. She pretended to study the map of the transportation network. Frau Wendt was a genuine Berliner: tart in speech but with a big heart. She felt no particular adulation for laws simply because they were laws. She was streetwise, with a knack for survival, and she was particularly fond of children. Her husband had been a staunch and militant Socialist until the day he was killed in a bus accident some six years earlier. Marianne felt a flicker of hope.

The next morning Marianne waited for Frau Wendt in the courtyard. She looked frequently at her watch and mentally tried to fabricate an excuse for being late to the factory. There was bound to be a scene, and being late was a serious offense. Workers who were late three times were reported to the police. But Marianne had never been late before.

"*Na*, Frl. Moldenauer, what are you waiting around for? I thought you had to work?"

"I have to talk to you first, Frau Wendt. It's urgent!"

"I can tell. Come up to the Feldburg flat, and I'll fix us some tea." The charwoman led the way unconcernedly. She unlocked the back door to the Feldburg flat, and Marianne followed her into the spacious kitchen. While the cleaning woman put water on for tea, Marianne spilled out the whole story. Frau Wendt soon stopped what she was doing and listened intently. When Marianne was finished, she nodded and resumed making the tea. "So that's why your mother looks such a wreck." She nodded again and got out cups and saucers, adding to Marianne, who was nervously dancing around as if on hot coals, "Late is late. If you're going to be punished, why not have a nice cup of tea first, and let's talk this through."

Marianne sat down. Frau Wendt made the tea and seated herself opposite Marianne. "The girl's five, you say?"

"Well, we don't know exactly, but that's what my mother guesses."

Frau Wendt poured the tea thoughtfully, decided it was too weak, and poured her cup back into the pot. She swirled the pot around. Then she looked at Marianne and declared, "I think we could manage. My sister has moved in with me, and she likes children. We'll say it is the illegitimate child of my sister's son Eddie. He was always a bit of a tomcat." Again she poured the tea. Satisfied by the strength, she poured for Marianne, too. "Yes, we'll say it is his child, and we didn't even know about it until the mother—you can play the mother—dumped her on us. The mother, we can explain, had a new friend and wanted to get married, but the boyfriend refused to take her illegitimate brat. That happens, you know," she said as she looked at Marianne. "Eddie's dead now, fell last winter at Leningrad, so he won't be able to defend himself. Yes, we'll manage. It might even be nice to have a child around again." She nodded, but then looked sharply at Marianne. "But you'll have to get a birth certificate. It has to be a birth certificate from another part of Berlin, Spandau perhaps, and it will have to list Eduard Springer as the father of the illegitimate child. Can you manage that?"

"Yes, yes. I can manage that."

"All right, then. I'll talk to my sister and leave you a note in your mail-box tomorrow with the time and address for bringing the child over."

"When will you need the birth certificate?"

"In about two weeks."

"Oh, thank you!" Marianne threw her arms around the cleaning woman and euphorically ran down the back stairs to her waiting bike.

The child moved in with Frau Wendt and her sister. Marianne, whose only strength at medical school had proved to be medical drawing, started her career as a forger.

*   *   *   *

Smolensk, Soviet Union
October 1942

Just after 7 am, Philip reported to the operations room to start preparing for the 10 am briefing. *Oberleutnant* Fabian v. Schlabrendorff, Tresckow's ADC, who had been on duty throughout the night, came yawning from the Duty Room as Philip entered. Schlabrendorff's junior rank was a function of his reserve status. In civilian life he was a successful lawyer, and he was several years older than Philip. As with other civilians in uniform, Philip did not find rapport with Schlabrendorff easy. Even when he had not been up all night, Schlabrendorff's uniform often looked as if he had slept in it. He apparently found it difficult to stand up without leaning against something, and his shoulders were permanently hunched. On account of the night duty and a cold, he was looking particularly bad just now. His nose was red and swollen and his eyes were watering.

Philipp asked politely, "Anything new?"

Schlabrendorff made a sour face and remarked haughtily, "New? No, the usual: we are trying to hold too long a front with too few troops, and the Soviets will eventually break through somewhere. On the basis of these reports," he indicated the telegrams of the previous night, "it will not be long before they overrun the 83rd ID."

"Isn't that the division the Field Marshal wanted to visit today?"

Schlabrendorff shrugged, either to indicate he didn't know or didn't care—Philip wasn't sure which. Given the fact that he had been up all night and was ill, Philip supposed his casual attitude was forgivable, but inwardly he disapproved. Although he had been on Kluge's staff barely three months and in that time had had only limited direct contact with the Army Group Commander, he respected Field Marshal v. Kluge. The Field Marshal was very intelligent, had a highly developed sense of responsibility for the troops entrusted to him, and set a good example of hard work and self-discipline.

"I need to prepare my weekly briefing on international affairs," Schlabrendorff told Philip as he blew his nose into his crumpled handkerchief. Tresckow had given Schlabrendorff the assignment of listening to enemy broadcasts and summarizing the news from around the world on a weekly basis. "I have the feeling something's brewing in America."

Philip nodded without comment. Schlabrendorff's briefings were fascinating, but as a good lawyer he never revealed anything in advance.

Suddenly *Feldmarschall* v. Kluge stood in the doorway. On days when he planned a trip forward to the front, as today, he usually set off in his personal train or by Fieseler Storch immediately after breakfast. His appearance in Headquarters was thus unexpected, and both junior officers came to attention in surprise.

"I just sent Boeselager back to bed," he announced, referring to one of his two ADCs. Along with many of the staff, Boeselager was suffering from some flu that was going around. The Field Marshal's other ADC was on a two-week leave, so his next request was not surprising. "I need someone to accompany me."

Given the fact that Schlabrendorff was ill and had been up all night already, Philip volunteered. "If *Herr Feldmarschall* would be satisfied with my services, I would be happy to accompany him."

Kluge looked at Philip critically and glanced at Schlabrendorff, but then nodded. "All right, Feldburg. Come along. I want to leave at once."

As they boarded the special train a few minutes later, Kluge asked without even looking at him, "Have you ever served as an ADC before?"

"No, *Herr Feldmarschall.*"

Kluge grunted to himself with apparent dissatisfaction, but said in a not unfriendly tone, "It's not difficult. Just try to anticipate everything I could possibly want, give precise answers to my questions, and keep your reports objective—unless I ask for your opinion. You will listen in on all telephone conversations and attend all meetings with me. Be prepared to tell me everything that was said in case I missed something."

The train consisted of a sleeping car, a dining car converted into an operations room, and a communications center. An anti-aircraft gun on a flatcar provided protection, and a freight car carried the armored staff car for mobility at their destination. Kluge led Philip into the mobile operations room, where all the relevant maps already hung. He indicated the telephones with which they could maintain contact with the staff in Smolensk and with all the HQs of all the armies belonging to the Army Group whenever they stopped at stations along the way. He suggested that Philip read the morning briefing that Boeselager had prepared but had been unable to deliver.

This summary of the information that had come in overnight confirmed what Schlabrendorff had already indicated: the Russians appeared to be preparing an offensive at the junction between the sectors held by Army Group North and Army Group Center. Such junctions were always weak spots, particularly since

Hitler prohibited the Army Group Commanders from having direct contact with one another. This made the coordination of operations between Army Groups particularly difficult.

"Just what units are located in Welikije-Luki?" Kluge asked as Philip finished reading the briefing.

Philip started. Welikije-Luki was a large town not far behind the front of the 83rd ID. "There are no fighting units in Welikije-Luki, *Herr Feldmarschall.*"

"I know that. I asked you what units *were* stationed there," the Field Marshal rebuked him.

Philip took a deep breath and did his best to remember. He started listing the various training and maintenance battalions until he had to admit, "That's all I remember, *Herr Feldmarschall.*"

"You forgot the experimental rocket unit," Kluge told him pointedly. Philip was already regretting volunteering for this duty.

The train stopped in Welikije-Luki, and there they transferred to the armored staff car. In this they traveled forward to the HQ of the 83rd ID. Kluge let the divisional commander describe the situation to him, and then insisted he be taken forward to the batteries that were allegedly exchanging fire with the Soviets. The divisional commander cast a glance at Philip uncertainly; it was one of the duties of an ADC to keep his "charge" out of unnecessary danger, but Philip was too uncertain in his temporary role to say anything. The divisional commander felt compelled to remark, "I cannot guarantee *Herr Feldmarschall's* safety that far forward. The enemy has sufficient forces mustered to launch an attack at any time."

"Our intelligence suggests he is still bringing up more units and will not attack immediately. If our intelligence is incorrect, then Major v. Feldburg will make sure I do not fall into enemy hands alive." He looked hard at Philip as he said this. "I trust you can shoot to kill, Feldburg." Without waiting for an answer, he strode out to his car.

They drove forward toward a front that hardly deserved the name. The battalions of the 83rd ID were spread so thinly that kilometer-wide gaps existed between them. With good reconnaissance, the Soviets would find those gaps and insert their cavalry through them, encircling and cutting off the isolated German battalions. The scenario sent shivers down Philip's back. Kluge seemed unperturbed. They drove from battalion to battalion and to the artillery batteries, which exchanged listless fire with the Russians. Kluge never took cover when enemy shells landed nearby, but rather watched them with professional interest.

Once he asked Philip the range of the Soviets firing at them. "I haven't the faintest idea, *Herr Feldmarschall*," Philip admitted, feeling like a schoolboy who had failed to do his homework.

"5-6 km," Kluge told him. Philip glanced toward the battery commander who, with obvious astonishment, nodded confirmation.

It was already dusk by the time they returned to Welikije-Luki. Philip's feet felt like blocks of ice in his boots and his hands were stiff with cold. Kluge, however, had by no means finished his inspection. They drove to the HQs of the training battalions, one after another. As Kluge was not expected at these units and an inspection by an Army Group Commander was anything but routine, Kluge's appearance provoked excitement bordering on panic. More than once Philip found himself trying to suppress a grin of amusement at the inept response of the flustered officers and NCOs. *Feldmarschall* v. Kluge turned on him and glowered reproachfully.

Finally, around 9 pm, they returned to their train and the journey back to Smolensk began. Kluge tossed his cap aside and removed his greatcoat and gloves. Then he sank down into a deep, soft chair and glared at Philip. "Well, Feldburg? What is your assessment?"

"*Herr Feldmarschall*, the 83rd ID alone cannot hold this sector. If the Soviets attack they will roll through—more than over—the 83rd."

"And Welikije-Luki?"

"*Herr Feldmarschall?*"

"What will become of Welikije-Luki?"

"It will be captured, of course. None of the training units have heavy weapons, much less training."

"Tell the train commander to stop at the next station and order the signals technician to prepare to patch through a call via Army Group to *Führer* HQ."

"*Jawohl, Herr Feldmarschall.*"

Usually calls to *Führer* HQ were scheduled well in advance. Because this was a special request, it proved more difficult than normal, but eventually—after several attempts—the connection was made. With Philip on the second phone, Kluge opened with an apology for the unscheduled call, and then explained where he was and what he had seen in the course of the day. "*Mein Führer*," Kluge stated in a firm, decisive voice, "under these circumstances it is irresponsible to leave the training battalions in Welikije-Luki. I hereby request permission to relocate these non-combat units."

Hitler's voice, so familiar from radio broadcasts, rasped directly in Philip's ear, a strange sensation. "*Herr Feldmarschall*, the abandonment of Welikije-Luki would be a serious lost of prestige for the German Armed Forces."

"*Mein Führer,* I am not suggesting the abandonment of Welikije-Luki, only the removal of the training battalions stationed there for the event—"

"You are anticipating the loss of Welikije-Luke, *Herr Feldmarschall!* That is defeatism! I had expected better of you, *Herr Feldmarschall!*"

"*Mein Führer*, it is the duty of every officer to anticipate the worst. I have described to you the situation of the 83rd ID. It is only reasonable to anticipate that the Red Army might break through—even if only temporarily—and reach Welikije-Luke. If they did, *mein Führer*, then these units—which lack all heavy weapons and combat experience—could be slaughtered before the situation could be restored—"

"*Herr Feldmarschall*, German soldiers must always be prepared to fight and die where they stand. I now have a map in front of me, *Herr Feldmarschall*. I want you to redeploy the 1st battalion of the 126th Regiment …"

Philip nearly dropped the receiver. The C-in-C of the combined German armed forces was ordering redeployment at battalion level? It was farcical. He looked toward Kluge, but the Field Marshal was apparently used to this. He was nodding, "*Jawohl, Mein Führer*. I'll give the orders at once, but that does not solve the problem of the training battalions in Welijike-Luki. *Mein Führer*, I am requesting orders to remove these units, which have no combat utility but are very important for future combat strength. Remember that one of the units is an experimental rocket unit. It would be very dangerous if this unit with its equipment were to fall into Russian hands—"

"Then you must see that it does not fall into Russian hands, *Herr Feldmarschall!*" Hitler shouted in his fanatical, raw voice. Philip held the receiver away from his ear and glanced toward the Field Marshal.

Kluge's face was grim, but he did not capitulate. "*Mein Führer*, I will do all in my power to hold the front in my sector—including the front before Welikije-Luki. The issue here is not whether we hold the front, but whether units of no combat value should be drawn into the fight. Their presence does not add to the effectiveness of my Army Group, but their loss would be a needless waste—"

"Then do not lose them, *Herr Feldmarschall*."

Philip had to admire Kluge's persistence. Hitler had not only given a clear answer, it was obvious that he was increasingly angry. Still, Kluge did not give up—although his tone became just a touch more desperate as he reported,

"These are very young soldiers for the most part, *mein Führer*, many of them barely released from the Labor Service. They have no combat experience whatever. In any critical situation, they will be useless. It is completely unnecessary to expose them to the dangers here."

"*Herr Feldmarschall!* I have made my decision! I forbid you to mention it again! You are to hold Welikije-Luki at all costs! At all costs, *Herr Feldmarschall!* Is that understood!?" And then, without the slightest transition, Hitler's shouting was replaced by a congenial tone and he remarked, "*Herr Feldmarschall*, I have allowed myself to send flowers to your wife for her birthday."

"Ah—um—thank you, *mein Führer*," Kluge stammered, baffled and out-maneuvered.

"Then good night, *Herr Feldmarschall*."

"Good night—*Heil! Mein Führer*."

Hitler hung up.

Philip replaced the receiver of his phone as silently as possible. Kluge was sitting opposite him at the other desk, and they were alone in the darkness. Philip slipped out to report that the conversation was over and they could proceed.

As the train rattled through the night, Philip returned to the operations car, but he didn't dare speak. Kluge was still sitting at his desk with his hand on the receiver of the telephone. He did not even glance at Philip when he returned. Philip felt like an intruder. No subordinate should witness such a humiliating dismissal of a senior officer, but he had had no choice. He sank down into a chair and waited.

After a long time, Kluge broke the silence. He spoke in a voice so soft that Philip almost didn't hear it over the clacking of the wheels on the rails. "You are one of Tresckow's officers, aren't you, Feldburg?"

"I'm assigned to the Ia-Section, *Herr Feldmarschall*."

"That's not what I meant," Kluge snapped back.

Philip held his breath. Kluge knew about the conspiracy.

"Well?"

"Yes, *Herr Feldmarschall*."

Kluge shoved back his chair from the desk so that he could stretch out his legs. He stared at Philip. "Do you know what's wrong with your plans?"

"*Herr Feldmarschall?*"

"You underestimate the bastard. You think you can arrest him and put him on trial and that then the rest of the fools will suddenly see him for what he really is—a cold-blooded murderer interested only in his own mad vision!" Philip had rarely heard anyone talk so bitterly about Hitler. "You're wrong! If he is left alive, he will always be able to enchant enough people to stop you. Not to mention the oath that binds the majority of officers like flypaper does flies!" Kluge snorted. "As long as he is alive, you will be outnumbered by the fanatics who believe in him, the criminals who have profited from him, and the fools who are stuck to the flypaper of a worthless oath."

"If numbers alone determined success, *Herr Feldmarschall*, the Red Army would have been in Berlin last spring."

Kluge made a sound that might have been a laugh. "Spare me your fantasies, Feldburg. I tell you: there is only one way for you to succeed. You have to kill the bastard."

"Better one bastard than the training battalions at Welikije-Luki...."

Kluge nodded as if satisfied by this answer. Then he pulled himself to his feet. "I need to get some sleep." Philip, of course, stood at the same time as the *Feldmarschall*.

At the door to the compartment he stopped and turned back to Philip. "Get some sleep yourself, and, Feldburg, you can tell Tresckow from me: if you kill him, you can count on me. But only if you kill him."

The train backed into position behind the wooden barracks that housed the *Feldmarschall's* quarters. He shared the wooden building with only the Chief of Staff and his ADCs. The rest of the staff was in a second, larger building some 200 meters away. Philip saluted and continued to the staff building between the tall, rustling pines. It was almost 6 am, but not yet greying with dawn. Philip went straight to Tresckow's room and knocked.

A groggy voice answered, "*Ja, bitte?* Who's there?"

"Feldburg, *Herr Oberst*. I've just returned from Welijike-Luki with the *Herr Feldmarschall*."

"Come in."

As he entered, Tresckow was swinging his feet out of bed to sit up and face him. Tresckow was dressed in pajamas. His feet were bare. But he looked up expectantly. It was obvious to him that Philip would not have woken him without a reason. "Has there been a breakthrough?"

"No, *Herr Oberst*. The military situation is unchanged. However, Kluge tried to talk Hitler into letting us pull the training units out of Welijike-Luki."

Tresckow raised his eyebrows. "And failed, I gather."

Philip nodded. "That's not why I'm here, *Herr Oberst*. I'm here because after Hitler had denied us permission to pull the training units back, Kluge asked me to convey the following message. I quote: 'You can tell Tresckow from me: if you kill him, you can count on me. But only if you kill him.'"

Tresckow reacted as if he'd been given an electric shock. He jumped to his feet. "He said that? 'You can count on me?' Do you realize what this means? With an entire Army Group behind us, we are no longer a little clique of officers trusting to a trick and the blind obedience of others for success! Olbricht has always insisted that his plans are weak because the Home Army—and its leadership—are weak. With the authority of a field marshal to make sure the orders of the post-Hitler government are respected and fighting troops to keep the SS in check, our chances are transformed! Completely transformed!"

Tresckow started pacing. "I've been wrestling with Kluge's conscience for almost a year. He's never been blinded by that madman, but he has shied again and again from the idea of being a traitor. He does not want to go down in history as the first Prussian field marshal who betrayed his country. No amount of debate on the essence of Prussia or treason itself could make him take the last jump. He's refused again and again."

"But he hasn't taken the fence yet," Philip insisted. "He set a pre-condition. He will only support us if Hitler is dead."

Tresckow stopped and stared at Philip intently. "Do you have a problem with that?"

Philip took his time answering. He understood Kluge's reasoning, and he had no difficulty seeing Hitler as a mad dog that had to be killed. But he had never shot a man face to face. It was not a pleasant thought. Nor was he certain he was capable of it. Hesitantly he explained to Tresckow, "I couldn't be sure of my aim. If I miss on the first shot, there will be no second chance."

Tresckow put his hand on Philip's shoulder. "I meant did you have a problem with the idea of assassination—not whether you were willing to carry it out personally."

"But the question is the same, *Herr Oberst*. I can't say I favor assassination only if someone else does the dirty work."

"Well said," Tresckow acknowledged, adding in an excited, almost euphoric tone, "but you've just given me an idea. If we could lure Hitler out here to Army Group Center, we could all shoot him. Between the half-score of us—particularly with crack shots like Boeselager and Gersdorff—one of us should be able to get in a fatal shot. Hitler's SS bodyguards will furthermore be forced to divide their attention among all of us as well."

"Tyrannicide *á là* Caesar."

"Yes." He smiled at Philip. "For the first time, Feldburg, we have a real chance of success."

CHAPTER 25

▼

Berlin
October 1942

Marianne had run into the new Freifrau v. Feldburg more than once in the entry
or on the stairs. The first time she introduced herself, the young Baroness had
seemed genuinely pleased to learn she was at university, and she had always had a
pleasant smile for Marianne since. Still, there is a world of difference between a
friendly smile in passing and doing someone a favor. But Marianne was desperate.

After her birth certificate for the Jewish girl was accepted without question by
the police, Frau Wendt had come to her with a request for a forged ID to help a
"friend" who was living "underground." This friend, it turned out, had been rescued from Gestapo arrest by a pastor of a Confessing Church. He and several
members of his congregation were active in trying to help "non-Aryan" members
and other victims of persecution. Marianne went to visit the church, and for the
first time in her life she was moved by religion. After she had gained the trust of
the pastor, she learned from him that the church maintained an entire network of
safe houses. Here Jews and other politically persecuted people could take refuge.
Marianne had explained to him that she could not help with a safe house, but on
the following Sunday she had taken him a sample of her "work": a forged university ID card filled out with semester and faculty and name—everything but the
photo and date of birth.

The pastor had stared at her, and she had asked, "Don't you know someone
who could use this?"

And so it had begun in earnest. One of the most important tasks, the pastor
soon explained, was getting extra ration stamps. The people who hid the "submarines" (people living underground) could not be expected to share their own—

often pitifully meager—rations indefinitely. He asked Marianne to mass-produce false ration stamps.

She agreed, of course, but it was easier said than done. The only place where she could work on her forgeries was in her own room at home. But of course, her parents viewed this room as part of the common apartment. Frau Moldenauer often entered the room without knocking, and she went in and out at will when Marianne was absent. Marianne lived, therefore, in constant fear of discovery, even in her own home. Not that her parents would ever betray her to the authorities, but if they learned what she was doing, they would forbid her to continue.

Marianne had been raised to be an obedient child, and she did not want to defy her parents. Nor did she want to endanger them more than necessary. But she was not willing to stop her activities, either. Since attending the services at the Confessing Church, she had become increasingly convinced that she had to help the persecuted. She felt she had been called by a Higher Authority to do what she was doing. Why else had she been given such an unusual gift? She often found herself quoting Luther in her head: Here I stand. I cannot do otherwise.

She had to find some place where she could work undisturbed and where the risk of discovery was minimal. She couldn't help but think of Jähring's atelier under the eaves. Peter Kessler had not rented it with the apartment, as he had no use for it. It was empty, unused. Why shouldn't the Baron—or since he was away at the front again, the Baroness—von Feldburg rent the attic room to her?

Of course, Marianne couldn't afford to pay rent. So what she was really thinking about was asking Baroness v. Feldburg to let her use the room free of charge. That was asking a lot of a stranger, and Marianne hesitated for days, feeling worse and worse as the persecuted waited desperately for the ration stamps she had promised to forge for them. Finally she realized that the worst that the Baroness could do was say "no"—in which case she had to come up with another solution. So she collected her courage, and after dinner knocked at the Feldburg flat.

Alexandra opened the door herself and smiled at once at the sight of Marianne. "Frl. Moldenauer, what can I do for you?"

"Good evening, Freifrau v. Feldburg. I'm sorry to bother you at this time of night, but I—I have a favor to ask of you."

"Come in out of the cold," Alexandra suggested, backing up and closing the door behind her. "Would you like to join me for tea?" She indicated the drawing room where she had just settled down at the secretary to write her daily letter to Philip. Tea was warming over the candle.

"Oh, that's not necessary," Marianne responded, embarrassed, but Alexandra was already on her way to fetch another cup and saucer. A moment later they were sitting at the low table with the tea between them and Alexandra was asking, "How are your studies coming?"

Marianne sighed. Her heart was no longer in her studies. It would be years before she could be qualified as a doctor, but what she was doing for the "submarines" was something immediate. She couldn't force herself to concentrate properly on things like chemistry when her mind was full of how to help the "submarines." "Not very well, I'm afraid," Marianne admitted. "In fact, I might well flunk out of chemistry."

"I hope not!" Alexandra countered sincerely. "It's so important for women to prove the Nazis wrong. Medicine is surely one of the most important fields for professional women." Alexandra risked these remarks because Philip had told her about Prof. Dr. Moldenauer's dismissal from the university, and intuitively she sensed that Marianne did not support the Regime.

Marianne straightened alertly. Supporters of the government never referred to Party members as "Nazis." She looked more closely at her landlady and then ventured, "Medicine is important, but it's not the only field that is important. We all have our limitations and callings. I think, maybe, I'm not meant to be a doctor as such." Marianne smoothed her skirt over her knees a little nervously and smiled timidly at Alexandra. "I've been told I have a gift for medical drawing, and so I want to major in it."

Alexandra had never heard of such a specialty, but was prepared to approve. "That sounds very interesting."

"It is—only, you see, it's hard to work in my bedroom at home. I don't have enough space or light. The work is very detailed and has to be exactly correct. That's why I was wondering about Herr Jähring's atelier." She looked up hopefully, holding her breath. Alexandra looked blank. "On the 5th floor at the back. Herr Jähring had an atelier there," Marianne explained. "I thought, since it isn't being used anymore, that maybe you wouldn't mind if I used it ..." Her voice faded off and she looked nervously at Alexandra, her hands clutched between her knees.

Alexandra liked Marianne and admired her for braving all the barriers put in her way. She was inclined to help if she could, but admitted, "Philip never said anything about an atelier. Let me see if I can find a set of keys." She left Marianne and went into the smoking room.

Philip had left a complete set of keys and all rental documents in his secretary. As one would expect of a good General Staff Officer, each key was neatly labeled, and there were two marked "Atelier."

"Let's go up and take a look," Alexandra suggested.

Together Alexandra and Marianne went to the back of the apartment and then out onto the service stairs. They climbed past Peter Kessler's apartment to the landing under the eaves. The left-hand door was open and one could see clothes hanging on lines, hampers, ironing boards and the like. The door to the right was closed and locked. Alexandra tried one of the keys and the door opened at once. She switched on the light inside the door and gazed around.

The atelier was neat and tidy. A stand waited—empty—before a wooden chair. Palettes and cases for paints, jars with "bouquets" of brushes, pencils and pencil sharpeners, rags, empty canvases, everything waited in neat rows for the return of the artist. Marianne felt her heart wrench. The room bore Peter's stamp. He—not Herr Jähring—was an orderly man who kept everything exactly in its place.

"It's completely unheated," Alexandra remarked with a glance at Marianne.

"Herr Jähring must have had—yes, look, there's an electric heater." Marianne pointed to a dusty heater on the floor under the window. "And I can dress warmly. There's lots of light." Marianne went into the room and turned on the bright standing lamp that stood behind the chair. There were several other lamps in the room as well.

"If you want to use it, I don't mind. You may use it, contingent on Philip's approval, and I can't see why Philip would object." Alexandra took the key off of the ring and handed it to Marianne.

"I—I can't afford to pay for it," Marianne admitted, blushing.

"I know," Alexandra told her, still smiling.

"Thank you, *Freifrau*—"

"Please call me Alexandra. I feel like I'm impersonating someone when I'm addressed as '*Freifrau*.'" They turned off the lights, closed and locked the door, and started down the stairs together. They only got to the next landing. Here the door cracked open, and Peter Kessler peered out of his apartment around the door. At the sight of the two young women he opened the door wider. "Marianne! Freifrau v. Feldburg! What brings you here? Is something wrong?"

Philip had warned Alexandra about Kessler, and she'd avoided contact with him up to now. Marianne, in contrast, smiled easily and told him happily, "Freifrau v. Feldburg has just agreed to let me use Herr Jähring's atelier! Now I can do all my studying and drawing there. Isn't that wonderful?"

Peter looked over at Alexandra and nodded. "That is very kind of you," he said, but his expression remained strangely worried. "If I'd known … Would you like to come in?"

"Thank you, no. I really must finish my letter to my husband. Good night," Alexandra nodded to both Marianne and Peter, instinctively aware that they wanted to talk. She continued quickly down the stairs, wondering how someone as nice as Marianne could let herself get involved with someone from the Gestapo.

Behind her Peter asked Marianne in a low, hurt voice, "Why didn't you tell me you wanted the atelier? I could have rented it for you."

"But Freifrau v. Feldburg is letting me have it for free," Marianne told him blithely.

"It's not good to be in debt to people like that," Peter told her in a low voice, his expression still clouded with worry.

"What do you mean, 'people like that?' I've never met nicer people than the Feldburgs."

"I know they're nice, but they're—well—they think they're better than us. And they're Catholic."

"Honestly, Peter, what difference does that make?"

Peter knew better than to argue with Marianne over politics, but in his circle the mistrust of Catholics was almost as great as the mistrust of Jews. Nor would he ever forget the arrogant way Major v. Feldburg had treated him on the day they met. It was obvious that Feldburg was not a convinced National Socialist, and Peter didn't want Marianne to associate with people who would only reinforce her own doubts about the Regime. "Come in out of the cold, and let's have a cup of *ersatz*."

Marianne slipped inside his apartment and into his arms. Leaning against the closed door, they kissed. Marianne was starting to feel better and better. She had found a place to do her forgeries where no one else in the world could disturb her. She had the only key! The fact that it was just upstairs from Peter was an added benefit. Now her parents would never know if she was up in her atelier studying or if she was visiting Peter. Her parents did not approve of her seeing Peter, and they certainly didn't like her going to his apartment. They would be shocked and distressed to see her now.

Not that things had gone "too far." Marianne had been raised too strictly, and had too many plans for herself, to risk going to bed with Peter. Nor had Peter tried to seduce her. He sometimes said that "if he got promoted" he would be in a position to marry, but he had not actually proposed. Marianne was just as happy. She did not feel ready to get married. She wanted to finish her studies. And given her parents' feelings about the Gestapo, she could hardly introduce Peter as their future son-in-law. Most importantly, it would be much harder to hide her activities with the Confessing Church if she were married to and living with Peter. No, things were better just the way they were.

Peter drew back from the kiss somewhat breathlessly. His glasses glinted in the hall light. His expression was very earnest. "Marianne, there's something I want to show you." He took her hand and led her down the hall to his meticulously neat office. Here he set his briefcase onto the secretary and turned the combination lock for each latch. He opened the briefcase and removed a file folder. He opened up the folder and removed a sheet of paper, which he handed to Marianne.

Marianne read: The White Rose Pamphlet. She frowned, unable to make anything of it. The next sentence read: "Nothing is more unworthy of a civilized people than to allow itself to be ruled by an unconscionable and evil clique of rulers without resistance." The word "resistance" made the blood rush to her face. There were others out there!

Peter was watching her face intently. "That was turned over to us today. A student brought it. He said it was circulating at the university. Have you seen it before?" he asked softly and urgently.

Marianne looked up and met his eyes. "Of course not, Peter. If I had, I would have brought it straight to you."

Peter searched her eyes. He wanted to believe her. He wanted with all his heart to believe she would come to him with anything like this, but some instinct said that she wouldn't. "Do you know who might have written something like this?" His eyes were large and pleading. If she would just help him, maybe he would get promoted, and then he would be able to afford a family. "It had to be a student," he explained to her; "it is full of quotes from Goethe and Schiller."

"Then it was probably a literature student," Marianne suggested lightly.

Peter frowned. "This is High Treason, Marianne. It's not something to joke about. These pamphlets bear no trace of Bolshevism, and none of our informers in known opposition circles know anything about where they came from. They are something completely new. We have to find out who is drafting and circulating these pamphlets and stop them, because they are very dangerous. Even if the perpetrators are only a small clique of foolish students, they are obviously trying to undermine the fighting morale on the Home Front and so aid the enemy. With our Armed Forces struggling for our very survival, people who write things like this deserve death, Marianne." Peter was very serious, and he looked at her with his eyes magnified by his glasses. He was afraid she might disagree with him.

Marianne, however, went onto tiptoe, and with one hand pulled his head down toward her to kiss him again. She whispered, "Peter, I haven't any idea who might have written these pamphlets. I think they are silly." Marianne was not play-acting. After her initial delight to discover that other people shared her opinion of the Regime, she had decided that distributing pamphlets was nonsense. They would help no one. All that mattered was helping the victims, not provoking the authorities to new repression.

*   *   *   *

North Africa
November 1942

The blistering heat of the equatorial sun lasted only as long as the sun burned down on the scorched landscape. By night the temperatures dropped to freezing, and then out of nowhere came a howling rainstorm that whipped through the tents and sent everything that wasn't tied down cartwheeling through the darkness.

Christian, wrenched from his sleep, first thought that it was one of the perpetual British bombing raids and made a dive for the ground. When the icy rain penetrated his consciousness, he got to his feet and ran out of his tent. He started shouting at anyone and everyone to grab every available container that could be used to collect water. They were so low on water that they had been rationing it, and one airman had been caught trying to drain water from a radiator for drinking. It was understandable, but unforgivable, because the vehicle hadn't been totally disabled.

Christian's orders were hardly necessary. The entire squadron seemed possessed with the same idea. Everywhere tents were turned—in some cases, literally—upside down to catch the precious rain.

But the rain did not last long. Minutes later the wind rent the clouds apart, revealing the glittering stars overhead. Christian automatically looked for a constellation or two and then, feeling the exhaustion, stumbled back to his tent and flung himself on his cot. The blankets he wrapped around himself were damp and gave off a distinctive wet wool smell, but he could no longer be disturbed by such details. He dropped quickly into a light sleep.

As had already happened twice since the news of Dieter's death reached him, Dieter appeared in Christian's dream. This time he shook Christian and woke him. "Sorry, Christian," he apologized with a slight smile, "but it's important."

"Every God-damned thing is important," Christian retorted irritably. In the dream, he did not remember that Dieter was dead and therefore had to be treated with respect.

"It's Yvette," Dieter continued, unperturbed by Christian's rudeness. "She's given birth to my daughter, and she's all alone. I want you to take care of them. You'll do that for me, won't you?"

"What the hell am I supposed to do? I'm half starving to death in this God-forsaken desert, and the RAF is bombing the shit out of us! I'll be dead in no time!"

Dieter smiled and shook his head. "Not you, Christian; you'll make it. Get money to Yvette, or get her a job at the base. You can manage it."

"Gabrielle—"

Dieter shook his head. "You know Gabrielle isn't worth it. Yvette and my little girl …"

As dreams are, without transition, Gabrielle was cuddling herself against Christian, complaining in a pouting voice about the dampness of the blanket. "That doesn't matter," Christian murmured, warmed by her mere presence. The feel of her satin nakedness against his skin excited him.

"It does matter," Gabrielle rebuked him. "I'm going to have a baby."

"*Whose* baby?" Christian demanded, feeling the cold and damp and roughness of the wool again.

Gabrielle laughed and was gone.

"Christian." It was Philip now, speaking urgently and in a low voice. "There's something I've got to tell you—"

They were interrupted by Walther, who came toward them beaming, "You fools! What are you doing freezing and dying out here for?—for a government you can't stand!" Walther evidently considered this a good joke and started laughing. "That's what I call over-breeding!" He laughed more heartily. "You've lost all your horse sense. We real Nazis aren't dumb enough to get our asses shot off in some foreign wasteland. We're making money hand over fist." Walther shoved his hands deep into his pockets and started pulling out fistfuls of paper money that he threw into the air like confetti. "That's what I call dumb," he said, laughing so hard that tears trickled from the corners of his eyes, "starving and dying for an Austrian corporal you despise! Too proud to join the Party and get rich."

Walther's laughter was still ringing in Christian's ears when he was shaken awake. The man leaning over him was *Oberleutnant* Scheel, his squadron adjutant. "*Herr Hauptmann*! A *Leutnant* has just arrived from Afrika Korps."

Christian's attention was directed to a drenched-looking Army lieutenant standing behind the adjutant. The lieutenant made a salute-like gesture and reported, "My orders are to prepare the airfield for demolition."

Christian sat bolt upright. "Could you repeat that?"

"I'm to prepare the airfield for complete demolition within the next 24 hours."

"Are things as bad as that?"

"Afrika Korps has only a dozen operable tanks, 5000 casualties and 8000 troops still missing. Italian losses are worse. It's unclear whether we have enough gasoline to get what vehicles we have left back to Tobruk. We can expect no supplies—not gasoline, food or water. Montgomery is trying to outflank us at every turn—"

Christian cut him off to address Scheel. "Reconnaissance patrol set for dawn—I want it doubled. Haven't we had word from *Gruppe?*" Scheel shook his head, stunned. "Try to establish contact." Christian turned back to the Army lieutenant. "You were saying?"

The *Leutnant* shrugged. "I believe *Herr Hauptmann* has correctly grasped the essentials."

Christian nodded. Outside, the torrential rain had started again.

The rain lasted two days, grounding all aircraft and bogging down the advance and retreat equally. Early on the morning of the 8th, however, *Luftwaffe* reconnaissance confirmed what Rommel already knew: the British 8th Army was biting at his heels with more than twice his strength and an intact line of supply. The orders to destroy the airfields and pull back, temporarily suspended, were now reissued—this time by *Luftwaffe* as well as Army commands.

Christian's squadron was used to moving rapidly. Up to now it had always been moving forward, but Christian soon decided that the mechanics were much the same regardless of the direction. Only the psychology was different.

Before the second reconnaissance patrol could get off the ground, the RAF swept in on a raid. Fighter-bombers came in low, seemingly without warning, strafed and bombed with impunity, and then were gone. Christian, picking himself up, hardly bothered to dust himself off. His gaze was fixed on the billowing black smoke of a fuel tank.

"Making my work easier," the engineer lieutenant remarked evenly, dusting himself off more thoroughly than his host.

Christian looked at him reprovingly. "That damaged fuel tank means I have to leave aircraft behind."

The lieutenant was not impressed. "The desert is littered with abandoned equipment. Some future archaeologist will wonder what was worth fighting for here," he gestured to the surrounding desolation. "Not so much as a water-hole."

Christian could only snort agreement, but there was no time for conversation. On the airstrip the second patrol was sitting with their engines turning over, unsure about risking the takeoff over a runway now littered with bomb craters. Ground crews were already setting up sticks with yellow flags to mark the craters, and Army engineers—the lieutenant's team—were cautiously circling a bomb that had failed to detonate on impact. Christian ordered the patrol into the air and went to check on the fuel situation.

In the motor pool the issue was how many vehicles could be made serviceable and how fast. The sun was climbing again, and the air grew hot. The mechanics stripped to the waist and wiped sweat from their greasy faces with the backs of their forearms. They held their black hands like limp claws except when they worked. In the kitchen the cooks worked only in their underpants, preparing the last hot meal the troops would get until God-knew-when. In the squadron orderly room, the adjutant was sorting through papers, burning anything he didn't want to transport.

The flak batteries opened up, and the RAF was back. A short incidental visit, it seemed. A quick strafe and then they flew on. The Army lieutenant nodded, "Must have better targets in range. Or they now realize they want the airfield as intact as possible."

The *Luftwaffe* patrol came back, and one of the pilots misjudged his landing. A wheel hit a crater and the plane whipped around and rolled over in the hole. The pilot was extricated with a broken collarbone and they siphoned off the remaining fuel; the aircraft was slated for demolition. The other pilot, meanwhile, reported the English positions. Christian gave orders to eat and start loading the vehicles. What they couldn't carry in the vehicles, they would simply have to destroy. "We'll start with the unserviceable aircraft at once."

"Please don't do that," the engineer lieutenant requested mildly.

Christian turned to him, stony-faced. "Why not?"

"Because I was planning to booby-trap it, along with the latrines and the file cabinets—in which I hope you will leave some inviting-looking papers."

It took a moment for Christian to shove aside his preconceived ideas and start to picture the implications of the engineer's suggestion. Slowly, however, the images started to take shape: curious English airmen crawling into the cockpits of his wounded Messerschmitts—and being blown to kingdom come; officious intelligence officers eagerly grabbing the "secret" documents from his safes—and the safes blowing up in their faces. As for the booby-trapped latrines....

Christian started to chuckle. The Army lieutenant joined him. And because laughter is infectious, particularly at such moments, the laughter of the one fed the laughter of the other until they were both guffawing in delight. It wasn't even that they felt any particular hatred for the English. The point was only to make the airfield unusable for a few days—maybe, if they were clever, even for a week. If they could give the Afrika Krops time to pull back to its bases, time to lick its wounds ... If Afrika Korps could only get back to Tobruk, back to Tunis, back to the aquamarine waters on the white sands below the pastel villages and fine minarets that Christian had (wrongly) imagined all North Africa would be ... If they could just delay the English advance for a couple of weeks—a couple of days!— surely they would have a chance to replenish their strength? Even now there must be convoys of ships on the way from Germany. Their holds must be filled with tanks and planes, fresh from the factories of the *Reich*. And tankers full of aviation fuel must also be rushing across the Mediterranean toward them.

"*Herr Hauptmann.*"

Christian, still grinning, turned his attention to the signals corporal, who had just come up beside him. "We've just intercepted the following message."

Christian took the cable and read: "Large Anglo-American task force landed near Casablanca and Algiers. Estimated combined troop strength: 100,000. Heavily equipped with armor and aircraft."

Once again Christian was moved to laughter, but this time it was a fraction hysterical.

CHAPTER 26

▼

Verchne Solonovski
November 1942

The orders that sent Philip south came out of the Army Personnel Office with a grade of urgency that was rare. Although his promotion to lieutenant colonel occurred simultaneously with the new assignment as Chief of Staff of the XXXII Korps, Philip was not given time to add the star to his shoulder tabs. Stadthagen would have to take care of that, along with packing and bringing his things to him by ground transportation. Philip's orders were for him to proceed "at once" and by air.

Because there was no direct link between Army Group Center and the newly established Army Group Don, much less to XXXII Korps, Philip had to make his way mostly by hitchhiking from one airfield to another, taking advantage of whatever happened to be flying in generally the right direction. In Rostov, how-ever, Philip's orders produced a Fieseler Storch to fly him personally forward. The courtesy was extremely unsettling. Such planes were usually available only for field marshals and commanding generals; when they were put at the disposal of a newly-baked lieutenant colonel, it could only mean that the situation at the XXXII Korps was disastrous. The pilot increased Philip's discomfort by flying at treetop level and admonishing Philip to keep a sharp lookout to ensure that they did not land on the wrong side of the lines.

They landed (on skis) without mishap in a clearing behind a factory that dou-bled as an improvised airfield. An *Oberleutnant* of the artillery was at the airfield to collect Philip in a battered staff car. The grave-looking young man had an ugly, discolored scar that ran from below his right eye to the center of his upper lip, his nose partially cut away: the mark of a Soviet cavalry saber, Philip guessed. He saluted and introduced himself. "Seydlitz, *Herr Oberstleutnant*."

"Feldburg," Philip held out his hand. "Are you the General's ADC?"

"I think I'm *Herr Oberstleutnant's* ADC. At least I was ADC to the former Chief of Staff."

"My predecessor is no longer here?" It was usual for an officer to await his replacement and introduce him to his new comrades and his duties. When possible, an overlap lasted as much as a week. Given the urgency of the orders, Philip had guessed that his predecessor might himself be under urgent orders to a higher posting and that the transition might be short as a result. Nevertheless, since he was coming from a totally different Army Group with absolutely no knowledge of local conditions, terrain or troops, he had hoped he would be briefed thoroughly, no matter how shortly.

"No, *Herr Oberstleutnant.* He was ordered back to Berlin at the same time as the commanding general."

"When was that?"

"Two days ago, *Herr Oberstleutnant.*"

"And the general's replacement?"

"Hasn't arrived yet; he's being sent from Berlin."

Philip stared at the serious *Oberleutnant,* but there was nothing more to say at the moment. All he could think was: this is worse than the last time.

At the provisional HQ, Philip went directly to the most senior staff officer still at his post, the Ia, Major Zimmermann. Zimmermann was an unusually tall officer with wavy blond hair and a boyish face turned prematurely old. He shook hands morosely and waited for Philip to ask questions, rather than taking the initiative of briefing. Philip was forced to remind him that he came from Army Group Center and had no knowledge of the situation or the corps' previous activities. Finally, since the Ia didn't seem to be making sense, Philip suggested, "Let's start at the beginning. What divisions are attached to this corps?"

"The First Romanian Panzer Division and the 13th German Light Panzer Division were attached to the corps."

"Were? And now?"

Zimmermann shrugged, "They don't exist anymore."

Philip took a moment to absorb that, but his urgent orders were not necessary for nonexistent troops. "What new units have been or will be assigned to this corps?"

Zimmerman shrugged again. "We've been promised a panzer division, three infantry divisions and a mountain division, but I don't know which ones or in what strength or when—if ever—they will arrive."

"So what troops are at this HQ's disposal as of today?"

"A flak battery and stragglers from various shattered divisions of this and other German corps."

They stared at each other, the major listless and Philip simply unable to grasp what was being said. Finally Philip asked, "What happened?"

"On Nov. 19, after a massive artillery barrage, the enemy threw 11 armies at the 3rd Romanian and 4th German armies. The 4th Army was torn in two, and the Romanians were overrun and obliterated. We, with one untested Romanian panzer division and the 13th Light Panzer—whose total armored strength amounted to 13 medium and 31 light tanks of French and Czech manufacture—were responsible for the counterattack against the ring the Soviets had meanwhile established around the 6th Army."

This statement would have produced laughter at a staff exercise, or even in the War Academy among green captains. Two weak divisions against 11 Soviet armies? "Who in God's name gave such an absurd order?" Philip demanded. *Generaloberst* Paulus had been one of his own instructors at the War College; he could not picture him giving such a stupid order.

"The *Führer* personally, *Herr Oberstleutnant*," Zimmermann answered tonelessly.

Philip noticed he wasn't breathing after several seconds. He forced himself to exhale. The mad dog was still at large, still wreaking havoc with his mindless orders and senseless "strategy," while Tresckow had not yet been able to lure him into the trap they had set at Army Group Center and kill him. Now Philip was afraid, truly afraid, and yet it was his duty not to show it. "All right. What happened to this corps after it made its attack?"

"We were ourselves encircled, but broke out to the west with everything we could scrape together. As soon as we had radio communication with Army HQ, the General Commanding and the Chief of Staff were relieved of command and ordered back to Berlin."

This no longer surprised Philip. They had failed, and Hitler expected of his troops only "victory or death." So he concentrated on essentials: "And the Soviets have left you in peace since?"

"Not exactly, *Herr Oberstleutnant*, but they don't appear immediately interested in pushing us out of our present positions. They will eventually attempt it, however, because our bridgehead at Nizhma Chirskaja remains the nearest point to the cut-off 6th Army. At present, however, they have given priority to consolidating the encirclement of the 6th Army rather than clearing us out of the bridgehead."

"Eminently sensible," acknowledged Philip before asking, "Who exactly is holding these positions if both your divisions were annihilated?"

"Oh, remnants of the 3rd Romanian Army that broke out with us, supply troops from other cut-off divisions, and stragglers, all thrown together in improvised units under whatever officers were available."

"This is madness," Philip concluded, unwilling to disguise his feelings any longer. Units made up of men who did not know each other under officers they did not know or trust were as good as nothing. The major in front of him made no reply. What could he reply?

The news that the General Commanding was flying in momentarily spared both Philip and Zimmermann the embarrassment of pursuing the "briefing" further. Philip went in search of Seydlitz and the staff car. He arrived in time to see the Fieseler Storch land and taxi over to the edge of the field. A man in a general's uniform, the red stripes of the trousers clearly visible in the dazzling afternoon sunshine, climbed out of the plane and then strode directly toward him.

Philip now underwent a different kind of shock. The man coming toward him was unmistakably General v. Rittenbach. In his stunned state he almost forgot to salute, and Rittenbach grinned, "What? Did you honestly think the Army Personnel Office picked you out of all the deserving General Staff majors? Don't be so arrogant!"

"A dubious honor, *Herr General,* when one knows what the situation here is," Philip countered, but he was smiling.

"*Dulce et decorum est pro patria mori, mein Lieber,*" Rittenbach retorted. Then he clapped Philip forcefully on the shoulder and strode purposefully toward the waiting staff car.

*   *   *   *

December 1942

The *Luftwaffe* lieutenant stopped shivering only after his second glass of cognac—and that although he was practically sitting on the tile oven in Rittenbach's office and wrapped in two blankets. It wasn't hard to conclude that the shaking of his hands had less to do with cold than with nerves. The lieutenant's Heinkel had been shot down on a return flight from Stalingrad just short of the Chir River. The pilot had not survived the crash, but the observer had managed to find his way to the German lines. The two days of cat-and-mouse with the pervasive Soviets in bitter cold and without provisions would only start to look like an "adventure" when he could talk about them to his grandchildren.

Rittenbach and Feldburg let him pour out his tale while the Ic, Hauptmann Jakob, meticulously took note of all the observations the *Luftwaffe* officer could make about the Russians he had encountered during his escape. Now and then Hauptmann Jakob pressed for more details, and it was clear that the Army intelligence officer found the *Luftwaffe* lieutenant hopelessly irresponsible in his failure to deliver more precise information. Rittenbach, too, demanded more details about what were, after all, the Soviet units facing his corps. Philip felt compelled to intervene with a reminder that the *Luftwaffe* lieutenant had not been on a reconnaissance patrol for the Army, but merely trying to get back with his life. "The lieutenant's mission was provisioning the trapped 6th Army," he pointed out.

The lieutenant cast Philip a grateful look, but Rittenbach, hardly stopping for breath, seized on the new topic vigorously. "Yes, do you really think you can supply over 200,000 troops with everything they need for survival and combat? It seems to me that what they need most are tanks—and not even the *Reichsmarschall* was fool enough to promise them that!"

The *Luftwaffe* officer sighed deeply, swilled the cognac in his glass, and then ventured, "*Herr General* will understand that I am not in a position to make such an assessment of the total picture."

"Well," Rittenbach countered, "start small. How many tons of supplies does your—did your—machine fly in?"

"1.5 tons per sortie."

"And how many sorties have you been averaging?"

"On good days, an aircraft goes in twice in 24 hours." Pride in this achievement rang in the lieutenant's voice.

"On good days," Rittenbach curbed him. "What about on bad days? And how many bad days do you have for each good one?"

"Bad days, *Herr General*, are when we're grounded by blizzards or heavy winds, but we must average a sortie a day—well, maybe a little less," he admitted.

"And when a plane gets shot down, how long does it take for a replacement to arrive—or is the *Luftflotte* getting smaller by the day?"

"We're taking heavy losses," the lieutenant admitted, looking down into his glass. "And not all are replaced."

Rittenbach turned to Philip. "I tell you, it can't be done. Göring was shooting off his mouth again. And on top of that, we've got that adventure in Africa around our necks, with Rommel screaming for materiel in light of the Allied landings in his rear." No one could contradict, so Rittenbach turned back again to the *Luftwaffe* officer, "And what is the situation inside the so-called 'fortress?'"

The lieutenant shook his head. "Indescribable. You've never seen anything like it. Men fighting over strips of frozen horse meat—they've shot all the transport and cavalry horses. They say some of the Russian volunteers have resorted to cannibalism—eating those of their comrades who drop of exhaustion, starvation or cold. The number of German desertions is climbing rapidly." Suddenly the lieutenant was shaking again, and he downed his last half-glass of cognac in one gulp. He continued his narrative without any prodding from his audience. "The wounded fight with one another for places on the returning planes. When they storm a plane, they leave a trail of blood and bandages and whimpering comrades behind them. They clamber over one another to fling themselves into the plane, oblivious to the screaming of the men under them. I saw one plane crash on take-off from overloading. Dreyer and I—Dreyer was my pilot—had to use our side-arms to stop more than 23 men getting aboard the plane."

"Why don't the doctors and medics maintain discipline?" Rittenbach asked in a shocked tone, but Philip asked softly, "Was your aircraft full of wounded when it went down?"

The lieutenant's eyes met his, and there were no words necessary.

Suddenly Rittenbach found his remaining questions about the combat readiness and mobility of the 6th Army superfluous and tasteless. After a thoughtful pause, he took a breath and told the *Luftwaffe* lieutenant, "You need to get some rest. We've already contacted your *Gruppe* with the news that you're alive. They will be sending a car for you later."

The *Luftwaffe* lieutenant was led off by the General's ADC, and Hauptmann Jakob excused himself to start correlating the data gleaned from the lieutenant's disjointed remarks. After ordering Zimmermann to request air reconnaissance to confirm some of the observations, commander and chief were alone.

Philip stood and, his hands jammed deep in his trouser pockets, started to wander about the narrow room. (As usual, Rittenbach had selected a modest Russian cottage on the edge of town for his personal quarters.) Rittenbach leaned back in his chair and crossed his arms. "Well, they're planning an offensive against us," he declared simply. "They want to roll us back from Nizhna Chir-skaya and so widen the gap between 6th Army and any relief. Furthermore, they want to unhinge us from our positions along the Rivers Chir and Don. A well-aimed thrust and they slice straight through to the Sea of Azov, thereby cutting off all of Army Group A in the Caucasus as well. And what have we got to stop them?"

"The 336th Infantry Division went into position today. It made a good impression and seems well led."

Rittenbach seemed about to say something, but then stopped himself. After a few seconds he asked, "And that's all?"

Philip shrugged, "There's the 7th *Luftwaffe* Field Division."

Rittenbach made a derisive gesture. The establishment of these divisions had been fought tooth and nail by the Army's High Command (OHK). They robbed the Army of desperately needed manpower and vehicles; and yet, due to the inadequacy of their infantry training and their inexperienced leadership, they were unreliable in combat. *Luftwaffe* Field Divisions contributed almost nothing to the Army's effectiveness, yet the troops in them died just the same—and in greater numbers. Hitler favored these *Luftwaffe* divisions, however, because he considered the *Luftwaffe* politically more reliable than the Army. At his most bitter, Philip even suspected Hitler liked these divisions precisely because they so readily died wherever he sent them, rather than struggling to survive like the Army inevitably did. Philip tried to suppress his hatred of Hitler now, however, because it was not productive.

"What divisions have we been promised?" Rittenbach demanded of Philip—as if he didn't know each unit by heart himself.

"3rd Mountain, 62nd and 294th Infantry, and the 11th Panzer," Philip recited the familiar litany. He could have repeated it in his sleep.

"They call us a panzer corps and assign us a single panzer division!" Rittenbach snapped irritably.

"*Herr General* is forgetting the 13th Panzer," Philip reminded him with a wry smile.

"Don't make me laugh! I need all 6 of their operational tanks for a HQ reserve," Rittenbach retorted. Then with a deep sigh he continued, "The relief of Stalingrad is supposed to be carried out primarily by the 4th Panzer Army under Hoth, but supplemented and strengthened by our entire corps—minus what we need to hold our positions here. The exact strength of the detached task force is more or less at our discretion—at least at the moment. If the Russians are about to attack us here with what sounds like an entire armored corps—assuming that the *Luftwaffe* lieutenant can be trusted—we'll be lucky to hold our own with everything we have. So what on earth do we have that we could offer the Task Force?"

"A motorcycle battalion is, I believe, still said to be relatively intact."

Rittenbach laughed appreciatively, and then cocking his head slightly he observed, "Marriage agrees with you, Feldburg. You're more relaxed and self-assured, even though the objective situation is undoubtedly worse."

"One can get used to anything, I suppose," Philip countered, shoving his glasses up his nose, embarrassed by the personal comment. He also returned to wandering about the room with his hands jammed in his pockets.

Rittenbach did not harass him, but returned to official business. "Unless I'm very much mistaken, the 4th Panzer Army is also dependent on reinforcements from Army Group A. All that takes time to collect and organize, and meanwhile the 6th Army gets weaker and less combat-effective. Another few weeks, and one wonders if they will even be capable of breaking out." Rittenbach was thinking out loud, and Philip felt there was no need for comment.

A knock on the door interrupted them and Zimmermann entered. "Forgive me, *Herr General*, but we've just received the following message from Army Group." He handed a decoded telegram to the General. Rittenbach read the message through, snorted, and handed it on to Philip. It read: "Withdrawal of 3rd Mountain and 62nd Infantry Divisions from present positions impossible. XXXII Corps must do without. Manstein."

Philip handed the telegram back and resumed his wandering without comment. Rittenbach thanked Zimmermann and the Ia withdrew. "I don't doubt Manstein has his reasons," Rittenbach resumed the conversation, "but really! The chances of us holding our own position are so precarious that one has to wonder how we can seriously think of relieving the 6th Army."

Philip was shocked. He stopped and stared at Rittenbach. "How can we abandon a whole Army?"

"We can't," Rittenbach agreed. "We have to get them out. But how? With what? *Ach*! If only they'd broken out immediately, when this corps did!"

"Paulus hasn't been granted 'freedom of maneuver' or the right to a 'flexible defense,'" Philip pointed out. "And apparently he lacks the moral courage of Hoepner and *Graf* Sponeck."

Rittenbach tapped absently at his desk with a pen. Then, realizing what he was doing, he threw the pen down irritably, as if it alone betrayed his unsettled state of mind. At last he announced, "It's water over the dam. We can't change what should have been done, and we can't persuade Paulus to sacrifice himself for the sake of his Army. We'll have to make do, as our honored Field Marshal suggests."

"This time ... And what about the next time?" Philip asked without looking at Rittenbach. He spoke softly, as if to himself, but they both knew he wasn't.

"What do you mean?"

Philip stopped pacing and removed his hands from his pockets. Facing Rittenbach almost at attention, he stated, "*Herr General* knows that the orders that produced this entire catastrophe can be traced back to a single source."

"Yes, I know that."

"We must assume that as long as that source continues to exercise supreme command of our armed forces, such orders are going to be issued again and again, with the same inevitable consequences."

"That's the logical conclusion."

"And does *Herr General* consider this situation tolerable?"

"Of course I don't consider it tolerable!" Rittenbach snapped. "But it is as unalterable as the weather!"

"*Herr General* cannot seriously believe that," Feldburg replied stiffly.

"Feldburg!" Rittenbach sat up straighter. "I've had months to think about it, and I've thought of very little else. But spending time in the *Reich* makes it all too clear: that man has the whole nation by the throat. Those who don't worship him as a saint and savior are afraid to sneeze too loudly! His power is boundless and his position unassailable."

"He could fall victim to an accident."

"That would be an act of God—or did you mean something else?" Rittenbach looked sharply at his Chief of Staff. "No! No, we're not some banana republic! We're German officers, not murderers, anarchists and madmen! God in Heaven, Feldburg, how can you even think of assassination?"

"Tyrannicide."

"I don't deny that. But murder is murder."

"If we can't save the 6th Army, that will be a quarter of a million men sacrificed to one man's vanity—"

"You don't need to remind me of that, but we have no choice! We cannot start a civil war in the midst of a world war. What do you think the Red Army would be doing while we tried to suppress the Party and SS? It's taking all we have to stop the Red Army from overrunning us as it is!"

"Under responsible leadership, it would be a good deal easier."

"Of course, but you underestimate the opposition to any change inside the *Reich*. You can't just kill one man and be done with it. Every corrupt Party official and every SS man with a guilty conscience is going to cling to power with a crazed survival instinct."

"*Herr General* cannot honestly think such elements are serious opposition for trained troops."

"Are you so sure of your troops, Feldburg? Are you sure they'll follow the orders of their officers if they are being asked to fight against the Regime? They don't blame him for the senseless orders, they blame us. You don't seem to appreciate the class hatred that sits deep in the breast of the average German worker and employee. I saw it all in '18. They tore the epaulettes off our uniforms. The Soldier Soviets ruled: officers were elected, the salute was abolished, and discipline could only be enforced with the approval of the soldiers' 'Councils'! In Leipzig they murdered ministers. In Munich they killed innocent hostages, including the poor Countess Westarp. You don't seem to realize how close we came to a German Soviet Republic. And Hitler didn't choose to call his party the National *Socialist* Workers Party out of love of socialism, but because he knows *they* love it."

"The Social Democrats were the only party to vote against the Enabling Law."

"Yes, the leadership saw the danger of Hitler, but the masses are just as happy singing Nazi marching songs as Communist ones. Whether it's the 1st of May or Hitler's birthday, it's all the same to them—so long as there is a parade."

"I don't think it's that simple, *Herr General.*"

"Perhaps not, but listen to the average man on the street. It's all 'our beloved *Führer*,' 'our precious *Führer*,' 'if only the *Führer* knew …' You murder him, Feldburg, and what are you going to offer in return?"

Philip had no answer to this. He had not thought that far. He knew only what Alix had said, that there were civilians working on plans for "afterwards." Rittenbach, meanwhile, was continuing, "You can't honestly think they'd take the Kaiser back?! No, they prefer their Austrian corporal precisely because he's the uneducated son of some second-rate customs official and never made it above the rank of corporal. They love him because he's one of them—and they don't trust us because we have a 'von' in front of our name!"

When Philip still found no answer, Rittenbach continued in a somewhat calmer tone. "It doesn't matter what we do, Feldburg. Whether we support Hitler or oppose him, we will always be reviled for 'pursuing our class interests.' Funny, isn't it?" Rittenbach leaned forward on his elbows. "If they pursue their class interests—even to the extreme of establishing a dictatorship of the proletariat—then it is noble and heroic. But let us defend our class interests—even in the context of democracy—and we are condemned as 'oppressors.'" Rittenbach shook his head sadly. "The fact is, they would rather have that man's demented dictatorship than any form of benevolent paternalism from the likes of us."

"Even when he is leading this country to a ruinous defeat and slaughtering their sons by the hundred thousand?"

"They don't believe he is responsible," Rittenbach insisted, sitting back in his chair again and gesturing vaguely with his arms. "Wait and see! When we lose the war, it will be because we evil, aristocratic generals failed to follow the inspired leadership of the great *Führer*! Mark my words, Feldburg; come the end of the war, you won't be able to wear that uniform without risk to your life. I saw it all in '18!"

"Doesn't *Herr General*—"

A knock on the door brought the discussion to an abrupt end. Both Feldburg and Rittenbach turned expectantly toward the door. Rittenbach called, "Come in!"

Rittenbach's ADC, *Oberleutnant* Hoerner, entered and announced, "General Pickert has just arrived, *Herr General*."

"Pickert? With his division?" Rittenbach could hardly believe the good news after so much bad. Pickert commanded the 11th Panzer Division.

"May the *Herr General* come in?"

"Of course! At once!"

General Pickert swept in, with a breath of cold that still clung to his greatcoat, and saluted smartly. He then shook Rittenbach's extended hand with ice-cold fingers, and Feldburg was introduced. Pickert announced, "I've come on ahead of my division" (Rittenbach's disappointment expressed itself in a slight sinking of his shoulders) "in order to get a good look at the bridgehead at Nizhna Chirskaya, from which the division will be expected to participate in the Stalingrad relief operation. Of course, I wanted to check in with you first."

"Excellent. I'd like to go forward to Nizhna Chirskaya myself. We'll look it over together." Rittenbach was already looking for his gloves. "You should be aware, however, that there are indications of an enemy build-up directly opposite our positions here on the Chir. We've only one infantry division and one *Luftwaffe* Field Division to hold the entire front from Surovikino to Nizhna Chirskaya—and your division, that is. When did you say your advance units would be arriving?" The two generals left together.

CHAPTER 27

▼

Verchne Solonovski
December 1942

Seydlitz woke Philip in the darkness of early morning. He was not fully dressed, his shirttails hung out, his tunic was open, and he was barefoot. "Excuse me, *Herr Oberstleutnant*, but the Duty Officer has more than one alarming report, which he thinks requires immediate attention."

Philip made no vocal answer. They had been more or less expecting this for days now. He pulled on his trousers and boots and then slung his greatcoat over his nightshirt before crossing to the operations room. The Duty Officer, the Id *Hauptmann* Neisse, looked up at him with a strained face. "I'm sorry to wake *Herr Oberstleutnant*, but the 336th is reporting a major breakthrough by Soviet armor, and there are two other breakthrough reports as well."

Philip took and read the decoded telegram, went to the situation map, and located the units and villages mentioned. "And the other breakthroughs?"

Neisse brought over the other two telegrams, and again Philip located the units and villages. Then he went to the nearest desk, picked up the telephone, and requested a connection to the 336th ID. He was connected with the Ia. "This breakthrough you're reporting …" The divisional Ia did not need any further encouragement to pour out a full report.

Two battalions of the 102nd Infantry Regiment had been totally overrun by armor in the night. Efforts by the regimental commander to restore the situation had failed. When Division tried to reinforce the 102nd with battalions from the remaining regiments, they discovered Russian infantry on their side of the river. The Soviet bridgeheads were being eliminated, but the armor breakthrough was beyond the control of Division.

"Understood," was all Philip said. He sent Seydlitz to wake Rittenbach.

By mid-morning Soviet armor was reported deep behind the lines of the 336th and sweeping rapidly, unopposed, to the south, in a move that appeared designed to cut off the entire corps and what was left of the 3rd Romanian Army. If successful, the Germans and Romanians would be pressed up against the River Chir with an inverted front. In short, rather than facing east with the river between them and the enemy, they would be facing west with the river at their backs and the Red Army between them and their lines of supply.

Towards noon, the corps' divisional commanders and their first general staff officers met at corps HQ. At least two, and possibly three, Soviet armor divisions had been identified as taking part in the attack. The entire force was designated, according to prisoners, the 1st Soviet Armored Corps. *Generalmajor* Zinsmeister, commanding the 336th ID, evidenced a certain nervousness, and stressed that his troops had only with difficulty destroyed the infantry bridgeheads. He expected the Soviets would try again in the coming night to put infantry across the Chir. His troops were under constant artillery fire. He demanded an immediate counterattack by the 11th PzD against the Soviet Armored Corps. Although the situation in the sector held by the 294th ID was quieter, the commander, *Generalmajor* Lenz, backed Zinsmeister's request that the 11th PzD move at once and directly against the armor threatening their rear.

Pickert argued against a frontal attack on the Soviets with his entire division. The Red Army, he insisted, always fought best when confronted directly. He preferred to let the Soviets come deeper into the corps' flank while he swung the bulk of his armored units around to take them in the rear.

Rittenbach sided with Pickert, with the modification that he ordered the panzer grenadier regiment into good defensive positions in front of the advancing Soviets to pin them down a little. Such positions offered themselves just north of Soviet State Farm (Khalhoz) 79. To ensure that the Soviets would not simply be deflected by this resistance and swing eastward to seize Corps HQ at Verchne Solonovski, Feldburg suggested that a pair of flak batteries from the *Luftwaffe* Field Division (the only really useful troops in these divisions) and the remnants of the 1st Romanian PzD be put into position east of State Farm 79. Rittenbach readily accepted the suggestion, and the divisional officers returned to their respective units to work out the details.

That same afternoon, Pickert's PzReg 15 made a frontal attack on the Soviets and allowed themselves to be driven back toward State Farm 79. The Soviets advanced confidently. The Germans gave ground. Leading units of the Soviet 1st Armored Corps reached the outer limits of the State Farm before sunset, but here were held up for several hours by the panzer grenadiers. During the night, how-

ever, the Soviet corps took control of the State Farm. They were greeted jubi-
lantly by the workers. Old women with tears streaming down their weathered
faces kissed the boys in the uniform of the Red Army. The Soviet commander,
with the approval of his commissar, allowed the peasants to hold a thanksgiving
service in the auditorium of the Khalhoz. The troops shared their rations with the
civilians and vice versa. Vodka in strictly limited quantities was distributed to the
troops. Meanwhile, the corps commander received written orders, delivered by
mounted couriers, to swing eastward, seize the German HQ at Verchne
Solonovski, and then push on to Nizhna Chirskaya to capture the German
bridgehead on the Chir from the rear.

Following this order, the Soviets ran into the first serious German resistance
since their successful crossing of the Chir. The German 8.8 anti-aircraft gun,
which had proved such a lethal tank-killer, broke the advance of the leading elements just after dawn. The Soviet commander called a halt so infantry units
could come up and clear away the Germans. But just at this point, with the short
winter's day still young, his trailing units found themselves attacked and overrun
by German panzers from the rear.

Pickert's panzers rolled through entire columns of Soviet motorized infantry,
setting one truck after another on fire. The Soviet infantry panicked. Trucks collided in an attempt to escape the panzers. Others overturned in the ditches or got
stuck in snow banks as they tried to flee. Those Soviet infantry that tried to reach
the woods on foot were cut down, so the bulk surrendered en masse. Pickert had
little time to deal with prisoners, so he requested that troops of the 7th *Luftwaffe*
Field Division assume responsibility for them and pressed on toward State Farm
79.

By now the remaining Soviet units knew what was coming and fought bitterly, but they found themselves encircled: the Romanians and the Flak on the
east, the panzer grenadiers to the south, and the panzers to the north and west. By
nightfall of the second day, Pickert could proudly report the destruction of 53
Soviet tanks.

Unfortunately, by the time this news reached XXXII Corps HQ, a new crisis
was distracting Rittenbach and Feldburg, robbing them of the chance to congratulate themselves. Soviet infantry was making such dogged and persistent attacks
on the bridgehead at Nizhna Chirskaya that the bridgehead—so vital for the
relief of Stalingrad—was in danger. There seemed no alternative but to scrape
together reinforcements for the bridgehead from other units. Before these reinforcements could have a beneficial effect on Nizhna Chirskaya, however, the Red
Army exploited the weakness all along the Chir front and launched two new

offensives, both of which succeeded. Pickert was called upon to clear up the new breakthroughs, the method and priority being left to the divisional commander himself. Pickert took his panzers to Lissinski first.

In the reoccupied State Farm 79, German panzer grenadiers found the corpses of 23 Soviet civilians. Their execution had been ordered by the Soviet commissar for alleged pro-German activities. The German officer making the report remarked, "I suppose this would be good material for a propaganda company, but who has time for that nowadays? And what are 20-odd civilians in this war anyway?"

"Their own people, Feldburg," Rittenbach stressed when he got the report, "and it's not even true. No one there was giving us any particular aid or information. No wonder so many of the Russian prisoner-volunteers (HiWis) don't try to escape. They know that all they can expect from their own government is to be shot." Then he lowered his voice and leveled his gaze at Philip. "Would you really risk a Soviet victory for the sake of eliminating that man? No, we've got to win this war first; then we can turn our guns around and wipe out the brown plague at home!"

"How can we win this war without eliminating him first?"

"With men like Pickert and Manstein—and you." Rittenbach was serious, and Philip fumbled with his glasses from embarrassment. Then Rittenbach continued in a lighter tone, "Besides, the German soldier is still the finest in the world."

Pickert moved his division by night and struck the Soviet bridgehead at Lissinski at dawn the next day. His attack was so successful that it completely decimated the Soviet bridgehead. Pickert was free to swing northwest to confront the next threat. After a march of 15 miles, his division attacked the second Soviet breakthrough at Nizhna Kalinovski the same day. By darkness, the Russian bridgehead here had been significantly compressed, but a pause was essential. Pickert's division had been driving by night and fighting by day for three solid days. No one at XXXII corps ventured to ask when the troops had slept or eaten.

Nor were they to get any rest that night. During their preparations for a continuation of their attack on the bridgehead, they were themselves attacked in the flank. Pickert reported that one of his battalions was completely encircled. Corps could only helplessly await developments, because they had already thrown their HQ reserve into the bridgehead at Nizhna Chirskaya. They also scrupulously refrained from passing on to the embattled 11th PzD the repeated reminders from Army Group Don and 4th Pz Army that they were expected to take part in the relief of Stalingrad.

General Hoth, Commander of the 4ᵗʰ Panzer Army, wired: "Anxiously expecting support of the 11ᵗʰ PzD."

Manstein wired: "11ᵗʰ PzD urgently required for relief of Stalingrad. It is to cross the Chir at Nizhna Chirskaya at the earliest opportunity and join forces with the 4ᵗʰ Panzer Army."

In the course of the next day, however, the bridgehead at Nizhna Chirskaya was lost to the Russians. After that, the remnants of the Romanian 1ˢᵗ Panzer and the *Luftwaffe* Field Division were sent to help the 11ᵗʰ PzD extricate itself from the fighting on the flank and prepare to fight its way across the Chir to join the 4ᵗʰ Pz Army. Pickert sent two captured Soviet officers back to XXXII Korps HQ; he had no time for the appropriate interrogations.

The Soviet officers were brought in a simple Russian sleigh pulled by a shaggy pony. At corps HQ there was some discomfort over the fact that one of the two officers was a high-ranking Soviet commissar.

"They shouldn't have sent him back without removing his rank insignia," one of the MPs at HQ murmured.

"Why not?" his comrade asked. "The orders to shoot them were rescinded ages ago."

The first MP jerked his thumb in the general direction of the rear and grumbled, "You never know what happens back there."

The news that a high-ranking Soviet commissar had fallen into their hands brought Rittenbach himself to the interrogation, but the commissar did not talk. He stared at his captors with a deadpan expression, betraying neither fear nor hatred, nor even contempt or curiosity. He answered not a single question, not even his name.

The second prisoner was a startling contrast. This Red Army major was highly decorated, missing two fingers of his left hand from a previous wound, and badly wounded in the thigh at the time of his capture. In contrast to the Commissar, his uniform was shabby, his boots all but worn out, his face unshaved; the only clean part of him was the thigh, which had been dressed by German medics. He did not wait to be questioned, but opened the interrogation with a question of his own: "Aren't you going to kill that bastard?! The only reason I let myself be taken prisoner was to have the satisfaction of seeing him shot!"

Hauptmann Jakob was so taken aback that he only managed a startled, "Sorry?"

"*Comrade* Vassily Sergeivitch Kozlov! A year and a half I've watched him cold-bloodedly order the burning of villages, watched him needlessly sacrifice whole battalions, watched his indifference to the neglect of wounded. Before scenes that would have made a stone weep, *Comrade* Kozlov did not bat an eye. Among the troops it was rumored he'd ordered his own mother's execution for anti-Soviet remarks. On his orders we bled and died, but when things went wrong, the commanders were shot or shot themselves! Koslov went right on giving orders, removed from the rest of us by his wall of silence, his new uniform, his leather and his fur." The Russian officer spat. "And you're going to let him live?" Then, after a baffled moment on both sides, the Russian officer started laughing hysterically. "But of course! He's your best ally, isn't he? He and his kind."

"There you have it," Rittenbach commented to his Chief of Staff when they were alone together. "Bad as the Brown Plague is, it doesn't interfere with us day to day. We don't have political commissars looking over our shoulders, giving orders."

"Only because our commissars haven't the courage of their Soviet counterparts," Philip quipped back. "They're too afraid of Soviet artillery to come closer than 50 km behind the front—and they're too intent on killing unarmed women and children to worry about fighting a real enemy. Besides that, we get enough interference from Hitler himself."

"You exaggerate, Feldburg. What we saw at Zubovo was bad, but it is simply not on the same scale as Bolshevik murders. My God! The whole of Siberia is one mass Concentration Camp. The entire class of independent farmers was wiped out. The officer corps was judicially massacred before the start of the war. We're caught between two evil—barbaric—systems. We have to choose which one is worse and concentrate on beating it before we turn our attention to eliminating the other."

"Agreed. Where *Herr General* and I disagree is on which of the two systems is the worse evil."

By Dec. 16, the 4th Panzer Army's advance units were within 60 km of the encircled 6th Army, and the 11th PzD stood ready to fight its way across the Chir on the next day. But on that day the Soviets launched a massive attack against the Italian Eighth Army, holding the flank of the extended Army Group Don west of XXXII Korps and the 4th Pz Army. This attack threatened to cut off the bulk of 4th Pz Army and XXXII Korps from their lines of communication and supply.

On the morning of Dec. 17, the Soviets also forced their way across the Chir directly opposite the XXXII Korps just north of Nizhna Chirskaya. The 11th Pz had to be diverted from its advance toward Stalingrad to deal with this immediate threat. While the 11th Pz was still engaging this threat, the Soviets broke through the weak Romanian units and the ill-trained *Luftwaffe* Field Division, which had been containing the bridgehead at Kalinovski ever since the 11th Pz had been sent to join the Stalingrad relief operation.

Rittenbach became convinced that the attack at Nizhna Chirskaya had been a diversion and that the breakthrough at Kalinovski constituted the real threat. 11th Pz had to be sent up to Kalinovski. Feldburg radioed Pickert, still in the midst of beating back the Soviet assault on Nizhna Chirskaya. "*Herr General,* General Rittenbach requests you to take your division north to Kalinovski immediately."

"What? I'm completely engaged here! I've got to clean up this mess first; then I'll go up to Kalinovski."

"*Herr General,* I'm afraid the situation at Kalinovski doesn't allow for any delay. We've determined that a Soviet motorized corps has broken through. The *Luftwaffe* Field Division cannot handle the situation. 11th Panzer must move at once."

By now, one month after his attachment to XXXII Korps, Pickert trusted Rittenbach and Feldburg's leadership. They had given him a long rein to do things as he liked up to now. If this once they made it imperative that he do what the General Staff generally condemned (breaking off a successful counterattack and leaving the enemy in possession of a strategic position it was on the brink of losing), then there had to be good reasons.

Pickert disengaged his troops, wheeled them about, and drove them through the darkness to Kalinovski. The troops of the division had not had a pause in 48 hours. Pickert drove up and down the column, asking his troops if they preferred to march or bleed.

By dawn, the remaining 25 operational tanks of Pickert's Pz Reg. 15 discovered Soviet tanks moving unperturbed southward in a stately column. Except for the fact that their hatches were shut, it might have been a peacetime maneuver. Hauptmann Lestmann ordered his own panzers to proceed in a similar orderly manner. They turned onto a parallel course and then—as if they only wanted to pass—started to overtake the column. When Lestmann was abreast of the lead panzer, he turned his cannon and opened fire. The other panzers followed his example. The Soviets didn't realize what was happening. Twenty-two Soviet tanks were destroyed without a single German casualty.

Hauptmann Lestmann's gunner remarked, despite the fact that his eyes were bloodshot and streaming tears from smoke and sleeplessness, "That was fun. Let's do it again."

"I hope you meant that, because there is another Soviet armor column over to our right."

The sergeant wiped his eyes on the back of his sleeve. "*Ja, Herr Hauptmann*; it's a lot better than looking into the barrel of a T-34."

In their second attack, they only managed to knock out 13 Soviet tanks. Then the Russian attack collapsed.

Rittenbach called Lestmann to HQ to give him the EKI. "It's not that we don't know you need sleep and hot food more than an Iron Cross," Philip remarked apologetically as he saw the *Hauptmann* out, "but it's the best we can do just now."

"Might I be allowed to see the situation map, *Herr Oberstleutnant?*" *Hauptmann* Lestmann seized the opportunity for a glimpse into the broader picture and the reasons behind the apparently senseless maneuvers. Philip took him back inside the operations room and narrated the situation, from the still precarious situation in the Italian 8th Army to the stalled 4th Pz Army 60 km outside of Stalingrad.

"They need us for Stalingrad, don't they?" the *Hauptmann* summarized, evidently shaken by what he'd seen.

"Yes—and all the other Mountain, Infantry and Panzer divisions that were promised and never came."

"That doesn't sound very optimistic, *Herr Oberstleutnant*." The young panzer captain was shocked.

"Should I pretend optimism when there are no grounds for it?" Philip countered with raised eyebrows.

"We must all show faith in the *Führer*. He has never let us down before. He is certain to master this situation as he has all the others."

"Like taking Moscow last year?"

"Feldburg!" Rittenbach roared from the adjoining room. "Let the *Hauptmann* get back to his panzers!"

The *Hauptmann* was relieved to go; he saluted hurriedly and disappeared. Philip stoically waited for Rittenbach's wrath. It didn't come. All the General did was come to stand in the doorway where he shook his head and warned, "Be careful, Feldburg. These younger officers are all more or less infected with the Brown Plague—and they can't be trusted to respect the fraternity of the officer corps, either."

During the next two days, 11th Panzer was subjected to a new attack. First the 110 Pz. Rgt was overrun and on the next day, the grenadiers. Although it was possible to restore the situation, the casualties were heavy and rest was imperative.

The division had temporarily reached the limit of its offensive capabilities, and XXXII Corps pulled them back into reserve.

This decision was colored by the fact that Manstein had pulled the 6th Pz out of the 4th Army because he needed forces to try to stop the gap over 100 km wide torn in the front of the Italian 8th Army. With that decision, a necessary one, the relief of Stalingrad had stalled irrevocably, and 11th Pz couldn't help anymore, anyway. Hoth could barely hold his own position 60 km short of Stalingrad, and he probably would not be able to hold on for long. The obvious imperative was for the 6th Army to break out in the direction of the 4th Pz Army. But Hitler personally and explicitly forbade General Paulus from attempting a breakout. Since in his mind surrender was unthinkable, the Supreme Commander of the German Armed Forces thereby consciously condemned a quarter of a million of his own troops to a slow death from cold, exhaustion and starvation.

Meanwhile, the situation behind the XXXII Korps had become catastrophic. The entire Soviet Guard Army was pouring through the gap torn in the Italian 8th Army and pushing unopposed toward Rostov and the Sea of Azov. The success of this operation would mean that, in addition to the 6th Army at Stalingrad, the 4th Pz Army, and large portions of Army Group Don (including XXXII Korps), all of Army Group A in the Caucasus would be cut off from their lines of communication and supply. Put another way, the Soviet offensive against Rostov threatened a million troops with the same fate as the 250,000 at Stalingrad.

Manstein had no choice but to abandon Stalingrad in order to save the rest, and this meant ordering disengagement from the enemy to the east and a redeployment of forces westward. The XXXII Korps correspondingly received orders to send the 11th Pz hurrying westward and to remove its own HQ to Tatsinskaya, 150 km to the west. The infantry, meanwhile, was to fight a rear-guard action designed to win time and deceive the Soviets about German intentions. XXXII Corps was, furthermore, to take command of the 6th Pz Division, which had been detached from the 4th Pz Army. The 6th and 11th Pz Divisions together were to form a task force entrusted with the vitally important counterattack against the Soviet Guard Army advancing on Rostov.

Strategically, the orders made perfect sense. XXXII Korps lay north of all other units of Army Groups Don and A, and so was in the best position to strike the first blow against the Red Army advancing toward Rostov from the north. But for the XXXII Corps HQ, the orders posed extreme difficulties. XXXII Corps was tasked with managing two distinctly separate operations being fought in two different directions almost 200 km apart: the defensive battle on the Chir (336

ID, 294 ID, 7 *Luftwaffe* FD and the Romanians) and the armored counterattack against the Soviet Guard Army (11th and 6th Pz Div). And somehow supplies, replacements and mail had to find their way to the correct units everywhere in time.

Rittenbach and Feldburg worked hard to avoid the natural tendency to neglect the unrewarding defensive struggle of the infantry on the Chir. Yet the task of restoring the front at Tatsinskaya seemed so urgent that a certain neglect did indeed result—especially since the HQ had also been moved westward.

Thus it came to some extent as a shock when in the midst of intense activity to organize the counterattack against the Soviet Guard Army, desperate pleas for help reached HQ from the 336th ID. The division reported that one of its regiments, the 102nd, had been cut off, encircled, and would soon be wiped out if it did not receive relief. The division's attempts to aid the regiment had been beaten off with heavy casualties. They did not have the strength for a new attempt.

Philip brought the message out to Rittenbach as he was on the porch of their command post, preparing to dispatch the two panzer generals, Pickert and Kitzinger. The two divisional commanders had just consulted and agreed on a plan for the counterattack against the First Soviet Guard Army. They were preparing to return to their own respective HQs to work out the details. "*Herr General* should perhaps see this before committing the 6th and 11th irrevocably," Philip suggested, handing him the telegram.

Rittenbach, as always when he felt a decision had been made and was in the execution phase, frowned irritably at the complication. He briskly took the telegram from his Chief of Staff while the divisional commanders waited with a mixture of impatience and unease. Kitzinger was slapping his gloves into the palm of his hand. Rittenbach took what seemed to be a long time reading the short message, and then Philip noticed he wasn't reading so much as staring. At that instant, Rittenbach thrust the telegram angrily back at Philip and announced, "You'll have to make that decision on your own, Feldburg, but I beg you to hurry so as not to delay the gentlemen" (the divisional commanders) "any longer than necessary."

For an instant, Philip was so astounded by this abrupt and inexplicable refusal to make a decision that he opened his mouth to protest. The keen interest on the faces of the two divisional commanders stopped him. He registered the concerned look of Pickert and the shocked, arrogant expression of Kitzinger, and realized that both generals feared that Rittenbach had just cracked. But Philip had seen Rittenbach go through worse situations, and had seen him more run down and nervous. It was simply inconceivable to him that Rittenbach had broken down now. Whatever was going on, seconds were wasting, and all three generals were awaiting his decision.

He passed the telegram to the divisional commanders so that they understood the situation and then remarked cautiously, "Only armor can cover the distance back to the Chir in time to be of any use. That means taking armor away from the offensive here and sending it back at once. If either of the two panzer divisions is to be weakened, then it should be the division blocking the Soviet withdrawal north, i.e., the 6th Panzer.

Kitzinger, as commander of the 6th Pz, at once protested vehemently. "The rescue of a single regiment is insignificant beside this operation! To weaken the forces here is to risk the collapse of the whole operation. It could mean sacrificing Army Group A and the 4th Panzer Army for the sake of a single regiment—a regiment that would then be lost in the general dragnet anyway!"

"If my colleague does not believe he can manage to block a Soviet withdrawal with his division minus a single battalion—because that is all this would take—then I'll give up one of mine," Pickert volunteered at once. He, after all, had been fighting alongside the 336th ID for over a month now; it wasn't a number to him, it was men.

"You have the more difficult task of encircling and taking the Soviets head on!" Kitzinger reminded his colleague angrily. "We're talking about the fate of an entire Army Group and more!"

"One battalion more or less isn't going to decide the fate of the Army Group. We're outnumbered many times as it is. Surprise, discipline and morale will decide this counterattack—not one battalion. That battalion might save a regiment, which we could very well need later on. More importantly: the failure to help it will do more damage to morale than can ever be made good!"

While the generals fought, Philip cast a pleading look to Rittenbach, but the corps commander might as well have turned to stone. Philip took a deep breath and with his eyes focused on Rittenbach, suggested, "Gentlemen, since General Pickert is willing to detach one of his battalions, may I suggest that the 11th Panzer assume the role of net, while the 6th Panzer assumes the encircling task?" He thus reversed the tasks just assigned the two panzer divisions, and also backed Pickert in favor of attempting the rescue.

The two divisional commanders glanced at Rittenbach, but he continued to ignore them.

"All right," Kitzinger agreed reluctantly. "You know my opinion. Let's hope you don't live to regret Herr Pickert's confidence, Herr v. Feldburg."

"I'll detach my 1st Battalion at once. Where does the 336th want it?" Pickert asked Philip.

"Lassinski is where the regiment is cut off, but your battalion will want to pick up more detailed information at Verchne Solonovski."

"Understood. Anything else?" Again the generals looked at Rittenbach, but he only shook his head woodenly. The divisional commanders saluted and, with an uneasy glance at Philip, hurried out to their waiting command vehicles.

Rittenbach stood on the wooden veranda watching them go, and continued to stand staring down the road long after the vehicles had disappeared. Zimmermann came out, but Philip waved him away. From the window to the operations room they could hear the ringing of telephones, and far away guns barked gruffly, lighting up the evening sky.

Abruptly Rittenbach pulled himself together and turned to Philip. "Thank you."

Philip shrugged uncomfortably. "Nothing to thank me for."

"Yes, there is. The regiment that's cut off—it's my son's."

"Mother of God," Philip murmured. Then: "What if I'd agreed with Kitzinger?"

Rittenbach laid his hand briefly on Philip's shoulder as he turned and went back into the operations room. "Then I wouldn't have told you."

At dawn, the counterattack against the Soviet Guard Army was launched. The Soviets were concentrated on a *Luftwaffe* base that they had conquered the day before, and were caught by surprise. They fell back automatically along their lines of communication toward the north, thinking to regroup when the German attack exhausted itself. Or perhaps the Soviet leadership believed the German attack was aimed solely at repossession of the airfield. As they pulled back hastily, they discovered to their horror that their lines of communication had been cut. The tanks they initially took to be reinforcements turned out to be Pickert's tanks. Caught between enemy armor and infantry from what seemed like all directions when only the day before the enemy had been demoralized, shattered and incapable of fighting, Soviet morale cracked. The radios of XXXII Corps picked up desperate pleas for instructions and relief from the Russian Guard Army. The Soviet High Command, however, remained silent and abandoned the Army to its fate. The two German panzer divisions pressed their advantage. In confusion, some Soviet units surrendered immediately, and others fought bitterly; but without determined leadership, the fate of the Russian Guard Army was sealed.

While Rittenbach appeared totally absorbed in directing or following the battle for the airfield, Philip went out to the communications center set up across the street. Addressing the corporal in charge of coded telegraphing, he requested contact with the 336th division and asked: "Status of 102nd Reg.?"

The answer came back: "102nd extricated with assistance of Pz Bn."

"Casualties of 102nd?"

"High."

Philip hesitated. On the wires came a message of congratulation from Manstein for the "brilliant" planning and execution of the counterattack against the Guard Army. The Commander of XXXII Corps, his Chief and all officers and men could "proudly note that their service had prevented a widespread catastrophe." Philip went over to the telephone operators and asked for a connection to 336th Division. The soldiers looked at him curiously; why didn't he use the phone in his own office or the operations room?

"Do you have the casualty lists from 102nd yet?" he asked the divisional adjutant. The Oberleutnant said no, it would take a day or two. "Can you make a special inquiry, please? The General has no idea I'm requesting this, but his son is in the 102nd. Can you please check and see if he made it out?" The divisional adjutant assured him he would do his utmost. Rittenbach was a popular general. "Thank you, and put the call through to me, not the General."

In the operations room, news had just reached the XXXII Korps via mounted courier that all the female *Luftwaffe* auxiliaries at the airfield had been brutally and repeatedly raped before they were murdered during the brief occupation of the airfield by the Soviet Guard Army. This news outraged the German soldiers far more than the fact that the male personnel of the base had also been slaughtered; that was war. The fate of the 26 female communications auxiliaries, by contrast, represented an intensification of the general barbarism that characterized the war in the East. More important, however, was the fact that despite all the jokes and rumors about the questionable virtue of women who volunteered for service with the armed forces, they were still German women—or rather, girls. They thus symbolized all the women and girls that each soldier wanted to keep safe and separate from what he was experiencing. In the ensuing angry expressions of helpless fury, there were not a few officers and NCOs who lashed out against the policy of assigning female auxiliaries to duty so far inside enemy territory. Then again, the airfield had been nearly 300 km behind the front just over a month earlier.

Rittenbach felt it was necessary that he show respect for the victims—and not incidentally, try to calm tempers—by going personally to the airfield. He insisted that Philip accompany him. Philip—very reluctantly—obeyed. It was nightfall before they returned to their own headquarters. Seydlitz was waiting somewhat anxiously for Philip. "I've had an informal message for *Herr Oberstleutnant* from 336th—"

"In my office, please." They withdrew to Philip's own office and closed the door.

"It concerns a certain *Oberleutnant v. Rittenbach*," Seydlitz continued, "I presume some relative of the *Herr General*."

"His son."

Seydlitz's shocked silence was answer itself, but Philip pressed him. "Did he make it out?"

"Yes, but he was severely wounded—lung and stomach wounds. He was dead on arrival at the field hospital."

Philip nodded and delivered the news to the father personally. Rittenbach took the news stoically, and then asked to be left alone. Philip and the General's ADC kept guard outside his chamber to be sure he wasn't disturbed. For much of the night the General wept.

CHAPTER 28

▼

Berlin
January 1943

The *Luftwaffe* liaison officer, who was generally thought to have his eye on Annie Lerche, put his head around the door and announced, "They're coming again."

Annie blushed, but she did not look up from her typing as she demanded, "How can you know that?"

"Buildup of aircraft over England."

"But they could be headed anywhere! Why should they bomb us two nights in a row after leaving us alone for nearly a year?" Annie could no longer keep her attention on her text and looked up. Her admirer rewarded her with a broad smile, revealing his rather too many gold teeth.

"Because, Beautiful, they think they'll catch us napping—but they won't. So have no fear."

"I don't have any fear anyway," Annie declared bravely (if unconvincingly), with a toss of her long hair. "And if you want my opinion—"

Alix did not get to hear Annie's opinion because the telephone rang. "*Allgemeine Heeresamt*, Feldburg."

The connection wasn't good and she had to strain to hear. "Army Group Center, *Oberst* v. Tresckow for General Olbricht."

Alix stiffened internally. The Ia of Heeresgruppe Mitte might have a perfectly official reason for calling Olbricht, but more likely it had to do with the conspiracy. "One moment; the General is in a conference. I'll have to see if he can take the call now." Leaving the phone off the hook, Alexandra stood and knocked on Olbricht's door. As she entered the office, General Thomas, Chief of the Armed Forces Economic and Armaments Department, was speaking: "… Goebbels is and will continue to make maximum use of the Unconditional Surrender demand, but that doesn't change the fact that the Allies have issued the ultimatum. Whether they meant to play into the government's hands or not, their demand is official policy."

Olbricht and Thomas were seated comfortably at the round table by the nearest window. The two generals looked up as Alexandra entered. "Baroness v. Feldburg?" Olbricht greeted her.

Alexandra let the door close behind her. "*Oberst* v. Tresckow is on the phone. Should I transfer the call?"

Olbricht, too, seemed to sit up a little straighter. "Please." He stood to take the call at his desk, but turned to address Thomas. "Policies have been known to change."

"Of course, but last time they promised negotiations on a clearly defined and reasonable basis, only to break their word and impose economically devastating conditions. What do you think we can expect if they start out demanding Unconditional Surrender?"

Alix could not delay her departure any longer. She left, closing the door behind her. Without bothering to go around her desk, she picked up the phone, still standing. "*Oberst* v. Tresckow? General Olbricht will speak to you now. I'll transfer."

As soon as she was finished, Annie stopped typing and asked, "Do you really think they might bomb Berlin two nights in a row? I didn't get any sleep last night at all. If—" The telephone on her desk interrupted her lament. She answered it, "*Allgemeine Heeresamt*, Lerche." She sat up straighter. "*Jawohl! Herr General* is with General Thomas—*Jawohl!* I'll tell *Herr General* at once!" Turning to Alexandra, who was still standing, "*Generaloberst* Fromm wants Olbricht and Thomas to report to him at once!"

Alexandra nodded, knocked again on the General's door, and stepped back into his office. Olbricht looked across at her, holding the receiver covered. "*Generaloberst* Fromm wants to see you and General Thomas immediately."

Olbricht nodded and Alix withdrew. The door to the hall opened and the *Luftwaffe Hauptmann* put his head in again. "Annie, I'm serious. They're coming for Berlin." His attention on Annie, he did not see Generals Olbricht and Thomas emerge from the General's office. He continued to Annie, "See if you can't sneak out early and get home safe, in the cellar."

"Sneaking out won't be necessary," Olbricht at once announced with a slightly ironic expression.

Startled, the *Luftwaffe* captain glanced toward the generals. In confusion he started to withdraw, and then thought better of it. He came fully into the office, saluted, and then darted away. Olbricht and Thomas laughed; then Olbricht turned to the mortified Annie and told her simply, "Really, you may leave now if you like. If this gets to be too regular, we'll have to be stricter, but as it is …" Then, turning to Alexandra, he added, "If you don't have any strong objections, Freifrau v. Feldburg, I would appreciate it if you would wait until I get back from General Fromm. There is something I need to talk to you about."

"No problem, *Herr General.*"

"Thank you." With that, the generals left, and Annie looked over, feeling guilty.

"Now I feel awful," she admitted. "I suppose I ought to stay, too …"

"Whatever for? Next time it's your turn, that's all."

Annie let herself be convinced, and at once started putting on hat and coat. "Maybe they won't come, and I'll have a nice long evening to rest up," she said wishfully.

"Probably," Alexandra agreed and waved goodbye.

By the time Olbricht returned from his consultation with Fromm, the Bendlerblock was emptying rapidly, as more and more officers and civilians got wind of the impending air raid and decided to try to make it home before the storm broke. Olbricht apologized for keeping Alexandra and asked her into his office. He closed the door and indicated the round table. After they were seated, he still hesitated. The heating was hissing, but otherwise the large office block had become unusually quiet. It was as if they were alone in the whole tract of offices housing the AHA.

At last Olbricht spoke. "This Unconditional Surrender demand comes at a very bad time for us. Just when the futile sacrifice of the 6th Army at Stalingrad had disillusioned everyone and the first signs of widespread war-weariness and even hostility to the Regime were evident, the Allies slammed the door in our faces. The call for Unconditional Surrender is like telling us that they intend to pulverize us whether we support our government or not. Even old and true opponents like Thomas question the wisdom of acting under the circumstances.

"Furthermore, as long as 'Unconditional Surrender' applies not just to Hitler but to a post-Hitler government as well, we have nothing to offer a nation still half-mesmerized by that maniac. People who two days ago were ready to throw Adolf out, along with the whole pack of corrupt Party bosses, are now saying: better to fight with Adolf to the last than to accept Unconditional Surrender. Hitler still promises them victory, after all. With this one announcement, the

Western Allies have won more support for the Nazi regime than twelve months of Goebbels' speeches could have done."

Olbricht paused, his gaze shifted to the bust of General Yorck v. Wartenburg that stood on his bookcase. Then he continued, "But Tresckow feels we must act despite the Unconditional Surrender demand, and I believe he is right. We have to act and hope that Unconditional Surrender isn't as ugly as it sounds. The sooner we act, the better. Which is why I asked you to stay—not merely to complain about the Western Powers," he added with a quick smile.

Serious again, he continued, "Hitler has agreed to visit Army Group Center sometime in the next two months. This will give Tresckow an opportunity to present his proposal for a change in the command structure. The problem is that we can't put his ideas into practice without preparation, or they could misfire. To try to avoid that, we've worked out certain supplementary plans."

"What Erich Hoepner and Generaloberst Beck were working on?" Alexandra asked.

"Exactly," Olbricht agreed as he stood to go to his safe. As he spun the combination lock, the air-raid warning started to wail. They both glanced instinctively toward the four windows lining the office. Despite the blinds that made them blank, the nearby searchlights lit up the opaque windows with lurid, wavering light. The General opened his safe and returned to the table with a manila folder, which he handed to Alexandra.

She opened the cover and found a neatly printed page opening with the words, "The *Führer* Adolf Hitler is dead!" She looked up at General Olbricht with a slight rush of adrenaline: they were planning an assassination. That was the "modification in the command structure" Tresckow would effect in the next two months. Her next thought was that handling these papers could no longer be justified as "just doing her job" or "following orders." If she typed up these papers, she had irrevocably crossed the Rubicon and become one of the conspirators. But she had been that in her heart all along.

"I would understand perfectly if you declined to have anything more to do with these," Olbricht assured her, misinterpreting her look.

"I would be delighted to type them—and even more to see them issued. But I can hardly type them in the outer office," Alexandra countered with a smile.

"No, you would have to do the work at home; and that means transporting the documents there and back, keeping them hidden for days on end in your apartment ..." He didn't have to voice aloud the entailed risk.

Alexandra flipped through the papers to estimate the amount of work required. The phrase "Concentration Camp commandants are to be arrested" caught her attention, but it did not surprise her. Uncle Erich had said that one of the first things they had to do was to rigorously move against all the accomplices of the Regime who had a reason to fear a post-Hitler government. He stressed that all such individuals had to be arrested and rendered harmless before they realized what was happening. A counterattack had to be prevented. The release of stalwart opponents of the Regime from the Concentration Camps would be an added benefit.

"When does everything have to be finished?"

"At the latest, within a month. That is the earliest date for a trip by Hitler to Army Group Center. However, *Gräfin* Schulenburg and Frl. v. Oven have also agreed to help."

"Then I'm sure we'll manage it in 10 to 15 days."

The renewed wailing of the sirens reminded them of the immediate danger, and the flak opened up beside the Bendlerblock. Olbricht took the folder back and locked it inside his safe. He urged, "Hurry," and they went together down into the bunker under the building.

After about an hour the sounds of bombardment and air defense faded. The bunker became still, but no "all clear" sounded. Someone went to investigate and came back with the news that a second wave of bombers was on the way. They would reach the city in about an hour. As General Olbricht had a car and driver waiting, he suggested that he drive Alexandra home in the lull.

The driver took full advantage of Berlin's empty streets, and raced along the broad avenues. The danger of driving too fast was easily subsumed in the impending danger represented by the lazily straying searchlights. As they reached the Feldburg apartment, distant flak batteries started to bark. Alexandra thanked the General and hastily climbed out of the car. From overhead came the drone of aircraft engines, presumably night fighters.

Alexandra unlocked the front door and ran for the cellar entrance. She knocked firmly on the door and was relieved when it opened nearly at once. As Theo Pfalz closed the door behind her, the first crumpf of detonating bombs could be heard some distance away.

Alix at once regretted the decision to leave the Bendlerstrasse. This was no bunker built to withstand bombs but rather an ordinary cellar—a place for storing potatoes, coal, old furniture and bicycles. Neither particularly deep nor concrete-reinforced, it would not survive a direct hit. Furthermore, the sound of the air attack penetrated the walls far more easily than in the bunker at the Bendlerstrasse. But Theo Pfalz greeted her with touching relief. "*Frau Baronin!* We were worried about you! Now if only Frl. Moldenauer would get here!"

Marianne had been on her way to deliver a forged ID card to the pastor of her church when the pre-alarm went off. It was then too far to go back. Furthermore, she knew how desperately the ID was needed. For someone living underground without documentation in Nazi Germany, every day—every hour—could bring discovery, arrest, Concentration Camp and death. On the street, in the shops, on subways or at the post office one could be asked to present ID. Anyone who couldn't was automatically suspect and often instantly "arrested" by their zealous fellow citizens. Every day without ID was a day living on charity and/or the black market. Without an ID, one had no right to food, clothing, coal, and soap— indeed, no rights at all.

Marianne never knew the stories of her "customers." She never saw them. Someone, one of the little circle of helpers in the congregation, would bring her a photograph, an example of the needed document, and the "data" to be filled in on the document. Sometimes she made marriage or birth certificates, sometimes factory IDs or draft exemption cards. But she never knew who the people really were or why they needed one particular form of ID rather than another—and she never asked.

Of course, she often wondered about them and even imagined stories as she worked late into the night doing her forgeries in the atelier, but what mattered most was not who they were but that they needed her. At twenty, Marianne had the rare privilege of feeling that her life was meaningful and that what she was doing was worthwhile. She was so convinced of the importance of her mission, in fact, that she did not break off her bike ride when the air-raid sirens wailed. She continued doggedly toward her destination.

When she reached the parsonage of the red brick church, however, she found it already locked and barred. The sirens screamed and the flak barked like hounds on the scent of quarry. Marianne shouted and pounded at the door and windows of the parsonage, but there was no one there to hear.

Only then did Marianne learn that fear is physical. Much as she wanted to be brave, she could not stop her limbs from trembling. As the drone of aircraft engines reached her senses, she was humiliated by the urge to urinate. Her thoughts began to drown in panic. She ran headlong into the street, pushing her bicycle. There had to be a public air-raid shelter near by. She knew she'd seen signs to one in the neighborhood, but in her panic she couldn't remember where.

The earth shook and leapt. Light flashed. The air itself seemed to flare up and roar. The second, third, fourth, fifth and sixth crashes shook her. In the midst of it, she threw her bicycle aside and flung herself onto the earth, her hands crossed over the back of her head. But no sooner had the first series of detonations ended than from slightly further to her right a new load was dropped. Marianne was screaming in terror and helplessness, but no one could hear her. The explosions and flak were too loud, and those people who might have heard her were themselves underground.

Before the second aircraft had fully disgorged its load, a third and fourth bomber opened their bays over the residential suburb. The night was lit up by the fires of the phosphorus bombs. A naked tree burst into flame and burned like the biblical burning bush.

Marianne, feeling the wind blow hot and seeing herself starkly white against the black pavement, picked herself up and started to run away. She ran hysterically, senselessly, with no thought to where she was going. She could escape the nearby fires, but she could not outrun hundreds of bombers as they droned steadily through the skies. For each squadron that turned off and started for home with the satisfaction of a job "well done," there were new squadrons still flying in.

Marianne ran, stumbled, fell, and cowered under her arms as the earth jumped and trembled, and then ran on. Finally, instinct or luck brought her to a familiar building: the Swedish Church. This refuge for "submarines" was known to her as an address for the most extreme emergencies. For a moment, the very sight of the familiar building calmed her worst terror. She ran around to the cellar door, confident of salvation, because she knew that there were people hidden in this cellar. The people here were hiding not from the bombs of the enemy, but from their own government and fellow citizens. Marianne pounded with her fists on the heavy wooden door. It did not open to her. She screamed and pounded harder, although her fists were soon black and blue and her knuckles scraped and bleeding. She knew there were people inside. She knew they could hear her, but only slowly did it dawn on her that they did not dare open the door. They did not know who she was, and so could not be sure she would not betray them. As this knowledge penetrated her consciousness, she collapsed in despair before the door. She curled up like a child and sobbed helplessly, as around her the attack reached its climax.

Nurse Gisela Tuchel was 33. She was a tall, dark-blonde, big-boned woman. She was efficient and orderly and none of her patients could complain about her, yet she was without particular devotion to her profession, viewing it merely as a job. When she arrived at the hospital for the morning shift, she was neatly and cleanly dressed. Her face betrayed no after-effects of the night's fierce bombing.

She went about her duties as she did every morning—without joy, interest, or particular ill humor. Everyone was startled when she cried out with evident interest, "Why, it's Frl. Moldenauer!"

The doctor on duty, Dr. Max Uhlenbrock, hurried over to her. "Do you know the girl?" he asked, surprised.

"Yes; she lives in the same house I do, in a big, second-floor flat. We all noticed she was missing last night. Her parents were silly with worry. Is she badly hurt?"

"No, not really. A broken baby finger on her right hand, smoke inhalation, cuts, bruises and shock. I gave her a sedative."

"Oh, well, that's good." Nurse Tuchel seemed to lose interest, but the doctor persisted, "You wouldn't happen to know why she was in possession of someone else's *Reichsbahn* ID card, would you?"

Nurse Tuchel frowned. "No; what are you talking about?"

Dr. Uhlenbrock led the nurse back to his small office beside the ward station. "These documents were found on her when she was brought in." He spread them out for Nurse Tuchel: Marianne's own ID, her student ID, and an employee card for the *Reichsbahn* made out for a certain Jens-Uwe Marks.

"Never heard of him," Nurse Tuchel declared.

"Not a friend or relative, perhaps?"

"No, no. Her father was a professor—but he was fired for political unreliability," Nurse Tuchel added the later information more to show off how much she knew than from conscious maliciousness.

Dr. Uhlenbrock considered her briefly, and then shrugged and gathered the documents together. "Well, I'm sure the girl will have an explanation when she's recovered from the shock. Apparently she was caught out in the open during the raid last night."

"A perfectly silly thing to do," Nurse Tuchel declared from a deeply entrenched sense of superiority.

Her curiosity aroused, however, she later asked the doctor what Marianne had said about the documents.

"Oh, she says she just found it lying in the street during the air raid and, thinking someone must have lost it, she picked it up."

"A likely story!" Nurse Tuchel scoffed. "It sounds very suspicious to me! I think we should inform the police. Perhaps the papers were stolen."

"What would a girl of 19 or 20 want with a man's *Reichsbahn* ID? You're making far too much of this. The girl must have been out of her mind with terror. She can't even remember where she was or how she came to be in the

Hohenzollerndamm. In her panic, she lost her bicycle and clung to a piece of paper she'd found. It's not an unfamiliar pattern for panic."

"I still think we should call the police and let them question Frl. Moldenauer. I'm sure they—"

"Save your indignation, Sister," the doctor answered with relaxed amusement. "I did turn the documents over to the police. The young man who just collected Frl. Moldenauer is a *Kriminalobersekretär* of the Gestapo. So that takes care of things, don't you think? And we have work to do, don't we, Sister?"

Gisela Tuchel opened her mouth to protest, but then thought better of it. What good would it do to point out that *Kriminalobersekretär* or not, Peter Kessler was known to be head over heels in love with Marianne?

CHAPTER 29

▼

Zaporozhe, Soviet Union
February 1943

Generalfeldmarschall v. Manstein spoke in a low, calm voice, sober and without pathos. The cadence and inflection would have been well suited to a university lecture hall. Nor did Manstein present a martial image; his hair was completely white, and he needed glasses to read or study a map. What commanded the respect of his audience was simply the strategic and operational genius that his fellow officers ascribed to him. Manstein's opinions commanded respect because they were Manstein's.

His audience now, the collected subordinate commanders of Army Group Don or their representatives, were not to be trifled with. Although prepared to respect the Field Marshal, they were all men with opinions and experience of their own. They were not prepared to accept everything the Field Marshal said without question, and they were in no mood for platitudes or false optimism.

Although the assembled officers could not know the details of their neighbor's position, there was little doubt about the overall situation. Manstein's dry and professional review of the Army Group's position was appreciated because of the detail it provided, but it was not necessary for the conclusions he drew. For roughly two months the Army Group had been defending itself against repeated enemy attempts to cut off them off. They had been fighting to keep open the lines of communication and supply and to enable the withdrawal of Army Group A—not to salvage the 6th Army at Stalingrad.

But that was not to say that the surrender of Field Marshal Paulus and the remainder of the 6th Army two days earlier left them unmoved. Inevitable as the surrender had been, the act of surrender itself still buffeted them with unwelcome thoughts and emotions.

On the one hand, it was a forbidden surrender—outright insubordination and disobedience from a man who had only been promoted to field marshal so that Goebbels' propaganda machine could announce that *Feldmarshall* Paulus had died with the rest of his Army. Hitler's war opera required the *Feldmarshall* to die for a lost city just as a captain went down with a sinking ship. But Paulus had failed to play the role cast him by the Propaganda Ministry. Instead, he had surrendered with what the Soviets claimed were 100,000 German troops.

On the other hand, that was less than half the number of troops that had been trapped in mid-November. If Paulus was not planning to perform the role the Dictator had written for him—if he was going to disobey orders—then why hadn't he done it ten weeks earlier? If he had disobeyed orders then by breaking out of the Soviet encirclement, he would have saved the bulk of the 6th Army. Or, alternatively, if he were too cowardly to face a court-martial for the sake of saving 200,000 lives, then why hadn't he at least surrendered to the Soviets six or four or even two weeks earlier? Every day he had delayed his surrender had cost hundreds of lives.

No matter how one looked at it, Paulus' surrender on Jan. 31 seemed a shabby and unworthy end for an Army that had suffered so long. Yet Manstein found a way to see it differently. "As you can see, gentlemen, the situation is grave. If we do not soon win the necessary permission to go over to a mobile defense, we could very well suffer the same fate as the 6th Army on a scale five times as great. I need hardly add that such losses would be irreplaceable and would signify the loss of the war here in the East. But let us not lose sight of the fact that the situation would look still worse, possibly hopeless, were it not for the fact that the 6th Army tied down enormous enemy resources by its heroic, selfless resistance. An earlier surrender would perhaps have saved more lives in the 6th Army itself, but it would have cost countless others in Army Groups A and Don. If the 6th Army had surrendered sooner, the Soviets would have launched much more forceful and determined attacks against our own flank. It goes without saying that those enemy forces, which up to now have been tied down by the siege of the 6th Army, will move against us at the earliest opportunity. It is this new situation that has induced me to insist on a personal interview with the *Führer*. I am confident that when I present him with the same facts I have outlined to you, our freedom to go over to a mobile defense will be granted. I would ask all of you to start preparing for this eventuality."

Manstein continued, "In the meantime, however, we must continue to hold the positions we have—as doggedly as possible. It is vitally important that I can assure the *Führer* that the Army Group is not in danger of being overrun or disintegrating. It is one of his most firmly held beliefs that Army Group Center was on the brink of collapse in December 1941, and that only his orders to stand fast prevented panic and rout from ensuing. Should the *Führer* have reason to see our situation as similar to that of Army Group Center last winter, his reaction will be identical: orders to dig in and stand fast at all costs."

Uneasily, the assembled generals and staff officers stirred in their seats. Thoughts went back to the individual sectors and the nearly impossible circumstances under which their troops were fighting. The prospects of holding their positions against even greater Soviet forces were nil. But Manstein had set a time limit. In three days he would talk to the *Führer* personally. Three days was a timespan they could grasp, and it was short enough to make the impossible task of "holding fast" seem possible—for that long. Not much longer, but certainly that long.

Philip, who had represented XXXII Corps at the briefing with Manstein, flew back from Zaporozhe to Donetz. At the airfield, *Oberleutnant* v. Seydlitz and Franz Stadthagen waited for him with a car to drive him the 230 km back to his own HQ. Seydlitz looked more weary and depressed than usual; his scar seemed unusually livid on his pale, strained face. Philip supposed he had lost even more sleep than the rest of them, seeing that his uncle had been one of the commanding generals in the 6th Army. Philip tried to cheer him up with Manstein's promise of a personal confrontation with Hitler.

"Does *Herr Oberstleutnant* think that will do any good?" Seydlitz asked, adding before Philip could answer, "Forgive my pessimism, but I know my uncle personally tried to talk the *Führer* into shortening the lines at Demyansk. Küchler, the Army Commander, and Halder both supported him, but it didn't do any good." The two officers climbed into the back seat of the staff car, and Stadthagen settled in behind the steering wheel. He was filling in for the usual driver, who had fallen ill just before Philip departed to Zoporozhe.

"Kluge sometimes had success," Philip pointed out, "and if there is any field marshal Hitler respects, then it is Manstein."

"*Herr Oberstleutnant* will forgive me for mentioning that my uncle had the Knight's Cross and Oak Leaves, and the *Führer* personally requested that he assume command of the relief operation for the units at Demyansk."

"And now, despite all his protests and appeals—both to Paulus and Manstein—he was not given permission to break out and is in Soviet hands," Philip finished the story. The car had left the airfield behind and started onto the icy, rutted road leading eastward. It was already dark, and the headlights were shaded.

It took considerable skill and concentration to navigate on the icy road past the slow-moving supply convoys that plodded eastward and against the stream of empty trucks, ambulances and sleighs returning the other way. The need to accelerate and brake frequently as they weaved in an out of the supply columns and the icy ruts made it a rough, uncomfortable ride.

Seydlitz sighed and asked in a low voice, "Does it make any sense? Does any of it make any sense?"

"Militarily?"

"No, not just militarily. Life in general; life at all?"

Philip hesitated. They had been together two and a half months. He liked the 23-year-old *Oberleutnant*, and for much the same reasons that Seydlitz was not generally popular. Seydlitz tortured himself with self-doubt and "too much profound thinking," as Rittenbach expressed it. Still, Philip was unsure if he should risk a discussion of this nature.

Seydlitz, however, seemed determined to provoke it. "*Herr Oberstleutnant* doesn't seem to me the kind of marionette who has never given a thought to what is going on out here."

"Thank you."

"The whole time I was waiting for you, I kept thinking: how is this possible? Millions of people bludgeoning one another to death in the most miserable conditions imaginable. The transports of wounded kept going by: vehicles laden with the mutilated remnants of humanity, people reduced to a sub-animal existence. And all our energy and intelligence is absorbed by thinking up ways we can best slaughter more of our fellow man ... Words fail me, *Herr Oberstleutnant*. I was raised to believe in a benevolent, all-powerful God. Can the God who said "Love thy neighbor as thyself," who said "The meek shall inherit the earth," want this war? But if He doesn't want it, why doesn't He stop it?"

"You forget I'm Catholic," Philip reminded his subordinate.

"No, I didn't forget. That's the reason why I'm asking you. The Lutheran chaplain I tried to talk to gave me nothing but platitudes about His "infinite wisdom" and our "need to have faith." Substitute the word "*Führer*" for "God," and it was like listening to one of Goebbels' speeches! I don't have faith and I don't believe in His infinite wisdom, or we wouldn't be in this mess. God—if there is a God—is not the God of my childhood, but something vicious and cruel and hateful."

Philip still hesitated. He removed his glasses and cleaned them meticulously, buying time to think. The gap between the two major faiths in Germany was as old as the Reformation and meticulously respected. The efforts to "convert" the adherents of one faith to the other had cost Germany one third of her population, depopulated entire provinces, leveled cities, brought trade to a standstill, and destroyed art treasures accumulated over centuries. Since the Thirty Years' War, an uneasy truce between the faiths had been maintained, but suspicion and even hostility remained. Philip had only to think of how his Protestant mother had been scorned and ostracized in Catholic Altdorf to be reminded of how profound the differences still were. "Rolf," Philip began cautiously, fitting his glasses back on his nose and behind his ears, "I'm not a theologian. I've never even been to university. I can only give you the answer that the priest in my home town gave me when I posed similar questions." He consciously used his ADC's first name and the familiar form of address.

"Yes?" the younger man insisted.

"He said: It's men who make wars, not God. Men do the killing. We can't pretend to have Free Will until a war comes along, and then suddenly blame everything on God." Philip paused, unsure if he should go on. As far as he knew, the Lutheran Church did not ascribe the same role to Free Will that the Catholic Church did. He feared his answer might be irrelevant to Seydlitz.

Almost as he'd expected, the younger man answered with vehemence, "I don't see that I have any Free Will. I feel like a pawn forced to commit crimes I don't want to commit."

"Crimes?" Philip's internal alarm signals rang. Surely this sober, conscientious officer had not been caught up in the SS atrocities?

"I put a pistol to the base of a man's head and blew his brains out," Seydlitz confessed.

Philip wasn't breathing as he asked, "A civilian?"

"No, a Red Army cavalryman."

Philip gently let out his breath. That wasn't necessarily outright murder. "Did you have a choice?"

"I don't know. I didn't take time to think about it. The man was hacking one of my gunners to pieces with his saber."

"You saved a man's life."

Seydlitz shook his head. "I was too late, I think. I don't know for sure. There were so many dead that day. So many wounded that never made it to the field hospital, much less home. I can't remember which of them survived. That isn't the point."

"What is the point?"

"That I'm being forced to kill other humans that I don't even know, and for reasons I don't understand."

"Forced by whom?"

"By fate, circumstances—or history, as the Bolsheviks would say. What else can I do but go on killing?"

"You could refuse to kill."

"That would be suicide. I'd either be shot by the enemy or after a court-martial. Besides, I know I will kill again. I'm compelled by training and society and the expectations of those around me to go on killing. Yet I feel like a murderer! And I feel like God hates me for what I have done! He hates me so much he has abandoned me completely."

"Do you want the Church's—sorry—my Church's answer to that?"

"Yes, I do." Seydlitz steadied his gaze at Philip as best he could in the swaying back seat of the staff car.

"The Church says that there is no absolute right or wrong answer to complicated moral questions. God knows that we are limited in our understanding and our insight. God, according to my priest, doesn't demand that we always do the right thing—only that we try to do the right thing as best as we can make it out. He does not abandon us for making mistakes. He asks only that we beg for guidance and open our hearts to His answer."

"That sounds easier than it is. He doesn't exactly speak out of burning bushes or thunder clouds anymore."

Philip laughed, "I've noticed. But, you see, that's where I—if I understand the difference between our faiths correctly—have it easier than you. My Church says that if I do my best, within my human limitations, to do what I think He would want, then I can expect to be forgiven, even if I am wrong. God does not blame us for things we cannot control, nor for our own weaknesses. He forgives us our mistakes, our misunderstandings, our confusion and helplessness. God, according to my priest, does not judge us on the basis of what we should have done in a world we don't live in, but on the basis of what we could have done in the world we're in. In a complicated world, God doesn't expect simple responses."

"Your priest said all that?" Seydlitz sounded so skeptical that Philip had to laugh again.

"He's an exceptional man."

"Then you wouldn't claim that every Catholic priest would give the same answer?"

"No, probably not," Philip admitted, aware of how lucky he had been in Father Matthias and Father Georg.

They were passing an artillery column. The guns were horse-drawn and the ponies seemed far too small for the load. The drivers were, without exception, Russian volunteers.

"I think that is all very interesting, *Herr Oberstleutnant*—"

"Between us, 'Philip,'" Philip corrected.

Seydlitz looked over to be sure this was really meant, and then nodded concurrence. "Thank you. I'll try to remember what you said next time I am faced with a specific dilemma. But what about life as a whole? I mean, is my life in any way meaningful? Can it really be that I was born to die out here in this senseless, filthy mess?"

"That may not be why you were born. You are as much a victim of human failure as everyone else born in this age. The question is: confronted by this deplorable reality, what can you do of your own Free Will to make your life meaningful?"

"Yes! That is the question: What?"

"Rolf! I'm 32 years old and a lieutenant colonel in the German Army, not the Delphic Oracle. I can't tell you what to do to give your life meaning."

"Too bad. I was beginning to think you had all the answers." Seydlitz cast Philip the closest thing to a smile that Philip had ever seen cross his tortured face.

When they reached the road junction at Antracit, the rumble of artillery had become incessant, and the sky was lit up by staggered flashes in a sweeping semicircle to the north and east of them. They stopped so that Stadthagen could check the oil and re-tank the car from a fuel canister carried in the trunk. The officers got out briefly to stretch their legs.

Seydlitz's attention was drawn to a group of Russian volunteers who were digging something at the side of the road. In the darkness, the exact purpose of their activity was unclear, but that it served their captors was self-evident. Seydlitz turned to Feldburg as if their conversation had never been interrupted. "Most people don't seem to need a purpose for living. Living itself, even under the most degrading conditions, seems enough for them. I don't understand that."

Philip, too, considered the Russians. "Perhaps it is the hope that if they just manage to survive, better times will come. Perhaps it is merely Darwin's 'survival instinct.'"

The roads were better for the next 90 km and Philip managed to sleep, waking only as they turned off the main road and headed for Schachty, where their HQ now stood. The artillery was nearer and it was possible to make a rough mental picture of where friendly and enemy batteries were drawn up. Schachty was at a junction of three roads from the east. The most southerly route of these was also the shortest route to the Don. Once the road had led to a bridge over the Don in the village of Razdorskaya, but the bridge had been destroyed by German engineers. The town of Razdorskaya had been held by units of XXXII Korps when Philip left for the conference at Manstein's HQ roughly 30 hours earlier. Now, from the red glow in the sky and the concentration of artillery, it was evident that the village was in flames and heavy fighting under way.

This alarmed Philip, since other elements of XXXII Korps were deployed much farther east at Utz Donetzskii and on the heights beyond the River Kundryushya. If the Russians broke through at Razdorskaya, the bulk of the Korps would be cut off. It sounded like a broken record.

With impatience to learn just what had happened during the last 30 hours, Philip mounted the steps of the run-down school building that served as Corps HQ. Though it was still dark outside, the lights burned here, and he sensed at once that a crisis atmosphere reigned. In the operations room he found Zimmermann crouched over the map, still in his stocking feet and looking bleary-eyed. "Thank God *Herr Oberstleutnant* is back," he greeted Philip.

"Where's Rittenbach?"

"He left for Razdorskaya hours ago—they're fighting in the town itself. God knows how they got across the Don. And now this; it just came in." He thrust the transcription of a radio message at his Chief of Staff. It read: "Under irresistible pressure from massively overwhelming enemy forces. Must pull back across the Kundryushya at Sadki." It was signed by *Oberst* Kramm, commanding one of the regiments of the 7th *Luftwaffe* Field Division.

Feldburg smelled panic in the message, and it infuriated him. It was clear from the sky and the sound alone that the Soviet focus was at Razdorskaya, not on the Kundryushya. Manstein's words still ran in his head: if Hitler had reason to think that the Army Group was on the brink of disintegrating, he would close his mind to all reason and insist on static defense to the death. If they were to have a chance of pulling back, regrouping, and resting, then their only hope was an orderly and prepared withdrawal, not headlong flight. More troops were always killed in a rout than in a retreat. And here was a colonel, a regimental commander, panicking under pressure and threatening to abandon a bridgehead vital for the withdrawal of other units. The weary and depleted but noble 336th was still deployed east of the Kundryushya!

"What the hell does Kramm think he's doing?" Feldburg broke away from Zimmermann and went directly into the communications center. "Get me radio communication to the 7th *Luftwaffe* Field Division's 94th Regiment immediately." The operators looked up at him as they hastened to obey. They could read the anger in his face and voice, and shared the amusement that soldiers always feel when they know one officer is about to chew out another.

The NCOs were not disappointed. As they later told Rittenbach, the "*Herr Baron* used language that we didn't think *Herr Baron* knew." Despite this, Feldburg failed to achieve his objective of stiffening the colonel's nerve. All he managed to do was confirm his worst suspicions: the colonel had panicked completely. Indeed, he'd panicked so completely that he was immune to orders, insults and threats from HQ. In a rage, Philip left the radio room and, shouting to Seydlitz to find Stadthagen and have him re-tank the car, he returned to the operations room. He told Zimmermann that he was going forward to Sadki to try to restore the situation. "Tell Rittenbach that *Oberst* Kramm has lost his nerve and is abandoning the bridge at Sadki!"

"He can't do that!" Zimmerman protested. "The 336th—"

"Why do you think I'm going forward myself? Be sure that Rittenbach understands the situation."

"*Jawohl!*"

Stadthagen and Seydlitz waited by the car, but Philip didn't even greet them. He just climbed in and barked at Stadthagen: "Sadki!" The other two hurried to get into the car after him.

The first greying of the eastern sky marked the approach of dawn as they reached the outskirts of Sadki. This was a Socialist town of grim, identical housing blocks that had become shabby and run down long before the war came to them. Troops in disorderly clumps were streaming toward them on the road, and Stadthagen automatically slowed down. Philip leaned forward. "Blow your horn and keep going. They'll get out of the way fast enough."

Stadthagen cast him a semi-horrified look and did as he'd been ordered. As the streets narrowed between the grim, grey blocks of concrete buildings, they became increasing clogged with soldiers, and the honking of the staff car seemed to have hardly any effect. Still Philip urged Stadthagen forward. "The faster you drive, the faster they'll get out of the way."

The angry, hateful looks of the soldiers forced aside by the honking staff car did not disturb Philip. They hated the man in the staff car forcing its way eastward because he represented all the stubborn, heartless staffs and higher headquarters that seemed never to take note of their exhaustion, hunger, cold or wounds.

Philip understood their feelings, but he did not let himself be confused by them. Knowing when to be ruthless was as much a part of being a good officer, a successful officer, as knowing when to spare the troops. Philip didn't consciously think all this as he urged Stadthagen against the current of fleeing soldiers; he knew it intuitively.

So the car forced its way forward against the increasing flow of troops until it reached the river embankment. Even here there was no sign whatever of the HQ—nothing but disorganized troops flooding back over the bridge and clogging the streets of the town on the opposite bank. Here and there, vehicles and motorcycles contributed to the chaos.

Philip flung open the door, stood on the running board of the car, and scanned the crowd for some symbol of authority. Finding none, he used his binoculars and directed them to the hills beyond the town where the regiment should have been in position. Dawn was breaking, and yet it was still gloomy enough for a flash of light to catch his attention at once. A few seconds later a shell crashed into the town on the other side of the river. What had been a disorderly but calm flow of troops across the bridge at once disintegrated into frantic panic. Some troops flung themselves down, some tried to turn back, and some tried to run forward faster.

To Stadthagen's horror, the next thing he saw was an enraged Baron v. Feldburg draw his pistol and plunge into the panicked crowd, shouting and waving his sidearm. Before Stadthagen's astonished eyes, the *Oberstleutnant* grabbed the arm of a fleeing officer candidate and shouted into his face, "How dare you, *Herr Fahnenjunker!*" He violently flung the young man around and set him moving in the other direction—eastward. Seydlitz, after a stunned moment, followed his chief, his pistol in his hand—but he only followed. It was Feldburg who grabbed here one and there another soldier. Physically, roughly, he turned one after another around and pushed them back against the flood.

Stadthagen watched in horrified fascination as Feldburg's mad gestures caused a clog in the rushing stream of soldiers flooding westward. Many of the troops he grabbed and tried to rally slipped away from him and ran for "safety" as soon as he had pressed on. But others seemed to have been brought to their senses. Once turned around, they followed in the *Oberstleutnant's* wake. The pebble in the stream became a rock, and then the unbelievable started to happen. As Stadthagen watched, awestruck, he could see the tide begin to turn. Suddenly there were more troops moving eastward across the bridge than fleeing to the west.

At that moment the Red artillery found the bridge. With a direct hit it obliterated what seemed like a half-dozen men still trying to run westward, and it cut down Feldburg and Seydlitz and the leading elements of those going the other way. The momentum that Feldburg had built up instantly dissolved. Everyone dived for cover or fled in panic to the west.

Stadthagen went berserk. He flung himself out of the car and plunged into the stream of troops rushing toward him. He screamed at them to go back, flailing the air with his rifle. But a crazy corporal could not drive panicked troops back into enemy fire. The Red artillery, having found the range, was leisurely lobbing shell after shell at the bridge. Most splashed into the river or landed on the embankment, but the artillery bombardment effectively forced the panicked soldiers to seek cover in nearby buildings. In the open area on both embankments and on the bridge itself, nothing stirred anymore. The victims of the first direct hit lay exposed in their blood on the bridge.

Stadthagen's fear overcame his berserker rage. He dropped onto his belly, but he was still obsessed with reaching Philip. He crawled forward on his elbows, closing his eyes and turning his head away from some of the corpses he had to pass. Still short of Philip, Stadthagen stopped, afraid of what he might find.

Then a voice called him by name. "Stadthagen! Here!"

He looked up and opened his eyes. Seydlitz had lifted his head and called. Stadthagen worked his way forward again. He could now see that Seydlitz had pulled himself forward far enough to half-shield Philip with his own body. "Is he alive?" Stadthagen called forward to the ADC.

"So far. You've got to get him off the bridge. I can't."

Seydlitz's right hand was blown away and his arm and shoulder bleeding profusely. Philip was more seriously wounded. His hips and lower body were drenched in blood. Stadthagen pulled himself into a crouch and told Seydlitz to roll Philip onto his back, but all they succeeded in doing was wrenching Philip from his merciful unconsciousness. He recognized Stadthagen. "What are you doing here?"

"We'll get you to safety—"

Philip shook his head. "Leave me—" He passed out again.

"You'll have to go back and get help," Seydlitz told Stadthagen.

Determinedly, Stadthagen crawled back to the west bank of the river and then ran to the shelter of the glowering apartment blocks that lined the embankment. But the soldiers who cowered in the filthy hallways shook themselves free of Stadthagen's grasp or violently flung him away from them. In their eyes, he was a madman.

Stadthagen became desperate. He hardly knew himself or what he was doing as he ran from building to building, trying to find someone willing to help him. Then suddenly out of nowhere, like a mirage, an eight-wheeler and a truck loomed up in the street in front of him. On the fenders of the eight-wheeler fluttered the pennants of a *Generalleutnant* and XXXII Korps. It was Rittenbach.

Stadthagen rushed forward and hauled himself onto the running board, sticking his head through the window. *"Herr General!* The *Herr Oberstleutnant! Freiherr* v. Feldburg!l He's on the bridge! Bleeding to death! We've got to—"

"Get hold of yourself, man!" Rittenbach ordered sharply. "I'll soon have things in hand."

CHAPTER 30

▼

Berlin
February 1943

The latest commotion had been caused by the announcement that women were now subject to industrial conscription. Only married women with small children were theoretically exempt. Henceforth, women who were not gainfully employed could be drafted to work in factories suffering from severe manpower shortages, despite the enslavement of most of Europe. The women already working in the Bendlerstrasse had every reason to be pleased with themselves. Their jobs were "essential" war work, but they were relatively pleasant, civilized and rewarding compared with factory or farm labor. Still, Alexandra had heard quite enough self-congratulation by mid-afternoon and was trying to get some work done. The ringing of the telephone and Annie's apparent deafness to it irritated her further. She grabbed the receiver and barked into it, "AHA, Feldburg!"

At the other end of the line a thin, distant, female voice remarked in a bored tone, "Stand by for a call from XXXII Korps. I'll connect you."

Alexandra heard the characteristic clicking to indicate a connection and jumped in excitedly, "Philip?"

There was no answer.

"Hello? Philip? XXXII Corps? This is the *Allgemeines Heeresamt*. Can you read me?"

A strange voice came across the wires and distance, "*Freifrau* von Feldburg?"

"Speaking."

"General v. Rittenbach here."

"One moment, please; I'll connect you with General Olbricht."

"No, please, I want to speak with *you*."

Even before he finished, Alix knew what he was going to say, knew what it meant. She felt instantly ill, physically ill, and she couldn't bear to hear it. She broke in, said the words herself: "He's dead."

"No, not yet. The surgeon says there is every reason to hope ... *Freifrau* v. Feldburg? Are you still there? Can you hear me?" It was a bad connection and the wires were rasping and clicking.

"Yes, I'm here," Alexandra confirmed, although the room was spinning around her.

"I'm going to see that he gets flown back to Berlin as soon as possible. He wouldn't approve of special treatment, but he doesn't have much to say about it right now. *Freifrau* v. Feldburg, I will do everything in my power—everything I would have done for my son...."

"Thank you."

"I'll keep you informed."

Alexandra put the receiver down and managed to push past the officer who had just entered with a mumbled, "One moment, please." She got to the door of Olbricht's office, knocked and—without waiting for an answer—got inside. Leaning against the inside of the door as she closed it, she couldn't get a word out.

She didn't need to. Olbricht jumped up, came around his desk and down the length of the room. He took her arm and led her to the sofa under the window. By this time she had broken down completely and was streaming tears, so he gave her his handkerchief. Then he stood by, hand on her shoulder, and waited until she had hold of herself enough to say, "There's someone out there who wants—"

"He can wait."

"I'm sorry. I'm overreacting. He's only wounded. They think there's some hope—the doctors, I mean."

Olbricht didn't answer. His hand, however, tightened convulsively on her shoulder, and she remembered that in the fall Olbricht's only son had been slightly wounded—"not in danger at all"—and then had died in a field hospital. The General, on a tour of the front, had stopped to visit his son, only to find that the 19-year-old had died three hours earlier. "I'm sorry," Alix sobbed, and the General's grip relaxed, became gentle again.

Slowly Alexandra pulled herself together. When she stopped crying, the General patted her shoulder and excused himself. He slipped out of the room and she could hear voices on the other side of the door. A moment later, Olbricht was back and handed her a glass of schnapps. "Drink this, and I'll see if I can get more concrete information."

"I'm sorry, I—"

"Drink that and let me telephone," he ordered, and Alix willingly obeyed.

✻   ✻   ✻   ✻

Altdorf

The sleet splattered against the window, and from the other side of the closed door came the sound of slow typing, a muffled tap-tap-tap. In the Police Chief's office, the heat was turned up, and the worn rug and battered wooden chairs seemed as war-weary as Sophia Maria felt.

The Police Chief himself was overweight and aging. Though he had been a member of the Party since shortly after the "seizure of power" in 1933, he had continued to do his duty in the same methodical and honest way in which he had always done it. What he privately thought of Hitler and the government, no one knew. As he took *Freifrau* v. Feldburg's statement regarding a reported case of black marketeering, he seemed vaguely tired.

Freifrau v. Feldburg said she could neither confirm nor deny any accusations of black marketeering against a neighbor, the widow Lehmann. In fact, the woman was known to be greedy and ill-tempered. It was rumored that she treated her forced laborers with meanness bordering on brutality. Sophia Maria did not doubt for a moment that she had been trading on the black market, and suspected that a good deal more than eggs and butter had changed hands illegally. But Sophia Maria was on principle opposed to the war and the controls, and she was certain that the worst corruption came not from the "little people" like Frau Lehmann. She was not inclined, therefore, to testify against Frau Lehmann. "Is the charge serious?" she asked the Police Chief.

The Chief of Police took a deep breath and fussed with the papers on his desk. "It carries the death penalty."

"But that's ridiculous! On account of a couple dozen eggs and some odd kilos of butter? That's simply absurd!"

"*Naja*, the highest penalty is hardly likely in this case," the Police Chief demurred. "But even if she gets only a mild prison sentence, who is going to run the farm? All five of her sons are in the armed forces, and two are already dead. Her girls can't manage alone, even with the help of the Poles."

"Is a prison sentence likely?" Sophia Maria asked.

"It's almost certain—or Concentration Camp—but as a rule these economic crimes are handled in a—ah—traditional manner."

Sophia Maria nodded. She felt sorry for the sons, who—if they survived the war—would return to find that their mother's greed had cost them their home, but there was nothing she could do about it.

"Oh, by the way." The Police Chief tried to sound casual, but he failed and had to clear his throat before continuing. "Um, I wanted to remind you that it is illegal for foreign workers to possess newspapers."

"Yes," Sophia Maria agreed, tensing inwardly.

"It was reported to me recently that your Pole, Jurek, had been seen in town with several newspapers under his arm."

"Oh, that," Sophia Maria sounded unconcerned. "He was picking them up for me."

"*Frau Baronin,* the law does not take into account the reasons *why* a foreign worker is in possession of newspapers. Forbidden is forbidden."

"But that's quite ridiculous. I'm sure the butcher in the Königstrasse has a Ukrainian girl helping him in the shop, and she wraps the meat in newspapers. Nobody objects to that."

"Well, old newspapers may be different, but Jurek was seen with the daily papers, which contain the latest *Wehrmacht* Reports."

"Oh, that doesn't matter; Jurek can't read German."

"*Freifrau* v. Feldburg, I'm afraid the law doesn't make any distinction between those foreign workers who can and those who can't read German—and I wouldn't be all that sure your Jurek can't read. He's been here two and a half years already."

"Herr *Meisterling,* you can't honestly mean that I am expected to drive into town myself only to pick up the daily newspapers?"

"You will have to send one of your German employees in the future."

"But they're the very ones I can spare the least. And Jurek comes to town regularly. I think this is all very unnecessary."

"Maybe it is, but the Imperial Defense Commissar" (this was the new title bestowed upon the *Gauleiters* since the fall of Stalingrad and was part of Goebbels' "Total War" campaign) "has expressly stated that he intends to crack down on lax compliance with the laws on foreign workers. He gave a lengthy and outraged speech in which he cited a large number of abuses. He says there have been instances of beer being served to French POWs in public bars—fortunately not in Altdorf!—and RAD girls have been seen dancing with Polish youth."

"Oh, we don't allow that!" Sophia Maria declared self-righteously. "The Poles were only teaching the girls the steps, but they didn't actually *dance* with them."

The Police Chief sighed deeply and looked wearily but sternly from under his bushy eyebrows. "*Freifrau* v. Feldburg, you and Father Matthias make my life very difficult. Did you know that priests have been arrested for saying prayers for the inmates of Concentration Camps and/or prayers for the Jews?"

"But I don't understand. Jesus himself was a Jew, and he prayed for them during the Crucifixion itself: 'Forgive them, Father, for they know not what they do.' How can we not pray for them?"

"*Freifrau* v. Feldburg, I have heard many complaints about Father Matthias' 'disloyal' or 'anti-National Socialist' remarks. What am I supposed to do with them?"

Sophia Maria shrugged. "Some people feel they have to go around making those kinds of reports to prove their own loyalty—probably the very people who have the most black-market dealings."

"Possibly, but did or did not Father Matthias publicly pray for the prisoners *on both sides* last Sunday?"

"Did he? I can't say I remember hearing such a prayer."

"No less than four parishioners wrote outraged letters over such a scandalous insult to our gallant troops. They point out that to pray for the prisoners on both sides is the same thing as saying that Soviet prisoners are equal to German prisoners, or that Slavs are the same as Aryans. I'm rather afraid the Gestapo would agree."

"Gestapo? Why should the Gestapo hear of this?"

"Because I am obliged to pass on all such reports to the Gestapo, *Frau Baronin*. These are political crimes and fall outside my jurisdiction."

"This is all ridiculous. Father Matthias is an old, beloved priest. If he hasn't grasped the finer points of National Socialist racial ideology, he is still a loyal citizen and beloved by his flock. Any attempt to remove him would cause an uproar in the community."

"No doubt led by you, Your Excellency." The Police Chief was very formal not out of sarcasm, but rather to express his own sincere respect despite the unpleasant demands of duty.

"No doubt."

"But in such an event, *Frau Baronin*, the 'dance lessons' and Jurek's newspapers might not look so harmless anymore. And where did your Ukrainian girls come by such sturdy shoes? They arrived with the same flimsy plastic shoes as the others, didn't they?"

"They couldn't work in those!"

"Please. There is no point in arguing with me. As far as I'm concerned, everything is in the best of order. But these reports against Father Matthias will have to be forwarded. You might want to tell him to expect the consequences."

The Police Chief saw Sophia Maria out of his office with a low "*Heil Hitler*" followed by a respectful bow. A little dazed, she went past his desultory secretary and the lounging policemen onto the doorstep. Sleet blew in under the shelter of the eaves, and she was wet before she could even tie her scarf around her head. A perfectly dreadful day!

To her surprise, on her return she found Father Matthias waiting for her in the manor kitchen. The bulk of the staff was gathered, too, all in a noticeably sober mood—and Father Matthias looked most depressed of all. Precisely because the priest made such an effort to cultivate cheerfulness wherever he went, it was a surprise to see him in this state. Sophia Maria at once guessed what was in the air: the Police Chief's warning had been too late. Most likely the Gestapo had received a number of reports directly, and had not waited for the Police Chief to forward his reports.

Father Matthias stood as he saw Sophia Maria. "Frau v. Feldburg, I need to speak to you alone."

"Of course; come up to my study." She pulled off her scarf and shook it out as she spoke.

In the study, Sophia Maria first turned up the heat and then turned solicitously to Father Matthias. "Father, I've never seen you in such a state. Let me have some tea brought up to us."

"No, I can't. Herr Amberg" (that was the local Party leader/*Ortsgruppenleiter*) "brought me some news, or rather brought me some news to bring to you."

Sophia Maria's heart missed a beat. So that was the way it was. Not the priest, but she herself, was to be the first victim of the Imperial Defense Commissar's new crackdown. "And he didn't have the courage to come himself?" she asked the priest with a certain bitterness.

"He thought—and I rather hope—that you would rather hear it from me." She looked at him, puzzled, and the priest continued gently, "Christian—"

The blow was so unexpected, it was like the time a young stallion kicked her in the gut with his hind hooves. Then she had been flung fifteen feet through the air and landed in a hospital, her insides mashed but repairable. Now she simply crashed to the floor as her legs gave out. She was not even granted the mercy of unconsciousness.

Consciously, she saw Father Matthias rush to her. Consciously, she felt him help her up, her whole weight on his old, thin arms. Consciously she noted how he trembled with the strain of helping her into a chair. Consciously she accepted the schnapps that Martha had thoughtfully sent up on a tea tray. She was conscious, too, that she was behaving badly. She was expected—and she expected herself—to be more dignified, more controlled, more aristocratic.

Her mind also registered that this time her insides would not be repairable. Never would they be the same again. She had seen it all with her mother. First her younger brother had fallen in 1915, and her mother had been crippled but gallantly tried to carry on. Then her elder brother had fallen early in 1918, and her mother had been broken. When Sophia Maria had seen her after a two-year break (because Ferdinand wouldn't let her travel through Berlin to visit her parents in the politically unsettled years 1918-1919), she had hardly recognized her. Her mother had become fragile and was always close to tears. She had cried at the mere sight of Philip and Christian because they reminded her of the boys she'd lost. She'd turned to religion and adopted Pacifism with embarrassing fervor. She'd even (to her husband's intense embarrassment) applauded the Provisions of Versailles that reduced Germany's armed forces to a ridiculous little troop bereft of modern weapons. Again and again, she had admonished Sophia Maria to stop her boys from having anything to do with the military. "You must teach them to hate uniforms and guns, Sophie," she had insisted with a feverish intensity. "You must see that they never, never kill other men."

But the allure of forbidden fruit had been far greater than the admonishments of a beloved grandmother. The boys treated their grandmother Walmsdorff with tenderness and respect. They had loved her enough never to flaunt their military ambitions, but both had wanted nothing more fervently than to be soldiers.

Not that it would have saved them if they had chosen other professions, Sophia Maria reflected. Even the self-proclaimed cowards like Franz Stadthagen or the peace-loving like Dieter Möller had been dragged into this inferno. The Nazi government had managed to create a conflagration so great that it was devouring even more young men than the Great War had done. And there was no end in sight. Then again, what good would an end to the war do her? Philip was on the critical list, and Christian was already gone. She couldn't bear it. She would go mad.

"Christian," the priest was saying, holding her hand in both of his, "didn't return from his last flight. He was on a patrol with three other aircraft. They were attacked by a superior enemy formation. The report said something about engaging a whole RAF wing, but I don't suppose we should take such things literally. What is certain is that the other pilots were too busy fighting for their own lives to see exactly what happened. He neither radioed nor returned to base. He's been posted missing."

"Missing? Is that supposed to be a comfort? Missing? God in Heaven, I want to scream!" she told the priest in an ice-cold voice. "Do you think I don't know what 'missing' means? It means the remains were never found. It means he burned up or blew up so completely they couldn't even find a piece of meat to identify him by! They didn't even look, from the way you tell it, and that means he might have bled or starved to death, parched by the sun to nothing. I wasn't born yesterday, Father. Missing means I'll never know."

Despite herself, she was crying. She wasn't sobbing. As with her own mother, the tears just streamed down her cold and bitter face. "Do you know what it is to be tortured by hope?" she asked the priest, but she didn't give him a chance to answer. "I had a cousin who was 'missing.' I saw my aunt go mad as a result. Every hungry, homeless vagabond fed her fanciful stories about seeing Hans here, seeing him there. British prisons, French prisons, American prisons, hospitals and insane asylums. Oh, yes, they all knew Hans—with a glance at the photos on the mantel—a tall, blond lieutenant of the infantry. Who could forget such a wonderful young man! He'd lost both legs and been ashamed to come home. He had amnesia from a head wound. He had fallen in love with a French peasant girl. Anyone who dared doubt these fairy tales was a monster who didn't love Hans or my aunt. Yes, I know what 'missing' means for a mother. My aunt went mad. Literally mad—digging in the graveyard with her bare hands because she'd dreamed they'd buried him alive!"

"But you're too strong for that," Father Matthias told her softly.

"Do you think so? I'm no so sure."

*   *   *   *

Berlin
February 1943

Philip's moments of lucidity were few and far between. He was briefly conscious as Rittenbach lay beside him on the bridge at Sadki. He'd tried to explain the situation—the 336th was still to the east—and Rittenbach had given him the worst rebuke of his career. ("Do you take me for an idiot or what? Shut up and obey orders for a change.") He remembered waking up briefly in Stadthagen's lap. Stadthagen was trembling and his teeth were chattering. He had a memory of being in an aircraft, feeling it sink sharply, and thinking of the *Luftwaffe* lieutenant whose plane full of Stalingrad wounded had crashed behind enemy lines. He'd woken up once during an air raid and found himself in a cellar under a shaking ceiling. Paint and plaster rained down on wall-to-wall stretchers and cots. The staff had apparently sought safer quarters and left the patients alone with their fear.

This time, as he came to, he was aware of the starched hospital sheets and the bustle of someone beside his bed. He kept his eyes closed. Medics and nurses were always bumping between the beds and administering unwanted food, injections and advice. He mentally pulled away from the fussing beside him—and then he smelled roses. The smell was so clear and pronounced that it tore his eyes open. He squinted in the dazzling white of the small hospital room—not a ward, he registered, but a small room. He strained to twist his head toward the insistent smell.

The sight stopped his breath and he lay stock still, afraid to move: Alexandra was arranging roses in a vase on a table by his bed. He could only see the side of her face, the back of her head and neck. The need to prove to himself that she wasn't a hallucination forced him to reach out his hand toward her. His arm was weak, and he only managed to lightly brush her elbow.

Startled, she spun around. Her eyes widened as they met his, and then she dropped on her knees next to the bed and held his hand in both of hers. Tears were brimming up in her blue eyes.

Philip's lips moved, but no sound came from them. Alix could not even guess what he was trying to say. It didn't matter. She reached out and stroked the side of his face. Yet even as they tried to communicate with their eyes, Philip started to lose consciousness again. He tried to fight for it, and Alexandra could see him trying, but he was too weak. He drifted back to sleep.

In Alexandra's eyes, sleep was suddenly no longer death's brother, but a necessary step to recovery. She kissed her husband's hand and for the first time since he had been wounded, she believed he would recover. She danced her way out of the Charité Hospital and down the steps to the waiting staff car with the general's pennants.

General Olbricht had arranged for Philip to be handled by the senior surgeon of Berlin's most prestigious hospital, the Charité—Dr. Ferdinand Sauerbruch. Olbricht had not even needed to draw on his prestige and power as the chief of the General Army Office, because Sauerbruch was a personal friend. Alix knew doctors weren't miracle workers. A fine title or high salary didn't necessarily make a doctor better than colleagues with lesser titles and lower salaries. Still, there was comfort in knowing that Philip was not at the mercy of some obscure Army doctor with perhaps only hasty wartime training. Furthermore, it didn't hurt for a doctor to feel he was treating a friend of a friend rather than some unknown officer, of whom there were so many.

"I can see there must have been some improvement," Olbricht observed as she climbed back into his car.

"He saw me and recognized me! I think he's going to make it!"

"Sauerbruch has been saying that ever since he survived the second operation five days ago."

"I know, but I didn't believe him."

"Well, now we have something to celebrate. Eva will like that." They were on their way to the Olbrichts' for dinner. Ever since Philip had been wounded almost three weeks earlier, the General and his wife had made a point of frequently having Alexandra for dinner. Usually there were other guests—Erich Hoepner, Dr. Sauerbruch or General Beck, Oster or Thomas—and there were almost always former comrades or subordinates of Olbricht on their way to or from the front. Tonight Alexandra was glad that it was only Uncle Erich, his wife and Generaloberst Beck.

Frau Hoepner gave Alexandra a hug and said with sincerity, "I'm so glad for you!" Frau Olbricht at once suggested champagne to celebrate Philip's recovery, and stood to go to the kitchen herself rather than ringing for the maid. Alexandra intuitively understood that she was thinking of her son and the champagne they had never been able to drink to his recovery. Impulsively she sprang to her feet and went after the older woman. In the kitchen she put her arms around her. The proud general's wife accepted the gesture in silence, but then with a jerk pulled herself together. She nodded to Alexandra, "Thank you. Now go back and celebrate. Nothing will bring Klaus back. All we can do is make sure this senseless slaughter is stopped as soon as possible! Your husband will help us with that, and that's reason enough to open the champagne."

In the living room, Olbricht, Hoepner and Beck were already discussing Philip's next assignment. "I'd planned to recall him to AHA and give him responsibility for Valkyrie, but we should consider whether he'd be more useful to us at OKW or directly with Fromm."

"Can you get him a position at OKW?" Beck asked softly. He was looking very weak, and Alexandra knew that he had been diagnosed with stomach cancer. Dr. Sauerbruch wanted to operate, but had postponed the operation once or twice already because of "unexpected" emergencies—one of which, of course, was Philip.

"I can recommend him to Keitel," Obricht started, but Erich Hoepner interrupted.

"Come now, Fritz," Hoepner glanced toward Alexandra, "our Alix has barely had three weeks with her husband. There is plenty of work for him right here in Berlin. There's no need to send him into the lion's den where—God knows—his influence would be minimal."

"That's true." Olbricht smiled at Alexandra, but it was an apologetic smile. He clearly felt a little guilty for even having considered it.

"Didn't you tell me Hitler will visit Army Group Center soon?" Beck asked Olbricht intently. His eyes seemed sunken into his face, and the dark circles under them made them seem larger and more demanding.

"Yes, the visit has been set for March 13," Olbricht confirmed.

Beck seemed to catch his breath and hold it. Then he let it out slowly and asked, "Is Kluge still committed?"

"Apparently, and Boeselager has committed his entire new cavalry unit to Tresckow."

Beck frowned. "He has no right to misuse innocent soldiers for political purposes."

"Georg Boeselager's soldiers would do anything he asked of them," Hoepner pointed out, with admiration bordering on envy.

"That is precisely why he has no right to ask it of them," Beck admonished the panzer general. Frail as he was, he still exuded moral authority as he sat stiff and uncompromising in his chair.

"The killing—if all goes according to plan—will be done by the officers of the staff," Olbricht interjected soothingly. "Boeselager's soldiers are simply to ensure the safety of the HQ and protect Kluge against the SS in the aftermath. That, I think, they can be asked to do in good conscience."

Beck nodded agreement and some of the stiffness went out of him, but the lines around his mouth betrayed the pain he was in. Alexandra wondered how much longer he could afford to delay surgery.

Frau Olbricht returned with a tray laden with champagne glasses and a chilled bottle of champagne. She set the tray down and gave the bottle to her husband. He smiled and deftly worked the cork free without either popping it or spilling any of the precious liquid. As he poured champagne into the waiting glasses, he remarked, "Coming back to Feldburg. If Tresckow's plan works, OKW won't exist anymore, and I can use him in the Ministry of Defense." (In a post-Hitler government, Olbricht was to be appointed Minister of Defense.) "But if Tresckow's plan—for whatever reason—fails, then we should consider the fact that Feldburg has proved so adept at getting along with difficult generals that he might even be able to keep Fromm in line."

The others laughed, and Alix protested, "Rittenbach isn't difficult."

"Not to you, my dear, but he had a history of chewing up and spitting out staff officers. Tresckow says he was nothing but trouble—a splendid troop leader but a perpetual powder keg—until your husband joined his staff. Manstein feels the same way; he explicitly praised your husband whenever the XXXII was mentioned because, he says, Rittenbach alone is too capricious."

Alexandra could only grin. Of course, she was so happy, she might well have grinned even if Olbricht had been telling her stories about how incompetent and cowardly Philip was. But Olbricht was continuing, "But my initial idea was probably the best. In the event that Tresckow's plan fails, I'll recall Feldburg to AHA and put him to work on keeping the Valkyrie Orders up to date. Having another officer with the Knight's Cross on the staff will increase the prestige and respect awarded the entire AHA."

"Philip doesn't have a Knight's Cross," Alexandra pointed out, still grinning as she took a glass of champagne from the tray Frau Olbricht was holding out to her.

"Oh, didn't you hear?" Olbricht sounded genuinely surprised. "Manstein approved it before your husband even left Russia—not for his efforts at Sadki, though I'm sure that didn't hurt, but for two months of holding the flank of Army Group Don under nearly impossible circumstances. Rittenbach told your husband about it personally, just before he was transported back to Germany. Apparently our dear Feldburg nodded without opening his eyes and replied, "My widow will be grateful.""

They laughed, but Alexandra felt uneasy. She had been so close to becoming a widow at 29.

CHAPTER 31

▼

Berlin
March 1943

When the all-clear sounded and they climbed from the cellar in the middle of the night, wearily and emotionally drained, they were shocked and frightened to find the sky lit up luridly. A vague, animal uneasiness ran through the little crowd of neighbors huddled in blankets and bathrobes as they stood bunched together at the top of the stairs to the cellar. Then shouting in the street induced Theo to go out. An officious character shouted at him angrily and hoarsely, "Don't just stand there gaping! Bring buckets and help!"

He reported to the others that phosphorus bombs had started a fire in the roof of the building just two houses to the left. Peter Kessler at once reached for two of the buckets waiting on their own stairs, and the other tenants followed his example, even Marianne. It was the bombing that terrified Marianne; she was prepared to deal with the aftereffects with a youth's sense of adventure.

In a little cluster, the residents from the Feldburg house set off down the street and joined the bucket brigade from the pump in the street to the burning apartment house. Even Alexandra was at first overcome by the excitement. The flames roared up out of the shattered attic and the windows on the fourth floor. The wind blew hot. Soon, however, the tedious strain of passing buckets back and forth overshadowed the excitement. Alexandra was still dressed for the office and realized she was sweating profusely under her winter coat, ruining her blouse. Soot, smoke and ash blew through the air, sticking to them, catching in hair and clothing. Glancing to either side of her, Alix saw that Nurse Tuchel's face was smudged with grime, and sweat drops made trails through it. Marianne looked no better, but she laughed and joked with Peter, whose glasses were slipping down his nose. He laughed back and looked at her soot- and sweat-stained face as if it were a beauty queen's. Love, thought Alix indulgently.

Nurse Tuchel hissed to Alexandra between pinched lips, "It's disgusting the way those two carry on! In the middle of all this! And he a police officer!"

Alexandra looked at the middle-aged nurse and felt the pity of a happily married woman for the old maid. She glanced again at Marianne and Peter and then at the respectable parents. The Moldenauers were clearly embarrassed by their daughter's behavior, but war had different rules, Alexandra reflected. Old codes of behavior seemed irrelevant when men were so scarce, and they all stood on the edge of their graves. It seemed as natural as the ash and smoke in the wind that a young woman in love—even one from a good family—no longer played coy or hid her feelings.

Alexandra's hands started to blister. Her back ached, and still worse was the growing thirst. She looked longingly at the slopping buckets as they were passed forward, but did not dare interrupt the rhythm even for a moment. The flames, meanwhile, seemed higher than ever. Frau Moldenauer dropped out of line and rested on the curb. She pressed her hands to her chest and drew deep breaths.

Excited, angry shouting from the head of the line was followed by a resounding crack and crash. A whole wall caved inward, and the fire sprang up from the third floor. A woman shrieked: "My parlor! My grandmother's furniture!" Someone else calmed her down. Orders were shouted to redirect the water to the neighboring houses. Light was creeping up from the east. A pre-dawn greyness hung over them.

"This is totally pointless," someone grumbled.

"Where's the fire department?"

"Where are the wonder weapons?"

"What's the matter with you?! Think what our troops have to suffer on the front!"

"Do you think they're fighting so we can spend the night like this?"

"Shut up or I'll have to report you."

"Everything I own," the woman sobbed; "everything."

Back in the Feldburg apartment, Alexandra accepted what she had feared; there'd be no time to sleep at all. She went directly to the bathroom and turned on the tap. Nothing happened. She turned further, turned the other tap, and went to the bathtub. Nothing. She went to the kitchen and tried the sink. No water.

At the office everyone asked if she had been hit, and she had to explain a dozen times that no, it had been two houses away, but there was no water. Others had their own tales. The northern and eastern sections of the city had been hit worst. There was neither electricity nor water nor streetcars there. At midday, Alexandra called Frau Wendt and asked if there was water yet. There wasn't. So Alix called her parents to see if they had water. Fortunately they did.

After work, she packed one suitcase with the dirty clothes Frau Wendt had been unable to wash and another with night things and a change. Then she took the bus to her parents' house. Here Alexandra was greeted by the Russian girl who helped in the house and kitchen. She was pretty, plump, and full of curiosity. Helga reported that she was a hard worker and a quick learner. Alexandra then went straight to the downstairs bathroom to wash her face and hands and then to the living room, expecting her family to be impatiently awaiting her. She was late.

To her astonishment, the room was empty. She wandered on to the dining room, but though the table was set, it too was empty. Then she heard voices behind the closed doors of her stepfather's study. She knocked.

"Who's there?"

"Me; Alix."

The door opened at once, and she found all four family members gathered. Frau v. Rantzow sat in the big reading chair with a sobbing Grete on her lap. Rudi, in his Hitler Youth uniform, was perched on the footstool, and Herr v. Rantzow had evidently been pacing. He had opened the door.

Grete, as always at the sight of her "big sister," leapt up and ran to her. "Alix! They want to send me away!" she wailed.

"That's not true!" her father corrected sharply. "This has nothing to do with what we want! The whole school with all the teachers is being evacuated. You have to go along, or you lose a whole year at school. Besides, it is a good idea to evacuate the young people. It should have been done long ago."

"But, Albrecht," his wife protested, "they'll be so far away, and we won't be able to visit. How can we be sure they'll be properly cared for?"

"Why shouldn't they be? No one has any interest in neglecting the children."

"No institution ever looks after children like a mother does, and this is all being organized by the Party," Alexandra's mother pointed out.

"It's going to be just like that awful camp!" Grete protested in a slightly whining voice, "drill, drill, drill, and inspections, and stupid songs!"

"Don't use that tone of voice!" her father ordered. "There is no reason to think this will be like that camp. This is your regular school, and your teachers will be there to continue your lessons. And really, Louisa," he addressed his wife in a kinder but still exasperated voice, "it will be much healthier for the children to get a full night's sleep every night rather than cower in cold cellars half the time."

"They could go down to Altdorf," Alexandra interceded. "I'm sure they could stay with my mother-in-law and go to the local school, if you prefer."

"Oh, yes! Please! I could learn to ride and take care of the horses!"

Herr v. Rantzow silenced his younger daughter with a frown and inquired of the elder, "You're sure *Freifrau* v. Feldburg wouldn't mind?"

"If you like, I can call and ask her right away, but I can't imagine she'd object. I think she'd enjoy having young people around."

"Would you prefer that arrangement, Louisa? You still won't be able to visit."

"But I'm sure they'd be in good hands," Frau v. Rantzow told him, with a grateful look to Alexandra.

"And what about you, Rudi?" Alix asked. "Would you prefer Altdorf?" Alexandra didn't really expect him to say "yes." He liked the drill and camaraderie that Grete hated.

"Oh, we aren't being evacuated," Rudi replied, with a nonchalance that could not disguise his pride. "We've been drafted into the *Luftwaffe*."

"WHAT???" both parents demanded simultaneously.

"Well, not exactly into the *Luftwaffe*, but we're going to be trained as flak helpers."

"No!" his father declared. "They can't draft 15-year-olds. Not even at the end of the Great War were we so desperate!"

"It will be just like being in the *Wehrmacht*," Rudi enthused.

"I can't believe this!" Herr v. Rantzow fumed. "I'm going to call the headmaster at once. We can't have sunk so low that we need 15-year-olds to man our anti-aircraft guns! What an unequaled failure of government!" And with this he left the study, apparently to telephone from somewhere else—or perhaps because he didn't want his family to be a witness to his own helplessness.

✳   ✳   ✳   ✳

Berlin
March 1943

Alexandra reported to her husband that Dr. Sauerbruch needed to operate yet again on Ludwig Beck. The first two operations had been "successful" but not "sufficient." Philip could only stare at her. He was intensely aware of how much Beck's participation in the conspiracy against Hitler meant to him. If it came to a coup, it was Beck—far more than Kluge, Witzleben or Hoepner—who would assure them the support of the General Staff and officers from the *Reichswehr*. The officers who had been commissioned since the expansion under Hitler might or might not be impressed by Beck, but virtually all senior officers were admirers of Beck. If Beck were too ill for active participation, they had no one of equal stature in the conspiracy.

But before Philip had even digested this news, Alexandra continued, "The *Führer* is giving a speech tomorrow that you must not miss. I've already asked the reception desk, and they assure me the radio in the lounge at the end of the hall will be tuned in. You only have to be wheeled down there in time."

Philip considered his wife from the perspective of his hospital bed and tried to imagine why he should ruin an otherwise normal day by having to listen to Hitler, but he didn't dare ask directly. He shared his room with a chemist who had given every indication of being a fanatical supporter of the Regime. All he could do was look at Alix reprovingly through his glasses and remind his wife, "I like to sleep after lunch. I need my sleep."

"I appreciate that; but when the speech is over, the *Führer* will inspect the exhibit in the armory, and I'm sure it will be very interesting. Key elements have been organized by Tresckow. If all goes according to plan, before the *Führer* even comes out of the Armory, we should all know the secret of how the war can be won quickly and gloriously."

The other patient in the room was listening so intently that his hands tightened on the edges of the magazine he was pretending to read. He knew Alexandra worked for the Head of the General Army Office, which—among other things—had responsibility for weapons development. He firmly believed that Alexandra knew something about the "miracle weapons" that would turn the tide in Germany's favor.

At about the same time, General Olbricht was saying to his son-in-law, a *Luftwaffe* staff officer, "Whatever you do, don't sit too near the podium. It will be bad enough for Eva and Rosemarie if *I* don't come home after Hitler's speech tomorrow."

The following morning, General Olbricht handed his secretary a slip of paper with "EW, EH & HT" scribbled on it. "For this afternoon, if something should prevent me from returning to the Bendlerstrasse after the speech. You have the telephone numbers?"

Alexandra deciphered the initials of *Feldmarschal* Erwin v. Witzleben, *Generalleutnant* Erich Hoepner, and *Oberst* Henning v. Tresckow, and nodded.

"And you know how to help *Oberst* Reinhard in the same event?"

Oberst Reinhard was Olbricht's Chief of Staff, a man who believed that the war could only be won "with Hitler," but who could be counted on to do his duty if—after Hitler was dead—the Valkyrie Orders had to be issued.

"I know what to do," Alexandra assured Olbricht. She was to take the Valkyrie orders to Reinhard and urge him to take them to Fromm for signature. Fromm could not be counted on to take the initiative on his own.

"Good. Then I hope to see you again mid-afternoon."

"So do I," Alexandra said sincerely—aware of the paradox of wanting the bomb to go off without killing too many of the "wrong" people.

Philip unwillingly obeyed his wife's instructions and joined the crowd of patients already gathered in the lounge. He was a little late and had some trouble finding a spot for his wheelchair. He jostled other patients, who cast him irritated and reproving looks. It was a disadvantage of being in pajamas, he noted, that he was not instantly identifiable as a major of the General Staff. Fortunately, the radio announcer was already commenting on the arrival of the dignitaries, and so the other patients were soon distracted. "… Field Marshal Keitel just left his staff car. He's going toward—no, he's just stopped to talk to General Olbricht of the *Allgemeines Heeresamt*. At last we can see the Deputy *Führer* and *Reichsmarschall* Hermann Goering with his staff. It can't be long now. Yes! The *Führer* himself!" Over the radio one could make out the background cheering, and a band struck up the Horst Wessel Song.

Philip glanced at the other patients and staff. All stared, transfixed, at the large radio on the shelf. The patients here at this civil hospital were predominantly civilians. They were wealthy and respectable citizens with the bent shoulders and creased faces of men used to shouldering responsibility. But as they stared at the radio, they reminded Philip of children listening to a fairy tale.

From the radio came the sounds of a hushed silence—only distant, muffled sounds reached the microphone. Then came Hitler's rasping, stringent voice. He spoke first about the "glorious and heroic sacrifice of the men at Stalingrad." Their example had "lit a torch for the German people to follow." He swore that their sacrifice had not been in vain, because Germany would replace the 6th Army ten—no—one hundred-fold.

Philip glanced over his shoulder to see if he could retreat. Alexandra might have her reasons for wanting him to hear this, but he was damned if he'd listen to such rot. From the radio, Hitler promised that Germany would fight on for the whole of Western Civilization or go up in smoke and shame. Philip's retreat was blocked by two latecomers, who cast him reproving glances for even starting to turn his chair.

Philip gave up trying to escape, but closed his ears and wished himself back in bed. He resented Alexandra for subjecting him to this, and concluded (self-pityingly) that she could not possibly appreciate how ill he still was or the pain he was in. As Hitler droned on and the audience around him continued to listen spellbound, his mood darkened even more. The conspiracy was pointless. How could you make a revolution with people like these? People who continued to idolize a man who had just sacrificed a quarter of a million young men? How could they adore a man whose policies had provoked the bombing that was slowly pulverizing their cities to rubble? Rittenbach was right. They were mindless sheep, Philip though bitterly, looking at his fellow patients as they gaped at the radio.

Hitler finally stopped speaking, and the commentator narrated that Hitler was entering the exhibit in the Armory. He promised to continue coverage in approximately a half-hour, when the *Führer* re-emerged. Meanwhile, they had the latest releases from …

A female voice wafted through the airwaves with a lilting, light melody. The patients turned to one another and agreed that it had been a very "impressive" speech—indeed, "inspiring" and "moving." "All the stronger for being so concise," someone said.

The female voice on the radio was brutally interrupted by the scratching of the needle on the record. A breathless commentator reported, "The *Führer* has just exited the exhibition, much sooner than expected. He and …"

Philip could stand it no longer. Ignoring the protests of those around him, he turned and wheeled himself back to his room with every intention of telling his wife exactly what he thought of her recommendations for entertainment.

Only a little over an hour after he'd left, Olbricht arrived back at his office in the Bendlerstrasse, surprising both his secretaries and his Chief of Staff. He bent over Alix's desk and scribbled on a piece of paper as if he were giving her a signature. "There wasn't time," the note said. Then he disappeared into his office without a word.

Alix handed her husband a get-well card. "From Henning v. Tresckow and *Freiherr* v. Gersdorff."

Philip, astonished, opened it. In Alix's own hand was written: "8 minutes short. Just as in the Beer Hall, 1938."

"Who did you say it was from?"

"Tresckow, sent via Gersdorff, who was here to explain the captured Soviet equipment to the *Führer* at the exhibition yesterday."

"I couldn't get near the podium," Gersdorff explained to Tresckow, "so I decided to carry the bomb in my pocket. I set the fuse the minute he entered the armory, but he didn't stop to look at anything. I chased after him, trying to draw his attention to one thing or another, but he didn't even spare me a glance. It was as if he could sense the danger ticking in my pocket. He made a beeline for the side exit, and I wasn't authorized to follow him any farther."

"It wouldn't have had much effect in the open, anyway," Tresckow comforted philosophically. "The bomb in his plane would have been so much better—if only it had detonated. Did your fuse work, by the way?"

"The fuse, yes; but whether the explosive would have detonated, we'll never know. The fuse in the aircraft ignited, too, remember."

"How could I ever forget? I called off the pistol attack because I was so certain the bomb in his plane would be better …" For a moment Tresckow sat, rubbing his high forehead with his long fingers as if he had a headache. It had seemed the perfect assassination: he had smuggled a bomb with activated fuse aboard Hitler's plane on March 13, and it should have blown up in the air while still over Soviet territory. First assumptions would have been that the plane was shot down by partisans or had blown up due to technical failure. The officers of Army Group Center would not have been implicated, and the issuance of Valkyrie would have been both legal and rational. The conspiracy would have been in control of the Army and state before a detailed investigation of the crash could take place, and the results could well have been kept secret until they were no longer relevant. At first all had gone according to plan. With the fuse already ignited, Tresckow got the bomb aboard Hitler's plane after Hitler had already boarded. The bomb was not discovered. But although the fuse functioned, the bomb failed to detonate. Schlabrendorff had to rush to *Führer* HQ to retrieve the unexploded bomb before it was discovered.

Then this ceremony to honor the dead at Stalingrad and display war trophies had presented a new opportunity for an assassination attempt. Gersdorff had volunteered, and explosives had again been obtained and prepared. But this time

Hitler's own instinct had saved him. It was hard to accept the failure of two assassination attempts less than ten days apart. It was hard not to see the hand of God in the failures. But how could God want Hitler to survive or want the war to continue? Tresckow drew a deep breath and managed a weary smile at Gersdorff. "At least you can face our Maker knowing you did your best."

"So did you, Henning," Gersdorff answered softly. "Even if you didn't carry the bomb yourself, you were the spirit and mind behind it."

Tresckow didn't answer immediately. He felt that he'd made a fatal mistake by preferring the bomb to the pistol attack, and that weighed heavily on his conscience and heart. As a result, he had squandered their best chance of success. Kluge's mood was volatile, the bulk of the population was recovering from the shock of Stalingrad, and it would be almost impossible to lure Hitler back to Army Group Center in the foreseeable future. Beck, furthermore, was now too ill to be counted on; he had been operated on no less than five times, and it was still uncertain if he would fully recover. In short, Tresckow's plans, so carefully developed over the last six months, had gone irrevocably wrong. "We need a new plan. We can't lure him back here a second time in the near future. We need to find other means of access to him."

"Can't Oster or Olbricht take care of that?"

Tresckow nodded. "I will request leave and return to Berlin. We need to rethink and regroup."

Gersdorff nodded, thinking to himself that Tresckow needed the rest, too.

＊   ＊   ＊   ＊

Berlin
April 1943

Alexandra did not like the look of Philip when she first came in; after weeks of steady improvement, he suddenly looked drawn and tormented again. Rather than sitting up as he had been for some time, he was lying flat on his back, and he only managed a half-smile as he reached out his hand. "If you'd been here half an hour sooner," he told her, "you would have seen how splendidly I can walk—so long as I'm supported by two heavyweight nurses."

Alexandra's eyes widened. "Are you serious?"

"Quite serious. They may call it walking; I don't think it was substantially better than when Rittenbach and Stadthagen dragged me off the bridge at Sadki. I told you that, didn't I? That Rittenbach himself helped carry me?" He paused. "At least, I think he did. Sometimes I think I confuse things."

"It doesn't matter."

"And Seydlitz came by to see me yesterday after you left." Philip couldn't meet his wife's eyes. "There's nothing left of his right hand. They had to amputate his arm just below the elbow. I get a Knight's Cross, and he loses his hand. Something's not right about that."

"Is Seydlitz bitter?"

"Not at all. That's what's so horrible. He says he wants to stay with me. I don't understand."

"I do."

Philip looked at her expectantly, and she laughed, "I married you, silly. How should I find it unbelievable when others are devoted to you?"

Philip looked down at her hand. "But so far I haven't ruined your beautiful hands."

The door to the room was flung open and a stout woman in heavy shoes, fur collar and a pheasant-feathered hat swept in. She did not even cast Alexandra a nod before assailing her husband in a deep voice, "Wolf!" Philip's roommate put his newspaper aside but did not get out a greeting before his wife continued, "It's absolutely impossible! Something has to be done. It can't go on another minute!"

"What, my dear?"

"This indiscriminate billeting of bombed-out people! The block warden has sent a whole family to us—the most common, vulgar people you can imagine! The kitchen is in a shambles. Mud has been tracked all over the house! And the gramophone! Wouldn't you know, the only thing they managed to save out of their whole apartment was the gramophone! I simply can't stand them in the house a day longer. You have to call what's-his-name!"

Philip and Alix were convulsed with laughter they were trying to suppress, even though Alix pointed out, when she had hold of herself, "It could happen to us, you know. It really isn't fair for me to be alone in the apartment when so many people are without a roof over their heads."

"I thought you said there weren't any windows in the apartment?"

"Only along the street. No one would think to call that damaged nowadays. Besides, the workmen promised to come next week."

"Seydlitz will need a place to stay. He's been assigned to an adjutants' training course that is held here in Berlin. After that, he hopes to get posted to AHA. If we take in friends, we won't have to take in strangers."

"Where can I reach him?" Alix asked, but before Philip could answer, a nurse entered.

"Freifrau v. Felburg? You're wanted on the telephone in Dr. Sauerbruch's office; a *General der Infanterie*." The nurse had forgotten the name, but she was impressed by the rank. Philip and Alix at once knew it could only be Olbricht, and exchanged an uneasy glance. Then Alix gave Philip a quick kiss and excused herself.

Olbricht apologized for disturbing her evening, but requested that she return to the Bendlerstrasse at once. There was no question of protest; Olbricht did not make unnecessary requests.

In the General's office, Alexandra found the General and Dr. Sack seated in armchairs around the round table. She joined them, and Olbricht wasted no time with small talk. "General Oster was placed under house arrest this afternoon."

Alexandra caught her breath. Oster was, after Tresckow, Olbricht's closest associate for Resistance activities still on active service. "Why?"

Olbricht looked at Sack, who sighed, "Ostensibly for trying to obstruct a lawful investigation into the activities of one of his subordinates."

Alexandra looked sharply at the General.

"Hans von Dohnanyi, one of us," he supplied the answer to the unspoken question.

"And what was the charge against Herr v. Dohnanyi?" Alexandra asked the military justice directly.

"Currency violations, misuse of office—and suspicion of treason."

Alexandra's stomach twisted itself in knots. Her brain reminded her that she'd known this could happen. She had accepted the risk consciously, although both Olbricht and Philip had given her ample opportunity to keep out. She had insisted on taking part. Only now did she appreciate how foolhardy she had been. In retrospect, she realized she'd put too much faith in the "invincibility and immunity" of the General Staff. But Oster was a general working in counterintelligence. If that wasn't protection enough ...

"At the moment, we do not appear directly endangered," Olbricht was commenting. "They have arrested two other agents of counterintelligence, Dietrich Bonhoeffer and Josef Müller. Both were involved in trying to establish contact with the Western powers in a futile search for reasonable peace terms after a change of government. This office was not directly involved. Indeed, I don't personally know either of the agents, although they, of course, may know of me."

"And they're in Gestapo hands?" Alexandra asked. It was said no one could withstand Gestapo torture longer than 24 hours.

"Not exactly. So far they are in military, not civil, custody."

"But," Dr. Sack put in, "the Chief Investigator is the *Luftwaffe Oberkriegsger-ichtsrat* Dr. Manfred Roeder, who broke the so-called *"Rote Kapelle"* spy ring." The *Rote Kapelle* had been an organization of anti-Nazis who had passed information, including military secrets, to the Soviet Union. Dozens of people associated with it had already been sentenced to death.

Olbricht's expression was serious but reassuring as he continued, "We're facing a potentially explosive situation. Very much depends on how cleverly and firmly the arrested persons withstand interrogation. But nearly as much depends on how effectively the Advocate General manages to thwart and slow proceedings—without, of course, being obvious about it. As Dr. Sack explained, it was a relatively obscure currency violation that attracted attention to Dohnanyi. At the moment, and unless the good Oster should totally crack—which I have no reason to expect—there is no reason why anyone should associate the scandal in the counterintelligence department with the *Allgemeines Heeresamt.*"

Alexandra nodded, her initial panic mastered. Valkyrie, she reminded herself, had been requested and approved by Hitler himself. As for the supplementary orders, no one had seen Olbricht give them to her, seen her type them in her flat at night, or seen her return them to the General. She could, in short, plausibly deny all knowledge of treasonable activity. And Philip was safe. He'd just been awarded the Knight's Cross. More importantly, he'd been wounded on the Eastern Front while physically enforcing one of Hitler's senseless orders—orders that Manstein had convinced the dictator to rescind just four days after Philip was cut down.

"… and that, as you can imagine," Dr. Sack was saying in his dry monotone, "is going to require nearly my full attention. On the other hand, I can't afford to neglect other cases, particularly not political cases, which might also blow up in our faces. I think you're the person who could help me in this. I've looked into your file, and you have the status of a legal intern on indefinite leave. I could employ you immediately, and your time in my department would be counted as part of your legal internship—to be exact, as time with the State Prosecution. If you then select Military Justice as your last optional post, you could be admitted to your final exam in roughly one year's time."

Olbricht watched his secretary's face as worry gave way to disbelief, and then to unadulterated delight. He laughed, "So that's how it is. And I always thought you liked it here." He waved Alexandra's protest aside before she even got it out. "Eva would never forgive me if I stood in your way. This is quite the best thing for both you and Dr. Sack—and for our joint project, although it comes at a bad time for me personally. The AHA will have to take over all the opposition activities which Oster's *Abwehr* previously managed. I need to concentrate as many reliable officers here in AHA as possible; most importantly, I need a Chief of Staff who actively supports me in this. The other day Hoepner was praising his former Ib to me, *Graf* Stauffenberg, but I know Moltke approached him about a year ago—and Stauffenberg thought we could still win the war!" Olbricht made a face to indicate what he thought of someone who held such an opinion. "I'll ask Tresckow for some recommendations when he's here. If your husband were a little more senior, I'd appoint him Chief, but he was only just promoted *Oberstleutnant*. I can't justify placing such a junior officer in such a prominent position. I hope you understand."

"Of course!" Alexandra assured him, still hardly able to grasp her good luck: an end to all the drudgery and the resumption of her legal studies in the only part of the justice system not entirely poisoned by National Socialism. She couldn't wait to tell Philip.

CHAPTER 32

▼

Berlin
April 1943

The atmosphere at Dimitri's had subtly but definitely changed again. The little student café was crowded as usual, but more smoke-filled than in the recent past, and the intensity of the conversations had increased noticeably. Not that the customers engaged in the loud, temperamental disputes and discussions typical of the Weimar years. Instead, the students meeting here in the spring of 1943 leaned forward and spoke in low, earnest voices. Rather than declaiming to the world at large, the different groups kept very much to themselves, and they frequently cast tense glances over their shoulders. Many of the students were in the uniform of the *Wehrmacht*, and there was also a marked increase in the number of women students. The latter no longer appeared as anxious to conform to the ideals of the Regime; several wore their hair short or wore makeup, while one girl was actually smoking.

Alexandra had the feeling that everyone looked at her as she entered, but then dismissed her as harmless. She looked about for a free table and spotted one way at the back. She started to squeeze her way between the other tables to reach it, and Dimitri caught sight of her. As always, he left the bar and came to bow over her hand. "Lady Alexandra! You're meeting your friend the singer?" Without awaiting an answer, he escorted her to the free table and promised tea.

On the empty table, a single white rose lay forlornly, and Alexandra caught her breath. Had Berlin students heard about the fate of their colleagues in Munich after all? Dr. Sack had told her about the little group of medical students who had published leaflets calling for an uprising. He had tried to intervene, since with the exception of the only girl involved, the students were all soldiers.

The Nazi courts had been faster, however, and the leaders of the little group were all beheaded before Dr. Sack had even learned of their arrests.

Alexandra glanced about at the other tables, wondering who had left the rose. But no one met her glance. Perhaps it had been left by someone who had already departed, she decided, and sat down, careful not to take the compromising rose in her hand. Dimitri arrived with her glass of tea—but rather than just setting it before her, he pulled out the chair opposite and sat down facing her. "How did it come to this?" he opened in a mournful tone. "I don't understand. My people greeted your *Wehrmacht* as liberators, with bread and salt. They said prayers of thanks for their liberation—and what have you done to them? You have enslaved and mistreated them. Turned them into Bolsheviks, when just two years ago they hated their oppressors. Why?"

"Oh, Dimitri! What do you want me to say?" Alexandra cried out. "Not all our troops behave badly. Many commanders treated the Russian civilians with respect and made sure that plunderers were severely punished. I know of so many officers who tried to help the population. My brother's division helped bring in the harvest in the sector they occupied. But the SS ..." She broke off and looked over her shoulder at the tables around her.

Dimitri sighed and patted her hand. "It's all right, Lady Alexandra. I know. I just can't understand. If you had only given us a chance to help you, there would never have been a Stalingrad!"

"I know, Dimitri," Alexandra sighed.

Dimitri patted her hand again, pushing himself back as he announced, "Here's your friend already."

Lotte was indeed squeezing her way between the tables toward Alix, but nothing about the way she was dressed today turned heads. She clutched a thin coat about her shoulders but wore no hat, lipstick, perfume, or earrings. "Lotte, what's wrong?" Alexandra asked at once, getting to her feet.

Lotte offered her both cheeks in a distracted way and sank into the chair Dimitri had just vacated. "Eberhard's been drafted, and I've been fired."

"What?"

Lotte met Alexandra's gaze, and it was clear she'd been crying. Her eyes were swollen, and red splotches were poorly hidden behind her makeup base. "It's part of the Total War," Lotte tried to explain. "They've reduced the entire company by 40%, and those of us who were let go are subject to conscription. Eberhard had to report to his training battalion yesterday—and it's not even a propaganda company! Infantry. Ordinary infantry. It's so unfair. Eberhard is perfectly useless as a soldier. He's sure to get killed."

Alexandra refrained from comment. She'd never managed to warm to Eberhard, although he had been "faithful" to Lotte longer than her previous lovers. Nor could she feel outrage at the thought of him finally facing the same unpleasantness and danger that Stefan and Philip and every other soldier had been facing for years.

"I know what you're thinking, Alix," Lotte said, reading her thoughts, "but he really has been good to me. He even said something about getting engaged."

Alexandra brightened. "Wonderful! When?"

"Oh, nothing definite, Alix. He can't commit himself now. Not when he's facing all these changes and has no idea what will become of him."

Alexandra bit her tongue. Eberhard always had a dozen reasons why he couldn't commit to Lotte.

"Alix, I was thinking. Maybe I should volunteer. You know the *Luftwaffe* is desperate to recruit female auxiliaries for air defense. They have thousands of communications auxiliaries stationed all over Europe. You remember Brigitte Köhler, don't you? I ran into her the other day, and she was on home leave from Norway. She says it's beautiful up there, and—"

"Lotte! You're crazy! If you join the *Luftwaffe* auxiliaries, you could just as easily end up in Russia! Philip told me about an air base that was temporarily overrun by the Red Army. All the auxiliaries had been raped and murdered in just 24 hours. Besides, even if you stay right here in the *Reich*, you'd have to wear a uniform and live in barracks, etc. The auxiliaries live just like common soldiers."

"Do you really think that the only thing I care about is my own comfort?" Lotte asked, her eyes swimming in tears and her voice strained. "Didn't it ever occur to you that I might love my country, too?"

"Lotte, that's not what I meant. But the auxiliaries don't exactly have the best reputation—"

"And what sort of reputation do I have?" Lotte shot back, her voice trembling.

"Lotte." Alexandra went around the table to put her arm around her friend. She hadn't seen her like this since the abortion four years earlier. "You're an artist. You're not some silly, half-grown girl. The auxiliaries are mostly straight out of the RAD. If you really want to volunteer, then volunteer for office work in the Army. You have the skills, after all—"

Lotte waved it aside, trying to smother her tears in a crumpled handkerchief and sniffling delicately, "I've forgotten all that. I couldn't take shorthand to save my life anymore."

Alexandra reseated herself and declared firmly, "Of course you could! I'll drill you, if you like. Lotte, seriously, you don't want to join the *Luftwaffe*. I'm sure I can get you an interview at the Bendlerstrasse. Olbricht is looking for a new secretary."

"Annie Lerche got married?" Lotte asked, staring at Alexandra over her handkerchief with bated breath. She had heard enough from Alix to know that Olbricht was the closest thing to a perfect boss that any one could hope for.

"No, I'm transferring to the Advocate General's Corps—as a legal intern."

"Alix! That's wonderful! Congratulations! What does Philip say?"

Alexandra hesitated. There was no denying he had been less enthusiastic than she had expected. He'd congratulated her, of course, but in a perfunctory way. He'd also let slip that he'd looked forward to working "with her" again. Dr. Sack's offices were in the maze-like Bendlerblock, but not just down the hall as when they were both at AHA. He'd also remarked that no doubt she'd have to work longer hours and would find it more difficult to get leave. All in all, his reaction had been disappointing. "He was pleased, but he has other worries right now," Alexandra excused her husband to her friend.

Lotte kept her opinion to herself, but she hadn't yet met a man who really rejoiced at a woman's career success. She had always paid for professional success with personal defeat. Even Eberhard had been noticeably more critical and difficult ever since she'd moved up from secretary to singer. But Alexandra had been so sure Philip was different that Lotte chose not to comment. Instead she asked cautiously, "And Olbricht doesn't already have a replacement for you?"

"No. I was only offered the new job two days ago. I'm supposed to arrange two to three interviews for him—"

"Alix, please!" Lotte grabbed her hand in supplication. "I promise you won't regret it."

Alix smiled faintly. "I know." Lotte only pretended to be empty-headed. Beneath her glamorous exterior was an ambitious, if not always single-minded, woman with the ability to work herself to the bone when she wanted something badly enough. She was a quick learner with good intuition regarding people (except when it came to lovers), and she was no Nazi. All of which made her a good candidate. Alexandra couldn't resist adding, however, "This is one boss you are not going to be able to seduce."

"Don't bait me!" Lotte retorted with a raised finger, and suddenly they were both laughing. Lotte, even without her makeup and her chic clothes, looked beautiful again.

*   *   *   *

Berlin
April 1943

Theresa was at her wits' end. She'd thought the journey to Warsaw had been bad, but conditions on the *Reichsbahn* had deteriorated dramatically in the three years since then. There were too few trains, and it was impossible to get reservations anymore, certainly not at short notice. Walther had tried to warn her. He'd tried to convince her that there was no reason for her to leave Warsaw at all. But Theresa was a mother, and she had a responsibility to her young children. When she learned that the Jews had managed to blow up several SS tanks and had killed dozens of SS troopers (and those were the official figures!), she packed her bags at once. Nothing could make her stay in Warsaw! In the first real fight of their marriage, she had shouted at Walther hysterically that their children's lives were a risk. If the Jews had weapons and homemade bombs, then God knew what the Poles had! The very fact that the Jews had made a whole SS battalion retreat from the Ghetto would encourage the Poles to revolt. Theresa insisted they had to flee while they still had the chance.

But then she found herself crushed with her three screaming children in the aisle of an overcrowded, run-down train, and no one—absolutely no one!—seemed willing to help. No one was even willing to give up their seats, so Theresa had to perch on a fold-down seat while Trude, Celina and the children sat on the suitcases. The children, of course, were soon crawling in the dirt of the aisle. The toilets were clogged beyond description and stank out into the hall. There was no water for her to wash her babies, much less herself. There was no diner, either. The other passengers—civil servants of the Government General, RAD and Employment Office and all kinds of policemen, customs officials and Party bosses—had all brought food with them, but Theresa had not thought to pack food. She was starving and her children were starving, and it was only natural that they cried and screamed.

In place of the gallantry Theresa expected of German men, a heavy-set, red-faced SS NCO shouted at her to shut her brats up before he did it himself. Other men stepped right over the children on their way to and from the stinking toilets, in one case tramping right on little Dietlinde's hand. When Trude berated the man for his carelessness, he told her off for traveling this route with small children. During the night, a man tried to steal one of their suitcases, and when Celina tried to stop him, he kicked her and called her a "Polish whore." A couple of men woke up and shouted at the thief, causing him to flee; but after that, none of the women dared even try to sleep.

Throughout the night Theresa's resentment built up, until she convinced herself that she hated Walther for having taken her to Warsaw in the first place—and even more for not letting her take the car to return home now. What sort of a monster was he, to let his own flesh and blood go through this hell just because he claimed he needed the car for his business? And was his business more important to him than his family?

Exhausted, filthy and hungry, they reached Berlin only to discover there were no taxis at the station. Theresa was advised to take public transportation. After all she'd been through, and with three small children! But the man from the *Reichsbahn* only shrugged at her outrage and turned away. There was nothing to do but follow his advice.

They arrived at the Feldburg apartment in the middle of the afternoon, absolutely at the end of their strength. Theresa was limping from the blisters on her feet, carrying Adolf in her arms. Trude was carrying Dietlinde and one suitcase, while Celina was struggling with two suitcases and Siegfried, who had to be dragged more than he walked. Theresa, who had last been to the family apartment in Berlin more than ten years earlier, had a hard time identifying it. She was confused by the gap in the row of houses left by a bomb. Furthermore, the façades of several other houses had been shattered and had fallen off, leaving their faces naked and unrecognizable. Even the Feldburg house was disfigured by boarded-up windows along the front.

Adding insult to injury, Theo Pfalz didn't recognize her. When she demanded that he let her into the Feldburg apartment, he flatly refused. She screamed at him, ordering him to let her in "this minute" or she'd make sure her brother fired him. He only looked at her as if she were mad, and then disappeared into his own apartment as if to get the key. In fact he put a call through to Alexandra and desperately asked for instructions. "There are three women here with three small children, and one of them claims to be the *Herr Baron*'s sister, but she looks a dreadful sight—fat and slovenly—and she stinks! What should I do?"

Alexandra told him to address her as "Frau Halle" and if she responded, to let her in. She would try to get home early, she promised.

Inside the apartment, Theresa was confused and angered to find that the large guest room was clearly already in use. Just who did her sister-in-law have living in the flat while Philip was in hospital? The uniforms and men's toiletries fueled her outrage. Her sister-in-law was apparently carrying on an affair right in the Feldburg apartment while poor Philip's life hung by a thread! It was so shocking it was almost unbelievable, but she comforted herself with the knowledge that she had discovered it in time. She could be sure Philip learned the truth. First, however, she and the children desperately needed a bath, a change of clothes and rest.

Theresa bathed herself first and then retired in the remaining large bedroom, leaving Trude and Celina to clean the children and then make up beds for the children and themselves.

Alexandra let herself in the door and called out at once, "Frau Halle? It's me, Alexandra. I'm sorry I'm so late. Have you been able to find everything you need?"

Theresa emerged from the dining room and gazed down the length of the hall at her sister-in-law. Alexandra had propped her briefcase against the wall and was removing her hat and coat. To Theresa, she looked thin and worn. Typical career girl, she thought disdainfully. She did not try to smile, nor did she move to meet Alexandra partway. Instead she waited in the doorway of the dining room, waiting for Alexandra to come to her.

Alexandra came down the length of the hall, smiling and holding out her hand. "Is everything all right?" she asked, as she registered Theresa's cool stance and disdainful expression.

"How should everything be all right? There are no toys for the children. There's no milk in the entire house. My maid had to borrow from your neighbors. And there is no one here to cook, either! This is hardly a proper household at all. I don't know why Philip stands for it."

"Because we have no children and so no need for toys or milk, and Philip has been on the Eastern Front or in hospital," Alexandra retorted in a firm tone, her smile gone.

"And you, of course, have been working." Theresa made it sound like an insult.

"Yes, I have been working—until 19:30. I just barely had time to stop and tell Philip you were here."

"Well, it's your choice to work, isn't it?"

"Yes," Alexandra answered, and continued to Theresa pointedly, "If I had been given warning of your arrival, then of course I could have made arrangements to be here earlier."

"How was I supposed to give warning?!" Theresa shot back. "Who would have dreamed the Jews would resist their deportation? Who could have dreamed they would smuggle arms into the Ghetto—much less manage to blow up SS tanks!

It's all a terrible nightmare!" In fact, Theresa had to make an effort to remember how frightened she had been in Warsaw. Somehow, here in Berlin, the Ghetto seemed very far away. Furthermore, after the trauma of the journey, the evidence of the bombing in Berlin, and the lack of comfort in the flat, the life she'd had with Walther already looked much better.

There were, Alexandra registered, disadvantages to no longer working at the AHA. In Dr. Sack's office the daily situation reports did not cross her desk. She had heard nothing of the Warsaw Ghetto uprising and had to ask, "You mean the Jews of the Warsaw Ghetto have started an armed insurrection?"

"I suppose you could call it that. All I know is that they have killed dozens of SS men and blown up several tanks. The SS had to withdraw. Of course, they could only have had the weapons from the Polacks. You can be sure the Polacks are planning a revolt of their own next. I had to bring the children to safety."

"Berlin isn't exactly safe these days." Alexandra indicated the boarded-up windows along the front of the house.

"I've noticed, but how could I know that? Besides, there are no train connections from Warsaw to Altdorf."

"Then you won't be staying long?" Alexandra could hardly disguise her relief.

"No; you can be sure I will continue home at the earliest practical opportunity."

"… She made it perfectly clear that my poor, displaced babies and I aren't welcome in our own home, Philip!" Theresa poured out her heart to her brother, sitting beside his hospital bed in a flowered print dress, white straw hat and white gloves. "She couldn't be bothered coming home at a decent time to greet us, and she left us to do all our own shopping today—although we don't know the shops or the schedules. She actually left the apartment before I'd even woken up! She just left a note on the dining room table with some food stamps. She doesn't have any interest in anything but her career, if you ask me. I wonder that she had time to marry you at all—although I daresay she probably thinks there is some professional advantage to be had from your title."

Any ambivalence Philip had felt about Alexandra's resumption of her legal studies was shattered by this assault from Theresa. The more his sister raged against Alexandra, the more he sided with his wife. The last thing he wanted was a woman like this, who thought that producing babies annually entitled her to luxury and privilege everywhere she went. Nor did he want a woman whose only interests in life were breeding and babies. To his sister he remarked, "You sound just like Grandmother Feldburg—going behind Mamá's back to complain about her to our father."

Theresa's mouth snapped shut. She could hardly remember her Grandmother Feldburg, but her brothers had consistently painted an ugly picture of her. There was no family insult greater than being compared to Grandmother Feldburg. Before she had a chance to digest this, Philip continued in a clipped "General Staff" tone (as Christian had always called it), "I married Alexandra precisely because she is intelligent, educated and ambitious. I am delighted she has this opportunity to resume her studies, and I'm extremely proud of the responsible position she has. I cannot see that a legal intern involved in cases where the death penalty is possible should stay around to help you do your grocery shopping. I should have thought that at your age—and with no less than two maids in attendance—you could have managed shopping on your own."

Theresa's face reddened. With the situation put like that, she was at first ashamed—but only for an instant. In the next second, she thought of how Philip always criticized her. She lashed out with tears in her eyes, "I should have known! You never take my side in anything! Not even now, when there's just the two of us left! Well, let me tell you something! Your fancy career girl is probably too busy to give you babies, so I hope you like the idea of my Siegfried inheriting everything at Altdorf!" It was an idea that greatly appealed to Theresa in her dreamy moments.

"You forget Christian. He's not the type to stay single, and I can't picture him married to a career girl, either," Philip reminded her dryly.

Theresa started violently. She stared, opened her mouth, and then covered it with her hand. All her anger dissipated and the blood drained from her face. He didn't know.

Philip felt as if the temperature in the room had just dropped twenty degrees. His sister was looking at him with pity. He found it hard to breathe. "What's happened to Christian?"

"Didn't Alexandra tell you?"

He shook his head.

"She should have told you. She had no right to keep it from you." Theresa spoke softly, and she looked ill. She hated being the one to tell him.

"What?"

"He—he was posted missing."

"When?"

"I don't remember exactly. The middle of February."

Philip calculated. He'd been wounded at the beginning of February and oper-ated on twice in the same month; the second operation had been on the 21st. He'd been on the critical list until early March. Alix probably had not dared to tell him about Christian for fear it would adversely affect his recovery. But in the six weeks since, there was no excuse. Then again, he remembered that Alexan-dra's father had been posted missing, but the body had been recovered months later. Maybe she had hoped for some definite news. Whatever her reasons, her intentions had been good. Why did he let Theresa's insinuations distract him? The issue wasn't when he'd been told. The issue was that Christian was probably dead.

He tried to conceive of that. He couldn't. Should he risk hoping? What were the chances that he'd survived a crash landing in North Africa and been picked up by either the enemy or natives? Slight, the General Staff officer concluded—maybe one in five. Me109 pilots sat on their gas tanks. It was far more likely that he'd blown up. Even if he had avoided an annihilating explosion, and the aircraft had simply been too badly damaged to return to base or Christian himself had been too badly wounded to fly any further, then he would have been forced to crash-land in the desert. That wasn't like a landing in England. Even if he'd sur-vived a crash landing in the desert, it was improbable that he'd received medical attention in time to survive.

But the brother said: Christian is a survivor. Philip had never seriously believed that Christian would die before him.

Philip thought back to the Battle of Britain and the evening they had spent together before Christian returned to his squadron. Christian had been so afraid to die, and so bitter about being asked to die for nothing. He thought back to Baden-Baden, and how Alexandra had convinced him that treason was better than letting the slaughter go on indefinitely. She had said they had to prevent Stefan and Christian from being sacrificed for nothing. But they had failed to act in time. Christian had already been sacrificed.

"I'm sorry, Philip," Theresa whispered, drawing him back to the present.

Philip looked at her blankly. His glasses glinted in the unrelenting hospital light so that his expression was unreadable.

"Maybe I should go and come back tomorrow?" Theresa suggested tentatively.

Philip nodded. Theresa was not the person he needed right now. "Is Mamá all right?" he remembered to ask.

"I suppose so," Theresa answered lamely. Her relationship with her mother was too superficial for her to know how Sophia Maria was doing. "She sounded very calm when she called me with the news—distant and controlled, as always."

"I'll call her," Philip said automatically.

Theresa stood, bent over Philip, and kissed his forehead. "I'll be back tomorrow and bring my babies. They'll cheer you up," she assured him with maternal pride, patting his shoulder.

Philip nodded absently. Theresa stopped once more in the doorway and looked back at him. He was staring across the room and didn't take any notice of her.

Philip was calculating: even Tresckow and Gersdorf's assassination attempts would have come too late for Christian. They had failed. They had failed the 6th Army, and they had failed Christian. But there were millions of other innocent young men still out there—starting with Stefan. Not just young men, he reminded himself. The bombing was increasing in intensity. Almost every night, one city or another was subjected to this so-called "carpet bombing," directed indiscriminately at military, public, industrial and residential targets. There were far too few night fighters and too few trained pilots to stop the combined Anglo-American air forces. Women and children, no less than soldiers, were being sacrificed night after night. It had to stop. Somehow they had to stop it!

With Beck still in hospital and Oster under house arrest?

Olbricht was the key. He had to get well and go back to AHA. But although the thought stiffened his resolve, it could not comfort him.

He sat silent and still in his hospital bed. Neither his roommate, who was reading his magazines, nor the nurse's aide that brought the evening meal, heard his heart crying out, "Christian, forgive me!"

CHAPTER 33

▼

Altdorf
April 1943

The entire household waited in the courtyard. The teams were already hitched to both the wagon and the small, open carriage. Only Theresa was missing. The clanging of the church bells was distant but insistent. The horses stamped in the traces and fussed with their bits. Sophia Maria exclaimed under her breath, "What is keeping the girl?" And then, "I'll go fetch her." She went back inside the manor and at the base of the service stairs called up, "Theresa! We're all waiting!"

There was no answer. In exasperation, Sophia Maria hurried up the stairs, calling again at the landing, "Theresa!" Still no answer. She continued to the top of the stairs and called down the hall, "Theresa! Where are you?!"

To her surprise, the door to the bathroom opened almost directly in front of her, and her daughter looked out. In a confused, slightly irritated voice, Theresa demanded, "What is it?" Theresa was still in a bathrobe and drying her hair on a towel.

"Theresa! Mass starts in 15 minutes. We'll all be late."

"Mass? You don't mean to tell me you all still go to Mass?"

Sophia Maria was taken aback. Ever since she had married in 1907, she had not missed Mass one Sunday. Even when she was in hospital for the birth of her three children, the sacrament had been brought to the patients. And what had started as a young bride's attempt to please her husband (and avoid the wrath of her mother-in-law) had become an integral part of her life. Sophia Maria honestly couldn't fathom Theresa's attitude. "Of course we go to Mass. It's Sunday."

"Oh. I didn't know. Walther and I never go to Mass anymore. Surely you know how bad it would look?" Theresa was scowling slightly, sensitive to the fact that—yet again—her snobbish family had failed to grasp just how important Walther had become.

"How can going to Mass make Walther look bad? Besides, it's not Walther we're talking about, but you. The whole household is waiting!" Sophia Maria spoke sharply. Ever since her daughter had arrived five days ago, she had been aware of feeling increasing anger against her. She had tried hard to suppress and disguise it, but with the clock ticking and the household waiting, her patience was nearing an end.

"Mother! Don't be so backward! Just what would Governor Frank think? Or all our SS friends? It's bad enough that we are Catholics. If we openly flaunted it, we'd lose everyone's respect! In the Government General, only the Polacks go to Mass!"

Sophia Maria had warned Theresa more than once not to use this term, and she felt that Theresa's choice of words was a willful act of open defiance. Furiously, Sophia Maria snapped back with the desire and intention of wounding her impudent and self-satisfied daughter, "I wish your father could hear you now!"

She achieved her objective. Theresa's father had been a demonstrative Catholic. He would have been mortified to hear any of his children say that "only the Polacks" went to Mass. But Theresa had been his darling, and she could not bear to look at herself through his eyes. She lashed out at her mother in self-defense, screaming, "What right have you to drag Papá into this! You never loved him—"

Sophia Maria slapped her with all her strength, and then fled back down the stairs. In the courtyard, Josef waited with the open carriage. The others had sensibly set off in the wagon. Josef took one look at his red-faced mistress and climbed up onto the box. He neither commented nor asked where Theresa was. He untied the reins, waited for Sophia Maria to settle in the seat behind him, and then whistled to the horse. They set off at a trot.

Sophia Maria was shaking with agitation. She had never struck Theresa before. She had never struck Philip, and although Christian had been spanked a number of times when he was little, she had never struck him in the face or in rage. The thought of Christian brought tears to her eyes, and she was far too weak to stop them. Why was Christian dead and that insufferable bitch alive?

For five days, Sophia Maria had been struggling with these thoughts. For five days she had been trying to find something of her little girl in Theresa. She had searched for something she liked about her. And all she had seen was her hated mother-in-law—self-righteous, complaining, arrogant and intolerant. Despite her youth (Theresa was only 25), she already had a striking physical resemblance to her grandmother because of the 30 pounds she had put on since her marriage.

She and Josef were late, of course. Mass had started. The voices of the congregation spilled out of the open doors. Sophia Maria and Josef slipped in and took seats at the back. Sophia Maria crossed herself and knelt with her folded hands pressed against her forehead. She felt a horrible, cold, knot in her stomach. Was there anything more unnatural than a mother who did not love her own child? She was responding to the Mass by rote, not really listening to the Latin.

And then Father Matthias was speaking in German. "I remember our sons and brothers, trapped in the vastness of the Russian winter, who after such endless misery and unspeakable sacrifice were forced to surrender at Stalingrad. They are prisoners now, and, dear God, we beg you to remember them all the more dearly because they are so far from home and those that love them. We pray, too, for the prisoners of war from so many nations who are captive here in Germany. They are no less isolated from their homes and families." There was an uneasy stirring throughout the church. Some of the congregation were outraged by these words, and others—like Sophia Maria—were horrified to hear Father Matthias yet again provocatively drawing the parallel. And then he went on, "And we pray for the poorest prisoners of all: the prisoners in the Concentration Camps. Regardless of what crimes they have allegedly committed, we beg You: Show Your infinite mercy to these poor souls in the hour of their greatest need."

"That is treason!" someone shouted out. "Treason!"

"Communists and Jews don't deserve our prayers! They hate God!"

Other voices called for the protesters to be silent. Father Matthias continued with the service as if he had not been interrupted. The organ came in a little prematurely and too loudly. The congregation sprang to their feet and sang with excessive enthusiasm. Some people were already slipping out of the church. "This is unheard of! This is intolerable!" someone was still insisting indignantly.

"He's an old man."

"He didn't say those prayers a year ago!"

I must talk to him again, Sophia Maria thought, and remained sitting as the church emptied. The acolyte doused the candles one at a time, and Sophia Maria found herself crying at memories of Philip. She didn't know exactly why. Philip, so the doctors said, was out of danger, but it had been a near thing. And the war wasn't over yet.

Father Matthias sat down beside her in the pew. He didn't speak. He waited patiently. Sophia Maria pulled herself together and smoothed the tears away from her face. "You shouldn't have done that."

Father Matthias smiled faintly. "'Here I stand. I cannot do otherwise.'" He'd said that the last time she'd warned him, when she'd told him the Police Chief passed on reports to the Gestapo. Now, as then, she did not know what to say, and Father Matthias wasn't giving her a chance. He was saying solicitously, "But that's not why you're crying. What is it? Or would you rather talk over tea?" He glanced over at Josef waiting patiently across the aisle.

"Yes, I could use a cup of tea."

They stood and sent Josef back to the manor.

Father Matthias had a pretty, sunny apartment in the baroque house directly beside the church. Here his housekeeper, Frau Becker, had already set the kettle on for tea. She was not surprised that he brought someone with him; he rarely returned from church alone. But it was a long time since Sophia Maria had been here.

She sat at the kitchen table and chatted with Frau Becker until the latter discreetly withdrew. By then Sophia Maria had a grip on herself again, but she was still grateful for Father Matthias' warm, dry hand on hers. "What is it?" he asked again gently.

"Theresa."

Father Matthias didn't seem surprised. He nodded and sighed. "You mustn't blame yourself."

Sophia Maria looked up astonished. "What do you mean?"

"Do you think Martha and Heidi and Ludmilla haven't already reported to me?" He smiled faintly. "Ludmilla was distressed by the way Theresa treats her Polish maid, because the girl is from one of the best families, as good—Ludmilla says—as the Feldburgs. Heidi was outraged by Theresa's laziness; she says she doesn't give a hand with anything, but rather expects to be waited on hand and foot. And Martha was in tears because, she says, Theresa treats her as if she were just an employee. But it's not your fault, my dear *Freifrau* v. Feldburg."

"It has to be," Sophia Maria countered. "At some level I must have failed." But Father Matthias was shaking his head firmly.

"It is very wrong for any of us to think we are to blame for the actions of others. Not even God is responsible for our actions." He looked hard at her as he said this. "We are free souls, and we choose every minute of every day what we are. We can choose to ask God for his help, support and advice, and we can choose to listen to the counsel of others, but we can also choose *not* to ask or *not* to listen. Whether we take advice or ignore it, we are alone responsible for what we do. You raised two exceptional young men to adulthood, Frau v. Feldburg, but you have no right to take credit for them."

"I know that," Sophia Maria snapped back. She did not need any more criticism at the moment.

But Father Matthias smiled faintly, and his hand closed firmly over hers, as he insisted, "But don't you see? You are no more to blame for Theresa than for Philip and Christian. I think, rather, that you should thank God for the great privilege of having raised such sons, and try to forgive Him for Theresa. It was perhaps the price you had to pay for your boys." He paused, considered this notion, and then added with a whimsical, light-hearted smile, "But surely it was worth it?"

Sophia Maria sat for a moment, uncertain how to react. Then she realized that the knot in her stomach was loosening. She was starting to feel better. She smiled faintly. "Thank you—yet again."

"My dear Frau v. Feldburg, if I couldn't help you see things a little more clearly after all these years, I would belong in the grave. Be true to yourself. Tell Theresa what you think of her—but don't be angry or feel guilty if she doesn't listen. It would be a lie and a capitulation for you to pretend you can like the woman Theresa has become. Your own sense of justice calls for you to protest against her petty tyranny—just as mine demands that I protest against a greater one." He smiled as he spoke, but this time his smile was sad—and it sent a shiver down Sophia Maria's spine.

When she returned to the manor, she found Theresa sitting stiffly at the breakfast table awaiting her. She was dressed in a navy and white polka-dotted suit with a white collar and cuffs. Her hair was braided around her head, and she held her head high. Sophia Maria took a deep breath and prepared for a confrontation. She even opened her mouth to apologize for slapping her, but Theresa forestalled her. "I've called Walther," she announced. "He says the uprising has been put down and everything is going back to normal. I've decided to return to Warsaw."

Sophia Maria considered her daughter. Although she looked very composed and distant, Sophia Maria suspected that what she really wanted was to be begged to stay. Ferdinand had done that, too: told her he had to leave whenever they'd had an argument. It was years before she'd called his bluff and not begged him to stay.

But she did not want Theresa to stay. The thought of her three innocent grandchildren made her hesitate, but she was not prepared to imitate her mother-in-law by trying to win her grandchildren away from their own mother. She had to accept that these grandchildren were lost to her—unless they one day came to her of their own free will. "When do you plan to depart?" was all she asked.

Theresa felt as if the last bridge had just been burned behind her. Even her mother didn't want her anymore.

*   *   *   *   *

Warsaw
April 1943

SS *Standartenführer* v. Aggstein had not been personally involved in cleaning out the Ghetto, but he still had better information than Walther. He explained in a low, earnest voice, "Most of the arms they used came from Polish sources. Can you imagine what they must have cost?! The Jews must still have enormous financial resources."

"I wouldn't be so sure the Jews had to buy the arms they used," Walther countered thoughtfully.

"But how else could they have secured them? They couldn't have stolen so many! You can't think that the Poles would give anything to the Jews? Not when their own partisans could use the weapons!"

"That's exactly what I fear. Polish hatred of the German occupation has reached such proportions that they may be willing to arm even Jews." Aggstein frowned in concentration as he listened. Walther continued, "I've been saying for months and years that you people have pursued the whole thing too ideologically. By alienating the Poles more than you had to, you've created embittered enemies, where a little enlightened despotism would have produced useful vassals."

Aggstein nodded, although his expression had not cleared. "You know I basically agree with you, but an alliance between the Poles and the Jews? Do you really believe that yourself?"

Walther shrugged. "It wouldn't surprise me. The Poles won't feel obliged to treat the Jews decently after they've driven us out, but letting the Jews die fighting us? I think that's very likely."

Aggstein sighed deeply, silently conceding that Walther was probably right. Walther had a very keen understanding of human behavior.

Walther went on, "What's the matter with Frank these days? His decisions make less and less economic sense. On Friday yet another 28 workers failed to show up. All rounded up and deported. What's the point of deporting workers already working in German factories? How am I supposed to keep factories running and meet production goals when I'm constantly short of workers? We've got some 40,000 German civil servants here in the Government General doing God knows what, but try to keep 400 workers on the shop floor! I tell you, it's absolutely crazy!"

Aggstein shook his head. "The real problem is the war—it's taking longer and consuming more manpower than we thought. The *Reichsführer* SS is not willing to accept that we have to delay the Final Solution until after the war is won. But regarding your immediate problems: we should be able to arrange for you to use KZ labor. Every time we clean out a ghetto, we end up with thousands of new inmates in the KZs, and they might as well be working as just sitting around. I'm almost entirely dependent on KZ labor these days."

"You mean the SS could lend me several hundred inmates?" Walther asked skeptically.

"Not exactly lend. If I remember correctly, the price per head is RM 1.50 for males and as little as 50 *Pfennig* for females—but of course, the females are a lot less valuable. They're always getting sick. You're much better off with males. Admittedly, you have to plan on more KZ inmates," Aggstein conceded. "They're not as strong as normal workers."

"All that matters is that I can count on them being there."

"We can guarantee that," Aggstein assured him confidently. "I admit that some of the camp commandants, particularly those from the Baltic States, can be arbitrary and thoughtless. They understand nothing about economics, but if you go and talk to them—take a good bottle of schnapps with you—they can usually be brought to see reason. Once you're on good terms with the KZ commandant, you can have him screen workers for those with qualifications. As a rule, the educated Jews and Poles—even the former partisans—are better than Gypsies and Homos. And political prisoners are less trouble than real criminals."

"Hmm. Are guards provided?"

"Yes. They escort the prisoners from the camp to your factory, keep an eye on them all day, and escort them back to the camp for the night."

"Would I have to pay for the guards?"

"No, I don't think so. They're Ukrainians for the most part—and bloody lucky to wear an SS uniform. Reliable Jew-haters, too."

"Which camp would supply me?"

"I'd have to check into that. Why don't you come 'round to my office tomorrow and I'll make some calls for you. By the time your gracious wife comes home next week, we'll have everything running smoothly again, and she'll forget there ever was a Ghetto, let alone an uprising."

*   *   *   *

Altdorf
May 1943

They were holding up the train for just for him, and never in his life had Philip felt so self-conscious. The crutches and the Knight's Cross: a fatal combination.

Stadthagen went down the metal steps first, dropped the suitcases, and then turned and looked back. He seemed to want to offer a hand, but a hand can't help a man struggling to support himself on crutches. Stadthagen was helpless unless Philip fell, and so he stood there as if waiting for Philip to fall.

But Philip didn't fall. Slowly, with grim determination, he placed first one and then the other crutch on the first step, the second step, the platform. His arms were trembling from the exertion, but he had to take another couple of steps so the conductor could board the train again and close the door. Then he had to make it down the platform to the exit. He turned his attention to this goal, but then stopped to watch his mother come toward him.

Why did he feel angry at his own helplessness? His mother, of all people, wouldn't care. No, he corrected himself: that was the wrong word. He could see how much she cared from the lines on her face. She looked old. Was that possible? Was 53 old? She had never looked old to him before. It was less than a year since he had last seen her. But last time he'd seen her, both her sons had been alive. Nor could he put all the blame on Christian. His life had hung in the balance for weeks. What madness had possessed him to try to turn the tide at Sadki alone? His hands on the crutches, he could only offer his cheek to his mother.

She let her hand linger on the base of his neck as she gazed up at him. "I'm so glad you could come home," she told him earnestly, adding only half sincerely, "and I'm sorry Alix couldn't come with you." In fact, she was quite pleased to have her son to herself for three weeks, but she knew that he missed his bride.

"Her new job. She couldn't take leave so soon."

"Of course not, and what are three weeks, really? If you had small children, you'd have sent her out of Berlin long ago. Then she wouldn't have been able to visit you in hospital daily, or return with you when you report back," Sophia Maria reminded him. "Her work actually helps you stay together."

Philip was slightly surprised to find his mother defending Alexandra, but it pleased him, too. If his mother had dared attack her as Theresa had, he would have been angry and defensive. Odd, this thing called love: at one and the same time he was angry with Alix for insisting she could not come with him, and yet angry with anyone who dared criticize her.

One of the Polish youngsters was holding the horses. He jumped up and took off his cap in respect at the sight of the "*Herr Baron.*" He even bobbed his head and smiled. Crazy world, Philip reflected. Why should this Polish youth, dragged from his home and family to do forced labor in a strange land, be glad to see him? Then his eyes went to the horses. They were young and impatient like the boy. "May I drive, since I can't ride?"

"Of course."

Philip handed the crutches to Stadthagen and then tried to pull himself onto the wagon. He failed. Stadthagen, the Polish youth, and his mother all had to help him. Finally, sweating, his eyes avoiding the others, Philip was in the driver's seat. His mother climbed up beside him, and the two servants clambered in the back. No one said anything.

When they reached the top of the drive and came out of the trees, Philip stopped and surveyed the scene. The formal garden had been converted into a kitchen garden for growing vegetables and herbs. Only the rose beds, gone wild, were not producing something "practical." The raked gravel of the drive had given way to a muddy, rutted road. The paint on the façade of the manor house was peeling. The window frames looked shabby. Lichen had started to take hold of the coat of arms over the carriage entrance. Rakes, pitchforks and an upended wheelbarrow were for some reason leaning against the front of the manor, robbing it of its dignity. "Could we sit in the rose garden for a moment?" Philip asked. "It's been so long since I've felt the warmth of the sun."

He turned the reins over to the young Polish worker, and with Stadthagen's help clambered down from the wagon. On crutches he made it to the lichen-gnawed bench and sank down, laying the crutches on the ground beside him. The two young men drove off, and Sophia Maria joined her son among the ill-kept rosebushes. At first they didn't speak. There was too much to say. Then Sophia Maria sighed and took Philip's hand. "I'm sorry to start with bad news, but you must be told. They arrested Father Matthias."

Philip stiffened and looked over sharply; the sun caught on his glasses. "When? Why?"

She stroked his fingers. "He was arrested three weeks ago, shortly after he said a prayer during Mass for those in the Concentration Camps—and now he's in Dachau."

Philip tried to grasp what that meant. The gentle, resolute old man stripped of his cassock and his cross—and given striped convict clothes instead. The respected "Father," advisor of widows, brides and hardened farmers, now a number to be abused and harassed by disinterested guards. The man of learning and sensitivity herded into an overcrowded, lice-infested hut and driven to do manual labor by swaggering youths and snarling dogs.

In Dachau no one would be interested in the priest or his former flock. And even if they were, Philip knew that not even dogs could have torn the secrets of the confessional from Father Matthias. The *Oberstleutnant* of the General Staff who had asked about treason would not be betrayed by the priest. But hadn't the priest been betrayed by the officer? Just as Christian had been betrayed by his brother? Nearly a year had passed since Philip had asked Father Matthias for advice, and there was nothing to show for it except a series of failed assassination attempts—and a Knight's Cross for carrying out the orders of the tyrant.

"I tried to warn him," Sophia Maria murmured. "Herr Meisterling told me he had to pass on the reports against Father Matthias, and I told Father Matthias that he had come to the attention of the Gestapo. I even suggested he should be more careful. Do you know what he did? He smiled a little wickedly and quoted Luther to me! 'Here I stand. I cannot do otherwise.'"

To Sophia Maria's horror, Philip laughed. For a moment she thought he'd gone mad, but then he put his arm around her shoulders.

How fragile and thin she had become. "Don't you understand?" he asked her. She shook her head. "If he said that, he knew perfectly well what he was doing. He was inviting arrest. He wanted it. He prayed for those in the Concentration Camps after you warned him, didn't he?"

"Yes; but, Philip, we don't know half of what goes on in those camps! They must be appalling! And Father Matthias is in his 70s! What if they send him to the stone quarries or—"

"Shhh," Philip soothed her, a finger on her lips and his arm more firmly around her shoulders. "Listen. I had a talk with him when I was last here—a long, deep, theological discussion. Or a political discussion, if you prefer. How do I tell you this? I complained that I wasn't doing enough to put an end to this criminal regime—and, Mamá, he not only approved of my intentions, he told he wanted to do more himself."

"What do you mean, 'do more'? You don't seem to realize what he's done here—for the Poles and now the Russians, and for all of us! I miss him everywhere. Lutheran that I am, I miss Mass and confession, and most of all I miss Father Matthias!"

"I admit I'm a poor replacement."

"Oh, Philip! I didn't mean that! You know I didn't mean that!"

"I know, but I wish I could at least help you understand that he really could not do otherwise—and still be true to himself."

"But that's silly; crazy. He'd worked in this community for more than 40 years. It was being true to himself to help us, serve us, guide us. Why on earth did he have to be provocative?"

"Perhaps to continue to guide us—to set an example. Or maybe he felt in his heart that he could do yet more."

"More? He can't do anyone any good in a Concentration Camp!"

"He can help those who are there."

Sophia Maria fell silent and then asked, "Do you really think he can do more good there than here?"

"What I think is not important. The only thing that matters is that apparently he thought he could. He stressed to me that we each have to work out in our own hearts what we think is right, and that sometimes that means we have to ignore everyone else and the laws and standards we were raised with. Just as a good officer has to know when to disobey, a good Christian has to know when to listen to his inner voice and ignore all others. Just as Luther and Christ did. They were both rebels in their own time and way."

Sophia Maria looked almost with disgust at her eldest and only surviving son. "Why in the name of God did you have to have a militarist for a mother? You'd have been a perfect candidate for the Society of Jesus—and then I wouldn't have to worry about you getting killed."

"But don't you think this cross is more attractive?" He flicked the Knight's Cross at his throat.

The unexpectedness of the remark forced a laugh from his mother, but then she scolded, "That's the kind of flippant remark I would have expected from Christian, not you!"

"Maybe he inspired it," Philip countered, so softly but seriously that she instantly regretted conjuring the ghost. Philip's gaze was distant for a moment, but he pulled himself together and focused on his mother again. Earnestly he told her, "Besides, even if I had become a Jesuit, I would probably have ended up in a Concentration Camp just as Father Georg did. But I have a strong feeling I am in the right profession—not because of any of the things I've done, but because of what I have yet to do. I, too, cannot do otherwise. Will you forgive me if it has the same result?"

Sophia Maria felt a chill go through her that the hot sun could not thaw and she stared, horrified, at her son. He was staring at her through his glasses, unflinchingly demanding understanding from her. She wanted to scream, to protest, to stop him. She wanted to remind him that she had already lost one son. But he knew that, and still he held her eyes and waited expectantly and confidently. She couldn't disappoint him. Against her will, she forced her stiffened neck muscles to nod. "Yes; whatever you do, I will forgive you." Her voice was a whisper, because it took so much to say these words.

*   *   *   *

Altdorf
June 1943

Alexandra almost missed the stop. From the window of the WC, she saw the station signs whisk past, almost too fast to read. She rushed back to her compartment to get her suitcases, but the train had already stopped before she'd wrestled them down from the overhead rack. She turned to the only man in the compartment. "Please help me. I didn't realize we were at Altdorf already, and with two suitcases—"

The man grunted, but he stood and took the larger of the two suitcases. "What have you got in here? Bricks?"

"Just some household things I wanted to save. I live in Berlin."

"*Ach*, so!" That explained everything. They pushed into the aisle and the man called for the gangway.

"What? You want to get off here?" an airman asked, astonished. With presence of mind, he stuck his head out the window and called, "Hallo! Someone still wants to get off!"

At the door the gentleman climbed down first, reached back for Alexandra's suitcases, and then gave her a hand. She thanked him sincerely. "I never would have made it without you!" He nodded and climbed back aboard the train. The whistle blew and the train started out again.

Alexandra did not have a chance to even turn back before she was all but knocked over by an exuberant Grete. "At last! At last!" Grete looked remarkably tanned and healthy. Her blonde hair hung in thick braids and her *Jungmädel* uniform looked starched and pressed.

"Since when do you go around in uniform?" Alix asked astonished.

"Oh, we all do. It's fun here."

"*Na*, weren't you expecting me?" Philip asked, intentionally echoing Alix's question of long ago, when she'd welcomed him home from Russia before their wedding.

At once startled and relieved, Alix nearly lost her balance as she turned to him. She reached out not so much to steady herself as from an irresistible need to be held by him. Philip was supporting himself on a single crutch and had a bunch of hand-cut roses in the other hand. With this arm he caught and encircled her. Then he pulled back and studied her critically. "You're still pretty," he decided, "but pale and overworked and in need of a long holiday."

"Two weeks is all I could manage," she admitted with trepidation.

He nodded with resignation. He hadn't really expected more. Then, with a formal bow and a magnificent smile, he presented her with the roses.

"*Ach*, Philip!" She couldn't resist another quick kiss. Only then, when she felt the lightness of her head and limbs, did she realize how much she had been afraid he would hold her three-week delay against her.

When it came time to go to bed, Alexandra insisted there was no need to call on Franz, and instead assumed the batman's role of helping her husband. The offer was lightly made and lightly accepted; but in Philip's boyhood room, with his horse-show ribbons and tin soldiers, awkwardness overtook them both. They had been married almost exactly a year, yet in all that time they had only slept together a score of times—all of them a year ago. Since then Philip had offered to be an assassin and Alexandra had typed up orders for the overthrow of the government, the air raids had started and Philip had tried to stop a panic single-handed, Christian had gone missing, and Alix had resumed her legal training. Hadn't they still been children a year ago? But what really hung between them was the wound that Alix had never seen and Philip never talked about. Alix was afraid to see the scars, and Philip was ashamed to let them be seen.

Alix helped Philip out of his boots and tunic and took his shirt and socks from him, but then they both, as if by agreement, stopped. Still in his breeches and undershirt, Philip flung open the turned-down comforter and slipped into bed.

"I'll turn in myself," Alexandra said, feeling uncertain and confused. She desperately wanted to hold and be held by this man she was treating like a patient or a child, but she had been warned by Dr. Sauerbruch that she must not "excite" or "strain" her husband. This might damage his recovery. "Should I turn out the light?"

"Please." The tone was unreadable, and Alexandra was afraid to look her husband in the face. She stepped to the bedside table, switched off the light, and hurried to the door. Behind her she could hear Philip wriggling out of his breeches while she fumbled for the door handle. "Alix."

She stopped. Fright and hope cramped her chest.

"Don't go."

She held her breath, still confused by what she felt. Damn! Was she some tramp? She tried to shame herself. Was she so desperate that she would put his recovery at risk? "Dr. Sauerbruch said—"

"Damn it, Alix! I can't, don't you understand? I can't! I just don't want to be alone!"

She was surprised by how fast she could rid herself of her inhibiting clothes and plunge between the cold sheets. For an instant she thought Philip, too, was surprised by her rapid and forceful arrival under the covers, because he seemed to gasp. Then the gasp came again, and with fathomless horror she realized he was sobbing.

She held him closer and tried to kiss him, but he snapped his head away and—biting back his sobs—said in a hard, bitter voice, "*Ja*, a Knight's Cross instead of children. No wonder you need a career, now that you have only half a husband."

"But Dr. Sauerbruch said—"

"What the hell does he know?"

The automatic answer would have been to say that Dr. Sauerbruch was a famous surgeon—or to say it didn't matter. Alexandra almost voiced the second absurdity, but she stopped herself in time. It was a lie, and Philip would have known it. "I almost lost all of you, Philip," she reminded him. "Do you think I can forget that for a minute? And I'm not working because I feel deprived. I thought I could make a positive contribution, but if you want me to quit—"

He closed his arms convulsively around her and held her tightly for several seconds before he could speak. "No. I don't. I don't want you to be any different than you are. It's just hard to accept what we've lost."

"But we still have each other. Whatever happens, from now on we'll be together," Alix told him.

He kissed her gratefully and they slept, clinging to one another in the narrow child's bed.

Word that a new priest had at last been assigned to Altdorf reached Sophia Maria, as so often, through the kitchen. Josef, who had been to town to collect the newspapers and the mail, reported that the mail had not been distributed yet, but he had met Father Johannes in the Post Office. "I told him he would be welcome to come 'round, Frau *Baronin*," Josef reported, "and he said he would call as soon as he could."

After Father Matthias' arrest, Altdorf had been without a priest of its own. Mass had been held only very irregularly, whenever a priest from one of the nearby towns had been sent. Many of the townspeople, particularly the older women, felt neglected and insisted that Sophia Maria complain to the Bishop. The Bishop had responded to Sophia Maria's letter by saying he would do what he could, but that Germany suffered from an acute shortage of priests.

"Not surprising," Sophia Maria told her eldest son indignantly over breakfast. "Half of them are serving with the *Wehrmacht*, and they throw the best of what remains in Concentration Camps. I wonder what the Bishop will have dredged up for us? No doubt either a man halfway to the grave or some boy straight out of seminary." The fact of the matter was that she didn't *want* a replacement for Father Matthias.

Philip cast Alexandra an amused glance but refrained from comment. He understood his mother and her feelings. He decided to change the subject. "Wouldn't you like to take Alix out for a ride, Mamá? She shouldn't go on her own yet—"

One of the kitchen maids was in the doorway. "*Frau Baronin*, Father Johannes has come to pay his respects."

"Already?" Sophia Maria asked incredulously.

"I wonder what Josef said to him," Philip muttered.

"Send him up," Sophia Maria agreed with a sigh, "and send up another place setting and make fresh *ersatz*."

The girl was gone, and they heard voices from the stairwell. Frau Opitz could be heard officiously giving directions to the breakfast room, and Martha was asking if the Father wanted *ersatz* or tea. Philip stood and went around the table to the door to meet the priest. He took one step out onto the landing and watched a tall and extremely thin young man work his way up the stairs, supporting himself on a cane. Philip offered his hand. "Father Johannes? Feldburg. A pleasure. Please join us for breakfast." He indicated the room behind him and the fourth, vacant side of the small table.

It did not escape Philip's notice that the priest had stiffened at the sight of him and seemed confused by the offered hand. For a moment his hand had hung halfway to his forehead before he reached out and shook hands without looking him in the eye. At Philip's gesture, he entered the breakfast room ahead of his host. From behind him, Philip made the introductions. "My mother, Sophia Maria Baroness von Feldburg, born Countess Walmsdorff, and my wife, Alexandra. My wife and I are only visiting from Berlin."

The young priest bowed first over Sophia Maria's hand and then Alexandra's before uncertainly taking the vacant seat at the table. Sophia Maria asked, "When did you arrive in Altdorf, Father?"

"Yesterday evening, Frau *Baronin*, quite late."

"Was anyone expecting you?" Sophia Maria asked. "I mean, the apartment has been locked ever since Father Matthias was arrested."

The priest seemed to jump at the word "arrested," and Sophia Maria cast her son a despairing glance.

"I was given the telephone number of the housekeeper," the young priest stammered. "The good woman was waiting for me when I arrived, and had even prepared a hot stew and made up the bed for me."

"Frau Becker was very devoted to Father Matthias—as we all were," Sophia Maria told him pointedly.

The young priest nodded. "Why was he arrested? Do you know?"

"Because he honored God more than the mad policies of this heathen government." Sophia Maria's tone was staccato and uncompromising.

Philip took his seat opposite the priest and answered mildly, "He said a prayer for the inmates of the Concentration Camps, Father."

The priest swallowed, stared at Philip, and seemed to want to say something, but he didn't get a chance. Sophia Maria was adding, "He also prayed for the prisoners on *both* sides." This time the priest seemed to twitch with discomfort. Again he looked to Philip while Sophia Maria continued forcefully, her eyes leveled unkindly on the young priest, "We have many prisoners of war serving in this community. May I ask when you got out of seminary?"

"Two years ago, *Frau Baronin*."

Sophia Maria gazed at him as if she did not believe him.

"And what was your last position?" The question came from Philip.

"Si-Si—"

And he stutters, Sophia Maria thought in despair. Mass will be interminable.

"Sixth Army?" Philip supplied the words.

"Jawohl, Herr Oberstleutnant."

Alexandra and Sophia Maria stared at Philip.

"Frostbite?" He nodded toward the priest's cane.

"Yes, but I didn't ask to be flown out, *Herr Oberstleutnant*; it was—"

"Please, Father, forget my rank and look at me as a mere parishioner. Furthermore, I assure you my mother is not as hostile as she is pretending to be," he glanced reproachfully at her. "Were you with the Army from the time you got out of seminary?"

"Yes, *Herr Ober*—" he stopped himself—"Yes, Herr von Feldburg."

Philip smoothed over the awkwardness, remarking, "Then I daresay you will find your duties here very challenging. Much more difficult than in the Army."

They all stared at Philip as if he had lost his senses. Philip looked from his mother to his wife and explained, "In the Army, Father Johannes only had to deal with men, mostly dying men or men afraid of dying. Here he'll have to deal with weeping widows and nubile young girls who have fallen in love with him—not to mention women of a certain age who want to confess to him all the details of their sexual misdemeanors—"

"How do you know what they confess?" Sophia Maria demanded indignantly.

"Mother," Philip leveled a gaze at her that suggested she was being naive, "I was an acolyte both here and at school."

Alexandra couldn't help giggling, and Sophia Maria suddenly had to laugh. The ice was finally broken. An hour later, when Father Johannes stood to leave, Sophia Maria was promising to help introduce him to the outlying farms.

Philip saw the priest down the stairs and out into the courtyard. The sun was high and hot. Philip nodded toward the workers' quarters and said in a low voice, "Father Matthias always had an open ear for the Polish workers. They are devout Catholics, and the arrangements made for them are wholly inadequate."

"I understand. I will do my best. But the Bishop warned me …"

"Not to follow in Father Matthias' footsteps?" Philip asked with raised eyebrows.

The priest sighed, but then he added intensely, "There must be some reason why God wanted me out of Stalingrad!"

Philip smiled faintly and nodded, "I'm sure you'll discover it." He held out his hand, and they shook hands. Philip turned back toward the house.

"*Herr Oberstleu*—Herr v. Feldburg," the priest called out. Philip looked back over his shoulder. The priest was coming toward him again, fumbling in the pocket of his cassock. "I almost forgot. After your man left the post office this morning, the mail arrived. There was this letter for your mother. That was my reason—or excuse—for calling here right away. In the excitement, I completely forgot." The priest smiled sheepishly.

Philip smiled and held out his hand. "No problem." He took the letter without looking at it and waved goodbye. "See you at Mass." Turning back toward the house, he glanced at the letter and stopped in his tracks. The handwriting reminded him—His heart stopped. In the upper left-hand corner was written in a neat hand: "CvF" followed by a series of incomprehensible letters and numbers ending with "USA."

He burst into the kitchen. "Mamá! Mamá!"

"There's no need to shout. I'm not deaf yet—"

He swept her into his arms and lifted her off the ground, causing both her and Alexandra to cry out, "Be careful!"

Philip ignored them. "He made it! Christian made it!" He shoved the letter into his mother's stunned hand and turned to the room at large. "My brother is alive. Frau Opitz, ring the gong. Call everyone together. My brother would want you to have a beer in celebration!"

"Christian?" Martha asked, disbelieving—and then suddenly the staff in the kitchen crowded around, talking at once, laughing, hugging each other. Herr Opitz came in from the front of the house, frowning until he heard what the commotion was about. One of the girls ran out to tell Josef and the others in the barn. Martha sank down at the table and started sobbing for joy. Franz called upstairs to his mother. In the midst of it all, Sophia Maria stood clutching the letter, supported by Alexandra.

Philip went over to her and gently kissed her forehead. He murmured to her, "Let me take you upstairs." She nodded. He took her elbow and helped her past Heidi and Franz, who congratulated them as if they'd had something to do with it. Philip turned as he started up the stairs and called back to Franz, "See that everyone gets beer, Franz."

Stadthagen nodded, grinning. "As ordered, *Herr Oberstleutnant!*"

In her study, Philip helped his mother into a chair, glancing at the photo that stood prominently on her desk. It was the photo from his wedding when he'd turned to congratulate Christian on his promotion. Philip and Christian were grinning at each other as if no one else existed. His mother had made two copies of it: one for here and one for her bedroom dresser.

He kissed her forehead and then withdrew, slipping his arm around Alexandra and guiding her toward the door with the remark, "My mother needs to be alone with my brother."

"Philip, wait!" Sophia Maria stopped him.

He and Alix turned back expectantly.

"What if he's been burned like Dieter or—"

"It doesn't matter. He's safe, Mother. They can't get their hands on him anymore. They can't sacrifice him to their damned madness. He's beyond their clutches. They can't waste him ever again!" The vehemence of his answer surprised even Alexandra. She tightened her hold on him to calm him, and he turned and dropped her a kiss of jubilation before leading her out of the room.

Christian wrote that the last thing he remembered was the dogfight. He'd woken up to the sound of sirens on a hospital ship. "They actually seemed to think a German U-Boat captain might fire torpedoes at a clearly marked hospital ship," he wrote. Continuing, "I told them they were crazy, and if they'd turn off the d-sirens I could go back to sleep."

The Americans, Christian wrote, claimed that he'd crash-landed his badly damaged Messerschmitt at one of their improvised airfields. They said they'd found him unconscious in the cockpit, a piece of shrapnel in the back of his head. He'd also broken both legs on landing. He reported that he was nearly recovered, and praised the medical treatment he had received. Here he broke off his own narrative to ask: "Is Philip all right? Did he get through the second operation? Please write, whatever the news. I can't bear not knowing." Then he went on to write with enthusiasm about the food (fresh orange juice, two eggs and "what they call bacon"—just for breakfast). He joked about the surprise of his captors when he volunteered to work. "They have some very strange ideas about aristocracy." All in all, he sounded very much himself.

The letter read, the Feldburgs went back downstairs and joined the staff for a beer. Then Sophia Maria called Theresa with the news. Afterwards each wrote a separate letter to Christian so he would get lots of mail, and they drove down together to the post office to send the letters off. And, of course, they opened a bottle of champagne in the evening. Sophia Maria kept insisting, "I'm so glad you're here to share this with me. It would be terrible to celebrate alone."

"Shall we lay bets on whether you have an American daughter-in-law before the war is over?" Philip asked his mother lightly, still hardly able to grasp that he'd been given a second chance. And whatever happened, his brother was safe.

Just before he drifted off to sleep that night, Philip admitted to Alix, "I can't help wondering if he really made a mistake on landing."

"What do you mean?" Alix asked sleepily, nestling her head on his shoulder.

"I mean: maybe he was flying more by instinct than thought. Maybe all he registered was that it was an airfield. But then again, at the time he did it, it was uncertain whether I would survive or not … I can't help wondering if Christian didn't know exactly what he was doing when he landed on an American airfield."

CHAPTER 34

▼

Berlin
August 1943

On the first day of Stefan v. Mollwitz's tour of duty in Germany, his principal emotion was disorientation. The orders sending him to a special three-month "heavy infantry weapons" training course at a military school on the outskirts of Berlin had surprised him on the Eastern Front. Mollwitz had grabbed his usual kit, reported to company and battalion commanders, hitchhiked on an ambulance heading to Divisional HQ, and from there joined an empty supply column until he reached a railhead and could board a leave-train. He reported to his new, temporary unit in the former Olympic Village at Döberitz without so much as having sent a telegram to his parents.

At Döberitz the cleanliness of the huts and the well-rested faces of the staff disoriented him. After 16 months in Russia, Stefan stood before tables in the Officer's Mess decked with white linen and silver, and honestly wondered if he still remembered the table manners such a setting demanded. It was with the awkwardness of a schoolboy or officer candidate that he stood stiffly in the club afterwards, holding his wineglass at the prescribed height and starting every reply "most obediently." When he went to bed that night and found the crisp white sheets with the ironed creases and a comforter bursting with feathers, he almost slept on the floor rather than defile such perfection.

It was also disorienting to be torn from that clean, warm bed in order to seek the safety of an air-raid shelter. First, the two things did not fit together. Second, the helplessness and unaccustomed fear shamed the young man, who had been drilled to think it was incumbent upon a lieutenant to show leadership and courage at all times.

And finally, for the young man who had spent the last four years almost exclusively in the company of men, it was disorienting to be confronted suddenly and everywhere by women. There were women bus conductors and women chimney sweeps. Women collected the garbage and women delivered the mail. Women in steel helmets from the last war acted as air-raid wardens, and women in head scarves and wooden shoes—forced laborers from the occupied territories—cleared the rubble after the air raids. Most unsettling, however, were the women in military uniform. These young women wore an eagle over their (often prominent) breasts and had rank and specialty badges on their sleeves. Worse still, they performed duties that soldiers usually performed.

When first confronted with this phenomenon, Stefan had been quite speechless. He hadn't the faintest idea how one was supposed to address such a curious creature. Was she a lady to be handled with respect and courtesy? Or was she a soldier to be addressed in a distant, authoritative tone? Confused and uncertain, he had retreated wordlessly.

By the fifth day of Stefan's tour of duty in the *Reich* the adjustment period was complete, and an intoxicating euphoria set in. The air raids were not really so different from artillery barrages—one's helplessness was no greater, and the fact that he shared the danger with civilians was no longer strange. Neither his fellow officers nor the civilians themselves seemed to think it was strange or incorrect that a lieutenant crouched in the earth with them at the sound of the sirens. No one expected leadership of him here.

The troops that depended on him were far away, pushed back into the subconscious recesses of his brain. In Döberitz he was just a trainee, and as such, free of all responsibility. When this at last sank in, he felt a weight lift from him.

The surprise he'd planned for his sister only partially succeeded, because his parents had betrayed his presence in Berlin. She'd been expecting him to call or drop by. Nonetheless, the unannounced ringing of the doorbell and his armload of *Sekt* did not totally lack effect. Nadja, a forced laborer they had been assigned because Philip, Alix, Seydlitz and Lotte all lived together in the Feldburg flat, answered the door, to the consternation of both parties. Stefan had been prepared for Alix or Philip, not a Ukrainian maid, and Nadja was not expecting a strange lieutenant bearing four bottles of champagne. The commotion brought Alexandra to the door, and Stefan unloaded the champagne onto Nadja to sweep his "big sister" off the floor and give her the kiss he unconsciously longed to give the girlfriend he'd never had time to find. Arm in arm, Alexandra led him to the study, where Philip was working at his desk on papers he'd brought from the office.

Not for a second had Alexandra doubted that her brother and her husband would become friends. Stefan, a victim of his own high spirits, defiantly ignored the senior rank and General Staff stripes of his brother-in-law, while Philip willingly fell victim to the younger man's effervescence. Rolf and Lotte joined them in the salon for the champagne, but they had only finished one bottle when the sirens sounded.

Somewhat brazenly, they carried the remaining bottles and a tray of glasses to the cellar. Here Stefan, mimicking a snotty waiter in a fancy restaurant, offered their fellow cellar-mates a glass of *Sekt*. As this rapidly depleted their reserves, Stefan decided to raid the Feldburg refrigerator in which, Stadthagen assured him, two more bottles of bubbly were carefully laid aside for this very occasion. The raiding of the refrigerator, of course, entailed going back upstairs, a violation of regulations and all rules of caution in the middle of an air raid. But Theo's protests as *Blockwarden* were quickly quenched by Philip who, for once, played the employer, senior officer and baron. He told his employee sharply that Stefan was a veteran of the Eastern Front who knew the dangers and could decide for himself. Stefan braved the dangers with impunity.

To the sound and trembling of distant detonations, they shared the remaining bottles. If Nurse Tuchel looked slightly disapproving at first, she soon capitulated in the face of Stefan's adept compliments, while Peter Kessler seemed outright flattered by the camaraderie of the lieutenant. Of course, Stefan didn't know Peter's profession as he chatted easily with the Gestapo inspector, his attention wandering now and again admiringly to Marianne. "Frightful, these air raids," he declared openly. "A scandalous type of warfare. We on the front really have no idea. And to think you have to take this night after night and still go on working!"

"It's the least we can do for the Fatherland," Peter assured him seriously. "Just because we have been designated u.k.—*unabkömmlich*—and aren't allowed to serve in the armed forces, doesn't mean we love our Fatherland less." Kessler meant every word.

"Of course not," Stefan agreed with him readily, adding, "Besides, the average soldier isn't terribly patriotic, either. We just don't have any choice."

Later, when Alexandra told Stefan about Kessler's profession, he stared at her wide-eyed and then laughed nervously. "But he looked so innocent and timid," Stefan defended himself.

"If criminals looked like criminals, there'd be no need for police," Alix pointed out.

"Or rather," her husband improved, "if police acted like police, there'd be no need for criminals."

Stefan laughed heartily, even if he didn't really get the joke. Then he remarked, "I can't have said anything frightfully stupid, or you wouldn't be standing there grinning at me."

"Brilliant deduction, little brother," Alexandra agreed. "Now give me a kiss and be gone. *We* have to work tomorrow."

"Silent, selfless work—didn't Seekt say?—is the virtue of the General Staff. Furthermore, staff officers have no names and should always be more than they appear to be."

"I hope so," Philip agreed, firmly taking his brother-in-law by the arm and guiding him to the door, "but sleeplessness is discouraged as counterproductive except in extremities." Then they shook hands and he added more seriously, "Come again soon—and as often as you like."

Stefan grinned, "I will—probably a lot sooner and more often than *you* like!" He started down the stairs at a run, stopped, and called up just before Philip closed the door, "Oh! And you can tell Alix I approve—even if you do have a damned Knight's Cross."

On the 12th day of Stefan's tour of duty in the *Reich*, he was in love. Her name was Klara Rademacher, and she was one of the female auxiliaries from the nearby *Luftwaffe* air-raid plotting center. Although she was a little plump, she looked neat and trim in her tailored uniform jacket and tie, and when she went out wearing her fore-and-aft cap perched jauntily over her shoulder-length hair, she looked very smart indeed. But she was not one of the "glamorous" girls, and her roundish face was always free of makeup—though not always free of blemishes.

When Stefan met her, she had just turned twenty. Since the female auxiliaries had a rather loose reputation, Stefan had at first been perplexed to find Klara behaving like a good girl of middle-class upbringing. Then again, he soon decided that this suited him. After all, who wants to fall in love with a girl that all your comrades have already slept with? Very soon Stefan had reached the point of finding everything about Klara uniquely charming.

Stefan bravely introduced Klara to his parents and his sister. If his parents seemed less than enthusiastic, he attributed this to their outdated snobbery. Weren't aristocratic titles irrelevant already? And Klara's father was a high-school teacher. What could be more respectable? Alexandra, as he had expected, accepted Klara at once and made her feel welcome. Seydlitz had treated her with so much gallantry, she'd gushed with enthusiasm about him, and Stefan would have been jealous if Seydlitz hadn't been so ugly. Lotte had been obnoxious and provocative, smoking and lounging about in her "movie star" manner, but that only made Klara seem more precious to Stefan. And Philip—well, Philip could be distant at times, but he was basically all right.

By the 40th day of Stefan's tour of duty in the *Reich*, being in love had started to lose some of its luster. Taking advantage of an official excursion of his class into Berlin, Stefan dropped by his sister's office in the late afternoon. Alexandra's new office was hardly more than a cubbyhole with a dirty window overlooking a small courtyard, whose only purpose was to provide natural light to the interior offices. But for all that, Alexandra was boundlessly proud of it, because it was hers.

In this dreary, patently legalistic, and expressly boring environment, Stefan viewed his sister like a rose in the desert. "It's not right to lock such beauty away in such a dingy corner," he announced, poking his head into the room. As he pushed the door to let himself in, it cracked against a bookcase and ricocheted back at him. The next thing he said was not polite.

"Stefan!" Alexandra leapt up in delight.

"Thought I'd come see this kingdom of yours—can't say I'm impressed." Stefan cast the room a disapproving look, rubbing his forehead where the door had hit him. He wrinkled his nose in distaste. "It's a glorious day outside. Wouldn't you like to come with me to the zoo?"

"The zoo?" she asked back, surprised, and then in the next moment she thought: Oh, to be children again! Brother and sister on an outing to the zoo. To Stefan she asked, "Will you let me feed the seals?"

"And the penguins."

"And will you buy me an ice-cream cone?"

"A double scoop."

Without further ado, Alix closed the books and binders on her desk and put them back on the shelves. She shoved her notes into the desk drawer and grabbed her coat and handbag. "Well, then, come on!"

Although it was after 5 pm, Philip rarely got away before 8 pm. Alix had time to go to the zoo with her brother before he wanted to go home. Her work would wait for her. But the opportunity to go to the zoo with her brother might never come again.

Stefan bought their tickets from the toothless old woman in the booth and handed them to the fragile old man at the gate. Alix wondered vaguely whether they thought Stefan too young for her, and found the thought amusing. Before them, the zoo was nearly empty. There were no children in neat school uniforms or toddlers with their nannies, as when Stefan and Alix had been children. Instead, elderly couples in shabby clothes went arm in arm and soldiers, alone and in pairs, wandered about listlessly.

Stefan bought Alix the promised ice-cream cone, and then they went to see the lions. The lioness had cubs, and she watched warily as the little crowd admired her playful offspring. "Typical," Stefan commented with a strangely serious face. "Even in Russia the children play, despite the sound of artillery and grenade throwers just a few kilometres away."

Sensitive to his change in mood, Alexandra tried to work out what might be preying on him. "How's Klara?" she asked, gently pulling him away from the lions and heading in the direction of her favorite animals, the seals.

Stefan sighed and Alexandra knew she'd hit a nerve, but Stefan did not elaborate immediately. They walked in silence, Alix holding Stefan's elbow, although he had his hands shoved deep into the pockets of his uniform trousers. "*Ach*, you know," he began at last, "Klara is a dear girl. I love her, really I do, but I don't know … Sometimes I just want to be with you or with some friends, or even alone."

"Quite understandable," Alexandra agreed, in a tone of voice meant to encourage him to keep talking.

"Then why does Klara take it like a personal insult? Why does she act like it's a denial of my love for her if I once say I want to go drinking with a couple of the others?" Stefan's voice and face were angry.

"Because she's just turned 20 and is in love for the first time."

Stefan glanced at his sister. "You make it sound so simple. Klara was in tears, and then she said all sorts of things … I don't know," he shrugged in embarrassment and didn't look at his sister as he added, "you know, about marriage and commitment and things like that."

"Ah hum," Alexandra nodded knowingly. What else could one expect from a simple, honest girl like Klara? "And you don't want to marry her," she added for clarification.

"It's not that! It's just that I haven't thought about anything that serious. For God's sake, I have to go back to the front in six weeks! And let's face it: my chances of surviving don't look all that promising. If I'm lucky, I'll only get an arm or a leg blown off. I don't see how a man can tie a girl down when he's in my position. It would be totally irresponsible!" Stefan spoke forcefully, with proud conviction.

"Ah hum," Alexandra nodded again. "Typical male rationalization."

"What?"

"Male rationalization. The fact is you don't want to marry her, but rather than being honest enough to say so, you pretend it's some virtuous gesture for her sake."

"But surely you see it would be irresponsible to tie a girl to me when the chances are so great of leaving her a widow?" Stefan insisted in an exasperated tone. He expected his sister, at least, to take his side.

"Why?" Alexandra shot back. "Do you think it will hurt her any less if you're not married? Ridiculous! Be practical: at least a widow is entitled to a pension. As a broken-hearted girlfriend, she gets absolutely nothing."

"Yes, but I mean she's free—"

"Oh, Stefan! Honestly. Don't be so naive! A widow is free, too. And if you think a girl like Klara is likely to even look at another man as long as her heart is engaged—whether it's official or not—you really are a poor judge of character."

"But marriage is planning for the future, and how can anyone plan for the future under present circumstances?"

"Marriage is the commitment of two people to face the future together— whatever it brings. It doesn't imply any sort of control over that future. We don't have that even in the best of times."

"But Alix! I don't feel ready to get married."

"That I can readily believe, and I would never advise you to marry against your instincts. But for God's sake, call a spade a spade, and stop this charade of only being responsible!"

Stefan sighed and then impulsively dropped onto a bench they were passing. He propped his elbows on his knees and held his head in his hands. "What am I going to do?"

Alexandra considered him from her standing position for a moment, her hands thrust into the pockets of her light coat as it flapped open in the wind. Then she sank down next to him and leaned her chin on her own fists so that they were shoulder to shoulder. "What's the problem?"

"Alix, I love Klara, really I do. And she's made the last month so wonderful. With her, I forget the war. She's what I've dreamed about: a girl to do things with, laugh with, to spoil and be spoiled by. I don't want to give her up—but I can't promise her marriage, either. It would be a lie. I mean, I might marry her after the war, but I can't commit myself yet. I'd go crazy. I can't explain it," he ended, exasperated with his own inarticulateness.

"And you can't just continue the way things were?"

Stefan sighed, "I don't think so. For almost a week Klara has been dropping hints, and then last night … She's so horribly jealous! If I so much as smile politely at one of her co-workers, she accuses me of cheating on her. I can't go anywhere where there might be other women without her accusing me of some tryst. It's driving me crazy!"

"I can imagine," Alexandra agreed. She understood better than Stefan that the reason Klara was jealous was the same reason that Stefan didn't want to commit himself: he was still looking. Klara was fine—for the moment—but she wasn't really the woman of his dreams. He still hoped, at least unconsciously, to find someone still better. But Alexandra kept this assessment to herself and asked instead, "And Klara thinks that being engaged will change all that?"

"I don't know—but she keeps coming back to it. How can she trust me, if she doesn't know where she stands? And if my intentions aren't honorable …"

"Have you slept with her?"

Stefan stopped breathing for a second and then answered slowly, "No." He did not look at his sister. His gaze was fixed between his boots.

"I wouldn't think the less of her if you had," Alix assured her brother, suspecting a lie. "I've lived to regret that I didn't sleep with Philip before our marriage."

Stefan glanced over his shoulder at his sister, startled by this confession. Then he sat upright and declared, "No, we haven't slept together, but I want to. I'm 25 years old, and I'm probably not going to see 26, and, yes, I want to sleep with the girl I love." His tone had turned defensive and defiant.

"If you were so sure you were going to die," Alexandra looked up at him, her chin still propped on her hands, "why not get engaged, even married?"

"Damn it!" Stefan sprang angrily to his feet. "Do you think I want to believe that? Do you think I can go on living with no hope at all?"

Alix stayed sitting, her chin propped on her hands and her face turned up to him. Her expression was strangely hard. She made Stefan feel embarrassed for his outburst, although he didn't know why. Wasn't he right? Shouldn't she be excusing herself to him? "Say something," he urged.

"You're right," Alix stated with a shrug, sitting upright and leaning against the back of the bench. She fixed a cold gaze on him. "Of course, you're right. How can we women dare to ask for anything in times like these? Your sacrifice is greater, your fate more bitter. Everything you face is more heroic and more tragic."

Stefan felt no better than before. He wasn't even sure whether she was sincere or sarcastic. Alexandra wasn't sure herself. "It's not that," Stefan started lamely.

"What is it, then? You want to have your cake and eat it too, don't you? You want Klara to love you and give you all she has—without complaint, without jealousy, without making the slightest demand or receiving the slightest payment—not even in the form of empty promises. You want to be free to go out with your comrades, and free to flirt with other girls, and yet be certain of Klara's unconditional love for you. And you think you can justify it all because an unjust regime is making unfair demands on you. But it's not the Regime that pays the price, is it? It's Klara—and she's as much a victim of the Regime as you are yourself."

Stefan looked down at the gravel and scuffed it with his boot, his thoughts in turmoil.

"It's most unfair to girls like Klara," Alexandra continued, "girls who have never wanted anything else out of life but love and marriage. With every day of this slaughter there are fewer young men, less hope. Pure statistics condemn her and millions like her to a fate that is hardly more dismal than that of their slaughtered would-be husbands—only the woman's agony is long and drawn out. Don't you remember the old maids that populated every family gathering, every café and every train compartment as we were growing up? Didn't you ever stop to think how empty, pointless and miserable their lives were? Maiden aunts with tiny incomes. Ladies' companions, governesses, needlepoint stores and copy work."

Stefan stared at his sister. "When did you notice all that?"

Alix laughed bitterly. "When? Until the day Philip married me! Why do you think I studied law? Or when I couldn't finish, took secretarial training? Because I never wanted to be like them—helpless, pitied, a failure with no purpose for living. But don't misunderstand me. You have to do what is right for you, and if Klara is the victim ..." She shrugged.

"You make me feel like a cad."

Alexandra smiled cynically and shook her head ambiguously.

"Mother of God! Don't just sit there like a sphinx!"

"Haven't I said enough already? Do you want me to become philosophical?"

"Anything but that sphinx expression!"

"A great genius, I think, might one day work out some formula for the multiplication of evil. I once compared it to an infectious disease that went out from Adolf and his crowd. I hypothesized that the infection attacked the moral and ethical fiber of the infected. At the time, I thought that only those in near or frequent contact with the carrier were affected, but now I realize that the system itself eats away at the moral foundations of society as a whole. Gradually, the continual use of devalued phrases and the organization of society on the basis of utility and "racial" necessity confuses even the most normal, healthy individual. Think of how many people walk past the forced laborers and don't register that they are forced. How often do we sit on benches like this"—she pointed to the lettering "for Aryans only"—"without asking what has become of all the Jews? Who asks if it was right that x or y was hauled off to a Concentration Camp?

"I guess it is too late to question. People who crawl exhausted from the air-raid shelters into the smoking morning to find that all they've saved, built and collected in years of honest living has evaporated in the wake of a phosphorus bomb don't have time to worry about KZ inmates, Jews or Russian prisoners, do they? People worrying about one son gone missing in the North Atlantic and the other son in Russia can't be expected to ask if we were right to start the war. People— the same people—working 60 hours a week in an armaments factory can't be asked to worry about what we're doing in the Occupied Territories. In short, it is too much to ask you to worry about Klara's fate when your own is so unenviable."

"You don't really believe that, do you?"

"What?"

"That it is too much to ask."

"*Doch, doch*," Alexandra assured her brother, getting to her feet and taking him by the arm. "Come on. Let's go feed the seals."

On the 85th day of Stefan's tour of duty in the *Reich*, a desperate depression lamed him. After a sleepless night, he called his brother-in-law and asked if they could meet alone. Philip had to go to the Berlin Commandantur for a conference, and suggested they meet afterwards in a bar near the Alexanderplatz.

Stefan arrived first at the appointed café. When Philip arrived, Stefan stood out of military courtesy and helped Philip out of his wet greatcoat. Philip, mystified by the telephone call, was further discomfited by so much respect. When they were seated and had ordered a beer from the surly waiter, Stefan couldn't help remarking, "Where did you come up with this joint?" The cheap, tasteless and run-down décor and proletarian clientele were no more attractive than the service. It hardly seemed the kind of locale where one would expect to meet a baron.

"Connections," Philip replied incomprehensibly; then, taking mercy on his brother-in-law, he explained, "I thought your call sounded as if you wanted a totally confidential talk. I think we can be sure that neither your friends nor mine are likely to show up here—much less a lady. What's more, the proprietor is an old Spartacus League member and spent years in a KZ, so you can even bitch about Adolf if you want. The Gestapo spies don't risk coming in anymore, not since the last one was found dead in the Spree. Drowned drunk, of course, but no one really believes it was an accident."

"How do you know all that?" Stefan wanted to know, completely amazed.

"Count Helldorf, *Polizeipräsident* of Berlin."

Stefan still wasn't sure what to make of this, but decided it wasn't his business. He started playing with the cardboard coasters praising Berliner Kindl—the beer sold in the bar. Finally he ventured, "I wanted to ask you something—as an experienced soldier." Stefan had been at the front more continuously than Philip, but Philip had no intention of making things difficult by quibbling. He just waited. Stefan asked, "Do you believe in premonitions?"

"What sort of premonitions?"

"You know, a premonition of one's own death."

"A specific dream, or just a vague feeling?"

Stefan shrugged. "Just a feeling."

"No," Philip answered unequivocally. "My brother, for example, had that, and he's now safe in American hands."

Stefan looked up, frowning. "I've had three friends who've had such premonitions, and they're all dead."

"The belief that one is going to die often induces a certain careless indifference to the normal rules of self-protection," Philip countered. "I've seen soldiers who stop wearing their helmets just because the weather is hot, and I've watched men only half-crouch when they should crawl, or light up a cigarette when they should maintain a strict blackout. Experienced soldiers, good troops, often decide at some point that they aren't going to survive anyway, and fall into bad habits. Men who are under stress too long start doing what is comfortable rather than making an effort to do what is safer. Hardly surprising if they get killed, is it?"

Stefan didn't answer, but he gratefully accepted the beer he'd ordered, took a big gulp, and continued, "I can't imagine ever coming back. When I try to picture the future, all I see is black nothingness."

It was clear that Stefan took this seriously, so Philip didn't want to insult him with a hasty or flippant reply. On the other hand, he wanted to dissuade Stefan from these dangerous, macabre thoughts. "Don't you think that could be simple uncertainty?"

"Can you picture the future?"

"I'm afraid to try."

"No," Stefan decided, angrily pushing his beer away. "No, it's not uncertainty. I'm going to die. I can feel it, sense it, in every bone in my body. I'm going to die in the next couple of months, and the worst of it is, I don't know why. Why should I die now? At 25? When I've just fallen in love for the first time in my life? What good is it going to do anyone?"

Philip was flattered that Stefan had chosen to confide in him, but he had to admit, "You know I can't answer that. Why do you ask me?"

"Because you—and Alix—seem to exude some sort of inner serenity that I don't understand. But I want to understand. You aren't cynical and bitter like many senior officers, nor naive and ambitious like the younger ones. And you aren't just stubbornly closing your eyes to everything around you, either. You know just exactly how stupid and futile this war is, and yet you aren't depressed." For a moment Stefan devoted his attention to his beer, and Philip watched him silently. Then Stefan looked up sharply. "You aren't going to play sphinx, are you? Why do you and Alix always have to play sphinx?"

"For your safety."

"What a joke! I just told you I don't think I'm going to survive the next few months!"

"But I think you are."

"What if I told you I'd just been promoted to Company Commander in Russia?"

Company Commander on the Eastern Front was the virtual equivalent of a death sentence, and Philip stopped breathing for a second. Then, after the initial shock, he answered, "You can't have been. You're too junior."

"Today I'm too junior. What about six months from now? Or twelve months? It's just a matter of time."

"Maybe the war will be over by then."

"How?"

"Leave that to the General Staff."

"They got us into this mess!"

"Do you believe that?"

"I don't know; didn't they?"

Philip refused to answer. Stefan dropped his head into his hands. "What am I going to do? God, the next four days are going to be hell! It'll be easier when I'm back there. On the front, there is always so much to do and worry about, and the others will be more important than me. That's the best part of being an officer— that there's someone else to worry about, no time for yourself."

"Alix said you had a letter from your platoon in which they said they missed you and hoped you'd come back soon."

A smiled crossed Stefan's face under the gloomy surface. "Yes; dated 'Paradise.'"

Philip laughed appreciatively and then added more seriously, "There's no higher compliment an officer can get. I envy you the trust of your troops." Stefan looked up quickly, suspecting insincerity or patronizing, but he found only unwavering earnestness. It was an odd feeling to be envied by a General Staff lieutenant colonel with the Knight's Cross. It forced Stefan to reconsider his lot again. "You know," Philip tried to explain, "the worst part of being a General Staff officer is not that we have no names, it's that we have no troops. An officer without troops is an abstraction, a sort of mutation. I know you didn't choose this profession. I know you would far rather have finished your studies and joined the Diplomatic Corps. But I hope you can agree that it is nevertheless a good profession. I firmly believe there is nothing nobler than being a good officer who has won the confidence and respect of his troops."

Stefan nodded, although he was not really convinced. Philip continued, "I envy you, Stefan, but I can't trade places with you. It's not just rank and this accursed wound. I'm serious when I say we're trying to stop the war as soon as possible. Like all General Staff work, it is done behind closed doors, namelessly and thanklessly—but I promise you, we will devote our last drop of blood to that goal if need be." He paused to lend weight to this statement. Then he added in a less solemn tone, "It is an immeasurable help that your sister supports me in this. I'd like to think you can return to the front a little strengthened by the knowledge that, despite our anonymity and distance, there are officers working with all their might to put an end to this senseless slaughter."

"*Ja*," Stefan nodded more definitively, although his face was still clouded. "*Ja*, that helps. It helps to think there might be an end at all—what's the Berlin expression? Better a terrible end than an endless terror?"

"God help us when that end comes."

CHAPTER 35

▼

Berlin
October 1943

Lotte was surprised by how much she liked her job at AHA. It wasn't music and it was strenuous and exhausting much of the time, but she found she liked being "in the middle" of things. She was the first to admit that she only understood half of what crossed her desk or was said between the doors opening to her office in three directions, but she liked the sense of excitement that went with it all. Furthermore, she was amazed by how friendly and helpful the other secretaries were. In her singing career, she had experienced other women only as rivals—which was why Alexandra had been her only female friend. At the Bendlerstrasse most of the girls were willing to help out, explain things, fill in and—in a pinch—even swap night or holiday duty. Annie Lerche, especially, had made an effort to see Lotte settle in and help her do a good job. Annie and Lotte were, meanwhile, better friends that Alix and Annie ever had been.

So, of course, Lotte agreed to cover for Annie while the latter went to register as "homeless." Her apartment had been so badly gutted by fire following the last raid that it was temporarily unlivable. She needed to report this fact in order to pick up the various forms entitling her to draw her rations from anywhere in the city, requisition temporary housing, and—most important—claim damages so she could get the materials necessary for repairs. What they'd both forgotten was that Oct. 1 was the day the new Chief of Staff was scheduled to start his duties at AHA.

Although Lotte arrived early, she didn't have time to remove her coat before the phone started ringing. A special briefing on the Italian situation had been scheduled at the Foreign Ministry, and she had to be sure Olbricht and his new Chief knew about it. Fromm's secretary wanted to know when Olbricht would bring his new Chief by to meet Fromm. The drivers' pool wanted the paperwork that authorized the new Chief to a duty car. The central telephone exchange wanted the full name, rank and title of the Chief for their lists. Lotte was steaming inwardly before she'd been at work a half-hour—and still in her coat.

She was bending over Annie's desk, to write down a telephone number before she forgot it, when the door opened behind her and an unfamiliar voice said, "Good morning—"

"Just a minute! Can't you see I'm busy?" she snapped irritably, finishing the note. Then, slapping the pencil on top of the pad, she turned around and caught her breath. The man standing in the door from the Chief's office, watching her with amusement, was wearing an eye patch over his left eye and had his empty right sleeve pinned to his tunic. He graciously reached out the remaining three fingers of his left hand. "Forgive me, *gnädiges Fräulein*. Stauffenberg. I've just arrived. Would you be so kind as to inform the *Herr General* that I am at his disposal."

Lotte later told Alix that it was hard to know which emotion was dominant in that moment. On the one hand, she was mortified to have greeted her new boss in such a tone and manner. On the other, she was shocked by the mutilation of his face and hand. Still she went on to exclaim, "Alix, you may not believe me, but despite his wounds he is one of the most attractive men I've ever laid eyes on. God, what he must have looked like before he was shot up! But of course, there are lots of handsome men who are utterly obnoxious. *Graf* Stauffenberg is like no one I've ever met before. He's got a charm that has nothing to do with mere good looks."

"He also has a wife and five children." Alexandra tried to bring Lotte back to earth.

Lotte smiled wickedly. "Not resident in Berlin, I wager."

"No, safely down in Franken somewhere, but don't let that deceive you. He lives with his brother and sister-in-law in Zehlendorf."

"Zehlendorf? No problem. That's the end of the world," Lotte assured her, laughing.

Stauffenberg and Olbricht had first met in August. Olbricht had tentatively selected Stauffenberg for the position of Chief of Staff after it was reported to him (via Halder and Beck) that Stauffenberg had at last changed his attitude toward both the war and Hitler. Stauffenberg's organizational talent was unquestioned, and even his predecessor at AHA, Oberst Reinhard, had recommended him for that reason. As soon as Stauffenberg was released from a Munich hospital in August, he'd reported to Olbricht in Berlin. At the time, he'd assumed his new assignment was routine, and had expressed a preference for reassignment to the front. Olbricht had countered by explaining what he expected of his new Chief—someone to coordinate all activities necessary for a military *coup d'état* against Hitler. Stauffenberg had been momentarily surprised, but he hadn't hesitated for a moment. On the contrary, he had been so eager to get started that it had taken considerable persuasion to convince him that he needed more surgery and two more months to recover.

Stauffenberg had stayed in Berlin and used the time to consult with Tresckow and a number of the civilian conspirators on the unofficial aspects of the coup planning. As he swept into Olbricht's office on the morning of Oct. 1, Olbricht was reminded of a racehorse going into the starting gate. Stauffenberg was laden with energy that was almost nervous.

Olbricht smiled and came around his desk. "*Graf* Stauffenberg, I'm glad to see you looking so fit and rested."

"*Herr General,*" Stauffenberg saluted and then took his superior's outstretched hand and hinted at a bow.

Olbricht indicated the round table. "I'm afraid I'll have to be brief. We are expected at the Foreign Ministry at 14:00, and I have a dozen other things on my desk that must be signed and sent out before then."

"Is the meeting at the Foreign Ministry important, then?"

"For us, yes. We're to be briefed on the plans to restore Mussolini."

That took even the debonair Stauffenberg by surprise. A second later he had guessed its significance. "With *Wehrmacht* support?"

"What else?" Olbricht countered with a cynical twist of his lips. "Which means we'll have to find the means to support yet another front with men and materiel that we do not have. Meanwhile, we must reckon with the fall of Kiev in the next few days. We can assume that Hitler will respond to the loss of such a prestigious object with new demands on the Replacement Army. However, as I presume you know, I was recently appointed head of the newly created Defense Replacement Office (*Wehrersatzamtes*). The duties associated with the new position include inspecting the production of armaments and particularly the development of new weapons. But these facilities must be located in areas less subject to bombing. I am increasingly required to conduct inspections at what seems like the end of the earth. You will therefore find your official duties here more than challenging, as you will be expected to represent me when I am away." Olbricht paused; Stauffenberg nodded.

Olbricht continued, "Furthermore, as you know, Hans Oster is still under house arrest. What you do not know is that the latest information suggests he will be expelled from the *Wehrmacht* and—if that happens—will be subject to civil justice, which means he could fall into Gestapo hands. In addition, Henning v. Tresckow has just been given command of a regiment on the Eastern Front. He is thereby completely removed from influence and planning with regard to Valkyrie."

"I should have started work two months ago."

Olbricht waved to Stauffenberg to calm down. "None of this would have changed if you'd started two months ago, and you are no good to anyone if you are too ill to think straight. The only point I am trying to make is that neither of the centers that in the past were responsible for planning, organizing, and triggering Valkyrie are operational any longer. This office must therefore assume full responsibility not only for Valkyrie, but for the initial spark as well. With my new duties requiring me to spend more time away from Berlin, that responsibility will fall primarily on your shoulders."

Their eyes met. "I hope that *Herr General* will never have reason to believe I have in any way betrayed the trust placed in me."

Olbricht leaned back in his chair. "I'm confident that you will not disappoint me, *Lieber* Stauffenberg. Now may I suggest that you go meet your Ia, Frhr. v. Feldburg. Feldburg was one of Tresckow's officers—until he got a front assignment and was badly wounded. He's had responsibility for Valkyrie—both the official and the unofficial aspects—since August. You can trust him one hundred per cent. And don't forget, we have to leave for the Foreign Ministry at 13.40 at the latest."

"*Na*? Working on High Treason?"

Philip jumped out of his skin, and then to his feet, at the sight of the officer in the doorway. He offered his hand across his desk. "Claus Stauffenberg, I presume."

"Philip Feldburg." Again Stauffenberg held out the only fingers he had left and shook hands, asking, "Which branch of the family is it?"

"Feldburg-Altdorf."

"I'm sure we must be related," Stauffenberg decided, sitting down uninvited. "Your mother?"

"Was a Gräfin Walmsdorff."

"Hm; I'll have to ask my brother Alexander. He's better at genealogy. So, how's the treason going?"

Philip considered his new Chief sidelong, and his disapproval was not completely disguised—which induced Stauffenberg to throw back his head and laugh. Then he got up, closed the door, and reseated himself. "Happier?"

"*Ja*. So," Philip started with a gesture to a row of ringed binders standing neatly in his bookcase, "Valkyrie is relatively comprehensive and provides an excellent framework for what we plan. Its greatest strength, however, is also its greatest weakness. Valkyrie exploits existing chains of command: namely, from *Generaloberst* Fromm as Commander-in-Chief of the Home Army to the various Military Districts (*Wehrkreiskommandos*) and to the various training and replacement battalions located inside the *Reich* and most importantly, in and around Berlin."

"You think that Fromm is not reliable?" Stauffenberg surmised with an amused expression.

"That, too," Philip readily admitted, "but I was actually driving at something else. The point is that the same orders, no matter how legally transmitted, will provoke very different responses in the recipients depending on their political inclinations and character." Stauffenberg leaned back and listened to his First General Staff Officer with a certain fascination. He found the contradiction between Philip's glasses, stiff posture and pedantic tone and the Knight's Cross at his throat intriguing. Here was a man who insisted on closing the door before talking to his direct superior about something they both knew they were doing, and yet he had been decorated for courage in the field three times. Stauffenberg had no field decorations, but he knew he was not afraid to do what had to be done here.

"Take, for example," Philip lectured, "an order to arrest the commanders of the Concentration Camps. An officer who has been outraged by the miscarriage of justice entailed in the establishment of such camps—or even more, an officer who has had the misfortune to know of someone unjustly confined in one of them—will inwardly applaud and carry out the order enthusiastically. But an officer who is convinced that such camps 'keep the streets safe' and help maintain the morale of the civilian population will ask: Why on earth should the KZ *Commandants* be arrested to help put down a forced laborers' revolt?"

"But an order is an order," Stauffenberg countered provocatively.

"Really?" Philip raised his eyebrows, and the harsh artificial light from the ceiling lamp glinted on his glasses. "I don't believe for a moment, *Lieber* Stauffenberg, that *you* would carry out an order you found immoral or illegal—just because it was signed by your legal superior."

Stauffenberg threw back his head and laughed appreciatively again. Philip waited for him to sober down. Stauffenberg's one eye finally met Philip's and he declared seriously, "I think we're going to work together splendidly. Now go on. What's your conclusion?"

"That the success of Valkyrie is not only a function of whether the orders go out by legal channels, but also a function of the reliability of the recipients—from our point of view."

"But we can't possibly control the personnel assignments of every recipient of Valkyrie!" Stauffenberg protested.

Philip gazed at him unwaveringly.

"Are you saying you think we have no chance of success?"

"No, not at all. Success can only be guaranteed by the reliability of the recipients, but we all know that there is never perfect success—or perfect failure. We live in an imperfect world. We cannot guarantee that all the recipients are reliable, but we can use what influence we have to establish contact with all recipients. The better the contact in advance, the more likely they are to trust us, whatever we order."

"Good. Do it," Stauffenberg agreed.

"But all the trust in the world is not enough if the preconditions have not been met. Valkyrie can only come into play at all if it has been triggered by the elimination of the C-in-C. For a start, without 100% certainty that he is dead, Fromm will not issue Valkyrie. Second, the response of the recipients is highly dependent upon that one fact. I'm not merely talking about the oath for apolitical officers—although that is undoubtedly a factor with many officers. I'm talking about the importance of this even for our supporters. *Feldmarschall* v. Kluge, for one, has personally made the elimination of the C-in-C an absolute prerequisite to his own cooperation. He made that very clear to me roughly a year ago. His reasoning is not to be dismissed: if Hitler is not dead, we will have civil war; because if Hitler is alive, we will not be in control of the armed forces—we will be fighting half of them."

"So let's shoot him," Stauffenberg returned with a shrug of his shoulders, but his one eye boring hard into Philip.

"I'm willing to try, but frankly I'm not an outstanding pistol shot—that was why Tresckow favored the joint attack, including good marksmen like Boeselager and Gersdorff. Still, if he comes through that door, I will do my best." Philip nodded to the closed door of his own office, leading out into the hall of the AHA.

Stauffenberg nodded seriously. It was obvious that Hitler was not likely ever to walk through the door.

"The problem isn't volunteers," Philip belabored the point; "it's access to him. Furthermore, I've been told all officers are required to remove their sidearms before entering the inner circle, so even those with access arrive naked of the means to take action."

Stauffenberg's three remaining fingers were drumming on Philip's desk, and his lone eye seemed to dart along the shelves. "There has to be a way," he declared fervently.

Philip nodded, but he did not share Stauffenberg's conviction.

When Alexandra still hadn't shown up to collect him at 8 pm, Philip put a call through to her office. She answered at once in a tense voice, "Feldburg, Advocate General Corps."

"Feldburg. Aren't you hungry yet?"

"Starving." She hesitated and then admitted, "Philip, I've got a new case here, and I want to finish reading the files. Go on home without me if you like."

"I have a better suggestion: I'll get something from the cafeteria and bring it up to you."

When Philip shouldered his way into her narrow office with a tray a half-hour later, Alexandra looked up gratefully. She quickly cleared a place on her desk, stacking the binders and file folders on top of each other, and then she sat back in her chair and combed her hair out of her face with her hand. "I don't know what I did to deserve you, Philip, but I am grateful."

"You look wrecked," Philip replied honestly. Since she had started working for the Chief Military Justice, Dr. Karl Sack, she not only worked longer hours, she was also more emotionally involved in her work. It was definitely taking its toll, even if her enthusiasm had compensated—at least at first.

"It's this case, Philip. It's not even something 'serious' like self-mutilation or desertion in the face of the enemy or whatever, but in a way that's what I find so depressing."

Philip indicated the tray. "Eat something before it gets any colder and dryer than it already is." Then he sat back, leaning against her bookcases and asked—to show he took her work seriously—"What is the case about?"

Alexandra spoke as she cut into the schnitzel on her plate, "A soldier on leave went to visit his girlfriend, who is doing her Labor Service. He'd sent notice in advance and had been assured that his girlfriend would be given the afternoon off. But when he arrived at noon, he was told to come back at 1:30, and then at 1:30 he was told it would be another half-hour, and then at 2 pm there was another excuse. In short, she was not released until 4 pm—for no reason. Sheer chicanery!"

Alexandra took a bite and continued, "Of course, he was supposed to have her back at camp by 9 pm. Of course, he didn't. Not that he abducted her or anything. They simply got back to the camp at around midnight. Not really such a terrible offense, do you think?"

Philip obligingly shook his head, while Alexandra managed another bite before continuing, "Of course, the camp leader made a scene. Our client—a veteran of you-know-what-better-than-I on the Eastern Front—lost his temper and called the busybody leader some impolite names. All deserved, in my opinion. And she reported *him* for insulting her uniform and thereby the NSDAP! And, Philip," Alexandra stressed, barely managing to chew and swallow in her distress, "rather than tearing up her report and telling the silly cow where to go, the Police Chief in this provincial town actually found it necessary to pursue the matter. Why? Who was really hurt?—Only our client and his girlfriend. But, no, the Police Chief felt it was his 'duty' to report the matter not only to us, but also to the Gestapo."

Alexandra pushed the empty plate away and irritably tucked her hair behind her ears. "The Gestapo not only took this ridiculous incident seriously, they decided to investigate the soldier's family. The logic was that he must have learned his disrespectful attitude toward the Regime from them. Aren't we suffering from an acute manpower shortage? Didn't you tell me recently that our divisions are on average at 65% of their required strength? How does the Gestapo have the time and resources to look into something like this?"

Philip could only shake his head. While the AHA was forced to call up older and older men for active service, and women were brought into the armed forces in ever-greater numbers to free up men for front service, the Gestapo and the Party organizations remained completely immune from the draft. For all that, Philip was more deeply moved by his wife's emotional involvement than by the facts; he was reminded that her passionate commitment to justice was one of the main reasons he was so in love with her. He was glad that he had not stood in the way of her transfer here.

"The Gestapo found 'evidence' of 'defeatism'"—Alexandra was continuing, gesturing angrily toward the files—"which they then attributed to our client. It seems that this soldier had had the nerve to tell his father that the Soviets were very good soldiers (according to the Gestapo, a lie). Furthermore, he said that the Soviets have 'limitless resources' (according to the Gestapo, a 'misleading distortion of the facts'). And worst of all, our client drew the conclusion that 'he didn't see how we could win the war.' This, of course is 'defeatism' and 'undermines the morale of the civilian population'—and so the Gestapo has told us we have to try him on both charges!"

She sighed and looked across at Philip. "I'm sorry. I know this must sound petty to you. I just can't grasp that people can be so vindictive as to pursue something as banal as this. I don't understand how we find the time and resources for this kind of thing when we are fighting for our survival on all fronts. The longer I sit at this desk, the more I realize that many of these denunciations are personal vendettas—people trying to eliminate a rival for a promotion or a job or a young man." Alexandra sighed and combed her hair out of her face with her hand again. "The leader who reported this soldier was probably only bitter about not having a boyfriend of her own!"

"Human nature can be extremely depressing, I agree, but we aren't going to change it tonight," Philip suggested with a faint smile.

Alexandra only then remembered how late it was, and noticed that Philip, too, looked exhausted. "I'm sorry!" she exclaimed sincerely. She at once stood and started efficiently putting her files away. "And I completely forgot! Your new Chief arrived today, didn't he? What's he like?"

"Charming, charismatic, an infectious laugh, sharp intelligence …" Philip fell silent, and Alexandra looked over her shoulder in the midst of putting away one of her file binders.

"Words of high praise, but I miss the enthusiasm. What is it?" She put away the last of her files and reached for her coat.

Philip stood and helped his wife into her coat before he took his own greatcoat off the hanger. "Maybe it's jealousy," he remarked as he pulled on the greatcoat.

"Because he was named Chief rather than you?"

"No, of course not!" Philip cast her a reproachful look. "I meant for his enthusiasm and optimism. He's not only completely committed to our plans, he's—" Philip paused, looking for the right word—"he's a fanatic. He seems to think that he alone can save Germany—despite the fact that better men than he have been trying for the last five years."

"Ah, one of those," Alexandra remarked, switching out the light and pulling the door to her office closed behind them.

"One of what?"

"Never mind; go on." She'd been thinking of Martin.

They started together down the dimly lit and deserted hall, Alexandra's heels providing a soprano accompaniment to the deeper thud of Philip's boots. "I don't know what else to say. He's undoubtedly competent, and he seems very adept at winning people. He had Lotte eating out of his hand in five minutes, fetching and carrying for him—she even made him *ersatz*."

"You've got to be kidding!" If there was one thing Lotte hated, it was having to "feed and clean up" after her employers. She had staunchly refused to do this for Oberst Reinhard for the last six months. (Annie took care of General Olbricht.)

Philip nodded and continued, "And not just Lotte. The same goes for the operators and the receptionists and the drivers. Quite amazing in a way—and not without its benefits for our joint project. But I hardly think it's enough to overcome the obstacles we face. When I think what Tresckow managed to organize— the explosives, Boeselager's brigade, Hitler's visit itself, and then smuggling a bomb aboard his plane unnoticed—only to have technical factors defeat his careful planning. Or when I hear from Hoepner how senior the generals and how comprehensive the plans were during the Sudeten crisis—only for the Western powers to snatch away the basis for action. It's hard for me to believe that suddenly everything is going to go our way just because Claus Stauffenberg is suddenly on our side."

"Didn't Uncle Erich say that Stauffenberg was an enthusiastic supporter of the *Führer* in 1940?"

"Apparently he even welcomed it when the *Führer* personally replaced Brauchitsch as C-in-C of the Army in December '41," Philip added in disgusted disbelief. "As late as the spring of '42, he was enthusiastic about the chances of an offensive from southern Russia and North Africa to seize Syria and Iraq!" Philip's contempt was so thick that Alexandra had to laugh. Then she put her finger to her lips as they descended the stairs to the grand exit, through the imposing square pillars and past the sentries onto the Tirpitzufer.

Outside it was dark and cold and windy, but Alexandra was happier in the open air than in the echoing corridors that seemed to have omnipresent ears. She hooked her arm through Philip's elbow and leaned against him, just to feel him warm and real beside her. "I'd say that explains a lot."

"What?"

"Your new Chief has a whole lot of mistakes and lost time he has to make up for, doesn't he?"

*   *   *   *

Berlin
October 1943

"For God's sake, be careful!" Alexandra called in alarm as, glancing up, she saw her husband climbing up a rickety ladder. She was on her hands and knees with a dustpan and sweeper, trying to clear away the chunks of plaster that had fallen from the ceiling during the raid of the night before. Much of the once heavy and elegant moldings now lay like crumbs upon the floor, and fine plaster dust iced everything.

Philip, who had started up an ancient and dubious-looking ladder, replied as he continued to climb (a none-too-heroic expression on his face), "If we don't board up these cracks, we'll freeze for weeks! You know how long it takes to get the permits for building materials and repairmen these days!" While the windows had been boarded up already, Philip's present concern was the window frames themselves, which under the pressure of nearby explosions had warped and started to come loose from the wall. Wearing an old raincoat of his father's to protect his uniform from the dust, he was intent on reducing the draft in the apartment. Dinner had been eaten in overcoats and their much-needed sleep before and after raids was endangered by the cold.

Alexandra watched uneasily as Philip worked his way up the ladder one step at a time, holding hammer and nails in one hand and with newspapers and plywood pinned under the other arm. "Couldn't Franz do that?" she asked cautiously.

"Stadthagen is hauling coal and seeing if we can't use some of these old tile ovens for the first time in 30 years." The central heating was increasingly unreliable and often off for extended periods after raids. Philip reached the second to the top step of the ladder and braced himself to start work.

Nadja, in an ill-assorted outfit of borrowed clothes, appeared in the doorway. Strands of hair were falling forward from her red print scarf, and her face was nearly as red as the scarf from evident exertion. "*Frau Baronin!* Herr Franz" (that was Stadthagen) "would like the *Herr Baron*" (Nadja for some reason was shy about addressing Philip directly and always made her requests through Alexandra if she could) "to come help him in the kitchen."

Philip cursed heartily and started his precarious way back down the steps of the ladder again. The two women watched him, Alexandra with concern and Nadja absently.

"What are you two staring at?" Philip wanted to know when he reached the foot of the ladder and noticed them.

"The Master of the House," Alexandra was quick to reply.

"You aren't exactly at your most elegant either, my dear," Philip reminded his wife, who was wearing a faded apron and a scarf tied at the base of her neck just like Nadja. They laughed.

Just then the sirens went off, and Nadja sucked in her breath in undisguised fear. Philip and Alexandra exchanged a look of unease. "Well, all right, no point in doing any more work until we see what they achieve tonight." Alix tossed down her sweeper in a gesture that could have passed for mere annoyance.

Stadthagen appeared in the doorway. He had stripped off his tunic, exposing his collarless shirt and suspenders. His shirt sleeves were rolled up and his armpits soaked. His hands and forearms were black with coal. "There's some sort of clog in the vent," he announced.

"Wash up for now and let's get to the cellar," Philip ordered mildly.

Lotte, in attire similar to Alexandra's, came out of the dining room, sweeping the scarf from her head and shaking loose her long blonde hair. She acted as if she were genuinely grateful that the impending air raid freed her of the tedious cleanup work. "We have time for a cigarette first, don't we?" she asked generally, adding with a sour look at Philip, "Your block warden is such a bloody tyrant about not letting anyone smoke in the cellar."

Philip's feelings for Lotte were mixed. He knew she was a loyal friend to Alix and not as stupid as she pretended, but there were times when her mannerisms grated on his nerves. This was one of them. In a polite tone he replied, "You're welcome to stay here and smoke right through the raid, if you like. It might even be a good idea. If something starts to burn, you'll be right here to put the fire out."

Seydlitz, arriving from the study at this moment, was quick to urge Lotte to think of her safety and volunteered to stay in the apartment 'if the *Herr Oberstleutnant*' wanted someone to put out fires. Philip accepted the rebuke from his subordinate silently, while Lotte quipped back, "Safety? In our cellar? You must be joking. That is nothing but a common grave. Safety can only be found in the bunkers they built for themselves, those bastards!" She lit up her cigarette and blew smoke from her nostrils like an angry dragon.

"Careful, Lotte," Alix warned despite her amusement; "that sounds dangerously close to treason."

Lotte only made a low growling sound in reply and then ground out her cigarette in a porcelain ashtray. In a group they collected their prepacked suitcases of vital necessities and precious possessions and traipsed down to the cellar.

Most of the other tenants were already in the cellar, including the Moldenauers, although Peter Kessler was notably absent this evening. A clatter at the door announced the arrival of two of the nurses who lived in one of the third-floor flats. They were still in uniform and evidently came straight from the hospital. "Thank God!" one exclaimed. "I couldn't bear the thought of another night in the hospital cellar!"

"Isn't it safer than here?" one of the other tenants, Frau Baumann, asked, astonished.

"What? Not a bit! Besides, if a nurse is there, no one asks if she's on duty or not. We're just expected to help regardless! What do they think we are? Saints? We're not even nuns!"

"Soldiers at the front don't have shifts and can't say they're off duty," one of the elder men, Herr Seeger, reminded them with a frown, admonishing with an upraised finger.

"That's their tough luck. We're only human, you know," the girl snapped back rudely, as she plopped herself down on a bench.

Outside, the flak had already started when Nurse Tuchel primly descended the stairs. She carried her suitcase of belongings and moved without haste. Lotte shook her head in admiration and Philip muttered under his breath to his wife, "Nerves of a plough horse."

Alexandra took a deep breath and held tight to Philip's hand. The mixture of emotions that possessed her was hard to sort out. She felt an undeniable fear that was cold and physical, but she also felt a selfish relief that Philip was with her. She even had the vaguely romantic thought that she would rather die with him than live on alone. Last but not least, however, she felt childish anger at the thought that they, who had never wanted this war and were doing all they could to stop it, might still be victims of it, no less than the fanatical Nazis around them.

Marianne's nerves started showing as soon as the familiar "symphony" of the air raid unfolded. The detonations came nearer and then veered off again. The light swayed and flickered to the distant bark of flak and then, out of nowhere, a series of explosions cracked and pounded, seemingly directly overhead. The ceiling plaster rained down on them, and everyone in the cellar grabbed someone else. The light went out entirely. "Hail Mary, full of grace," a female voice prayed in a high whine, while a flood of words in Ukrainian came from Nadja.

"Where's the torch, Pfalz?" Philip demanded of the block warden.

A trembling flashlight came on and then jumped and flickered as a new series of explosions shook the room to a new shower of dust and plaster. The baker's assistant, who had recently been billeted with the Moldenauers along with her mother and aunt, got down from one of the bunk beds set up in the cellar. She sat herself between her mother and her aunt and all three waited, locked in an embrace. Marianne was visibly trembling from head to foot, despite her mother's attempt to soothe her by stroking her arm and hand. Stadthagen had his arm around Nadja, who was virtually sitting in his lap.

Then again the explosions receded. A collective sigh of relief swept the cellar as they registered they had been spared this time. Even the regular light came on again, and Theo could switch off the flashlight. An irrepressible need to talk seemed to seize half the inmates of the cellar; they started talking at once. The nurses debated whether this had been as bad as some other raid they'd experienced in the hospital. Herr Baumann, an aging insurance company employee from the fourth floor, remarked in an ambiguous tone, "If they don't hurry up with the Miracle Weapons, there won't be much of Berlin left!"

"Then we'll rebuild more grandly than ever," Frau Gieseler informed her neighbor definitively. "And *their* cities will be leveled, absolutely leveled, so there's nothing left to rebuild!"

"We've been waiting for that for years!" Marianne exploded, not yet recovered from the effect of the raid on her overwrought nerves. Her voice and hands still trembled. "A year ago we were before Stalingrad, and now the Russians have recaptured Kiev!"

"Calm down, child, calm down," Prof. Dr. Moldenauer tried to calm his daughter. "You're overwrought, that's all." Turning to the others, he reminded them pleadingly, "You know she was nearly killed in an air raid, and ever since ..."

"Understandable," Frau Bauman agreed.

"Yes, but she should still have more faith in the *Führer*," Frau Gieseler declared reprovingly. "*You* should have given her more faith in the *Führer*," she pointedly told the grey-haired professor, feeling smug and superior.

"Yes, yes, I'm sorry, I know." Prof. Dr. Moldenauer gratefully took the blame on himself—anything to stop Frau Gieseler from making a scene about Marianne's foolish remarks.

Frau Gieseler nodded smugly and readjusted herself on the hard bench, but Nurse Tuchel wasn't satisfied. "How do you know Kiev has fallen?" she asked in a slow, ominous voice. "It wasn't in the *Wehrmacht* Report."

Suddenly one could have heard a pin drop in the cellar, despite the distant rumble and roar of the still ongoing air raid. Marianne sat between her parents, pale and trembling. Her parents were paralyzed, lamed by the accusation—the fatal accusation—that hung in the dusty air. If the fall of Kiev hadn't been announced by the *Wehrmacht*, one could only have heard about it by listening to enemy broadcasts—a capital crime.

"Maybe it wasn't Kiev," Marianne muttered unconvincingly. "Maybe it was someplace else. I don't remember exactly. And now the Italians have declared war on us as well," she tried to change the subject.

"That's only because those filthy traitors threw out Mussolini!" Frau Baumann declared, adding eagerly, "Now that we've rescued Mussolini, things will turn around again."

"Yes, exactly," Alexandra picked up the unwitting lead. "And we're sending first-rate divisions there, too, experienced divisions from Russia. They'll put things right."

"The Italians aren't bad fighters," Philip made his contribution, "just poorly led."

"They're so temperamental," Lotte proclaimed; "their defeatism was probably just a mood. I once sang with an Italian opera singer; you must have heard of him …" Lotte launched into a story, leaning forward and gesturing dramatically. In a moment, she had them all enthralled—whether with wonder or disapproval didn't matter. Her tales from the glamorous world of opera distracted everyone from Marianne. Only Nadja, who could not follow so much German, contented herself with snuggling deeper into a corner with Stadthagen. The latter, his back turned to the others, devoted himself entirely to her. Lotte's diversion was so successful, in fact, that by the time the all-clear sounded, Alexandra was more concerned about Stadthagen's all-too-obvious flirting with Nadja than about Marianne.

Upstairs they found new layers of dust and new chunks of ceiling plaster, and saw that many of the pictures had fallen from the walls. Worst of all, the last of the chandeliers lay smashed in the middle of the salon.

For a horrified moment Philip stood staring at the shambles, and in his mind he saw the way this salon had looked when his grandfather had entertained *Graf* Zeppelin in the fateful summer of 1914. He'd only been five at the time and should have been in bed, but he'd sneaked out of bed to catch a glimpse of the great man. The guests had been in formal dress, and the light from the chandelier had glinted on the ladies' jewels and on the epaulettes and braid on the uniforms. Compared to the glitter of the *Kaiserreich*, his father's parties had seemed sober and modest: the men in black tails and the ladies' dresses tailored and under-stated. And now there was nothing but a heap of shattered crystal coated with plaster dust in the middle of a boarded-up and dilapidated room.

Alexandra went down on her knees in distress, desperately looking for intact pieces.

Philip held out his hand to her. "Leave it. We need to get some rest."

"Doesn't it hurt?" she asked, looking up at him. "They're your family's trea-sures."

"Yes," he admitted, "but I try to remind myself they're just things."

"What good does it do to destroy innocent things?" Alexandra burst out. She was feeling guilty for not having dismantled all the chandeliers and sent them home to Altdorf. It hurt, too, to see things she had never been able to afford shat-tered and broken like this. "This destruction—this senseless destruction—doesn't shorten the war a single day! Don't they know that? The English claimed that the bombing of London only strengthened civilian morale. Why do they think we're any different?" She seemed close to tears, and Philip loved her for that. He was suddenly aware of just how much he loved her, and his body responded with desire.

He held out his hand again, answering her protest automatically, "Because they can send 10 times as many planes and drop 100 times the explosives, they think they can break us."

"Us—but not them. They have their safe bunkers, just as Lotte said," Alix flung back, her fingers taking now one and now another of the crystals in her hand in despair.

"Come, Alix, we can't change anything here tonight," he repeated more urgently.

With a sigh, she left the shattered crystal behind and went to Philip. He put his arms around her, hardly daring to breathe. For a moment they stood together, Alix resting her head on his chest and Philip gazing over her shoulder, aware only of the familiar but almost forgotten quickening of his loins.

"We could at least remove the paintings from the frames and send them to safety, "Alexandra suggested.

Philip bent and kissed her. "Don't worry about it," he muttered as he closed his lips over hers.

Alexandra felt as if an electric shock had gone through her. His kiss was hot and demanding, not at all like the brotherly kisses she had become accustomed to. Alexandra pulled back a little and looked up at him questioningly. Philip met her gaze, a smile playing at the corners of his lips. "There are things more important than things, don't you think?"

"Philip?"

He took her hand and led her to their bedroom. Here, too, a layer of dust and broken plaster lay like a light snow across the furnishings and floor, but because the moldings were more modest, they had not fallen down yet. The window here was still intact, making the room comparatively warm. Philip closed the door behind them and pulled Alexandra back into his arms. They kissed again, and Alexandra started to feel dizzy as the blood rushed through her veins. Philip led her to the bed. "I guess Dr. Sauerbruch knew what he was talking about after all."

CHAPTER 36

▼

Berlin
November 1943

The Moldenauers had just settled down to Sunday lunch when the doorbell rang.

"Now who can that be at this time?" Frau Moldenauer asked, annoyed. It was just after 1 pm—a time when civilized people were expected to be sitting down to the midday meal and, therefore, a time when civilized people did not disturb their neighbors or friends. The bell rang again, loudly and insistently.

"Marianne, go and see who it is, and tell them we are just sitting down to lunch," Prof. Dr. Moldenauer ordered. Marianne dutifully went to the door.

From the dining room, as Frau Moldenauer ladled out the soup into the china bowls, they listened. They heard what sounded like several people push past Marianne into the hallway where their voices—loud and harsh—rang out clearly. "We're looking for Marianne Moldenauer."

The parents exchanged a horrified look. Frau Moldenauer dropped the ladle and didn't even notice that it splashed soup onto the clean tablecloth. Prof. Dr. Moldenauer got to his feet, his face pale.

"I'm Marianne Moldenauer," Marianne admitted uncertainly.

"Secret State Police!"

"Oh my God!" Frau Moldenauer collapsed, and though her husband tried to catch her, he wasn't quick or strong enough. She sank onto the floor.

"Help! Marianne! It's your mother! Come quick!"

Marianne appeared, saw what had happened, and ran across the room to help her father. The two strange Gestapo officials stood in the doorway watching.

"My God! My God!" Marianne's father was beside himself. "It's her heart. She has a weak heart!"

"No, I think she's just fainted." Marianne tried to calm her father.

From the doorway came a sharp voice. One of the two men ordered the other to call an ambulance. At once the second man crossed to the telephone and dialed the emergency number. He gave the address and hung up.

"Leave her there," the first man ordered Marianne. "The ambulance will be here shortly. Come with us."

"But—"

"Do you want to be charged with resisting arrest?"

The room started to swim around her. Marianne got to her feet only with difficulty. "But I've got to get some things," she stammered.

"We'll send for them if necessary. Hurry up."

"You can't just come in here and take my daughter away," Prof. Dr. Moldenenauer protested. "Where is the warrant for her arrest? What are the charges?" The Gestapo men were leading her out of the room, and Prof. Dr. Moldenauer couldn't leave his unconscious wife to follow them. He had to raise his voice to call after them, "My wife has a heart condition. My son is serving in the *Wehrmacht*. My daughter—doesn't she have the right to a lawyer?"

Marianne couldn't help her father. It took all her strength and self-control to go with the two Gestapo officers, to take her coat off the hanger and pull it on. She did not even hear or register what her father was saying, much less the short, unfriendly replies of the police. Her mind was numb. How had this happened? Had one of her forgeries been inadequate? Had the man or woman caught with false ID revealed where they had gotten it? But that was never Marianne herself. Had the pastor of her church himself been arrested? The door opened before her, and one of the men took a firm hold of her arm above her elbow. His grip was so harsh that it hurt her even through her winter overcoat. He pushed her down the stairs. He pushed her past Theo Pfalz's open door and down the icy, ash-covered walk to the street. Here he shoved her into a waiting BMW.

In the back seat of the BMW she sat squeezed between the two officials. Neither was as young as Peter Kessler. Glancing at them sideways, Marianne saw men in long leather coats with turned-up collars and brimmed hats. One had cropped grey hair and heavy jowls. The other had a Hitler mustache and a mole on his ear. They were staring straight ahead as if they were driving the car themselves. Neither said a word or spared her a glance. The driver apparently already knew their destination.

Marianne was relieved when she registered that they were not driving to Gestapo headquarters in the Prinz-Albrecht-Strasse. They stopped instead before an elegant apartment house on a residential/commercial side street near the Kurfürstendamm. Marianne was hustled out of the car and stood before the door, still gripped harshly by the one official and flanked by both of them. They rang the bell long and insistently—from habit, no doubt. There was a long wait and then the buzzer sounded. One of the escorting officials pushed open the door and they entered a cool, dark marble entryway that seemed completely intact. Was the Gestapo even immune from Allied air raids? Marianne wondered in amazement.

The door fell shut behind them, and Marianne was pushed into the iron cage of the elevator. The elevator groaned up two flights and then the door rolled open. The Gestapo escort rang another bell, and another buzzer announced that the lock had been released from the inside.

Marianne found herself in a reception area. A woman shoved some papers toward the two officials. They signed. Marianne was required to hand over her ID and then told to take a seat. The men who had brought her disappeared. She sat alone in the room, ignored by the woman at the reception desk. The clock ticked loudly.

Marianne's thoughts went back to trying to imagine who had been caught and how she had been discovered. She tried to think of some defense, but it was impossible without knowing what they already knew. If she denied something they could document, she would only discredit herself. If she gave away facts or names they hadn't already discovered, she would endanger the freedom and lives of others. Did she dare ask to see Peter? How would he react if he learned she had lied to him, misused his trust, compromised him? Would he be able to forgive her? Was his love so great? Or had he ordered the arrest? A chill went through her.

For months Peter had been urging her to give up her atelier because—under the rafters—it was the most endangered of all locations in an air raid. Houses not directly hit by the bombs often caught fire from blown sparks. Peter kept urging her to bring her "things" down and store them in his apartment. He had room enough, he insisted. They'd had several spats and one real argument about it in which he'd threatened to go to the air-raid warden and get her "officially expelled." Had he maybe obtained a key from Frhr. v. Feldburg? Had he been to her atelier and seen what she really did up there?

Or was it the ID she'd lost in the air raid that had never been reclaimed? But that had been almost a year ago. Surely they couldn't be that inefficient. Or had they been shadowing her all this time, waiting for enough evidence to arrest her? Had Peter been writing regular reports about her?

Marianne was so hot she was nearly nauseated. She took off her coat and folded it over her arm on her lap.

The telephone on the receptionist's desk rang, and the woman picked it up. "Yes … yes." She hung up. "You are to go in to Inspector Zielinski now." She indicated a closed door with a brass nameplate.

Marianne entered a large rectangular room with a Persian carpet covering nearly the whole floor. On the fresh white walls hung gold-framed pictures of Hitler and Himmler. A huge desk, which stretched nearly the width of the room, faced her at the far end. The only windows were behind the desk, so that the man sitting in front of them was an ominous silhouette.

To one side, under the picture of Himmler, was a smaller, utilitarian desk with a sour-looking secretary. Apparently she was to record the interrogation. She sat with sharpened pencils lined up next to her steno pad. A typewriter was pushed to one side.

Marianne walked the seemingly eternal distance from the door to the chair that was placed at a slight angle before the large desk. She sat down at a gesture from the Inspector.

From close up, Marianne could make out the Inspector's features: a handsome man in his mid-forties with short salt-and-pepper hair over a square, tanned face.

"Frl. Moldenauer?"

"Yes."

"Resident in Berlin-Kreuzberg?"

"Yes."

"I presume the date and place of birth on your ID are correct."

"Yes."

"Are you still enrolled at the university?"

"Yes."

"School of Medicine?"

"Medical drawing is my actual field of specialty."

"Um hum. You aren't a member of the *Nationalsozialistische Studentenbund.*" (National Socialist Student League)

"I don't have time. I've had a lot of trouble with my studies."

"Girls don't have the brains to study—much less medicine. You would do more good for your country by getting pregnant and giving the *Führer* a child every year."

As this was not a question, Marianne chose not to respond.

The inspector returned to the questioning. "If you have no time for the *Studentenbund*, how is it you have time for the Church?"

"Man does not live by bread alone."

"Why the Confessing Church?"

"I'm a devout Christian."

"But why the Confessing Church? Why not the German Church? Aren't you a patriotic German?" For the first time, the inspector's tone was aggressive, hostile.

"Of course I'm a patriotic German."

"Then why don't you belong to the German Church?"

Marianne shrugged, but she swallowed at the same time. Her face betrayed that her pretence of nonchalance was sheer bluff. "I prefer the pastors of the Confessing Church."

With a sneer the inspector retorted, "Because they are all pacifists and Jew-lovers?"

"Are they?"

"How many of the parishioners of your church are Jews?"

"None of them. All parishioners are Christians, or they wouldn't be in church at all."

"Jews will do anything to save their own fat skins. Hypocrisy and blasphemy are nothing to them."

Marianne forced herself to appear indifferent, to sit calmly. Regardless of what this man said, regardless of how crude or odious he became, she had to retain the appearance of indifference. But the Inspector realized that she had steeled herself against his provocation and changed tack at once.

"How did you know Kiev had fallen on the night of Oct. 6 when it wasn't announced in the *Wehrmacht* Report until Oct. 10th?"

"I didn't know. I was upset and I got confused. The reports had talked about fighting near Kiev."

"Have Smolensk and Kremenchug fallen?"

"No."

"Yes, they have! It was announced in the *Wehrmacht* Report on the 19th of this month!"

"I don't know Soviet geography very well."

"What does that have to do with it? Don't you listen to the *Wehrmacht* Reports?"

"Yes, but it just doesn't mean that much to me."

"WHAT?" The man roared and half-leaped out of his chair in apparent rage. Marianne gasped in surprise and pulled back in her chair. "What?" he repeated in outrage. "The news of our glorious Fighting Forces and their courageous struggle to protect you 'doesn't mean very much' to you?"

"I only meant that the various Russian names don't mean much to me."

And so the interrogation went on for the next two hours. The inspector's tone ranged from bored to furious, from contemptuous to patronizing, and through it all, Marianne didn't know if she were behaving correctly or not. She wasn't sure if her stupid slip about Kiev during the air raid was the core or the periphery of the interrogation. If it were the core it was bad enough; it could cost her and her parents their heads. But the questions kept coming back to the Confessing Church, too, and Marianne began to fear that something about her activities there had been discovered.

"Where did you get to know so many Jews?"

"I don't know any Jews."

"No?" the inspector mocked surprise. "Then how is it that you sent off 23 packages to Jews in the Riga and Warsaw ghettos in the last 4 months?"

Marianne opened her mouth, but no answer came out. Trapped! If she didn't know the people she had sent the packages to, where did she have the names and addresses?

"Well?" the man barked louder.

Marianne swallowed. "I knew one family …"

"These packages weren't to one family! What do you think we are? Idiots?" He slapped his hand on the desktop. "Stop lying and start cooperating, or your life is going to get much more unpleasant!"

"I'm not lying. You didn't let me finish. I knew one family and they sent me the names of their friends."

"And you spent your money and time collecting things for Jews you didn't even know?!"

Marianne felt her throat cramp. The packages came from all sorts of well-meaning Christians who wanted to do their little bit to help the Jews, but were too timid to send the packages themselves. They had brought her extra food, soap, detergent, toothpaste and aspirin—all the desperately needed necessities of daily life that the Jews could not obtain in their overcrowded ghettos. If Marianne admitted that, she would betray all those well-meaning people. But if she said she had sent it all on her own, they would know she was lying, because she could never have obtained so many rationed goods in four weeks—unless she was dealing on the black market. But how could they know what was in the packages? "Yes," Marianne managed to croak out. "Yes, I did," she admitted, adding daringly, "It's not illegal."

"Why are you so interested in the Jews? What kind of a pervert are you?" the inspector retorted. "How does a good German girl get so corrupted by this filth? This racial pest! Did some Jew rape you perhaps? Turn you into his whore?"

Marianne blushed so violently that the inspector backed off, apparently embarrassed by his own crudity. "Go wait in the hall!" he ordered with a wave of his hand.

Marianne virtually ran out of the room. She could hardly believe her good luck. But sitting opposite the disinterested receptionist, her euphoria faded. She hadn't really escaped the question about her interest in the Jews. He would ask it again. And she didn't have an answer. Her stomach growled aloud. The receptionist cast her a disgusted look.

"I was brought here just before I sat down to lunch," Marianne explained.

"What's that to me?" the woman responded sourly.

"Please, may I be allowed to get something to eat?"

"No," the woman told her brusquely and turned her attention back to the novel she was reading.

Marianne forced herself to concentrate again on the question about the packages and her interest in the Jews, but the door to Inspector Zielinski's office opened, and the secretary who had taken the notes called Marianne back into the office. When Marianne was seated before the Inspector's desk again, he pushed a typed transcript of her interrogation at her and told her to sign it.

"May I read it first?"

"Of course." He leaned back in his chair.

Marianne read carefully. She searched for some thread that revealed what they knew about her—and she tried to memorize her own answers so that she would not contradict herself in the future. When she came to the end, she found that the last set of questions had been deleted. She signed the transcript.

The inspector pushed a button on his desk, and the two men who had arrested her reappeared. The inspector nodded his head in their direction and Marianne obediently went to them. They gestured her out of the room, past the receptionist and out into the hall. "But I don't have my ID back," she protested.

The stocky man with close-cropped hair laughed outright. The man with the melancholy Hitler mustache looked at her pityingly. The former gripped her by the arm again and directed her into the elevator. As it sank back down the center of the stairwell, her brief hope of release faded.

Outside, the car waited. Again she was hustled inside, again flanked by her silent escort in the back seat. When the car turned left from the Anhalter Bahnhof in the direction of the Prinz-Albrecht-Strasse, a terror so powerful gripped Marianne that she stiffened, and both her companions turned to stare at her. Neither of them laughed this time, and the one with the mustache really seemed to pity her. But they did not stop at the Prinz-Albrecht-Strasse with its notorious cellars. Instead they drove on to the women's prison in the Lehrter Strasse. The two police officials brought her to the reception area and turned her over to the female warden.

Marianne could grasp this situation even less than her arrest. Ever since she had started her illegal work, she had accepted the possibility of being picked up by the Gestapo. She had half imagined interrogations—and imagined them to be much worse than what she had just experienced. She had imagined windowless rooms with bright lights directed at her. She had imagined being tied to a chair while men in boots with riding crops prowled around her, shouting questions at her. She had imagined being slapped and spit at. But she had never imagined herself as a criminal.

But here she was confronted by hardened, professional prison wardens who looked at her as if she were a thief, a murderer or a prostitute. She was ordered to strip. Hesitantly she removed her clothing down to her underwear, but this was not enough. "All the way," one of the women told her coldly.

Marianne removed her underwear and stood stark naked in the cold room, her feet cringing on the dirty, cement floor and her arms crossed helplessly across her nubile breasts.

"Bend over."

"What?"

"Deaf or just dumb? I told you to bend over."

Marianne bent over, never imagining what would happen next. One of the wardens went behind her and with her cold, calloused hands pulled Marianne's buttocks apart. She slipped a gnarled finger inside her vagina and felt around inside, apparently looking for something. The unexpectedness of this humiliating probe made Marianne gag in revulsion. Not even in the RAD had she undergone such degradation!

The inspection of her body complete, the woman moved away. Marianne stood upright again, but was so ashamed she could not meet the eyes of the wardens. She was handed rough but clean prison garments and told to put these on. She was allowed her own underwear. After she had dressed in the striped prison clothes, she was ordered to sign a chit listing all the belongings that she had brought with her. These were sealed in an envelope. "Any questions?"

"What are the charges?"

The woman behind the desk shrugged.

"Do I have a right to make a telephone call?"

"Don't make me laugh."

"Can I write a letter? At least send for a toothbrush and comb?"

"I'll have to check."

"May I have something to eat? I haven't eaten since breakfast."

"You'll get the regular evening meal."

With that, the formalities were over. Marianne was led out of the office, up two flights of metal stairs and along an iron balcony lined with cells—numbers and barred windows. She was halted before the door numbered 548. The guard opened the door with her key and held it open for Marianne. She went in. The door clanged behind her. The key turned in the lock.

There was a fold-down desk, a stool, an iron-framed, fold-down rope bed that had no mattress or blankets, a wash basin and an open, seatless toilet. There was a barred window over her head with filthy glass and one broken pane that let in the bitter November air. Over the wash basin was posted a list of regulations (according to paragraph so-and-so of such-and-such law, the inmate was forbidden from and required to …) Marianne sank onto the stool and stared around herself in disbelief. It couldn't be true.

It took Peter Kessler a whole day to secure Marianne's release. At every stage of his struggle, he kept Marianne's parents informed. And as soon as he got word that she'd signed out of the Lehrter Prison, he put a call through to Prof. Dr. Moldenauer, saying that Marianne was on her way home. Frau Moldenauer sat watching from the front window, and at the sight of Marianne climbing out of a taxi in the street below, she jumped up and ran to open the door. When Marianne saw her standing in the open door, she ran the rest of the way upstairs and flung herself into her mother's arms. Then she turned to her father, who assured her that her mother had indeed only fainted, not had a heart attack. Guiltily, Marianne registered that she had not given her poor mother a thought during her more than 24 hours in Gestapo custody.

"Herr Kessler called as soon as he knew you were on your way," Professor Dr. Moldenauer was continuing. "I can't say enough for that young man. I'll never be able to thank him enough."

"And how he loves you, dear," Marianne's mother put in proudly. "There aren't many girls who can win such selfless devotion. I swear, he was nearly as distressed as we were. A gentleman, a real gentleman. He'll be here for dinner—if he can't get away sooner."

"Here?" Marianne asked for confirmation. Her parents had up to now studiously avoided inviting Peter into their apartment.

"Yes, and now that you're home and I've seen you with my own eyes, I'll go buy some things before the shops are empty." Frau Dr. Moldenauer hugged her daughter again in relief.

Alone with her, Prof. Moldenauer looked more sternly at his daughter. "I hope this has taught you a lesson. From now on I trust you will be more careful about what you say, although I honestly don't know how I'll ever be able to face Nurse Tuchel again without spitting in her face!"

"Nurse Tuchel reported me? For the remark about Kiev?"

"Didn't they tell you that?"

"No. And—and how did Peter get me out?"

"He didn't tell us how. You'll have to ask him yourself."

When Peter rang the bell for dinner, Marianne went to the door herself to let him in. She had bathed and washed her hair and put on her best silk dress. Her hair was pulled back from her face by little gold barrettes, but fell long and wavy to her shoulders. She even brushed some rouge on her cheeks and applied lipstick.

Peter stood on the landing holding the largest bouquet of flowers she had ever seen in her life. At the sight of her, however, he forgot everything except his relief. He flung his arms around her and pulled her close. "Marianne!"

She clung to him and lifted her lips for his kiss, but her heart pounded with fear. His relief was too great for comfort. It suggested that he had not been sure his influence was great enough to get her out.

He held her to his chest and murmured, "Marianne, Marianne. Promise me that you will NEVER listen to enemy broadcasts again. Please. I know your father does it. I—I know you don't see anything wrong with it. But look what happened. If this happens again, I don't know if I can help you. Please promise me!"

Marianne nodded. She could not only promise this—she was willing to keep her promise. This wasn't her important work. "I promise, Peter. Now come in and meet my parents properly. They are so grateful to you."

The dinner went very well indeed. The Moldenauers could find no fault in Peter Kessler after what he'd done. Indeed, once they had removed the blinders of their own prejudice, they discovered what their daughter had seen in him all along. He was polite and earnest, but with a love of life and flashes of shy humor that were endearing. Frau Moldenauer would later tell everyone that she had never met such a well-brought-up young man in all her life. He'd jumped to help her carry things, and he at once offered to help with the various repairs, left unfinished from the last bad raid, which the professor could not manage himself.

Prof. Dr. Moldenauer was endeared by the way Kessler admired the library and showed concern for saving the "precious books" from the raids. Kessler even offered to find some place to store the books in safety, if the Moldenauers did not themselves have friends or relatives willing to store the books.

Alone in the library (while Marianne and her mother cleared away the dinner dishes), Peter at last found the courage to broach the subject nearest to his heart. "Prof. Dr. Moldenauer, I—I have been meaning to talk to you for some time, and I'm sorry that—that there had to be this terrible incident first, but I—I think you know that my interest in Marianne is not just some light fancy."

"No, Herr Kessler, you've proved that."

"Then you understand, Prof. Dr. Moldenauer, that my intentions are very much the best. I—with your permission, Prof. Dr. Moldenauer—I would like to marry your daughter."

"That pleases me, Herr Kessler." Prof. Moldenauer held out his hand and, when Kessler put his own in it, he clasped his other hand on top. "It really pleases me to think that my Marianne has won the heart of such a good man. Furthermore, I want to apologize to you for my earlier reticence. I hope you can forgive me—as an old man—for being too stiff-necked and stuck in my ways."

"But of course, Prof. Dr. Moldenauer. I understand perfectly. I mean, Marianne has told me how unfairly you were treated by your colleagues and students. I don't approve of such crude methods at all, Prof. Dr. Moldenauer. It is perfectly normal that after such unpleasant experiences you would—ah—be reluctant to trust someone in my position."

"Can I offer you a cigar to celebrate? And, of course, you must use the familiar form of address with me now."

The sirens went off.

The raid that night concentrated on points farther west in the city, and when the all-clear sounded, the residents of the Feldburg house returned to apartments which had suffered no new damage. As it was not yet midnight, Peter asked his future in-laws if they didn't want to join him in his flat for a glass of wine to celebrate the engagement. Prof. Dr. Moldenauer, with a glance at his wife, declined. They could celebrate on another night. For now, they needed their sleep.

"You don't mind if I go up to Peter's for a glass of wine, do you?" Marianne asked.

"No, of course not, dear." Her parents kissed her good night. Marianne and Peter climbed the stairs arm in arm.

As soon as they closed the door behind him, they were in each other's arms. Marianne went on tiptoe and pressed up against Peter. "I love you," she kept whispering between kisses. "How can I ever thank you enough?"

Peter had an answer which he did not dare put into words, but he had the feeling she knew it before she asked. After all, she had asked to come up here. They found their way to the bedroom without a light. Marianne dispensed with her clothes even before Peter finished undressing. She lay back on the bed and held her arms out to him with an expression that was eager and excited. Peter was a little nervous, but she so obviously wanted this that he overcame his embarrassment.

Their inexperience heightened their excitement. For Marianne it was the first time, and for Peter very nearly so. He'd only had two rather pathetic sexual encounters during his studies. They knew only enough to get the mechanics right, and were both separately surprised by how soon everything seemed to be over. Marianne assumed that she was different from other girls, too intellectual, etc., to really enjoy sex the way they seemed to. Peter, when he recovered from the sheer mind-blowing ecstasy of it, was frightened by his own courage. "Marianne? Are you all right?" he asked timidly.

"Yes, fine." But she got off the bed and disappeared in the direction of the bathroom with her clothes. She reemerged fully dressed. "I'd better go back downstairs, or my parents might start to wonder."

Peter nodded; he pulled on his trousers and saw her to the door. "I'll get you a ring and we can publish an announcement in the papers," he told her.

She nodded, gave him a quick kiss on the cheek, and started to open the door. Then she closed it again. "Peter?"

"Yes?"

"How did you spring me?"

"Oh," he shrugged a little nervously, "I said you had the information about Kiev from me. But it won't work a second time," he warned at once. "They didn't really believe me. Why *do* you go to the Confessing Church?"

"I like the people," Marianne countered, avoiding his eyes by turning away from him.

"When we marry, you'll have to give up the Church," Peter told her firmly. Now that she was his, he felt it was time he clarified a few things.

"Why?" Marianne demanded sharply, turning back.

"You know the Leadership disapproves of religion. It would be disastrous for my career if you were a practicing Christian—much less in the Confessing Church!"

"Well, then, maybe we shouldn't get married after all!" Marianne decided.

Peter was flabbergasted. "Marianne! You can't mean that!"

"I'm not going to give up the Church for you or anyone!"

"Marianne!"

She opened the door and ran down the steps without a backward glance, leaving Peter in frustrated confusion behind her.

*   *   *   *

Warsaw
November 1943

The news that the Red Army was within just 100 km of the eastern border of the Government General sent Theresa into a new panic. "Why doesn't the *Wehrmacht do* something?" she demanded in a voice strained from a sleepless night. "Where is the SS? Where are the Miracle Weapons?"

Walther refolded his newspaper with a crack and set it down next to his place setting at the breakfast table. He considered his wife silently and—for the first time in a long time—objectively. Theresa had put on roughly 30 pounds in the last five years—almost as much as he had. Her once perfect oval face was now marred by a double chin. The thick, dark hair that had crowned her head with glistening braids at their wedding hung in ill-kept strands. Her eyes, once so wide with admiration for him, were filled with fear.

"You know perfectly well that the *Wehrmacht* and the SS have fought magnificently, but the Russians are now being supplied by the Americans and have limitless resources. We have had to give ground so we can regroup and go over to a flexible defense," he told her patiently, quoting his friends from the Party.

"Flexible defense? What's that supposed to mean? Just how much more land are we going to surrender? When are we going to finally stop the Red Army?!" Theresa was hoarse, the start of a head cold induced by the sleepless night. Her head ached. Her throat ached. Her limbs ached. She was at the end of her strength, and all she got from her husband were these empty phrases. "Why can't we go home?" Theresa asked in tear-filled voice. She wanted to go back to Stuttgart, back to the little factory safe inside the *Reich*. She wanted to go back to being a happy young bride.

"You know why," Walther snapped back, his face closed to her as he got to his feet to indicate he refused to discuss this again. He spoke bluntly. "Everything we have is here. In the *Reich* we would be paupers—not to mention that I'd be eligible for the draft. I expected more courage from a woman with your blood. Your brothers, whatever else one can say about them, are not cowards." Theresa had disgraced him when she'd fled for home during the Ghetto uprising. Aggstein had warned him then that her flight had been viewed as "defeatism" and noted negatively throughout the senior ranks of the Administration of the Government General. Walther did not want a repeat of that. He did not want Theresa to leave Warsaw now.

"I have three young children to think of," Theresa whined, her breath catching and her nose starting to run.

"Good heavens, Theresa, you'd think you were the only mother in all Warsaw! I don't see the wives of the other German officials fleeing in panic. Now I have to get to the office." Walther strode out of the breakfast room, calling for his driver, leaving a shattered Theresa behind him. No matter how she looked at it, it was clear that Walther cared more about his factories and his status than he cared about her and the children. Being married to an ambitious man didn't look so desirable anymore.

Seated comfortably in the back of his car, Walther consciously turned his thoughts away from Theresa and her increasing hysteria. He focused instead on another pressing problem: the decreasing efficiency of his KZ workers. Whereas just six months ago, the average weight of his male workers had been roughly 120 lbs, it was now down to 110. With female workers the drop was even more dramatic, from 100 to 85 lbs. Furthermore, despite a sharpening of discipline and an increase in the number of Latvian overseers, actual production had dropped on a per capita basis.

Walther was more and more convinced that he was going to have to invest in measures to improve the physical condition of his laborers, or else face a continued decline in productivity. He was, however, extremely reluctant to invest at this time, because he was not fool enough to believe the official assessment of the military situation. It was, of course, possible that the new Miracle Weapons would send the advancing Red Army to oblivion. It was considerably more believable that the new weapons and German courage would bring the enemy to a halt and force Stalin to negotiate a separate peace. But it was not certain that either of these scenarios would occur. Walther, therefore, was anxious to hedge his bets.

Rather than investing more in his facilities here in Warsaw, he would have preferred to build up his secret Swiss bank account.

The guards at the gate to this factory recognized his car as it came around the corner, and one of the sentries, a submachine gun over his shoulder, opened the gates for *Herr Director*. As Walther's car swept in through the 8-ft. barbed-wire gate, the sentries in steel helmets saluted. Walther didn't notice; he was thinking thoughts he did not dare share with anyone. He was thinking that if the worst-case scenario became reality, he might not be able to make use of a Swiss bank account—at least not at first. If for some reason he couldn't get out in time, he would need to come to terms—at least temporarily—with a Polish government. And if he was going to get along with a Polish government, then some certified display of "opposition" to the Nazi regime would be very useful. Somehow he had to distance himself from the occupation government—or at least its most excessive policies.

It wouldn't hurt, he found himself thinking as he passed the skeletal figures in striped clothing mopping down the stairs up to his office, if he demonstrated "pity" or "humanitarianism" toward the KZ inmates. There were many Polish Communists among them and—realistically speaking—the Communists stood the best chance of forming the next Polish government. If his own KZ workers reported that he had been a "good capitalist," he might be given a chance to salvage something of his empire. The Poles would desperately need the products of his factories, too. After all, the Polish population had gone virtually without any new clothes for almost 6 years now; their shoes were long since worn out. His factories, however, could switch production from uniforms and military boots to civilian clothing in a very short time. Besides, all the former owners were dead. Why shouldn't he be allowed to continue running them until he could get away to Switzerland? Or if the war went the other way, and the *Wehrmacht* managed to hold the Eastern Front while negotiating with the West, then it would be just as well if he had been good to the Jews, because everyone knew the Jews controlled the American press.

Looking at the situation that way, he had to admit it would not really cost him that much to increase the bread ration of the KZ workers to, say, 100 grams a day. Or even more important, he could provide barracks for them right on the factory grounds, thereby saving them the long march to and from the camp. Both measures would do much to improve the strength and alertness of the workers— a clear economic as well as a political advantage.

In his own office, one of the KZ women was dusting. At the sight of him coming in the door, she ducked down to make herself smaller than she already was and scuttled out as fast as she could. All skin and bones, with huge eyes in a meat-less face under a shaved head, the woman was sexless. Indeed, she reminded Walther of an insect more than anything else; but he could just picture the way the Jew-friendly American press and the Soviet propaganda machine would turn women like this into martyrs. It would definitely be better to do something to mitigate their current lot than to continue to exploit them beyond their strength.

His assistant and his secretary had both followed him into his office. His assis-tant was helping him out of his coat, and his secretary was standing with a steno pad in her hand and asking which of the various calls she should place first. Walther waved her silent, telling her to leave him alone with his assistant. The secretary withdrew and Walther turned to the eager young man who acted as his personal assistant.

The young man was, of course, the son of a Party boss. In exchange for some useful favors from his father, Walther had agreed to give the boy this safe job. Otherwise he would have been drafted into the *Wehrmacht*—on account of his wonderful Party credentials, most probably into the SS. The young man was 28 and had a degree in philosophy or history or some such useless field; Walther couldn't remember which one. It didn't matter. All that mattered was that he clearly had no desire to die for Greater Germany, and he therefore did his very best to please Walther.

Walther hesitated to confide in him, but ultimately he would need his help. So he launched into a lecture on why he had decided to build barracks for his KZ workers directly on the factory premises. He confined his arguments strictly to the economic advantages.

The young man nodded dutifully at each of his conclusions, but at the end he still ventured to say, "*Herr Director* Halle? If I may?"

"Yes?"

"I—I feel it is my duty to point out that—ah—the SS will—ah—not approve of this measure."

"I know," Walther told him, adding bluntly, "the SS is building an empire while the *Reich* bleeds to death." The young man caught his breath and looked up at Walther with a mixture of shock and admiration. It was blasphemy to say something like that—certainly in the Government General. But Walther contin-ued, "Well, I don't see any reason why we should help them. What I propose is good for the *Reich*, and it is good for Halle Industries, Inc., and it is good for the workers. That's enough for me," he told his assistant firmly.

"*Jawohl, Herr Halle!*"

∗   ∗   ∗   ∗

Berlin
November 1943

The young officer burst out of Stauffenberg's office and almost ran Philip down in the hall. He was nearly two meters tall, blond and blue-eyed, and moved with strong, forceful steps. His salute was smart, but his eyes met Philip's directly—bore into him—as if looking for something. He nodded once and was gone.

Philip turned to watch him go and then knocked and went into Stauffenberg's office. Stauffenberg was leaning back in his chair, daubing with his handkerchief at his empty eye socket under the black patch. He smiled at the sight of Philip and announced without introduction, "He'll do it."

"Who will do what?"

"Bussche. Didn't you see him? He just left."

"The *Hauptmann* who just left your office?"

"Yes, Axel *Freiherr* von dem Bussche-Streithorst. He's just agreed to blow himself up with you-know-who."

"And how is he going to do that?"

"He declined the English explosives. He says anything with a long fuse only causes uncertainty—see what happened the last two times. He says the same explosives as in a German hand grenade are good enough for him. He says he feels confident that he can hold onto him for 30 seconds."

"And how is he going to get close enough to hold onto him at all—with a hand grenade?"

"Didn't you notice how good-looking he was?" Stauffenberg teased.

"I didn't notice, but I'll take your word for it. Since when did our C-in-C show an interest in pretty officers?"

Stauffenberg threw his head back and roared with laughter. When he'd finished, he explained, "Not the C-in-C. We need a good-looking man to model the new uniforms. You know the *Führer's* interest in details. He's insisted on seeing the new uniform before it goes into production. The prototype is finished and Bussche is on his way to obtain the explosives he needs. When he has the explosives, he will proceed directly to the *Wolfschanze* and the uniform will be sent to him there. Since he has to model the equipment, he'll have his arms with him. Good, no?" Stauffenberg was evidently feeling very pleased with himself.

Philip had to give credit where it was due. He nodded, "Yes. It's good." By which he meant it sounded like a plan with a chance of success—certainly after the look Bussche had given him in the hall. "What's the earliest date? I'll want to check over Valkyrie."

"Three to four days from now—at the most, a week." Philip nodded without further comment. "Was there something you wanted, by the way?" Stauffenberg asked, remembering that Philip had come seeking him.

"Yes, my wife wanted to have you to dinner Saturday—if you're willing to risk our cellar rather than the safety of the suburbs."

"I'd be delighted."

Alexandra had never seen Lotte so nervous. She occupied the bathroom for almost an hour and emerged looking like she was performing at the opera. "Lotte, this is supposed to be a casual dinner party for colleagues. You see him every day, after all."

"I know, but he only sees me as an extension of the typewriter, telephone or steno pad. For which you can hardly blame him when I'm in "practical" clothes. I thought—don't give me that look!"

"Lotte, you're riding for a fall. Even if you succeeded in seducing him, he's Catholic and can't divorce his wife—even if he wanted to. Why—"

"Who said I wanted to seduce him? I just want to flirt with him a little—or rather, for him to flirt with me."

Alexandra shook her head, admitting, "I'll never understand you, Lotte," and then pushed past her to get bathed and dressed for dinner.

Stauffenberg arrived shortly afterwards, while Alix was still combing out her wet hair, so Philip escorted him into the smoking room for a cigarette. This corner room, with only one window overlooking the courtyard, had suffered the least bomb damage. Except for broken moldings and the somewhat bent and crooked brass chandelier (which had fallen and been rehung twice), in here one would not have known there was a war on.

As Lotte brazenly swept into the dim room, she caught the words, "Bussche has been at the *Wolfschanze* for two days now, waiting for the uniform to arrive—"

Stauffenberg broke off as he sensed someone in the doorway and turned around sharply—almost guiltily, she thought. At the sight of Lotte, he turned instantly gallant. "Ah, *Fräulein* Koch." He swept forward to bow over her hand.

Lotte smiled up at Stauffenberg. "I hope you don't mind me joining you for a ciggy. Alexandra won't let me smoke anywhere else in the apartment."

"Our pleasure," Claus assured her graciously. With amazing dexterity, given that he only had three fingers, he extracted and offered her one of his own cigarettes. The slight trembling of his fingers could easily have been exertion rather than overwrought nerves. He turned to Philip with an apologetic smile. "Would you perhaps have a light for the lady?"

Philip brought a lighter and flicked it for Lotte. Her perfume was far too strong and her makeup too heavy, he thought with disapproval. He then offered a light to Stauffenberg as well, looking at him closely. The strain of the last few days was starting to show on Stauffenberg, too. This waiting for the call from *Führer* Headquarters was getting to all of them. It was hard to imagine what Bussche must be going through—waiting for the opportunity to kill himself.

Rolf Seydlitz emerged in the doorway. "*Herr Oberstleutnant?*"

"Rolf, come in. Claus, I don't think you've met Rolf Seydlitz yet. He will be joining us in AHA as soon as he finishes the adjutants' course."

"Seydlitz? You're related, then—"

"My uncle," Rolf cut off the senior officer almost rudely, "and I haven't heard from him since the fall of Stalingrad." He'd had more than enough questions about his uncle ever since the first leaflet of the *National Kommittee Freies Deutschland* (NKFD) and the *Bund Deutscher Offiziere* had been dropped over German lines. It included an appeal to German soldiers, signed by his uncle General Walther v. Seydlitz.

Stauffenberg glanced at Feldburg but then told Rolf disarmingly, "I greatly admire General v. Seydlitz—and I agree with everything said in the appeal." (Lotte sighed loudly. Couldn't these men talk of anything other than the war? Did they truly have no other interests?) Stauffenberg was continuing with enthusiasm, "How did Seydlitz word it? 'Hitler as a statesman has caused the most powerful nations on earth to join together in an anti-Hitler coalition. Hitler as warlord has led the German Army to its most catastrophic defeats.' He even says the war is being fought only in the interests of Hitler and his clique without the slightest regard for the people or the nation. The appeal is very well written. Do you think it genuine?"

"*Herr Oberstleutnant?*" Rolf glanced from Stauffenberg to Philip, the glance at the latter one of censure for submitting him to this. Rolf resented being interrogated about the NKFD. He was angry with his uncle for putting them all in such an awkward situation. His aunt was being pressured to divorce him in his absence, his cousins were being treated like pariahs, and some of his own alleged friends and comrades refused to give him their hands or pointedly turned their back on him when he entered a room.

"Do you think your uncle wrote the appeal himself? Does it sound like him?" Stauffenberg persisted.

"The last letter I had from my uncle was very bitter, *Herr Oberstleutnant*. More I cannot say."

"But that the line about the League's goals being not only an overthrow of Hitler but also an 'honorable' peace? Would he have suggested that if he had no reason to believe the Soviets might back away from Unconditional Surrender?"

"I have no idea, *Herr Oberstleutnant*," Rolf insisted doggedly.

"What Stalin says to Seydlitz and what Stalin means can be very different," Philip pointed out, taking Rolf out of Stauffenberg's line of fire.

"The entire appeal will have been approved by Stalin," Stauffenberg insisted.

"And Stalin will say what serves him without feeling in any way compelled to keep his word. Why should he seek a separate peace with us now that the Red Army is on the advance and we are clearly beaten? It's only a matter of time until we are utterly defeated."

"Even a cornered and fatally wounded boar can kill—or should I say, *especially* a fatally wounded boar, when brought to bay, can kill. I think that Stalin is afraid of what may happen when his armies cross into the *Reich*. He's seen what damage we can do fighting in his country, and may dread the thought of what we will do when we're fighting on our own territory, defending our homes and families."

"And perhaps he fears that that is what the Western Allies want—and intend to let happen," Rolf suggested softly.

The two senior officers turned to him, surprised, and Rolf was almost embarrassed. Stauffenberg seized on his words, "Yes! Exactly! And on top of that, Stalin may be as afraid of successful generals as our own dictator is. If he lets the Red Army win the war militarily, he has to share the limelight with Zhukov and Voroschilov. If he comes to a political agreement with a post-Hitler government, then he can take all the credit for himself."

"The only post-Hitler German government that Stalin is going to accept is a Communist one," Alexandra declared. She had entered unseen, but at once joined the conversation.

If Claus had been surprised by Lotte's appearance, he was completely taken aback by Alexandra's. She had changed into a black velvet cocktail dress that was simple, elegant and modest—except for having only one sleeve and leaving the other shoulder naked. She wore only a string of pearls and pearl-stud earrings, but Lotte's heart sank at the sight of her. She watched jealously as Stauffenberg bowed low over Alexandra's hand and was acutely aware of the difference between this hand-kiss and the one he'd given her; the latter had been flattery bordering on mockery, while the bow to Alexandra was genuine admiration. And Alexandra didn't even value it, Lotte noted in despair. Already she was combing her fine hair away from her face and continuing, "Stalin is not going to negotiate with reactionary General Staff officers and aristocrats."

"He made a pact with the *Führer* once before. If the toll in blood is high enough, I'm sure he will be willing to treat again," Claus assured her in a soothing, patronizing tone.

Philip opened his mouth to point out that his wife did not need to be talked down to, but then changed his mind and watched Alexandra defend herself.

She smiled up at Claus Stauffenberg and cocked her head. "Stalin has never scrupled to shed blood for the sake of his objectives. We have not yet inflicted anywhere near the losses that the forced collectivization caused." (She knew that from Dimitri.) "Nor did Stalin scruple to kill his former associates or supporters—even tracking Trotsky down abroad and having him assassinated in exile. He is not a man who will make half a peace for half a victory. If we have any chance of a separate peace, then this can be only with Churchill, who has no love for Communism. He alone may be able to recognize just how dangerous it would be to Britain's interests if Germany were governed from Moscow, via a man like Wilhelm Pieck."

"My wife's stepfather is a diplomat, Claus," Philip remarked from the background to counter Stauffenberg's apparent astonishment.

"I see," Claus managed, although he seemed slightly disoriented nevertheless—something Alexandra did nothing to alleviate as she added, "Furthermore, you'll gain far more support for your government among the field marshals if you promise to hold the Eastern Front."

"I wouldn't be so sure of that. Many of our field marshals remember the days of the *Reichswehr*-Red Army secret cooperation." Claus again made the mistake of talking down to her.

"And they also remember what happened to the officers they learned to respect in the 20s," Alix countered more sharply than before. "The mock trials of the Soviet officers quite outdid anything Hitler has done. So far Hitler has confined himself to dismissing difficult officers, not murdering them."

The arrival of Nadja, announcing dinner, put an end to the discussion. Alexandra turned back into the gracious hostess and Claus gallantly took her offered arm. Philip escorted Lotte and Rolf brought up the rear.

The dining room was in notably worse condition than the smoking room. The chandelier here had once been crystal, but Alix had dismantled it in time, sending the separately wrapped pieces down to Altdorf. Electric lighting was provided only by a bare bulb hanging from the cracked ceiling. In order not to draw attention to this, the light was not on, and the room was lit entirely by candlelight. The table was covered with linen, but on the buffet deep gouges revealed the places where the frames from the pictures had fallen. The doors to the buffet hung open, as the door frames had sprung and warped so that nothing quite fit anymore, and many of the glass panes of the china cabinet were cracked or broken. The pictures had been removed so that the walls were blank, but the darkened squares on the wallpaper recorded where once pictures had hung. Still, the room was warm from the tile oven in the corner, and the candlelight hid many of the blemishes. Set with linen, china and silver, the table presented a gracious, almost peacetime picture in the gentle candlelight.

Stauffenberg turned the conversation to the bombing, asking how they had managed to save so much. Lotte, however, was relieved by the change of subject, as here she could join in. She, after all, had been completely bombed out of her own apartment and had lost virtually everything. "Fortunately," she explained, leaning closer to Stauffenberg, "I had all my winter clothes in a trunk in the cellar, and my better summer things I kept in the suitcase with me, but everything in the apartment was lost—the top floors of the house collapsed completely."

"It is fortunate that you were not in the apartment at the time," Claus Stauffenberg agreed.

Nadja and Franz served the soup and hot rolls while Philip poured wine. Lotte managed to turn the conversation to music. The telephone rang. Philip glanced at his watch. What emergency couldn't wait 'till morning? Valkyrie? He shoved back his chair, but already Franz was in the doorway looking amazed. He declared in an awed tone, "*Führer* Headquarters for *Oberstleutnant Graf* Stauffenberg."

Stauffenberg sprang to his feet. "That can only be Bussche! I gave him this number just in case." Franz led Stauffenberg to the phone.

Philip and Alexandra waited, gazing at one another, unable to continue eating. In case of what? If Bussche had been successful, he would not be in a position to telephone. The news of Hitler's death should have come through official channels, not from FHQ.

"What's the matter?" Lotte asked.

Alexandra shook her head once to indicate she couldn't answer. She was straining to hear something of the conversation, but the phone was too far away. Fortunately it was only a short conversation. Stauffenberg re-emerged in the door, looking paler and more dazed than Stadthagen two minutes earlier. He reseated himself with an automatic, "Forgive me." He replaced his napkin and only then met Philip's gaze. "The uniform that Bussche was due to model was destroyed by Allied bombers during the transport to *Wolfschanze*. Bussche must return to his unit."

"I see." Philip nodded and picked up his spoon. Just as with Tresckow's attempts, the assassination had failed because of factors beyond their control, but somehow it didn't surprise him. On the contrary, he found it increasingly hard to believe they would ever succeed.

CHAPTER 37

▼

Berlin
January 1944

The news spread like wildfire through the offices of the Replacement Army and AHA. Soon everyone was talking about it. At a meeting of the Senior Commanders at Hitler's HQ, Hitler had made an impassioned speech that Feldmarschall v. Manstein found so insulting he had called out something in the middle of it. Hitler, unused to having anyone interrupt him, ended his speech abruptly and asked to see Manstein alone. Most of the officers discussing the incident expected Manstein's dismissal momentarily, while the minority argued that Hitler would have done that already if he intended to.

Claus Stauffenberg paced back and forth in his office, while Philip watched him calmly. "Maybe Manstein is coming around."

"To what?"

"To our point of view. I visited him almost exactly a year ago—just before the surrender of the 6th Army. He agreed that the entire campaign in the East had been badly planned."

"He had nothing to do with it, as I remember," Philip remarked dryly.

Stauffenberg laughed and agreed. "Modest he is not, although he is by no means arrogant. He let me speak my mind openly—a mere major to a field marshal—and he agreed that the command structure had to be changed. He promised he would do all he could to make Hitler see this, but he absolutely refused to see that a change in the command structure might have to be accomplished against Hitler's will."

"And what he apparently objected to at this last meeting is that Hitler questioned the loyalty of the assembled generals and field marshals. Not exactly the reaction of someone who is considering disloyalty," Philip argued.

"Maybe." Stauffenberg stopped pacing and paused to look at Philip directly, his one eye alive with energy. "But maybe it is because loyalty has become so difficult for him that he was so furious to have it called in question. You know Manstein!" Stauffenberg waved what remained of his left hand toward Philip. "Out of uniform, you'd take him for a kindly old gentleman farmer. By nature he is reticent—not to say, shy. If he is provoked into rudely shouting something in the middle of his C-in-C's speech, he must have been truly at the end of his patience. And a man at the end of his patience may be ready to cross the Rubicon."

Philip considered this, remembering what Alix had said about Stauffenberg himself. Stauffenberg, too, had believed in and supported the Regime for years; but when he made the break, he did so with a determination that Philip admired. Even now, although Stauffenberg daubed irritably at his empty eye socket, he was pacing like a caged lion. "Don't we have an excuse to send you to see Manstein? My excuse a year ago was the creation of Russian volunteer units. Surely we could come up with something like that again?"

Lotte put her head in the door. "*Graf* Stauffenberg, Freiherr v. Feldburg, General Olbricht wants to see both of you in his office immediately."

Philip got to his feet, and together they crossed through the secretary's office to Olbricht's office.

Olbricht was standing behind his desk, and the look he gave his subordinates as they entered was a warning. With a gesture of his hand he indicated they should close the door behind them. Then, without introduction, he announced, "*Graf* Moltke has just been arrested by the Gestapo."

Philip neither knew Moltke personally nor understood the significance of this announcement, but Stauffenberg caught his breath. "Why? Do we know the charges?"

"Not yet. Nor do I intend to inquire. I do not intend to show the slightest interest in *Graf* Moltke, and nor will Dr. Sack. Moltke is a civilian employee of Counter Intelligence, and as such this office officially has no interest in him whatsoever. To show even the slightest concern could be fatal." He let this hang in the air for a moment and then said in a gentler tone, "*Lieber* Stauffenberg: as Yorck's cousin, you could of course visit Yorck and his wife without arousing suspicion. See what you can find out—most importantly, if the Gestapo searched the Yorck/Moltke residence. Find out what material they found or might have found. I want your report tomorrow morning. Feldburg, ask your wife to be in touch with *Gräfin* Moltke. I expect she will come to Berlin and try to see her husband; *Gräfin* Yorck is a lawyer by training, but since she is not practicing at present, they do not have the access to the various chambers and libraries. Your wife may be able to help them develop a line of defense."

"May I ask, *Herr General* ..."

Olbricht waited expectantly.

"I gather *Graf* Moltke knows about our plans."

"Yes."

"What else does he know?"

"Too much."

Alexandra met with both *Gräfin* Yorck and *Gräfin* Moltke to discuss the situation. She also accompanied them to Gestapo HQ, where *Gräfin* Moltke requested permission to visit her husband. She was denied. By the end of the day Alix had learned all about the circle of civilians, from a variety of professions, who had been working for almost four years on writing a post-Nazi constitution.

Although Alexandra took an instant liking to *Gräfin* Yorck, she found *Gräfin* Moltke's—and her husband's—firm opposition to an assassination hard to understand. That night when she collected Philip in his office, she found herself arguing passionately against the absent Moltke. "We can't just sit and wait for the Allies to end the war!" Alexandra declared in agitation, glancing to be sure the door to the hall was closed. "The cost is too high. And why should we have any say in what comes afterwards if we have done nothing to free ourselves?" She was sitting in Philip's visitor's chair. "It's all very well for *Graf* Moltke and his friends to draft a future constitution, but if we have done nothing to end the war, then the only constitution we can expect is the one Stalin imposes on us. Do they think that they can let others do all the dirty work, and then come in and take over?"

Philip removed his glasses and wiped them clean on his handkerchief. "More or less. In my experience, most civilians expect the military to do all the unpleasant tasks and then, when we are no longer necessary to their immediate safety, they turn up their noses at us because we are 'bloodthirsty,' 'brutal' and 'aggressive.' As I recall, your own attitude toward the General Staff was not very different."

"Don't remind me!" His wife cast him an exasperated look as she combed her hair back with her hand. "But it doesn't make sense to draft a constitution if one has no way of implementing it!" she insisted. "Don't they see that if Stalin wins this war he is going to impose Soviet-style Socialism? And if the Western Allies win, Roosevelt and Churchill will write our constitution for us. Why should any one of the victors pay any attention to what a circle of German intellectuals dreamed up while waiting for the Allies to act?"

"Why should they believe that there are any decent Germans at all, if we have done nothing to stop him?" Philip added softly.

"Exactly!" Alexandra agreed.

"But, Alix, I hope you see where this leads us?" her husband insisted softly, replacing his glasses and leaning forward.

Alexandra hesitated. Something about his mood and look sent a chill down her spine. "What do you mean?"

"I mean that the logical consequence of what we just said is that a demonstration of our existence may be necessary—even if the chances of success are nil."

Alexandra took a moment to register what he'd said, and then asked, "What are you planning now?"

"Nothing new, but even Claus is beginning to get discouraged. The day may come when we have to take a chance very much against the odds."

They stared at one another. What was she supposed to say?

"Let's go home," Philip suggested, getting to his feet and reaching for his greatcoat. "The sirens could sound any minute."

*   *   *   *

Berlin
February 1944

"Congratulations, *Freifrau* v. Feldburg," the doctor told her with a routine smile. "The tests are positive. You are at least three months pregnant. I estimate the child will be born in mid- or late July." He stood and held out his hand to her.

Alexandra shook it limply, not daring to meet the doctor's eyes. Somehow, to the very last she had hoped it wasn't true. She didn't want to be pregnant. Now she would have to give up her legal training at the last minute, just months short of her Second Exam. And Philip would probably send her away from Berlin. She would be expected to go to Altdorf and live with Sophia Maria until the war was over. But by then Philip might be dead. If the coup failed, the Nazis would arrest him and kill him. And if the coup never took place, the Allies would arrest him. And if—as seemed likely—the Soviets reached Berlin first, they would very likely shoot him. Even if the coup succeeded, who was to say that Philip would survive the bombing until then? It was getting worse all the time. Alexandra knew it was irrational, but she felt certain that if she left Philip in Berlin alone, it would be the last she ever saw of him.

"You can now get a work exemption and leave Berlin," the doctor assured her—assuming that she, like the rest of his patients, was still in Berlin only because she was compelled to work in some job in the city by the ever more draconian laws about industrial conscription.

Alexandra didn't bother telling the doctor that she felt very differently. He was already handing her a signed form on which he had just filled in her name and added the date. "Take that to the Employment Office, and they will give you the certificate of exemption needed for your employer."

"Thank you," Alexandra said automatically, and left the doctor's office.

In the waiting room, a score of other women waited anxiously for the piece of paper that would free them.

Alexandra went back to her office, but found she couldn't work. It was also pointless. Why start anything when she wouldn't be able to finish? She would have to turn over all her cases to someone else. Dr. Sack would be displeased. He was short-staffed, and at least one of the other young legal interns was untrustworthy—he kept complaining about how "reactionary" the officer corps was and how they needed more National Socialist spirit. His favorite phrase was, "We should introduce NS Commissars similar to the Soviet Commissars—you'd be surprised how fast the front would stabilize then!"

Alexandra reached for her phone, started to dial Philip's extension, and then changed her mind. Instead she put a call through to Olbricht's reception desk.

"*Allgemeines Heeresamt*, Koch."

"Lotte, it's me, Alix. Is there any chance you could get away for lunch?"

"In the cafeteria?"

"Heavens, no, Philip might see us there. I need to talk to you alone. Can you meet me at the Esplanade? I'm buying."

It was two hours before Lotte could get away, and by then the dining room of the Esplanade was almost empty. They were given a table for two in a corner. Alexandra ordered a sherry for both of them, adding with an apologetic smile to Lotte, "If you don't want one, I'll drink both."

"What's wrong?" Lotte asked, but her mind had been trying to work out what this could be about ever since Alexandra had called. The best explanation she could think of slipped off her tongue before Alexandra could answer. "Philip isn't having an affair, is he?

Alexandra managed a short laugh and shook her head. "No, it's not that ... I'm pregnant."

Lotte, dearest Lotte, did not say "wonderful" or "congratulations"—and for that, Alexandra loved her. Instead Lotte considered her in silence for a moment and then stated matter-of-factly, "That's really not so terrible, Alix. I mean, you are married to the father—aren't you?"

"Lotte! Of course it's Philip's! How could you—"

"Calm down. I just meant if it's Philip's child, then why shouldn't you have it?"

"Because it means giving up my job, and that means not taking the Second Exam and never finishing my training, and never being a lawyer. And it means leaving Berlin and maybe never seeing Philip alive again. And it means I'll be just another widow trying to raise a fatherless child on her own without any kind of proper qualifications ..." Alexandra was close to tears, and Lotte reached out and covered her hand with her own until Alexandra got hold of herself. Alexandra nodded and took a handkerchief out of her handbag to blow her nose.

The waiter arrived and set a glass of sherry before each of them. When he had withdrawn again, Lotte raised her glass. "*Sieg Heil*, Alexandra—whatever that's supposed to mean."

"*Ja, ja.*" Alexandra raised her glass and drank the meaningless toast, grateful that Lotte hadn't made it "to the youngest Feldburg" or some such thing.

Lotte sipped the topaz liquid slowly, trying to decide what to say next. She couldn't help remembering when she had been pregnant. The father of her child had been a married man and her benefactor. He was a senior official of the Propaganda Ministry who had arranged the auditions that had enabled her cabaret career. He had been her most enthusiastic fan, reserving a table near the front night after night and bringing various friends and colleagues to "admire her talent." They made love in her dressing room more often than anywhere else—sometimes during intermission in frantic, nervous haste because Lotte was afraid of missing her cue. But he had reacted to her pregnancy as if he didn't know that the one had to do with the other. Next he had been quick to put the blame entirely on her. "You mean you didn't take precautions?" he'd asked, outraged. Next he'd accused her of sleeping with "God knew how many" other men. Only one thing was absolutely certain: the father of her child refused to recognize it, much less take any responsibility for it. Before she caused him any "embarrassment," he also made sure she lost her job. He did not answer her calls. He returned her letters unopened, and he made sure that she was turned away at the Ministry. She had never seen him again.

Lotte had wanted to kill herself. It wasn't just a matter of hopelessness; it was a sense of worthlessness. Alexandra, however, had spent countless hours talking to her, building up her self-esteem. Alexandra had insisted that she move into Alix's little apartment to keep her from "doing something silly." Alix had suggested going back to the Music Academy, and when Lotte insisted she wanted to learn something "practical" instead, Alix had helped her enroll in a secretarial course. The only thing Alexandra had not helped her with was the abortion.

Lotte put down her empty sherry glass and said very softly, "You know I can give you the address of a doctor—if that's really what you want."

Alexandra sat for a long moment, turning her empty sherry glass around on the starched linen tablecloth. Slowly she shook her head. Without lifting her eyes to look at Lotte, she admitted, "I could never kill Philip's child. It may—all too soon—be all I have of him."

Philip had never seen Alix look so tired or depressed before—not having seen her when he was himself still on the critical list. He took her briefcase from her. "Some new case?"

She shook her head.

He thought again. "Not Stefan?"

"Do I look that bad?"

"Almost. What is it?"

"Not here. I'll tell you when we get home."

But the sirens sent them to the cellar before they could talk. It was a bad raid. The detonations seemed to be directly overhead, and Alexandra clung to Philip's hand so hard it hurt. Philip put his arm around her and kissed the top of her head, wondering if it was the bombing that was starting to get to her. Yet she didn't tremble the way Frl. Moldenauer did, nor wince at the sound of the nearest detonations. Philip had seen—and smelled—fear often enough to be able to distinguish various degrees of it. Alexandra's fear was still very much under control. More than that, when the old woman who had been billeted with the Baumans started whimpering prayers and moaning, "We're all going to die in here. We're all going to die," Alexandra was the one who distracted her with questions about her home and family. Whatever was upsetting Alexandra, he decided, it wasn't the bombing. That was just an added burden that was wearing them all down gradually.

It was past the darkest hour of the night when the all-clear sounded—or it should have been. But the sky to the northwest was ablaze with so many strong fires that the whole city seemed to be trapped under a glowing orange dome of cloud. They went out in front of the house to stare and Alexandra, trying to guess what part of the city had been so badly hit, asked uncertainly: "You don't think they were trying for the Bendlerstrasse, do you?"

Philip had to agree that it looked that way. He put a call through to the duty officer as soon as they went inside, and was told that the Bendlerstrasse was intact. Potsdamer Platz appeared to have borne the brunt of the raid, the duty officer said. They went to bed, and Alexandra put off telling Philip about his baby until the next day.

The next morning they took the bus to work together with Lotte. The fire department was still fighting fires in the remnants of buildings all around the Potsdamer Platz. The Platz itself appeared to have been completely leveled. Huge heaps of smoking rubble marked what had only yesterday been movie theaters, department stores and office buildings. The famous heart of Berlin was unrecognizable.

Back at her desk, Alexandra still could not work. She moved files around from place to place, pretended to read, doodled on her notepad, and then jumped like a cat when the phone rang. Dr. Sack wanted to know the status of several cases. She forced herself to concentrate, and even managed to write the opinion he requested. She left it with his secretary and retreated back to her office. The phone rang again. This time it was Philip. "Alix, why don't you ask your mother if you can sleep down in Dahlem? It's quieter there, and your parents' cellar is not as crowded."

"I didn't marry you to sleep alone," she snapped back—and then bit her lip, ashamed of her own irritability. She could hear Philip stiffen on the other end of the line and wanted to apologize, but he was speaking already. With admirable calm he said, "Then ask your mother if we can both come. You need to get a good night's sleep after last night."

The last place Alexandra wanted to be was with her mother. When her mother found out she was pregnant, she would gush and fuss and insist on Alexandra taking the next train to safety. But Alexandra was exhausted, and the house in Dahlem was still so marvelously untouched by the war—or at least by the air raids. Alexandra swallowed and said, "We'll need to collect our things."

"I'll send Franz to collect our suitcases" (he meant the ready-packed suitcases they took down into the cellar every night) "and I'll try to get away early. All right?"

He kept his word and they were both out of the Bendlerstrasse by 7 pm. Alexandra's mother had dinner waiting for them when they arrived an hour later. It was like a return to another world or age: no broken windows, no sprung doors, no cracked or fallen plaster, no naked bulbs. Without the children (Rudi slept with his flak unit), the atmosphere was also less tense. Herr v. Rantzow seemed strangely mellowed, Alix registered. He no longer had to set an example, perhaps, or else he had lost all hope of influencing anything. Frau v. Rantzow was happy to have at least one of her children with her. She did most of the talking. Didn't Alix and Philip want to move in permanently? She feared getting homeless people imposed on them by the Housing Office, and it was safer and quieter here than in the heart of the city—even if the occasional stray bomb landed here. Philip looked at Alexandra. "We'll think about it," she answered.

Herr v. Rantzow went out to walk the dog.

"Do you see much of Klara Rademacher?" Frau v. Rantzow asked Alexandra.

"Nothing at all. We have so little time for socializing."

Frau v. Rantzow sighed. "I wish Stefan had committed himself before he went away. Although Klara …"

"Forgive us, Mutti, but I'm really exhausted." Alexandra did not want to get into a discussion with her mother about the pros and cons of Klara Rademacher. "I need to go up to bed."

"Yes, of course, dear," Frau v. Rantzow said, disappointed. Alexandra stood and gave her a hug. "We'll give serious thought to moving in with you, Mutti," Alexandra promised and smiled, knowing that tomorrow, when she told her the news, she would make her mother very happy. That at least was something: knowing that she would make at least one person very happy. She looked at Philip, who was standing to go upstairs with her.

Alexandra waited until they were in bed, and then she drew a deep breath and plunged in. "Philip, I have something to tell you."

"*Ja?*"

"I'm carrying your child."

His arms tightened around her and he kissed her, but he took a few moments to answer. When he'd thought he was permanently impotent, he'd been bitter and realized how much he wanted children. And yet a child now—in the middle of this war, with so much uncertainty, death and destruction all around them— seemed mad, or at least misplaced. But worst of all, it would mean being alone after he had come to depend on Alexandra being with him. "When is it due?" he asked cautiously.

"In mid or late July, the doctor said."

Philip eased his hold a little, but stroked her shoulder. "And when is your Second Exam scheduled?"

"The first week of May," Alexandra told him, shifting her head on his chest to look up at him, holding her breath hopefully.

"Then it probably makes sense for you to stay for that and then go down to Altdorf afterwards, don't you think? If you feel up to it, that is?"

"I do. I want to finish, Philip. You understand, don't you?"

He nodded. That would give them three more months together. Three months in which—maybe—Claus would find someone who could carry out the assassination, and they could stop the war.

CHAPTER 38

▼

Berlin
May 1944

The week after Alexandra took her Second Exam, they organized a party to celebrate. Of course, she didn't have the results yet, but she wouldn't have them for
another 6 to 8 weeks anyway. Since she was leaving for Altdorf at the weekend (so
Philip could take her down on the night train on Saturday and return on the
night train on Sunday to be at work Monday morning), this was also a goodbye
party. They invited everyone they knew and liked, and Franz made sure that the
windows had been reglazed (for the second time) before the party.

Lotte insisted on evening dress (so she could wear one of her pretty things for
Claus, she said), and General Olbricht contributed a case of champagne from his
wine cellar. They flung open the French doors between the front rooms and in
the drawing room, pushed all the furniture to the side, and rolled up the carpet
for dancing. In the salon around the grand piano, extra chairs were arranged for
those not interested in dancing. The dining room was set up as a buffet. Rolf proclaimed himself "disk jockey" and moved the collection of records from the
library into the salon, where he set up the record player on the piano bench.

Theo Pfalz was warned to expect the guests starting at 8 pm and was tipped
handsomely for the extra duties. He decided on a small party of his own and
invited his buddies for a night of *Skat* and beer. They sat in the porter's lounge
listening to the radio, playing cards and answering the door in their various uniforms of block warden, SA man, air-raid warden and train conductor.

Shortly before 8 pm Rolf put on the first record, and Philip opened the first
bottle of *Sekt* to get the evening going. Lotte and Alix emerged from the bed-
rooms. Alexandra, at seven months, felt awkward and ugly in a made-over gown
of her mother's from the twenties. The gown was of beige lace in two layers,

waistless of course, and trimmed with black velveteen. Lotte looked stunning in an off-the-shoulder satin gown with a low décolleté and tight-fitting waist and hips, but flared below the knees.

Rolf let his eyes scan Lotte with appreciation, but he gave her only a nod of approval. He knew she would never take an interest in a mutilated man, and he felt he only made of fool of himself when he fawned on her. Philip, knowing how awkward Alexandra felt, went and put his arms around her. "Whether you believe it or not, you look lovely in my eyes." Alix gave him a kiss in thanks, and then Philip brought Alix and Lotte each a glass of *Sekt*.

The first of the guests to arrive were Annie Lerche with her *Luftwaffe Hauptmann*. The *Hauptmann* had a bottle of cognac, which he'd "organized," and Annie brought homemade meatballs, still hot and savory-smelling. They were followed almost immediately by the Sacks and the Olbrichts. Franz was taking the guests' coats, while Nadja collected the food and drink donations of the guests and set them up in the dining room.

Klara Rademacher arrived in a dirndl and fringed silk shawl. She was a little nervous; it was the first time she'd been invited to a baron's party. "I don't own anything you can really call 'formal,'" she apologized to Alexandra breathlessly.

"But you look lovely," Alix assured her. "What do you hear from Stefan? He hasn't written *me* in weeks."

"Oh, I had a letter Monday. But didn't you hear? His division was praised in the *Wehrmacht* Report yesterday!" Her eyes glistened with pride.

Alexandra had not heard—she'd been too preoccupied with her exams and the trip to Altdorf, and her unborn child—and the words struck her unprepared. She recoiled and groped hopelessly for an answer. Didn't Klara know that the units praised in the *Wehrmacht* Reports had been mauled, gutted, 'burned up,' as the soldiers put it? She shied away from the implications and so from Klara. "We'll have to talk later, when things have settled down a bit." Turning away, she said, "Philip, Klara needs a drink."

The doorbell was ringing. Since Franz was nowhere to be seen, Alix went to the door herself. She was startled by the towering figure of a stranger in a black uniform. After her heart missed a beat, she registered that the uniform was not SS, but Panzer. The tall red-haired major introduced himself: "Robert Kleinschmidt, Frau von Feldburg; I served with Philip in France."

"Of course." Now she remembered. "My husband was so pleased to learn you were now adjutant at the Panzer School in Krampnitz. Come in, come in."

On the stairs Alexandra could hear more guests, and so she waited for Berthold Stauffenberg, Claus's brother, and his wife. Berthold was in navy uniform;

he served as a legal advisor on international law to the *Seekriegsleitung* (Navy High Command). His wife was loaded with homemade applesauce and pickled pears. "Not exactly appropriate for a party, I know," *Gräfin* Stauffenberg apologized, "but these days one brings what one has."

"Of course! Thank you! Where's Claus?"

"Oh, he had some meeting in Lichterfelde and said he'd come on from there." Alexandra understood. Lichterfelde was where *Generaloberst* Beck lived. Nadja took the jars while Franz relieved the guests of their coats. Philip emerged to greet them and offer drinks. They started together toward the music, and the bell rang again. Alexandra turned back and opened it.

Crowded on the landing she found no less than six young people in rather ill-matched, casual clothing. One was in a worn-out suit that he appeared to have inherited from his father or grandfather. Another youth wore a tweed blazer over a roll-neck sweater. Rudi himself was in corduroy trousers with a pullover—anything but formal attire. The three teenage girls with them had evidently made an effort to dress up, but had only succeeded in making themselves look cheap. One girl was wearing second-hand clothes with an over-large bodice that hung on her flat chest. One of the others looked like she'd intentionally bought her velvet vest two sizes too small, so that her bust all but burst it. The third girl wore an old flapper gown with sequins on it.

Rudi grinned at his sister and held up a bottle of cheap *Sekt*. "You said I could bring friends," he reminded her.

Alexandra thought she'd said "a friend," but it didn't matter, really. The more the merrier. "Of course; come in."

"Oh, the introductions," Rudi remembered. "My sister, *Freifrau* v. Feldburg; and my comrades from the 114th Flak battery, Ulli and Michael. And the girls, too—they work the spotlights and the observation equipment: Ruth, Doris and Gabi."

"You can take your own coats and things into the library," Alix indicated the room where the coats, hats, sidearms and ladies' purses were being stacked, "and then come help yourselves to refreshments."

"Is there somewhere where we can fix ourselves up a bit?" the girl in the tight vest asked. Alix directed her toward the bathroom with a smile. The slogan "The German woman doesn't drink, smoke or paint herself" had limited appeal these days, but teenage girls still risked considerable unpleasantness if they broke its injunctions in public.

"I hope you have some records besides waltzes," Rudi remarked with a disdainful glance toward the drawing room, where several couples were waltzing to Strauss.

"Yes, but you'll have to negotiate that with *Oberleutnant* v. Seydlitz. He's in charge of the music."

"Seydlitz? Not related to—"

"If you mention that to him, I'll throw you out. Understood?"

"Hey, what do I care? The NKFD's got it right, if you ask me. Besides, it's not the Russians who are bombing the shit out of us. You don't mind if we smoke, do you?"

Young people under the age of 21 were forbidden from dancing, smoking and drinking in public. Alexandra was perfectly aware that the only reason Rudi and his friends had come to her party was to partake in these forbidden activities. She couldn't blame them. But an older-sister streak couldn't resist rubbing in the transformation that a year in the Flak had effected. "But, Rudi, I didn't think good Hitler Youth members had such decadent habits?"

"Shit on the Hitler Youth! I've had enough of that crap! Tough as leather and hard as Krupp steel—makes me want to puke! Why the hell should we be hard as steel? So they can use us like Krupp steel in their shitty war while telling us we can't drink or smoke? The Party bosses are a bunch of bastards!"

The remarks took Alix so by surprise that her first impulse was to laugh. Her upbringing got the better of her, however, and she rebuked, "Mind your language, Rudi! This is my home, not some barracks!"

"*Ja, ja*, I'll be good. Promise." Rudi brushed his lips against her cheek in a gesture of reconciliation and smiled from under his shock of blond hair. With a start Alexandra registered that he was turning into a young man and looked very much like Stefan had at the same age. Oh, God, keep Stefan safe, she prayed silently.

Just after nine, Marianne left her parents' apartment in a rush to get some medicine for her mother. The doctor had called in the prescription to the only apothecary open at this time—fortunately, one on Gneisenau Strasse. Marianne rushed out, pulling on her coat as she went. The light in the stairwell didn't work anymore, but she knew her way, and with one hand on the banister she ran down the stairs.

Suddenly, at the second landing, she careened into a man holding onto the banister as he worked his way up the stairs. The first shock of the collision was followed by a second shock when she looked up into the face of a man wearing a black eye patch. She found herself steadied by a mutilated, three-fingered hand. She next registered that his other hand was missing altogether.

She'd hardly taken in the extent of the damage before all shock melted under the warmth of a smile and a deep, gracious bow. "Forgive me, *gnädiges Fräulein*; it is frightful to be startled in one's own home. I'm afraid I couldn't find the light switch."

"It doesn't work anymore. I shouldn't have been running, but I need to get some medicine for my mother. She has a heart condition." Marianne poured it all out in an unthinking rush.

"May I be of some assistance? My car and driver are out in front."

Marianne hardly knew how to react. Such gallantry was not something one ran into every day—much less officers with cars and drivers at their disposal. Even Baron v. Feldburg didn't have that.

"Forgive me. I should introduce myself," he bowed slightly. "Claus Stauffenberg."

"Marianne Moldenauer," she replied automatically, holding out her hand.

Stauffenberg smiled, took her hand in his mauled one, and bowed over it again. "Now, to my car?"

"Yes, thank you! There's an apothecary on Gneisenau Strasse that is still open. The doctor's already called in the prescription," she explained as she continued down the stairs beside the officer.

"A good sign," Stauffenberg remarked. "Gneisenau was one of my ancestors, on my mother's side."

They reached the front door just as Stauffenberg's driver was about to come in. "I'm sorry, Graml," Stauffenberg told the driver, "we have a short errand. The young lady needs to pick up some medicine on Gneisenau Strasse."

"I can take care of that, *Herr Graf*, if you and the young lady wish to go back up." Marianne started at the title. As far as she could remember, Stauffenberg was the first count she had ever shaken hands with.

Stauffenberg turned to Marianne. "What do you say?"

"I think I'd better go. The people at the apothecary might not understand why a *Wehrmacht* corporal was collecting my mother's medicine. My father is just a retired professor. But there's no need for you—"

"I wouldn't think of sending you out alone—not even with Graml." He opened the door for her and Marianne gave Graml the address.

By the time they returned from the apothecary, Marianne was totally under Stauffenberg's spell. By then she also knew that Stauffenberg worked with Philip and had been invited to Alexandra's goodbye party. Marianne thanked Stauffenberg profusely, and he insisted it had been his pleasure. Then she hurried up the next flight of stairs, unconsciously repeating his name to herself. *Graf* Stauffenberg. Claus *Graf* Stauffenberg.

At the Feldburg flat, Stauffenberg was greeted like the prodigal son by his host, commander and brother—all of whom had been more or less anxiously awaiting his arrival. Graml was welcomed to the kitchen party, where Nadja was dishing out borscht and Stadthagen was pouring beer for Olbricht and Sack's drivers as well as for Nadja and himself.

Claus Stauffenberg, Olbricht and Philip disappeared into the library for a few moments, but no one thought it odd that the Chief of Staff might want to have a word with his commander and Ia in private before joining the festivities. Rudi meanwhile had talked Seydlitz into playing jazz records, and the young people dominated the dance floor. Many of the other guests had drifted into the dining room and were standing about, chatting comfortably.

Just after 1:30 am, the air-raid sirens went off. Rudi and his friends at once rushed out onto the balcony to give a commentary on the danger. Asked if they didn't have to return to their unit, they claimed it was too late. They were AWOL anyway, Rudi admitted, but Alexandra had no time to digest this information.

Meanwhile a contingent of guests, led by Annie Lerche's *Luftwaffe Hauptmann*, advocated staying above ground. "If it's got your number on it, it's going to get you no matter where you are," he reasoned.

"Better to go out like a light in an explosion than suffocate and melt in some caved-in cellar," was Robert Kleinschmidt's opinion.

It was only with difficulty that Philip and Alexandra managed to herd everyone into the cellar. The other residents of the apartment house were none too pleased by the overcrowding caused by the guests, and found their alcohol-induced light-heartedness perfectly obnoxious. Frau Gieseler particularly expressed her disapproval of "strange young men" being brought into a cellar where "decent women" were only half dressed (she was in her bathrobe). Other residents were more outraged to discover that their air-raid warden had enjoyed Theo Pfalz's hospitality to such an extent that he was the drunkest of them all.

As the usual trembling and rumbling began and swelled, Rudi and his friends provided a running commentary on the events overhead. "That's one of the new batteries." "That's the one on Belle Alliance Platz." "They must be Halifaxes—" "*Na*, Lancasters." "Listen! Night fighters." "There's the battery on Kottbusser Damm."

Then the explosion crashed against them with a single jolt, splitting the ceiling, and the door to the cellar blew inwards—followed by a roaring wind, heat, and a timid flame that almost at once grew confident. The secondary explosions racked them before they had recovered from the first. The plaster dust swirled. Someone was shrieking, until someone else slapped them silent. Theo fell backwards into the room; but Robert Kleinschmidt, followed by Philip, Berthold Stauffenberg, and Annie's *Luftwaffe Hauptmann*, pushed past Theo Pfalz to the buckets of sand on the stairway. In the next instant, Rudi and his friends crowded toward the door to fight the flames as well. "Here! Get these blankets wet!" one of them ordered, and the girls from the Flak Battery at once set about pouring water onto a pile of waiting blankets and then distributing them to the stunned occupants of the cellar. Seydlitz joined the other officers near the door.

"It's the house next to us," Seydlitz informed the other occupants of the cellar reassuringly. "The first explosion was probably an air mine, and the second was the phosphorus bomb that went in next door. We've only got some burning debris in the courtyard."

"Oh, my God!" With that, the officers at the door were out of the cellar and into the air raid. Alexandra sprang to her feet, but Claus Stauffenberg held her back. "Not in your condition," he admonished. But Peter Kessler left Marianne with her parents and followed the officers into the night. Stadthagen, Graml and the other drivers followed him.

Seydlitz was back in the doorway. "Give me those wet blankets. People are trapped next door!"

The three flak helpers collected the blankets in a jumble and handed them up to Seydlitz, but they hung back, not venturing into the inferno outside. The three nurses, on the other hand, moved swiftly and purposefully past the teenage girls in their ruined party dresses. Now General Olbricht, Dr. Sack, and two of the other male tenants also left the cellar to help with the rescue. From across the city came the rumble and croak of bombers and flak.

When the all-clear sounded, an ambulance had already cleared away the dead and wounded. A fire truck and crew were dousing down the burning building and the houses on either side with streams of dirty water from the canal. The wind was blowing hard away from the Feldburg house. At the sight of his wife, Philip limped over to her. He could hardly stand straight for pain, and his dress uniform was ruined by smoke, dust, and sweat. He smelled of all three. Alexandra caught him in her arms. "Philip?"

"We were very lucky," he remarked simply.

The ringing of the telephone brought Philip from a sleep so deep he wasn't sure where he was at first. Then, registering the gurgling ring of the telephone, he rolled painfully out of bed and stubbed his toe against the door frame. Still the telephone rang and rang. Hobbling down the hall, Philip wondered what could be so urgent that Olbricht or Stauffenberg would want him despite knowing what they'd been through last night. They knew, too, that he was taking Alix down to Altdorf tonight. Had the Anglo-Americans opened a second front at last? Because his voice was still raw from the smoke inhalation of the night before, it was hardly recognizable as he barked into the receiver: "Feldburg."

There was a pause. "Who's that?" his father-in-law asked in a tight voice.

"Philip, Herr v. Rantzow. I was fighting fires until early morning—if my voice sounds a little strange." Mentally he was swearing, because whatever it was Herr v. Rantzow wanted, it wasn't as important as some sleep. Transferring the phone to his right hand, Philip looked at his watch. It had stopped.

"Is Alexandra available?" Herr v. Rantzow insisted.

"She's sound asleep. The house next to us burned to the ground and we didn't turn in until 6 am," Philip repeated, annoyed that his father-in-law still hadn't grasped the situation.

"Well, maybe you can break it to her best."

Philip tensed, his irritation gone. "What?"

"Stefan's dead. We just got the news."

Philip stood very still and silent. It hit him harder than he expected. He'd failed Stefan, and in so doing he'd failed Alix. How was he going to tell her this?

"Philip? Are you still there?"

"Yes, of course."

"Her mother needs her. Do you think you could delay your departure for a few days?"

"Yes, we'll put it off a week," he agreed. That was easier said than done, but he would worry about the details later.

"And you'll come over as soon as you can?"

"Yes, but it will be hours. Alix needs her sleep—especially in her condition. I'll tell her when she wakes, and then we'll come straight over. I'll bring Alexandra's things so she can stay with you all week."

"Yes, that's a good idea. Thank you." Herr v. Rantzow hung up.

Philip returned to his bedroom and stood for a long time staring down at his sleeping wife. She had gone to bed without washing, and her face was smudged with smoke. Her hair was dirty with it. Lying curled on her side, her dirty face resting on the back of her hand, she reminded Philip of a child. His eyes went to her swollen belly, and gently he reached out and felt it. It was hard to believe there was new life in it. It was hard to believe that a new person might be growing there who one day would be as complex and delightful as Stefan had been. But it was good, he thought; not because anyone could ever replace Stefan for Alexandra or her mother, but simply because it was good that a new person would be born into their lives.

Exhaustion overtook him. He too needed sleep. He'd completely overdone it last night, and the pain was worse than it had been for months. Slowly and carefully he went back around to the other side of the bed and gently lowered himself down. He closed his eyes and slept. He dreamed that Christian was dead, and woke with a start. For a second he wasn't certain what was reality: was Christian dead, or Stefan?

"Is something wrong?" Alexandra asked, reaching out to him sleepily.

Philip could not find an answer.

Alexandra sat up and looked down at him. "Something is wrong."

"We had a telephone call while you were sleeping."

"From whom?"

Philip knew he had to tell her, but his courage failed him.

Alexandra's eyes were uneasy. They searched his face, bored into him, while her mind worked through the possibilities. Olbricht and Stauffenberg had been with them last night, knew that they were leaving for Altdorf tonight—and if it had to do with Valkyrie, Philip would be gone already, not lying here beside her. News from Altdorf? Or from her own family? The *Wehrmacht* Report! "Philip?"

"I'm sorry, Alix. I've failed you. Your stepfather called …"

Alexandra's eyes widened. She knew, but she cried out for help. "Philip!"

"Stefan's dead."

It was several hours before Alexandra managed to pull herself together enough to bathe, dress and go to face her mother. Watching her struggling to get her crying under control and then breaking down again and again, Philip finally understood why she had failed to tell him when Christian had gone missing. She cried so hard she was physically ill, and Philip started to get concerned for the baby—though he didn't dare hint at that, fearing it would only upset her more.

"I—I know I'm behaving badly," Alix said to him from the bathroom floor; "not the way a Feldburg behaves, no doubt." She was hiccuping from crying so hard.

"That's not the point," Philip assured her, helping her back up onto her feet. "If only crying would bring him back." He led her back to their bedroom.

By now Nadja, Lotte and Rolf knew what had happened. Nadja was crying out of sympathy for Alix. Lotte at once went out to buy flowers for Frau v. Rantzow, and Rolf set off to "organize" a car so Philip and Alix wouldn't have to take public transportation to the Rantzow villa.

Eventually the sobbing subsided and Alexandra sat in Philip's arms, sniffling more calmly. She kept shaking her head, but was unable to put into words what she was thinking. Nadja brought her a cup of tea. When Alix saw that the Ukranian maid was crying, too, she flung her arms around her and they cried together for a bit. That seemed somehow to do her good. After Nadja had withdrawn, Alexandra announced that she would bathe, dress and go to her mother.

By the time she was ready, Rolf was back with General Olbricht's car. Since the Rantzows lived very near to the Olbrichts' villa, Rolf could return the car after dropping them off and then take the bus back to the flat. Lotte pressed a huge bouquet of flowers on Alexandra, and Rolf drove the General's car over to the Rantzow villa.

Herr v. Rantzow opened the door himself, and Alexandra followed the sound of her mother's sobbing. In the entryway an obviously distraught and helpless Herr v. Rantzow murmured to Philip, "She hasn't stop crying since the news came. Nothing I can say seems to comfort her at all. She's making herself ill!" For the first time since they had met, Philip and his father-in-law understood one another completely.

Alexandra went down on the floor before her mother and laid her head in her mother's lap. Her mother bent forward, wrapped her daughter in her arms and sobbed, "Oh, Alix, only you understand. I've lost your father all over again. But at least your father had time to marry and have children—and they took all that away from Stefan. Stefan's been killed before he's had a chance to live!"

"That's not true, Mutti," Alexandra told her gently but firmly. Sitting up, she looked her mother in the eye. "I don't know anyone who was as alive as Stefan or who loved life more. That's why it's so hard to lose him. But you can't really believe that so much life and energy and love are really gone? He's here with us right now—and we're probably making him feel terribly guilty for causing us so much grief." Tears were streaming down her face as she spoke, but her voice was steady.

Frau v. Rantzow clutched her daughter's hands in hers, her lips trembling, and her face was glistening with tears as she asked, "Do you really think so?"

Alexandra nodded, "Yes."

Her mother flung her arms around her and cried some more, but the worst was over for the moment. By dinnertime, Alexandra had coaxed her mother into eating something and Helga, red-eyed and sniffling, managed to make a hot meal. Philip, meanwhile, had relieved Herr v. Rantzow of the duty of calling Rudi, Grete and Klara Rademacher. Rudi was under arrest for being AWOL the night before and not available, but the duty officer assured Philip he would be given the news.

Shortly after dinner, Alexandra took her mother up to bed and stayed with her until she fell asleep. She returned downstairs and joined Philip and her stepfather in his study. They were drinking cognac, and Alexandra asked for sherry. Her stepfather poured, standing in his perfectly tailored suit, even now the elegant diplomat in a winged collar with greying sideburns. "I must thank you, Alexandra," he admitted as he brought her the sherry. "You've been wonderful."

Alexandra took the sherry in the cut crystal glass and smiled sadly up at her stepfather. "It isn't me, really. I'm just a bit of Stefan still alive."

"Nonsense," her stepfather contradicted; "you've been a great help. It's just all so pointless! This whole stupid war and all the senseless sacrifice!" Herr v. Rantzow's nerves, kept in check by the need to support his wife, now cracked. His hands clenched around his heavy tumbler until his knuckles were white. "If only the Western Allies would land! Why are they taking so long? Don't they realize that if they wait too long, the Eastern Front will collapse and the Russians will win the war without them?! The sooner they land, the sooner the war will be over!" Without giving anyone a chance for comment, he continued in an angry voice, "You can be sure it's the damned Americans who are hanging back. They're so afraid of casualties! Afraid that public support for the war will crumble as soon as the bodies start coming home. You know they ship their dead soldiers home, don't you?" Herr v. Rantzow asked Philip. Philip hadn't known; he shook his head. "They're that rich and that spoiled that they actually collect their dead and send them home all the way across the Atlantic at government expense! What a bizarre people—so spoiled and soft and naive, and yet so dangerous. Once they land, the war won't last more than a few weeks. They have more men, armor and ammunition than the Soviet Union, and because they cannot afford a long war, they will throw everything they have at us. I tell you, once the Americans land in France, the war will be over in weeks. If only they had landed months ago!" Herr v. Rantzow's voice cracked, and it took Alexandra a second before she realized he was crying.

She had never seen him cry before, and she hesitated. She cast Philip a helpless glance and then went over and gently laid her arm around her stepfather's waist.

He had dropped his face into his long, elegant hands with the signet ring and he left it there, accepting but not returning Alexandra's gesture. Between clenched teeth he managed to say, "I'm so sorry, Alix. I'm so sorry Stefan will never know a better Germany than the one he died for."

Alexandra asked Philip to go for a walk with her around Lake Grünewald in the fading light of the long summer day. They took the bewildered family dog with them. The sky was luminous and the stars were coming out; the forest was black. Alexandra could walk neither fast nor far in her condition, but she needed the fresh air. Soon they found a bench and sat down. Alexandra had her arm through Philip's. "Philip, don't be angry with me," she started timidly, "but I've started to wonder if *Graf* Moltke is right after all. I mean, what if we make our coup and then get blamed for losing the war? Won't all the Nazis then be stronger than ever? Won't they destroy whatever government we try to establish? I don't even know what Moltke and his friends have thought up; do you?"

"I've heard some things. There is no one plan, really—just a lot of ideas. That is, everyone agrees we have to have a government based on the Rule of Law—a constitution that guarantees basic human rights such as equality before the law and freedom of religion, association and movement. Almost everyone agrees that we have to have a state based on the fundamental principles of Christianity, such as respect for life and for our fellow man and responsibility toward the weak and poor. But as you know, the devil is in the details. There are some people who argue that we need to restore a monarchy, because Hitler's success demonstrates that Germans need a 'leader,' and if they don't have a hereditary one, they will follow every megalomaniac that comes along. Others want to see American-style democracy, and others want to see more Socialism. Claus is throwing his weight in with the Socialists at the moment."

Alexandra actually managed a smile, even if it was a sad, weary smile. "The Revolutionary Count—it suits him. Can't you picture Claus with Robespierre?" Philip looked at her in astonishment, unable to follow her intuition when she gave it free rein like this. "And where does General Olbricht stand?" she asked.

"As so often, we have much the same opinion."

"Which is?"

"Olbricht told Claus: first act, then let's see who's left over."

"But, Philip, if my stepfather's right—if the war isn't going to last more than a few weeks after the Americans land in France—then why not let them win the war? Why risk the lives of the very best men Germany has? Beck and Tresckow, Olbricht and Uncle Erich—and you? Why not let Hitler sign this merciless

Unconditional Surrender and take the blame for the war he started and lost? Why should Beck or Olbricht—who were always against the aggression—be forced to swallow the bitter pill?"

Philip held her closer to him and kissed the top of her head. He understood her thinking. With Stefan already dead, her compulsion to shorten the war—even if only by a single day—had eased. Instead, she saw that he was in a relatively safe staff position and was at greater risk from a failed coup than a marginally prolonged war. Her logic was impeccable, as usual, but he shook his head nevertheless. "First of all, your stepfather underestimates us. The Americans may have endless material resources, but their troops and officers are inexperienced. I think we may be able to hold both fronts for as long as six to eight months after the Americans land—and they haven't done that yet. So the war could go on another nine to ten months. In that time, we could have lost another half-million men on the front and maybe half that again in our shattered cities." He dropped his voice. "And then there are the Concentration Camps and the death camps. We're systematically slaughtering people, Alix—as if they were animals with an infectious disease ..." His voice faded into the darkness.

"You mean the *Einsatzkommandos*?" Alexandra asked.

"No, I mean we've built special slaughterhouses for people. The SS is diverting rolling stock—which we desperately need to keep the Eastern and Italian Fronts supplied with ammunition and other war materials—to transport people to these camps. They transport people in freight cars and then herd them into large chambers and gas them."

Alexandra wanted to say, "That can't be"—but it was too horrible for Philip to have made it up. "How do you know?"

"Olbricht told me. I don't know his source. It doesn't matter. After what I saw the *Einsatzkommandos* do, it's impossible to question this. And we have to stop it. Or at least try to stop it. Or maybe just to demonstrate before God and the Allies and history that *German officers* opposed these measures. The coup isn't just about stopping the war—at least that's not what it's about for Olbricht or Tresckow or me anymore. It's about taking a moral stand against a regime that is morally depraved. It's about—if you like—trying to save Sodom and Gomorrah by finding ten just men who are willing to stand up and be counted—even if it costs them their lives."

Alexandra gazed at her husband in frightened awe. It was almost completely dark, and his face was in shadow. She could make out the curve of his dark hairline against his high forehead, the glasses hiding his eyes, and the set of his lips. She was frightened and she shivered, but she could not protest. She had set him on this path. She had supported him at every step. What right did she have to lose heart now?

Philip took her hand and entwined his fingers in hers. "Now do you understand why I've been so selfish? So reluctant to let you take our child to safety in Altdorf?"

All her nightmares were true. After she left Berlin, she would never see him again. "When?"

"Just as soon as our current volunteer assassin with access to Hitler finds the right opportunity."

CHAPTER 39

▼

Berlin
June 1944

Marianne tagged along behind the other students a little uncertainly. Ever since she had returned Peter's engagement ring and told him their relationship was over, she had been making desperate efforts to find new friends. Rainer was an overly tall and unattractively thin engineering student, but she had met him at her church. His father owned coal mines in Silesia and now in the Government General. Somehow his father had also obtained for him an exemption from military service, and he made no bones about being extremely grateful. None of the students in this crowd—not even those in uniform—made any pretense about being "heroic." Their motto was "survive"—at any cost, it seemed.

They had taken her to a small, old, somewhat run-down café with Russian décor. A fragile old man with white hair nodded a greeting to them and took their orders in exchange for their food stamps. Outside the sun shone brightly between large clouds that rapidly marched across the sky. The dingy café brightened and darkened irregularly.

Jens-Uwe, a *Luftwaffe* sergeant recovering from a lung wound, leaned closer to the table and lowered his voice. "Have you heard that Göring recently suggested to Goebbels that they reintroduce 'good day' as the official greeting?" Marianne almost opened her mouth to exclaim in surprise, but caught herself just in time. The others, knowing it was a joke, shook their heads and waited for the punch line. "Goebbels, of course, refused, saying that 'as long as Hitler lives, there will be no 'good day.'"

The little circle of students laughed appreciatively. One of the others leaned closer and lowered his voice. "Did you hear this one? 'When will the war finally end?' 'When Göring can fit into Goebbels' pants.'"

Again they laughed. Jens-Uwe had another joke ready. "In the air-raid shelters these days, people use three different greetings. Those that say 'good evening' are on their way to bed, and those that say 'good morning' have slept in the cellar, and those who say '*Heil Hitler*' haven't woken up yet."

This got the biggest laugh yet. Rainer slapped his hand on the table-top in delight, and one of the others was laughing so hard he had to wipe tears away from his face.

"Isn't it amazing how time flies?" Jens-Uwe asked his circle of friends. "A thousand years has gone by already!"

They dissolved into laughter again, and this time even Marianne joined in. The next thing she knew, a brawny man was standing right beside her chair, roaring from his red, fleshy face, "That's enough! You filthy cowards! You defeatists! I've heard enough of this talk! Not one of you leaves here until the police arrive! Dimitri! Call the police!"

Marianne never knew if it was because the pretty offices off Kurfürstendamm had been damaged or destroyed in the raids, or if it was because this was a different crime or district, that she was taken somewhere else. In any case, this time she found herself facing an interrogation in a gloomy, old brick building in Moabit, an industrial part of the city. There were bars on the ground-floor windows, apparently to keep thieves out as much as to keep prisoners in. The whole building stank of mold, clogged toilets and unhappy humanity. The other people she encountered in the halls as she was marched roughly along were in faded, worn working clothes. Most smelled of sweat. The room they thrust her in had boarded-up windows and a naked light bulb. A single wooden chair, rather like the kind used by schoolchildren, waited in the middle of the room in front of a heavy old desk, which was scratched and discolored from years of careless use. Behind the desk was a middle-aged, heavy-set man in civilian clothes.

The door clanged shut behind her. This time there were no formalities. "So you think the Thousand-Year Reich is over, do you?"

"No," Marianne started. At least this time she knew exactly what the charges were, but her voice almost failed her nevertheless. She had to clear her throat before adding, "Not at all."

"DON'T LIE TO ME!" the man behind the desk roared at her. He had an ample belly and heavy jowls. In fact, he looked very much like the man who had arrested them, Marianne noted. But he wasn't the same man, just the same kind of petty bourgeoisie busybody. "There were witnesses that you laughed."

"It was just a joke—"

"JUST A JOKE! You think it is funny to suggest that our Thousand-Year Reich has collapsed? You think the fate of your nation and race is an appropriate subject for stupid jokes?"

"Yes," Marianne insisted as bravely as she could. "One can joke about anything. It doesn't mean anything."

"Oh? It doesn't mean anything to suggest '*Heil Hitler*' is only said by people who 'haven't woken up yet?' Woken up to what?"

Marianne shrugged. "I don't know. I didn't make the joke."

"But you laughed at it!"

"Is that a crime?"

"Don't be impudent with me! Do you think I don't know you've been arrested before? Do you think I don't know you listen to enemy broadcasts? Do you think I don't know you go to the Confessing Church—just like your friend Rainer?"

Marianne was getting hotter. It was, she noticed, oppressively hot in this room. It was hard to breathe. The questions came thick and fast, and no matter what she said, they could twist her answer into something sinister. She was sweating, but the questions didn't stop. She was thirsty, and it was hours since she had been to a toilet. Her bladder was getting heavy, almost painful. She asked to be allowed to go to the toilet.

The interrogator stopped as if surprised by the request. It made her blush. But he pressed a buzzer on his desk, and a woman in SS uniform appeared. He ordered her to take Marianne to the toilet. The woman led her away down the long corridor, down a half-flight of stairs, and through a scratched, dirty door. The toilet was dingy. Mold darkened the cracks of the discolored tiles. The whole place stank. Marianne was taken to a dirty toilet stall and told to leave the door open while she "did her business."

When she returned to the interrogation chamber, it was empty. She was told to sit down and wait. She waited. And waited. What could they do to her for having laughed at a few simple jokes? She had heard it whispered that Judge Roland Friesler at the People's Court had sentenced people to *death* for telling jokes. But how could they do that? Besides, she hadn't told any jokes; she had only laughed at them.

Marianne tried to dry her sweating hands on her skirt. Her skirt was sticking to the chair. She stood up a little to try to make herself more comfortable, and at once the SS guard at the door ordered her to sit down again.

The problem wasn't the jokes: it was her "criminal record." She'd been arrested before. And she belonged to the Confessing Church. If they followed that lead far enough … Marianne couldn't think about it. She couldn't deal with the consequences. And what about Rainer? How much did he know? She hardly knew him. She'd met him at church. They had chatted after services. He'd found out she was going to university and suggested they meet after a lecture. She'd been happy for the distraction, happy to meet other young people. She was having a hard time getting over Peter … That was another topic that didn't bear thinking about.

Since her last arrest, their relationship had become completely crazy. On the one hand they slept with one another, and on the other they fought more and more violently. Peter seemed to think that just because he had possessed her physically he could control everything about her—where she went, what she did, whom she associated with. He thought she had to account to him for every minute of her time. He thought he owned her. The very memory of his behavior made her angry, even here and now.

Yet in the next instant Marianne froze, in the cold knowledge that Peter had saved her last time. If she didn't have a Gestapo inspector willing to speak up for her now, how was she ever going to get out of here?

The interrogator returned. He walked around behind his desk. He sat down and gazed at her. He drummed his fingers on the top of the table as he considered her. Then he started a new line of questioning. "These friends of yours—like Rainer—they're cowards, aren't they? Draft dodgers, not willing to fight for their Fatherland."

"I don't know, really. I hardly know them."

"You hardly know them? You are willing to sit around in a café with a bunch of men you hardly know? What sort of slut are you?"

Marianne sighed inwardly. Apparently it was standard procedure for Gestapo interrogators to insult female prisoners. She treated the question as rhetorical, and after a moment the interrogator did, too. He continued, "Who are your friends? This Pastor Költz of the Confessing Church?"

Oh, no! Marianne's whole body stiffened in terror. Pastor Költz was the man to whom she delivered all her forged documents. If they moved against Pastor Költz, it would be the end. Not just for her and for him, but for all the people dependent on them. She licked her lips and nodded stiffly. "Yes, I consider Pastor Költz a friend." She tried to sound calm. "But not like I want."

"What do you mean? What do you want?"

The diversion seemed to have worked. She shrugged, "I mean, not like a young man. You know." She shrugged again, avoided his eye, and looked down at her hands like a modest middle-class girl ashamed of admitting her desire.

"Oh, that. And Rainer?"

"We're just getting to know each other. That's why I went along with him. That's why I wanted his friends to like me. That's why I laughed at their jokes."

"Aha." The fingers drummed on the table again. The interrogator nodded. "We will continue tomorrow." He stood and left without another word. This time there was no protocol to sign; she was simply taken to prison.

There were advantages to being a "repeat offender," Marianne decided. This time she was prepared for the probing finger up her vagina, the prison clothes, and the cell. Since it was a warm June evening, she did not even mind the broken windowpanes above her head. At least they let in a little fresh air.

She sat down on the fold-down bed and waited in a curiously numbed state of mind. Part of her thought she ought to be more frightened. She had been more frightened last time. This time it was bound to be worse. But the mere fact that she'd been released once made her hope—irrationally—for that again. At least as long as the daylight lingered.

With the darkness, her mood changed. She started to go over all the things she had said to Peter in various fights—most notably the last time she had spoken to him. That had been when she returned the engagement ring he'd given her. She'd told him that she was an adult woman and she didn't need him telling her what to do. She'd told him that he was worse than her father had even been. She'd told him—and she cringed at this memory—that she didn't want his "so-called protection" if it meant "giving up her very soul." The fight, as always, had focused on his insistence that she stop going to church.

So, she told herself in the grim darkness of her prison cell, she had her soul—but no protection from the "Devil's servant." (Yes, she'd used that phrase to Peter in one argument or another.) Suddenly she wasn't so sure she'd made the right choice. Then the sirens went off.

She hadn't been expecting them. The last time she'd been imprisoned, there had been no raid. It wasn't part of the "routine" here. But the effect they produced in her was the same as always. Her nerves instantly went on alert. She got to her feet and went to the door. She listened for the sound of footsteps. They had to hurry if they were to open all the cell doors one by one. Marianne tried to remember how many doors there were between the stairs and her own cell. She was roughly in the middle of the long hall. There must be at least a half-dozen cells that would have to be opened first. If only they would start! What was taking them so long? She couldn't hear anyone moving outside at all. Did they start on another floor? But then the bombers would be here before they got through the whole building! But there was no sound anywhere! Was she the only prisoner in the whole tract? Had they forgotten her?

She knocked on the cell door. She called out, "Hello! Hello! Come let me out!"

The second warning was blaring. The light from the probing searchlights brightened the cell. Marianne banged louder and shouted more furiously. "Hello! Hello! You've forgotten me! Help!"

The flak started to crumpf, and then with a whistle the first stick of bombs rained down. Marianne screamed at the top of her lungs, "Guards! Come quick! They're already here! Let me out!"

The knowledge that the guards were long since safe in the air-raid shelter reached her brain, but she didn't want to believe it. She screamed and screamed, no longer articulately, as the first detonations shook the old prison building. The cell was gradually turning red from the light of the flames outside. She could hear the droning of the aircraft overhead—when she didn't scream to drown out the sound.

She couldn't take any more! She had to get underground! How could they leave her exposed like this? She hadn't been sentenced to death yet! Didn't they realize that if they let her die up here, they could never get any information out of her?

That was it! They would only let her go to safety if she cooperated with them! "Guards! Guards! I'll tell you everything, anything! Just let me out of here! Let me into the cellar! I'll name names. I'll tell you everything!"

It worked! She heard someone coming. A key turned in the door. They had heard her the whole time. It was part of their torture methods to leave prisoners exposed to the air raids. They had waited intentionally until she was so terrified that she said she would name names.

She stepped back from the door, terrified of what she had done, but behind her the bombs still rained down on the battered city and the flak barked like a pack of helpless terriers. She was trembling from head to foot.

In the doorway stood a hideous, toothless hag with wisps of grey hair and one eye that rolled down to the right under a half-closed lid. "You stupid girl!" the hag shouted at her, in a raw voice that spattered evil-smelling saliva with each word. "How dare you promise to betray others just to save your own skin? What good is that going to do you? Even if they let you out of here, you could die tomorrow out there!" She pointed toward the window, which glowed red and then brightened and dimmed again. "Hold your stupid tongue, you spoiled brat—even if your friends are as stupid and selfish as you!" And with this, the witch was gone.

Stunned, Marianne stood in the middle of her cell, afraid she had lost her sanity. Outside, the crescendo of the aircraft, flak, bombs and flames raged. Sirens wailed. The prison trembled and the earth seemed to jump. Marianne's terror continued to mount, but she was now afraid of the "witch," too. She did not dare cry out. She paced about her cell and flung herself up and down until she exhausted herself.

She went to the interrogation the next day with a throat raw from shouting. Her hands and wrists were black and blue from pounding on the door. She had bags under her eyes and her lips were chewed raw. At the sight of her the interrogator raised his eyebrows and asked, "What happened to you?"

"I was left in my cell during the air raid," Marianne told him, and there was a trace of indignation in her voice.

"Oh, that. Of course. We have to leave the prisoners above ground. There's no time to get them all handcuffed, and if they aren't, they might overpower the guards. Now, let's go back to your friend Pastor Költz. How long have you known him?"

"I don't know exactly. As long as I've been going to his church."

"How long is that?"

"A couple of years."

"Why do you go to his church?"

God help me! Marianne prayed. "He's not like most pastors. He's different."

"He's not patriotic, perhaps? He doesn't believe in our *Führer*? He thinks the Thousand-Year Reich is already over, for example?"

"No; I mean he's a real Christian. He says we should help our fellow man."

"Doesn't National Socialism teach us that? Did you never learn anything from all your Labor Service? What do you think National Socialism is all about, if not everyone helping our Great Fatherland? Why do you need all this mumbo-jumbo about resurrection and wine turned into blood? An intelligent girl like you should laugh at that—not the size of the *Reichmarschall's* trousers! What is it about this superstitious nonsense that appeals to you more than the wholesome principles of National Socialism?"

"It's more personal," Marianne tried to explain. Keep it harmless, she told herself. "I don't like groups and marching and uniforms."

"You don't like uniforms. I see. So that's why you hang around with the draft dodgers?"

"No. I mean I don't like uniforms for girls."

"But you hang around with draft dodgers, don't you?"

"Not very much."

"No, right, not very much. You prefer Pastor Költz and his friends. What do you do with these older people, anyway?"

Marianne's heart was pumping in double time, and the worst of it was knowing that she was blushing. She couldn't control the flow of blood in her veins. Marianne swallowed, but her throat was dry as a bone. "May I have a glass of water?"

"NO! Answer my question!"

"I—we—it's just that—"

To the evident annoyance of the interrogator, the telephone rang. He tried to ignore it. "Answer me! What do you do with a bunch of old people?" The telephone was too loud and too insistent. Marianne stared at it, praying for it to continue.

With a scowl, the interrogator lifted the receiver and shouted into it. "What is it? ... Yes. I'm in the middle of the interrogation right now The telephone rang ... Yes ... As you order!" He smashed the receiver down and glowered furiously at Marianne. Then with an exasperated gesture he rang a buzzer, and the door opened behind Marianne. She was escorted back to her cell.

In her cell a cold cup of substitute coffee and a hard white roll awaited her. She devoured the roll, but poured the coffee down the sink. The worst was over, she told herself. She could sense it.

Along the hall she could hear someone collecting the coffee cups. She held hers ready as the door opened. To her amazement, it was the witch of the night before. Only now did Marianne notice that she was dressed like a prisoner. By daylight she looked no less hideous, but Marianne realized she was not really as old as she looked. The woman squinted at her with her good eye. "You'll get used to the raids. Be thankful you're here and not in a KZ!" She pointed to her damaged eye and was gone.

Stunned, Marianne stood rooted to the floor for several seconds. KZ. What if she were sent to a KZ? Prison was humiliating, but it was somehow still part of the old, legal order. There were regulations—not just for her, but for the guards as well. But in a KZ, everyone knew the SS did what they liked. There, they had no one to account to except their own superiors.

She sank onto her bed. God help me! She wasn't strong enough for this. She had been arrogant and proud to think she could help others. She had been playing God. She had believed that because she was doing His will, he would protect her. She had believed in a Guardian Angel. It was all silly—what had the Gestapo man said?—superstitious bunk. Others who were doing His will—Pastor Bonhoeffer, Paster Stellbrink in Lübeck, many others—had been caught in the Devil's net. Why should she have thought herself safe? Peter …

This time her parents collected her at the prison gate. Her mother rushed forward and clung to her. Her father, looking very grey and bent these days, patted her helplessly on the back. They said nothing. In silence they took the *S-Bahn*, changed to the bus, and walked the last block. Marianne and her mother clung to each other the whole way. They went up the stairs. The banister had been shaken loose during the repeated raids, and it swayed dangerously rather than offering support. Plaster dust and crumbs littered the floor. The door to the Moldenauer apartment didn't fit properly into the frame anymore, and a new bolt had been improvised. Her father let them in. They walked, still silent, into the kitchen and sank down. They stared at one another.

"What did you do this time?" her father asked bitterly.

"*Vati*!" Frau Moldenauer protested before Marianne could answer.

But her father burst out angrily, "Can't you see that you endanger us all with your nonsense? Your mother and me and even your brother! Why can't you be more careful!"

"Can't *you* see that she's been through enough?" countered Frau Moldenauer indignantly to her husband. "She's been punished already! But," she turned on her daughter with a pleading look, "Marianne, you must make up with Peter! When we found out what had happened and turned to him, the first thing he said was: 'Marianne doesn't want my help.' Of course, he helped anyway. Your father begged him, and he—he was so gallant, and told your father not to humiliate himself." She glanced at her husband as she admitted this, but Marianne's father looked away, ashamed. "He said he would help for our sake, Marianne. You've hurt him badly, and he's such a good man. You've got to make up with him!"

Marianne did—because she knew that she could not go through another arrest. She had learned that her faith was not strong enough. She knew that the raids would wear her down until she named names. Her release had saved the others as much as it had saved her.

So she humbled herself before Peter. She admitted she had been wrong. She promised to do everything he asked of her. She even said she would not go to church again, although she didn't say why. She let him think it was to please him.

In reality, she didn't dare. She knew how close she had come to betraying the others, and she could not risk that. She told herself that the war would soon be over and no one would need her forged documents anymore. She told herself she had done as much as she could.

But when they had finished making love that night with the passion that usually followed reconciliation, Marianne asked Peter timidly, "How did you manage it this time, Peter?"

He stiffened. "Does it matter?"

"Yes," she told him steadily. "I need to know how much I owe you."

"I ..."

"Yes?"

"I told my colleagues that I knew you belonged to an opposition circle—one involved in helping the Jews and the like. I—I said I was using you as bait, and I didn't want you arrested until I had identified as many of the others as possible. Then, I promised to make a big, multiple arrest."

Marianne lay paralyzed in her lover's arms, and their heartbeats merged so powerfully together that she could not distinguish hers from his—no more than she could disentangle her fear of him from her love.

∗   ∗   ∗   ∗

Berlin
June 1944

"Freiherr von Feldburg!" Annie Lerche called out as she saw Philip go by in the hall.

He put his head in the office. "*Ja?*"

"*Herr General* wants you to report to his office immediately. He's been looking for you for the last fifteen minutes."

"Something unusual?" he asked, surprised by her tone, with a questioning glance to Lotte.

Lotte shrugged to indicate she didn't know, and continued with her typing. Annie said, "You'll see. General Fromm just left here five minutes ago." She made a point of not looking at him and resumed her typing even as she spoke.

General Fromm was a thoroughly unpleasant superior, and far too puffed up with his own importance to visit his subordinate's office unless he had some particular reason. Philip knocked and Olbricht called, "Come in."

Olbricht welcomed him with a broad smile and an easy, "Ah, there you are. We've been looking all over for you."

Stauffenberg was already there, leaning against the General's desk. Now he stood up straight, remarking, "I'll be right back—if *Herr General* will excuse me, that is."

"Of course. Take a seat, Feldburg." Olbricht indicated a chair near the window and sat opposite, his legs stretched out comfortably. "Fromm was just here. He wanted a favor of me."

"*Generaloberst* Fromm?"

"Yes." Olbricht was obviously pleased with himself. "He came to ask me if I could bring myself to part with *Graf* Stauffenberg—he wants him as his own Chief of Staff."

Philip was a little confused as to why Olbricht should seem so pleased by this development. Olbricht and Stauffenberg not only worked flawlessly together, they had developed a good personal friendship. Olbricht had gone to considerable trouble to get Stauffenberg assigned to the AHA in the first place. Now the search for a new Chief of Staff would start over again. "Don't you see the implications for Valkyrie?" Olbricht asked, amused.

"You mean that if Fromm refuses to co-operate, Stauffenberg—as Fromm's Chief of Staff—can sign the orders with apparent full authority."

"Precisely. It should make the whole thing run more smoothly. And there's always the chance he'll have more influence on Fromm once he starts working for him directly. In any case, when Stauffenberg told him bluntly he no longer believed the war could be won and favored a 'change in the command structure,' Fromm replied that such sentiments were no obstacle to his being Chief of Staff of the Home Army!" Olbricht slapped the table with his hand in delight, adding, "Then he made a most intriguing remark. He said—as if incidentally—'and don't forget Keitel when you make your coup.'"

Philip started.

"In short, I think Fromm can be counted on to play along until the attempt is made—and then to jump on the bandwagon. Assuming the assassination is successful, I think he'll even sign Valkyrie himself; but one way or another it would be a good thing to have his Chief a reliable partner in this. You and I will sit a little to one side once Valkyrie is actually issued. Stauffenberg will—starting July 1—be at the very nerve center of the Home Army, with full authority to issue orders to all the *Wehrkreiskommandos.*"

At this moment Stauffenberg returned with a bottle of *Sekt*. "Gentlemen, may I suggest a small celebration is in order?"

"Absolutely. Ask the ladies to join us."

Stauffenberg went back and stuck his head into the secretariat. "Ladies, if you would be so kind as to join us ..."

In a moment the cork cracked against the high ceiling and the foam frothed down the neck of the bottle. Five glasses were quickly filled and lifted. Olbricht offered at toast to "*Oberst* i.G. *Graf* Stauffenberg" (apparently a promotion went with the new assignment), Chief of Staff of the Home Army." The others seconded and drank. He continued, "And, of course, to my own new Chief of Staff, Baron v. Feldburg."[1]

Philip literally choked on the champagne bubbles from sucking in his breath in surprise. Everyone laughed. "Come now," Olbricht teased; "it can't come as a surprise."

"*Doch!*"

"*Na*, cheers!" They drank again.

"Before you assume your duties, Feldburg, I want you to tour all the Military Districts in person and check on the preparations for Valkyrie. Try to get a feel for each and every commander and chief, so we know roughly where we can expect the most trouble. I think we can assume that Valkyrie will be issued within the next two months—that, or the Americans will be in Berlin."

*   *   *   *

Paris
June 1944

High summer in Paris: the wide avenues and the stately buildings of the Second Empire, the trees and parks and pigeons, the lamp-lined bridges arching graciously over the Seine, and the stubby, rather dirty towers of Notre Dame against a pale blue sky.

It was the last stop of Philip's tour of Military Districts, and it put him in a nostalgic mood. He'd last been here on a whirlwind visit following the French campaign. Both he and Paris had been somewhat embarrassed by the rapid turn of events. He'd felt strange with the brand-new Iron Cross dangling on his chest, and he'd been sensitive—perhaps over-sensitive—to the searing looks of passing strangers. Now, however, Paris was run down. The streets were almost empty of

---

1. In fact, Oberst i.G. Ritter Mertz v. Quirnheim replaced Stauffenberg as Chief of Staff to Olbricht.

vehicles and what traffic there was came from bicycles, horse-drawn contraptions, and *Wehrmacht* vehicles. Much of the *Wehrmacht* traffic was horse-drawn, too, or had curious contraptions for wood-burning fuel. The sight of German officers, even ones with a Knight's Cross, was so commonplace that Philip attracted no attention—not even hostility—from the population. The sidewalk cafés were grey with customers—both male and female *Wehrmacht* personnel. Even the Parisiennes failed to impress. With their too-short skirts and too-big hats, they looked far less elegant than Alexandra before she was pregnant.

Philip found himself wondering where Alix had lived in Paris and what it had been like then, before the war. He tried to picture her eight years younger, fresh from college, enjoying the freedom of the French Republic after years of National Socialism at home. He pictured her shopping and sitting in the cafés and wandering along the street-side art shows. He wished they could have known each other then. He wished they had been allowed to share the good times as well as the bad.

He called her every night—a highly unsatisfying procedure of difficult and often bad connections. Even worse was the sensation of being listened to by the operator, the Duty Officer, or the communications sergeant of whatever Military District he was visiting. Alexandra always assured him everything was "fine." She was being "spoiled," she insisted, by so much attention from the staff and the Polish women. Neither he nor she felt free to say what they were really thinking or feeling. Philip ended each telephone call feeling lonelier than before.

Before the Hotel Majestic with its intact, elegant façade (something bomb-scarred Berlin could no longer offer), a black Mercedes with the flags of a three-star general waited. Soldiers in steel helmets, instead of bellboys in braid, stood guard at the door. The soldiers presented arms to Philip as he passed through.

In all the other Military Districts, only the occasional staff officer was initiated into the real purpose of Valkyrie. Here, however, the military governor himself, General Heinrich v. Stülpnagel, was one of the conspirators. Indeed, Stülpnagel had been one of the officers who, along with Generals Halder and Witzleben, had been prepared to remove Hitler from power in 1938 to *prevent* a war. Unlike Halder and others, Stülpnagel's opposition to the Regime had not wavered since. In a post that others would have coveted and exploited for its luxury, ease and security, Stülpnagel chafed under a sense of isolation and helplessness. He particularly suffered under the apparent responsibility for policies he could not change, much less control. His time in Paris was a constant struggle against the excesses and arrogance of civilian (Party) and SS officials, who often possessed authority of an overlapping or ambiguously similar nature to his own.

In the hotel's grand reception hall, one of Stülpnagel's staff officers, Caesar v. Hofacker, greeted Philip. Hofacker was a cousin of Stauffenberg's and, like his boss, fully informed about Valkyrie. "*Herr General* is awaiting you, *Herr Oberst-leutnant.* He's about to set off for La Roche Guyon and requests that you join him."

"He's on his way to see Rommel?"

"Yes."

In his office, Stülpnagel—tall, straight, grey-haired and strikingly hand-some—accepted Philip's salute and then shook hands, announcing that they had to leave for La Roche Guyon at once. His adjutant brought him his greatcoat even as he spoke, and he hung it over his shoulders. "Herr v. Hofacker tells me you are to replace *Graf* Stauffenberg as Chief of Staff at AHA," he remarked as they headed back down the carpeted stairs.

In the waiting Mercedes, Hofacker took the seat next to the driver and Philip was seated next to the General in the back. "You can speak freely," Stülpnagel announced as they set off down the broad streets in the direction of Normandy. "Are there any new developments in Berlin?"

"Only that *Graf* Stauffenberg hopes to play a more direct role."

"But the problem remains ignition, doesn't it?"

Philip sighed and agreed simply, "*Jawohl.*" A successful assassination was the unavoidable, unyielding, uncompromising necessity. Without it, all the planning in the world did not help—and nor did having the right people in the right places.

"The situation here is becoming increasingly difficult," the military governor explained crisply to the visiting staff officer from Berlin. "I'm sure you're fully informed of developments on the invasion front, so I won't go into that. But in addition to that, the *Résistance* gains in audacity and strength daily. Four out of every five former collaborators are now trying to whitewash their collaborationist past with some dramatic gesture of anti-Germanism. At the same time, the Party demands a dramatic increase in the number of 'volunteers' for service in the *Reich*. I also get constant complaints about the slow pace of the Jewish deporta-tions. If I drag my feet much louder and longer in either of these areas, I'm going to get cashiered." He paused to let this sink in.

Philip felt compelled to admit, "We thought that General Stieff would be will-ing to do it himself. He kept the explosives with him for weeks, but eventually he admitted," Philip looked for a way of wording it that was not too insulting, "that he wasn't capable of it."

Stülpnagel turned his well-proportioned face to Philip, and his deep-set eyes were piercing. A grey eyebrow twitched, but then he continued, "Then I presume Olbricht and Stauffenberg will find an alternative—soon. Events are moving very rapidly. That is what I want to talk to you about.

"You will soon hear from Rommel's own mouth his extremely pessimistic assessment of our ability to contain the Western invasion forces. We must give some serious thought to whether holding the Western Allies back serves anyone's interests other than Stalin's."

Philip started. He was still too much of a soldier to have considered the possibility of *not* resisting an enemy invasion. Stülpnagel noticed the shock that went through him and nodded. "It is not an easy thought, but—as Beck said back in '38—exceptional times demand exceptional measures. Every soldier and every tank we burn up in a futile rear-guard action against the British and Americans is a soldier and tank that might otherwise be employed to stop the Soviet invasion. If it is painful to imagine Germany occupied by the Americans and British, it is nonetheless preferable to a Soviet occupation. The only chance we stand of stopping the Soviets before they cross into Germany is to throw everything we have—from Norway to Italy—at them.

"There are some elements in the Armed Forces here who believe that the Anglo-Americans are as horrified by the prospect of the Soviets in Berlin as we are. These elements argue that the Western Allies, particularly now that they have a foothold on the Continent, will make common cause with us against the Soviets." He paused and added, "It might interest you to know that a number of SS commanders belong to this school of thought."

"Do we want *them* as allies?" Philip asked, discomfited by the very thought. As he had said to Alexandra just over a month ago, he did not see this coup merely as a means for ending the war. He saw it as a political statement against the policies of Hitler's regime—most especially the SS.

Stülpnagel answered, "Do we have a choice? What matters is that we succeed in ending the slaughter. It would be an unforgivable vanity to risk failure for the sake of keeping our hands clean. Rommel is no ideal ally, either. He was a devoted follower of Hitler. He is vain in the extreme and he possesses, at most, mediocre intelligence. But he is a good soldier. Once he makes a decision, he'll stick to it—and of course, he's very popular.

"It would, of course, be a fatal mistake to discuss our plans with Rommel, but I believe he can be won over to the idea of 'opening the Western Front' to the Anglo-Americans *after* a successful action in Berlin—if Generaloberst Beck is willing to pursue this option."

"You believe Rommel would be able to negotiate an armistice with the Western Allies?" Philip asked skeptically.

"Possibly—particularly if he is Head of State of a non-Nazi Germany." Again Stülpnagel paused to let this sink in. Then he continued, "Rommel taught the English to respect his tactical abilities in Africa, and he has a reputation for fairness and decency that is not undeserved—even if it is less exceptional than the Anglo-Americans seem to think. That's the message I want you to take back to Beck and Olbricht. With Rommel as titular Head of Government after a coup, we might be able to get the separate peace we desperately need. Furthermore, he might secure us the backing of the bulk of the population."

Philip knew Olbricht was relatively indifferent to who filled what post in a post-Hitler government. Although slated to take over the Ministry of Defense, Olbricht was not politically ambitious. Still, Rommel's credentials as a leader of a democratic opposition were nil. That made Philip somewhat reluctant to embrace the idea, but in any case it was not his decision. He nodded and promised to pass on the suggestion to Beck, Olbricht and Stauffenberg.

When Philip reached Berlin late in the afternoon of the following day, the city had suffered two daylight raids in succession, and smoke and dust hung in the summer air. Train and tram connections were badly disrupted, and fires still raged in some districts. Whole battalions of Concentration Camp inmates had been brought into the city to help with the removal of corpses from collapsed cellars and incinerated apartments. Before the rows of shops with shattered windows, policemen patrolled to prevent looting. On public announcement pillars, a huge poster announced the execution of a man—his photograph provided—for plundering. "He who plunders sabotages Victory!" shouted the poster in large red lettering.

Theo Pfalz must have been watching out of his window, because he rushed out as soon as the staff car stopped in front of the house. Philip stepped out and waited for Stadthagen to get his suitcase from the back. "*Herr Baron! Herr Baron!* A telegram! It came this afternoon," Theo called to him, waddling down the walkway with his arm outstretched.

Philip put his briefcase down and took the telegram from Theo. His face and gestures were fully controlled, but his tension was obvious in the fact that he opened the telegram on the open street. Theo and Stadthagen watched him as he opened the envelope. The telegram was from Altdorf, and Philip held his breath. It was much too soon. The baby wasn't due for another 2-3 weeks. "Friedrich v.

Feldburg born at 8.15 this morning. We're both healthy and happy. Thinking of you. Love, Alexandra."

"Stadthagen, do we have any *Sekt* left in the cellar?"

"Congratulations!" Theo and Stadthagen burst out simultaneously. Theo offered Philip his hand and pumped it vigorously. "Congratulations, *Herr Baron*," he said again. "A son or a daughter?"

"A son."

"Splendid, splendid; and the *Frau Baronin*?"

"Fine. Stadthagen, bring up whatever you can find—for Theo, too." Turning to the porter he said, "You can share it with your friends tonight. It's your *Skat* night, isn't it?" While Theo nodded and thanked him, Philip continued to Stadthagen, "Bring up two bottles. If there's no champagne, bring a good wine."

Philip entered the house and started up the stairs two at a time, anxious to put a call through to Altdorf, but the pains came so sharply that he had to grab the precarious banister and wait a moment. No, he wasn't fit, and the travel of the last two weeks had weakened him, he registered. Since Stadthagen was on his way to the cellar, Theo picked up Philip's suitcase and started up the stairs with him. "*Herr Baron*, there is another officer waiting for you. He arrived almost an hour ago. I told him you weren't back yet, but he insisted on waiting."

"No problem, Herr Pfalz. Do you know who it is?" Philip started up the stairs again, slowly now and in pain. Beside him, Theo huffed and puffed from the exertion of carrying the suitcase.

"The one-eyed colonel, *Herr Baron*."

"*Ach*, Stauffenberg. He'll be happy to join the celebration. Any other news?"

Theo stopped to catch his breath, unable to climb stairs carrying a suitcase and talk at the same time. "*Ach*, I don't know. If I did my duty and reported every disloyal remark I hear these days, the whole house would be empty. It makes me so angry the way everyone is turning against the *Führer* now." Theo hastened to add, "I don't mean you, *Herr Baron*! You were always anti-Nazi; I can respect that. It's these selfish cowards who were all 150%-ers as long as the going was good! And now they turn on the *Führer* when he needs our support most. They make me sick!" With this he picked up the suitcase again and led an astonished Philip up the rest of the stairs.

Philip thanked Theo for carrying the suitcase and let himself into his apartment. "Claus! Rolf! Lotte! Everyone!" He put the pain out of his mind.

Nadja emerged. "*Herr Baron*?"

"The mistress has had a son. This morning. Where is everyone?"

"Herr v. Seydlitz has duty tonight and Frau Lotte was invited out—"

"There you are, Claus!" Philip greeted Stauffenberg as the latter emerged from the smoking room. "Did you hear? Alexandra had a son this morning. I've already sent Stadthagen for something decent from the cellar. You don't mind if I make a call first, do you? Make yourself at home and I'll be with you in a moment."

Stadthagen brought Philip a glass of warm champagne while he was still trying to get through on the telephone. The lines were overloaded and the connection bad. "Alix?"

"Philip? Are you back?"

"Are you all right? I thought the baby wasn't due for weeks."

"It wasn't, but your son was impatient. He's beautiful, Philip. I always thought babies were ugly—but not Fritz. He's all yours—dark hair—I can't wait for you to see him. Can you get leave?"

"I'll try. You're sure you're all right?"

"I miss you—"

They were cut off. Philip tried to put the call through again, but it was impossible. He decided not to keep Stauffenberg waiting any longer, and to try again later. He took his glass back into the smoking room. Even as elated as Philip was, the sight of Claus pacing around the room, his face drawn and pale, drained the joy out of him. Stauffenberg tried to smile as he turned to him, but it was so forced that it failed to overcome the lifelessness of the left side of his face. "Congratulations," he offered, lifting his glass, "to the youngest Feldburg."

Philip joined the toast, but his unease was not stilled.

Claus made a further effort. "Do you have a name?"

"Friedrich Stefan Paul Maria," he rattled it off easily. Alexandra and he had agreed on names for both a son and a daughter long ago.

"Send my best wishes next time you talk to Alexandra. And your trip? Was it productive?"

"Yes, I think so. We can talk about it later. What's bothering you?"

"Something terrible." Stauffenberg put his half-empty glass down and, taking his handkerchief from his pocket, daubed at his empty eye socket under the patch. He took a deep breath. "They've arrested Leber."

"Julius Leber? Again? On what charges?"

"He and Adolf Reichwein decided to meet with representatives of the Communist underground. He and others felt we should widen the base of support, tap the KPD personnel and organizational resources. I agreed," Stauffenberg admitted, even as the question formed on Philip's tongue. This was a point on which Philip knew Olbricht vehemently disagreed with Stauffenberg. Olbricht had forbidden it precisely because he suspected all KPD underground organizations had been infiltrated by the Gestapo. Stauffenberg had been acting on his own in this—as he seemed increasingly willing to do of late. Philip didn't like it. Stauffenberg was continuing, "The KPD presented a program so moderate that Leber became suspicious. He chose not to attend the next meeting, so Reichwein went alone. Reichwein was arrested immediately with the Communists, and Leber was picked up today."

"Two Social Democrats, then. No clear connection to us." Philip made the remark more to himself than to Stauffenberg. He was trying to assess the immediate damage and danger.

Stauffenberg responded angrily, "That's not the point! Leber is going to be subjected to the worst abuse possible! A Socialist! An old enemy! They'll try to take him to pieces!"

"I don't think they're likely to succeed." Philip spoke out of the deepest respect for Leber. Leber had been such an outspoken opponent of the Nazis even before their seizure of power that he was 'arrested' almost immediately afterwards—despite being a Member of Parliament and so legally immune from arrest. He had been in a Concentration Camp when the *Reichstag* passed the Enabling Law. When he was released in mid-March 1933 (after massive workers' protests on his behalf in his native Lübeck), the evidence of abuse was still visible on his body. He had been too weak to speak at the rally organized for him, but he had gone to the microphone and shouted one word: "Freedom." Shortly afterwards he was arrested again, and he spent the next four years in various prisons and Concentration Camps. Yet he had emerged more determined than ever to bring down the Regime. Philip believed that if anyone in the world could and would stand up to Gestapo torture, it was Julius Leber.

Stauffenberg, however, responded with outrage—or was it guilt? Did he at last understand why Olbricht had so vehemently opposed contact with the Communists? "How do we know what he can take?! The French *Résistance* believes no man can hold out longer than 24 hours; their agents are told they have that long to disappear after a contact has been picked up. And Leber's not a young man. Besides, he had been weakened by years of abuse in KZs already. We can't just leave him in their clutches! We can't expect him to sacrifice himself for our sake! We've got to get him out!"

Philip had never seen Stauffenberg so worked up. He paced fretfully about the room and kept dabbing at his empty eye socket. Then, in a gesture of irritation, he pulled the eye patch off altogether and stuffed it in his trouser pocket.

"How?" Philip asked calmly, lowering himself onto the arm of his father's large leather reading chair.

Stauffenberg didn't answer right away, but he continued to pace, his expression grim. "How often is Fromm required to brief Hitler?"

"Roughly every ten days—you know that as well as I."

"But he only occasionally attends personally."

"He hates Keitel," Philip responded flippantly, and then it dawned on him what Stauffenberg was driving at. He sat up straight in his chair and said firmly, "No, Claus. Don't even think about it. You can't sign the Valkyrie orders and answer all the incoming calls from the Military Districts if you've just blown yourself up with Hitler."

"But I won't have to. If Hitler's dead, Fromm will gladly sign them himself."

"We can't be sure Fromm will answer questions the way we want them answered."

"Then you and Olbricht will have to handle that."

"That won't work. Valkyrie must be issued by the C-in-C of the Home Army, and any confusion or hesitation can only be eliminated by him or his Chief of Staff. No one is going to even ask to talk to Olbricht or me once those orders are on the wires."

"You said yourself that the assassination was the most important thing."

"It is, but I don't see why you have to be the assassin. Why can't your adjutant do it?"

"First, because they don't always let adjutants in—one of our attempts failed already precisely because of that. Secondly, my adjutant only attends the meetings I'm at, so I'd still get killed anyway—whether I carried the thing myself or not. There's no advantage in it."

"There would be with a time fuse. You could accidentally forget your coat— or better still, your briefcase—with the bomb in the bunker."

Stauffenberg stopped pacing and considered this option, but then shook his head. "No; if I've left, Hitler will have left, too. Bussche had the right idea. Shortest possible fuse, fling yourself on Hitler, and hold on like the devil until the thing goes off."

"Bussche was a man nearly two meters tall, built like a lion and—at the time he was going to make the attempt—he still had all his limbs." (Bussche had since lost a leg in combat.)

"Touché," Stauffenberg conceded; "but there has to be more than one way to skin a cat. Up to now, the principal problem has been access to Hitler. I now have regular access to him. We can't afford to waste this opportunity. Sometimes

I think it was the only reason I was born, the reason I chose this career, the reason I was spared in Africa. Everything in my life has led me to this point and place—so I can kill him. It is my destiny."

Philip considered the wreck of a man before him, who had once been called the 'Darling of the Gods' because he'd been endowed with all possible blessings: pedigree, good looks, charm and intelligence. Undoubtedly many coincidences had combined to bring him to this point. Yet destiny nullified the significance of Free Will. It turned men into mere puppets in a divine theater. And if one considered all the coincidences that had served to keep Hitler alive up to now, then to accept destiny was to accept that Hitler, too, was God's will. Philip refused to accept that possibility.

Stauffenberg, sensing the lack of agreement, changed the subject. "The best aspect of the plan is that because I'll have repeated access to him, I'll have the chance to reconnoiter the situation before I make my attempt. My first briefing at *Führer*-HQ will be a dry run. On the second, I'll do it." Stauffenberg said this with so much conviction that Philip realized further protest was pointless. Instead he warned with all the gravity of foreboding, "Be careful. If you make an attempt and anything goes wrong—for whatever reason—there'll be no second chance. We'll all hang."

"Nothing will go wrong."

CHAPTER 40

▼

Berlin
July 15, 1944

"Issue Valkyrie at Alarm Level One," General Olbricht ordered his Chief of Staff, with a look at his watch. The General showed not the slightest sign of strain. In his white summer uniform, he appeared cool despite the oppressive heat.

After all that had been said and all the efforts that had been made to ensure that the orders went out legally, from Fromm or his Chief of Staff, Olbricht was issuing them on his own after all. Even though Philip had been warned, he still found himself countering, "Already? But I thought the daily briefing wasn't scheduled until 13.00?"

"Correct; but we agreed he would go through with it regardless, so there'll be no repeat of what happened four days ago." Stauffenberg had gone to *Führer* HQ equipped with a bomb on July 11, but because neither Himmler nor Göring attended the meeting, he had—in accordance with instructions—not set it off. Unhappy about this, however, Stauffenberg had insisted that the next time, he should act regardless. Beck and Olbricht had agreed. Furthermore, because Fromm planned to go to *Führer* HQ with Stauffenberg for the next meeting, Olbricht agreed to risk issuing Alarm Level One on his own authority. The Western Allies could not be confined in Normandy much longer, and Leber might break any day.

Olbricht was continuing, "I estimate that the Valkyrie units in and around Berlin need two to three hours to get operational. If we want those units to be ready at the critical moment, we have to alert them now."

Philip thought of a thousand objections. What if Hitler himself didn't show at the briefing? What if Stauffenberg didn't have time to set the fuse? What if he were prevented from attending the briefing? Or what if he had to present his own briefing? What if the Valkyrie units questioned orders signed by Olbricht? But he realized this was just an attack of nerves and said, "*Jawohl, Herr General.* Anything else?"

"Not at the moment. Join me for lunch today. We should depart at 11.45 and be back at 13.00 sharp. Fellgiebel is supposed to confirm the action before closing down the communications from *Führer* HQ. As soon as we know the trigger has been pressed, we can issue Alarm Level Two."

Alexandra was dozing on the terrace. The book she had been reading slipped onto the flagstone floor beside her, and her head rolled to one side. With a violent start, she was shaken from her sleep and half leapt out of her chair. She looked around, frightened by the suddenness of her awakening. Her heart pounded fast and forcefully. The mother instinct drove her first to the cradle, but Fritz was sound asleep on his belly, his tiny fists curled beside his head with its mass of fine, dark hair. The peaceful sight only increased his mother's unease. She looked about frantically for some tangible object that might have woken her. But the entire valley and household seemed sound asleep, as if under a magic spell.

What was she doing here? She ought to be in Berlin. Why had she waited so long? Fritz was in the best of hands. Ludmilla was nursing him. She had given birth to a daughter a couple of weeks earlier and had much more milk than Alexandra herself. The whole household doted on little Fritz, and Sophia Maria would ensure his welfare. Here in the peace of Altdorf, he was safe. But his father was alone in hell.

When was the next train to Frankfurt? Did she have time to make the connection to the fast train to Berlin? She had to try.

Frau Olbricht served lunch on the back terrace, and the garden bloomed peacefully before them. She did not try to force conversation on the two men with her, her husband and his Chief of Staff, who were both singularly silent this lunch. She poured the coffee when their cups were empty and offered cake with a minimum of interruption. At the distant gurgling of a telephone, both men jumped, but waited immobile until the General's orderly brought the message. "*Führer* HQ for *Herr General.*"

Olbricht stood and disappeared inside the house. Philip looked at his watch. It was 12.26. The briefing couldn't have started yet, so it was too soon for Fellgiebel's call. Stauffenberg? Frau Olbricht, straight and controlled as a soldier, started to clear the things away onto the waiting rollaway tray-table.

The orderly reappeared. "*Herr Baron. Herr General* requests you to join him."

Philip tried not to hurry too much. The General was still on the telephone, his expression clouded and tense. His forehead gleamed with sweat, his glasses slipped down his nose, and he pushed them back into place irritably. As he caught sight of Philip, he said into the phone, "Here's Feldburg." He handed the receiver to Philip.

"Feldburg," Philip identified himself.

"Himmler and Göring are not going to attend today's briefing either," Stauffenberg said in an exasperated, nervous voice. "Do you think it is still advisable to present the briefing I prepared, or should I wait for an occasion when they can hear it, too?"

Philip was startled by the question. The decision had been made—largely at Stauffenberg's own insistence, but certainly with Olbricht's and his own approval. "Yes, of course," he answered emphatically. My God! We've already issued Valkyrie Alarm Level One illegally, he was thinking. His hands were suddenly sweating. There would be hell to pay if Fromm or Hitler discovered they had issued Valkyrie. There would be no second chance.

"Good," Stauffenberg answered at the other end of the line. He sounded relieved. "I'll do it, then." He hung up.

Philip too hung up, and looked at General Olbricht, perplexed. "I don't understand."

Olbricht shook his head. "Neither do I—unless Stieff and Fellgiebel were so persuasive against an attempt that he really had doubts." Olbricht did not say what they were both thinking: that Stauffenberg himself had lost his nerve at the last minute. Who were they to judge him? Could they be so sure they would not be plagued by similar doubts on the brink of committing murder?

"He said he'd do it," Philip remarked, to try to counter the increased unease that the telephone call had produced.

In Frankfurt they gave Alexandra a queer look when she asked for a ticket to Berlin. "Do you have orders there? A job?"

"No, my husband is stationed there."

"Are you crazy? They're bombing Berlin day and night! No one in his right mind would go there voluntarily! And any husband who would expect it is a monster."

Olbricht and Philip did not go directly to the Bendlerstrasse, but stopped by the Berlin Commandant to tell General v. Hase that Valkyrie had been issued. They also made a brief call on *Graf* Helldorf, Chief of Police in Berlin, with the same message. From there they called one of the "insiders" down at Infantry Regiment 9 in Potsdam, where several young officers had volunteered to act as aides to the principals in the coup. The young officers were told to come up from Potsdam and take a table at the nearby Esplanade hotel, ready to come over to the Bendlerstrasse as soon as the coup was in progress. In Beck's living room, several of the conspirators no longer on active service collected and went through—yet again—the draft of the message that was to be delivered over the radio explaining the coup. It was a means of keeping themselves distracted while they waited for the *Wehrmacht* car that was to collect them and take them to the Bendlerstrasse.

The troops of the alerted Valkyrie units were assembled and confined to barracks. Few of them knew even the official purpose of Valkyrie, and—as the Saturday afternoon wore on—they grew restless on account of an alert that seemed to serve no purpose.

The only passengers on the fast train to Berlin were indeed those "under orders" for the capital: soldiers returning from leave, soldiers with posts in Berlin, couriers both civilian and military taking messages to institutions still located in Berlin, businessmen with business in the capital, civilian employees of companies and government organizations with jobs in the capital. An atmosphere of grim combat readiness accompanied them as they rolled steadily northward.

No sooner had Olbricht and Feldburg entered the reception hall than Annie jumped to her feet with a message in her hand. "An urgent call from *Graf* Stauffenberg!" She stretched across her desk to hand Olbricht her scribbled message. Olbricht's face blanched. "Could you join me, please," he muttered to Philip and went into his office.

Philip closed the door behind him, and Olbricht handed him the message in Annie's hand without comment. "No—repeat—NO opportunity to carry out extra briefing." The message was logged in at 14:35. It was now after 16:00.

For a moment they both stood in Olbricht's office, lamed by the implications of the renewed failure and, above all, the unauthorized issue of Valkyrie. Olbricht pulled himself together first. "Call in the new Ia—Harnack, isn't it? Tell him we issued Valkyrie as an exercise and now intend to inspect the various units. Ask him to join us. And ask Frl. Lerche to order my car again."

Harnack, who had succeeded Philip as Ia, was now officially responsible for Valkyrie. His face stiffened, and it was obvious he was furious to hear that his two superiors had issued Valkyrie without even informing him. It was an apparent affront to his competence. "Am I to understand that *Herr General* and *Herr Oberstleutnant* are dissatisfied with my handling of Valkyrie?" he asked stiffly.

"Nothing of the kind," Philip assured him. "I worked out the orders as they now stand—unless you have made changes in the last 15 days?"

"The opportunity to review Valkyrie had not yet presented itself, but if *Herr Oberstleutnant* had warned me that an exercise was imminent, I would have given Valkyrie higher priority."

"Major Harnack, you are missing my point. We wanted to test the orders as they stand. Your job is to make improvements after we see how the exercise went today. Are you ready?"

Harnack took his cap and sidearm and followed Philip. Together they went to Olbricht's reception hall to await the General who, Annie told them, was still on the telephone. Lotte, although also on the phone, waved at Philip frantically when she saw him. She tore a piece of paper from a note pad and handed it to Philip as she said into the receiver, "Yes. I'm still waiting." Covering the receiver, she said to Philip, "Your mother tried to reach you."

Philip's heart stopped. He read the message. "Alexandra arrives Berlin-Anhalter Station at 22.50 tonight. Love.'

"Gentlemen." Olbricht emerged from his office, his pistol in place, pulling his cap on. The trio went quickly down the pink granite stairway to the staff car waiting in the cobbled court.

There were no other women in Alexandra's second-class compartment, and the men took full advantage of the "smoking permitted" notice. The jackets of her fellow passengers swayed with the train, and the racks overhead creaked under the weight of the luggage piled onto them. Every one of them, whether soldier or civilian, traveled with as many edible provisions as he could carry. Only Alix, travelling with a single overnight bag, went virtually empty-handed toward the battered metropolis. Her companions took pity on her when the dinner hour struck. Each provided her with a bit of this and a bit of that from his own supplies. "Camaraderie of the front!" an elderly civilian called it.

At Doeberitz the state of readiness left a good deal to be desired, and Olbricht's face clouded with concern. Olbricht was not the type of general to shout and stamp, but the commander at Doeberitz felt his displeasure. He ran his finger uncomfortably between his neck and collar and tried to explain, until Olbricht cut him short with a reminder that in war there was no adequate excuse. He then called the troops together and gave a short speech about the importance of Valkyrie. "The enemy can reach Berlin with more than his bombers. He can send paratroopers as well. Remember how we rescued Mussolini. We cannot exclude the possibility that they might imitate us and try to kidnap the *Führer*. Furthermore, there is a genuine risk of riots by forced laborers—or more precisely, the danger that Communist agents will incite riots. You know what conditions are like in Berlin. Do you think it will take so much to turn the dissatisfaction into outright revolt? And who is going to keep order in Berlin or protect our government against enemy paratroopers and Communist riots, if not you?" To Philip's ears the official purposes of Valkyrie sounded ridiculous, but the troops were apparently used to any sort of nonsense out of Berlin, and accepted it all with resignation.

Olbricht left it at that, and they continued to Krampnitz. Here the readiness was exemplary. Panzers and personnel carriers had been checked out and stood in order of march before the barracks, oil and gasoline tanks full. The troops had been issued their equipment and kept within call, without so strictly confining them that their nerves and patience were frayed. Philip nodded his thanks to Robert Kleinschmidt as Olbricht thanked the troops and their officers for their performance. Again the General gave a short speech about the importance of Valkyrie. The commander ordered a quick march-past, and Robert Kleinschmidt grinned widely at Philip behind his commander's back.

Finally they headed for Potsdam to inspect the cadet school. Olbricht's inspection of the cadets was somewhat perfunctory. He gave roughly the same speech as before, but the General was evidently tired. His words rang hollow, and the cadets were disinterested and bored. As they stepped out into the gathering darkness, Philip felt the deep depression that had gripped the General as well. They had failed again. Stauffenberg, in whom they had placed so many hopes, had failed.

Harnack drew their attention to the north and noted, "Air raid on Berlin again."

"Let's have a civilized meal here in Potsdam," Philip suggested, checking his watch to be sure Alexandra's train was not due for several hours. He suggested a restaurant and they went together. Driving back to Berlin after the meal, however, they were stopped by police at the Glienicke Bridge. The all-clear had not yet been given in Berlin. Philip anxiously looked at his watch. It was 22:25. He would be late meeting Alexandra's train.

"The train will be held up, too," Harnack reasoned. "If we'd thought of it sooner, we could probably have met your wife's train in Potsdam. It might even still be there." Olbricht told the driver to take them back to the Potsdam train station. But here they were told that the all-clear had been given after all, and the train had gone through. Harnack transferred to a commuter train, but Olbricht told his driver to take them to Anhalter station. They raced up the autobahn to the heart of the city and then drove on the wide east-west axis almost to the Brandenburg Gate; but the closer they got to the Anhalter station, the more intensive the bomb damage was. Olbricht observed dryly, "I doubt that any trains have come in."

Philip didn't answer. As the road ahead was blocked, the driver backed up and tried a new approach. Fires still raged, and fire trucks doused them with streams of water. The sirens of the ambulances filled the air, along with thick smoke and blowing ash. When they could get no closer because of the fire engines blocking the street, Philip announced he would continue on foot, and flung open the door.

"Wait," Olbricht ordered. "I'll come with you." He got out of the car, after giving the driver instructions to park and wait for them.

Even on foot, the firemen would not let them through. They pointed to the tall walls flanking the street. Wrapped in flame and bathed in hose water, these were teetering on the point of collapse. Olbricht and Philip retreated, turned into the next alley, and tried to work their way toward the station along the next street. They were going against the stream. Toward them came people still wrapped in damp blankets, people wearing gas masks, people pushing wheelbarrows and baby carriages with a few salvaged possessions. They looked at the two officers with unseeing eyes. Ambulance sirens wailed and whined.

When they at last reached the intersection before the Anhalter station, they could see that the station itself had been the victim of a direct hit. Behind the grand portal of the entryway, flames roared as in an inferno. From three sides, fire engines pumped water into the collapsed main hall, but the real activity was the loading of what seemed like dozens of ambulances lined up inside the fire engines. The arches of water reached gracefully over the heads of the medics, who carried stretcher after stretcher out of the darkened platform area behind the inferno to the waiting ambulances.

Olbricht stopped Philip. "There's no point in it. The train is sure to have stopped someplace else—maybe Wannsee or Dahlem."

Philip freed himself of Olbricht's grasp and continued forward. Olbricht followed. They passed between the fire engines. Here the firemen were too busy to stop them. Under the arching water, spray and spume fell like a heavy drizzle. Philip went to the first ambulance. "Who are the victims?"

"God knows! Poor souls!" came the medic's answer without a glance. He was an elderly man, wrinkled with age and care.

"Were they in the station or on a train?"

The man shrugged. "Does it matter?"

Philip went to the next ambulance. "Do you know where the victims come from? Were they on a train?"

"Most of them. Two trains were hit."

"Which trains?"

"Platforms 1 and 2."

"From where?"

The man shrugged, and with a grunt heaved the stretcher into the back of the ambulance.

"Philip, don't," Olbricht warned, but Philip continued. Now he was searching the faces on each stretcher, stopping each medic. "Which trains were hit?"

He got different answers: Münich, Vienna, Basel, Frankfurt …

On the platform itself, the victims were laid out waiting to be transported, the living beside the dead. The stretcher crews went down the line until they found someone still alive, and then they loaded the stretcher. The dead were left on the platform for the time being.

The only light here was the uneven glow of the fire. Sometimes Philip had to bend down to assure himself that the corpse was not Alexandra. "Philip, if she's alive she's probably already been transported to hospital. It would make more sense to go home and telephone the hospitals from there."

Philip continued down the platform, farther and farther from the heat and light of the fires. Here the medics were still engaged in trying to clear the dead and wounded out of the twisted and charred remains of the railway cars. The interchangeable metal sign identifying the route was still in place on one of them: the train was from Frankfurt.

Olbricht caught his arm and held him back. "No, Philip!"

"What if she's in there bleeding to death?"

Olbricht let him go, and together they searched to the last car. They did not find her.

"She must be alive," Olbricht concluded. "They've only been able to remove the living. For all we know, some of the passengers even managed to walk away."

"Yes," Philip agreed, but his face was petrified. He would never forgive himself for wishing she were with him in Berlin.

They stepped back onto the platform, where the smoke-filled air was welcome after the stench of death in the devastated train.

"Come." Olbricht took Philip by the arm and led him up the platform, past the ambulances and fire trucks, to the waiting staff car. He told the driver to take them back to the Olbricht villa. "First thing you do is call your flat and see if she isn't already waiting for you there. Then we'll call the hospitals."

Frau Olbricht met them at the door of the Olbricht villa. For all her self-control, she was evidently relieved to see her husband. "I've had a call from the *Reichsführer* SS—personally—and from Generaloberst Fromm. They both want to know what right you had to issue a Valkyrie exercise without even informing them. Himmler says he'll be very interested in your report tomorrow, and Fromm was much less polite. He wants you to report to him first thing in the morning. What went wrong?"

"Stauffenberg was unable set off the bomb. More I don't know, but we have a more urgent concern right now. *Freifrau* v. Feldburg's train was caught in the raid. We have just searched the dead on the platform, and now need to call the hospitals."

"No, you don't," Eva smiled. "*Freifrau* von Feldburg is at the Stauffenberg villa in Nicolasee." Olbricht and Philip could only stare at her. "When the train stopped in Wannsee, your wife transferred to the *S-Bahn*, thinking she'd be home faster that way," Eva explained. "But she only got as far as Nicolassee when the air-raid sirens went off, so she got out and took refuge in the Stauffenberg villa."

Inside the villa, Claus removed his eye patch and pressed his handkerchief into the eye socket while his brother fixed him another drink. Their low, urgent voices—Claus still agitated, his brother trying to soothe him—spilled out onto the doorstep, where Alexandra waited in the dark for Philip. Claus had sent his car to collect Philip at the Olbricht villa.

Now that she knew what had happened today, she was blaming herself bitterly for her spontaneous decision to come to Berlin. She was just an added burden. Another thing for Philip to worry about. All Claus's politeness had not been able to disguise his disapproval. With just a look and a few words, he had given her a guilty conscience.

She sat tensely on the doorstep while overhead, the tall spruce trees swayed and rustled. At last a car turned into the street, and Alexandra jumped up and ran down the walk to meet Philip as he stepped out of the back. "I'm sorry; I—"

He wrapped his arms around her and held her fast, relief and exhaustion making his hold tight. Alexandra waited. Philip just held her, gazing across the neat lawns of the neighboring villas. Gradually the tension eased and he admitted, "I've missed you. Thanks for coming." Then he bent and kissed her.

CHAPTER 41

▼

Berlin
July 20, 1944

A second "exercise" of Valkyrie was impossible. Fromm had raged and threatened, and Himmler's suspicions had been aroused. So the next time Stauffenberg took his bomb to *Führer* HQ, all that the other conspirators could do was wait. In Paris and Vienna, the informed conspirators awaited word from Berlin. In Berlin the various civilian conspirators awaited word from the Bendlerstrasse. And in the Bendlerstrasse, Olbricht and Feldburg awaited word from the *Wolfschanze*.

The daily briefing was scheduled for 13:00, and Olbricht went home for lunch as usual. They decided, however, that since the Valkyrie orders could not be issued in advance this time, it would be better for Philip to remain in the Bendlerstrasse, ready to go to Fromm the instant the news came in. General Hoepner dined with Olbricht—in uniform for the first time since his dismissal more than two years earlier. Alexandra packed a picnic lunch and sent it to the Bendlerstrasse with Stadthagen.

All proved to be an unnecessary precaution. No news came form Hitler's HQ. Olbricht returned from lunch with Hoepner. The hot summer day passed in agonizing slowness, filled only with the routine crises associated with trying to fight a lost war with too few reserves and too little materiel. More than once, Philip found himself reading items presented to him for signature several times. Once or twice he caught himself signing things whose contents he could not remember. The bells from St. Matthew's church struck three. *Oberstleutnant* Herber came by to ask if Feldburg had had a chance to review a proposal he'd made regarding munitions deliveries. Philip apologized and said no, he hadn't had time yet.

From the receptionist's office next door he heard Annie say, "General Olbricht, *Generalleutnant* Thiele from *Führer* HQ." Philip froze and waited. Behind the General's closed door on the far side of the reception desk, Olbricht took the call. It didn't take long before Annie knocked on Philip's open door and asked him to go into the General.

Philip walked through the reception hall, past Lotte and Annie, with a melodramatic sense of going toward his destiny. On the other side of the General's door was the news if Hitler was finally dead or not. He knocked and entered, closing the door behind him. "*Herr General?*"

Olbricht shook his head, his lips tight. "Thiele reports an explosion and several casualties. When I asked if the *Führer* was safe, he couldn't give me an answer."

They gazed at one another; was that success or failure?

"I'll try to get through to Rastenburg myself. Please have a seat." He gestured to the chair before his desk and picked up the receiver. The clock moved slowly forward. The angle of the light through the windows shifted ever so slightly. The church bells struck 3:30, 3:45. Olbricht stopped trying to get through. He hung up the phone and sat for a moment with his hand still on the receiver. Philip waited. The General sat up straighter, pulled his hand back from the phone and turned to his Chief of Staff. "Issue Valkyrie at Alarm Level Two."

Philip got to his feet. He saluted as he answered, "*Jawohl, Herr General.* At once." They were going to make the gesture—regardless of what had happened and regardless of their chances of success. This was not so much a coup, Philip reflected, as a gesture of defiance in the name of decency.

By the time Stauffenberg himself arrived back in the Bendlerstrasse, the first cables with the news "The *Führer*, Adolf Hitler, is dead" had been sent to the communications center for distribution by wire to the Military Districts. The *Commandant* of Berlin, General v. Hase, had alerted all troops under his command, including the only regular combat unit in Berlin, the Guards battalion "*Gross Deutschland.*" Feldburg had alerted the various training units belonging to the Home Army, including the Panzer School at Krampnitz. Alarm Level Two not only required the readiness alert of these units, but put them under orders to actually proceed to the destinations assigned to them by the Bendlerstrasse. While the Guards battalion received orders from General v. Hase to seal off the government district, the Infantry School at Doeberitz was ordered to occupy the radio station, and the panzers from Krampnitz were ordered to Berlin to await further instructions. Generaloberst Beck arrived at the Bendlerstrasse.

Stauffenberg did not report to his own commander, but went directly to Olbricht in the AHA. He swept into the reception hall with energy that was electric. No one could remain immune to it. At the sight of him, Philip jumped and came forward to greet him. Stauffenberg beamed at him. "He's dead. I saw myself how he was carried out." Then he added, "But Haeften" (Stauffenberg's ADC) "says you only had the news just over an hour ago. Have you only just started giving the orders?"

"We had no choice."

Stauffenberg frowned but nodded, "Well, it can't be changed." Together they went into Olbricht's office as he answered their knock.

Olbricht got to his feet at the sight of Stauffenberg. He came around his desk toward them, his expression worried. "What happened?"

"We learned on arrival that the briefing had been moved forward by half an hour to 12:30, to enable Hitler to meet with Mussolini in the afternoon. As a result, Keitel was even more nervous than usual. He tried to herd us all into the briefing hut—the briefing took place in a hut rather than a bunker because of the heat, I presume—and I had to ask to excuse myself. Haeften and I went into one of the small waiting rooms and started to pack the explosives into my briefcase." As he related this, the nervousness and urgency of the moment was still so vivid that his breath shortened. "First Keitel called through the open window for me to hurry; then he sent a sergeant to stress the urgency of punctuality. At Keitel's call I activated the fuse, but the sergeant burst in on us before we could pack the second explosive.

"I then went directly into the briefing hut, where the briefing had already started. Keitel suggested I should start my briefing at once, but Hitler waved the suggestion aside. Another officer indicated I should stand not far from Hitler's right, and even asked a rear admiral to make room for me. I managed to place my briefcase under the table. Then, muttering that I still had to make a telephone call, I left the hut. I went to the communications hut, pretended to place a call, and then crossed over to the general administration block and stood out front talking to General Fellgiebel. *Oberstleutnant* Sander joined us to say that a car for my return had been organized, and just then a massive explosion took place.

"Almost immediately, Haeften arrived with the car. I at once took leave of Fellgiebel, climbed in next to the driver, and ordered him to take us to the airport. As we drove toward the exit, we had a good view of the briefing hut through the trees. It was as if a 155mm shell had made a direct hit. Smoke billowed up. Ashes were blowing through the air. People were working feverishly to remove the casualties.

"We reached the first control point before an alarm had been issued, but the lieutenant in charge had heard the explosion and closed the gate on his own initiative. We had valid papers, of course, and I pretended I had "*Führer* Orders" to get to the airport at once. He allowed himself to be intimidated.

"At the second control, the alarm had been given, and the sergeant was unimpressed by everything I said. I had to get out of the car, telephone to the commander, and request permission to pass. The sergeant didn't take my word for it, but telephoned himself to confirm. Only then were we let through. On the way to the airport, Haeften threw the remaining explosives and the unused 30-minute fuse out of the car window. In Rastenburg the aircraft was ready and waiting for us as ordered. We hadn't even finished climbing when the pilot informed us that the tower at Rastenburg had just grounded all further flights. We made it out by one minute." Stauffenberg could hardly hide his sense of triumph, and it was infectious. Philip, too, was elated, but Olbricht remained surprisingly serious. "Fromm has refused to sign the orders."

"Coward," Stauffenberg scoffed.

"It's not that simple, *Graf* Stauffenberg," Olbricht's formality warned. "I told him we had word the *Führer* was dead and suggested we issue Valkyrie. He said he wanted confirmation from *Führer* HQ—not an unreasonable demand in light of the fiasco on Saturday. Furthermore, I assumed that the communications blackout had been instigated by Fellgiebel as planned, since I had not been able to get through myself. Fromm, however, not only got through, he talked to Keitel personally. Keitel says Hitler survived the blast." Olbricht's eyes were fixed on Stauffenberg.

Stauffenberg made a gesture of irritation. "He's lying, as usual. I saw the explosion myself. Hardly anyone could have survived it."

"Keitel did," Olbricht observed dryly.

"It's possible Keitel wasn't in the hut when the explosion occurred. He's often called out for this or that. Hitler was in the briefing hut, and he's dead."

Olbricht took just a second more to think, and then he appeared to be satisfied. "All right; come with me to Fromm."

They left, and Philip returned to his task of sending out the various orders prepared long in advance. These orders stated that the Army had assumed executive power in the wake of an SS coup attempt. They named former Chief of Staff *Generaloberst* Ludwig Beck as Head of State. Field Marshal v. Witzleben was appointed C-in-C of the Armed Forces and the military districts. The arrest of SS, Party and Gestapo officials, the occupation of the Concentration Camps, and the arrest of their commanders were ordered.

"Baron v. Feldburg?" Lotte stood in the doorway. "*Generaloberst* Fromm wants you to report to his office at once."

Philip handed the next batch of orders to Seydlitz, who was again acting as his ADC, and told him to take them to the communications center for issue. He went down the hall, walked up the five steps to the main building, and turned right into the corridor leading to Fromm's office.

Generaloberst Fromm was a tall, thickset man, and he glowered at Philip from behind his desk as Philip saluted. He wasted no time on preliminaries. "Have you issued Valkyrie?"

Philip glanced at Olbricht. "Yes."

"You're under arrest!" Fromm barked, adding in an outraged tone, "How dare you issue orders for which you have no authorization! Insubordination of the most unheard-of kind! If not treason," he added ominously.

"I don't think you've grasped the situation," Olbricht remarked calmly. "We're arresting you."

Fromm's face grew livid. He sprang to his feet, but he didn't manage to get out his protest.

"I set the bomb myself," Stauffenberg announced. "I know Hitler's dead. I saw him carried out."

Fromm's fury switched from Feldburg and Olbricht to Stauffenberg. "Then you'd better shoot yourself!" he shouted. "Your assassination has failed!"

"On no account do I intend to shoot myself."

Fromm lunged at his Chief of Staff as if he wanted to strike him physically. Olbricht and Feldburg jumped between the two men, and he turned on them with all his strength and rage. They struggled with him, forced his hands behind his back, removed his pistol, and turned it against him. Fromm was instantly still. Philip was panting and in pain. He was glad that Olbricht held the pistol.

"We'll give you five minutes to think about it," Stauffenberg decided.

"I don't need five minutes. Hitler is alive, and you're making a fatal mistake."

"Call one of the ADCs to keep a watch on Fromm," Olbricht ordered Feldburg.

With Fromm confined to quarters, Beck—wearing a simple grey suit—and Erich Hoepner, who had been named C-in-C of the Home Army in Fromm's place, took over Fromm's office. Beck declared simply, "For us it doesn't matter if Hitler is actually dead or not. We must proceed as if he were."

Half an hour later came the first radio announcement of an "unsuccessful assassination attempt against the *Führer.*" A speech by the *Führer* was promised for later. Officers in the Bendlerstrasse loyal to the government viewed the radio announcement as a sophisticated means of preparing the population for the shocking news of Hitler's death. Philip heard them talking in the hall. "First they mention an unsuccessful attempt. Then they'll admit that he was slightly wounded. Then they'll say there are medical complications or some such thing. Only after that will they admit he's actually dead. Otherwise it would be too much of a shock, especially for the fighting troops."

Officers who were opponents of the Regime saw the announcement as a ploy by the Propaganda Ministry in the ongoing power struggle between the Army and the SS/Party. "They're trying to confuse us."

"They can find an actor who imitates the *Führer's* voice and have him read a speech Goebbels writes him."

Philip wondered why the Infantry School hadn't seized the radio station yet and silenced it.

By 6:30 pm the government district, including the Ministries of Interior and Propaganda, the HQ of the SS and SA, and the Chancellery had been sealed off by the Guards battalion. Training units of the Home Army under Valkyrie orders had occupied the armory and the Royal Palace in their central Berlin locations. The panzers form Krampnitz had reached the outskirts of Berlin.

But a teletype from Keitel to General Olbricht ordered him to personally suppress the "mutiny" by Fromm and his Chief of Staff, Stauffenberg. Another order from *Führer* HQ, issued directly to the subordinate commands of the Home Army, denied that Hitler had been killed and appointed Himmler C-in-C of the Home Army. Telephone calls started to come in from the subordinate commands: What was going on? Which orders were valid?

Olbricht, Feldburg and Stauffenberg fielded these calls and repeatedly insisted that the orders from Hitler's HQ were SS machinations. The Army had to respond vigorously to put down an SS coup.

In addition to *Generaloberst* Fromm, General Kortzfleisch, Commander of the Berlin Military District, refused to cooperate with the coup and was arrested. An SS officer appeared to arrest Stauffenberg, and was himself arrested instead. One of the young officers from IR 9, *Oberleutnant* Ludwig Frhr. v. Hammerstein, was assigned to guard him, while some of the civilians who had started to collect in Stauffenberg's and Olbricht's offices expressed doubts about such "gentlemanly" behavior. A pistol-toting churchman asked, "If the roles were reversed, do you think they'd handle you so correctly?"

Another civilian said more bluntly, "A little blood has to be shed if we are to be taken seriously."

Philip didn't have time to reply. His phone was ringing. "Feldburg," he identified himself.

"Fellgiebel here, calling from Rastenburg. The *Führer* is alive." Fellgiebel hung up. Philip stood for a moment, stunned. Fellgiebel was one of the conspirators. He had no reason to perpetuate an SS lie. Fellgiebel was also the man who should have immediately informed the Bendlerstrasse of the assassination, and then closed down communication to and from *Führer* HQ. Philip now understood why he had failed to do so: he knew Hitler had survived the blast. Stauffenberg had lied.

The noise from the outer office came through a haze. Herber, one of the many staff officers of the AHA not involved in the coup, was demanding of Annie, "What the hell is going on here? Who are these civilians? What is the *Herr General* up to?"

Annie answered loyally, "Whatever General Olbricht and *Graf* Stauffenberg are up to, it must be all right!"

Feldmarschall v. Witzleben swept into the reception hall in full dress uniform and demanded to see Olbricht, Beck or Stauffenberg. He sounded angry. Olbricht came out and escorted him to Fromm's office, where Beck and Stauffenberg were to be found.

The telephone rang again. "Feldburg."

"Cadet School, Potsdam. We have counter-orders from *Führer* HQ. What is going on?"

"As far as we can make out, the SS is trying to seize control. Follow your military orders."

"Is the *Führer* dead or isn't he?"

"Our information says that he is dead." Did he lie convincingly?

"But you can't be sure?"

"Orders are orders!" Philip snapped.

"Yes." The other party hung up. They would obey orders, of course, but which orders?

A colonel in the uniform of the panzers loomed in the doorway. "What's going on here? Is Hitler dead or isn't he?"

"Hitler's dead."

"Don't misunderstand me." The colonel gave him a sharp, piercing look. "When I heard the news, I had my orderly break open a bottle of champagne. Hearing the bastard was dead was the best news I've heard in four years. But if he's not dead …"

"The Army is trying to take control of the country away from the Party and the SS. Whose side are you on? Ours or Himmler's? It's that simple."

The colonel grinned and was gone.

In the hallway, someone had apparently run into Olbricht. A man with a strange voice announced that he refused to carry out any further orders from the Home Army or AHA. Philip heard Olbricht reply brusquely, "You'll carry out your orders or I'll have you court-martialed."

The next minute, Olbricht stepped into Philip's office from the hall and closed the door behind him. "Witzleben has just jumped ship."

"Why?"

"He thinks Hitler is still alive."

Philip said nothing, but his face betrayed him.

"You think so, too."

"Fellgiebel just called with that message."

Olbricht nodded and then asked, "How did Tresckow word it? 'The assassination must take place, come what may. Should it fail, the coup attempt in Berlin must nevertheless be made. It is no longer the practical effect that matters; what matters is that the German Resistance movement demonstrates to the world and to history that it was willing to risk the decisive gesture. Everything else is unimportant.'"

"You memorized it."

Olbricht smiled wanly and used the door from Philip's office into the reception hall.

On impulse, Philip picked up the phone and asked for a connection to Paris. Stülpnagel's Chief of Staff answered, and Philip identified himself. "Regardless of what you hear from *Führer* HQ, you must continue to carry out Valkyrie."

"The *Herr General* has already assured Generaloberst Beck of his unconditional support."

"Even if Hitler should be alive?"

"*Generaloberst* Beck informed us that that was likely. General v. Stülpnagel remains committed. The Valkyrie orders will be carried out in their entirety."

"Thank you." Philip hung up. So the "Western Solution," Stülpnagel's proposal for opening the Western Front to the Anglo-Americans, might yet be attempted. Although Rommel had been wounded three days ago, his replacement was none other than *Feldmarschall* v. Kluge. Kluge, unlike Rommel, had never been a supporter of Hitler, and he had committed himself to the coup almost two years ago. Unfortunately, he had also made Hitler's death an absolute precondition of his participation ... However, maybe Stülpnagel could talk him into the Western Solution ...

Ludwig v. Hammerstein put his head into the reception hall and announced, "The Guards battalion has been ordered to withdraw from the government district and move against the Bendlerstrasse!"

Philip stepped out of his office into the reception hall. "Who gave that order?"

"The *Führer* personally."

Olbricht was standing in his door on the far side of the reception hall. Annie and Lotte sat frozen in the middle.

"How did he do that?" Olbricht asked Hammerstein.

"Major Remer went into the Propaganda Ministry to arrest Goebbels; but instead, the Minister put through a call to *Führer* HQ. Apparently the *Führer* talked directly to Remer, promoted him to *Oberst* on the spot, and ordered him to crush the revolt in the Bendlerstrasse."

Olbricht's face hardened. "Remer!"

Philip remembered that both Olbricht and Beck had expressed doubts about Remer's reliability, but Stauffenberg had insisted he was the kind of young front officer who had been totally indoctrinated with the National Socialist "Leadership Principle"—i.e., the kind of officer who never thought for himself and never questioned orders. True enough, perhaps, but it didn't help now that he had orders direct from Hitler. If the assassination had succeeded, of course, he would undoubtedly have been a fanatical supporter. Philip found himself remembering the dark train trip back from Welikije-Luki and *Feldmarschall* v. Kluge's warning.

"The Guards battalion is only one infantry battalion," Olbricht observed. "The Panzers must be in position by now, and they are still following our orders." He glanced across the room to Philip. "Send a courier to the Panzer Commander and order him to seal off the government district at once."

"*Jawohl.*" Philip turned to the harassed, frazzled and frightened-looking Lotte and said, "*Gnädiges Fräulein*, please type out the following order for *Oberst* Röggner, Panzer School Krampnitz: Proceed at once to occupy and seal off the government district. All—underline all—resistance is to be put down with force if necessary. Arrest the Minister of Propaganda and send him under escort to the Bendlerstrasse." Lotte's hands were visibly shaking as she ran the appropriate form into her typewriter and started to type. She kept making errors, but Philip stood over her until she was finished.

"How do you want to sign this?" she asked, looking up over her shoulder.

"On the orders of *General der Infanterie* Olbricht. *Freiherr* v. Feldburg, *Oberst-leutnant* i.G."

Lotte pulled the form with its duplicates from the typewriter. Philip bent and signed it at her desk, and then he put his head back into his own office. "Stadthagen!" Franz sprang to his feet. "Take this order to the commander of the Panzer troops now collected at the Siegessäule. No, wait." Philip went to his desk, took the first sheet of paper, and scribbled a note to Alexandra: "Thank you for everything. Without you, these last years would have been meaningless hell. Give my love to my mother. Take care of our son. Try to explain what we wanted and why. Love, Philip." He folded the paper, stuffed it in an envelope, and sealed it. He addressed the envelope simply "Alexandra" and handed it to Stadthagen. "When you've delivered that order, drive home, give this to my wife, and help her get out of Berlin *tonight*. Do you understand?"

"Yes, of course; can't I—" Franz cut himself short, pulled himself together, and delivered the smartest salute of his life.

As soon as Stadthagen was gone, Philip picked up the phone and tried for a connection to Altdorf, but there were no lines free.

From the reception hall, Herber's raised voice was demanding to know, "Who are we supposed to defend the building against? Who are we protecting here? Who is behind this supposed coup against the *Führer*?"

Philip rose and went into the reception hall, where he found a half-dozen non-involved staff officers of the AHA confronting Olbricht. The civilians who had previously filled the office had all disappeared. The secretaries looked exhausted and more frightened than ever. Philip's attention was attracted to a *Luftwaffe* uniform and recognized Friedrich Georgi, Olbricht's son-in-law. He registered that the General, too, was taking leave of his loved ones.

"Gentlemen," Olbricht addressed the indignant delegation of staff officers in a level voice, "let's not discuss this here. Come into my office."

No sooner had the crowd moved into the General's office, however, than a young lieutenant appeared in the doorway, looking somewhat bewildered. "I'm looking for General Olbricht."

"I'm his Chief of Staff. Can I help you?"

"I've been sent by *Oberst* Röggner. We have orders from you to occupy the government district and arrest the Minister of Propaganda, but counter-orders to withdraw to Fehrbelliner Platz and await further orders."

"One moment, please. Let me consult with the General." Philip left the panzer lieutenant where he was and went into Olbricht's office.

"… that's true." Olbricht was evidently answering a question. "But we have also heard the contrary. To be safe—" Olbricht interrupted himself, his attention on Philip.

Philip excused himself, went around the cluster of hostile officers, and reported to Olbricht, in a murmur inaudible to the others, what the panzer lieutenant had just told him.

Olbricht nodded. "You have a friend with the unit, don't you?"

"The Adjutant and I were in France together. He commanded one of my platoons."

"See what you can achieve face to face."

"*Jawohl.*" Philip went back into the reception hall. The panzer lieutenant was evidently trying to get information out of Lotte, who was steadfastly shaking her head and saying doggedly, "I don't know."

"*Herr Oberleutnant,* how did you get here?"

The panzer lieutenant was surprised by the question. "I beg your pardon?"

"Did you walk? Drive a panzer? Take a streetcar?" The question was sarcastic.

"I came by motorcycle—"

"Good. I'll come along and talk to your CO personally."

"*Jawohl, Herr Oberstleutnant.*"

The panzers were no longer collected at the Siegesäule. They had already started back for Fehrbelliner Platz. With the motorcycle's superior speed, Philip and the lieutenant overtook the panzers on the Hohenzollerndamm and waved the lead panzer to a halt just abreast of Hohenzollernplatz.

The last light of the day lingered in the Western sky at the end of the long, tree-lined avenue. Around them the five-story buildings—those not already reduced to rubble—loomed dark and ominous. Not a light showed; not a creature stirred. Perhaps, Philip imagined, people peered timidly from behind their blackout blinds at the unusual sight of an armored column right in the heart of Berlin. Perhaps they were indifferent.

Philip climbed out of the sidecar and approached the lead panzer. The turret was open. The commander wore his black fore-and-aft field hat. In the darkness, Philip could not distinguish the rank insignia or the face. "*Oberst* Röggner?"

"*Ja.*"

"*Oberstleutnant* Freiherr v. Feldburg, AHA."

"One moment." The colonel climbed out of the turret of his panzer and scrambled down agilely. In a moment he was joined by Robert Kleinschmidt. The colonel took Philip by the arm and led him to the side of the street, out of hearing of the crews. The engines of the panzers hummed in the background. "You want us to bring down the government, don't you?" the colonel asked.

"Yes, *Herr Oberst*."

"Is Hitler dead or isn't he?"

"Hitler is alive—but he is also a madman leading this country to certain destruction. The only chance Germany has for a future of prosperity and self-respect is if we eliminate him and his accomplices and reestablish a state based on the rule of law." Philip sensed that he lacked the necessary eloquence. He was not like Goerdeler or Leber, who could move men with their inspired speeches—much less Hitler or Goebbels, who could blind men with words until they wanted what was worst for them. He had never felt his own inadequacies more clearly.

The colonel nodded. "You want me to bring down this pack of criminals with a battalion of ill-trained, green youngsters?" He gestured toward his tanks. Philip had no answer. "Do you have any idea of what a massacre it would be the moment the SS panzers—and there are plenty within range—arrived?"

"The war is senselessly costing thousands upon thousands of lives every day," Philip countered.

"I know. But can you honestly promise me that by turning my panzers around this minute, I could stop the war?" He gave Philip only a second, and then proceeded. "If you could, I would do it. But I don't believe your coup has the slightest chance of success now. Do you? Do you honestly want to be responsible for further senseless bloodshed? If you asked me to turn my guns against the Concentration Camps, I'd do it. If you asked me to move against the SA and the Gestapo and the fat party bosses, no problem. But against the Guards Battalion?"

"Philip, we can't be sure our troops would obey our orders even if we gave them," Robert admitted.

The colonel continued, "Hasn't this country seen enough fratricide? Does *Generaloberst* Beck really want Berlin to become a battleground? I don't believe it."

Philip thought of the fine-featured man with the deep-set eyes and the marks of internal agony on his face. Beck had wanted to see Germany restored to international prestige and power, an equal partner with France and England. But Hitler's megalomania had perverted his dream. Now Beck was trying to salvage a fragment of self-respect and a flicker of hope for a better future. Would that future be served by German troops shooting one another on the Kurfürsten-damm? Philip thought of Olbricht's order to him: see what you can achieve … Did he want to achieve more bloodshed at this stage? Even if he could? He shook his head, took a step backward and saluted smartly. "Thank you, *Herr Oberst.*"

The colonel returned his salute and started back to his panzer, but Robert Kleinschmidt lingered. "Philip, do you need somewhere to hide?" Without wait-ing for an answer, he added hastily, "Go to my apartment. Wait for me there. I can get you civilian clothes or, better still, one of my brother's SS uniforms. False papers—"

Philip shook his head. "Thank you, but I'd only endanger you. I'm too deep in this to get out now."

"What are you going to do?"

"Go back to the Bendlerstrasse and die with my comrades."

Robert was silent for a moment; then he reached out and shook Philip's hand. "It has been an honor and a pleasure to know you."

"You, too."

Robert ran back to the waiting panzer.

Philip stood and watched the panzers, one after another, shift into gear, groan, and clatter toward Fehrbelliner Platz.

It was now 10.40 pm. Darkness was nearly complete. Philip was on foot, with no means of transportation except the public buses and trams. He walked to the Underground station and descended the steps. To his astonishment, after the empty streets above ground, there were people in the station. They all stood star-ing toward a loudspeaker from which the voice of Goebbels cursed. The voice drove him back into the night air. He continued on foot. From many of the open windows and balconies, the sound of Goebbels' voice ridiculed him. He could not make out the words themselves, only the tone of threat and hatred—and he knew that both the threats and the hatred were directed at him, very personally.

In the Bendlerstrasse there were now plenty of troops, and an indefinable commotion reigned. Philip moved automatically forward, limping badly from the long walk. The pain was almost unbearable. No one took much notice of him. Orders were shouted in the routinely angry tone of NCOs the world over. At the entry to the Bendlerstrasse courtyard, a sentry sharply asked for his identi-fication and what he wanted.

"I've spent the day on an inspection in Potsdam and was ordered to report. What the hell is going on here?" He tried to sound both confused and authorita-tive.

"A coup attempt against the *Führer!*" came the sharp reply. The sentry called the sergeant over. The sergeant studied Philip's face and looked at his papers again; then, saying he wanted to consult his superior, he went off with Philip's ID. Philip knew he was trapped. Troops in the service of Olbricht and Stauffenberg would have let him pass at once. He looked around with a fleeting thought of escape, but that wasn't what he'd come here for. A commotion in the courtyard beyond the iron railing of the gate drew his attention.

From the side entrance came two helmeted soldiers pushing General Olbricht before them. The General's hands were tied behind his back. He was followed by Stauffenberg. Stauffenberg's remaining arm was bound with a crude and bloody bandage. *Oberleutnant* v. Haeften followed, struggling stubbornly between his guards. Olbricht was positioned before some sandbags against the south wall of the courtyard. The firing squad was drawn up, their target lit only by the headlights of some cars drawn up on the opposite side of the courtyard. The General, perfectly calm, faced his execution. Philip found himself thinking, "I must remember to write this down for his wife." Mentally he even formulated the letter: "He died with the greatest dignity." The guns crackled.

Stauffenberg was quickly placed as the next target. Even in death, the different temperaments flared to the surface. Stauffenberg was defiant. He cried out "Long live Holy Germany!" A curious phrase, but it was half drowned in the volley, and perhaps he hadn't heard it correctly. Haeften lay at Stauffenberg's feet. Apparently in the last moment, he'd jumped before his colonel. Madness, Philip thought. The next volley brought Stauffenberg down.[1]

Philip turned away.

"Hey! Where is *Herr Oberstleutnant* going?" the sentry called after him. "I thought *Herr Oberstleutnant* had to report?"

"Yes, to General Olbricht—and you just shot him." This so stunned the sentry that it silenced him, and he let Philip walk away.

Just as he reached the canal and wanted to cross the street, a truck roared up from behind him, stopped cautiously at the intersection, and then proceeded. As it started over the bridge, Philip could see clearly into the back: a jumble of corpses on the flat bed. He made out the red stripes of the General Staff on the

---

1. Four officers were shot in the courtyard of the Bendlerstrasse on the night of July 20-21: General Friedrich Olbricht, Oberst Claus Graf v. Stauffenberg, Oberstleutnant Ritter Mertz v. Quirnheim (Olbricht's historical Chief of Staff) and Oberleutnant v. Haeften.

uniform trousers, a general's bloodied tunic, and a fragile man in a grey civilian suit. Beck! The truck pulled away in the darkness.

Philip stood for a long time, supporting himself on the railing of the bridge. Here, for a few minutes, he thought he was going to be sick. He didn't know why, considering all the things he'd seen over the past few years, from the murdered infants of Zubovo to the victims on the train just five days ago. Then the faintness passed, and with a deep breath he managed to drag himself across the rest of the bridge to the bus stop. There he sank onto a bench and rested his head in his hands. The pain in his hips was worse than it had been in months. Almost as bad as when he'd first been released from hospital. Maybe that was where the nausea came from. He wanted to lie down, to rest for an hour or two before he attempted to do all the things he still wanted to do. Pray God that Stadthagen had managed to get Alix safely out of Berlin!

The sound of the bus wheezing up to the stop brought him to his feet. He hobbled to the door and pulled himself into the bus with such obvious difficulty that the conductor came and helped him. Clinging to the railing, he started to pull out his wallet, but the conductor waved it aside, and helped him instead to one of the seats reserved for the handicapped. At his own stop, one of the other passengers, with a Party badge pinned prominently on his lapel, stood and helped the wounded lieutenant colonel with the Knight's Cross out of the bus. Philip thought: if he knew I was one of the officers who just tried to kill Hitler …

Since one air raid or another, the front door of the apartment house could no longer be locked. Philip pushed it open and was brought up short by the unmistakable sound of Hitler's own voice hissing and snarling at him. It was coming from Theo's apartment. He'd left his door open, apparently to let in the cool night air after the long, hot day.

Hitler was saying: "… a tiny clique of ambitious, unscrupulous and criminally stupid officers plotted to kill me and at the same time eliminate the entire leadership of the German Armed Forces. The bomb laid by Colonel Count von Stauffenberg exploded only meters away on my right. I am completely unhurt, except for some completely insignificant cuts and bruises. I take this as a sign from Providence that I must continue to pursue my life's goals as I have up to now…."

Philip tuned out the sound of the voice and dragged himself with difficulty to the first landing. Here he had to pause, leaning against the window overlooking the courtyard until he had the strength to continue. The pain was almost unbearable. Hitler promised to "mercilessly exterminate" those who had tried to kill him. That drove Philip up the next set of stairs. When he reached the landing before the doorway, he leaned heavily against the door as he went to extract his keys from his pocket. By accident he leaned against the bell. He moved away and was still trying to pull out his keys when Nadja's timid voice came thinly through the door. "Who's there?"

"It's me, Najda; I'm—"

The door was wrenched open, and Philip half fell inside. Alexandra and Nadja caught him. Stadthagen was there, too. "You've been wounded!" Alexandra cried out in horror.

He shook his head. "The old wounds. I've walked too—" She was helping him to the leather couch in the smoking room. "What are you doing here? I told Stadthagen—" he looked reproachfully over his shoulder at his orderly.

"I tried, *Herr Baron*, but what was I to do—"

"I refused to leave, Philip," Alexandra told him directly, matter-of-factly. She grabbed a pillow and stuffed it behind his head and neck as he sank down.

"Alix!" He caught her arm and made her look at him. "You can't stay here! The Gestapo could be here any minute. Our beloved Herr Kessler will no doubt rush to earn some laurels!"

"Do you think I could run away? They know who I am. If I'm not arrested as kith and kin, I'll be arrested for having worked for General Olbricht and for being legal intern to Dr. Sack. I'm in this as deep as you are. Whatever happens, we're in this together. We decided that on our honeymoon, remember?"

"We didn't have a son then, Alix."

"But he's in good hands, Philip. Do you really think the Gestapo won't follow me to Altdorf?" She was right, of course; and as Philip recognized it, he was paralyzed with despair. Philip," she said as she took his hand in hers, bending over him as he lay flat on his back. He gazed into her face and was amazed by her calm. There was nothing hysterical or melodramatic about her expression or tone of voice. "Whether they arrest me here or there makes no difference to them, but I'd rather be with you. I'm afraid to be alone. Can you deny me the comfort of being with you?"

Philip continued to look into her beautiful but mature face. It was something he'd sensed and loved from the start. Alexandra, for all her childlike brightness and optimism, had a mature soul. For a moment the strength of her love for him made him waver in his resolve. Maybe she was right. Maybe they should stay together to the very last possible moment. But the pain that burned up from his hips smothered the thought. He didn't have the strength to withstand abuse at the hands of the Gestapo.

"You're going to shoot yourself." Alexandra read it in his eyes and sank onto the floor beside him, still holding his hand. Her gaze was fixed and empty, directed at nothing across the room.

Philip had to twist onto his side and prop himself on his elbow to see and talk to her. "Alix, try to understand. I know too much. More importantly, I know too many names. There isn't a prayer that I can get anything but execution, but there are others who can only be associated with us and endangered by being named by one of the known conspirators. Wringing the names of our accomplices from us is going to be their principal objective. They feel they have to eradicate us all—or live in constant danger of a new attack. They will not rest until they have wrung every name from us that they can—and better kill ten innocent men than let one guilty man go free. You know that is how they think—and how they operate."

With his free hand he stroked her cheek. She would not meet his eyes. She sat with her head bent and her eyes shielded by her lids. "Please understand. I can't save myself. All I can do by letting myself be arrested is endanger others and prolong my agony. The end result will be the same, but this is more merciful."

"Is there no hope we could hide? Escape somewhere?" Alexandra asked, turning to look at him at last. She was still calm, but her eyes were swimming in tears.

"For you! For you alone there is a chance! But I can hardly hold myself upright. I can't walk another step."

"But when you're rested …"

"I'll be able to walk again, but not far, not long. I can't run." Alexandra didn't answer. She swallowed, and he knew she understood him. "That's the other reason I wanted you out of here," he admitted. "I'm sorry you'll be alone when they come—sorry you'll be alone at all. But you can't—I can't—I don't want you here when I—" The tears brimming in her eyes caught the light from the hallway and glistened and glimmered in the darkness. "It's not really that tragic, Alix. I could have been killed so many times in the last four years—in France or Greece or Russia—or even here in Berlin. That would have been an insult—to die for that man. This way I have the rare privilege—perhaps it is the last privilege allowed the remnants of the feudal aristocracy—of dying for an obsolete honor. It would be nice to think that perhaps, one day, this sacrifice will even do some good. Maybe our gesture will not entirely be forgotten—even if it is not entirely understood. But that is probably too much too ask—"

"What do you mean? I will never forget! I will never let them forget! I will scream it from the rooftops if I have to!"

"You have to be alive to do that, Alix."

She started.

"I promise," he continued gravely, "I'll do it right. If you aren't here to have to deal with the mess, I'll do it in a way that's quick and absolutely certain. Will you promise me in return to try to survive?"

He could see her thinking; different emotions swept across her face. Philip waited patiently, too exhausted to feel the press of time anymore. Finally she curled her fingers more tightly in his and answered steadily, "Yes, I promise. I want to raise our son to understand. I want to give him respect for the things you'll die for. I want him, too, to subscribe to your 'obsolete' code of honor."

Philip sank back onto his back, exhausted. "Thank you." He closed his eyes. He would have liked to sleep. Just half an hour! But there really wasn't time. His eyes opened again with a start. He turned his head to the side. Alexandra was gazing at him. "Did I sleep?"

"Only for a couple of minutes."

"But I mustn't. There isn't time. You promised me you would try to survive, and the Gestapo could be here any minute. You have to leave at once."

"Yes, I know. I was trying to decide where to go and how."

The doorbell rang long and loud. Both Feldburgs shrank back in horror. They had waited too long. The bell rang again and again. Then a thin female voice came, muffled, through the wooden door. "Let me in! It's me, Marianne Moldenauer. Please! I want to help!"

Alexandra responded intuitively to the urgency and pleading. She opened the door and Marianne stepped inside, breathless. Her hair was in disarray and she looked as though she had flung on the first clothes that came to hand. "Baroness von Feldburg. Your husband—"

Alexandra gestured toward the smoking room. Marianne peered into the dark room and could barely see Philip lying on the couch. She saw his polished riding boots and the Knight's Cross, which caught a gleam of light. Then she saw his eyes gazing at her solemnly. Marianne moved into the smoking room and went down into a crouch before the sofa. "Baron v. Feldburg, I heard the *Führer's* speech. I heard him mention *Graf* Stauffenberg by name. Forgive me if I'm wrong, but I thought—you were his friend, his closest associate. From the moment I met him, I sensed—I knew—if there is anything I can do to help! You see, I'm experienced in these things! I've been helping Jews go underground for years. I can even get you forged papers. I know safe addresses."

Philip pulled himself half upright, propped on both his elbows. His face had the tense alertness that Rittenbach knew so well: the General Staff officer concentrating all his knowledge, intelligence and instinct on the problem presented. "Addresses even for tonight?"

"Yes, for tonight, too." Marianne did not hesitate for an instant. Peter might betray her, but before he did, she would save one more deserving soul. And who could be more deserving than someone who had tried to put an end to the whole system of exploitation and murder? She had done what she could, but what Stauffenberg and Feldburg had done was much, much more. If this was the last thing she did on earth, she wanted to help Philip survive.

"What does your friend Herr Kessler think of these activities?"

"He doesn't know. Of course he suspects something. That's why he's made it very hard for me to be active recently. But this one last time, I'm sure I can manage it—precisely because he knows how frightened I am of a new arrest. He thinks he's tamed me."

Philip had enough combat experience to know that there are times when the risks are huge, but you simply have to take a chance. This was one of them. He turned to his wife. "Go!" he ordered. In a single motion he swung his feet down and called into the apartment, "Stadthagen! Nadja!"

The frightened servants were evidently hovering just outside the door and appeared at once. "Pack a suitcase for the mistress at once! Stadthagen, help the mistress pack. Nadja, put every ounce of food that can be packed and carried into my suitcase—and all the ration stamps we have in the house. Go, get started," he ordered his wife and the servants imperatively. When they were gone, he turned to Marianne. "I'm too ill to go underground. I'm going to shoot myself, but I'm entrusting my wife to you. She is as endangered as I. She typed up the secret orders. She—never mind. She was one of us, and they will find that out very soon." He removed his wallet, and Marianne backed away.

"I'm not doing this for—"

"I know. I'm not questioning your motives, Frl. Moldenauer; but in these times if one lives illegally—or helps those who do—money is necessary. I know another address in case you need it. Can you remember? Robert Kleinschmidt, Panzer School Krampnitz. He offered to help me. If you need to, get in touch with him. Can you remember or should I write it down?"

"I can remember. I have experience in these things."

"If I didn't believe you, I'd have shot you." He smiled, but Marianne always wondered if it had really been a joke. His pistol was in his hand.

Nadja was finished first. She could hardly drag the suitcase she had filled. "Good," Philip praised her. "Stadthagen, you go with the ladies, but I'd like you to come back. There will be at least one letter I want you to mail. On no account is it to fall into the wrong hands. You *must* see that it gets into the mail before the house is searched."

"I'll be back as soon as possible, *Herr Baron*," Stadthagen assured him.

"I go with the mistress," Nadja announced.

"What? But—"

"It's all right," Marianne assured him.

"All right, then," Philip agreed, relieved. Then she wouldn't be confronted by the mess, either—and Alix would have someone to hold her. He remembered how they'd cried together at Stefan's death. Yes, Nadja was a blessing. God protect her. "Go! Hurry!"

Alexandra ran to him and gave him a last fierce but hurried hug. He kissed her quickly, and then pushed her gently but firmly away. "Go!" They started toward the door in a crowd. "Remember your promise, Alix!" he called after her, just as the door fell shut.

He listened to them going down the stairs. They were hardly quiet. Theo would be sure to hear them. Philip sat, straining his ears and holding his breath, during their progress. He heard the front door close, and then no more. He was alone. Rolf and Lotte wouldn't be coming home tonight. They would be held by the Gestapo at least overnight, and more likely for days, weeks, months … He couldn't think about that now.

Slowly he let out his breath. He lay back on the sofa, his eyes closed, gathering his strength. He still had so much to do before the dawn.

Epilogue

Alexandra survived the war, sheltered by various individuals and families in Berlin—who did so at the risk of their own lives. Philip's prominent role in the Resistance even assured her respect and good treatment from the Soviet authorities when they entered Berlin. Alexandra was allowed to travel to Altdorf shortly after the end of the war with a safe-conduct from the Soviet authorities. There she started the search for her son and her in-laws. She eventually became a highly respected judge in the Federal Republic of Germany.

Sophia Maria was arrested under the kith-and-kin order for Philip's role in the Resistance. She was imprisoned and interrogated. Her unwavering pride in her son and her contempt for the Regime won her the respect of her wardens and interrogators. It also caused her to be sent to the Dachau Concentration Camp rather than being released. In April 1945 she and other prominent prisoners, including Stauffenberg's widow, Stalin's son, and Pastor Niemöller, were removed from Dachau and liberated by German troops sent to arrest the SS guards. Shortly afterwards, the prisoners were turned over to the US Army and treated to a very mild, short-term internment. On returning to Altdorf, Sophia Maria found the manor occupied by the US military. Here, because of her membership in the NSDAP and her position as leader of the local *Frauenschaft*, she was again arrested and treated with suspicion. Eventually, however, she was allowed to live with Heidi in one of the servants' rooms of her manor. The majority of the Polish workers had already returned to Poland, but Jurek and his two children chose to stay in Germany rather than return to a Soviet-run Poland.

Alexandra and Philip's son, Fritz, was taken away from Altdorf at the time of his grandmother's arrest on July 23, 1944. Only with difficulty and the help of the Red Cross and the US military authorities was it possible to locate him again, under the name of Adolf Fischer in an SS foster home.

Peter Kessler was arrested July 21 by his own colleagues, who could not believe he had failed to notice anything suspicious about Philip. After three weeks in custody and numerous interrogations, he was able to convince them of his innocence. As punishment for his incompetence, however, he was sent to Romania, where he disappeared in the confusion at the end of the war.

Peter never betrayed Marianne, and after his transfer away from Berlin, she increased her humanitarian efforts to help the persecuted. Her efforts brought her no benefit. In the early days of the Occupation, she was denounced to the Soviet authorities by Nurse Tuchel as a "Gestapo" agent and arrested. Efforts by the pastor of the Confessing Church to locate her and secure her release all failed. She disappeared in the impenetrable Gulags of Stalinist Soviet Russia.

Although Stadthagen could not entirely convince his interrogators that he knew nothing of Philip's sentiments and activities, he was given the "opportunity" to prove his loyalty on the front. He eventually managed, with the remnants of his unit, to surrender to the Americans, and was repatriated after two years in a POW camp in the US.

Nadja disappeared altogether. She greeted her countrymen with enthusiasm, only to be deported back to the Soviet Union. There she—as a "volunteer" worker in the *Reich*—was treated as a traitor and sent to Siberia. Nothing more is known about her fate.

Rolf v. Seydlitz, as a relative of the General Walther v. Seydlitz, a resident of Philip's house and his ADC, was arrested on July 20 in the Bendlerstrasse. Under torture he confessed knowledge of Philip's and Stauffenberg's sentiments and vague suspicions that they were 'planning something.' This was sufficient grounds for the death sentence in the Nazi courts, and he was hanged.

Lotte, in contrast, readily convinced her interrogators of her complete ignorance and innocence. She continued to work in the Bendlerstrasse under the new SS bosses until the end of the war. She continued to live in the Feldburg apartment, which—except for one side wing—was completely gutted in an air raid in March 1945. Her arrest in the Bendlerstrasse by the Soviets saved her from the lawlessness of the first days of the occupation. After her release, she met and married an American officer. Although the marriage was not a success, by the time of her divorce she had US citizenship and lived in California, where she remained the rest of her life.

Alexandra's mother and stepfather were briefly taken into custody because of their daughter's outlaw status. Herr v. Rantzow was released for duty in the Home Guard and, during the last battle for Berlin, was hanged for desertion by an SS patrol as he tried to slip home to his family on April 30, 1945. Frau v.

Rantzow was released sooner and assigned to work in an arms factory. She died there of heart failure just before the end of the war.

Following Sophia Maria's and her parents' arrests, Grete was sent to a Nazi school for "delinquent children." The harsh discipline, work, and punishment in the school were aggravated by frequent evacuations as the front drew ever nearer. In the last days of the war, the school was overrun by the Soviet Army. Grete was raped 23 times in succession. She never fully recovered. She did not finish high school, got vocational training as a seamstress, and then worked as a shop girl, but could keep no job for long. She eventually married, but was divorced two years later. She became increasingly dependent on alcohol, and died at the age of 45 from an overdose of pills.

Rudi, with the rest of his flak unit, was thrown against the advancing Red Army in the final struggle for Berlin. He was one of the few to survive, but the price was the loss of both legs. He had just turned 17. He studied accounting after the war and worked as a bookkeeper the rest of his life. He married only late in life, but the marriage was not a success. His wife left him after seven years, taking their two children with her.

Theresa and her three children disappeared in the last months of the war. They joined one of the treks and probably either were killed by strafing Soviet aircraft or died of hunger, exhaustion and exposure along the way. They shared this fate with roughly 3 million of the more than 12 million Germans forcibly expelled from German settled territories east of the Elbe.

Walther, on the other hand, neither witnessed nor shared his wife's and children's fate. He escaped first to Czechoslovakia and then to Austria, where he convinced the American authorities of his unblemished record as a staunch anti-Communist. With the money accumulated in his Swiss bank account, he was able to reinvest in production facilities and raw materials, and reopened a textile and then a leather-making factory. In the '50s he remarried, and eventually had four children by his second wife. He died an extremely wealthy and respected West German industrialist. In his obituary his "heroic efforts to mitigate the fate of his forced laborers during the war" were particularly highlighted and praised.

Father Matthias lived to witness the liberation of Dachau by American troops, but died shortly afterwards from the effects of undernourishment and maltreatment.

The Silbers were murdered in Auschwitz.

Christian was released early from prison as a result of his mother's efforts, her good connections with the American military authorities, and his brother's undoubted participation in the July 20th Plot. Rather than returning home directly, however, he went to France and located Yvette. As a "collaborator," she had been subjected to displays of hatred, humiliation and discrimination at the hands of her fellow citizens. Her head shaved, she was living in a cold-water, one-room slum with Dieter's three-year-old daughter when Christian found her. Gabrielle, Yvette told him, could be seen in silk and satin at the finest restaurants and theaters, on the arms of British and American officers.

Christian took Yvette and her daughter, Danielle, with him to Altdorf, hitch-hiking and walking most the way. On arrival, Christian rapidly got into trouble with the Americans occupying his house for his "arrogance" and made problems for his mother by insisting that he, and not the occupation troops, was the owner of the estate and manor. Eventually, with much diplomacy on the part of Sophia Maria and Alexandra—and changing circumstances—Christian did manage to regain control of almost all the Feldburg properties. He gradually repaired the damage done to the manor and estate until these provided an increasingly respectable income for the extended family. Although he married Yvette, the marriage was never really a success. They had only one daughter together.

Christian turned down the opportunity to help rebuild a German air force for the Federal Republic of Germany. Instead he acted in various consulting capacities to the West German Ministry of Defense. In all his activities, whether public, professional or private, he was tireless in reminding his fellow citizens about the significance of July 20. Like Alexandra, he was often frustrated and angered by the tendency of his fellow citizens to criticize the German Resistance for having done too little, too late or for not having "politically correct" attitudes—i.e., not subscribing to the exact same political program as the critic. Christian was particularly offended by the self-righteousness of the younger generation—who had never faced the difficulties of National Socialism—for regarding his brother as a "militarist" and a "reactionary." The suggestion that his brother was a murderer, because "all soldiers are murderers," caused him to lose his temper completely, and he became increasingly discouraged about the future given the "bigotry and blindness" of the younger generation of Germans.

But as Alix pointed out to him, shortly before she died at the age of 86, she too had once accused Philip of being a militarist and a reactionary—but had learned better. "All we can do, Christian, is to keep telling the story, and hope that now and then someone does understand."

*   *   *   *

Historical Note

Altogether, roughly 7,000 people were arrested in the aftermath of the July 20 coup. Nearly 5,000 people were executed in consequence of its failure. People were executed not only for direct participation in the Resistance, but also for hiding participants, or for having knowledge of their sentiments or suspicions about plans and not reporting these to the authorities. In some cases, people were arrested for doing no more than whispering, "Too bad it failed."

More people died—in air raids, on the fronts, and in the death camps—in the months between July 20, 1944 and the end of the war than in the preceding five years of war altogether.

Of the 800 General Staff officers serving at the time of the coup, 150, or almost 19%, lost their lives in connection with the July 20 Plot. No other institution in Germany, with the exception of the leadership cadres of the Communist and Social Democratic parties, can claim a comparable sacrifice, in percentage terms, in the fight against the National Socialist dictatorship and terror.

The fate of the historical figures who appear in this novel was as follows:

- Beck, *Generaloberst* Ludwig: assisted suicide, July 20, 1944.

- *Generaloberst* Johannes Blaskowitz: although relieved of his command in Occupied Poland so that the SS would have a free hand to pursue the policies of the Regime, was later given important military commands, notably an Army Group in France in 1944.

- Boeselager, Georg Freiherr v.: killed in combat, August 26, 1944.

- Boeselager, Philipp Freiherr v.: role in the Resistance not discovered; survived.

- Bussche, Axel Freiherr v. d.: was still in possession of the explosives he had planned to use in his assassination attempt when the coup attempt was made. He was in an SS hospital at the time, awaiting treatment for his amputated leg. He managed to have the incriminating explosives removed and destroyed. His role in the Resistance not discovered; survived.

- Fellgiebel, Fritz Erich: executed, Sept. 4, 1944.

- Fromm, *Generaloberst* Friedrich: executed for cowardice, Aug. 30, 1944.

- Georgi, Friedrich: arrested but not expelled from the Luftwaffe and so not turned over to the Nazi courts; survived.

- Gersdorff, Rudolf-Christoph Freiherr v.: role in the Resistance not discovered; survived.

- Greiffenberg, General v.: fate unknown by the author.

- Groscurth, *Oberst* Helmut: captured at Stalingrad; died in Soviet prison camp, April 7, 1943.

- Guderian, General Heinz: appointed Chief of General Staff July 21, 1944, he expelled military members of the Resistance from the armed forces enabling their interrogation by the Gestapo and persecution by the People's Court instead of courts-martial. He survived the war.

- Göring, Hermann: tried and sentenced to death at the Nuremburg Trials; committed suicide to avoid execution.

- Hardenberg-Neuhardenberg, Heinrich Graf: survived an attempted suicide, arrest and confinement in a Concentration Camp. Survived the war.

- Harnack, *Oberstleutnant* Fritz: survived.

- Haeften, *Oberleutnant* Werner v.: executed without trial, July 20, 1944.

- Hammerstein, Ludwig Freiherr v.: survived underground in Berlin despite being on publicly-posted wanted posters.

- Hase, General Paul v.: executed, Aug. 8, 1944.

- Helldorf, Wolf Heinrich Graf v.: executed, Aug. 15, 1944.

- Herber, *Oberstleutnant* Franz: decorated and promoted for his part in suppressing the Coup of July 20.

- Hoepner, General Erich: executed, Aug. 8, 1944.

- Hofacker, *Oberstleutnant* Caesar v.: executed, Dec. 20, 1944.

- Kleist, *Oberst* Bernd v.: survived.

- Küchler, General (later *Feldmarschall*) v.: relieved of command by Hitler in January 1944; survived.

- Kluge, *Feldmarschal* Gunther v.: suicide to avoid arrest by the Gestapo, Aug. 19, 1944.

- Leber, Julius: executed, Jan. 5, 1945.

- Leeb, *Feldmarschall* Ritter v.: relieved of his command by Hitler, January 1942; survived.

- Lehndorff-Steinort, Heinrich Graf von: executed, Sept. 4, 1944.

- Lerche, Annie: survived.

- Manstein, *Feldmarschall* Erich v.: condemned to 18 years imprisonment by the victorious Allies; pardoned after 3½ years.

- Model, General Walter: survived.

- Moltke, Freya Gräfin v.: arrested, interrogated and temporarily imprisoned; survived; lives in the US.

- Moltke, Helmuth James Graf v.: executed, Jan. 23, 1945.

- Olbricht, General Friedrich: executed without trial, July 20, 1944.

- Olbricht, Eva: arrested and interrogated by the Gestapo; imprisoned but later released; survived.

- Oven, Margarete v.: survived.

- Reinhardt, *Oberst* (later General) Hellmuth: survived and served in the *Bundeswehr*.

- Roeder, Dr. Manfred: survived.

- Rommel, Erwin: forced to commit suicide, Oct. 14, 1944.

- Sack, Dr. Karl: hanged, April 9, 1945.

- Sauerbruch, Dr. Ferdinand: survived.

- Schlabrendorff, *Oberleutnant* Fabian v.: survived despite arrest and torture, trial before the People's Court, and confinement in a Concentration Camp.

- Schrader, Major Werner: suicide to avoid arrest by the Gestapo, July 28, 1944.

- Schulenburg, Ehrengard Gräfin v.d.: survived.

- Seydlitz, General Walther v.: survived.

- Sponeck, General Hans Graf v.: murdered on Himmler's orders, July 23, 1944.

- Stauffenberg, Berthold Graf v.: executed, Aug. 10, 1944.

- Stauffenberg, Claus Graf v.: executed without trial, July 20, 1944.

- Stülpnagel, General Carl-Heinrich v.: executed, August 30, 1944.

- Tresckow, *Oberst* (later General) Henning v.: suicide to avoid arrest by the Gestapo, July 21, 1944.

- Tresckow, Erika v., his wife: survived.

- Trott zu Solz, Adam v.: executed, Aug. 26, 1944.

- Wartenburg, Marion Gräfin Yorck v.: survived, became a judge in the Federal Republic of Germany.

- Wartenburg, Peter Graf Yorck v.: executed, Aug. 8, 1944.

The military engagements described in this novel are based on first-hand accounts of the fighting on the respective fronts, and represent a synthesis or modified version of these real events. The conversation between *Feldmarschall* von Kluge and Hitler is based on a conversation that Philipp Freiherr von Boeselager actually experienced as his ADC. Because the date or location of the fighting has been altered to meet the needs of the novel, all unit designations below Army Group have been changed. The descriptions of bombing in Berlin are moved forward somewhat; the RAF did not begin its "Battle of Berlin" until August 1943.

German Military Ranks

German Army	British Army	US Army	SS	SA
Generalfeld-marschall	Field Marshal	-	Reichsführer SS	Stabschef
Generaloberst	-	General (4*)	Oberstgruppen-führer	-
General der (Branch of Service, e.g. Infantry or Artillery)	General	Lieutenant General (3*)	Obergruppen-führer	Obergruppen-führer
Generalleut-nant	Lieutenant General	Major General (2*)	Gruppenführer	Gruppenführer
Generalmajor	Major General	Brigadier General (1*)	Brigadeführer	Brigadeführer
Oberst	Colonel	Colonel	Standarten-führer	Standartenführer
Oberstleutnant	Lt. Colonel	Lt. Colonel	Obersturmbah-nführer	Obersturmbahn-führer
Major	Major	Major	Sturmbahn-führer	Sturmbahn-führer
Hauptmann/ Rittmeister	Captain	Captain	Hauptsturm-führer	Hauptsturm-führer
Oberleutnant	1st Lieutenant	1st Lieutenant	Obersturm-führer	Obersturm-führer
Leutnant	2nd Lieutenant	2nd Lieutenant	Untersturm-führer	Untersturm-führer
Feldwebel	Sergeant	Sergeant	Obers-charführer	Truppführer
Gefreiter	Lance-Corporal	Corporal	Rottenführer	Rottenführer

German General Staff Positions

Abbreviation	Position	English Explanation
Ia	Erste Generalstab-soffizier	First General Staff Officer—Operations
Ib	Zweite Generalstab-soffizier	Second General Staff Officer—Support
Ic	Dritte Generalstab-soffizier	Third General Staff Officer—Intelligence
Id	Vierte Generalstab-soffizier	Fourth General Staff Officer—Training
IIa	1. Adjutant	Adjutant, Officers' Affairs
IIb	2. Adjutant	Adjutant, NCOs and Other Ranks
III	Gericht	Advocate General's Corps
IVa	Rechnungswesen, Verwaltung	Paymaster and Administration
IVb	Arzt	Chief Doctor
IVc	Veterinär	Veterinarian
IVd	Geistlicher	Chaplain
	Oberzahlmeister	Senior Pay Master Civil servant, serving with the Army. They had their own uniforms and ranks within their branch of service, similar to military ranks, but were not considered officers.
	Justizinspektor	Legal Advisor See above

Glossary

Abbreviation	German Term	English Equivalent
	Abitur	Equivalent of a high school
AOK	Armee Oberkommando	Army Command
AK	Armeekorps	Corps Command
BDM	Bund Deutscher Mädel	League of German Girls
d.G.	der Generalstab	An officer belonging to the trained elite corps of the German General Staff
	Ersatz	Coffee substitute
	Einsatzgruppen/ Einsatzkommandos	SS special forces deployed behind the front lines to exterminate Jews and Gypsies
	Frauenschaft	National Socialist women's organization
	Freifrau/Freiin	Baroness
	Freiherr	Baron
	Freikorps	Military units formed to fight the German revolutionaries in 1918-1920, after the Army itself had largely disintegrated after the defeat in WWI
	Fieseler Storch	Small, light aircraft with short takeoff and landing runs, making it an ideal aircraft for the transport of VIPs
FüHQ	Führer Hauptquartier	Hitler's headquarters
	Gauleiter	Regional party official
Gestapo	Geheime Staatspolizei	Secret state police
	Graf	Count
	Gräfin	Countess
HJ	Hitler Jugend	Hitler Youth

Abbreviation	German Term	English Equivalent
ID	Infantrie Division	Infantry Division
i.G.	im Generalstab	Officer serving in a staff position
IR	Infantrie-Regiment	Infantry Regiment
KPD	Kommunistischer Partei Deutschland	German Communist Party
KZ	Konzentrationslager	Concentration Camp
	Kreishauptleute	Occupied Poland was divided into Districts (Distrikte), each headed by a Governor (Gouverneur), which were divided into rural regions (Kreise) headed by a Kreishauptmann. These were usually simultaneously the local party leader, or Standortführer, for their region.
	Kreisleiter	Local party official
	Kübelwagen	VW car, frequently used as a staff car
NKFD	National Kommittee Freies Deutschland	Organization of German POWs in the Soviet Union
NS	Nationalsozialistisch(e/er)	Nazi (adjective)
NSDAP	Nationalsozialistische Deutsche Arbeiterpartei	Nazi Party (noun)
MG	Maschinengewehr	Machine gun
OB	Oberbefehlshaber	Commanding officer/CO
OKH	Oberkommando des Heeres	Army High Command
OKW	Oberkommando der Wehrmacht	Armed Forces High Command
Ord.O	Ordonnanzoffizier	Aide de Camp—ADC
	Polizeipräsident	Chief of Police

Abbreviation	German Term	English Equivalent
PzD	Panzerdivision	Armored Division
RAD	Reichsarbeitsdienst	Labor Service
RB	Reichsbahn	National Railway
	Reich	The German Empire; common term for Germany at the time
	Reichskanzler	Chancellor/Head of Government
	Reichswehr	100,000-man army allowed by the Treaty of Versailles; politically neutral and highly trained
	Staffelkapitän	Squadron Leader
SA	Sturmabteilung	SA—"Brown Shirts"
	Sekt	German champagne
SD	Seicherheitsdienst	Secret police of the SS
	Skat	German card game
SS	Schützstaffel	SS
	Waffen-SS	SS units engaged in military operations rather than racial policies and police work
WK	Wehrkreis	Military District
	Wehrmacht	Armed Forces; the expanded military forces of Germany after the Treaty of Versailles was abrogated by Hitler

978-0-595-49088-2
0-595-49088-3

Printed in the United Kingdom by
Lightning Source UK Ltd., Milton Keynes
137821UK00002B/57/P